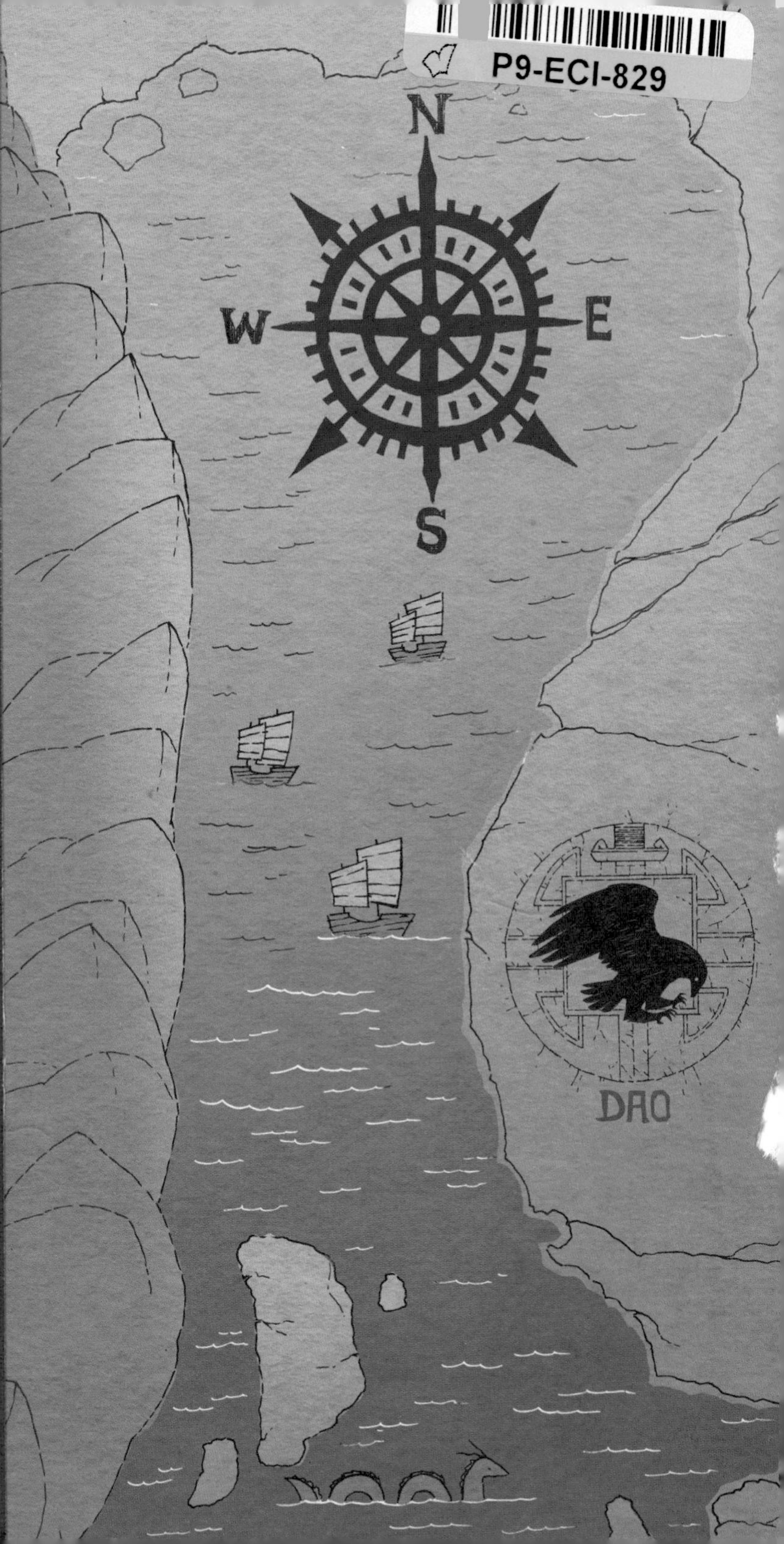
N
W
E
S
DAO

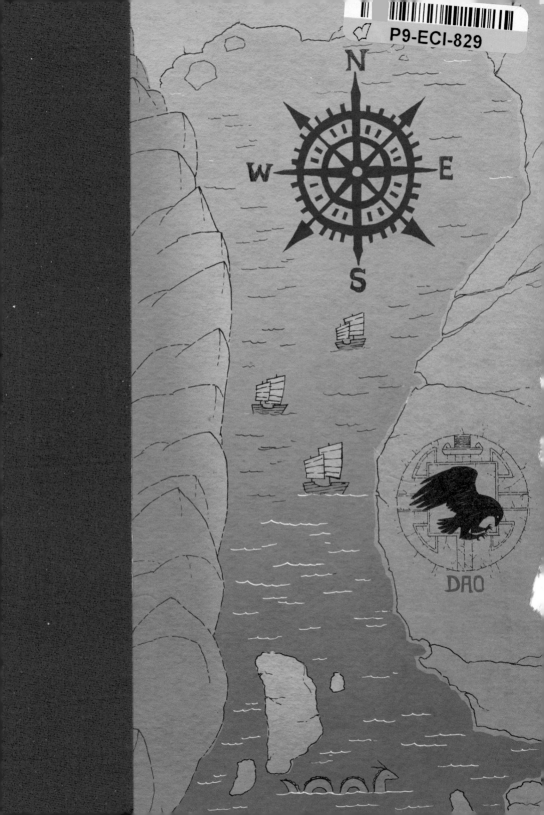

THE DIVIDED EARTH

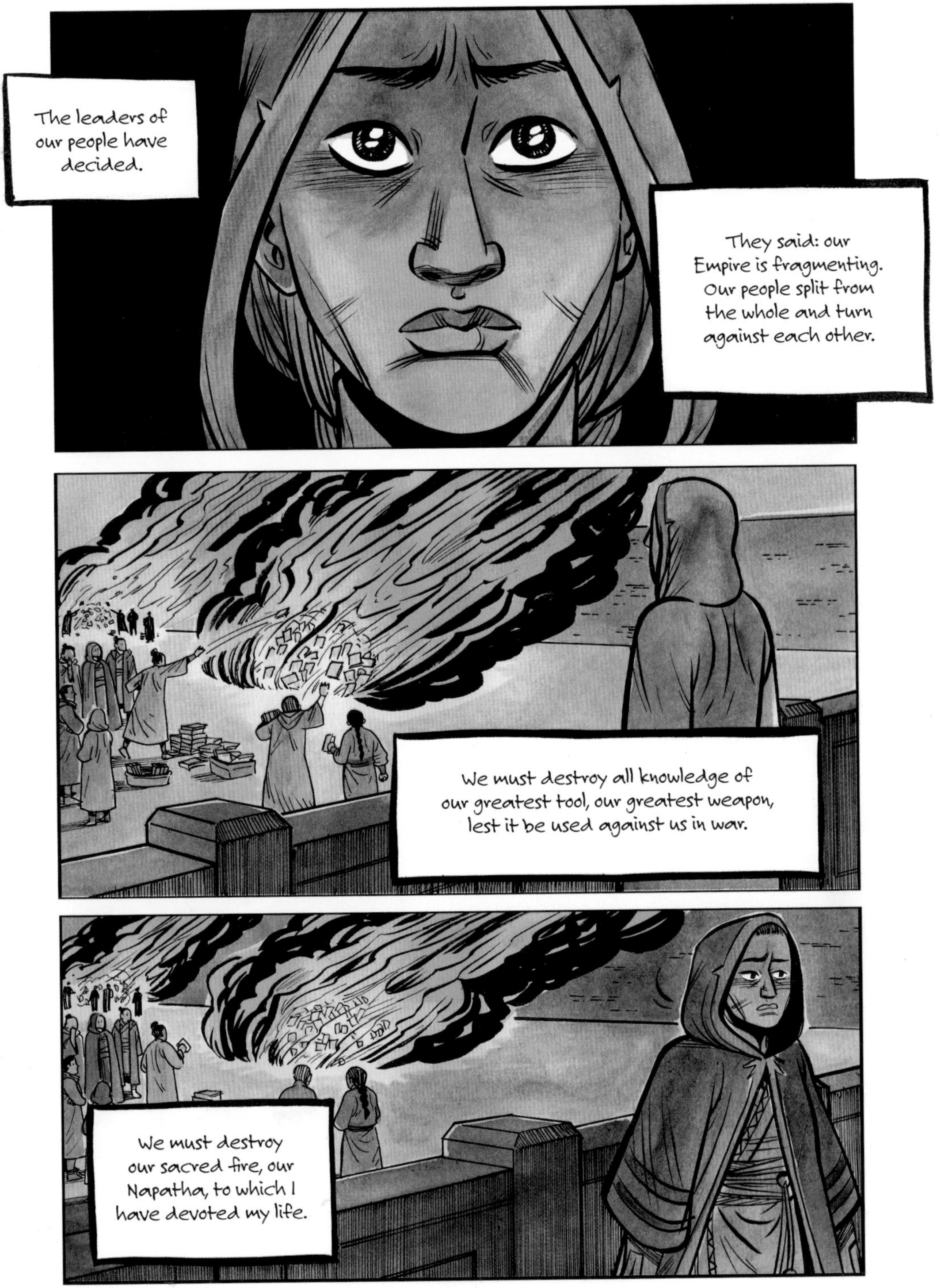
The leaders of our people have decided.
They said: our Empire is fragmenting. Our people split from the whole and turn against each other.
We must destroy all knowledge of our greatest tool, our greatest weapon, lest it be used against us in war.
We must destroy our sacred fire, our Napatha, to which I have devoted my life.

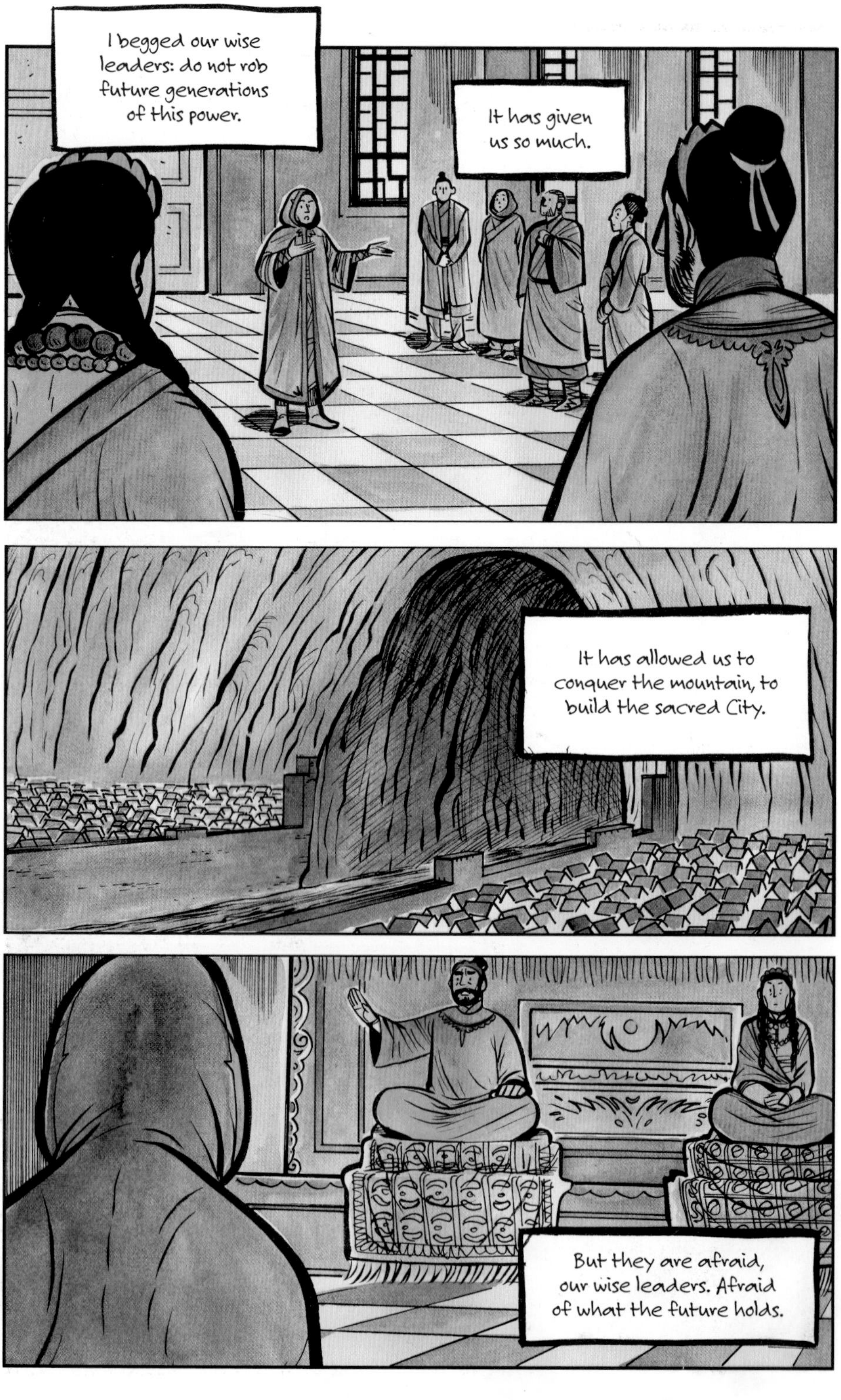
I begged our wise leaders: do not rob future generations of this power.
It has given us so much.
It has allowed us to conquer the mountain, to build the sacred City.
But they are afraid, our wise leaders. Afraid of what the future holds.

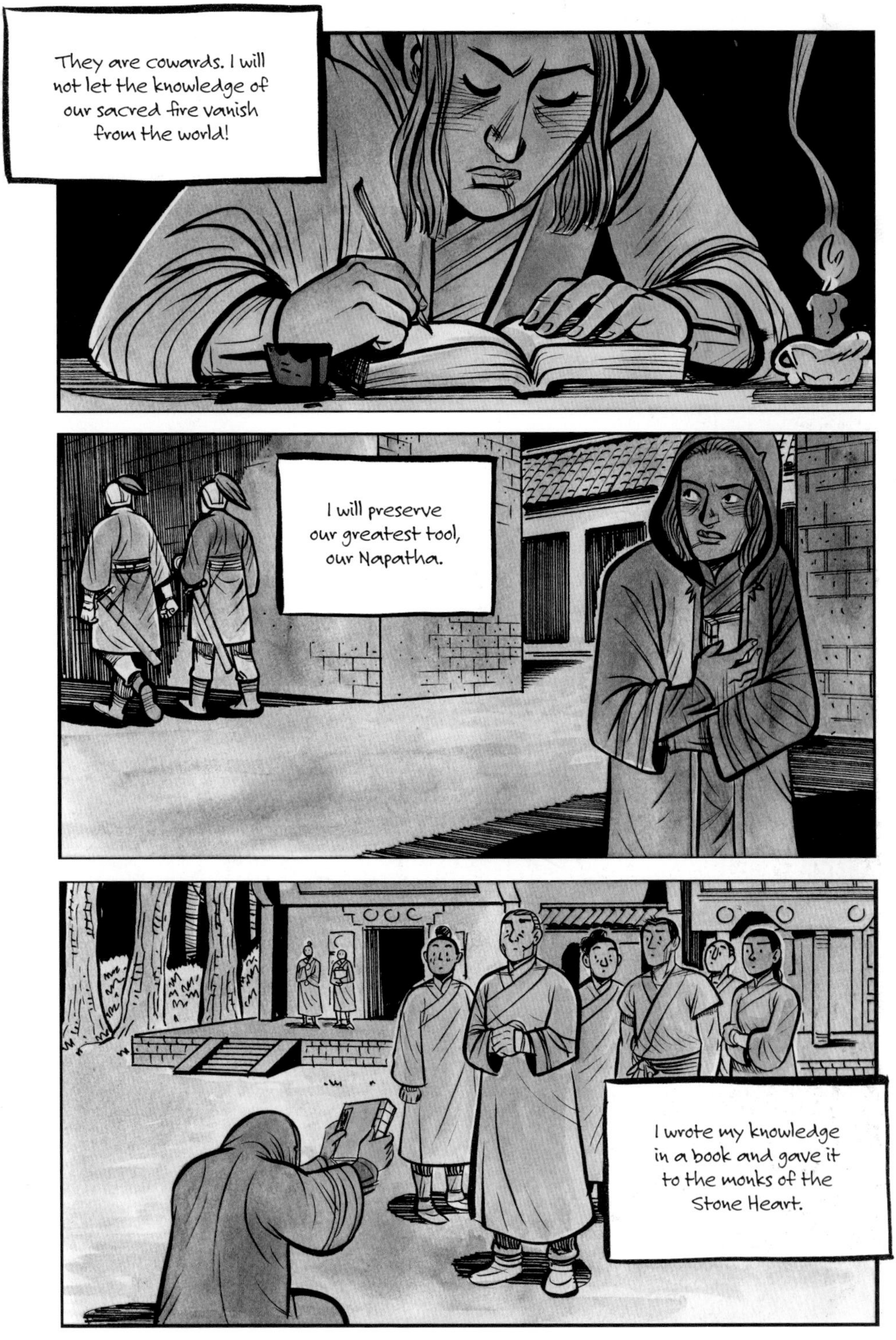
They are cowards. I will not let the knowledge of our sacred fire vanish from the world!
I will preserve our greatest tool, our Napatha.
I wrote my knowledge in a book and gave it to the monks of the Stone Heart.

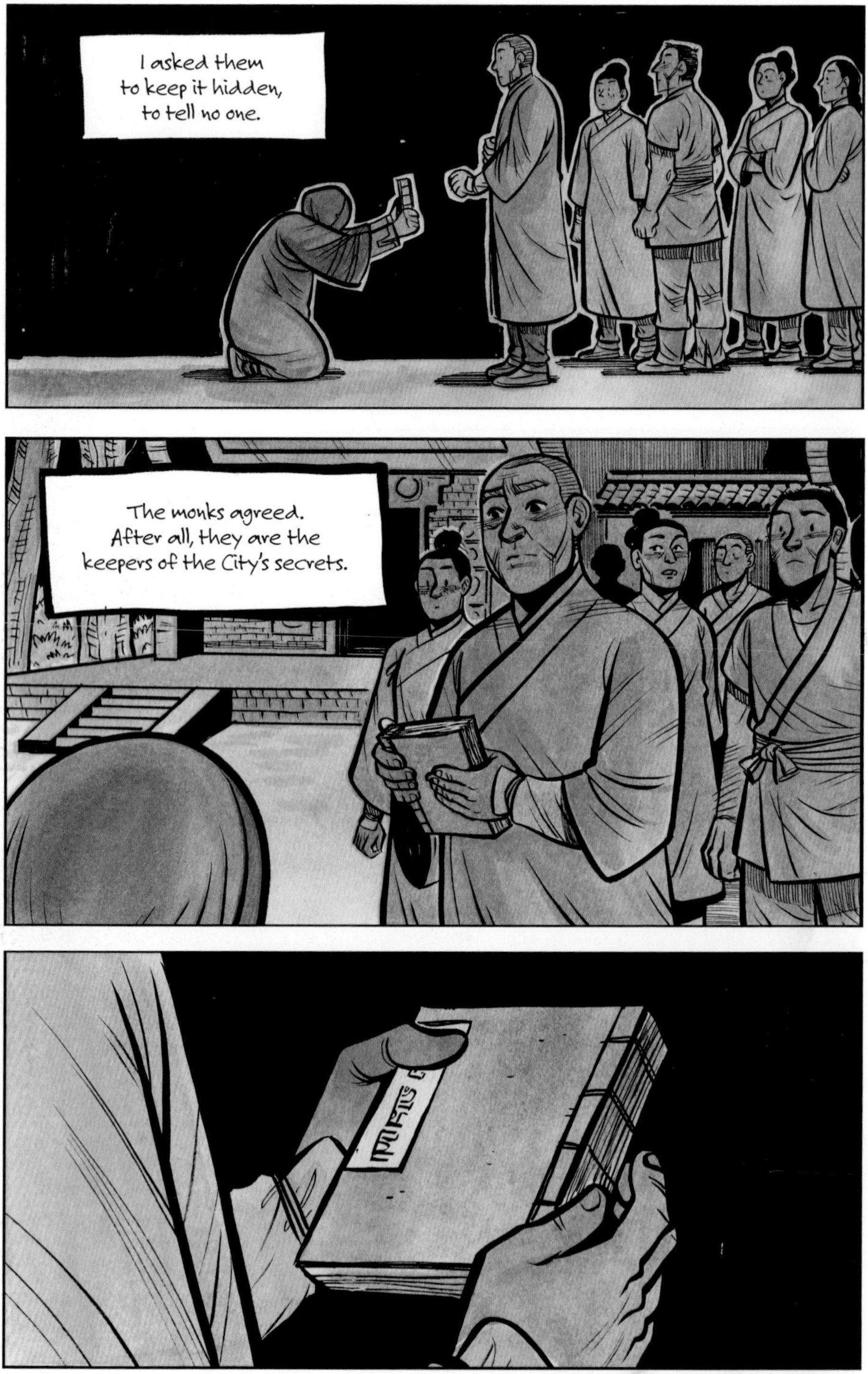
I asked them to keep it hidden, to tell no one.
The monks agreed. After all, they are the keepers of the City's secrets.

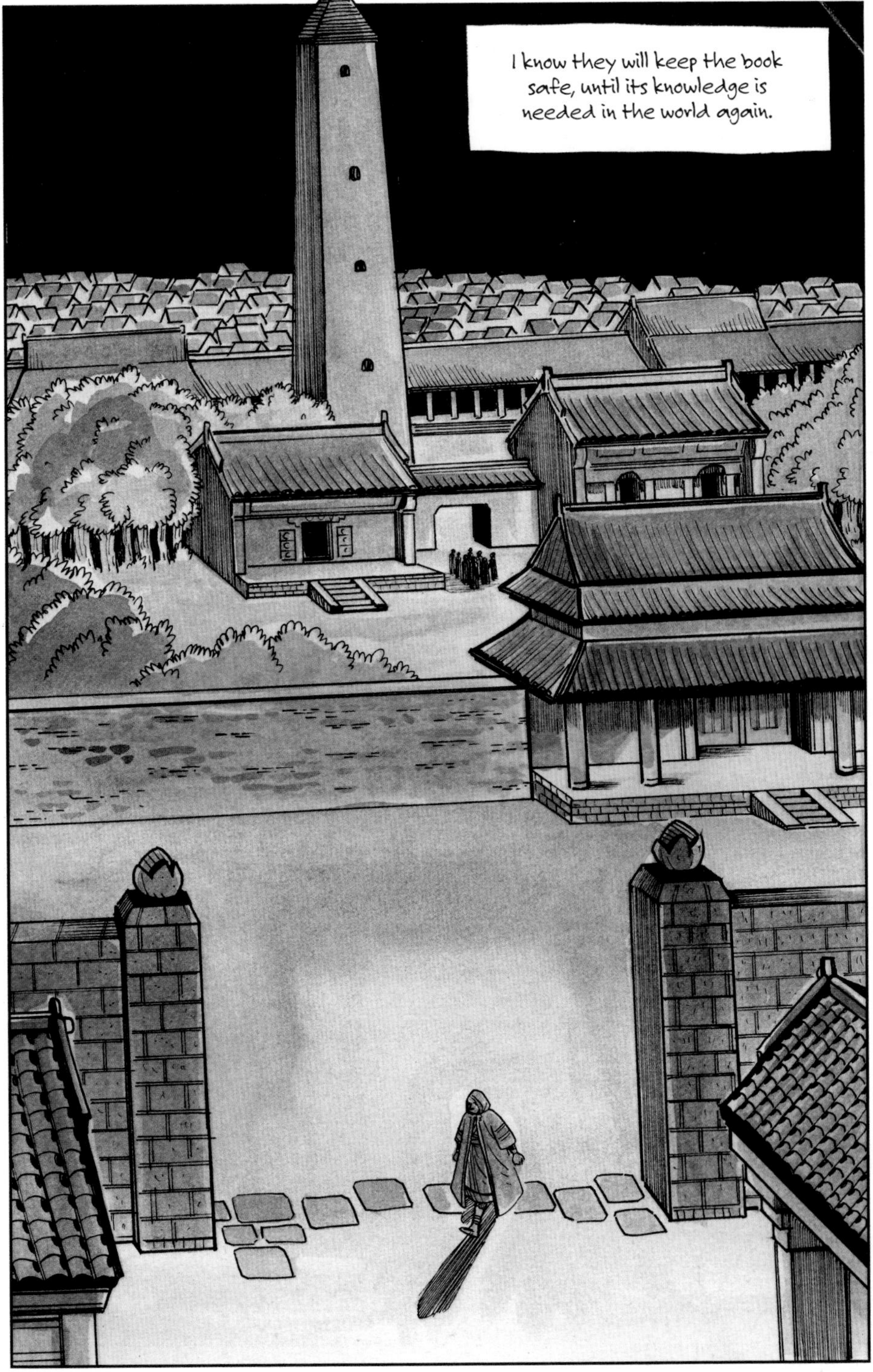
I know they will keep the book safe, until its knowledge is needed in the world again.

THE DIVIDED EARTH

THE NAMELESS CITY

FAITH ERIN HICKS

COLOR BY JORDIE BELLAIRE

:01

First Second

NEW YORK

DAY 1

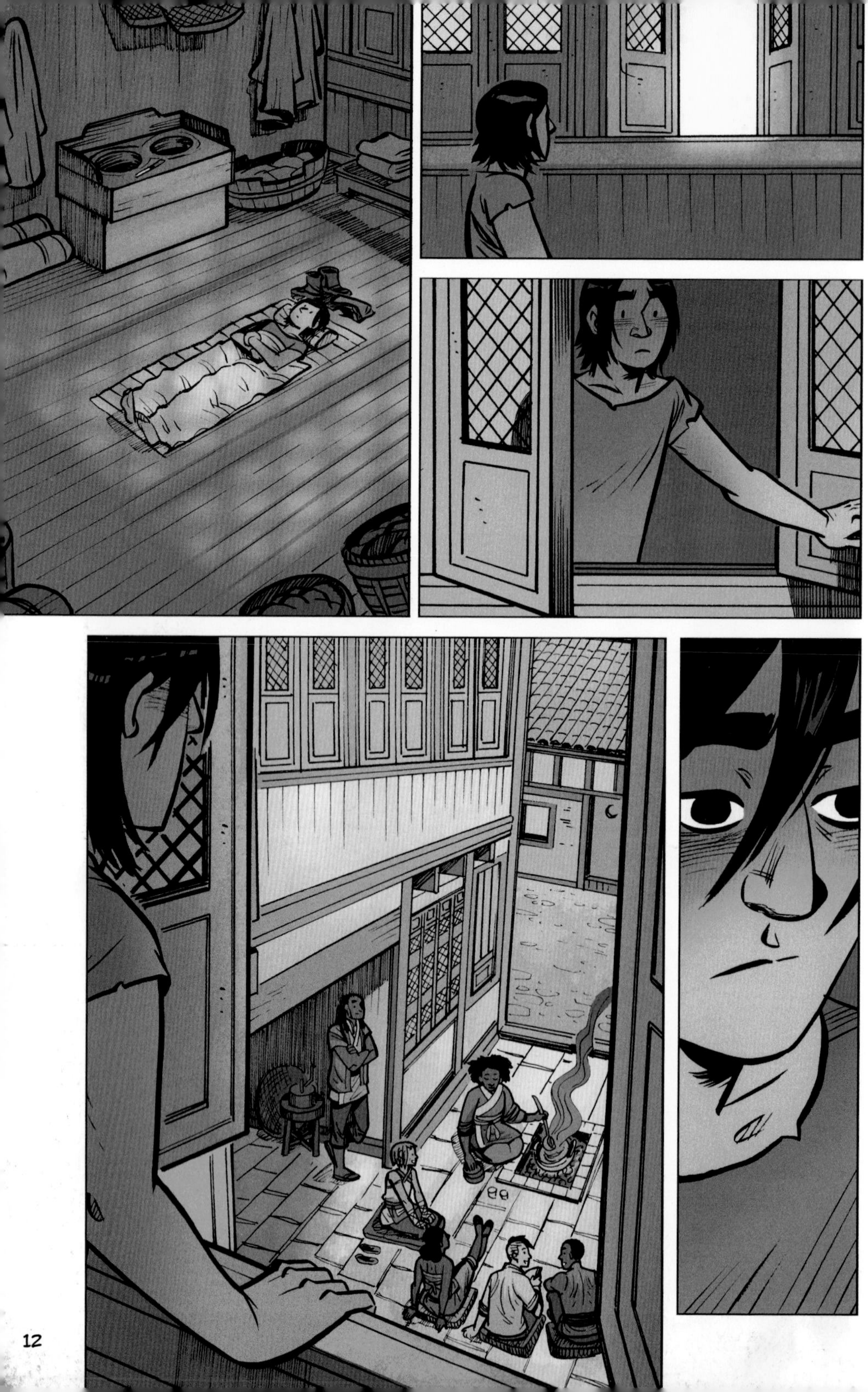

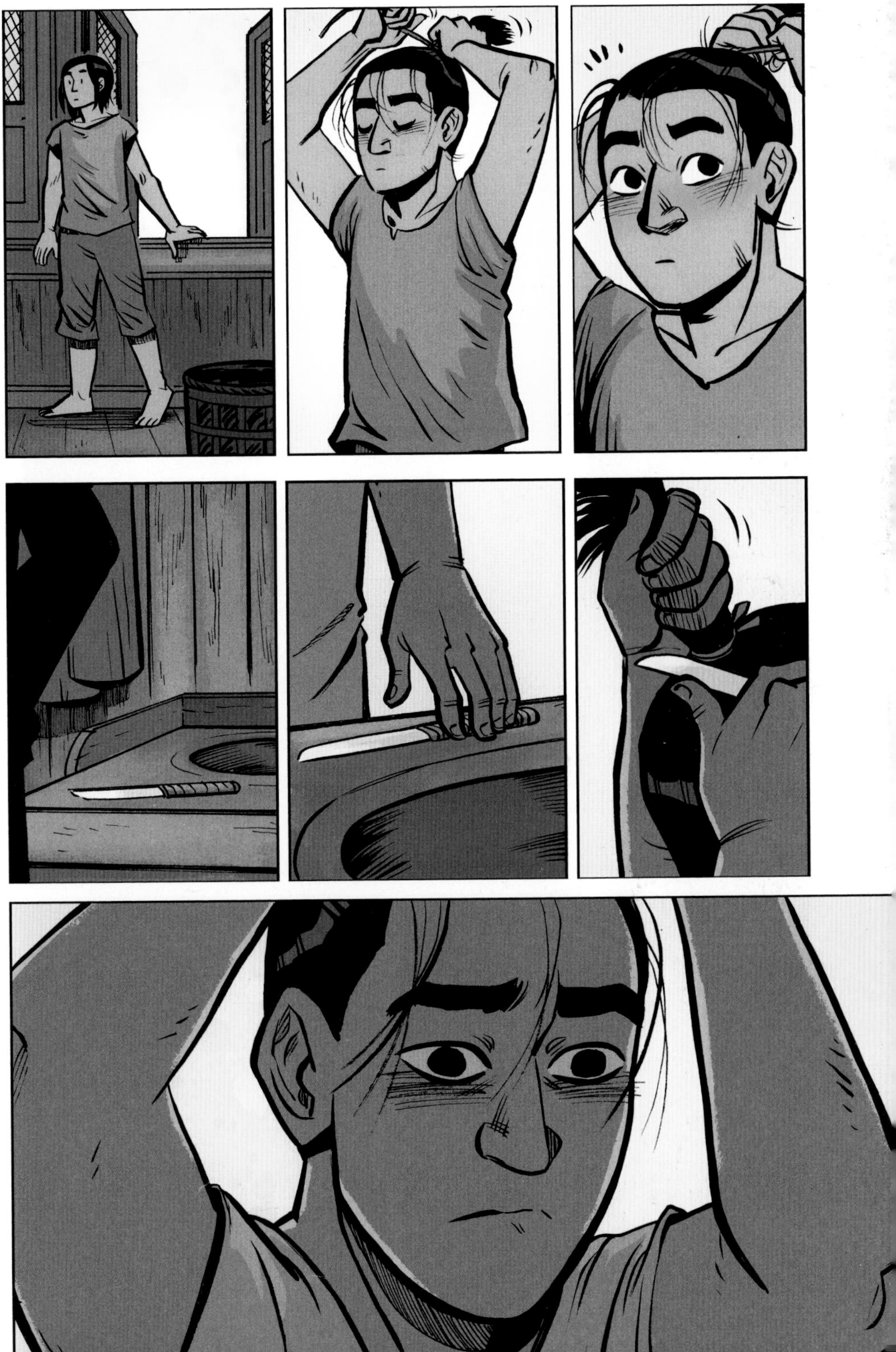

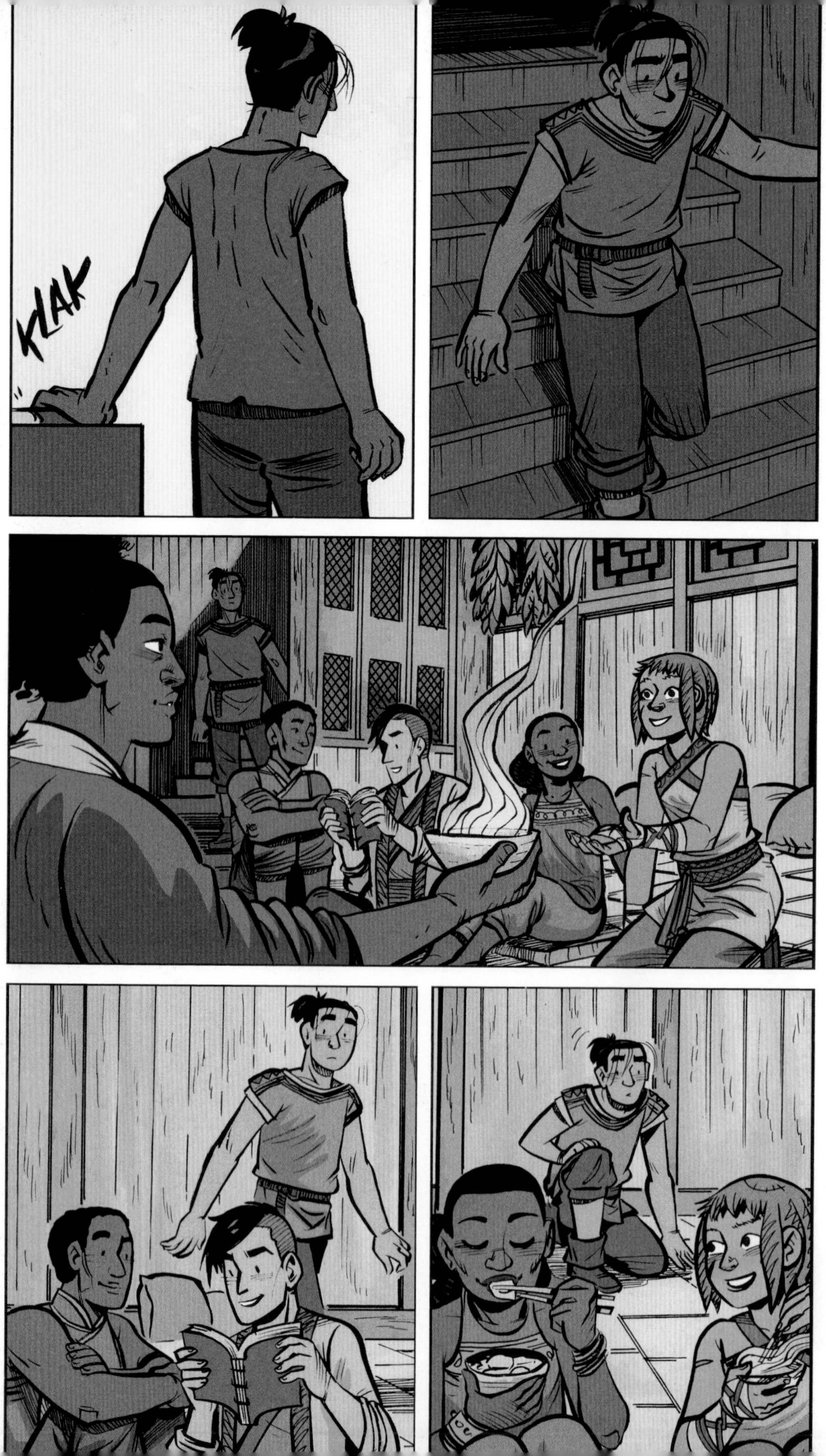
KLAK

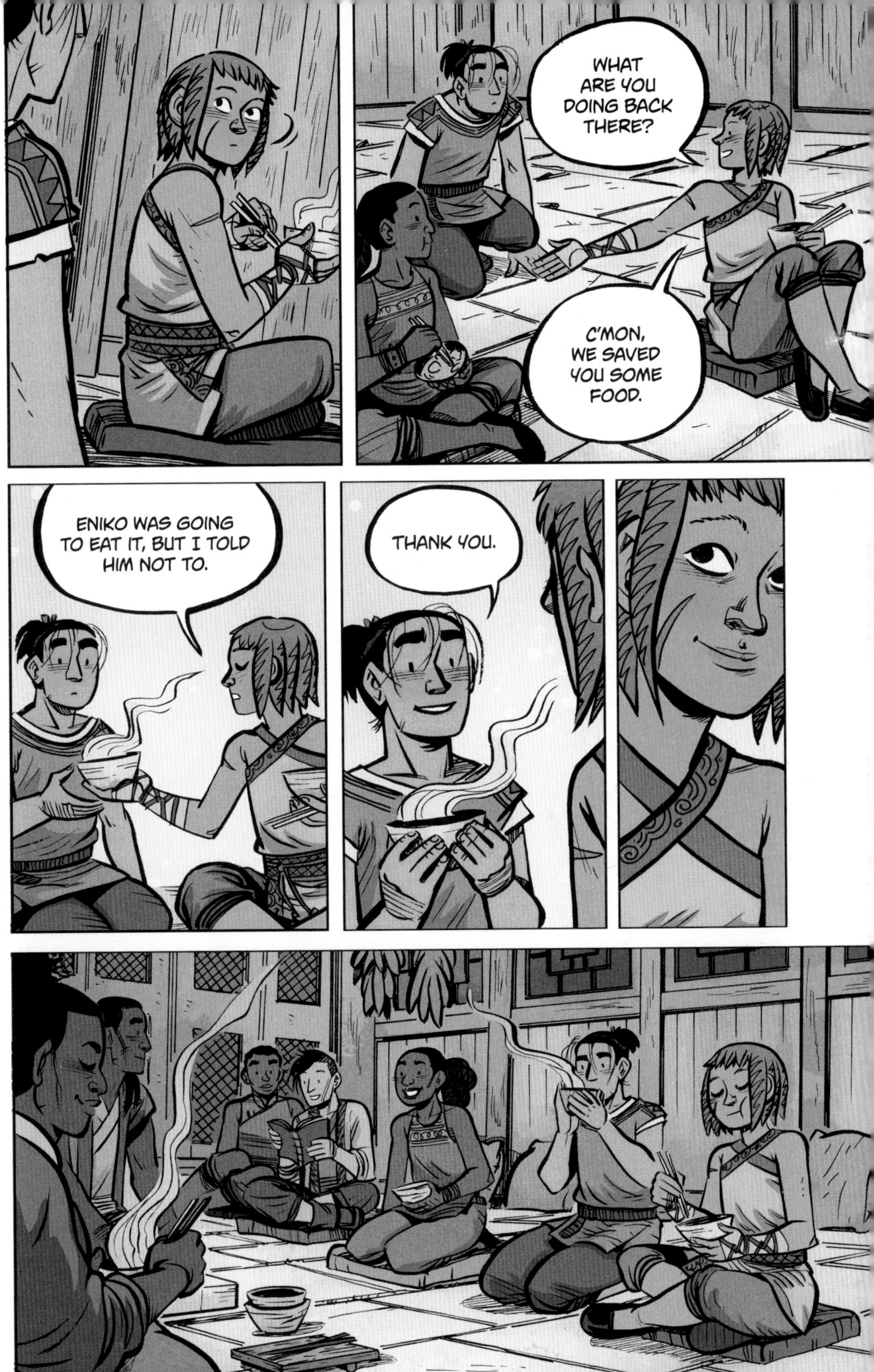
WHAT ARE YOU DOING BACK THERE?
C'MON, WE SAVED YOU SOME FOOD.
ENIKO WAS GOING TO EAT IT, BUT I TOLD HIM NOT TO.
THANK YOU.

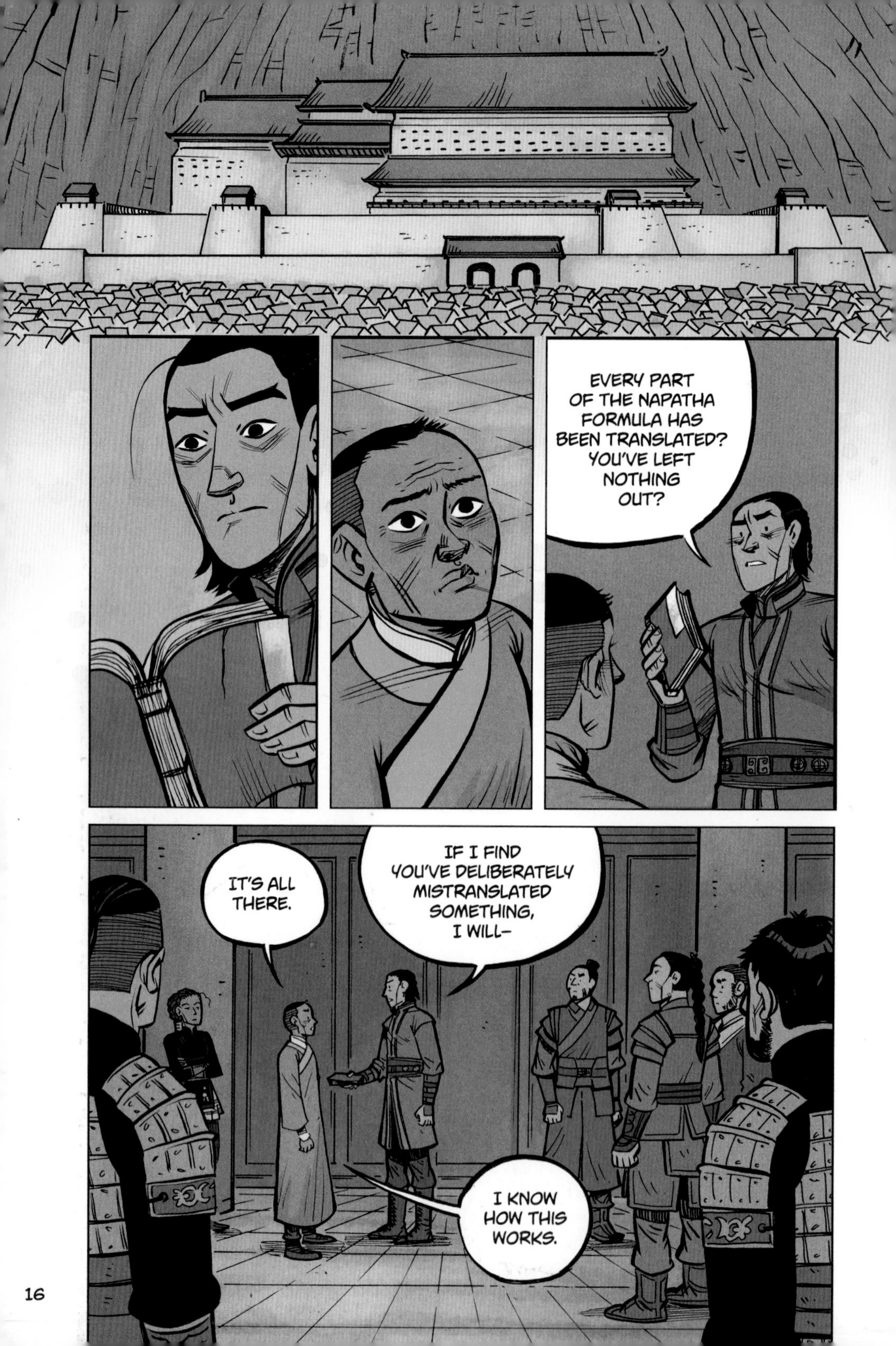
EVERY PART OF THE NAPATHA FORMULA HAS BEEN TRANSLATED? YOU'VE LEFT NOTHING OUT?
IT'S ALL THERE.
IF I FIND YOU'VE DELIBERATELY MISTRANSLATED SOMETHING, I WILL-
I KNOW HOW THIS WORKS.

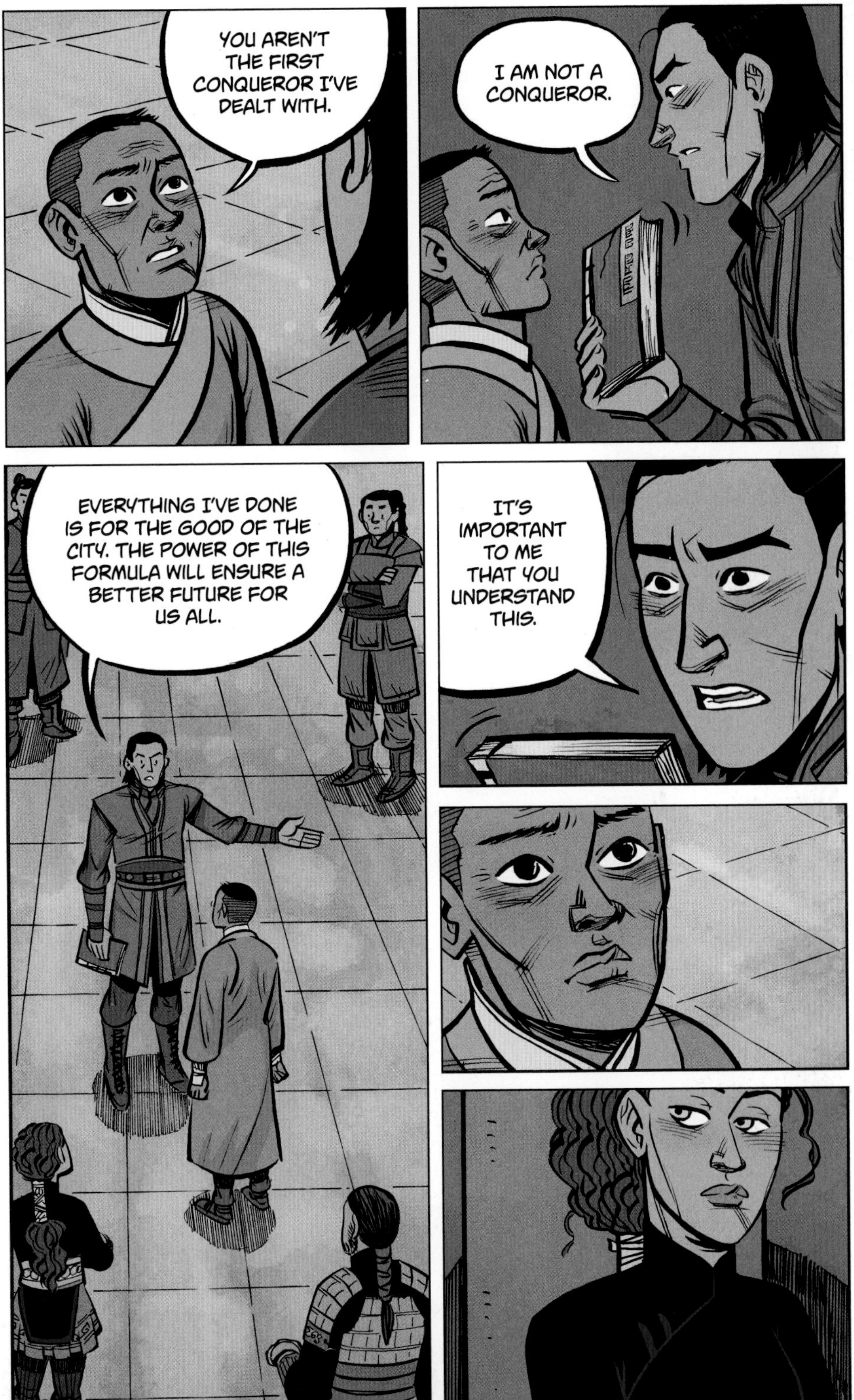
YOU AREN'T THE FIRST CONQUEROR I'VE DEALT WITH.
I AM NOT A CONQUEROR.
EVERYTHING I'VE DONE IS FOR THE GOOD OF THE CITY. THE POWER OF THIS FORMULA WILL ENSURE A BETTER FUTURE FOR US ALL.
IT'S IMPORTANT TO ME THAT YOU UNDERSTAND THIS.

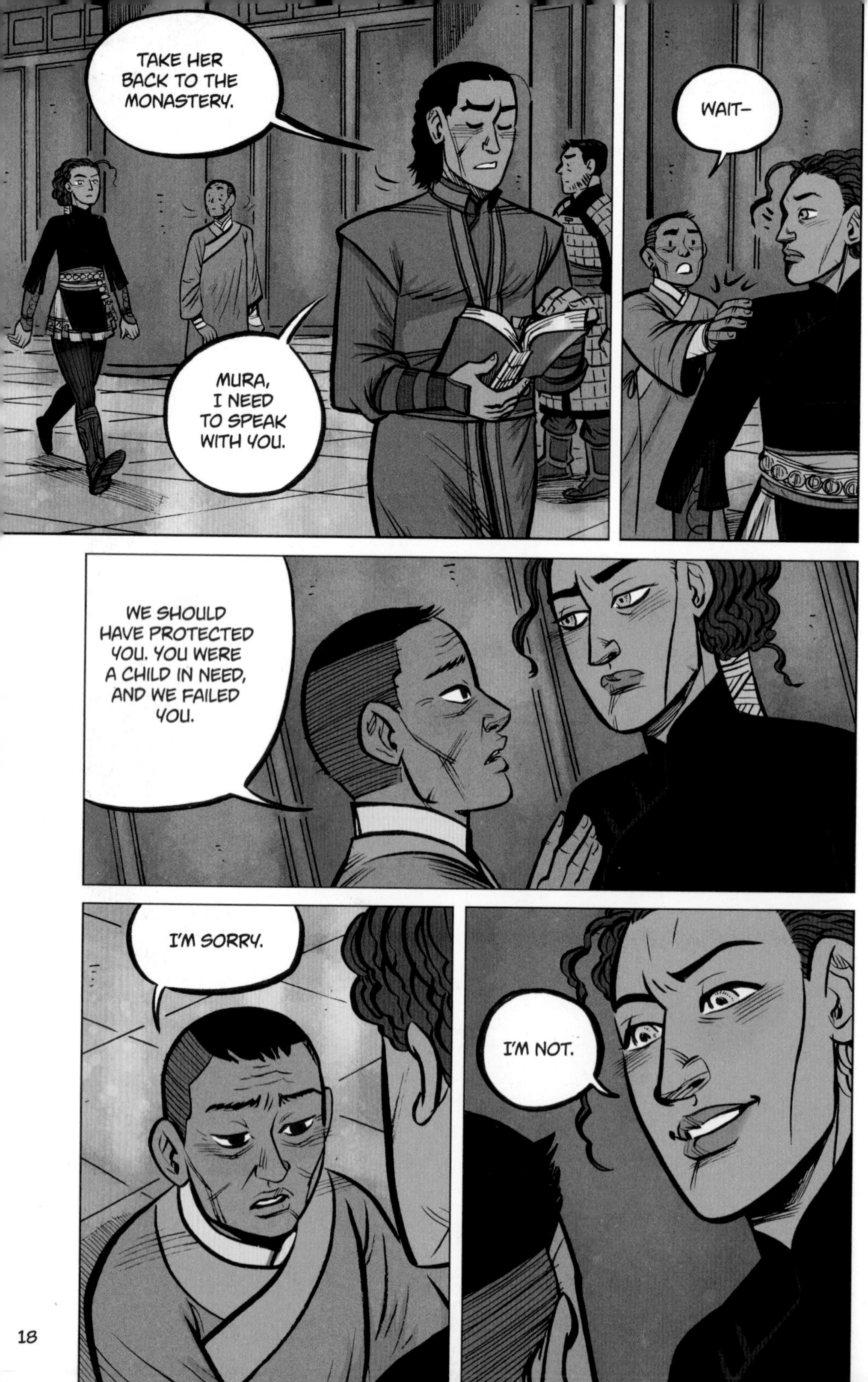
TAKE HER BACK TO THE MONASTERY.
MURA, I NEED TO SPEAK WITH YOU.
WAIT-
WE SHOULD HAVE PROTECTED YOU. YOU WERE A CHILD IN NEED, AND WE FAILED YOU.
I'M SORRY.
I'M NOT.

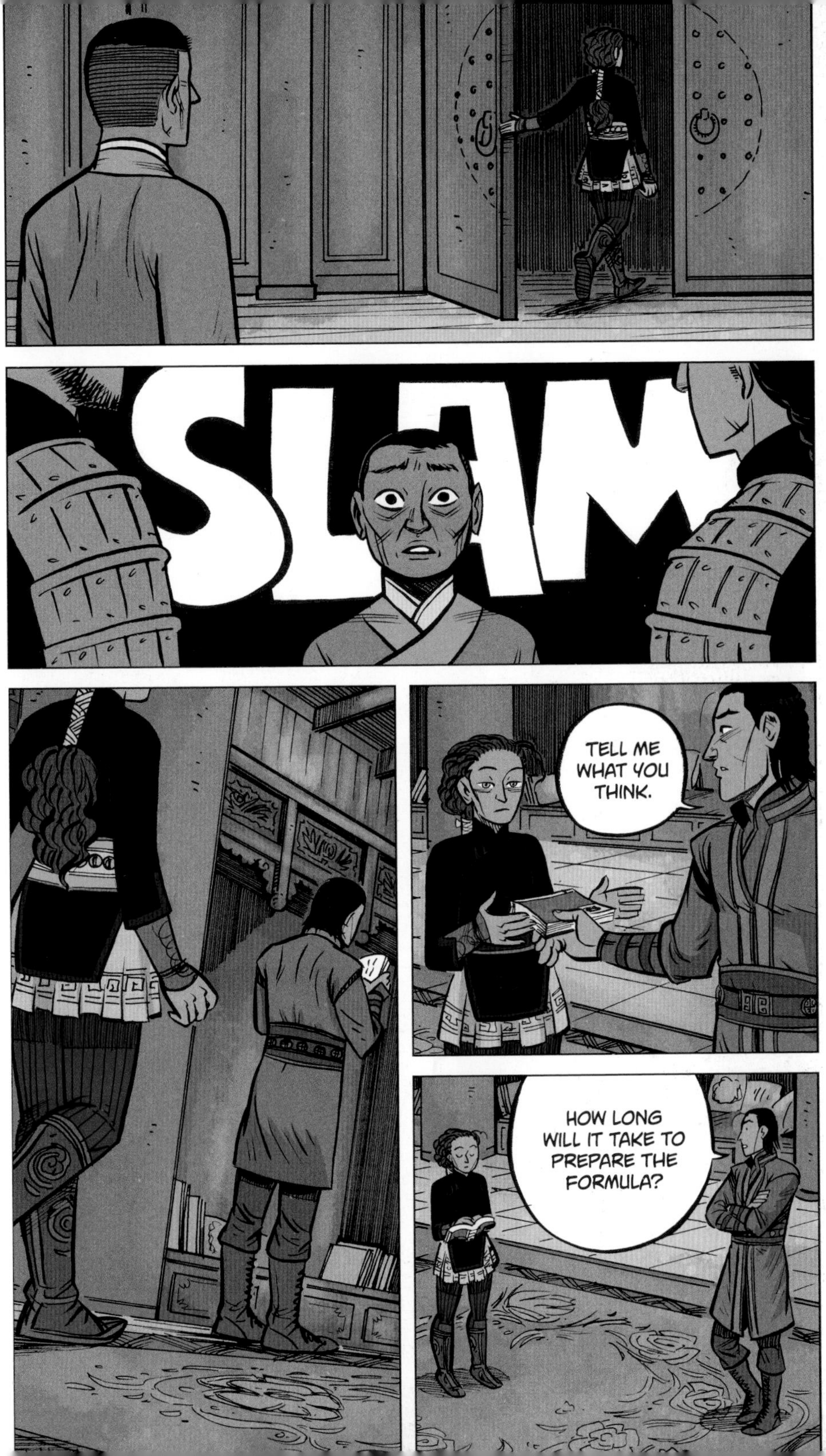
SLAM
TELL ME WHAT YOU THINK.
HOW LONG WILL IT TAKE TO PREPARE THE FORMULA?

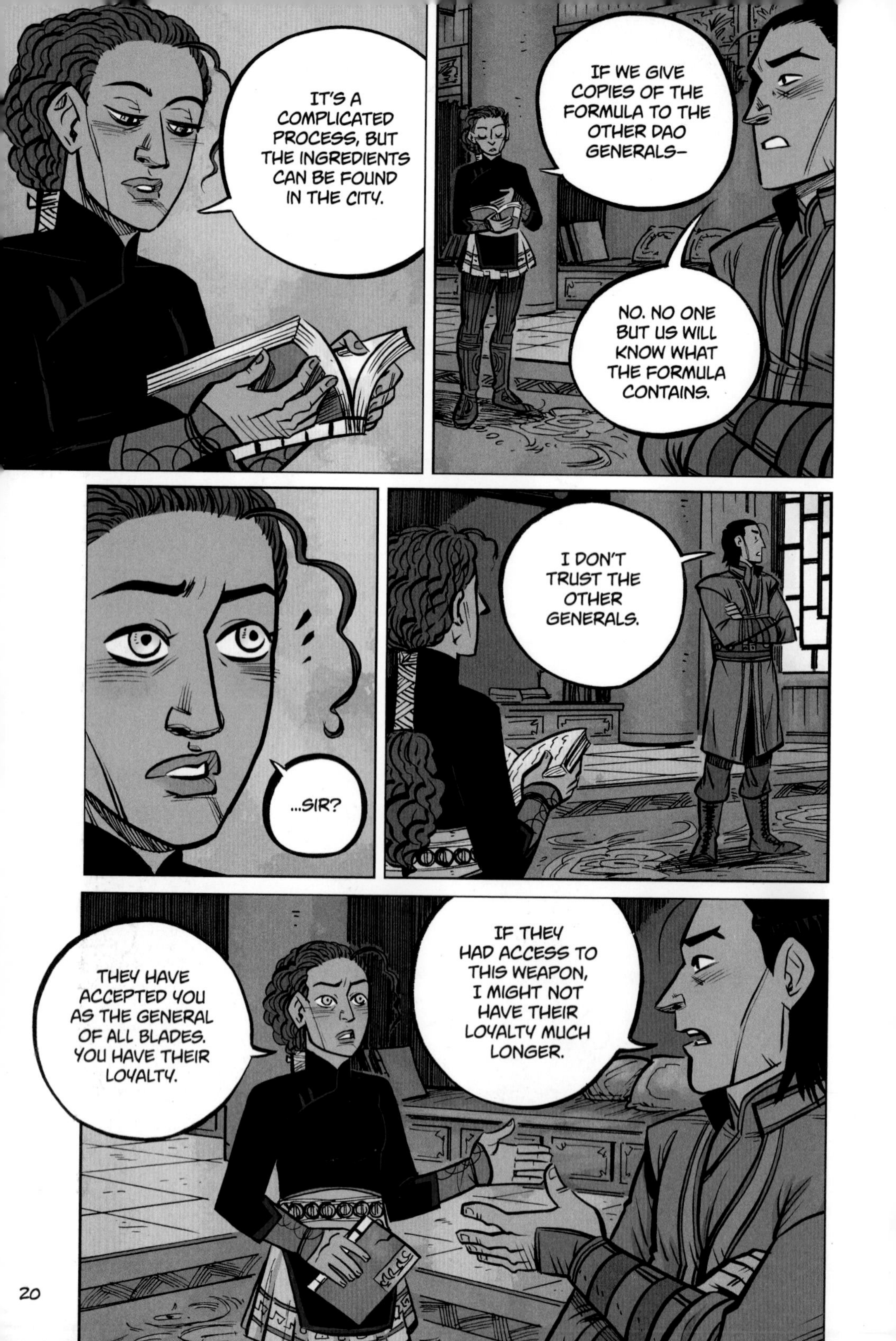
IT'S A COMPLICATED PROCESS, BUT THE INGREDIENTS CAN BE FOUND IN THE CITY.
IF WE GIVE COPIES OF THE FORMULA TO THE OTHER DAO GENERALS–
NO. NO ONE BUT US WILL KNOW WHAT THE FORMULA CONTAINS.
...SIR?
I DON'T TRUST THE OTHER GENERALS.
THEY HAVE ACCEPTED YOU AS THE GENERAL OF ALL BLADES. YOU HAVE THEIR LOYALTY.
IF THEY HAD ACCESS TO THIS WEAPON, I MIGHT NOT HAVE THEIR LOYALTY MUCH LONGER.

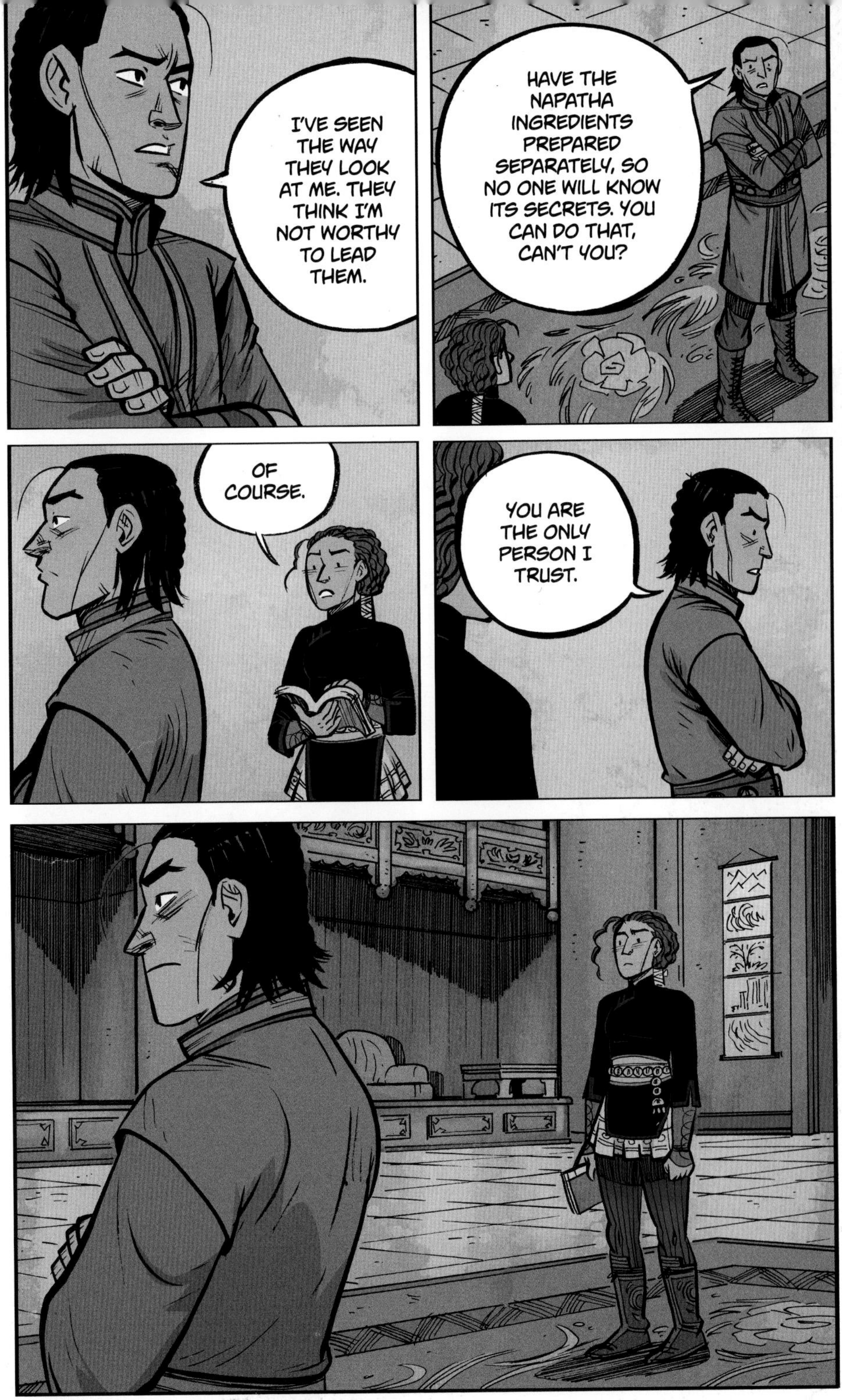
I'VE SEEN THE WAY THEY LOOK AT ME. THEY THINK I'M NOT WORTHY TO LEAD THEM.
HAVE THE NAPATHA INGREDIENTS PREPARED SEPARATELY, SO NO ONE WILL KNOW ITS SECRETS. YOU CAN DO THAT, CAN'T YOU?
OF COURSE.
YOU ARE THE ONLY PERSON I TRUST.

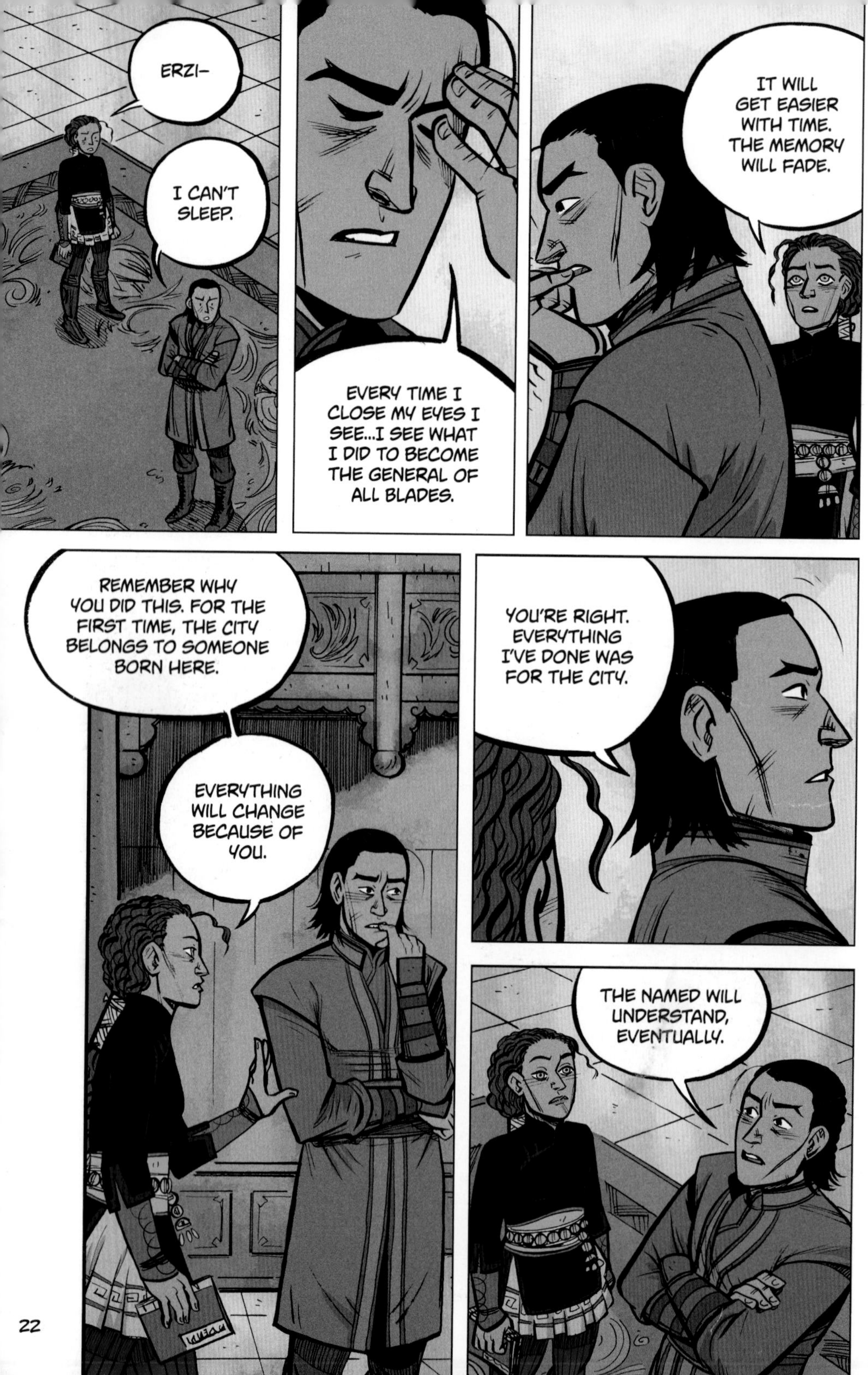
ERZI–
I CAN'T SLEEP.
EVERY TIME I CLOSE MY EYES I SEE...I SEE WHAT I DID TO BECOME THE GENERAL OF ALL BLADES.
IT WILL GET EASIER WITH TIME. THE MEMORY WILL FADE.
REMEMBER WHY YOU DID THIS. FOR THE FIRST TIME, THE CITY BELONGS TO SOMEONE BORN HERE.
EVERYTHING WILL CHANGE BECAUSE OF YOU.
YOU'RE RIGHT. EVERYTHING I'VE DONE WAS FOR THE CITY.
THE NAMED WILL UNDERSTAND, EVENTUALLY.

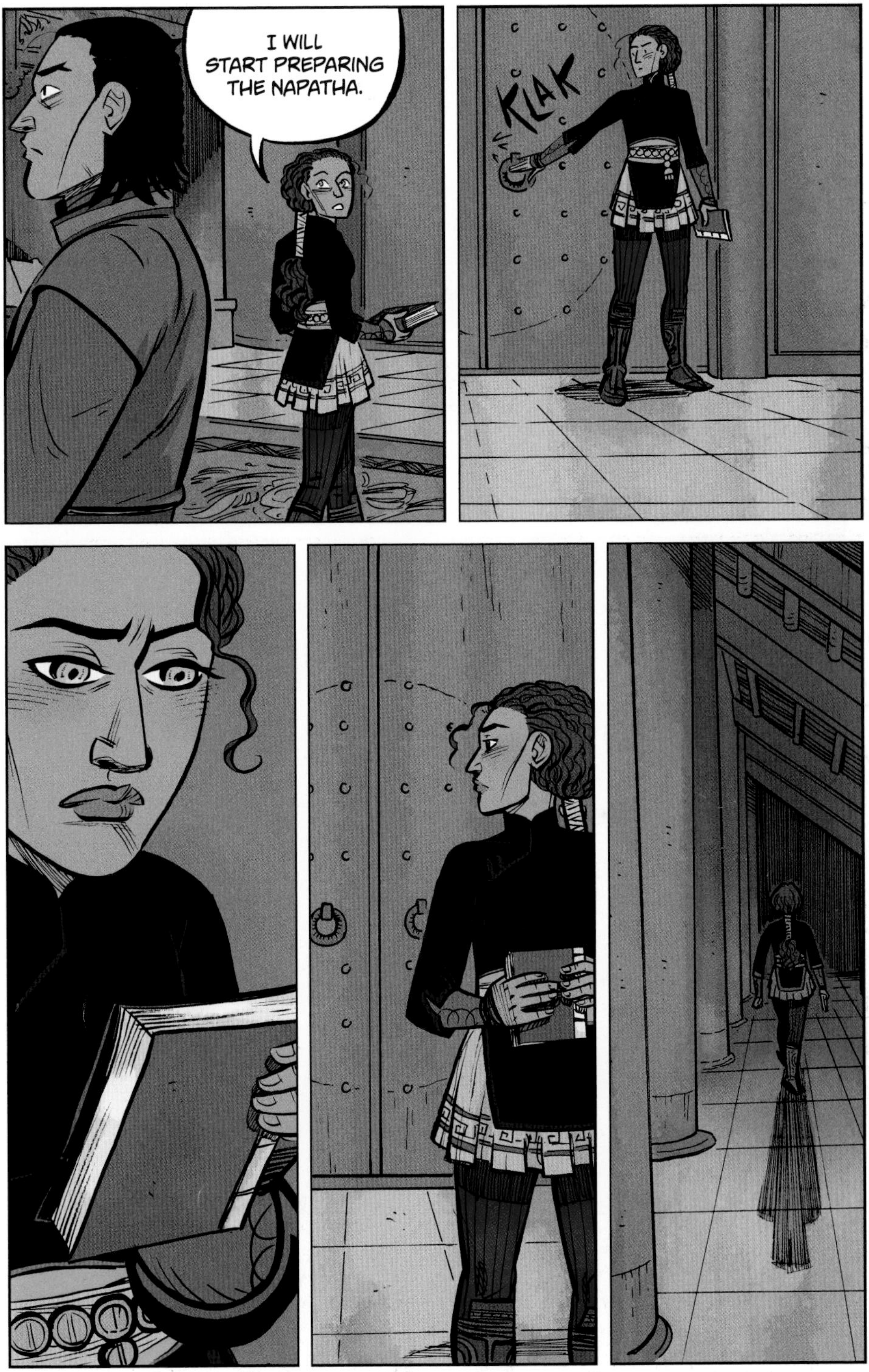
I WILL START PREPARING THE NAPATHA.
KLAK

DAY 2

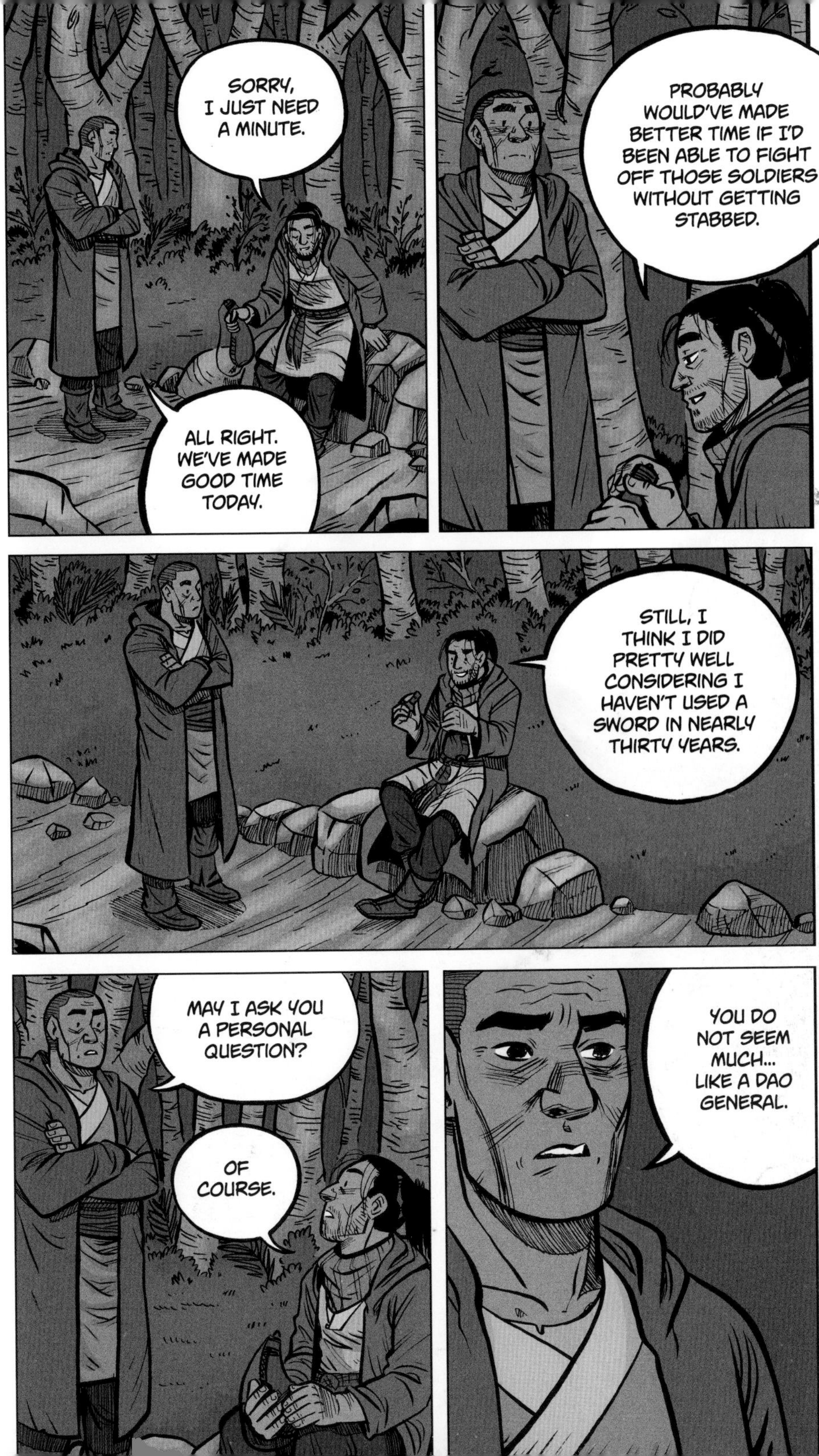
SORRY, I JUST NEED A MINUTE.
ALL RIGHT. WE'VE MADE GOOD TIME TODAY.
PROBABLY WOULD'VE MADE BETTER TIME IF I'D BEEN ABLE TO FIGHT OFF THOSE SOLDIERS WITHOUT GETTING STABBED.
STILL, I THINK I DID PRETTY WELL CONSIDERING I HAVEN'T USED A SWORD IN NEARLY THIRTY YEARS.
MAY I ASK YOU A PERSONAL QUESTION?
OF COURSE.
YOU DO NOT SEEM MUCH... LIKE A DAO GENERAL.

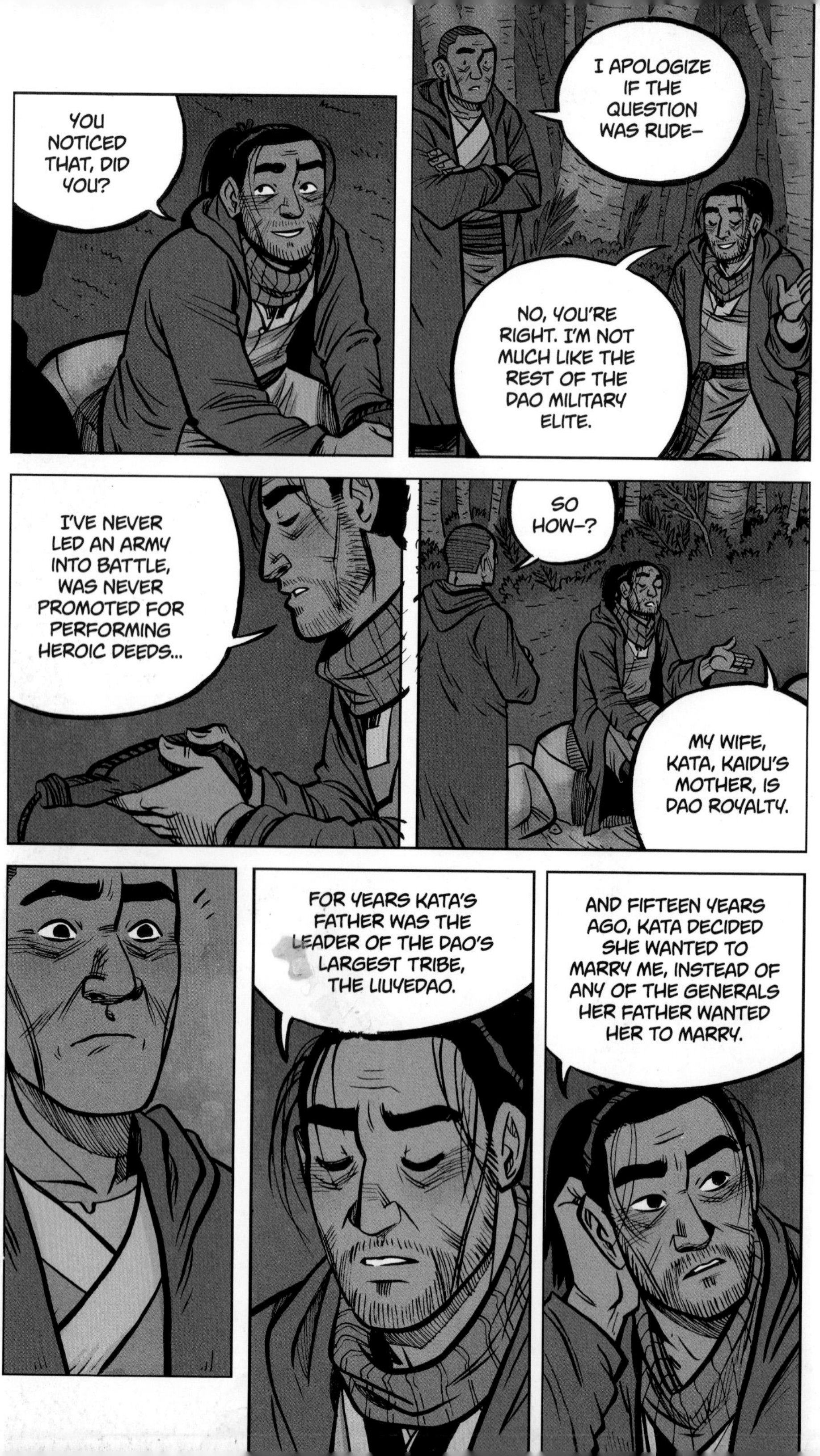
YOU NOTICED THAT, DID YOU?
I APOLOGIZE IF THE QUESTION WAS RUDE–
NO, YOU'RE RIGHT. I'M NOT MUCH LIKE THE REST OF THE DAO MILITARY ELITE.
I'VE NEVER LED AN ARMY INTO BATTLE, WAS NEVER PROMOTED FOR PERFORMING HEROIC DEEDS...
SO HOW–?
MY WIFE, KATA, KAIDU'S MOTHER, IS DAO ROYALTY.
FOR YEARS KATA'S FATHER WAS THE LEADER OF THE DAO'S LARGEST TRIBE, THE LIUYEDAO.
AND FIFTEEN YEARS AGO, KATA DECIDED SHE WANTED TO MARRY ME, INSTEAD OF ANY OF THE GENERALS HER FATHER WANTED HER TO MARRY.

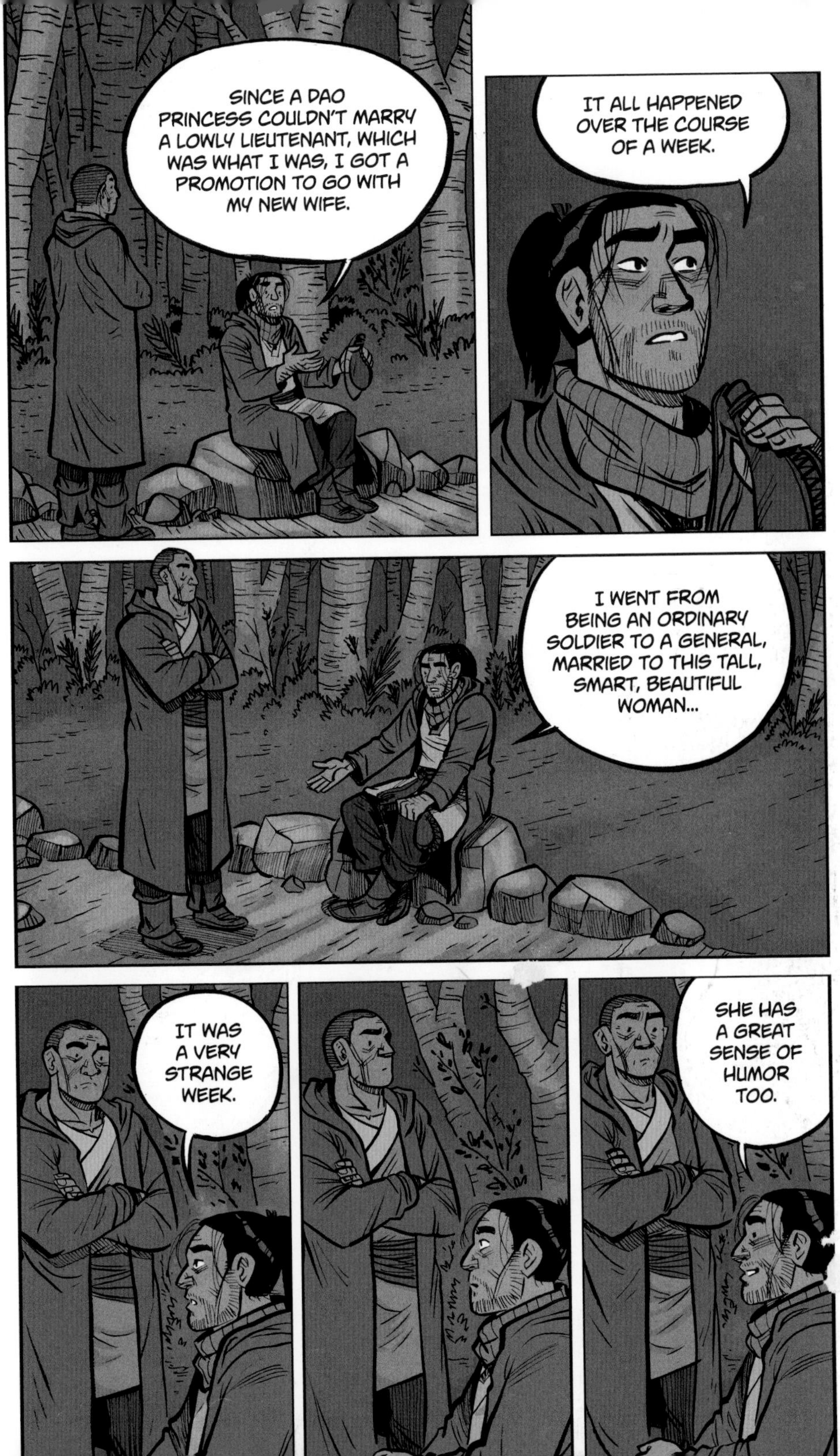
SINCE A DAO PRINCESS COULDN'T MARRY A LOWLY LIEUTENANT, WHICH WAS WHAT I WAS, I GOT A PROMOTION TO GO WITH MY NEW WIFE.
IT ALL HAPPENED OVER THE COURSE OF A WEEK.
I WENT FROM BEING AN ORDINARY SOLDIER TO A GENERAL, MARRIED TO THIS TALL, SMART, BEAUTIFUL WOMAN...
IT WAS A VERY STRANGE WEEK.
SHE HAS A GREAT SENSE OF HUMOR TOO.

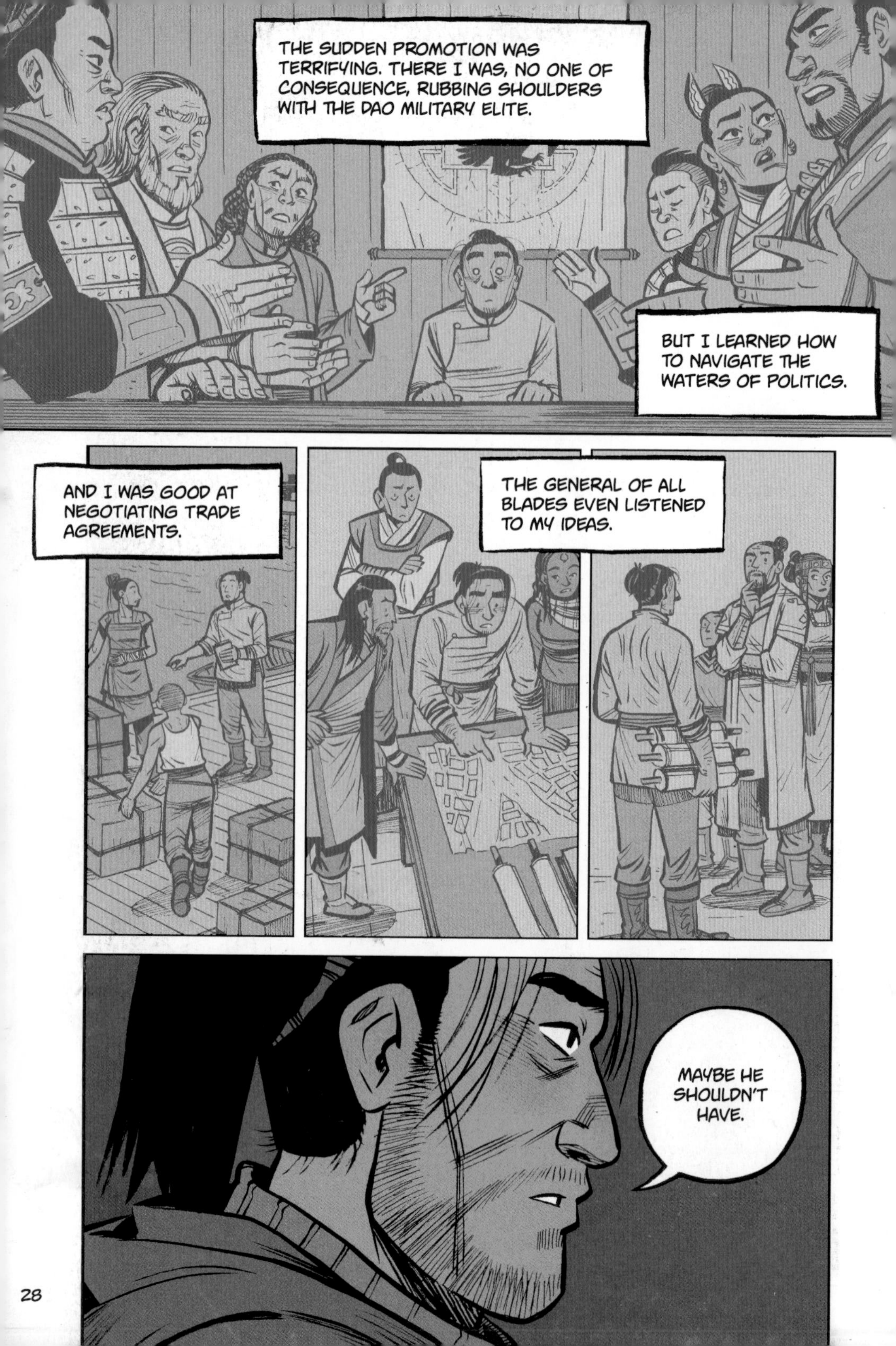
THE SUDDEN PROMOTION WAS TERRIFYING. THERE I WAS, NO ONE OF CONSEQUENCE, RUBBING SHOULDERS WITH THE DAO MILITARY ELITE.
BUT I LEARNED HOW TO NAVIGATE THE WATERS OF POLITICS.
AND I WAS GOOD AT NEGOTIATING TRADE AGREEMENTS.
THE GENERAL OF ALL BLADES EVEN LISTENED TO MY IDEAS.
MAYBE HE SHOULDN'T HAVE.

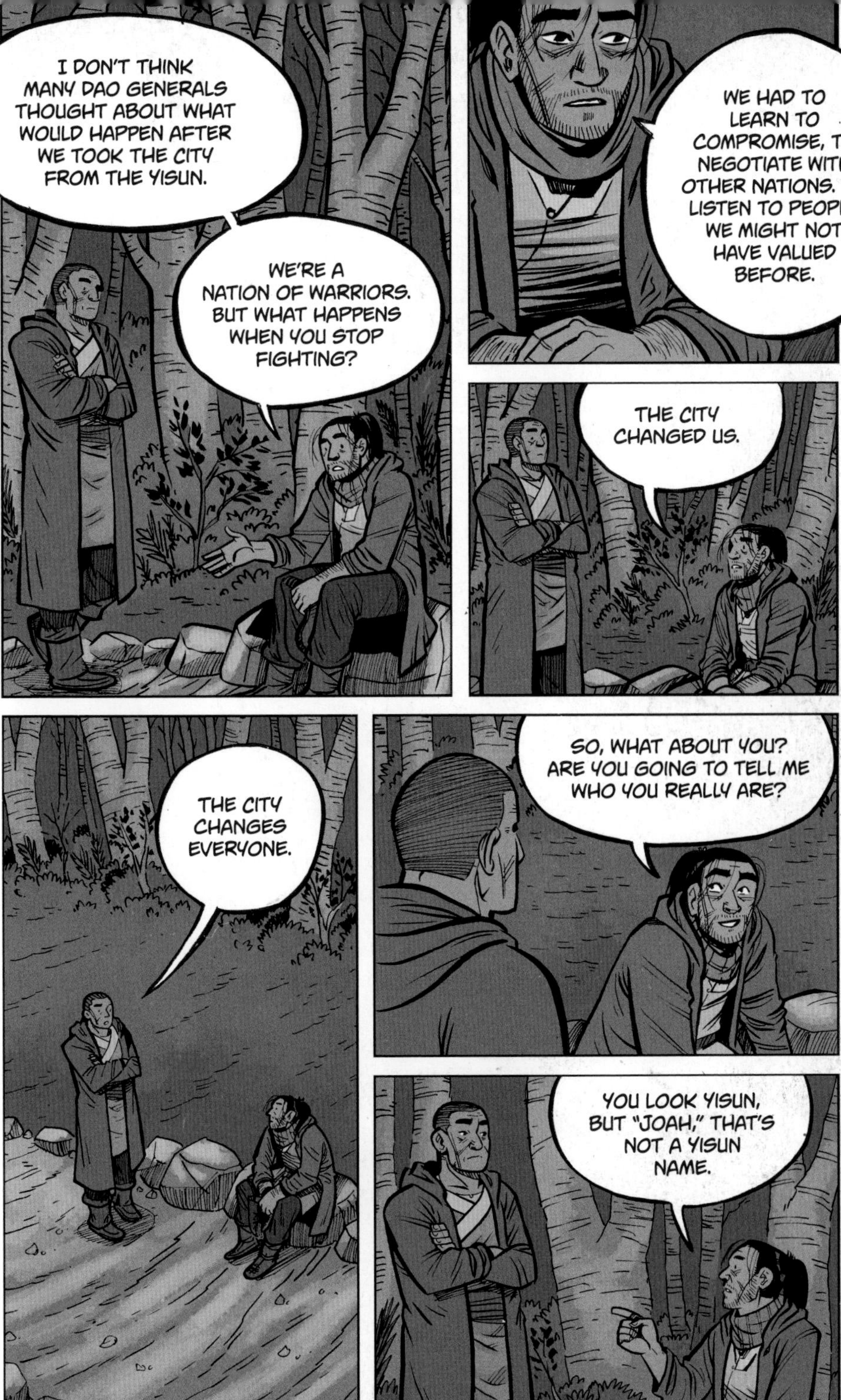
I DON'T THINK MANY DAO GENERALS THOUGHT ABOUT WHAT WOULD HAPPEN AFTER WE TOOK THE CITY FROM THE YISUN.
WE'RE A NATION OF WARRIORS. BUT WHAT HAPPENS WHEN YOU STOP FIGHTING?
WE HAD TO LEARN TO COMPROMISE, TO NEGOTIATE WITH OTHER NATIONS. TO LISTEN TO PEOPLE WE MIGHT NOT HAVE VALUED BEFORE.
THE CITY CHANGED US.
THE CITY CHANGES EVERYONE.
SO, WHAT ABOUT YOU? ARE YOU GOING TO TELL ME WHO YOU REALLY ARE?
YOU LOOK YISUN, BUT "JOAH," THAT'S NOT A YISUN NAME.

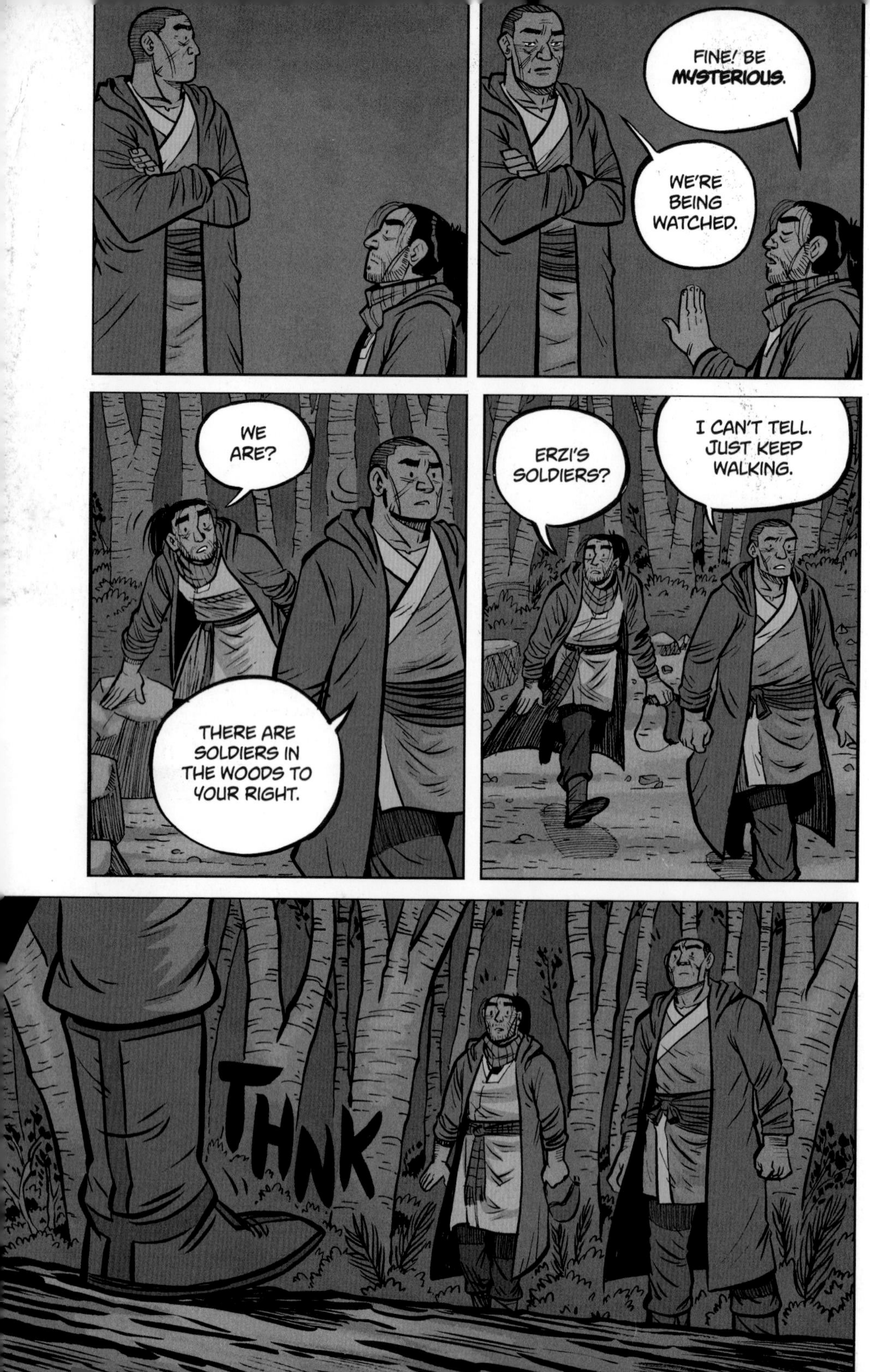
FINE! BE MYSTERIOUS.
WE'RE BEING WATCHED.
WE ARE?
THERE ARE SOLDIERS IN THE WOODS TO YOUR RIGHT.
ERZI'S SOLDIERS?
I CAN'T TELL. JUST KEEP WALKING.
THNK

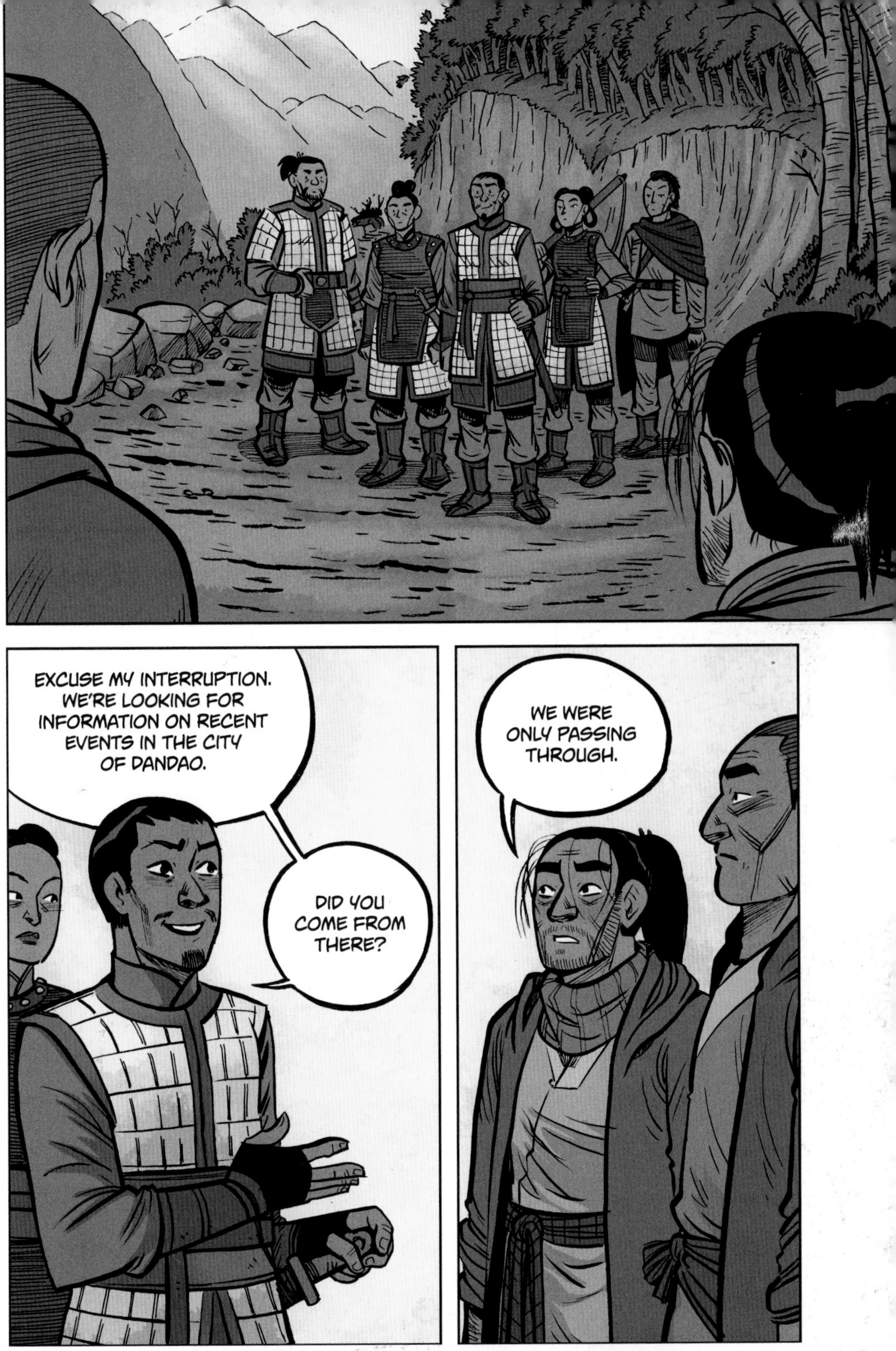
EXCUSE MY INTERRUPTION. WE'RE LOOKING FOR INFORMATION ON RECENT EVENTS IN THE CITY OF DANDAO.
DID YOU COME FROM THERE?
WE WERE ONLY PASSING THROUGH.

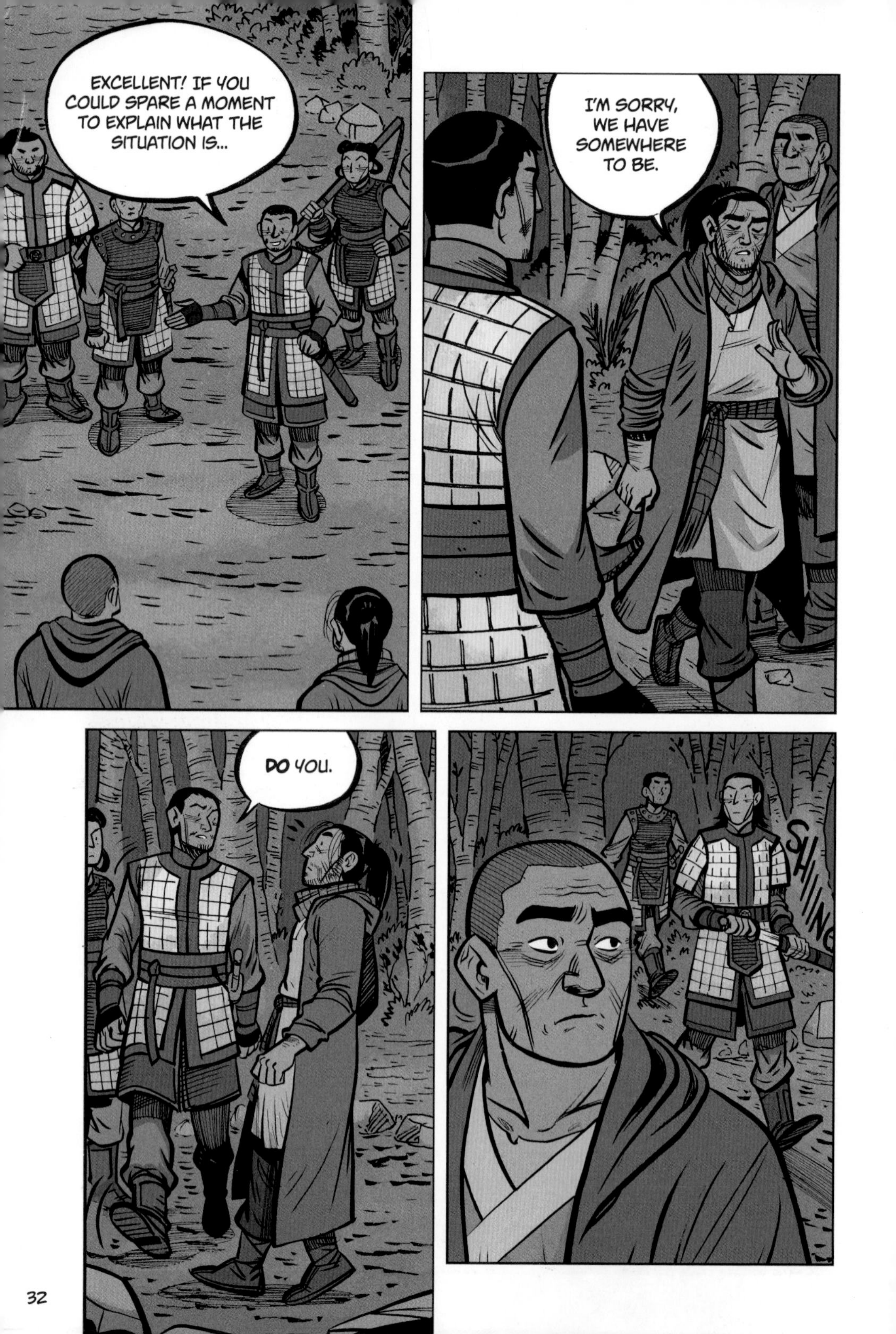
EXCELLENT! IF YOU COULD SPARE A MOMENT TO EXPLAIN WHAT THE SITUATION IS...
I'M SORRY, WE HAVE SOMEWHERE TO BE.
DO YOU.
SHING

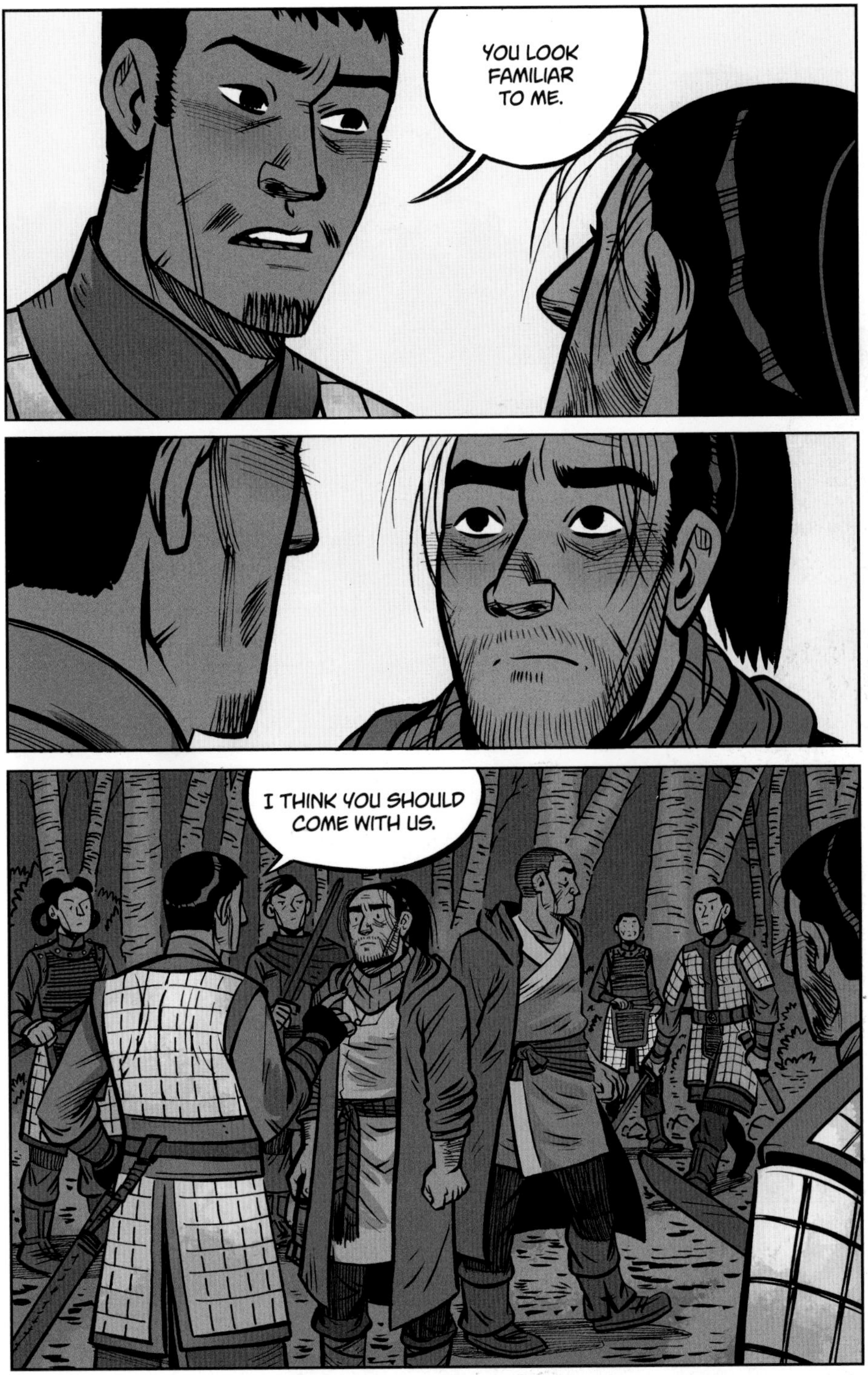
YOU LOOK FAMILIAR TO ME.
I THINK YOU SHOULD COME WITH US.

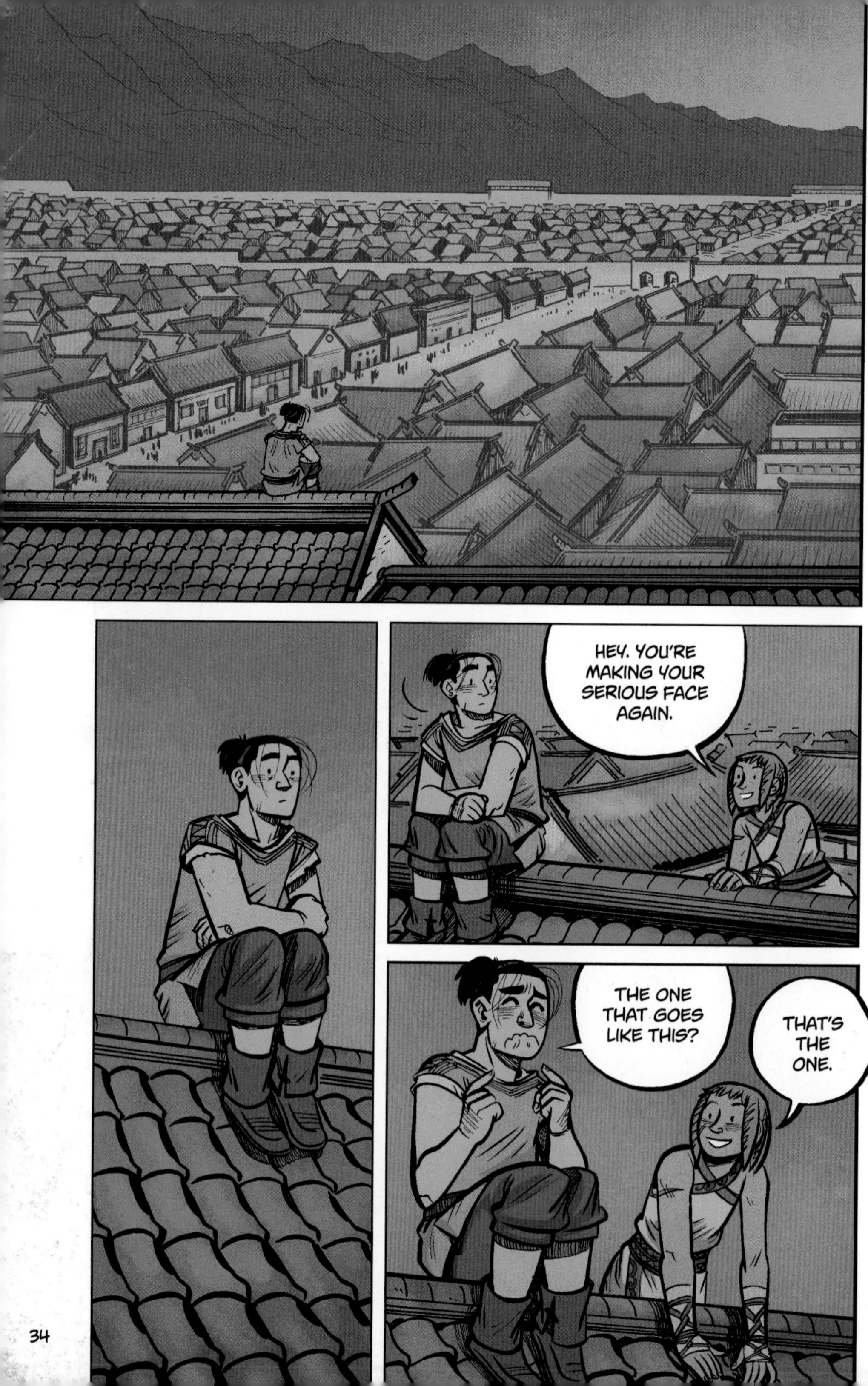
HEY. YOU'RE MAKING YOUR SERIOUS FACE AGAIN.
THE ONE THAT GOES LIKE THIS?
THAT'S THE ONE.

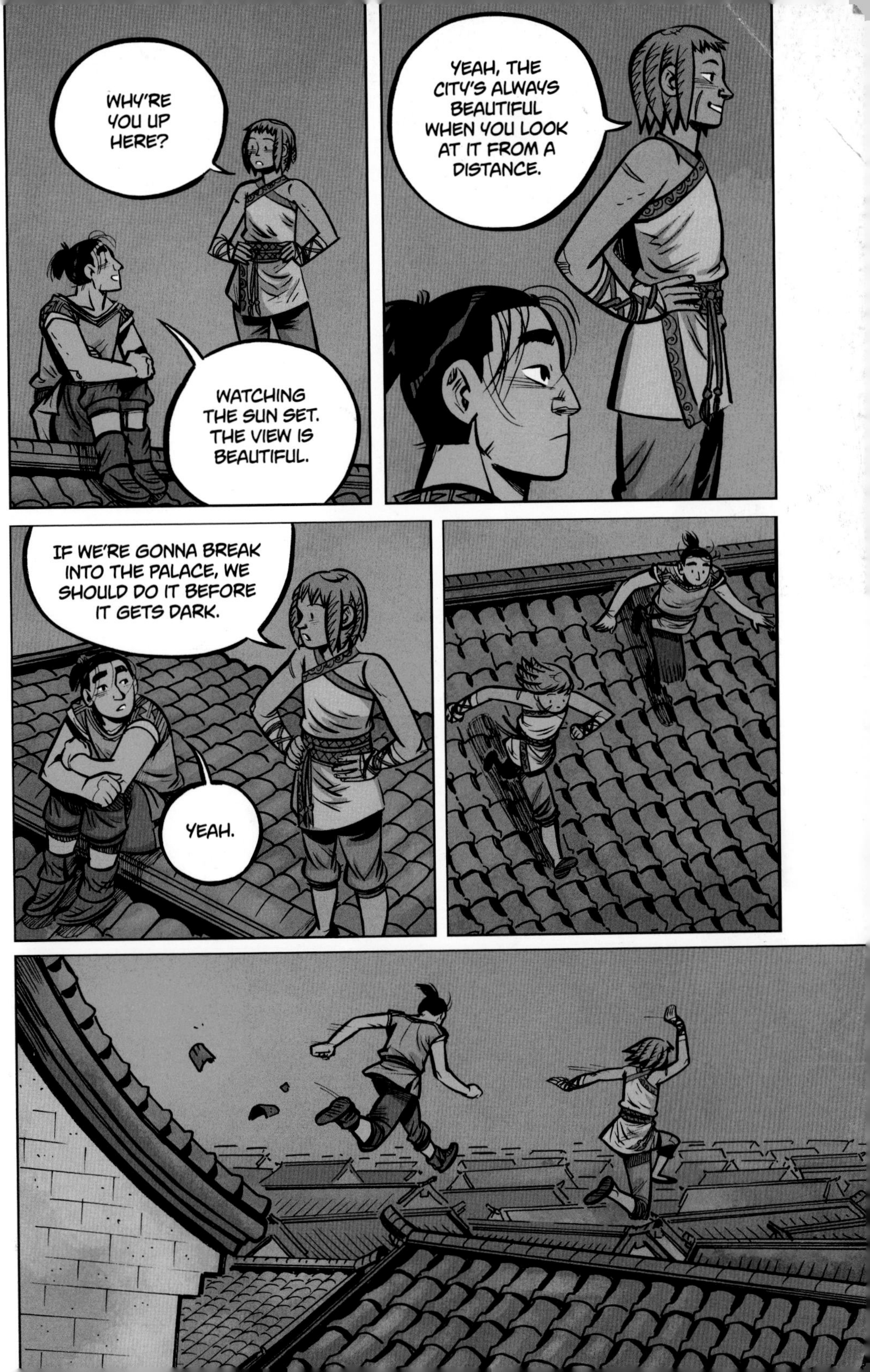
WHY'RE YOU UP HERE?
WATCHING THE SUN SET. THE VIEW IS BEAUTIFUL.
YEAH, THE CITY'S ALWAYS BEAUTIFUL WHEN YOU LOOK AT IT FROM A DISTANCE.
IF WE'RE GONNA BREAK INTO THE PALACE, WE SHOULD DO IT BEFORE IT GETS DARK.
YEAH.

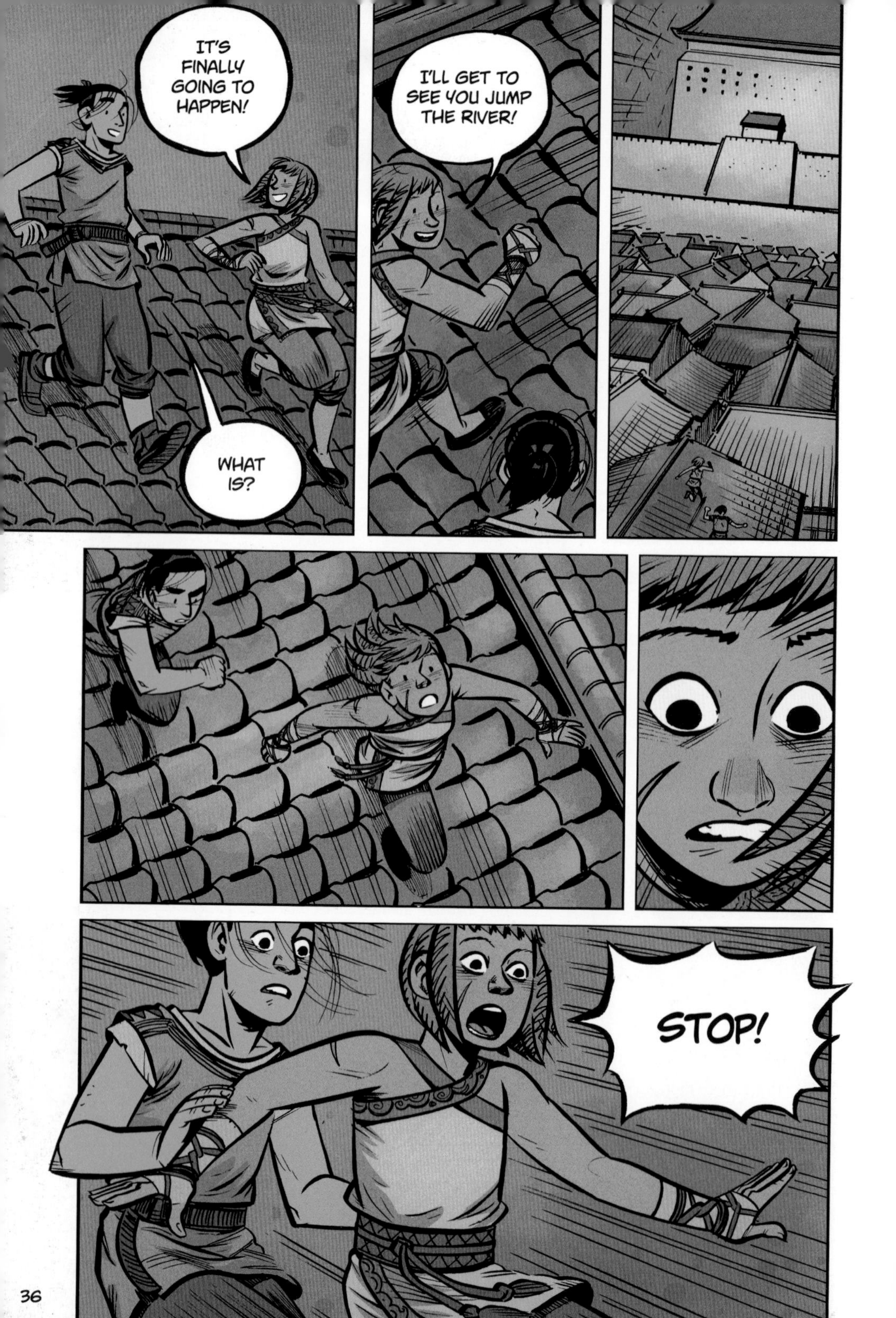
IT'S FINALLY GOING TO HAPPEN!
WHAT IS?
I'LL GET TO SEE YOU JUMP THE RIVER!
STOP!

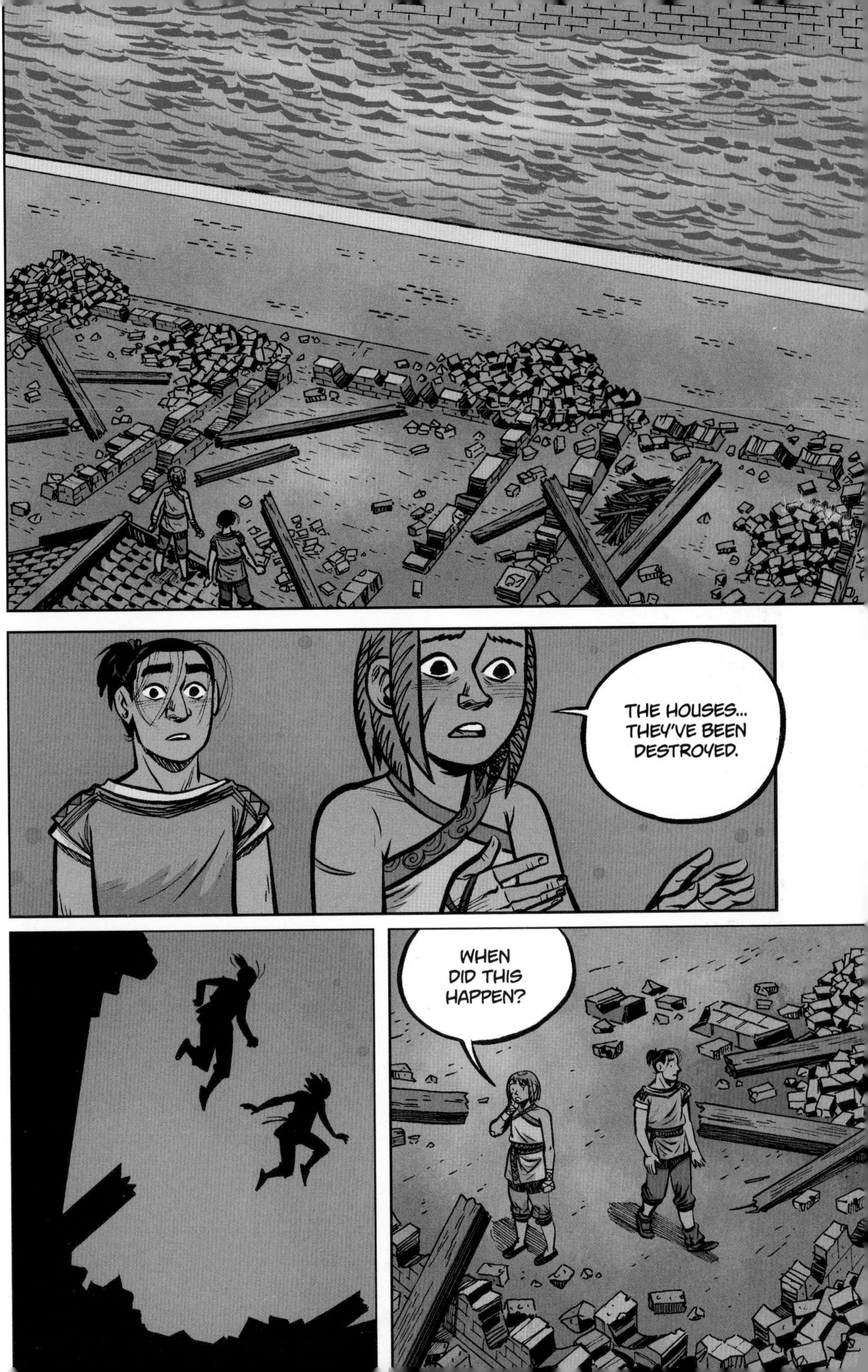
THE HOUSES... THEY'VE BEEN DESTROYED.
WHEN DID THIS HAPPEN?

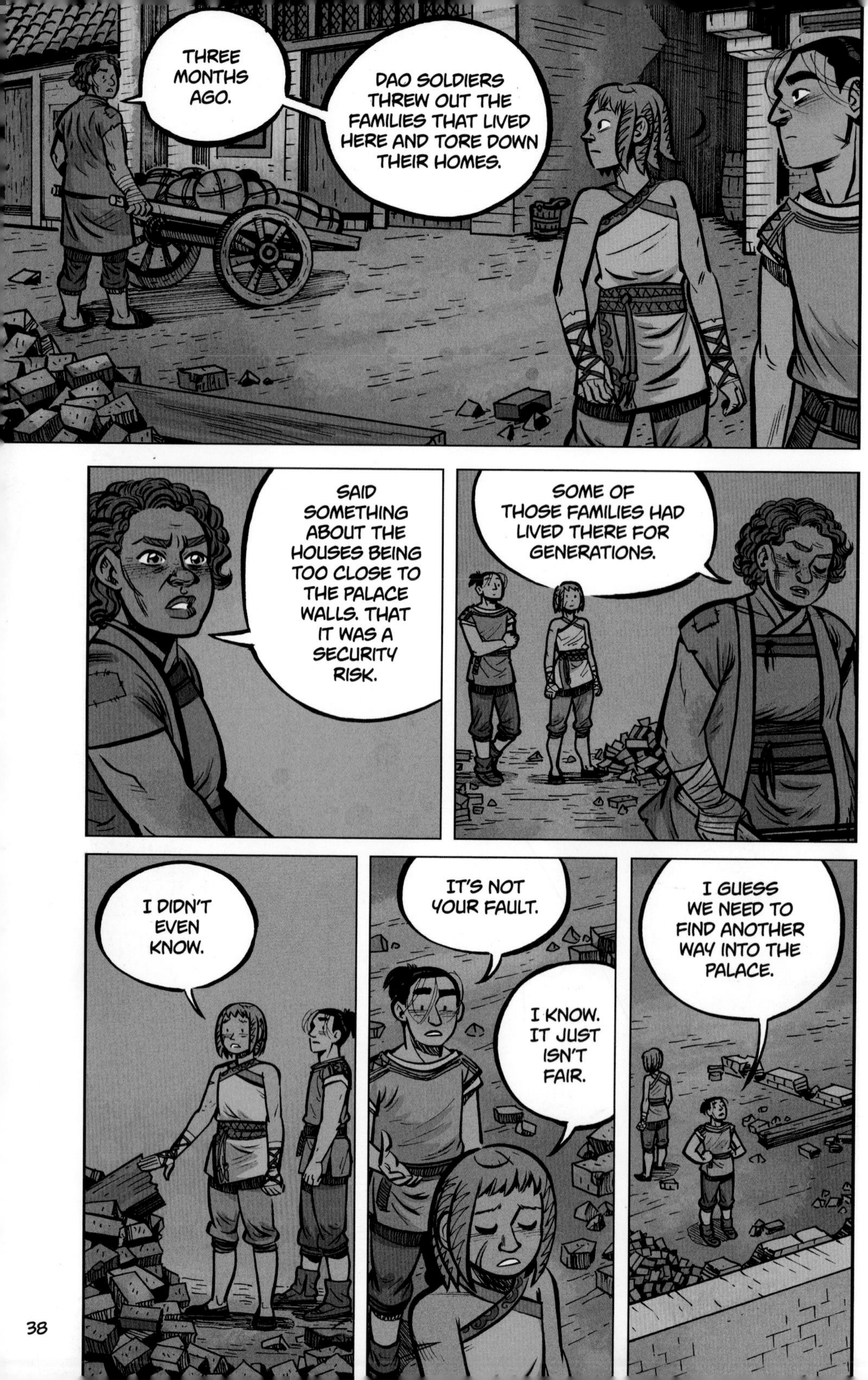
THREE MONTHS AGO.
DAO SOLDIERS THREW OUT THE FAMILIES THAT LIVED HERE AND TORE DOWN THEIR HOMES.
SAID SOMETHING ABOUT THE HOUSES BEING TOO CLOSE TO THE PALACE WALLS. THAT IT WAS A SECURITY RISK.
SOME OF THOSE FAMILIES HAD LIVED THERE FOR GENERATIONS.
I DIDN'T EVEN KNOW.
IT'S NOT YOUR FAULT.
I KNOW. IT JUST ISN'T FAIR.
I GUESS WE NEED TO FIND ANOTHER WAY INTO THE PALACE.

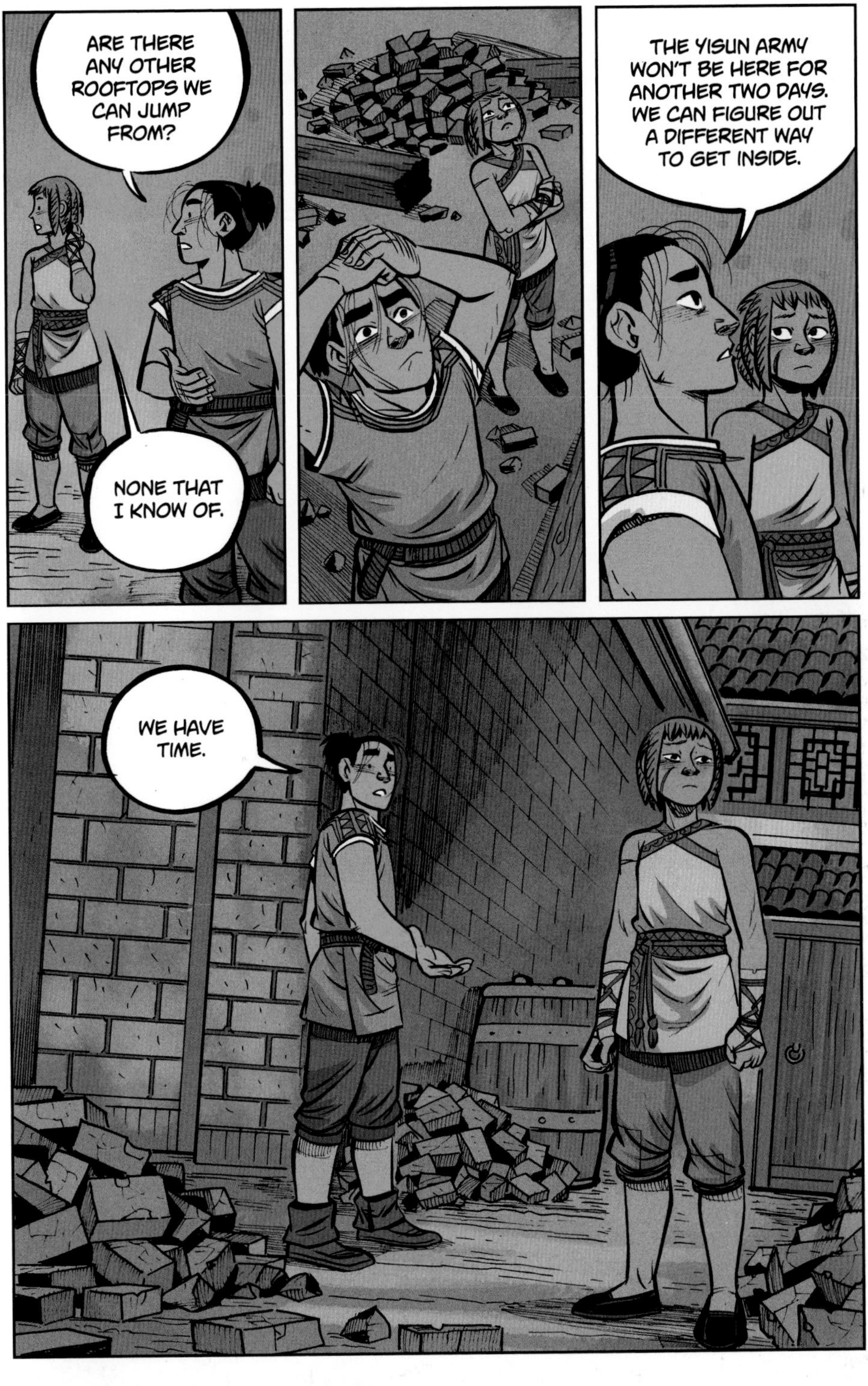
ARE THERE ANY OTHER ROOFTOPS WE CAN JUMP FROM?
NONE THAT I KNOW OF.
THE YISUN ARMY WON'T BE HERE FOR ANOTHER TWO DAYS. WE CAN FIGURE OUT A DIFFERENT WAY TO GET INSIDE.
WE HAVE TIME.

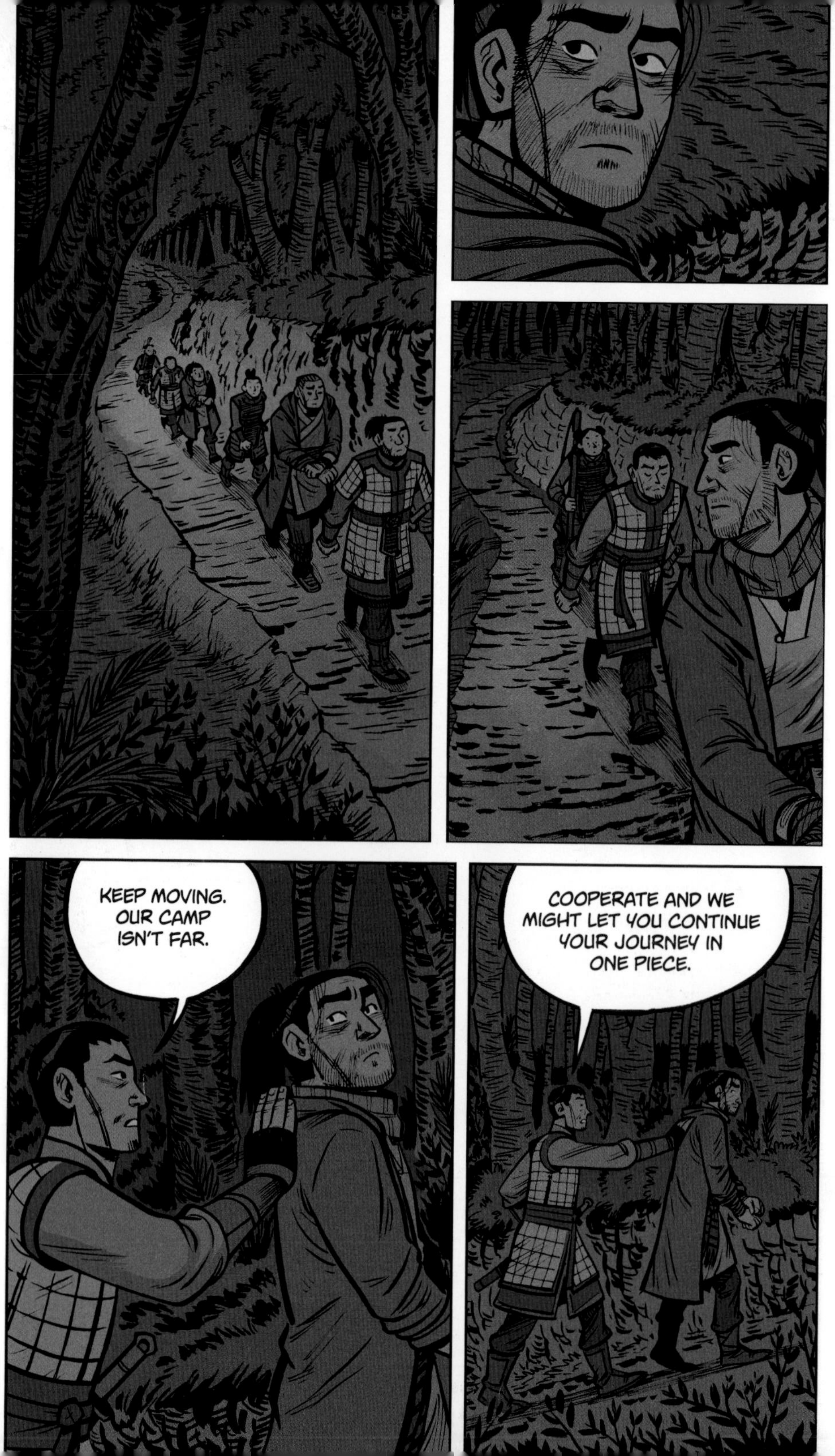
KEEP MOVING. OUR CAMP ISN'T FAR.
COOPERATE AND WE MIGHT LET YOU CONTINUE YOUR JOURNEY IN ONE PIECE.

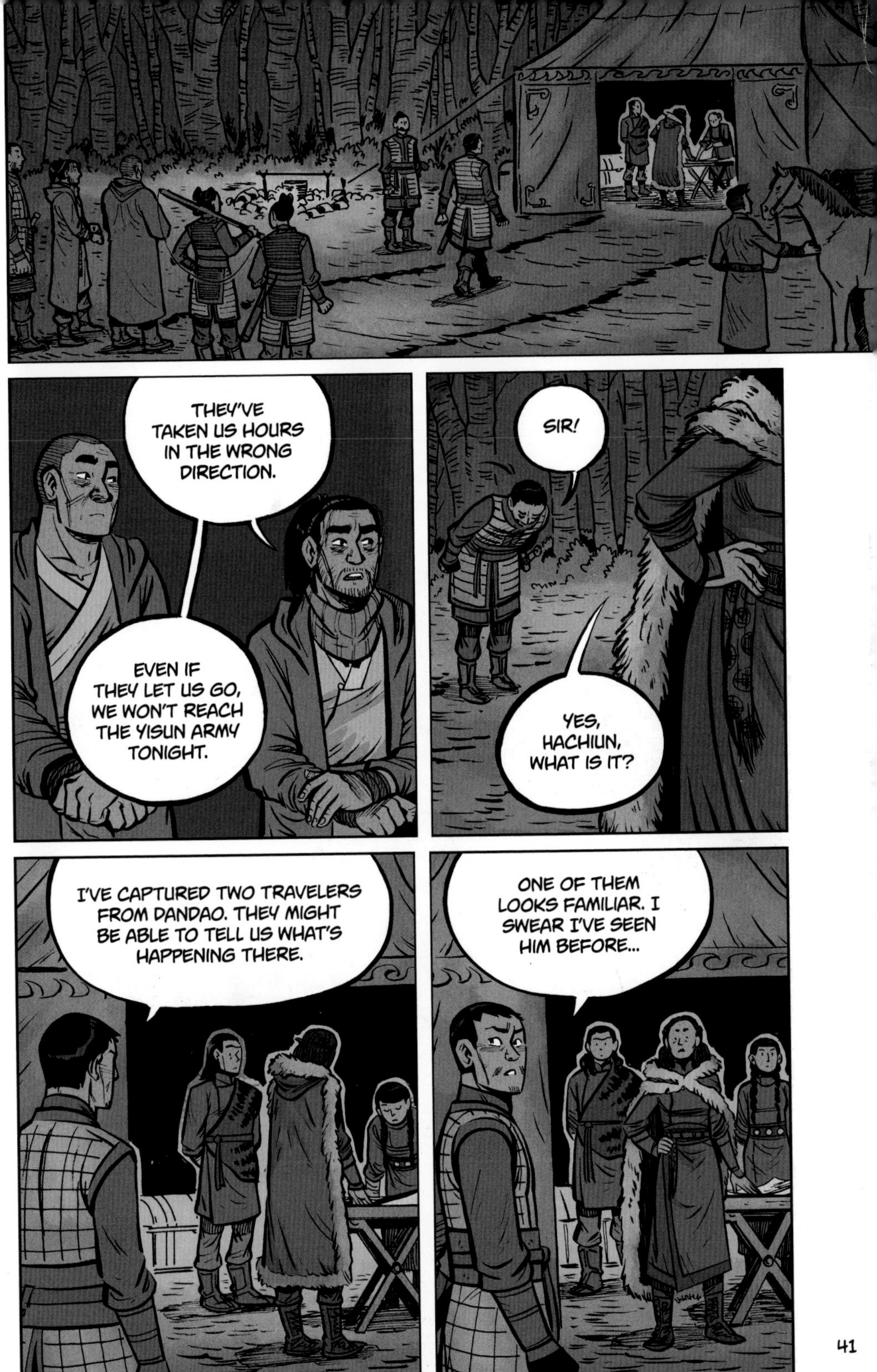
THEY'VE TAKEN US HOURS IN THE WRONG DIRECTION.
EVEN IF THEY LET US GO, WE WON'T REACH THE YISUN ARMY TONIGHT.
SIR!
YES, HACHIUN, WHAT IS IT?
I'VE CAPTURED TWO TRAVELERS FROM DANDAO. THEY MIGHT BE ABLE TO TELL US WHAT'S HAPPENING THERE.
ONE OF THEM LOOKS FAMILIAR. I SWEAR I'VE SEEN HIM BEFORE...

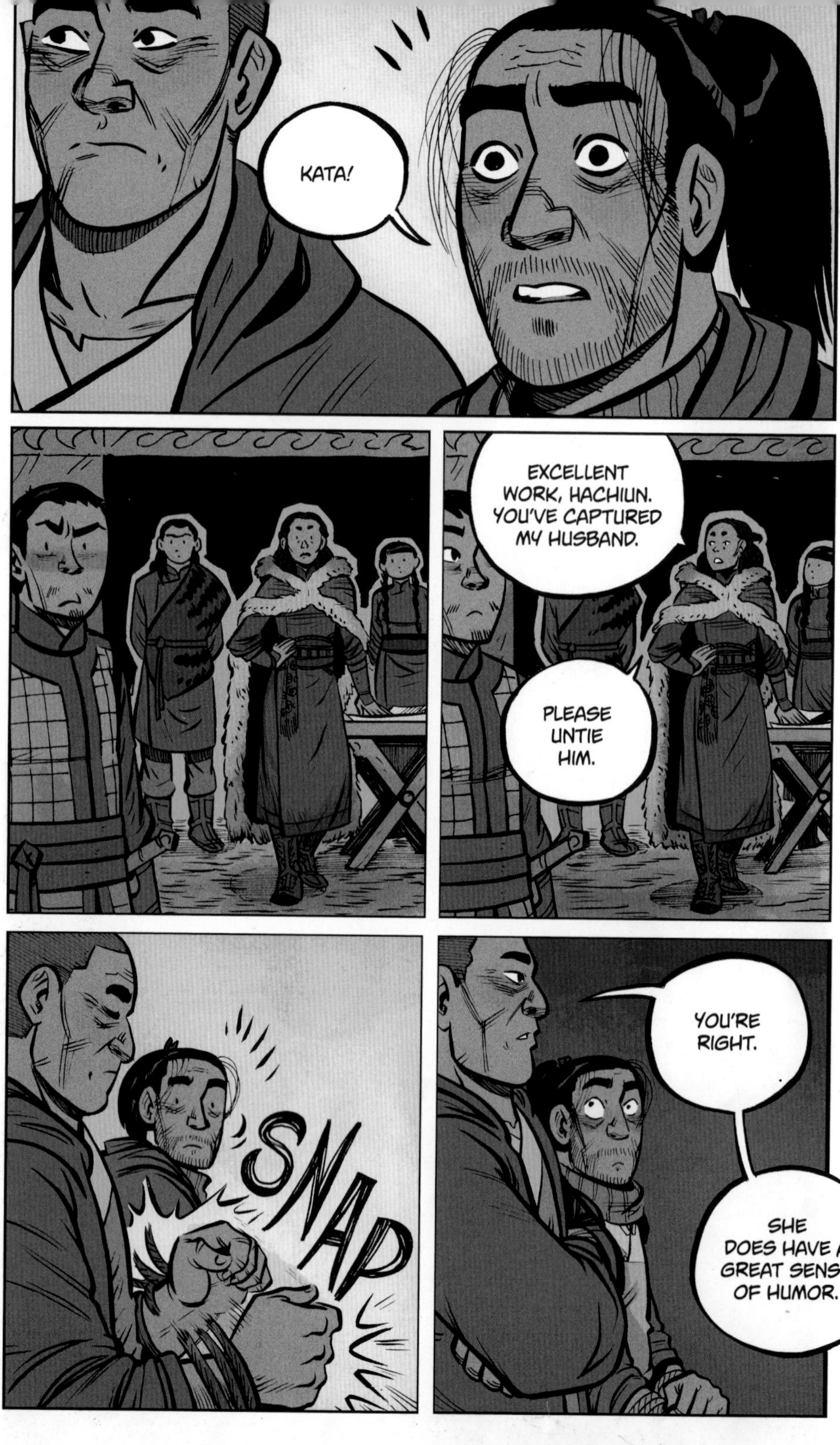
KATA!
EXCELLENT WORK, HACHIUN. YOU'VE CAPTURED MY HUSBAND.
PLEASE UNTIE HIM.
SNAP
YOU'RE RIGHT.
SHE DOES HAVE A GREAT SENSE OF HUMOR.

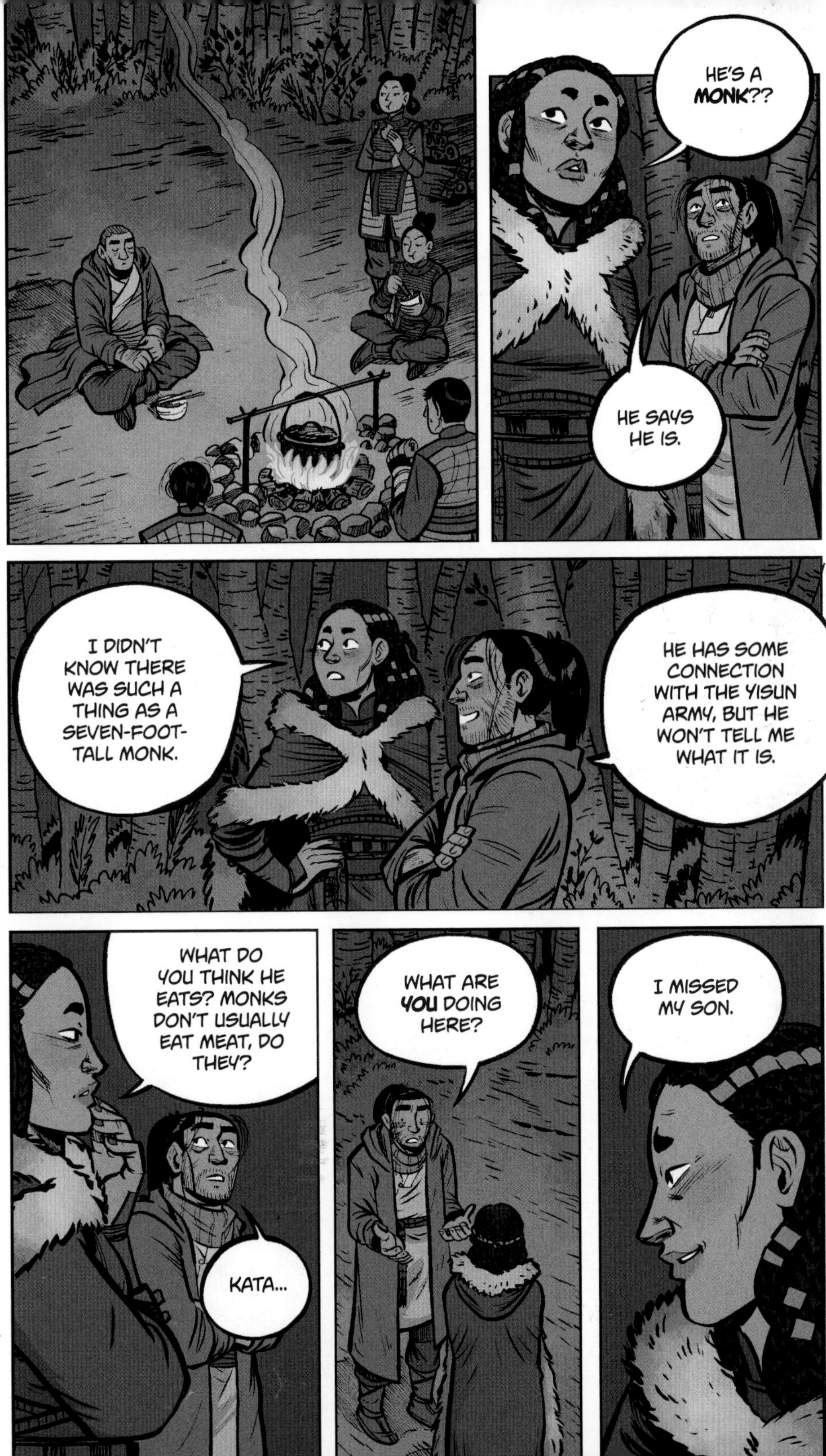
HE'S A **MONK**??
HE SAYS HE IS.
I DIDN'T KNOW THERE WAS SUCH A THING AS A SEVEN-FOOT-TALL MONK.
HE HAS SOME CONNECTION WITH THE YISUN ARMY, BUT HE WON'T TELL ME WHAT IT IS.
WHAT DO YOU THINK HE EATS? MONKS DON'T USUALLY EAT MEAT, DO THEY?
KATA...
WHAT ARE **YOU** DOING HERE?
I MISSED MY SON.

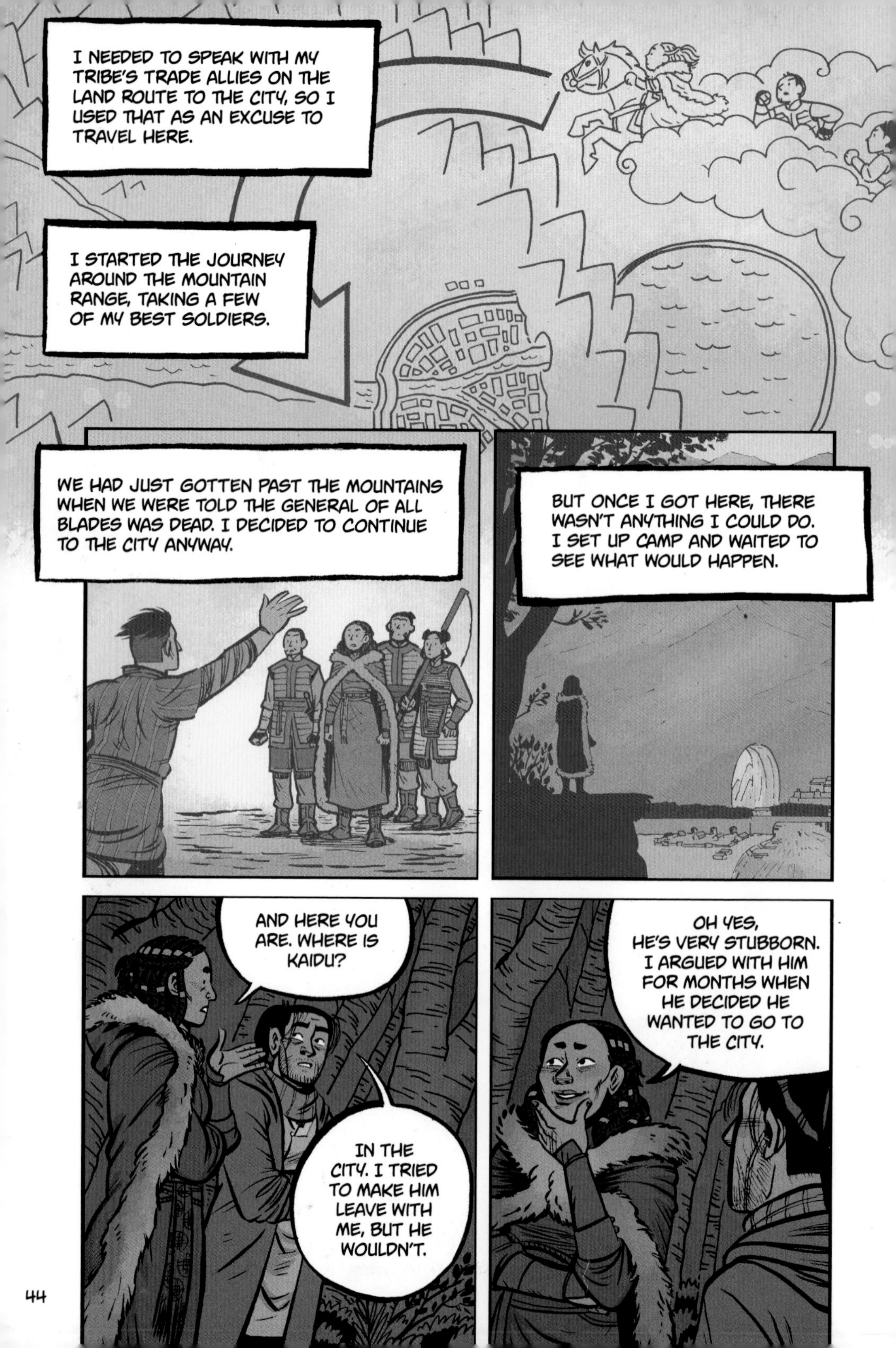
I NEEDED TO SPEAK WITH MY TRIBE'S TRADE ALLIES ON THE LAND ROUTE TO THE CITY, SO I USED THAT AS AN EXCUSE TO TRAVEL HERE.
I STARTED THE JOURNEY AROUND THE MOUNTAIN RANGE, TAKING A FEW OF MY BEST SOLDIERS.
WE HAD JUST GOTTEN PAST THE MOUNTAINS WHEN WE WERE TOLD THE GENERAL OF ALL BLADES WAS DEAD. I DECIDED TO CONTINUE TO THE CITY ANYWAY.
BUT ONCE I GOT HERE, THERE WASN'T ANYTHING I COULD DO. I SET UP CAMP AND WAITED TO SEE WHAT WOULD HAPPEN.
AND HERE YOU ARE. WHERE IS KAIDU?
IN THE CITY. I TRIED TO MAKE HIM LEAVE WITH ME, BUT HE WOULDN'T.
OH YES, HE'S VERY STUBBORN. I ARGUED WITH HIM FOR MONTHS WHEN HE DECIDED HE WANTED TO GO TO THE CITY.

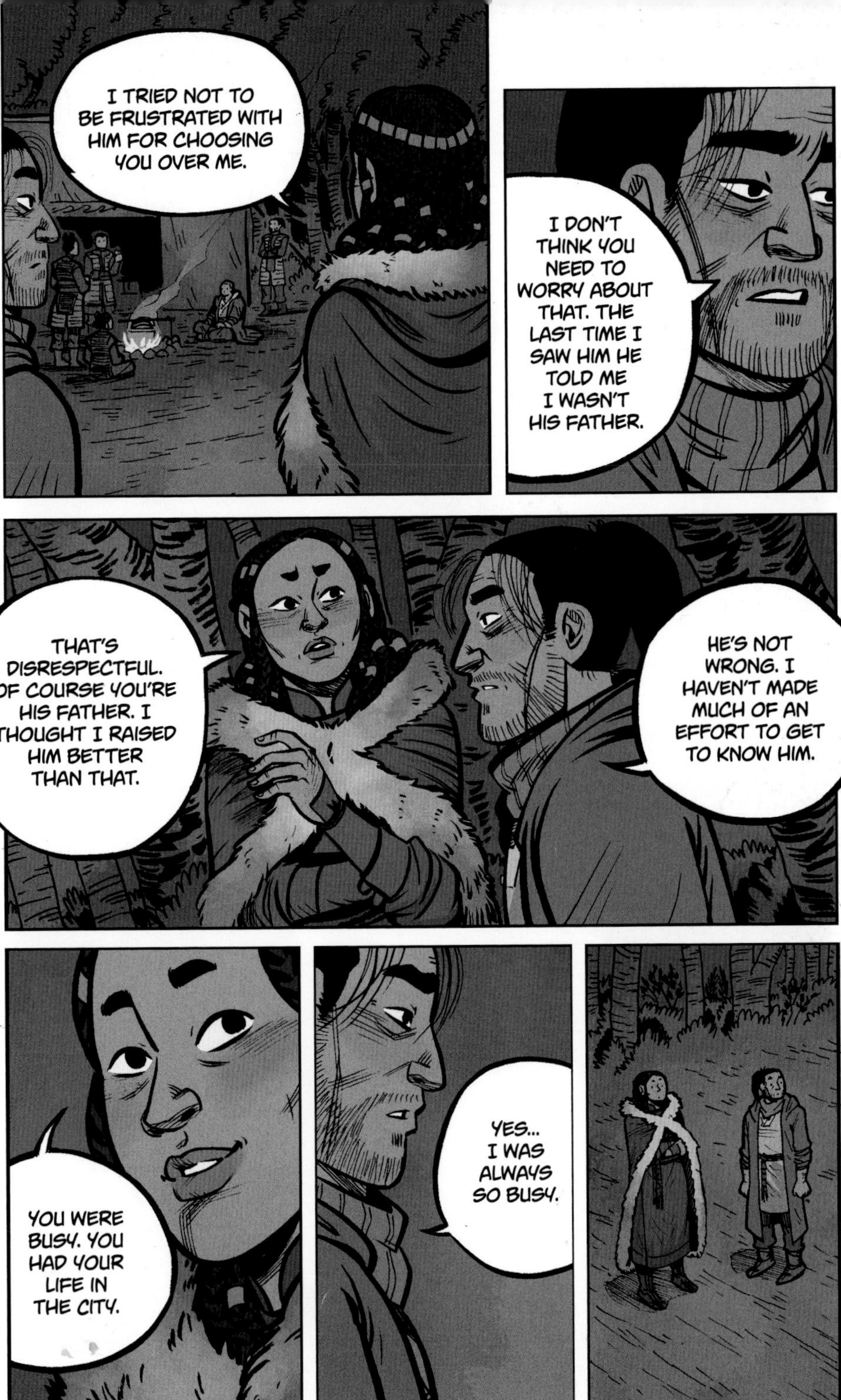
I TRIED NOT TO BE FRUSTRATED WITH HIM FOR CHOOSING YOU OVER ME.
I DON'T THINK YOU NEED TO WORRY ABOUT THAT. THE LAST TIME I SAW HIM HE TOLD ME I WASN'T HIS FATHER.
THAT'S DISRESPECTFUL. OF COURSE YOU'RE HIS FATHER. I THOUGHT I RAISED HIM BETTER THAN THAT.
HE'S NOT WRONG. I HAVEN'T MADE MUCH OF AN EFFORT TO GET TO KNOW HIM.
YOU WERE BUSY. YOU HAD YOUR LIFE IN THE CITY.
YES... I WAS ALWAYS SO BUSY.

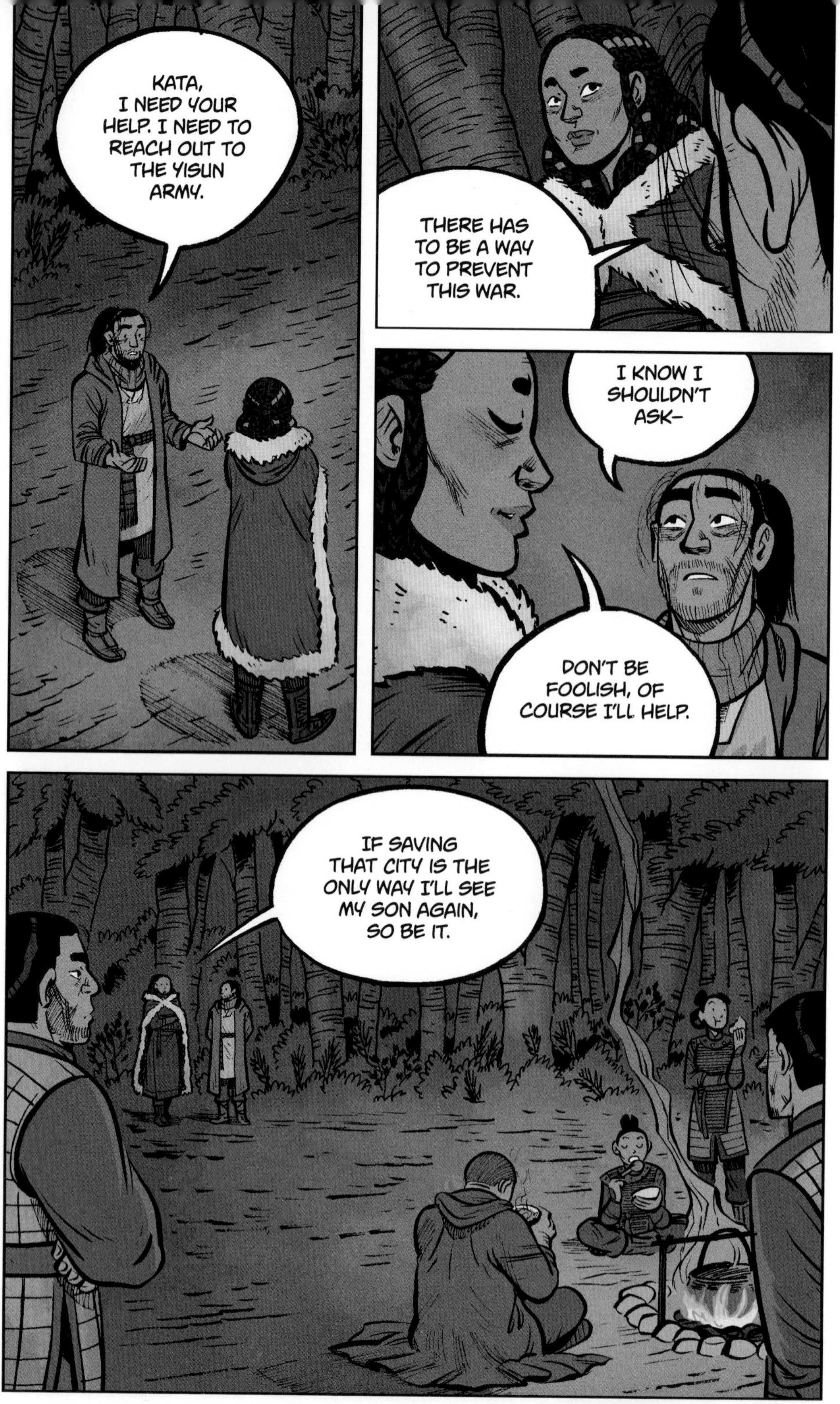
KATA, I NEED YOUR HELP. I NEED TO REACH OUT TO THE YISUN ARMY.
THERE HAS TO BE A WAY TO PREVENT THIS WAR.
I KNOW I SHOULDN'T ASK–
DON'T BE FOOLISH, OF COURSE I'LL HELP.
IF SAVING THAT CITY IS THE ONLY WAY I'LL SEE MY SON AGAIN, SO BE IT.

DAY 3

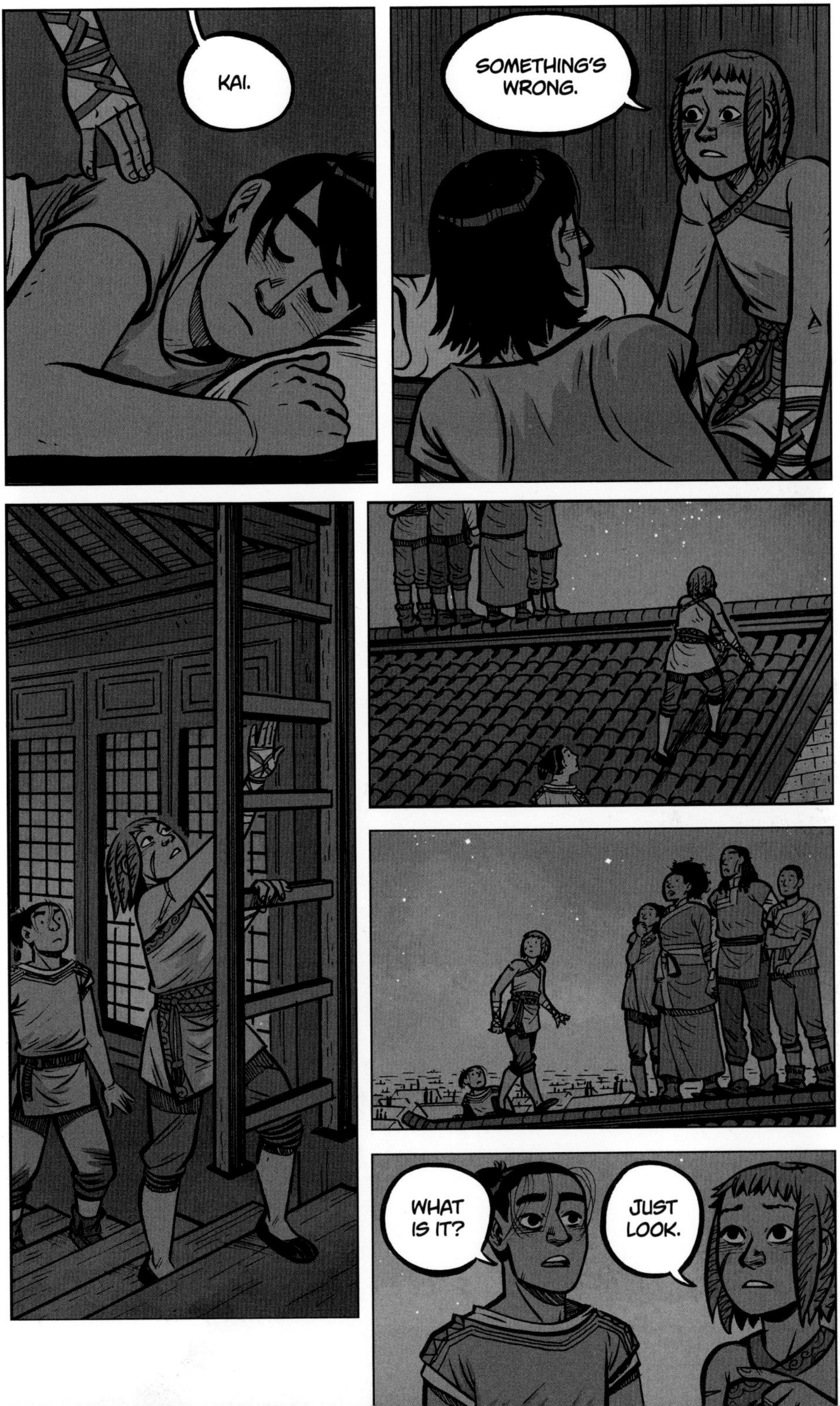
KAI.
SOMETHING'S WRONG.
WHAT IS IT?
JUST LOOK.

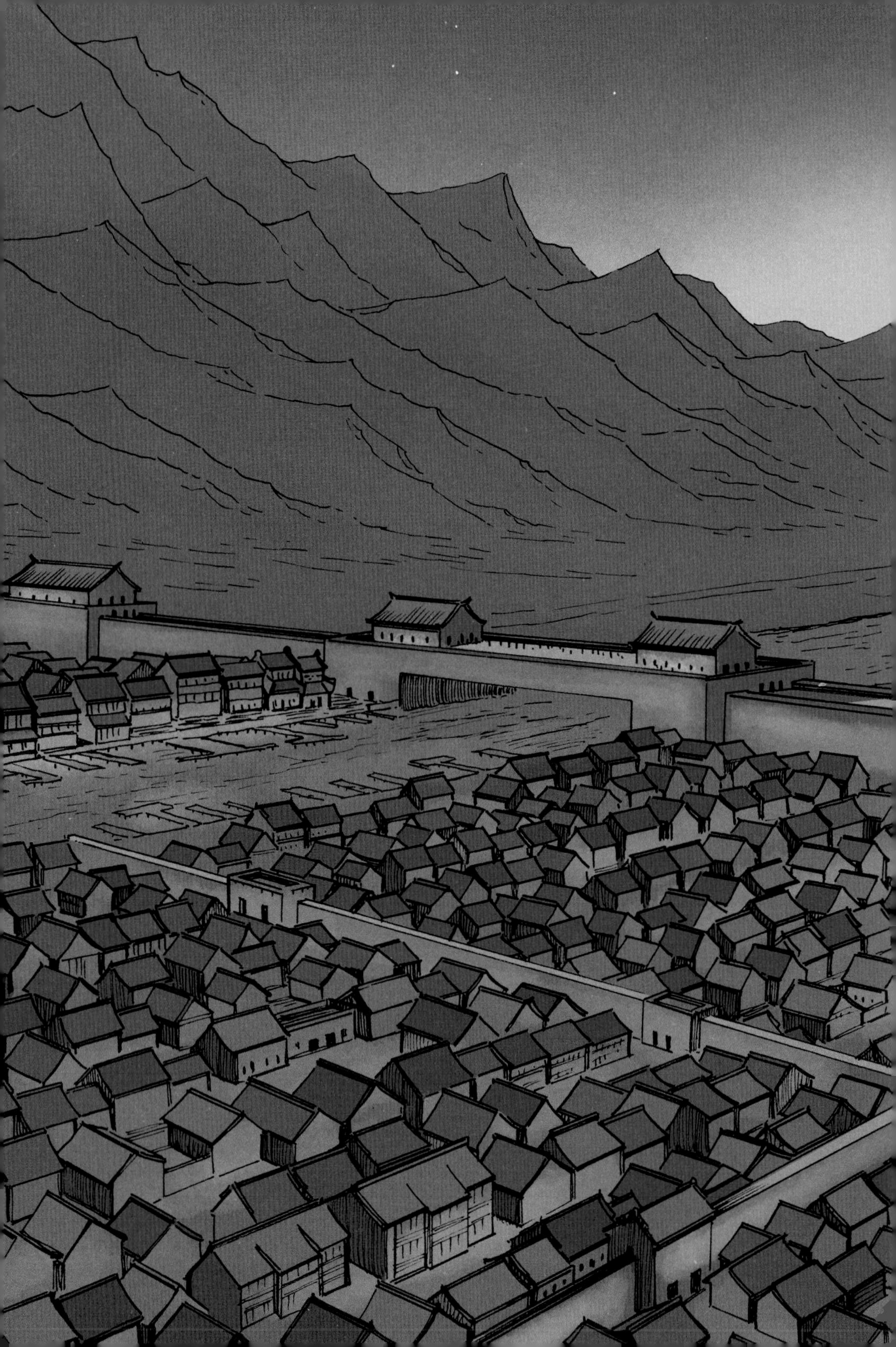

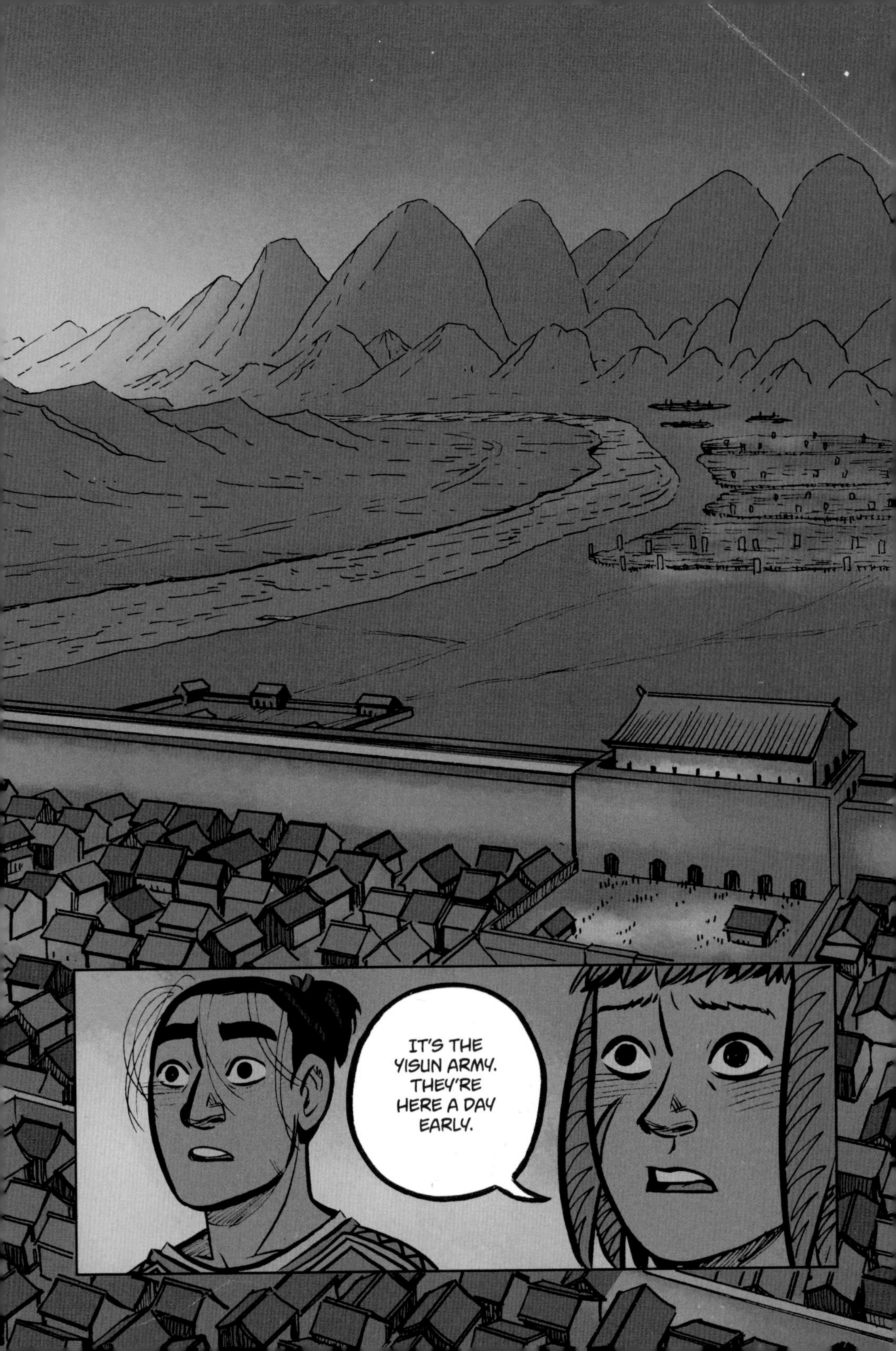
IT'S THE YISUN ARMY. THEY'RE HERE A DAY EARLY.

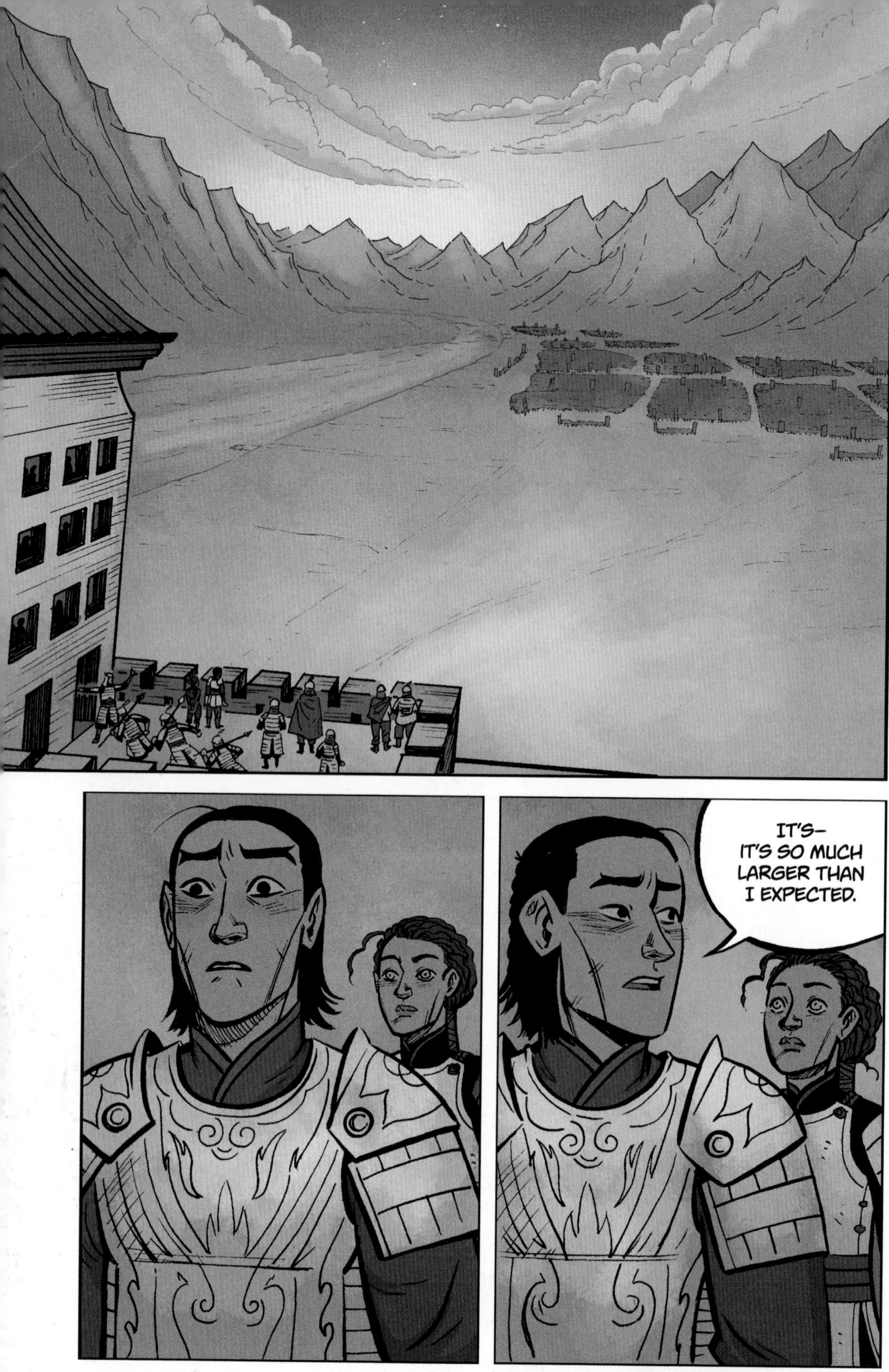
IT'S—
IT'S SO MUCH LARGER THAN I EXPECTED.

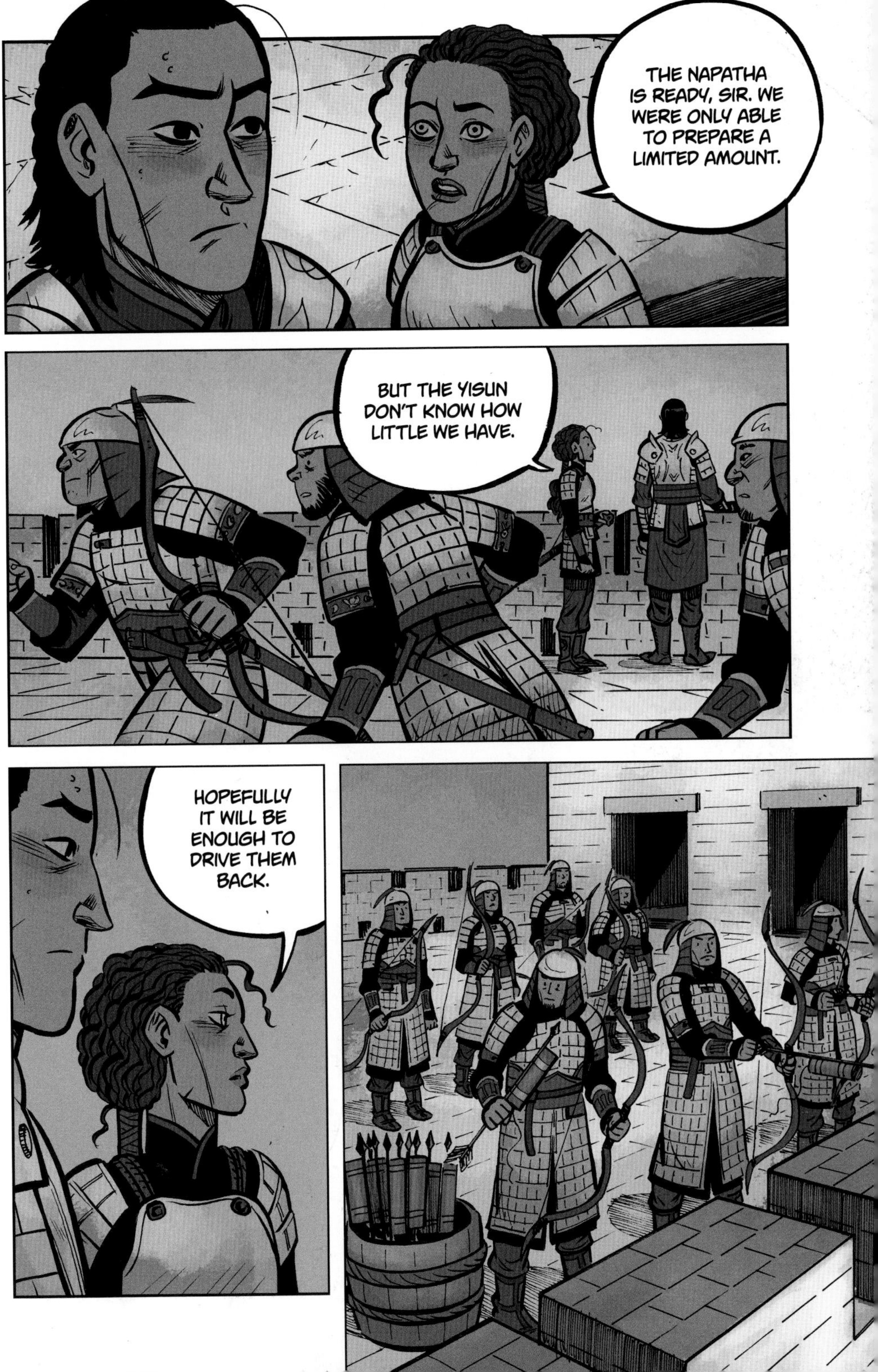
THE NAPATHA IS READY, SIR. WE WERE ONLY ABLE TO PREPARE A LIMITED AMOUNT.
BUT THE YISUN DON'T KNOW HOW LITTLE WE HAVE.
HOPEFULLY IT WILL BE ENOUGH TO DRIVE THEM BACK.

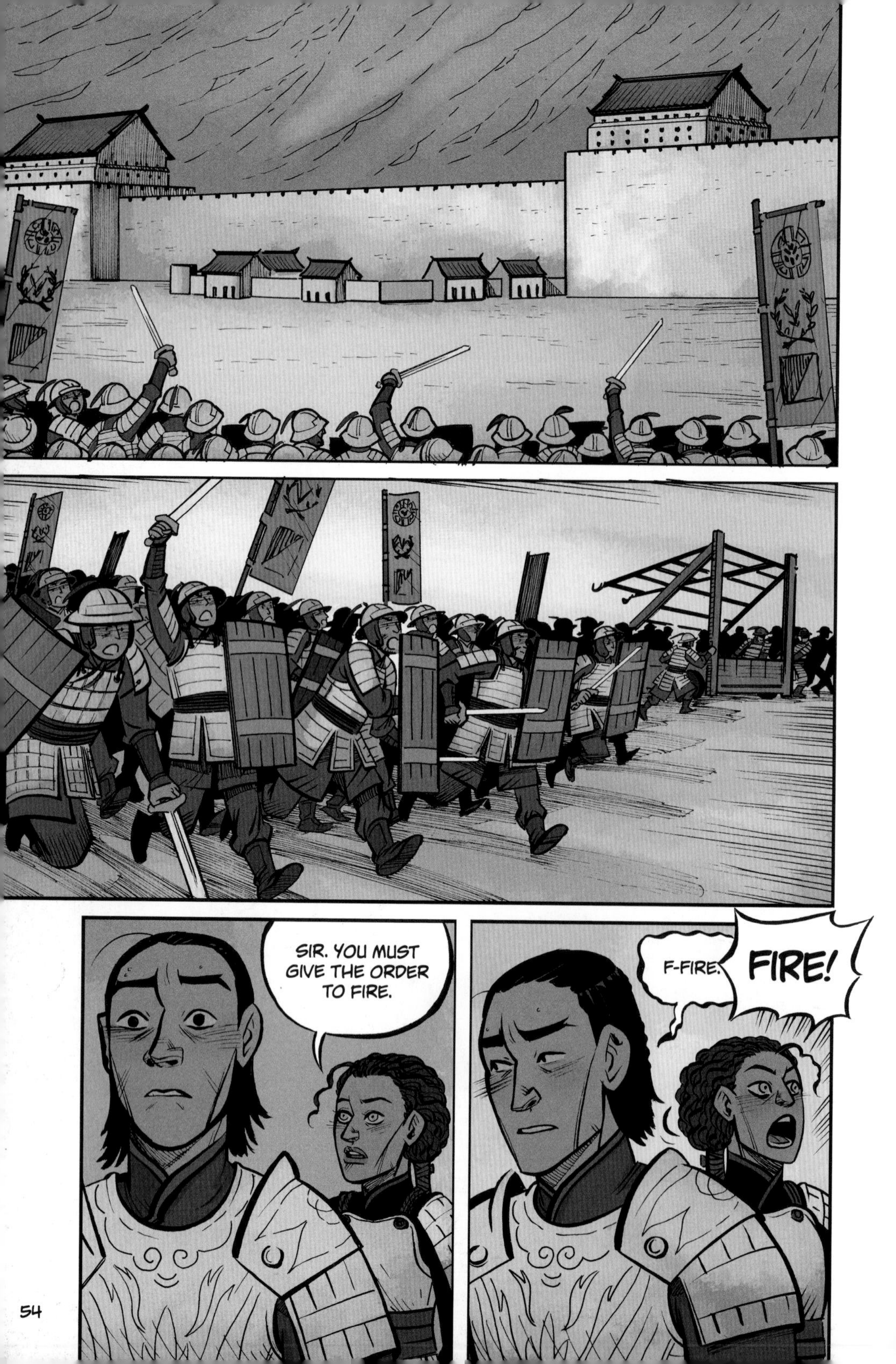
SIR. YOU MUST GIVE THE ORDER TO FIRE.
F-FIRE.
FIRE!

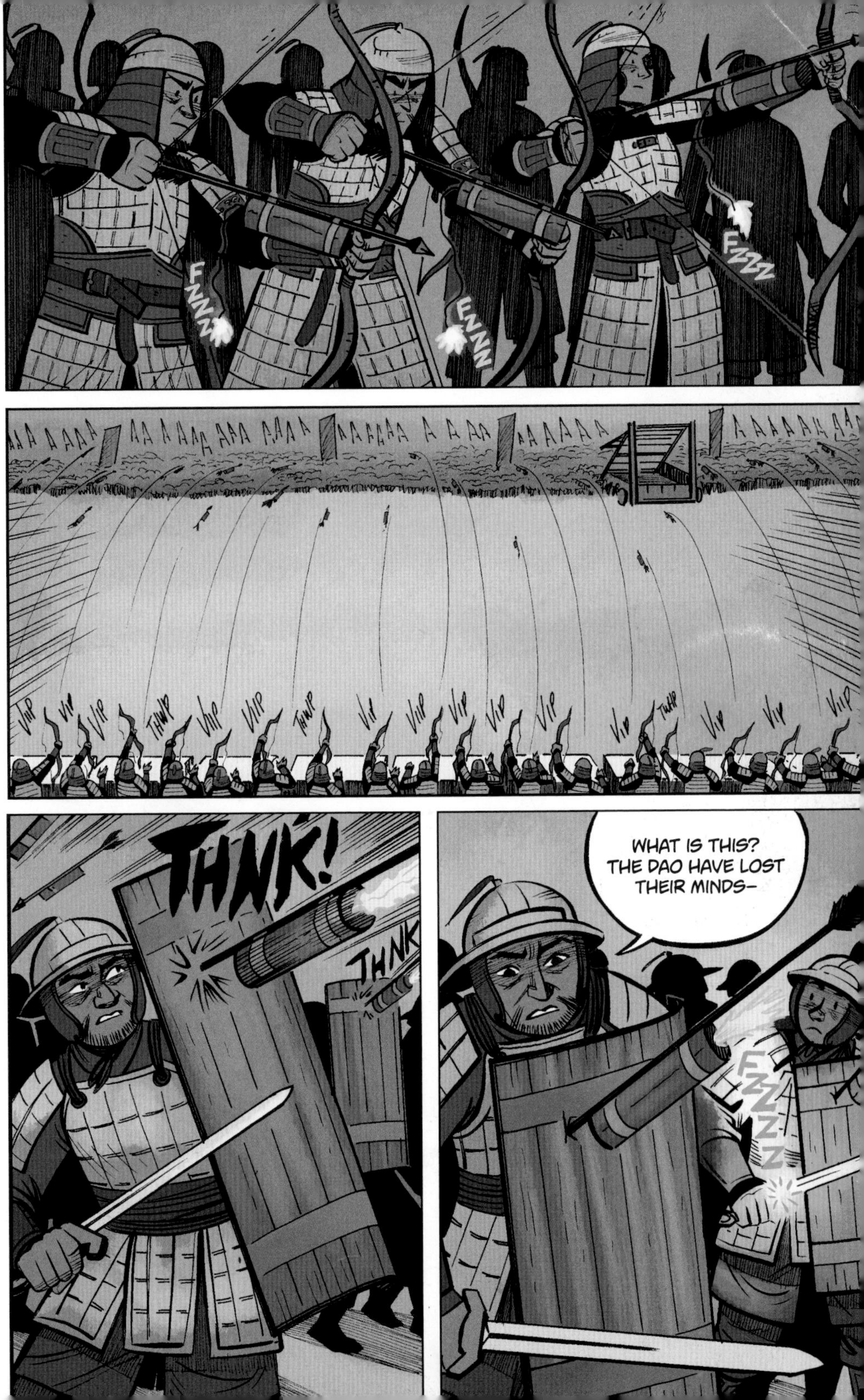
FZZZ
FZZZ
FZZZ
VIP
VIP
THWP
THNK!
THNK
WHAT IS THIS? THE DAO HAVE LOST THEIR MINDS–
FZZZZ

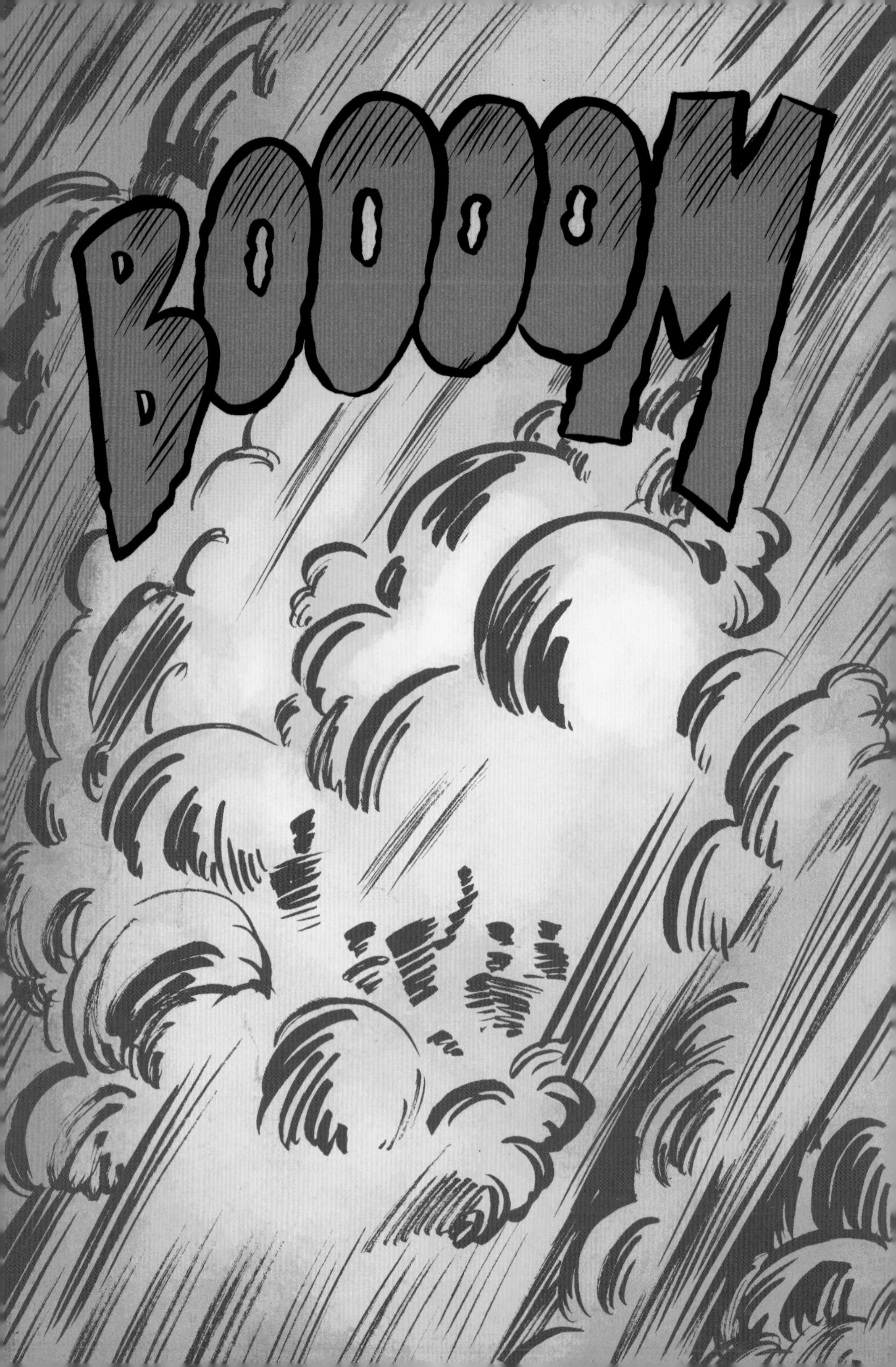
BOOOOM

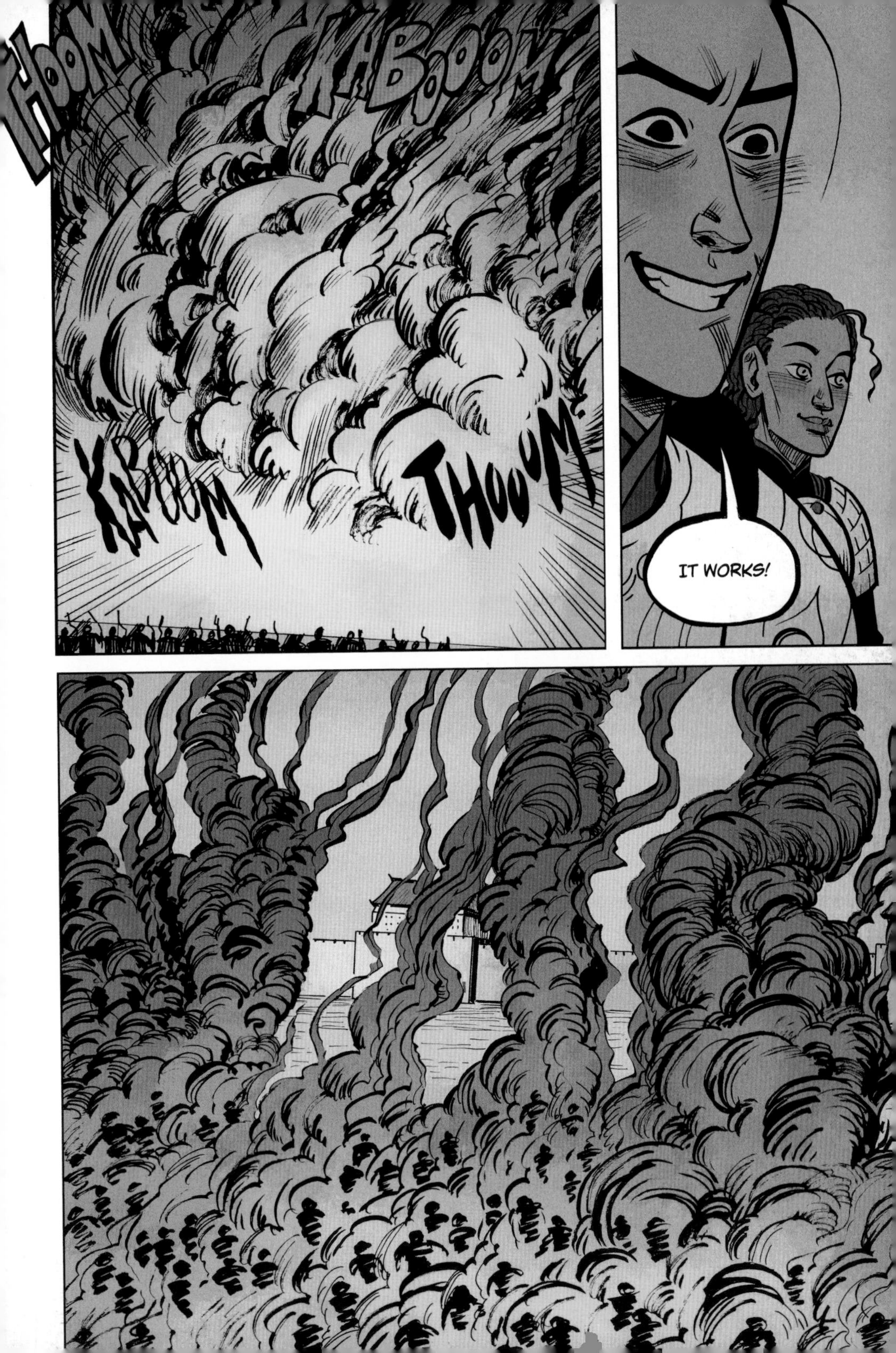
THOOM
KABOOOOM
KABOOM
THOOOM
IT WORKS!

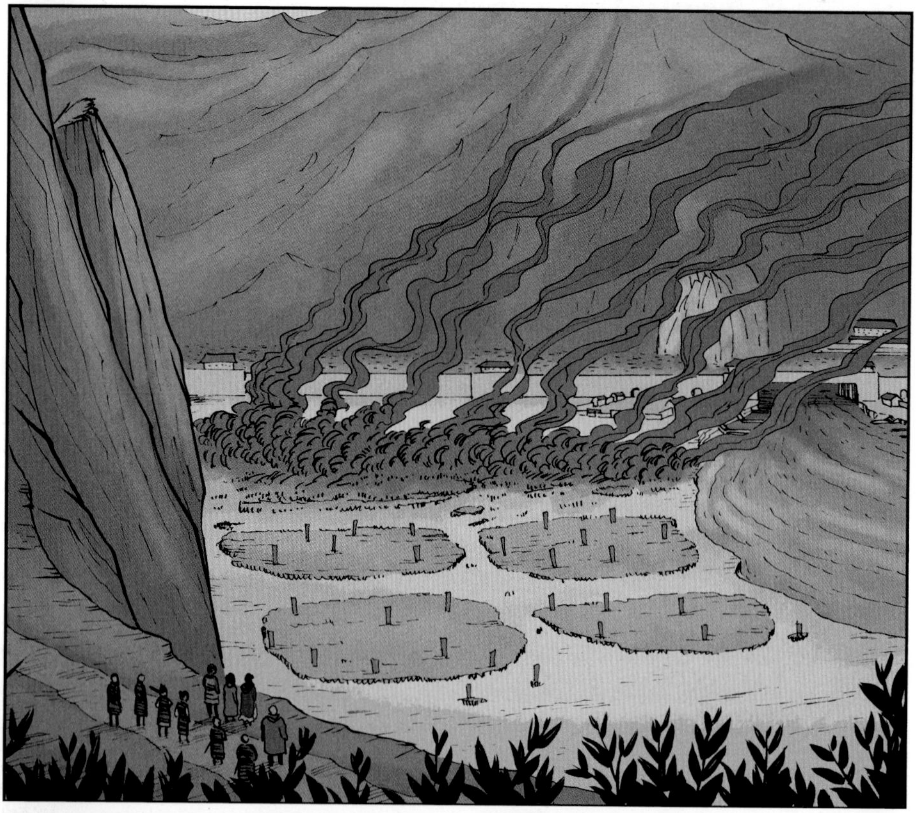

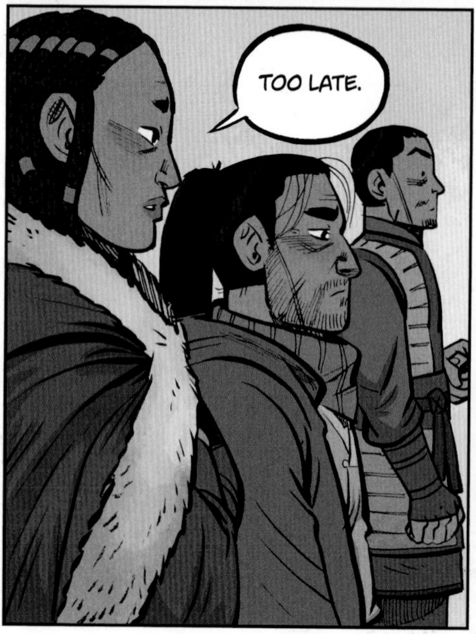
TOO LATE.

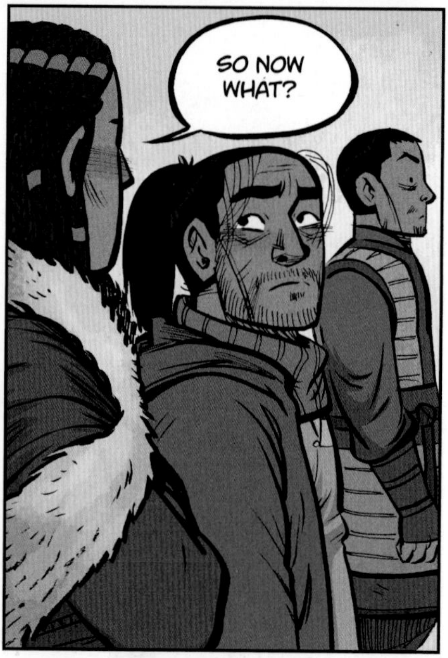
SO NOW WHAT?

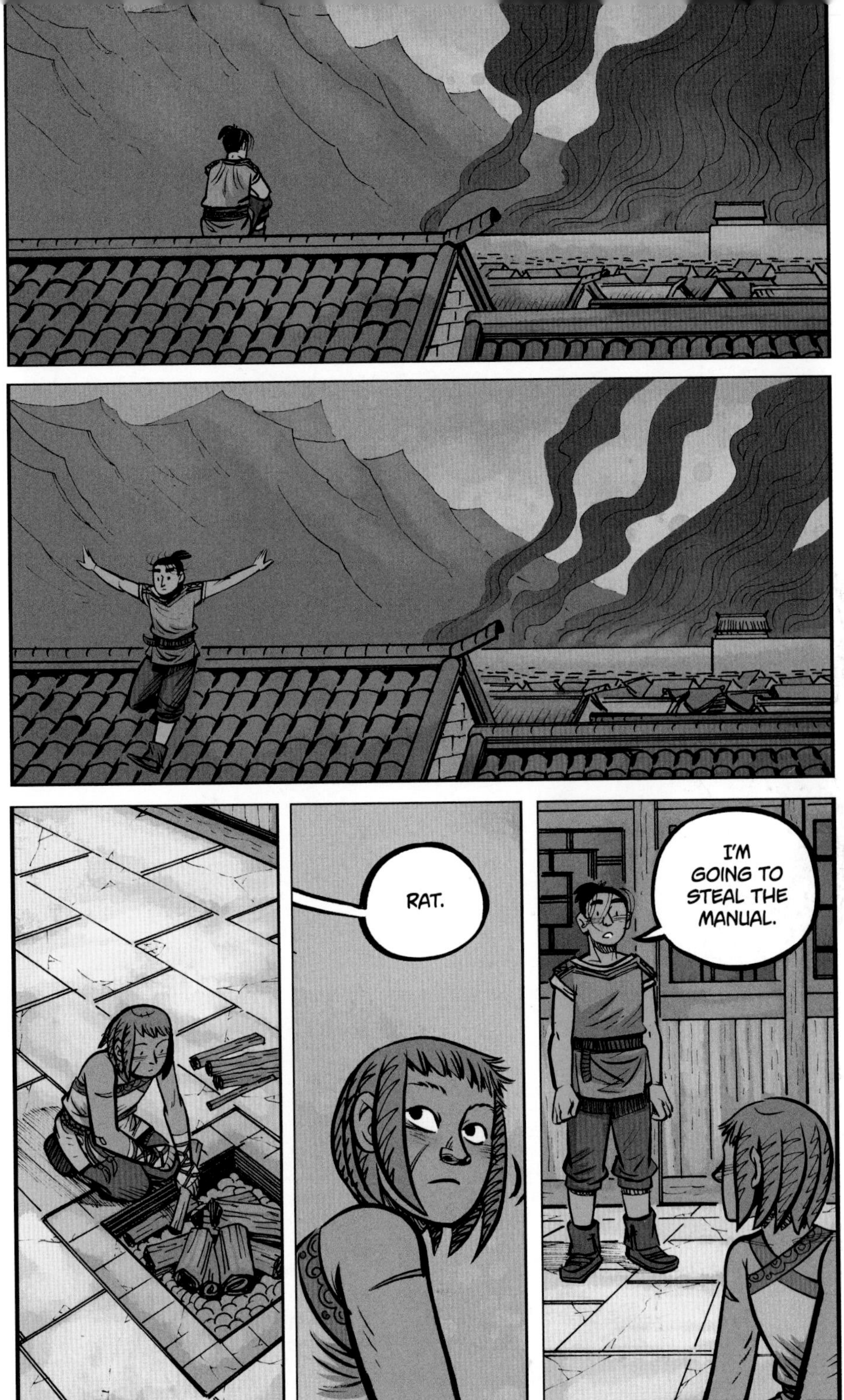
RAT.
I'M GOING TO STEAL THE MANUAL.

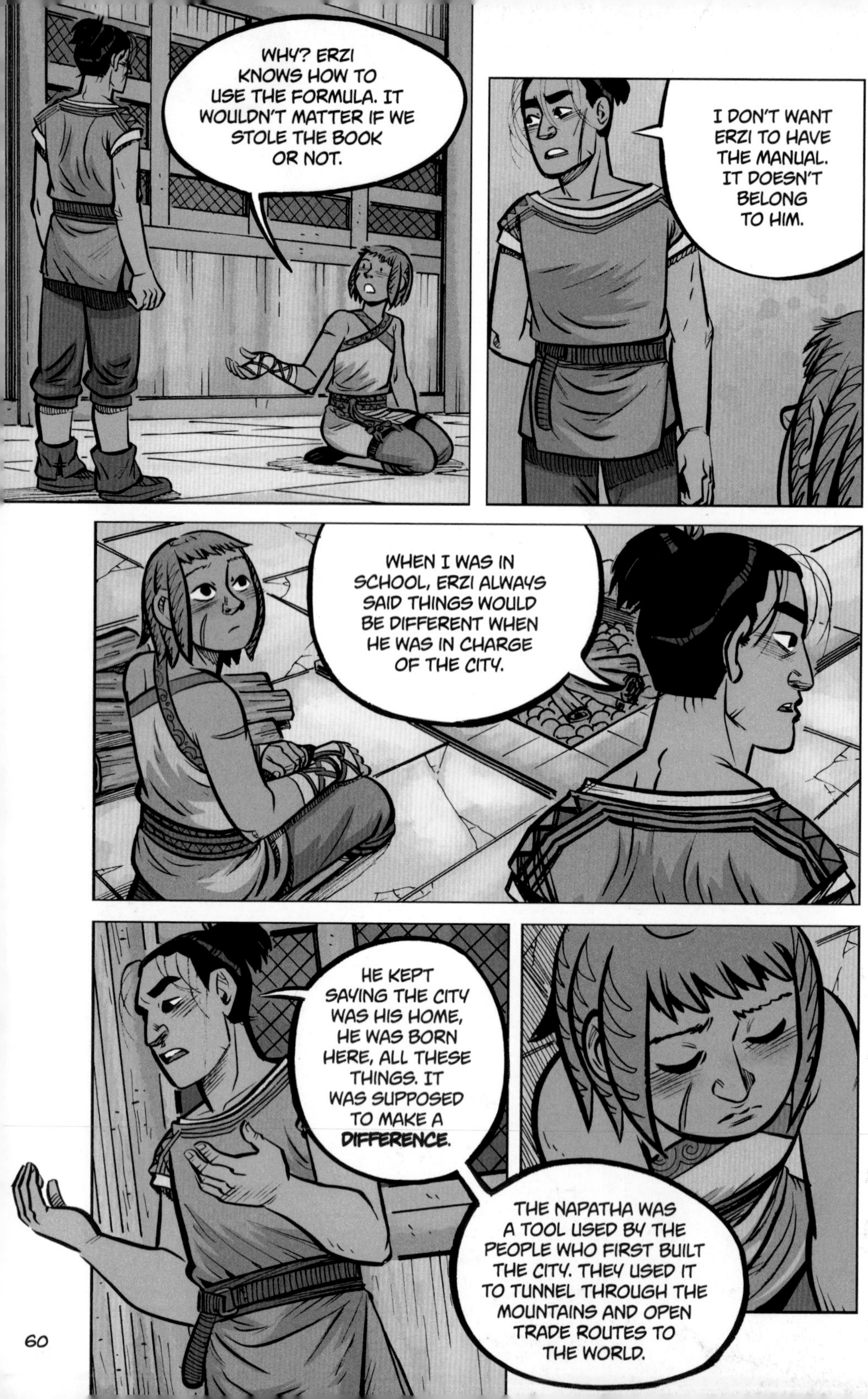
WHY? ERZI KNOWS HOW TO USE THE FORMULA. IT WOULDN'T MATTER IF WE STOLE THE BOOK OR NOT.
I DON'T WANT ERZI TO HAVE THE MANUAL. IT DOESN'T BELONG TO HIM.
WHEN I WAS IN SCHOOL, ERZI ALWAYS SAID THINGS WOULD BE DIFFERENT WHEN HE WAS IN CHARGE OF THE CITY.
HE KEPT SAYING THE CITY WAS HIS HOME, HE WAS BORN HERE, ALL THESE THINGS. IT WAS SUPPOSED TO MAKE A **DIFFERENCE**.
THE NAPATHA WAS A TOOL USED BY THE PEOPLE WHO FIRST BUILT THE CITY. THEY USED IT TO TUNNEL THROUGH THE MOUNTAINS AND OPEN TRADE ROUTES TO THE WORLD.

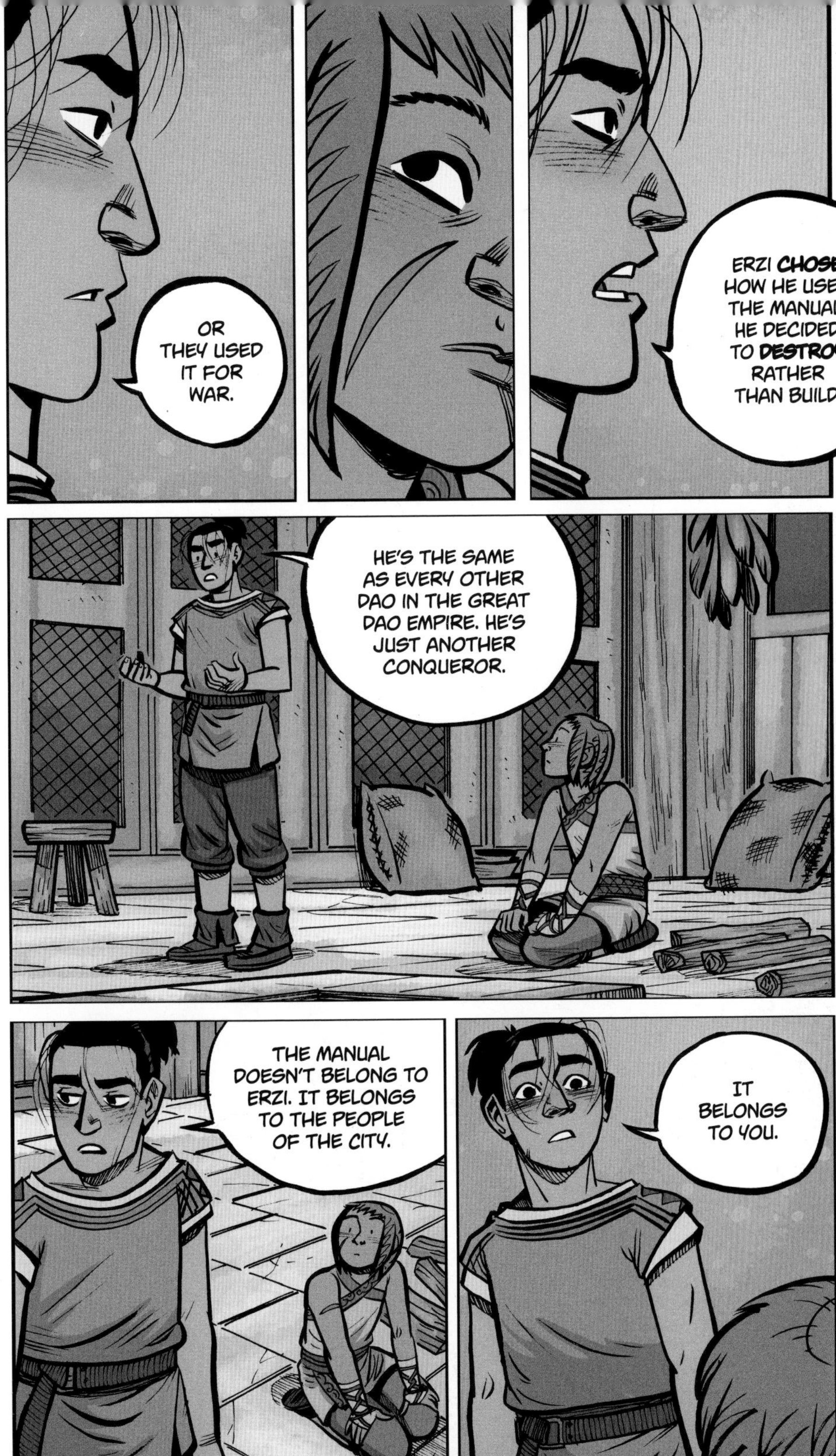
OR THEY USED IT FOR WAR.
ERZI CHOSE HOW HE USED THE MANUAL. HE DECIDED TO DESTROY RATHER THAN BUILD.
HE'S THE SAME AS EVERY OTHER DAO IN THE GREAT DAO EMPIRE. HE'S JUST ANOTHER CONQUEROR.
THE MANUAL DOESN'T BELONG TO ERZI. IT BELONGS TO THE PEOPLE OF THE CITY.
IT BELONGS TO YOU.

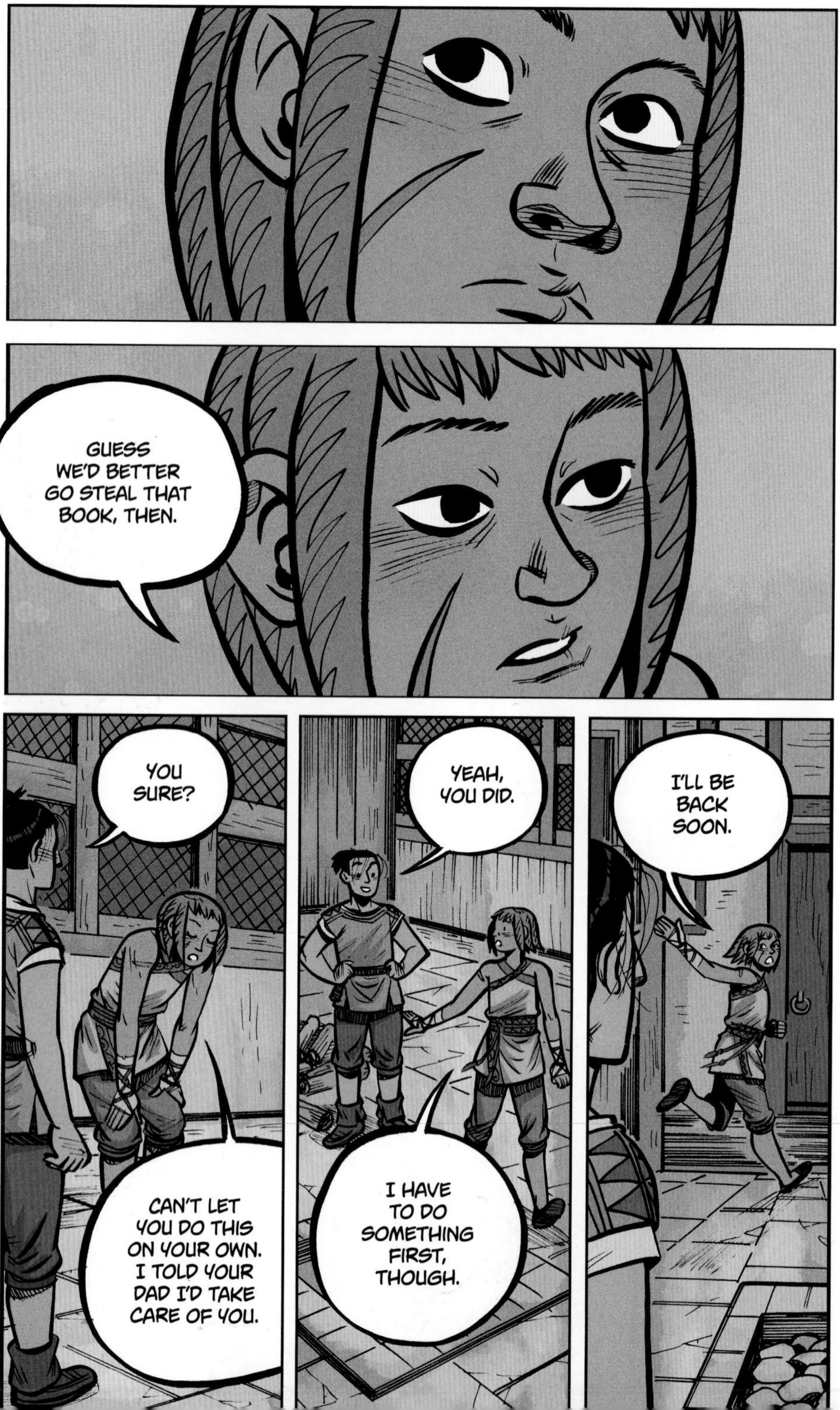
GUESS WE'D BETTER GO STEAL THAT BOOK, THEN.
YOU SURE?
CAN'T LET YOU DO THIS ON YOUR OWN. I TOLD YOUR DAD I'D TAKE CARE OF YOU.
YEAH, YOU DID.
I HAVE TO DO SOMETHING FIRST, THOUGH.
I'LL BE BACK SOON.

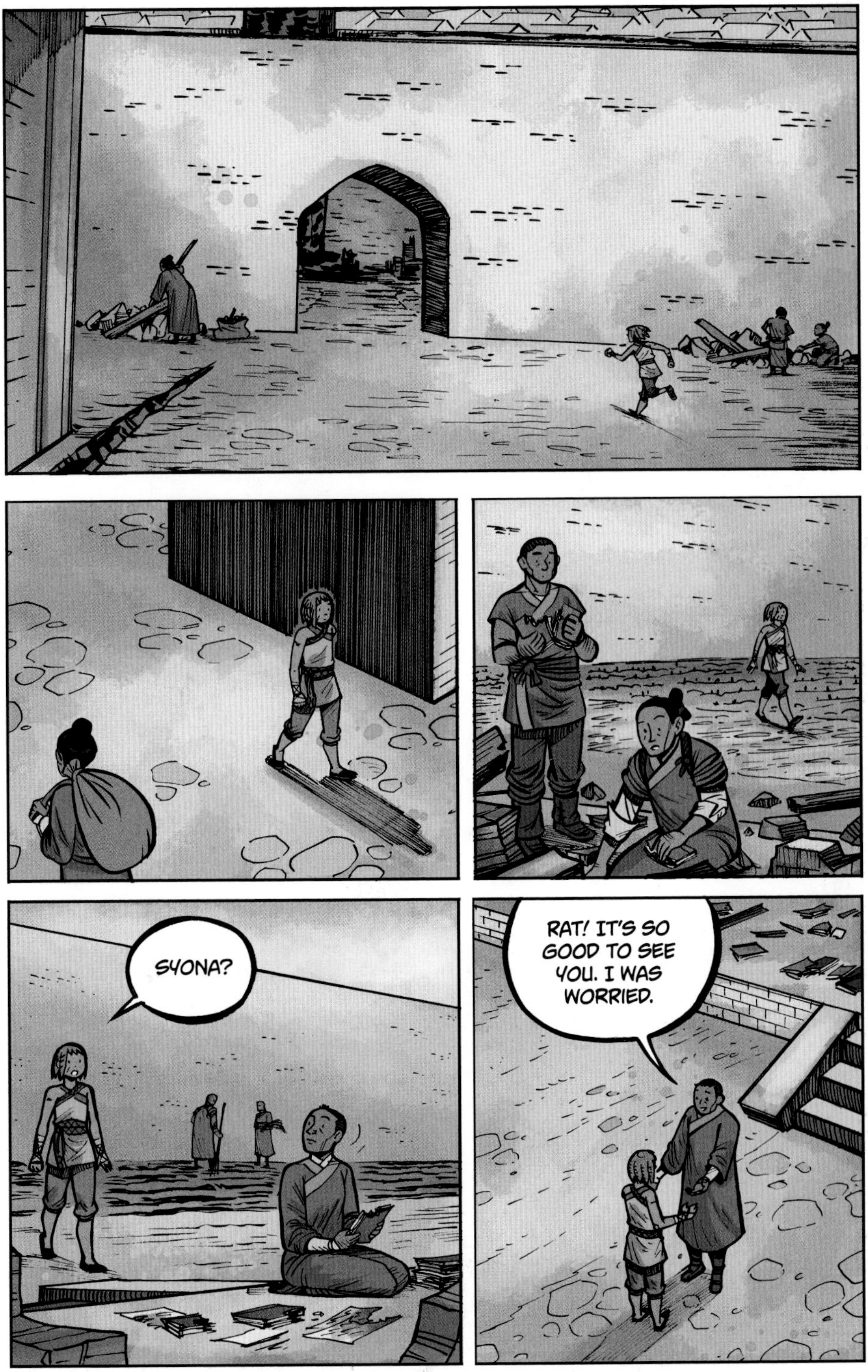
SYONA?
RAT! IT'S SO GOOD TO SEE YOU. I WAS WORRIED.

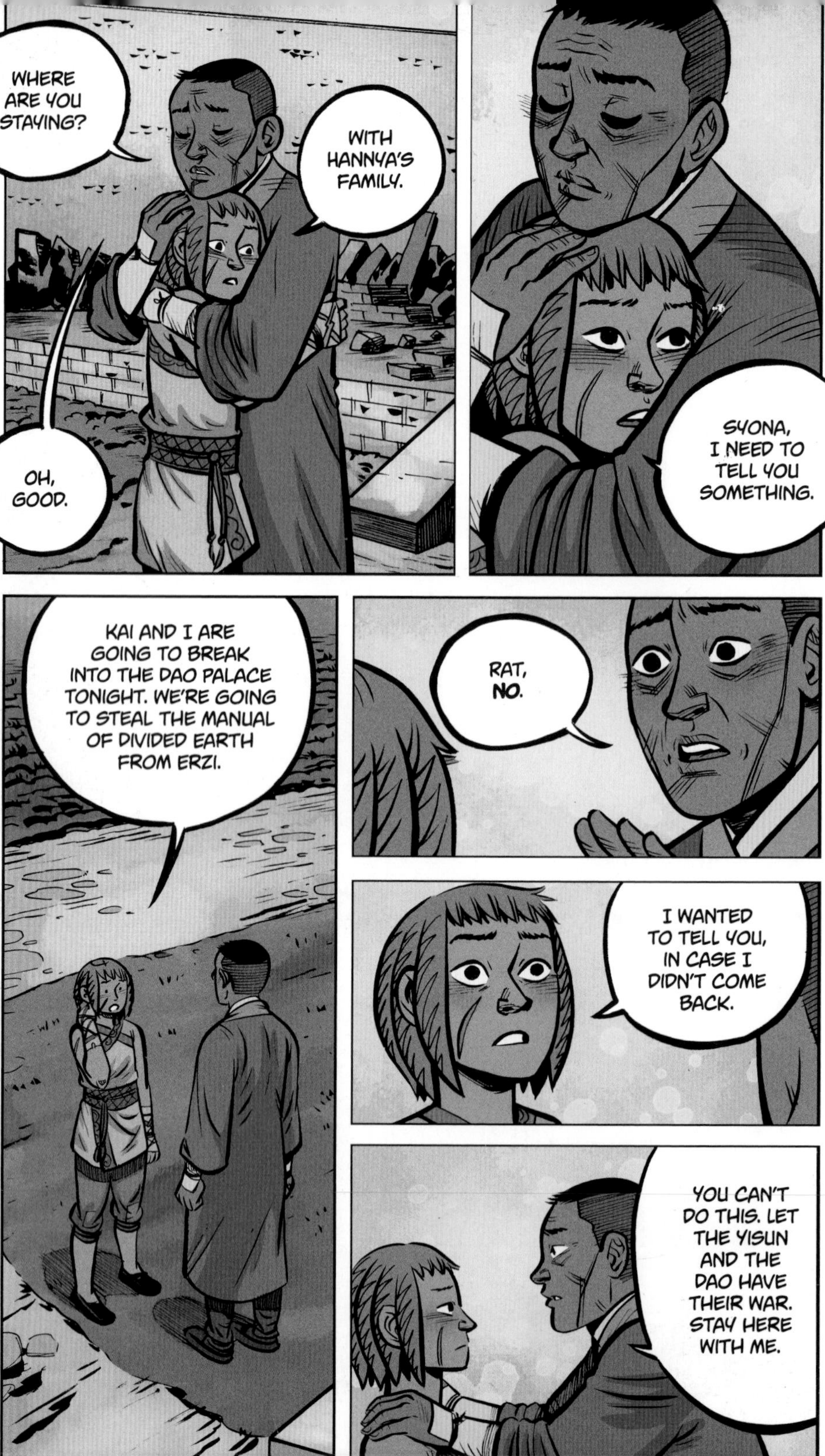
WHERE ARE YOU STAYING?
WITH HANNYA'S FAMILY.
OH, GOOD.
SYONA, I NEED TO TELL YOU SOMETHING.
KAI AND I ARE GOING TO BREAK INTO THE DAO PALACE TONIGHT. WE'RE GOING TO STEAL THE MANUAL OF DIVIDED EARTH FROM ERZI.
RAT, NO.
I WANTED TO TELL YOU, IN CASE I DIDN'T COME BACK.
YOU CAN'T DO THIS. LET THE YISUN AND THE DAO HAVE THEIR WAR. STAY HERE WITH ME.

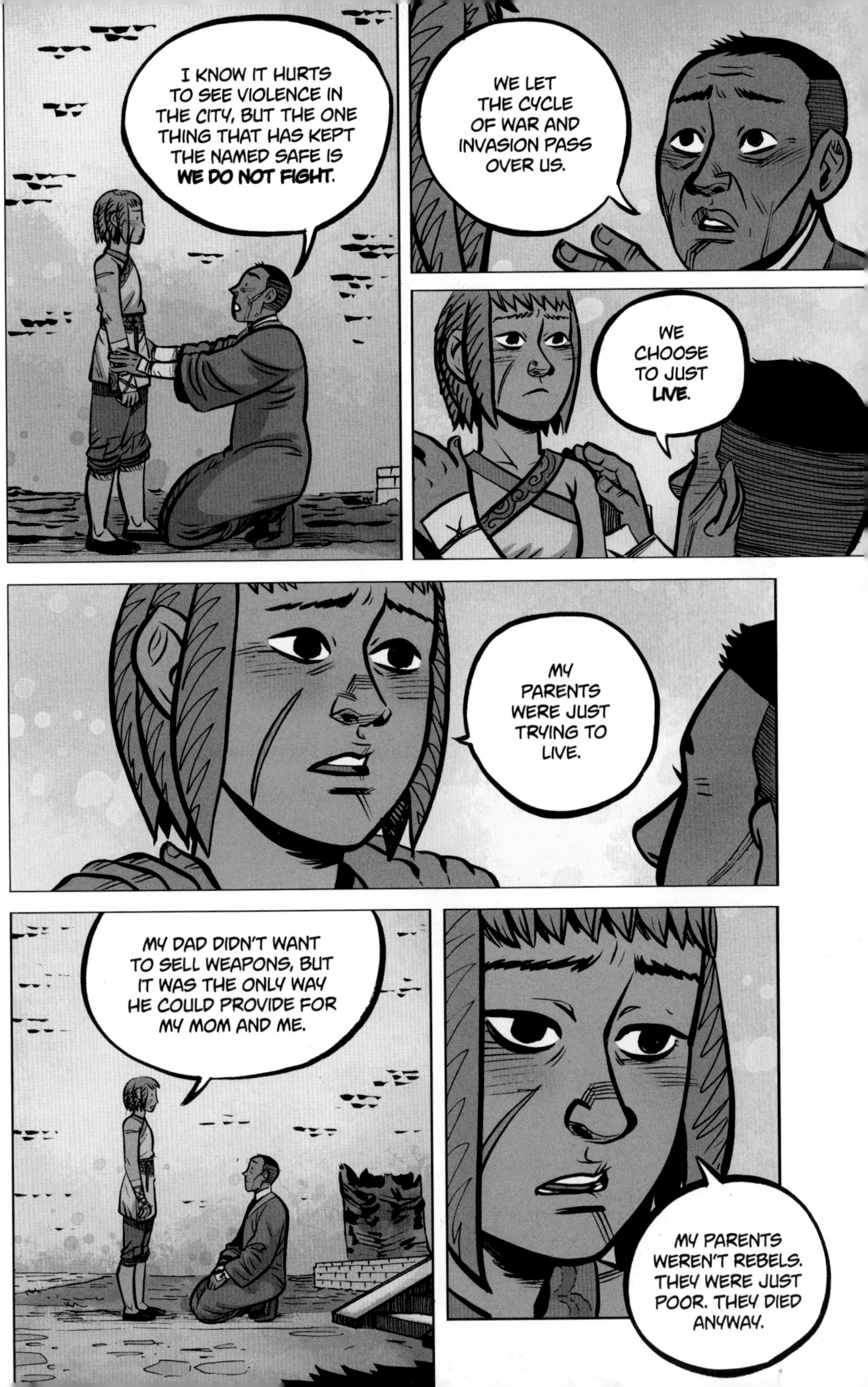
I KNOW IT HURTS TO SEE VIOLENCE IN THE CITY, BUT THE ONE THING THAT HAS KEPT THE NAMED SAFE IS **WE DO NOT FIGHT**.
WE LET THE CYCLE OF WAR AND INVASION PASS OVER US.
WE CHOOSE TO JUST **LIVE**.
MY PARENTS WERE JUST TRYING TO LIVE.
MY DAD DIDN'T WANT TO SELL WEAPONS, BUT IT WAS THE ONLY WAY HE COULD PROVIDE FOR MY MOM AND ME.
MY PARENTS WEREN'T REBELS. THEY WERE JUST POOR. THEY DIED ANYWAY.

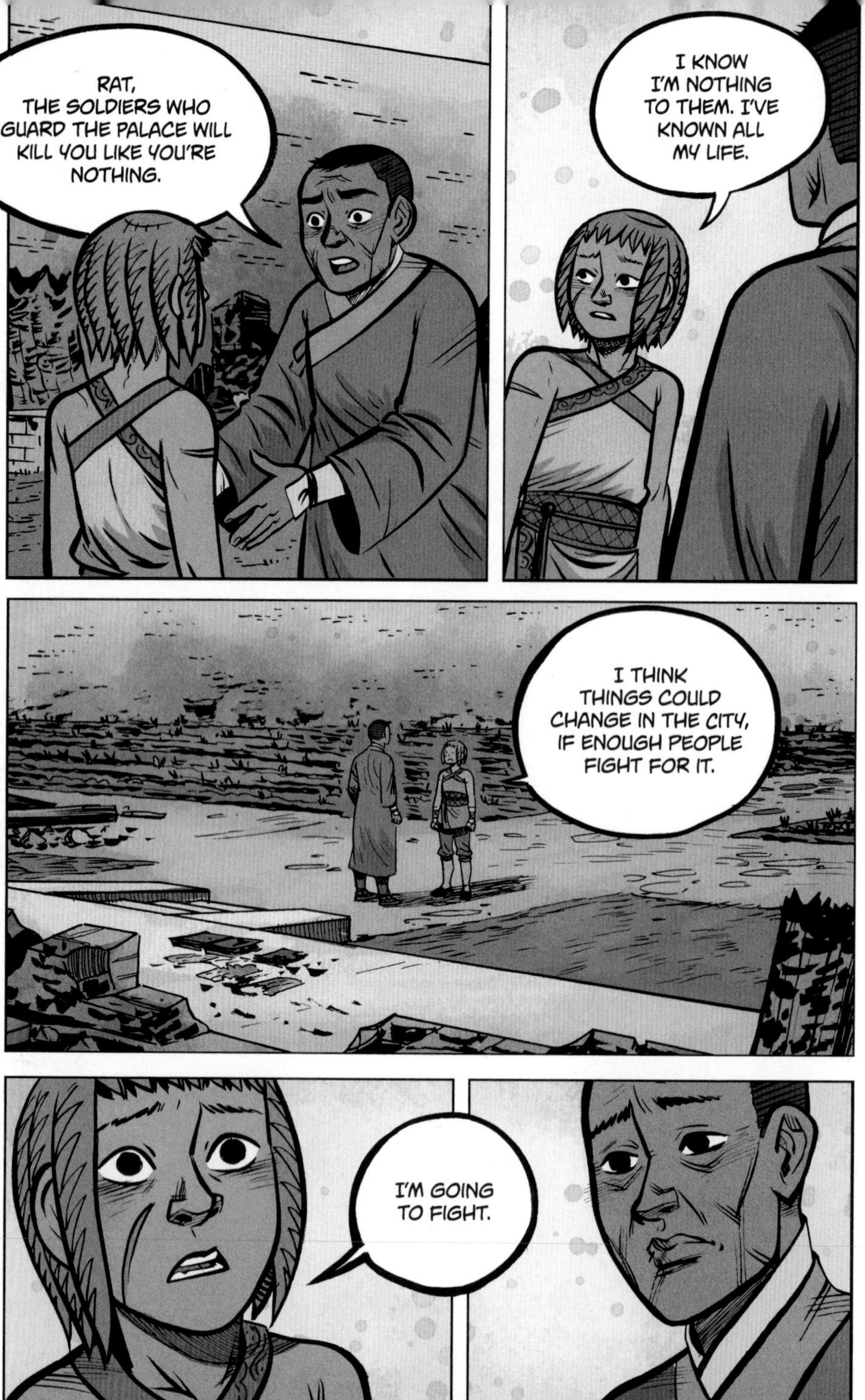
RAT, THE SOLDIERS WHO GUARD THE PALACE WILL KILL YOU LIKE YOU'RE NOTHING.
I KNOW I'M NOTHING TO THEM. I'VE KNOWN ALL MY LIFE.
I THINK THINGS COULD CHANGE IN THE CITY, IF ENOUGH PEOPLE FIGHT FOR IT.
I'M GOING TO FIGHT.

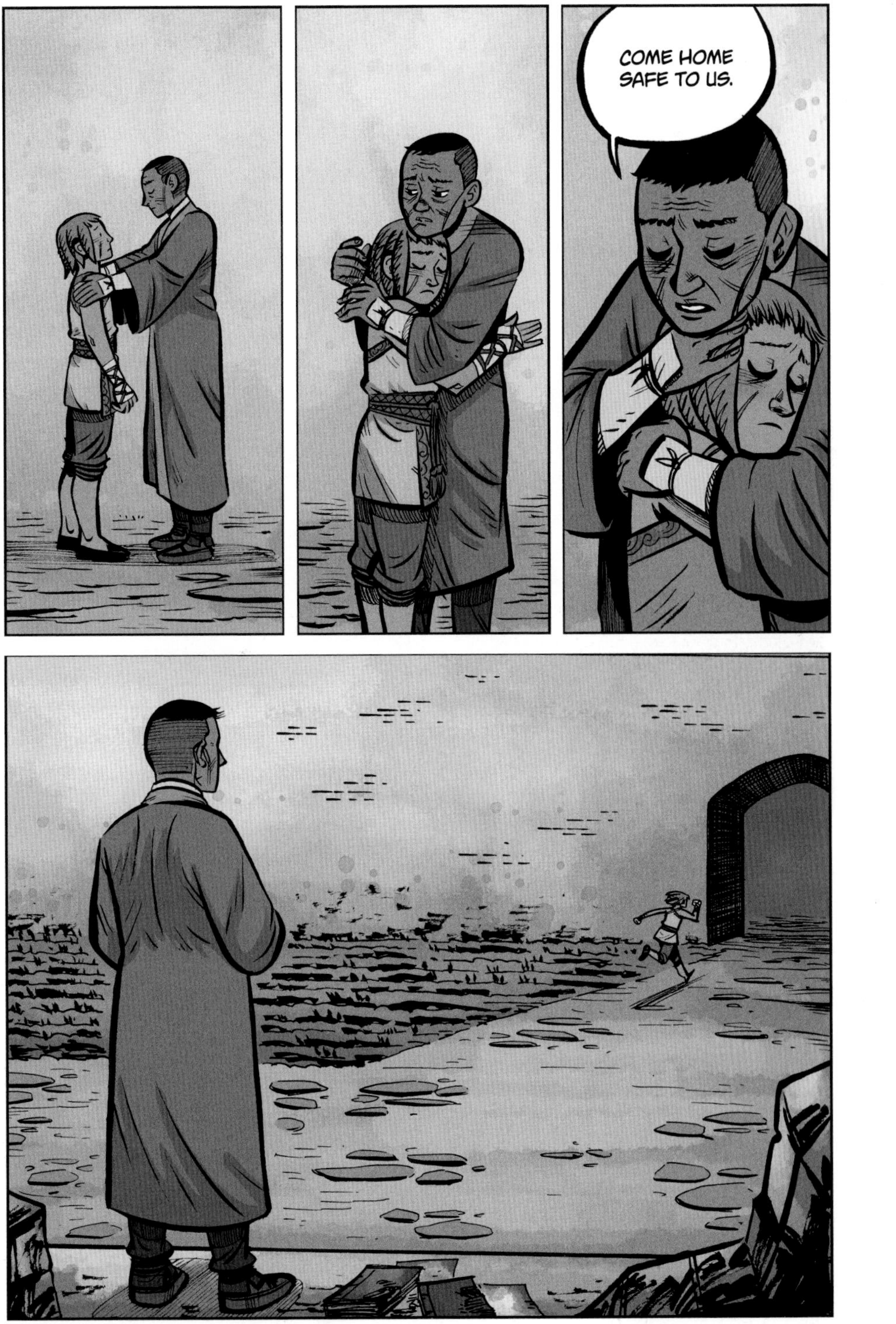
COME HOME SAFE TO US.

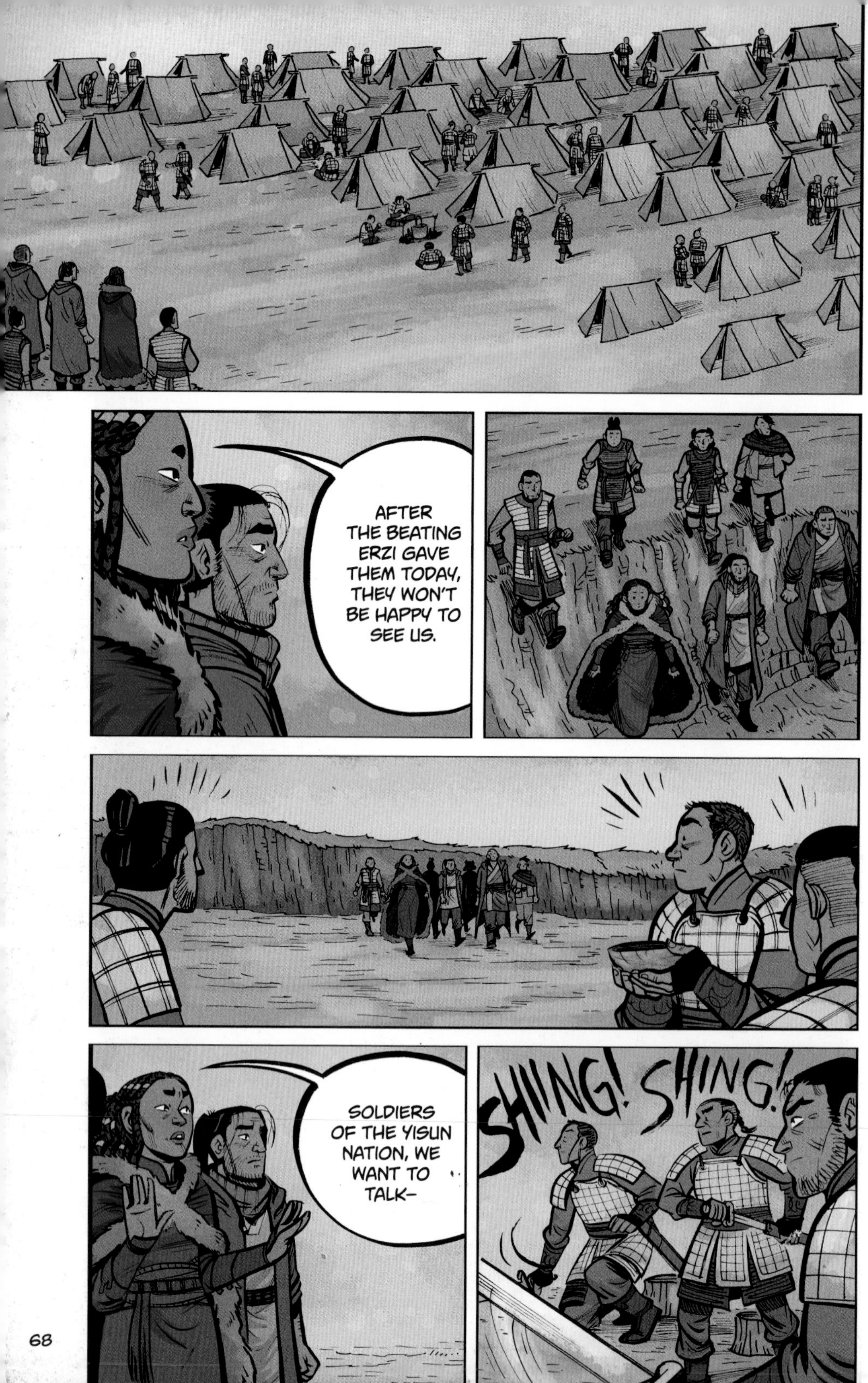
AFTER THE BEATING ERZI GAVE THEM TODAY, THEY WON'T BE HAPPY TO SEE US.
SOLDIERS OF THE YISUN NATION, WE WANT TO TALK–
SHING! SHING!

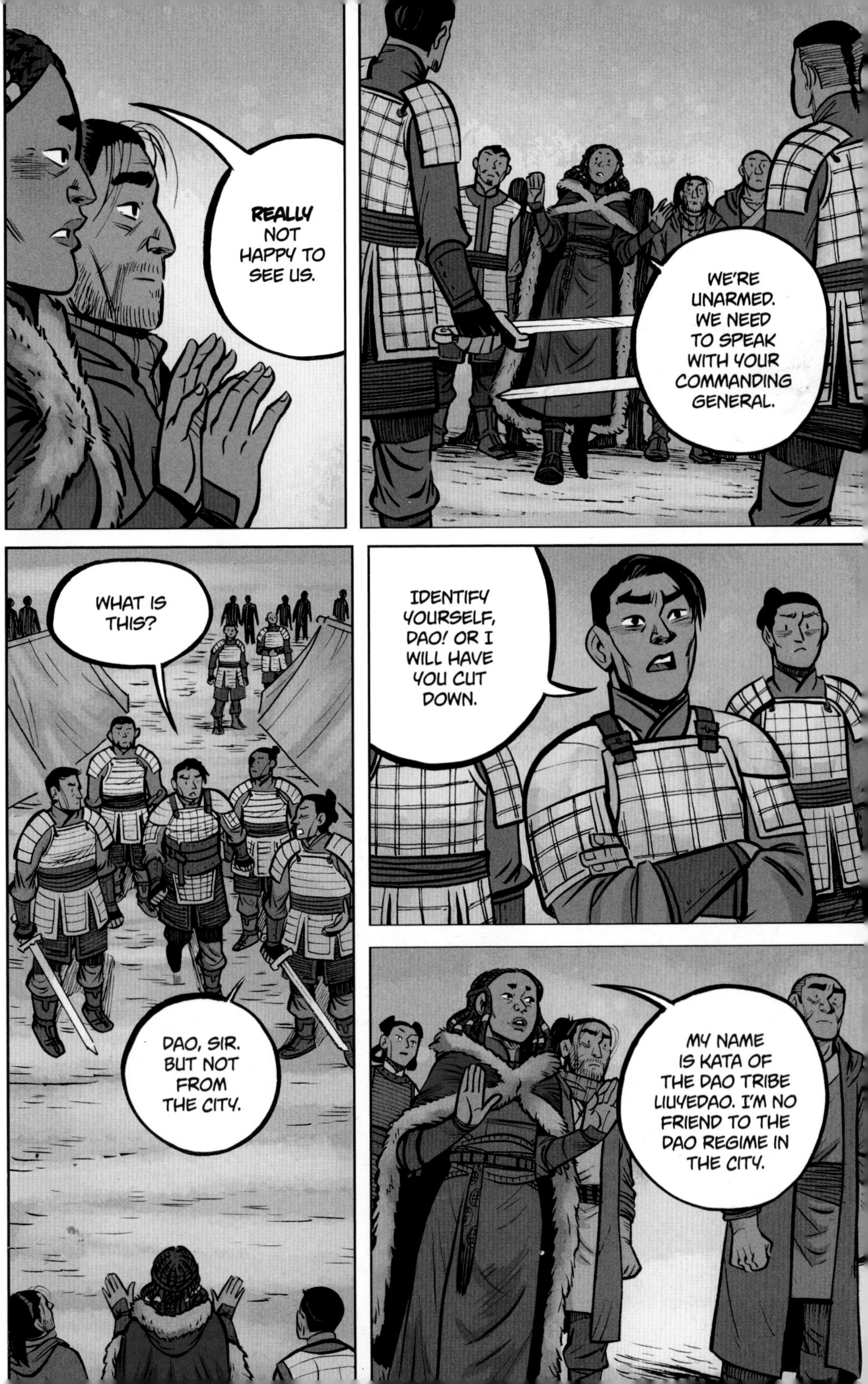
REALLY NOT HAPPY TO SEE US.
WE'RE UNARMED. WE NEED TO SPEAK WITH YOUR COMMANDING GENERAL.
WHAT IS THIS?
DAO, SIR. BUT NOT FROM THE CITY.
IDENTIFY YOURSELF, DAO! OR I WILL HAVE YOU CUT DOWN.
MY NAME IS KATA OF THE DAO TRIBE LIUYEDAO. I'M NO FRIEND TO THE DAO REGIME IN THE CITY.

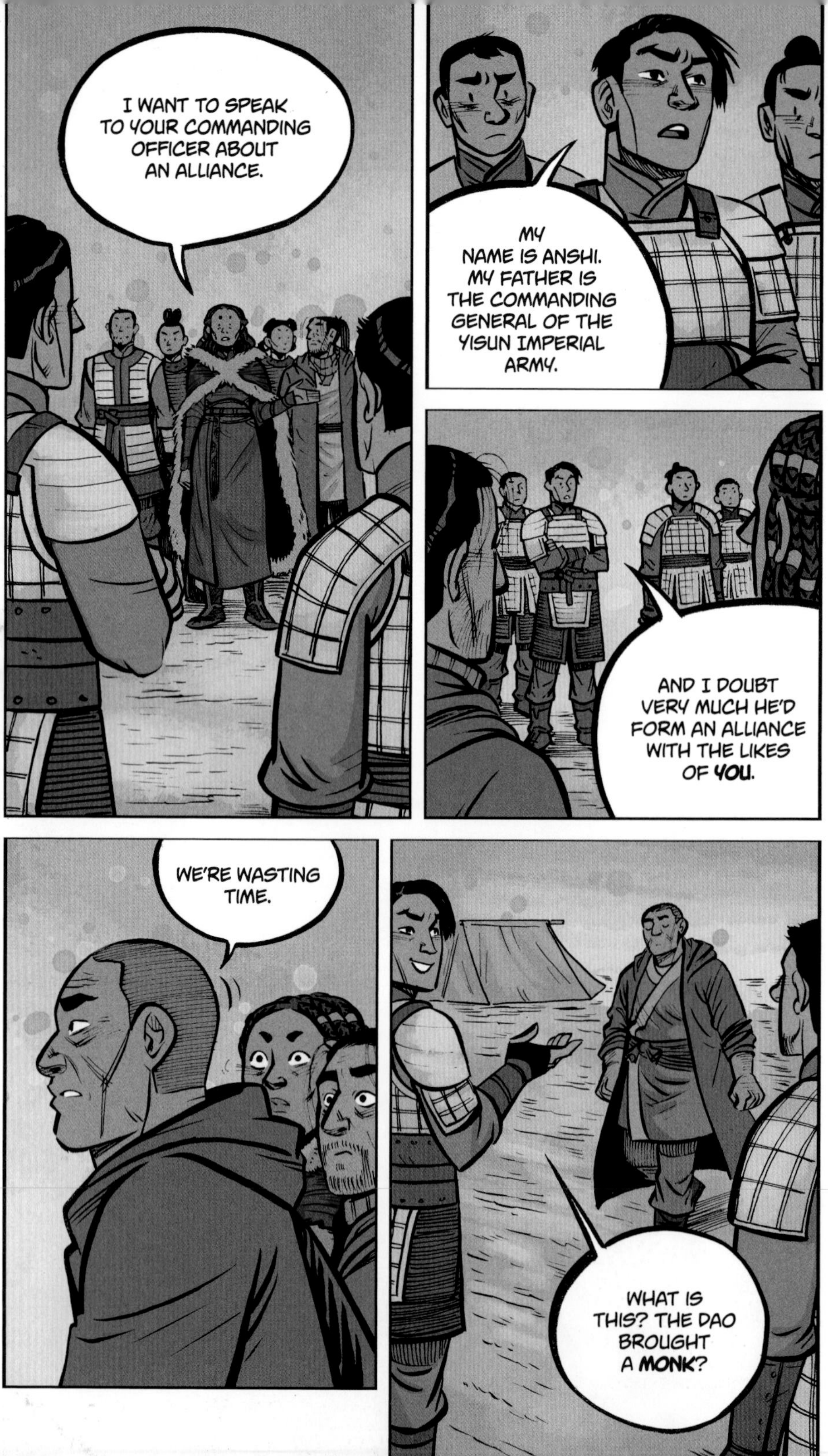
I WANT TO SPEAK TO YOUR COMMANDING OFFICER ABOUT AN ALLIANCE.
MY NAME IS ANSHI. MY FATHER IS THE COMMANDING GENERAL OF THE YISUN IMPERIAL ARMY.
AND I DOUBT VERY MUCH HE'D FORM AN ALLIANCE WITH THE LIKES OF **YOU**.
WE'RE WASTING TIME.
WHAT IS THIS? THE DAO BROUGHT A **MONK**?

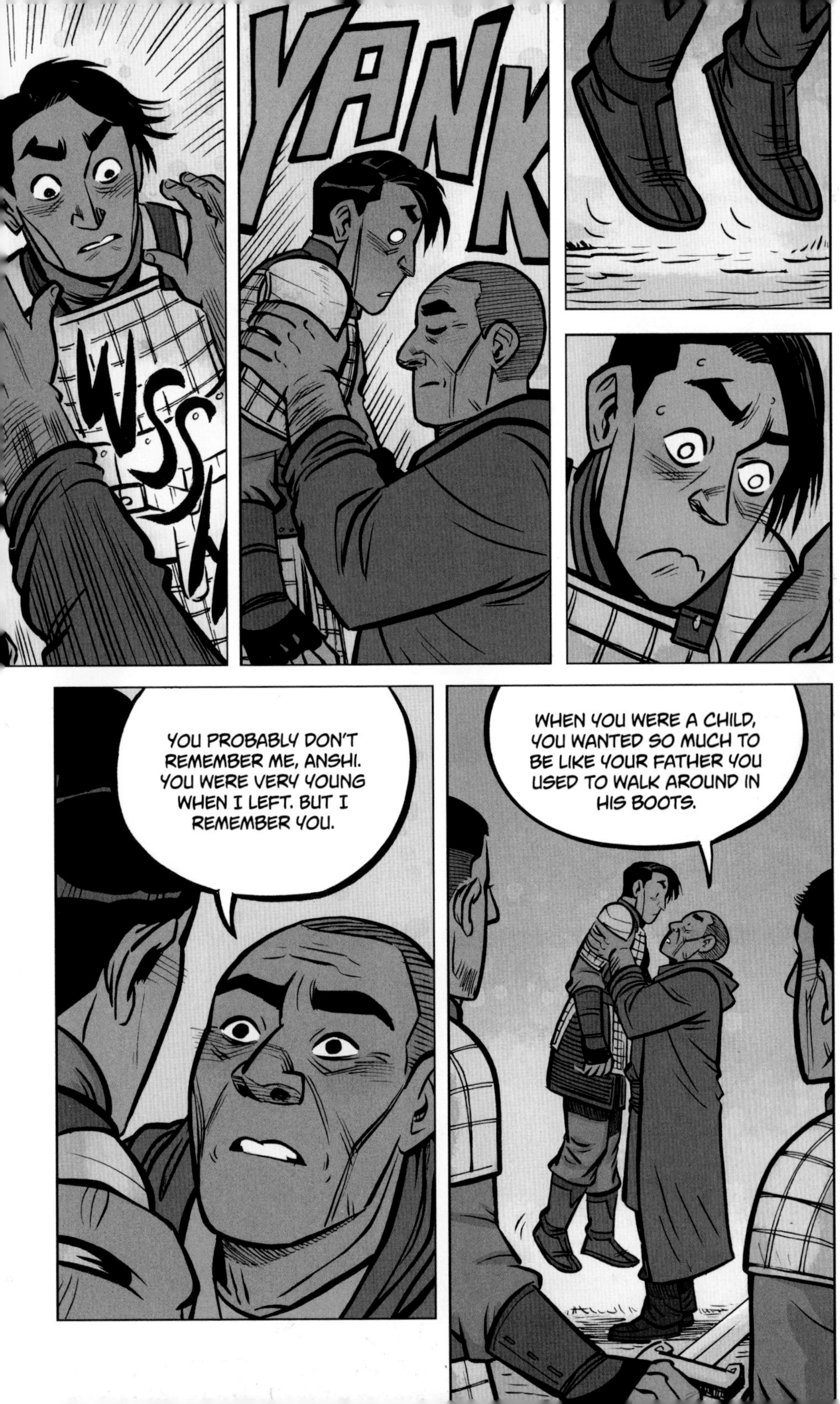
WSSH
YANK
YOU PROBABLY DON'T REMEMBER ME, ANSHI. YOU WERE VERY YOUNG WHEN I LEFT. BUT I REMEMBER YOU.
WHEN YOU WERE A CHILD, YOU WANTED SO MUCH TO BE LIKE YOUR FATHER YOU USED TO WALK AROUND IN HIS BOOTS.

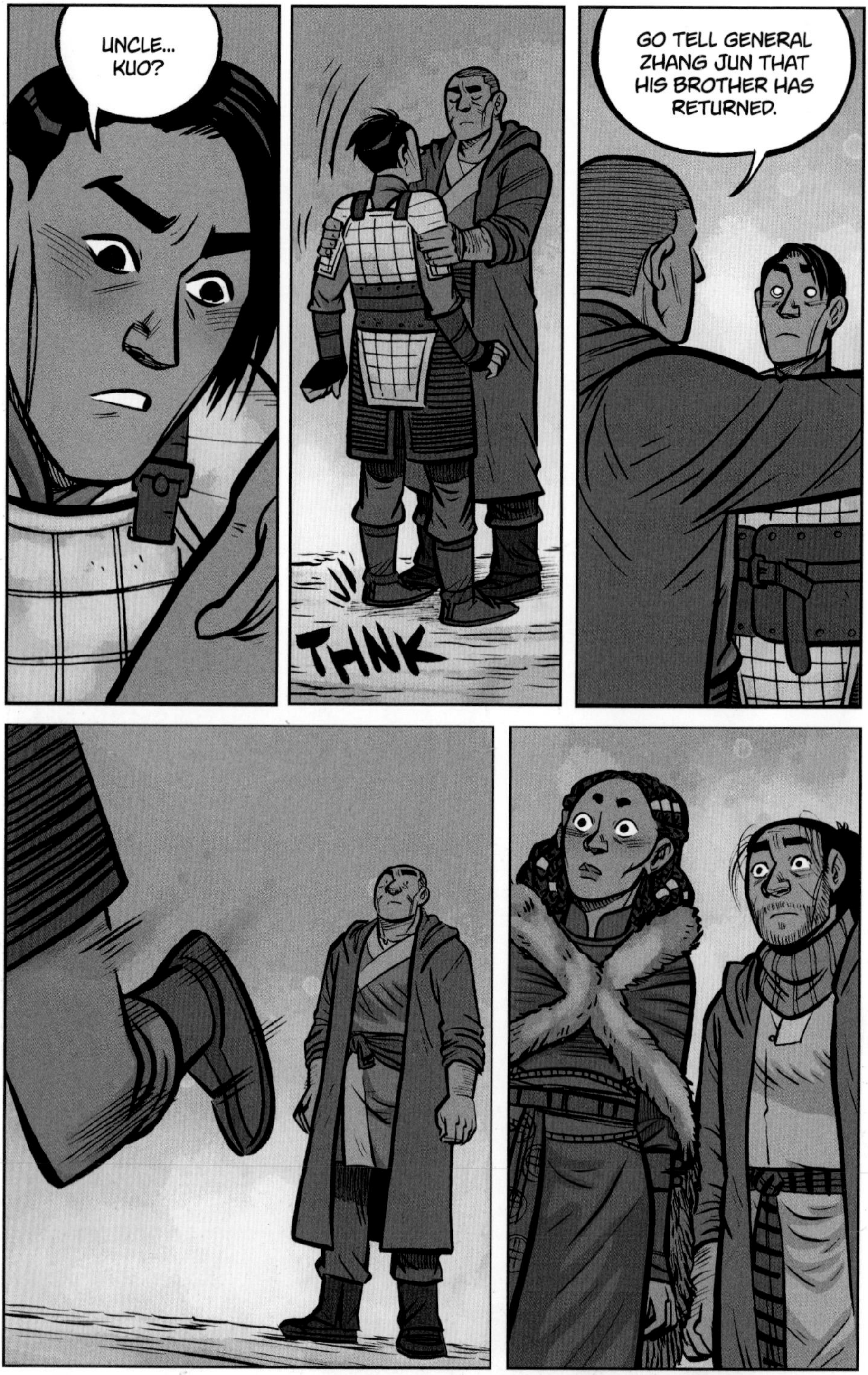
UNCLE... KUO?
THNK
GO TELL GENERAL ZHANG JUN THAT HIS BROTHER HAS RETURNED.

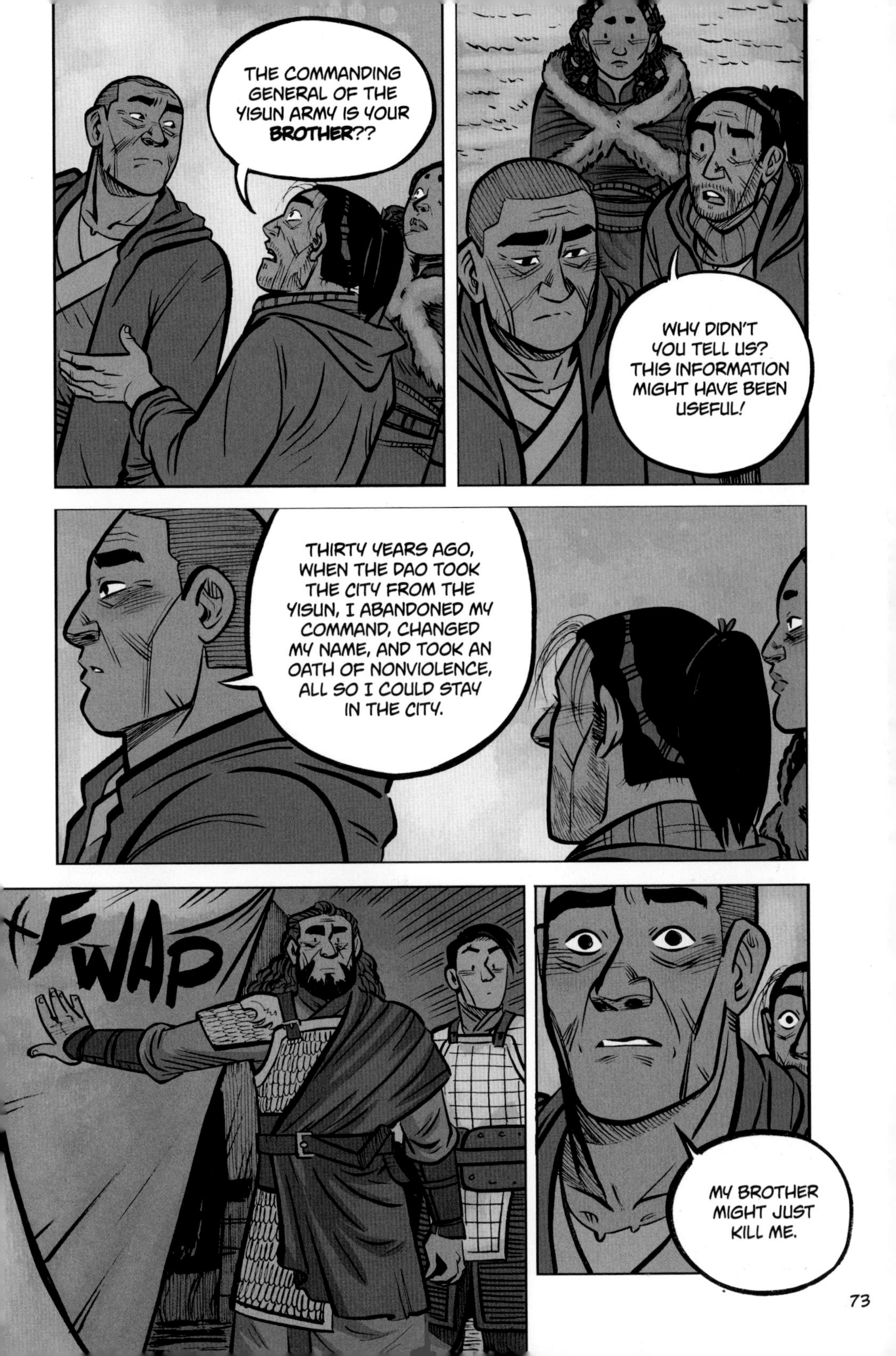
THE COMMANDING GENERAL OF THE YISUN ARMY IS YOUR BROTHER??
WHY DIDN'T YOU TELL US? THIS INFORMATION MIGHT HAVE BEEN USEFUL!
THIRTY YEARS AGO, WHEN THE DAO TOOK THE CITY FROM THE YISUN, I ABANDONED MY COMMAND, CHANGED MY NAME, AND TOOK AN OATH OF NONVIOLENCE, ALL SO I COULD STAY IN THE CITY.
FWAP
MY BROTHER MIGHT JUST KILL ME.

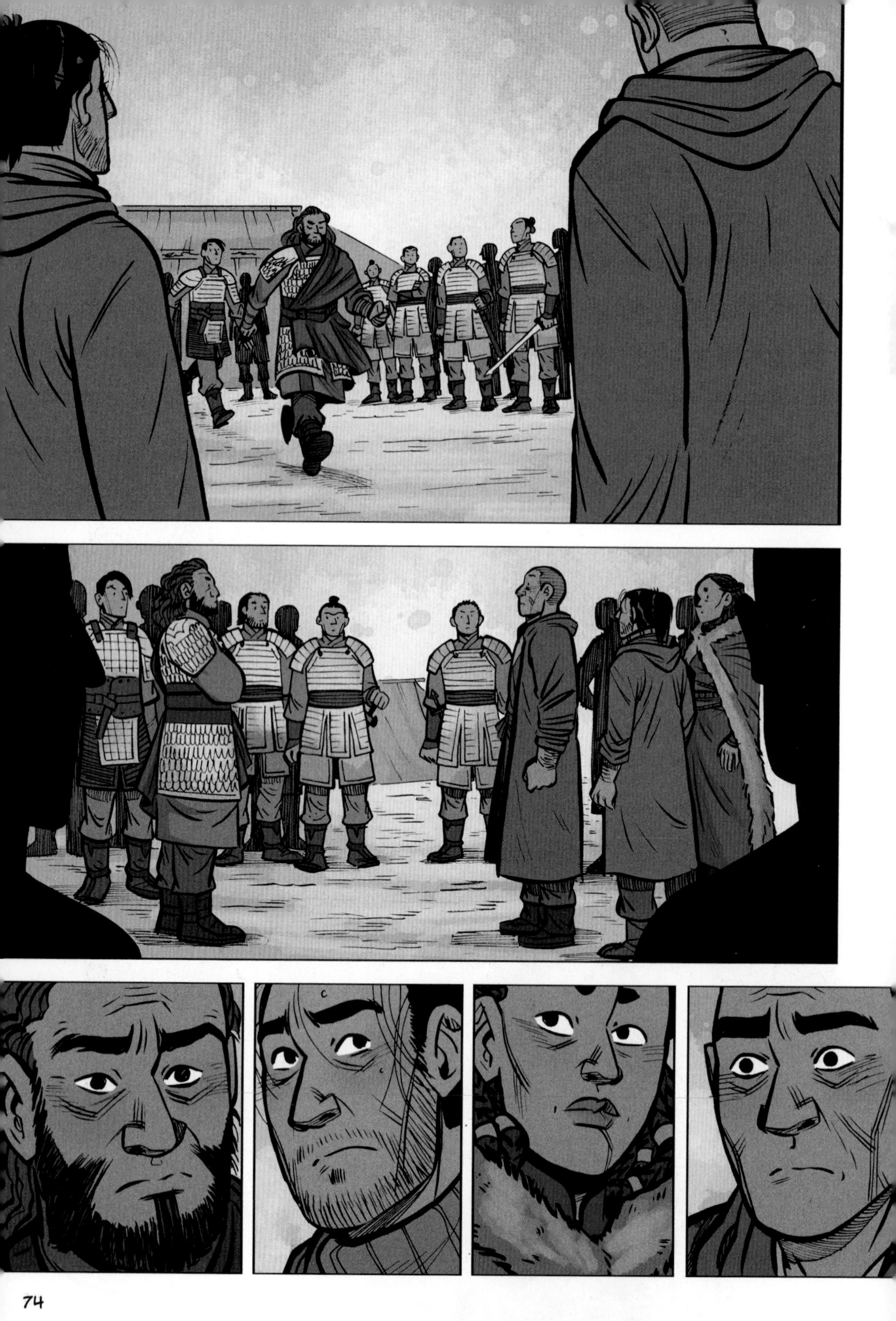

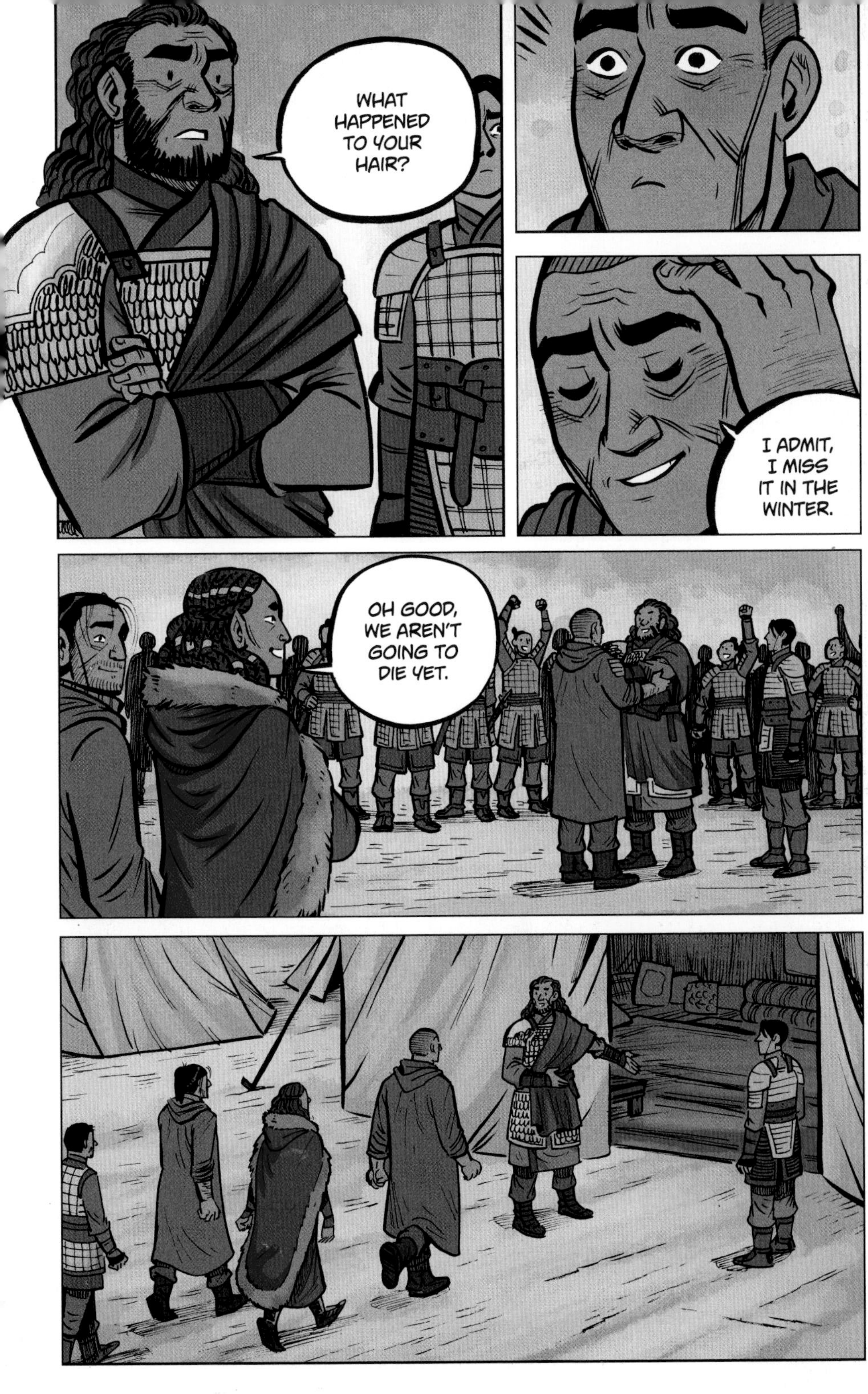
WHAT HAPPENED TO YOUR HAIR?
I ADMIT, I MISS IT IN THE WINTER.
OH GOOD, WE AREN'T GOING TO DIE YET.

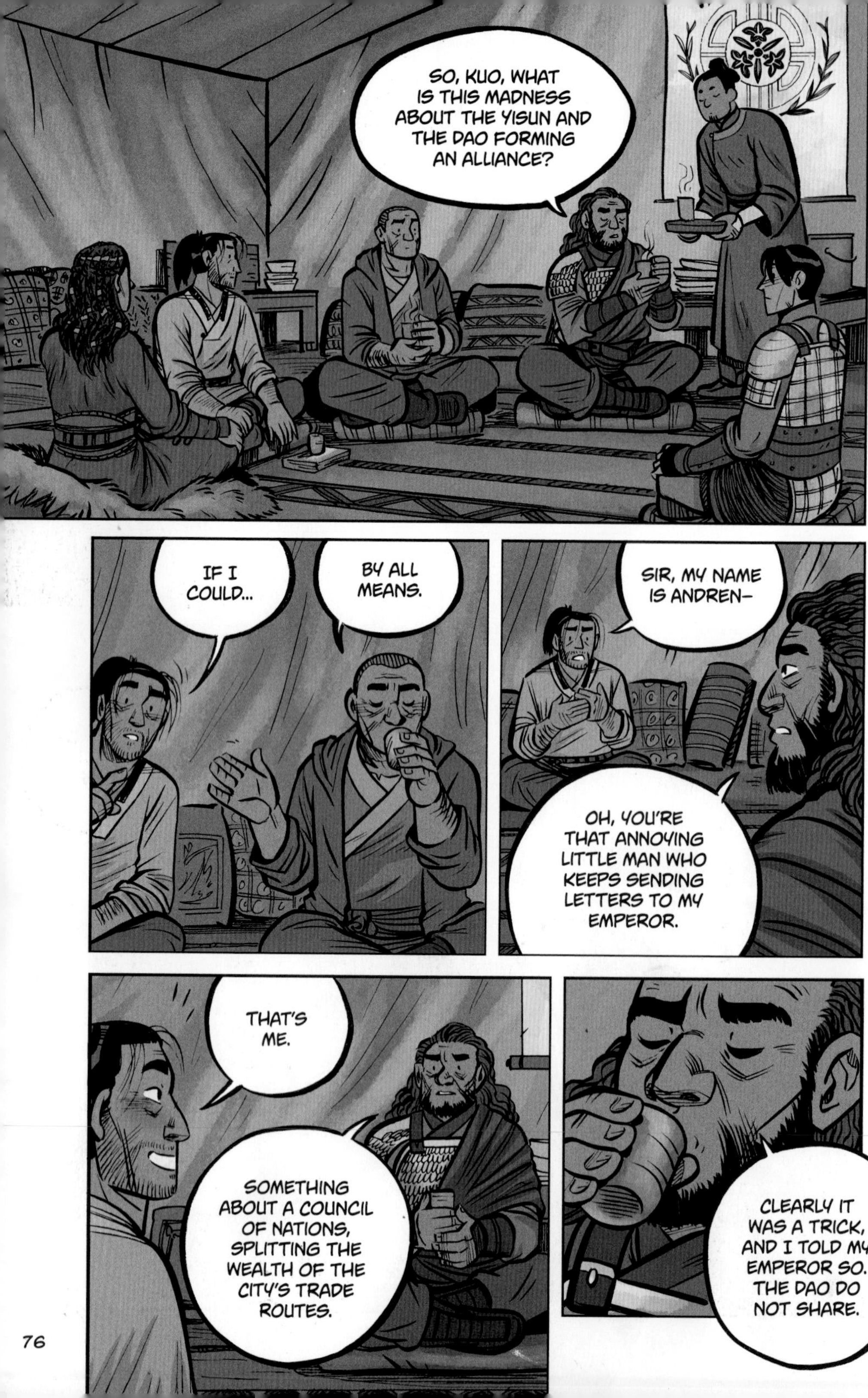
SO, KUO, WHAT IS THIS MADNESS ABOUT THE YISUN AND THE DAO FORMING AN ALLIANCE?
IF I COULD...
BY ALL MEANS.
SIR, MY NAME IS ANDREN–
OH, YOU'RE THAT ANNOYING LITTLE MAN WHO KEEPS SENDING LETTERS TO MY EMPEROR.
THAT'S ME.
SOMETHING ABOUT A COUNCIL OF NATIONS, SPLITTING THE WEALTH OF THE CITY'S TRADE ROUTES.
CLEARLY IT WAS A TRICK, AND I TOLD MY EMPEROR SO. THE DAO DO NOT SHARE.

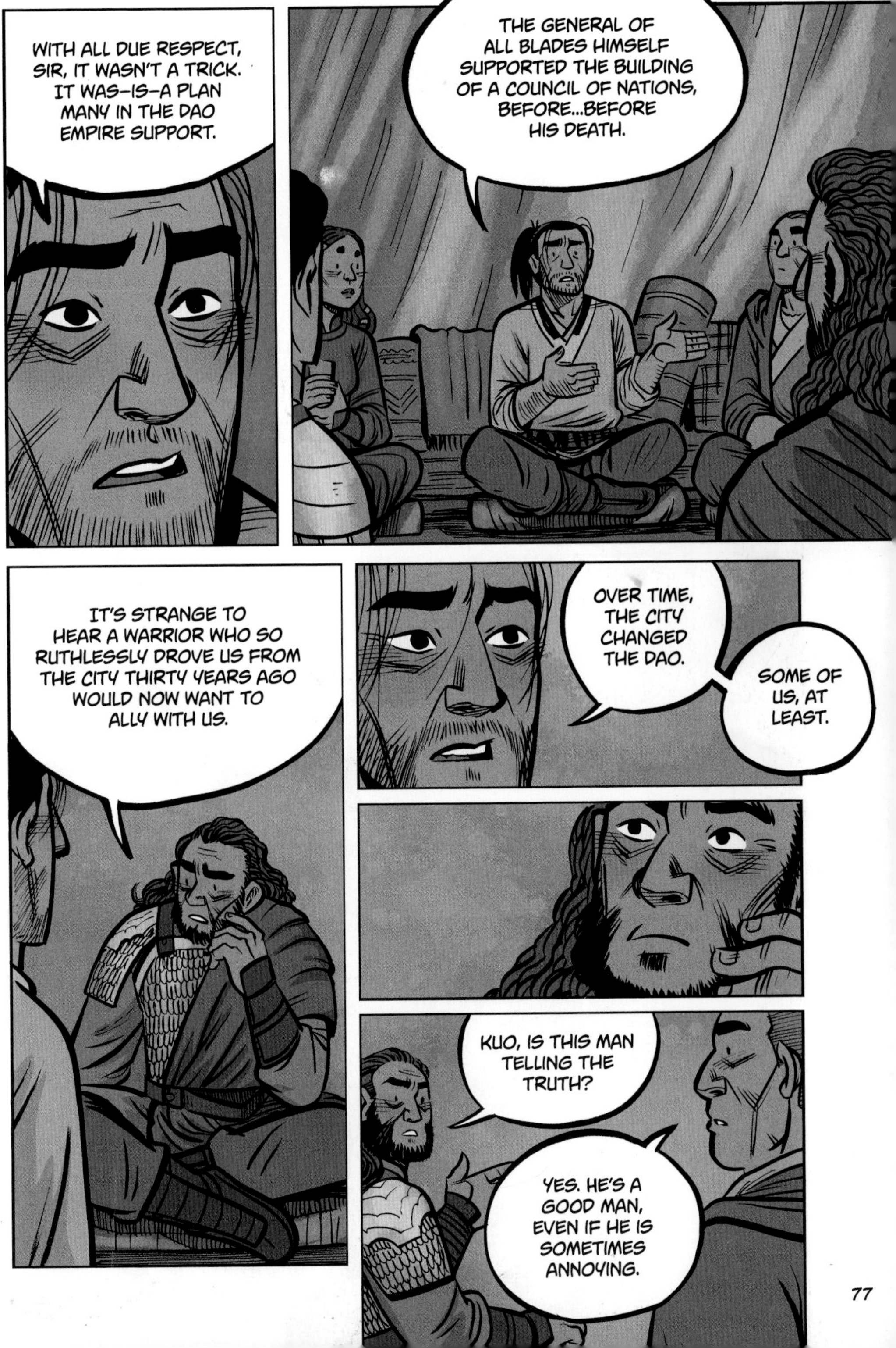
WITH ALL DUE RESPECT, SIR, IT WASN'T A TRICK. IT WAS—IS—A PLAN MANY IN THE DAO EMPIRE SUPPORT.
THE GENERAL OF ALL BLADES HIMSELF SUPPORTED THE BUILDING OF A COUNCIL OF NATIONS, BEFORE...BEFORE HIS DEATH.
IT'S STRANGE TO HEAR A WARRIOR WHO SO RUTHLESSLY DROVE US FROM THE CITY THIRTY YEARS AGO WOULD NOW WANT TO ALLY WITH US.
OVER TIME, THE CITY CHANGED THE DAO.
SOME OF US, AT LEAST.
KUO, IS THIS MAN TELLING THE TRUTH?
YES. HE'S A GOOD MAN, EVEN IF HE IS SOMETIMES ANNOYING.

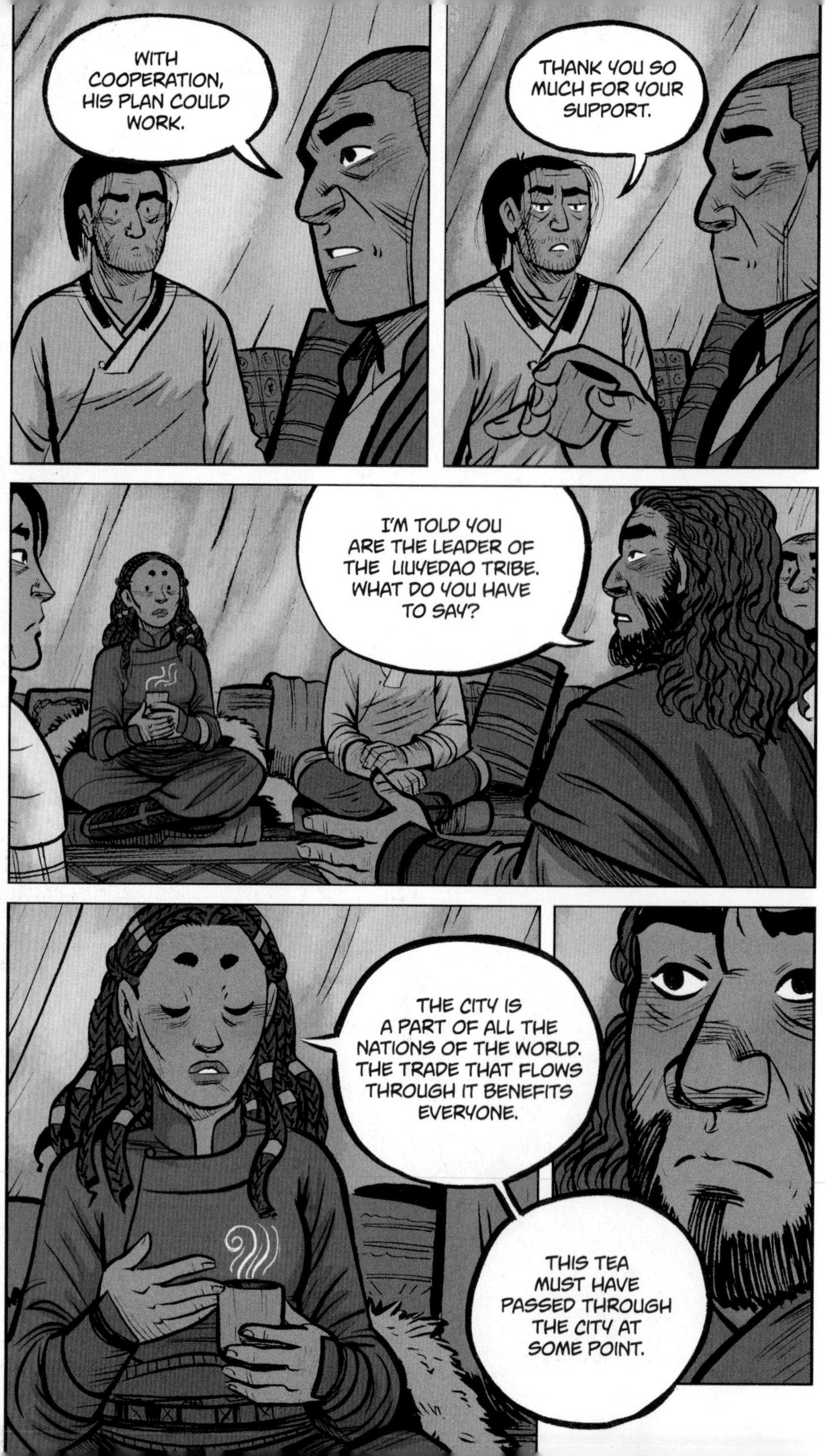
WITH COOPERATION, HIS PLAN COULD WORK.
THANK YOU SO MUCH FOR YOUR SUPPORT.
I'M TOLD YOU ARE THE LEADER OF THE LIUYEDAO TRIBE. WHAT DO YOU HAVE TO SAY?
THE CITY IS A PART OF ALL THE NATIONS OF THE WORLD. THE TRADE THAT FLOWS THROUGH IT BENEFITS EVERYONE.
THIS TEA MUST HAVE PASSED THROUGH THE CITY AT SOME POINT.

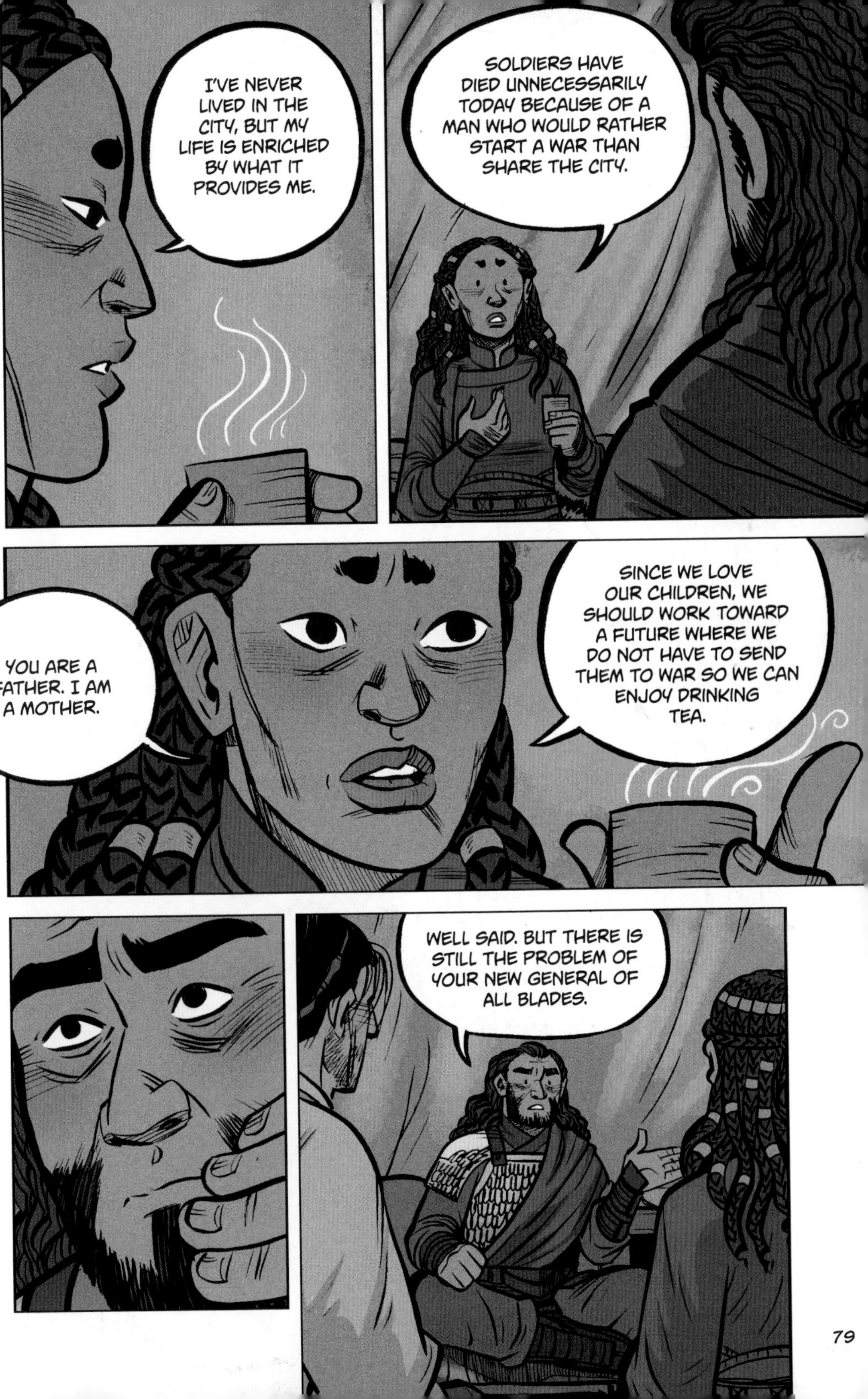
I'VE NEVER LIVED IN THE CITY, BUT MY LIFE IS ENRICHED BY WHAT IT PROVIDES ME.
SOLDIERS HAVE DIED UNNECESSARILY TODAY BECAUSE OF A MAN WHO WOULD RATHER START A WAR THAN SHARE THE CITY.
YOU ARE A FATHER. I AM A MOTHER.
SINCE WE LOVE OUR CHILDREN, WE SHOULD WORK TOWARD A FUTURE WHERE WE DO NOT HAVE TO SEND THEM TO WAR SO WE CAN ENJOY DRINKING TEA.
WELL SAID. BUT THERE IS STILL THE PROBLEM OF YOUR NEW GENERAL OF ALL BLADES.

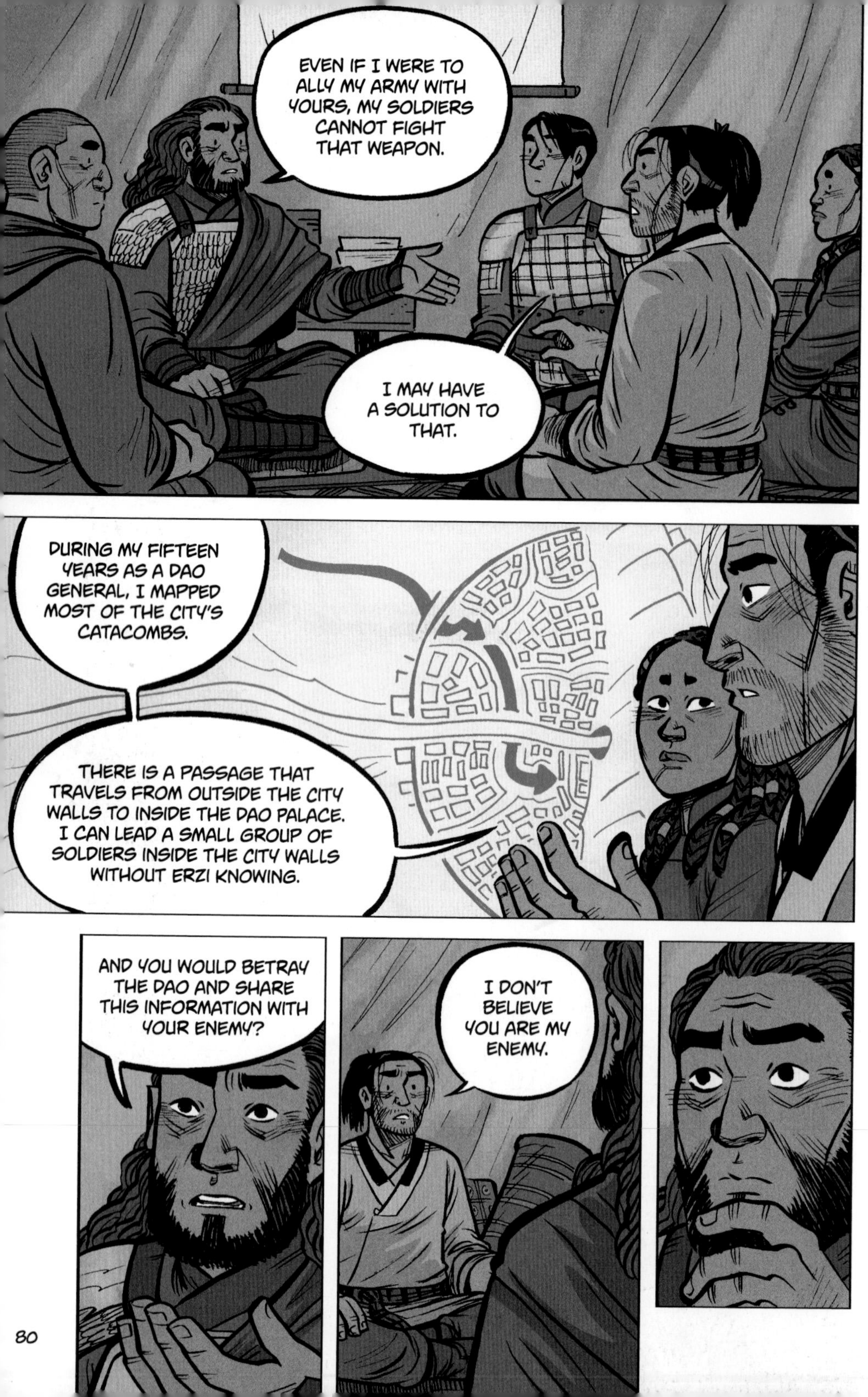
EVEN IF I WERE TO ALLY MY ARMY WITH YOURS, MY SOLDIERS CANNOT FIGHT THAT WEAPON.
I MAY HAVE A SOLUTION TO THAT.
DURING MY FIFTEEN YEARS AS A DAO GENERAL, I MAPPED MOST OF THE CITY'S CATACOMBS.
THERE IS A PASSAGE THAT TRAVELS FROM OUTSIDE THE CITY WALLS TO INSIDE THE DAO PALACE. I CAN LEAD A SMALL GROUP OF SOLDIERS INSIDE THE CITY WALLS WITHOUT ERZI KNOWING.
AND YOU WOULD BETRAY THE DAO AND SHARE THIS INFORMATION WITH YOUR ENEMY?
I DON'T BELIEVE YOU ARE MY ENEMY.

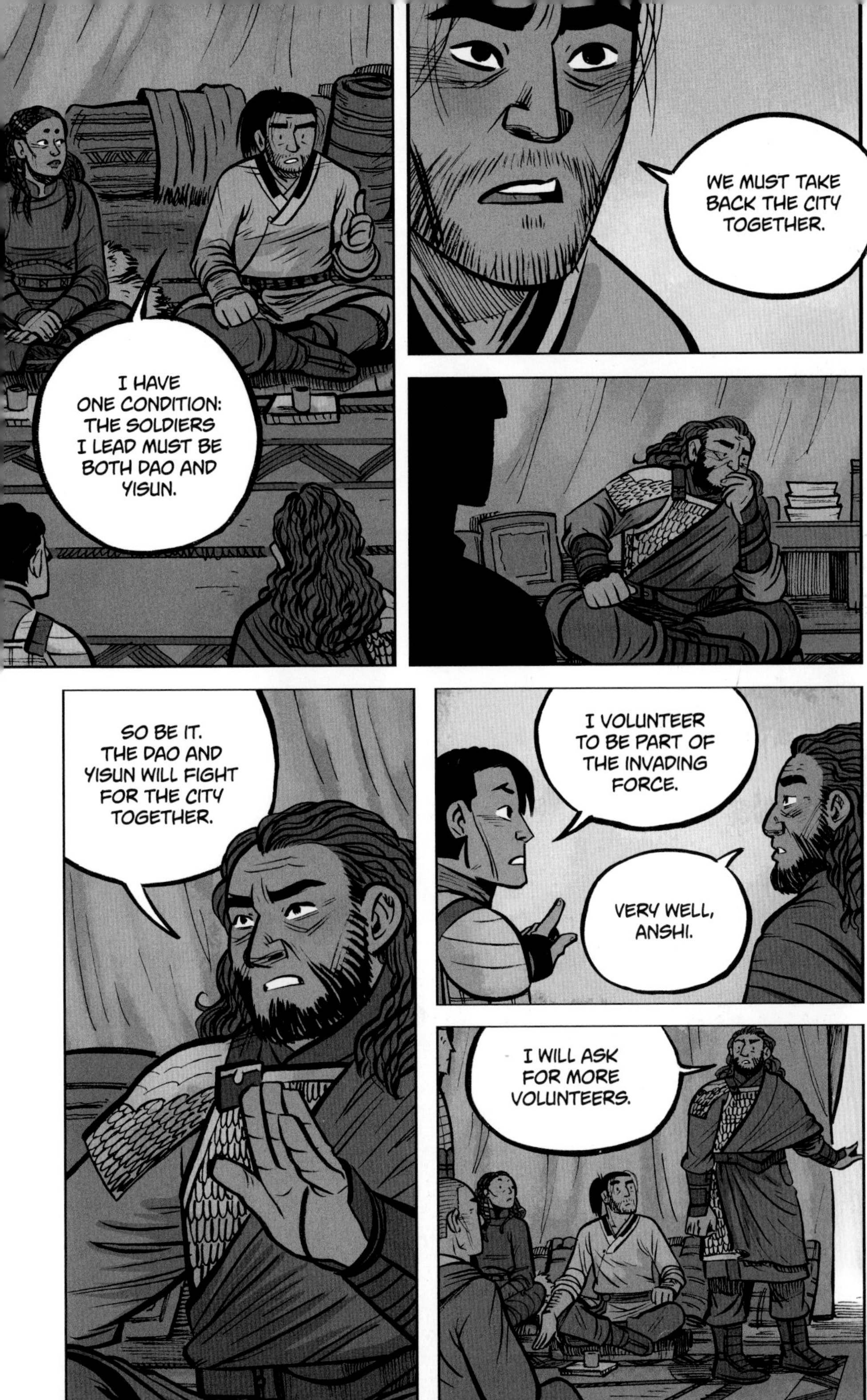
I HAVE ONE CONDITION: THE SOLDIERS I LEAD MUST BE BOTH DAO AND YISUN.
WE MUST TAKE BACK THE CITY TOGETHER.
SO BE IT. THE DAO AND YISUN WILL FIGHT FOR THE CITY TOGETHER.
I VOLUNTEER TO BE PART OF THE INVADING FORCE.
VERY WELL, ANSHI.
I WILL ASK FOR MORE VOLUNTEERS.

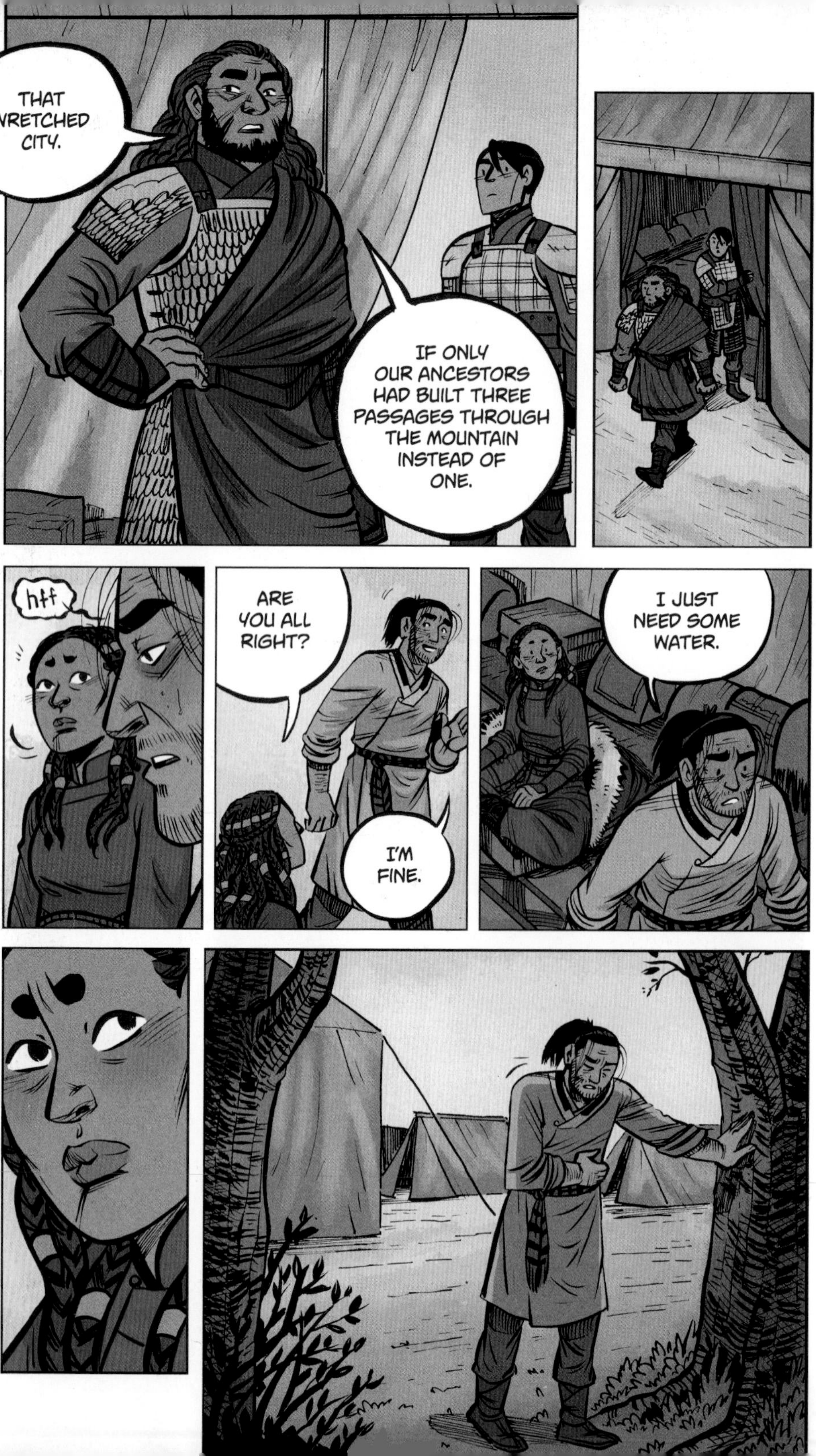
THAT WRETCHED CITY.
IF ONLY OUR ANCESTORS HAD BUILT THREE PASSAGES THROUGH THE MOUNTAIN INSTEAD OF ONE.
hff
ARE YOU ALL RIGHT?
I'M FINE.
I JUST NEED SOME WATER.

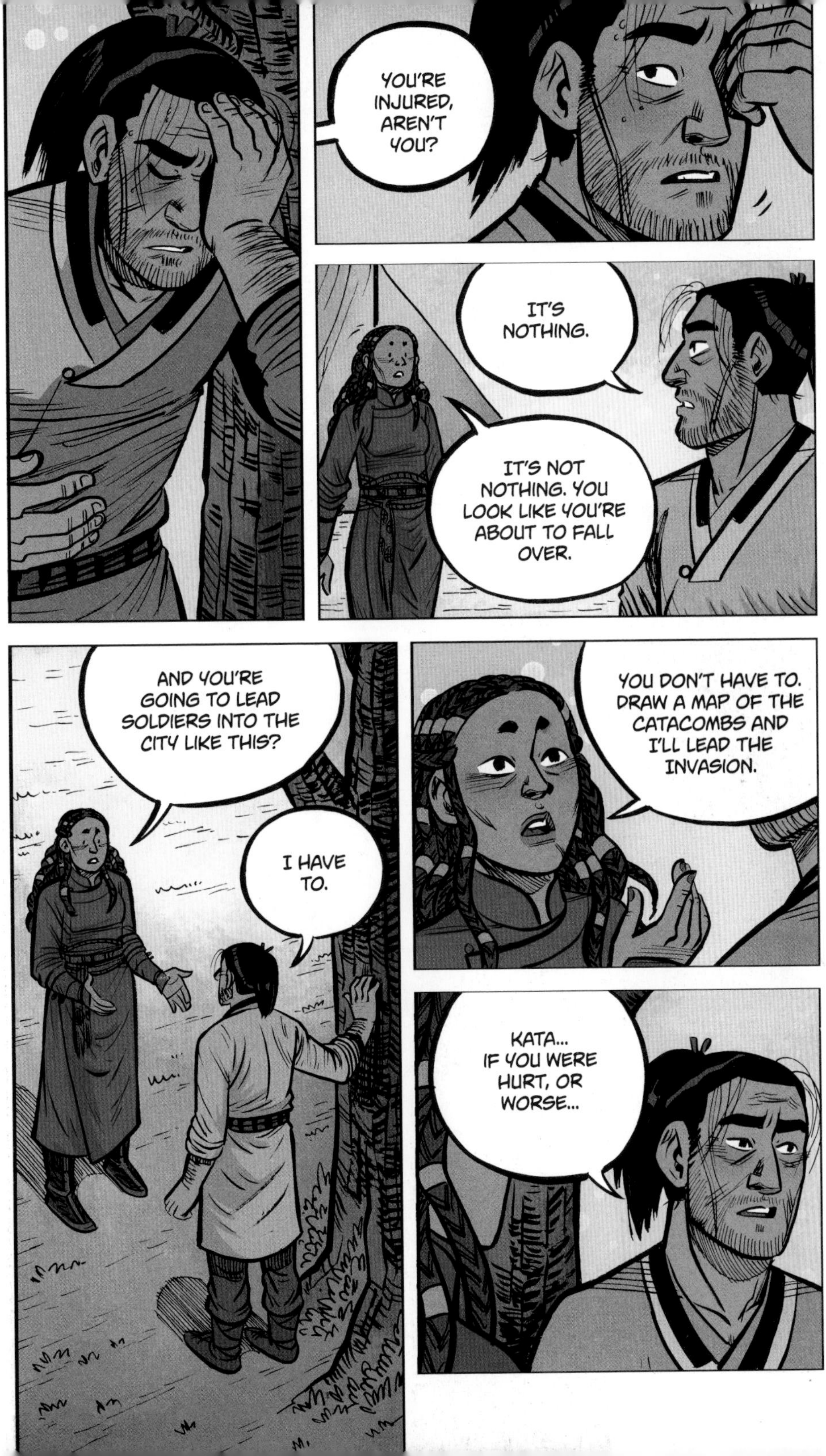
YOU'RE INJURED, AREN'T YOU?
IT'S NOTHING.
IT'S NOT NOTHING. YOU LOOK LIKE YOU'RE ABOUT TO FALL OVER.
AND YOU'RE GOING TO LEAD SOLDIERS INTO THE CITY LIKE THIS?
I HAVE TO.
YOU DON'T HAVE TO. DRAW A MAP OF THE CATACOMBS AND I'LL LEAD THE INVASION.
KATA... IF YOU WERE HURT, OR WORSE...

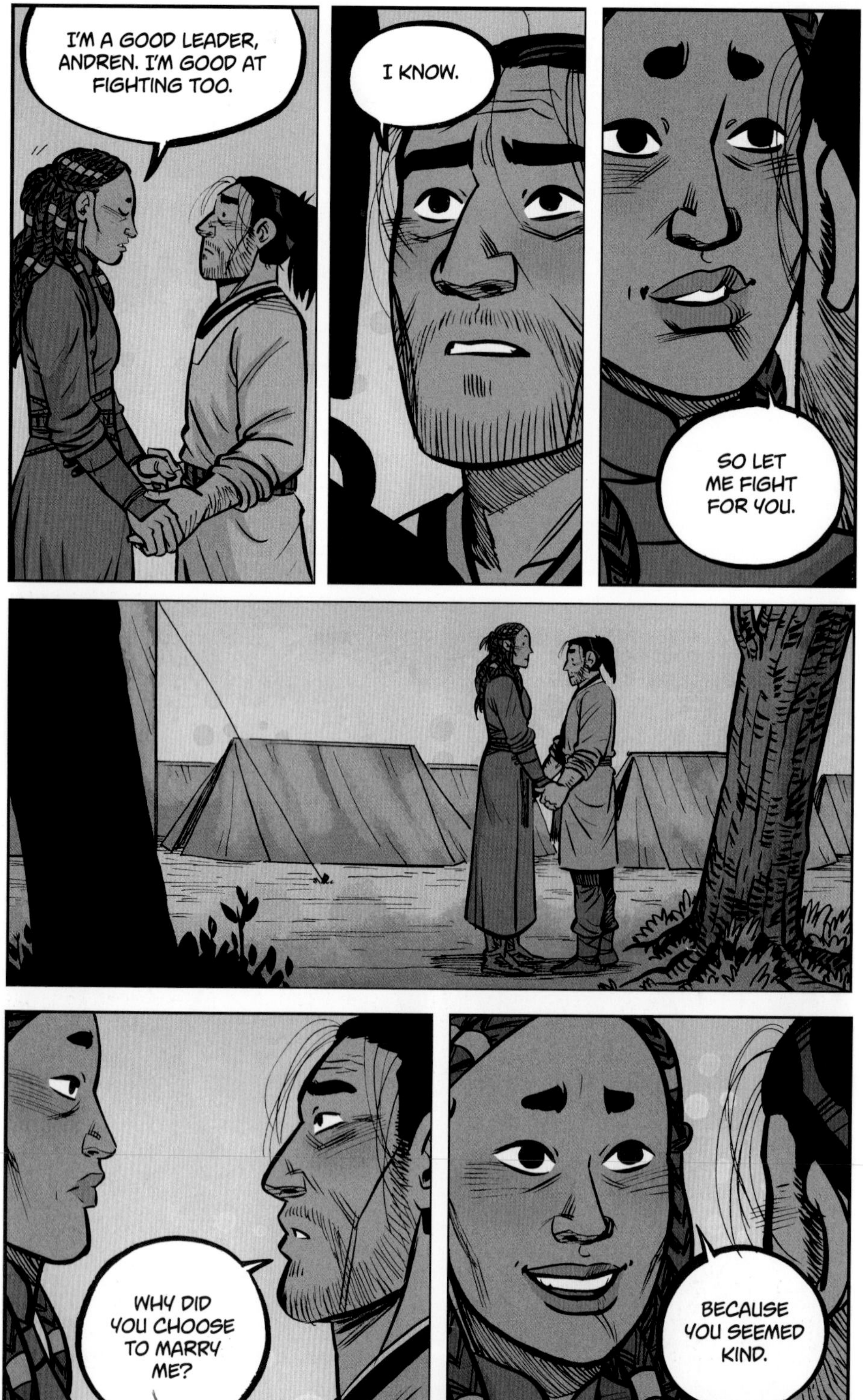
I'M A GOOD LEADER, ANDREN. I'M GOOD AT FIGHTING TOO.
I KNOW.
SO LET ME FIGHT FOR YOU.
WHY DID YOU CHOOSE TO MARRY ME?
BECAUSE YOU SEEMED KIND.

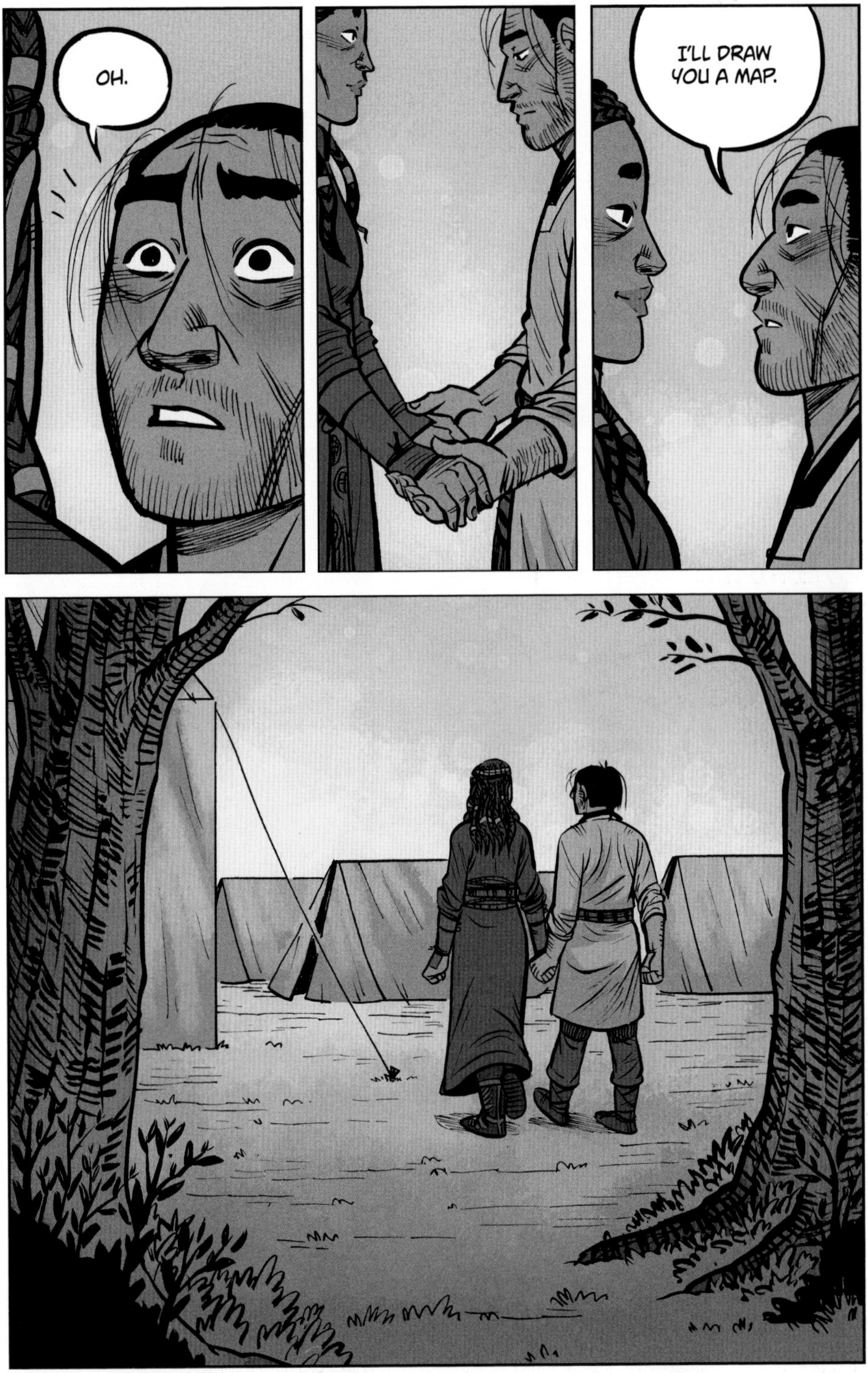
OH.
I'LL DRAW YOU A MAP.

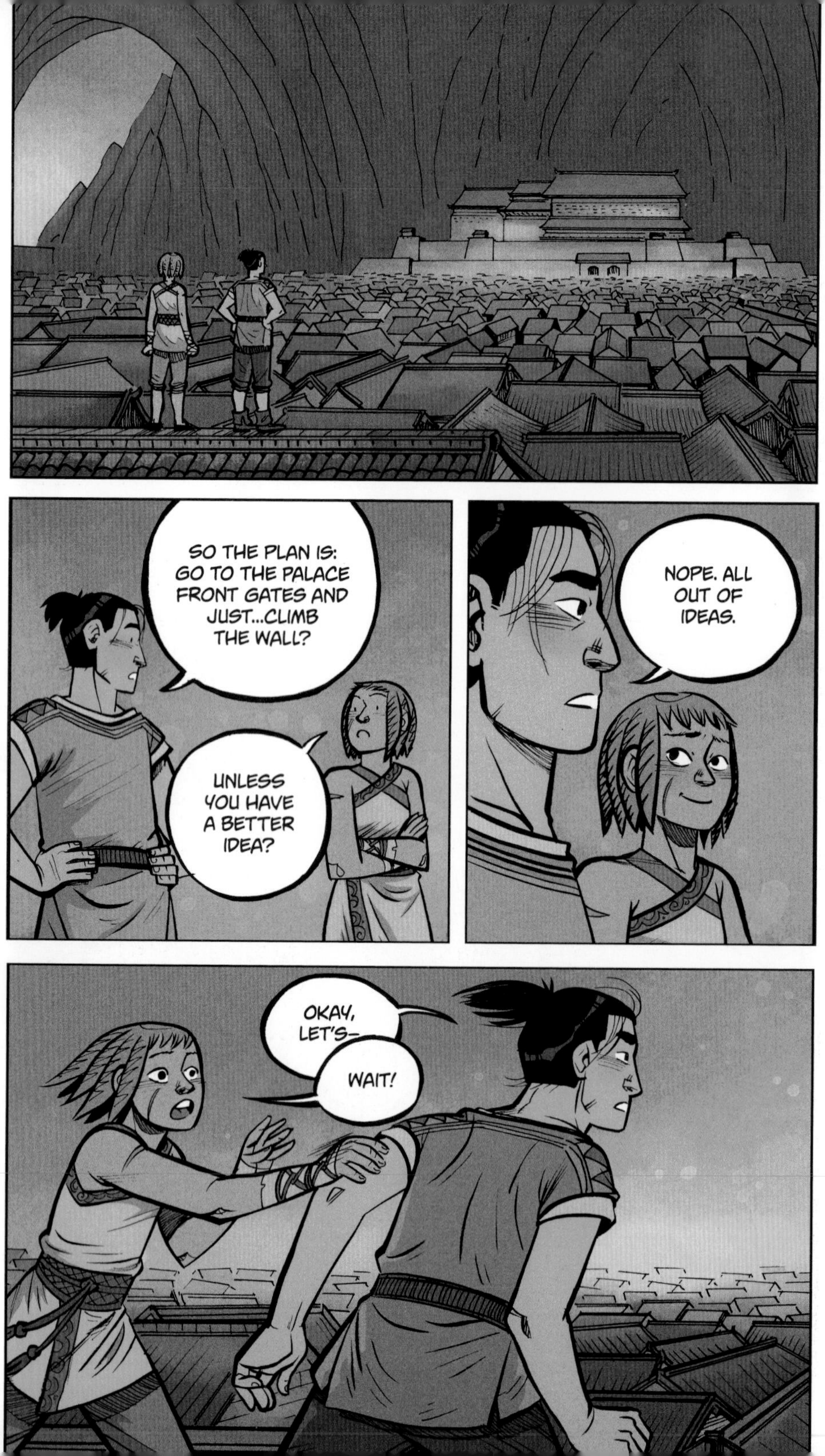
SO THE PLAN IS: GO TO THE PALACE FRONT GATES AND JUST...CLIMB THE WALL?
UNLESS YOU HAVE A BETTER IDEA?
NOPE. ALL OUT OF IDEAS.
OKAY, LET'S—
WAIT!

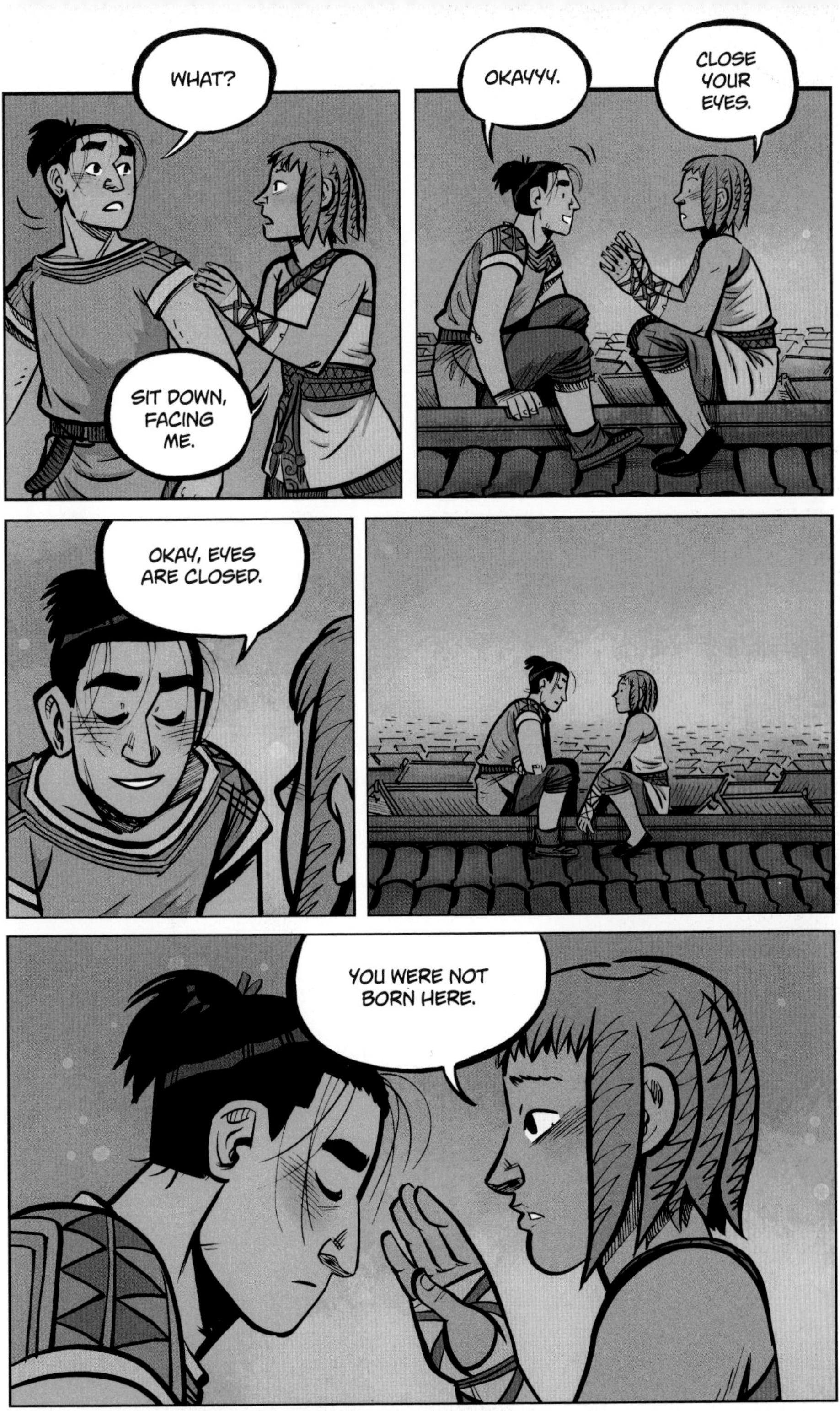
WHAT?
SIT DOWN, FACING ME.
OKAYYY.
CLOSE YOUR EYES.
OKAY, EYES ARE CLOSED.
YOU WERE NOT BORN HERE.

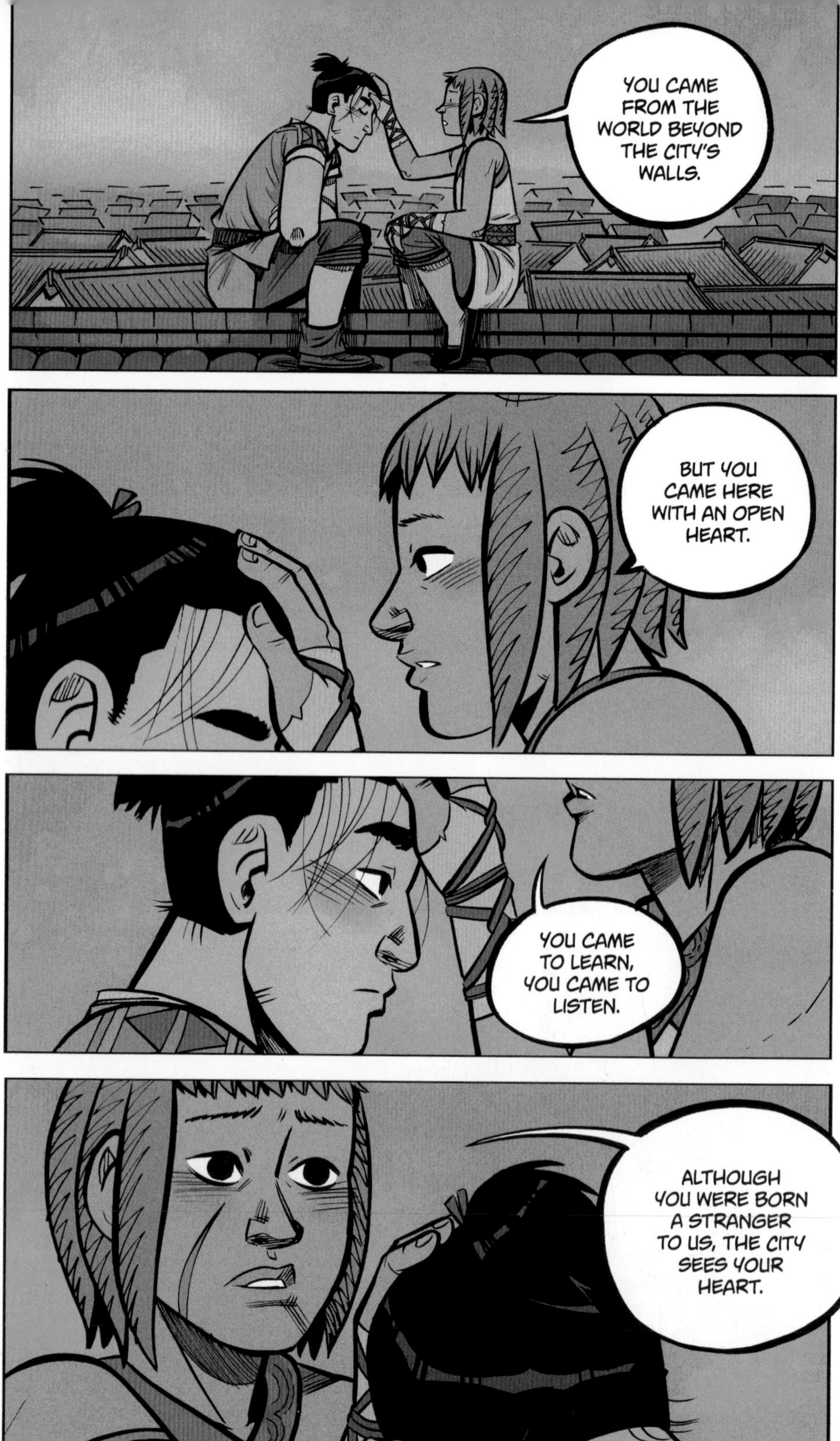
YOU CAME FROM THE WORLD BEYOND THE CITY'S WALLS.
BUT YOU CAME HERE WITH AN OPEN HEART.
YOU CAME TO LEARN, YOU CAME TO LISTEN.
ALTHOUGH YOU WERE BORN A STRANGER TO US, THE CITY SEES YOUR HEART.

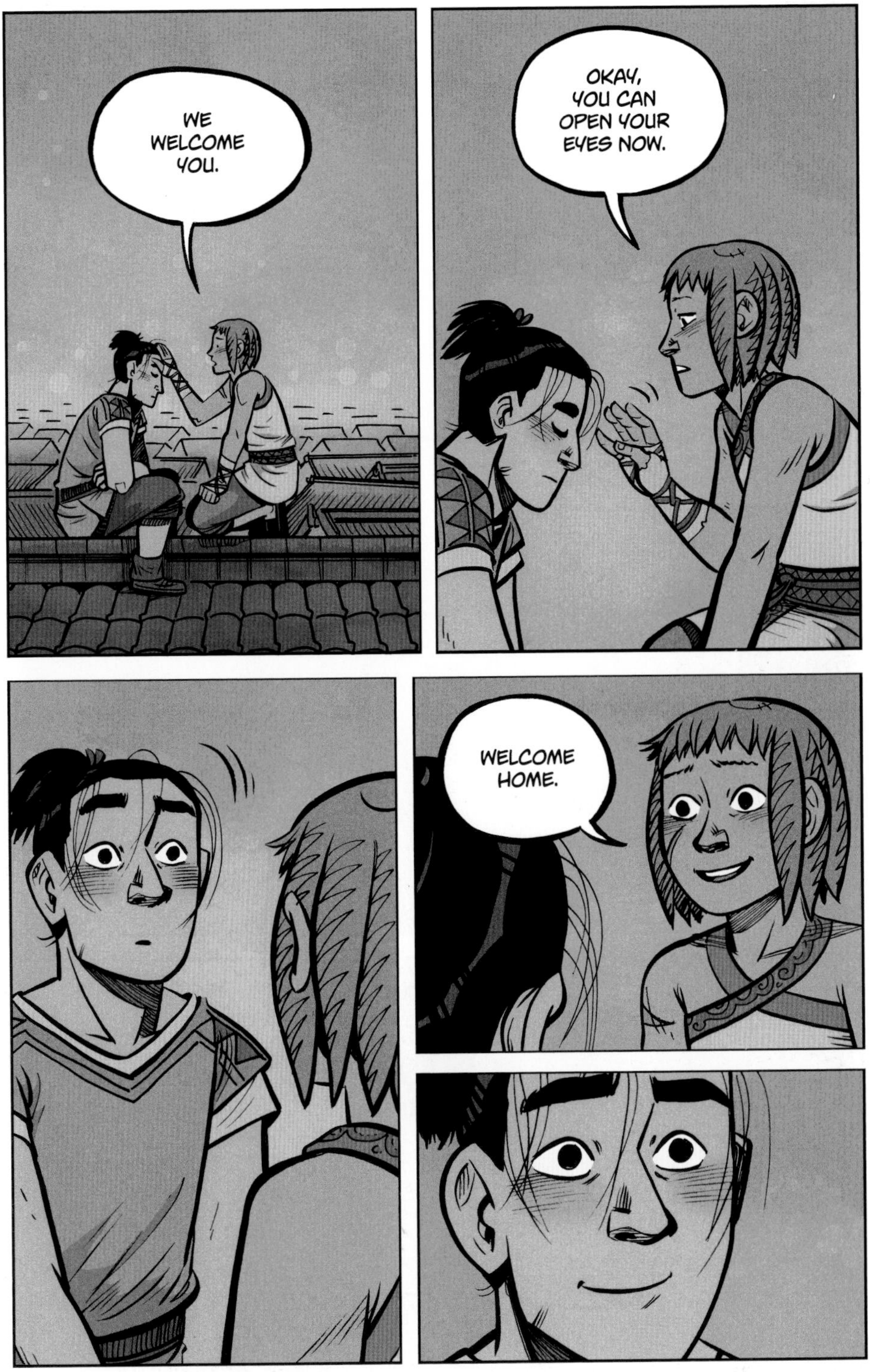
WE WELCOME YOU.
OKAY, YOU CAN OPEN YOUR EYES NOW.
WELCOME HOME.

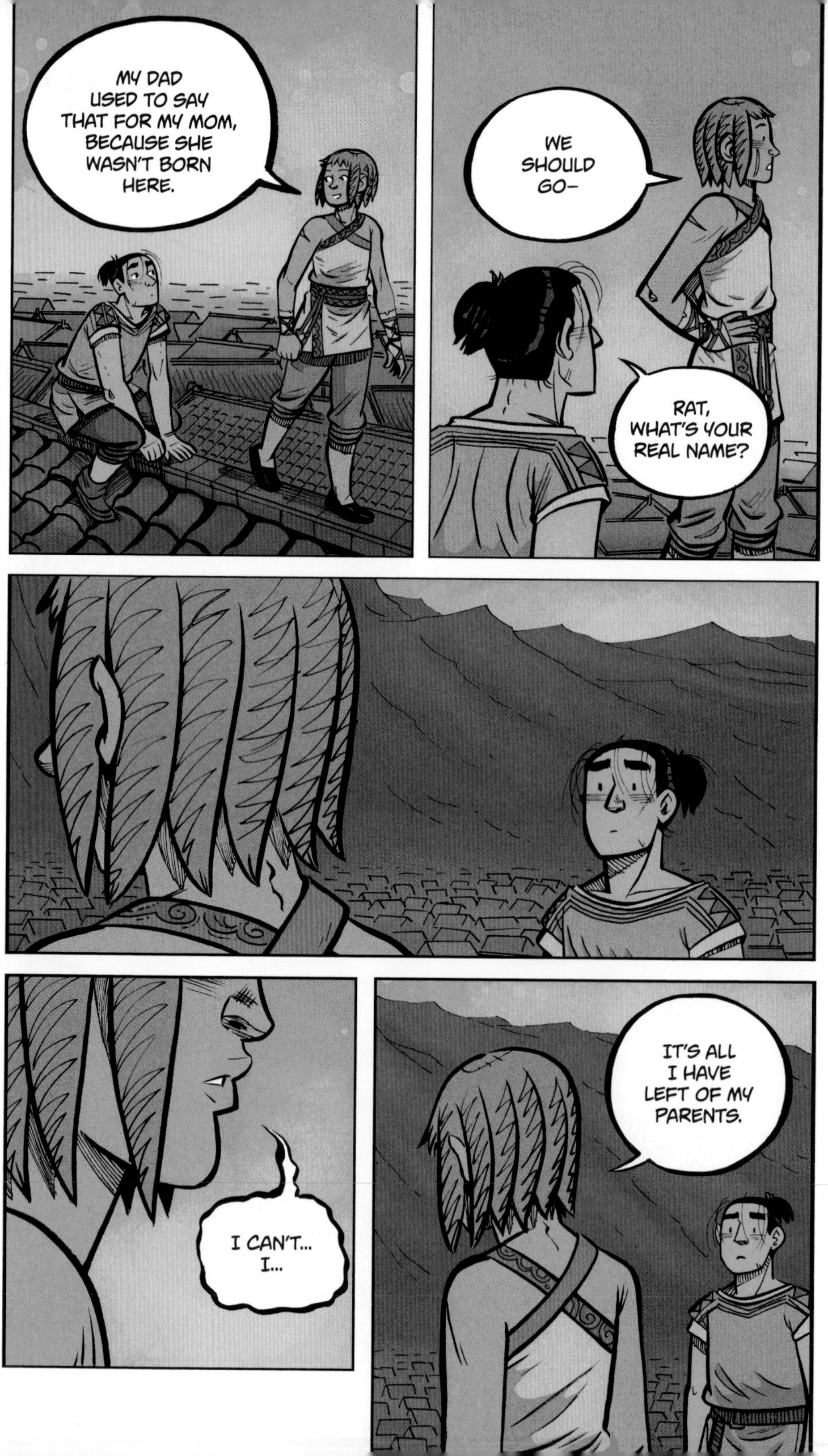
MY DAD USED TO SAY THAT FOR MY MOM, BECAUSE SHE WASN'T BORN HERE.
WE SHOULD GO–
RAT, WHAT'S YOUR REAL NAME?
I CAN'T... I...
IT'S ALL I HAVE LEFT OF MY PARENTS.

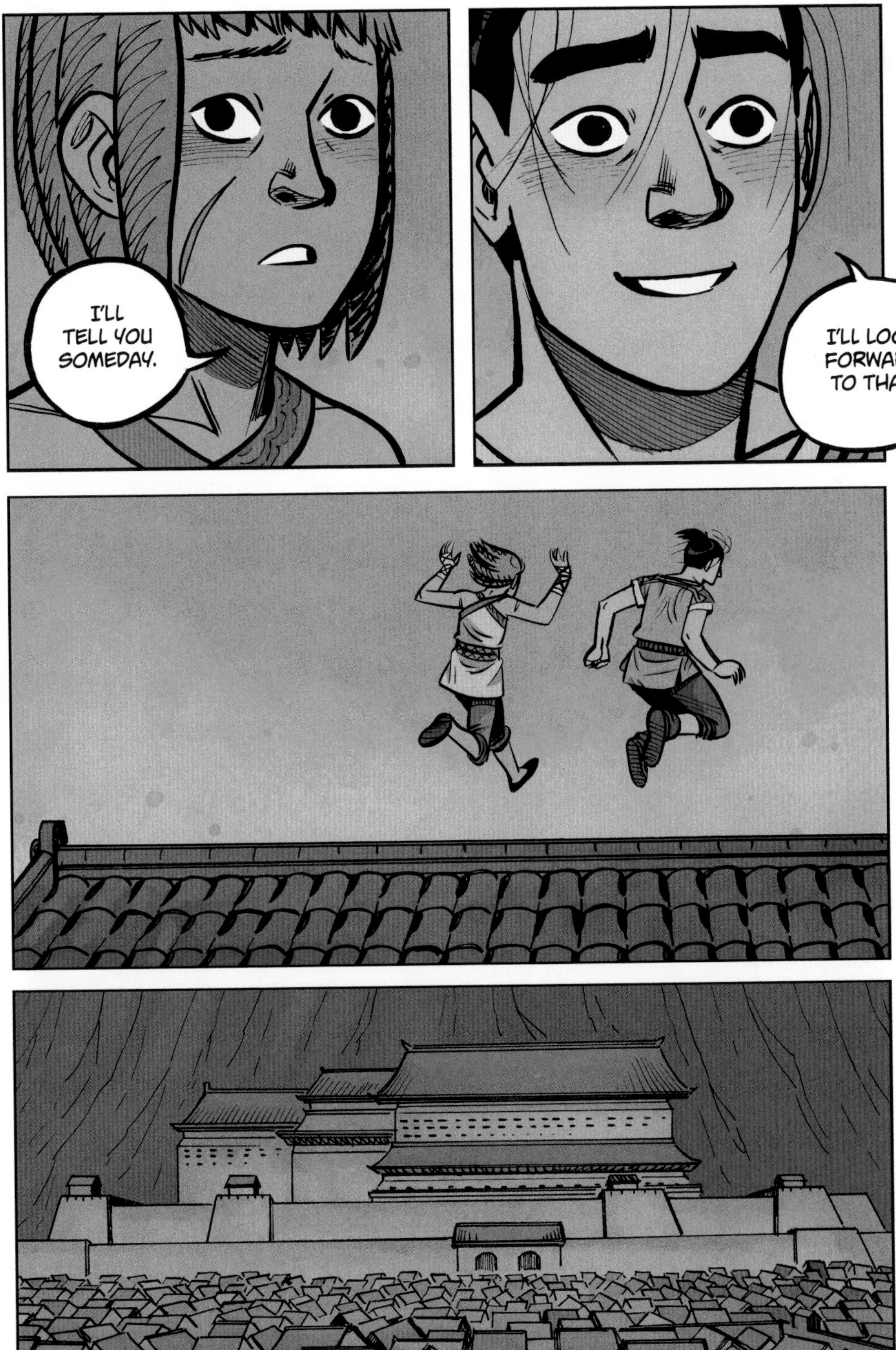
I'LL TELL YOU SOMEDAY.
I'LL LOOK FORWARD TO THAT.

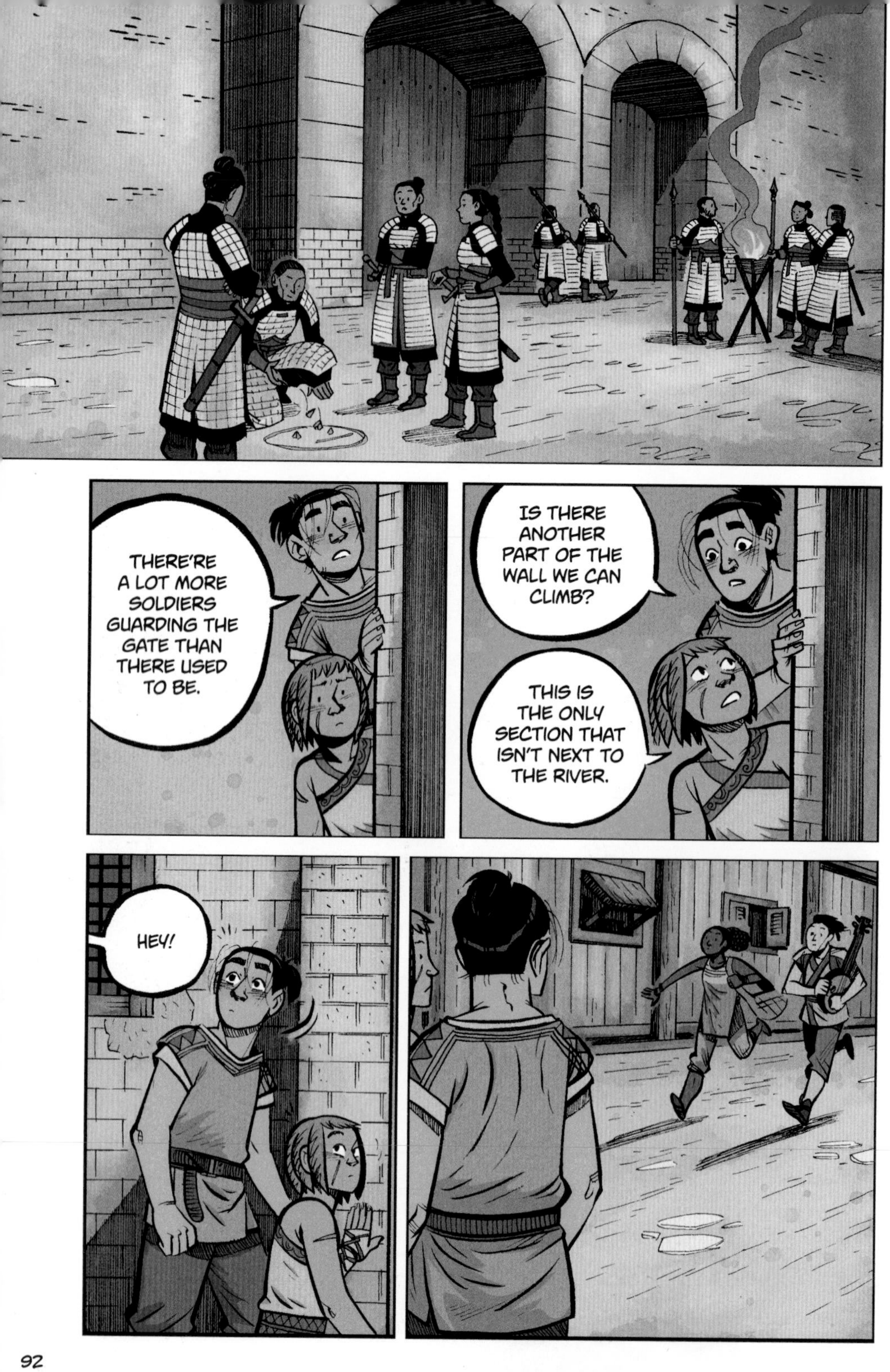
THERE'RE A LOT MORE SOLDIERS GUARDING THE GATE THAN THERE USED TO BE.
IS THERE ANOTHER PART OF THE WALL WE CAN CLIMB?
THIS IS THE ONLY SECTION THAT ISN'T NEXT TO THE RIVER.
HEY!

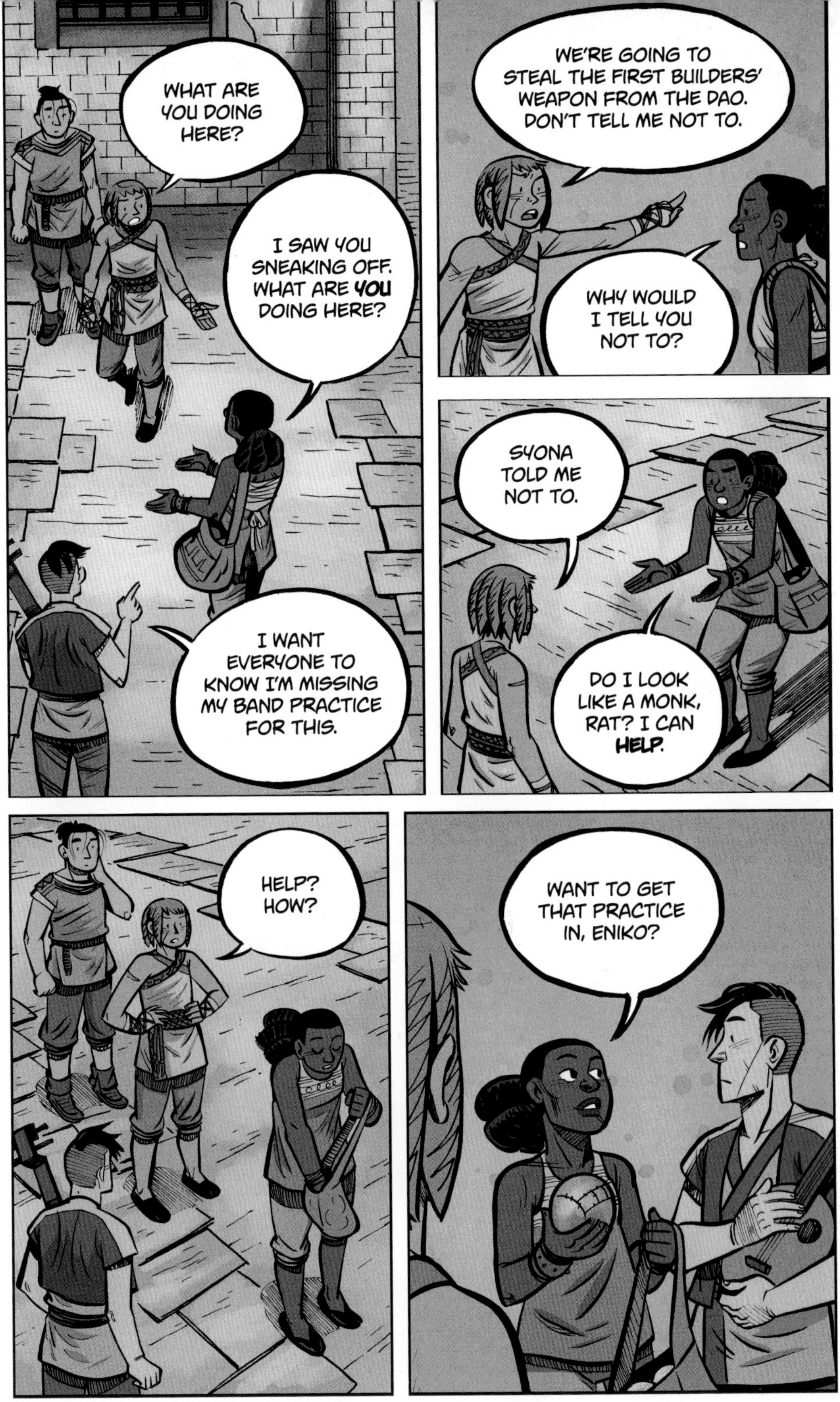
WHAT ARE YOU DOING HERE?
I SAW YOU SNEAKING OFF. WHAT ARE **YOU** DOING HERE?
I WANT EVERYONE TO KNOW I'M MISSING MY BAND PRACTICE FOR THIS.
WE'RE GOING TO STEAL THE FIRST BUILDERS' WEAPON FROM THE DAO. DON'T TELL ME NOT TO.
WHY WOULD I TELL YOU NOT TO?
SYONA TOLD ME NOT TO.
DO I LOOK LIKE A MONK, RAT? I CAN **HELP**.
HELP? HOW?
WANT TO GET THAT PRACTICE IN, ENIKO?

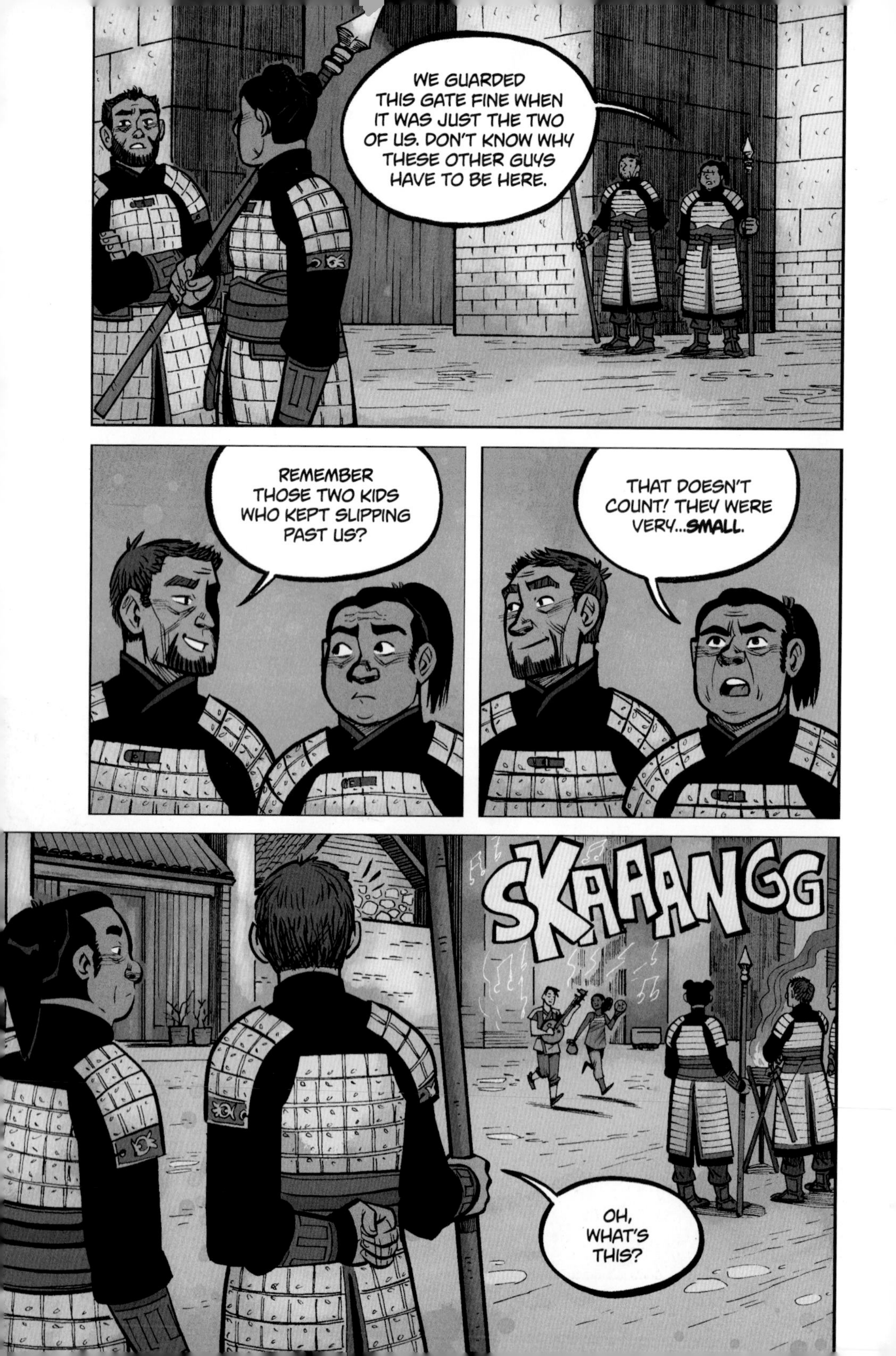
WE GUARDED THIS GATE FINE WHEN IT WAS JUST THE TWO OF US. DON'T KNOW WHY THESE OTHER GUYS HAVE TO BE HERE.
REMEMBER THOSE TWO KIDS WHO KEPT SLIPPING PAST US?
THAT DOESN'T COUNT! THEY WERE VERY...**SMALL**.
SKAAANGG
OH, WHAT'S THIS?

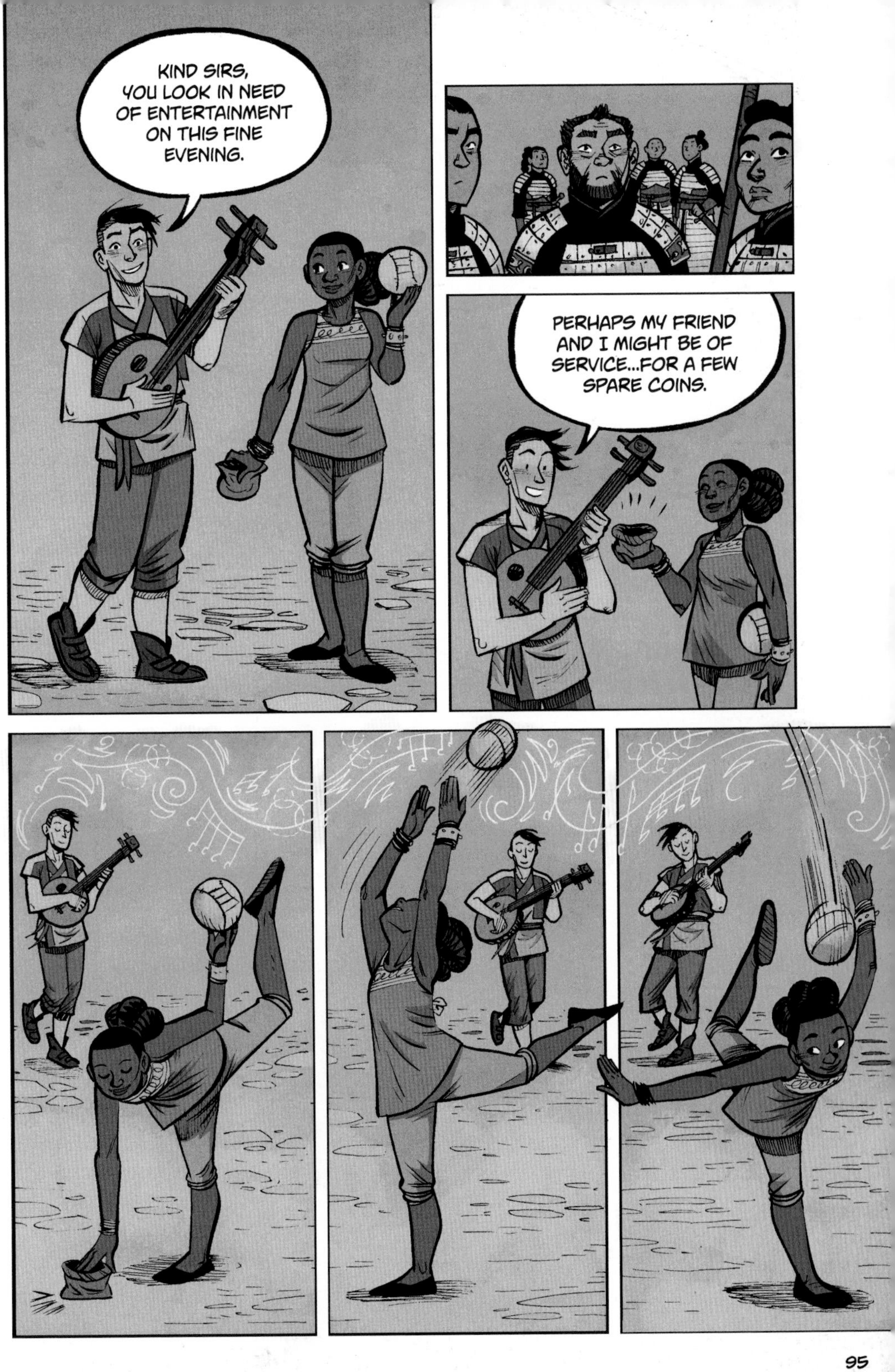
KIND SIRS, YOU LOOK IN NEED OF ENTERTAINMENT ON THIS FINE EVENING.
PERHAPS MY FRIEND AND I MIGHT BE OF SERVICE...FOR A FEW SPARE COINS.

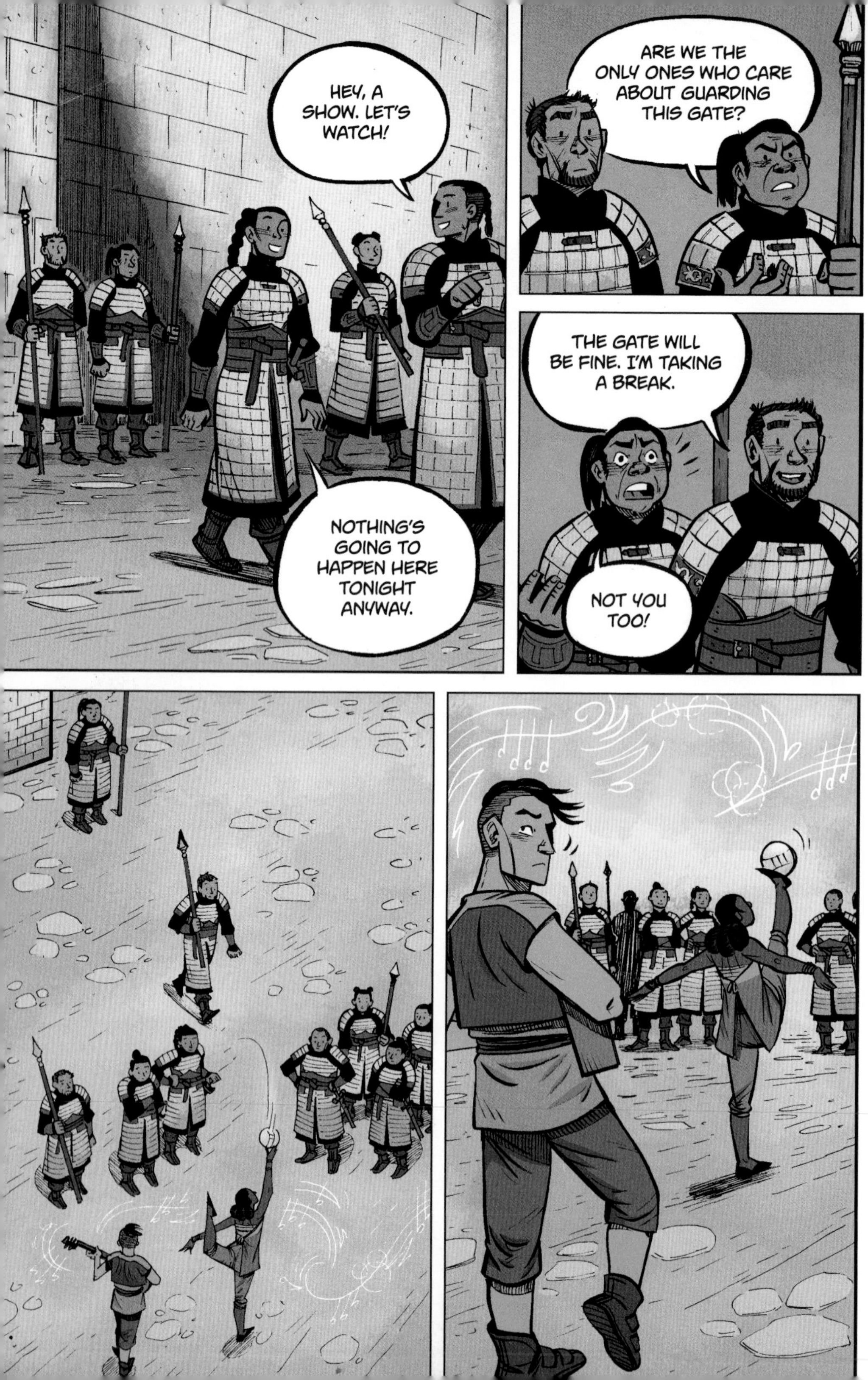
HEY, A SHOW. LET'S WATCH!
NOTHING'S GOING TO HAPPEN HERE TONIGHT ANYWAY.
ARE WE THE ONLY ONES WHO CARE ABOUT GUARDING THIS GATE?
THE GATE WILL BE FINE. I'M TAKING A BREAK.
NOT YOU TOO!

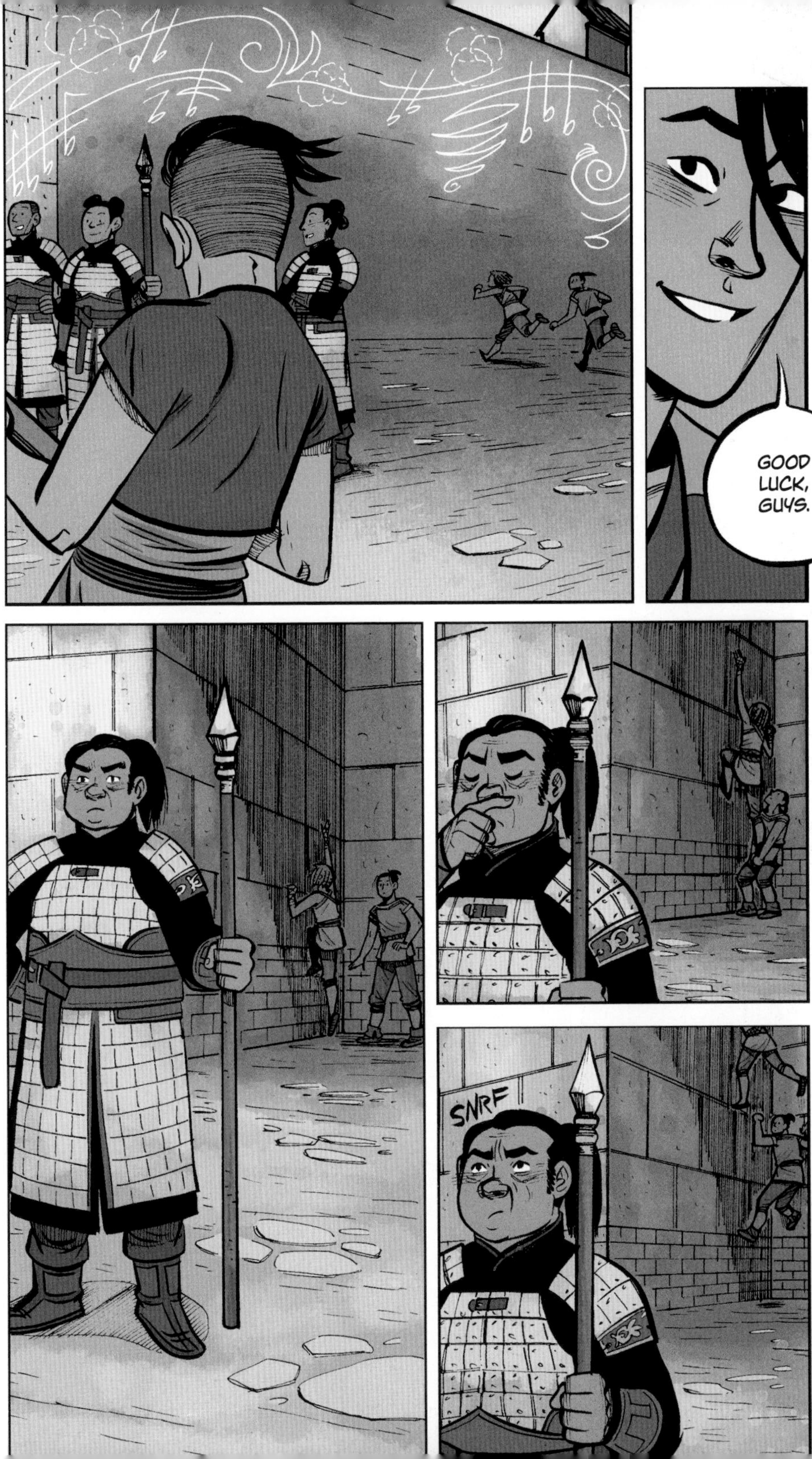
GOOD LUCK, GUYS.
SNRF

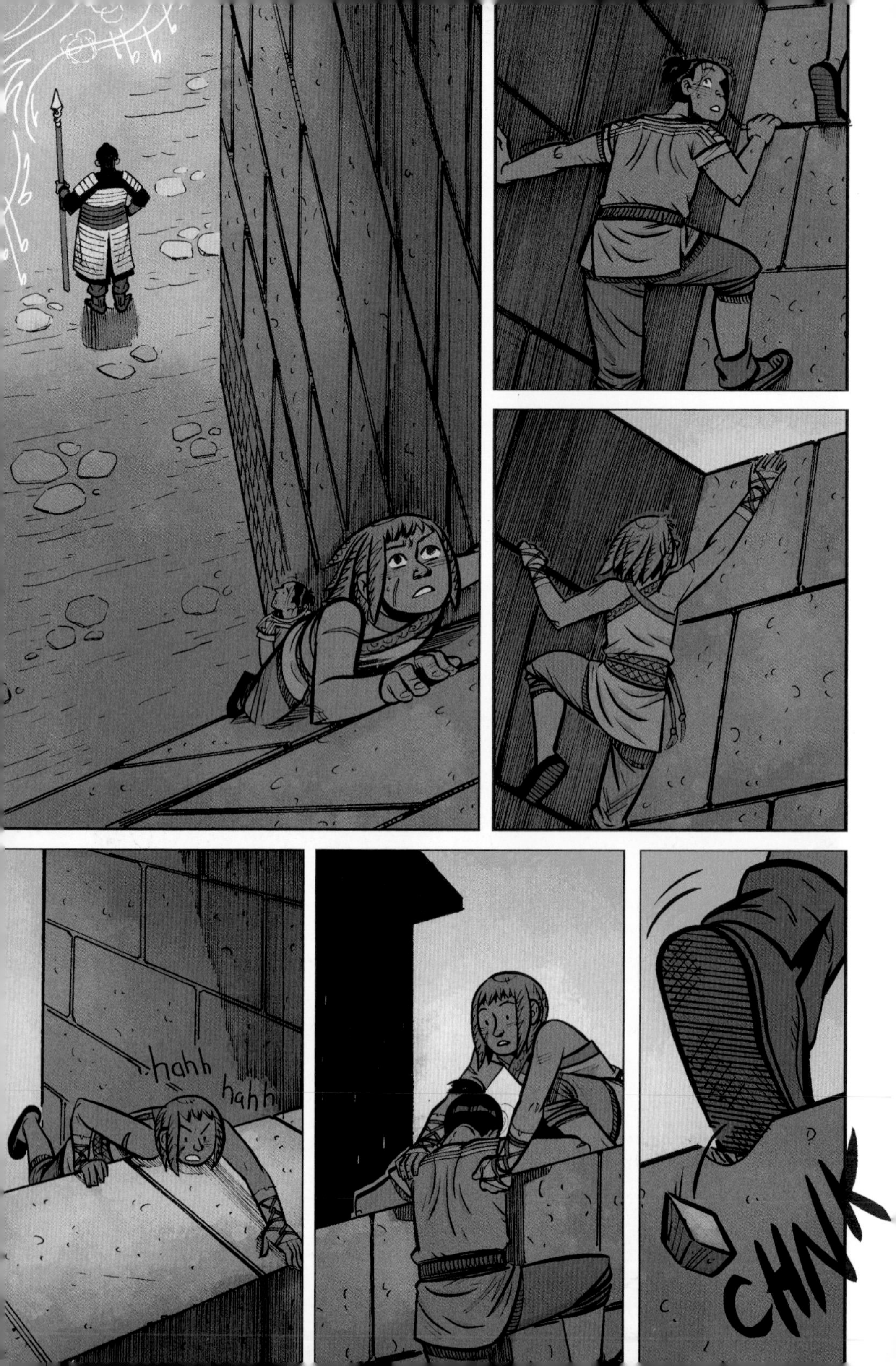
hahh
hahh
CHNK

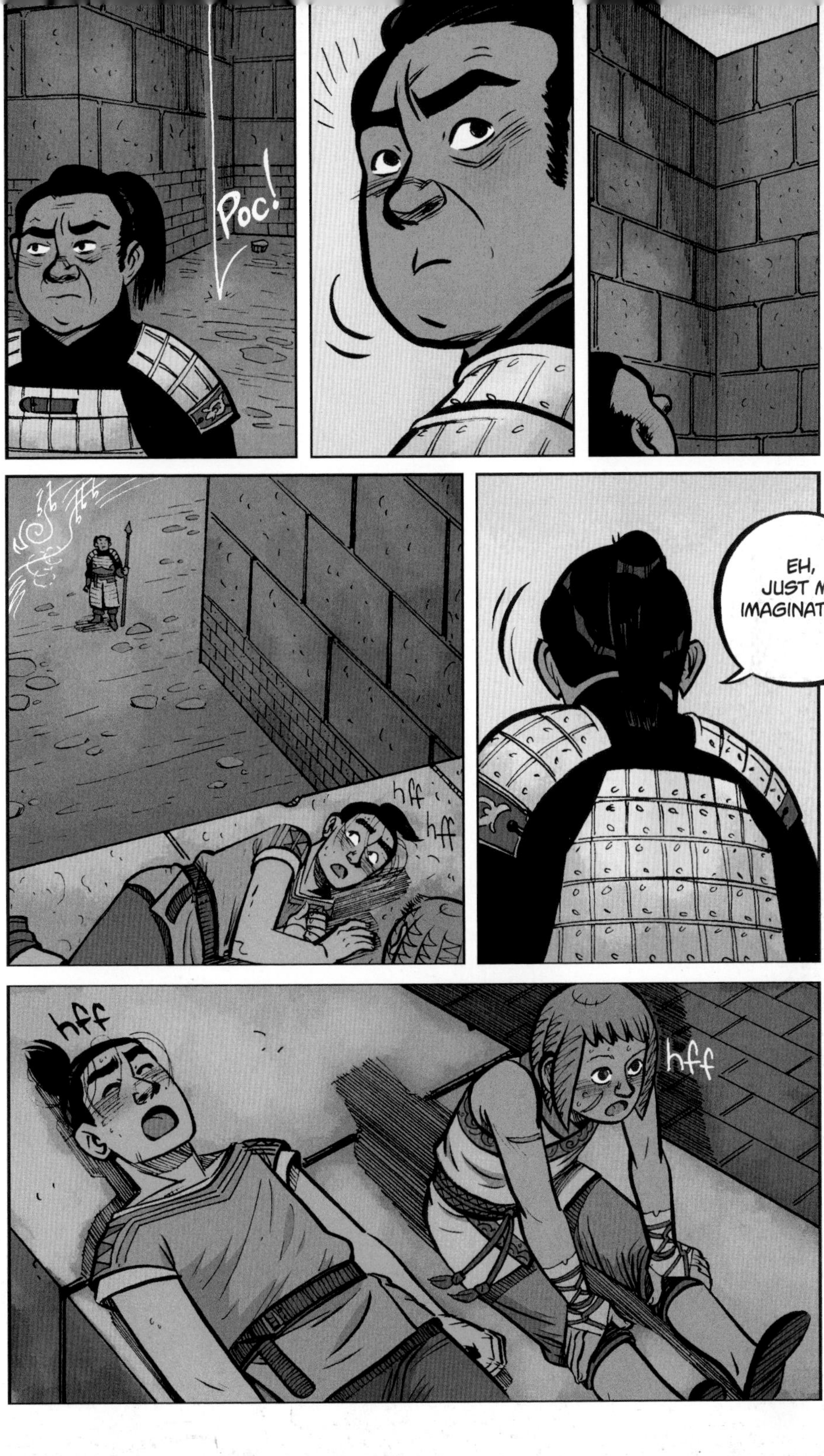
Poc!
EH, JUST MY IMAGINATION.
hff
hff
hff
hff

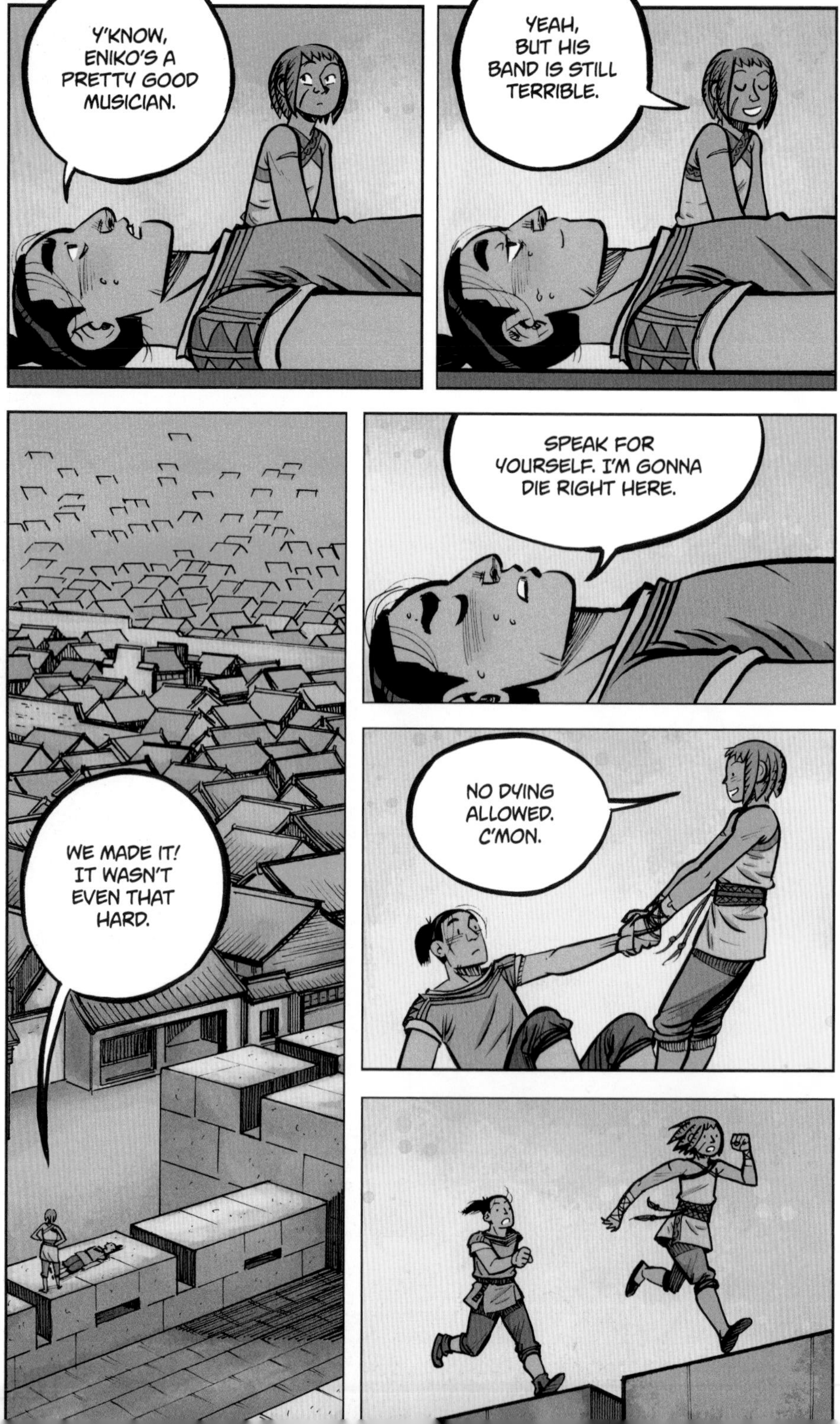
Y'KNOW, ENIKO'S A PRETTY GOOD MUSICIAN.
YEAH, BUT HIS BAND IS STILL TERRIBLE.
WE MADE IT! IT WASN'T EVEN THAT HARD.
SPEAK FOR YOURSELF. I'M GONNA DIE RIGHT HERE.
NO DYING ALLOWED. C'MON.

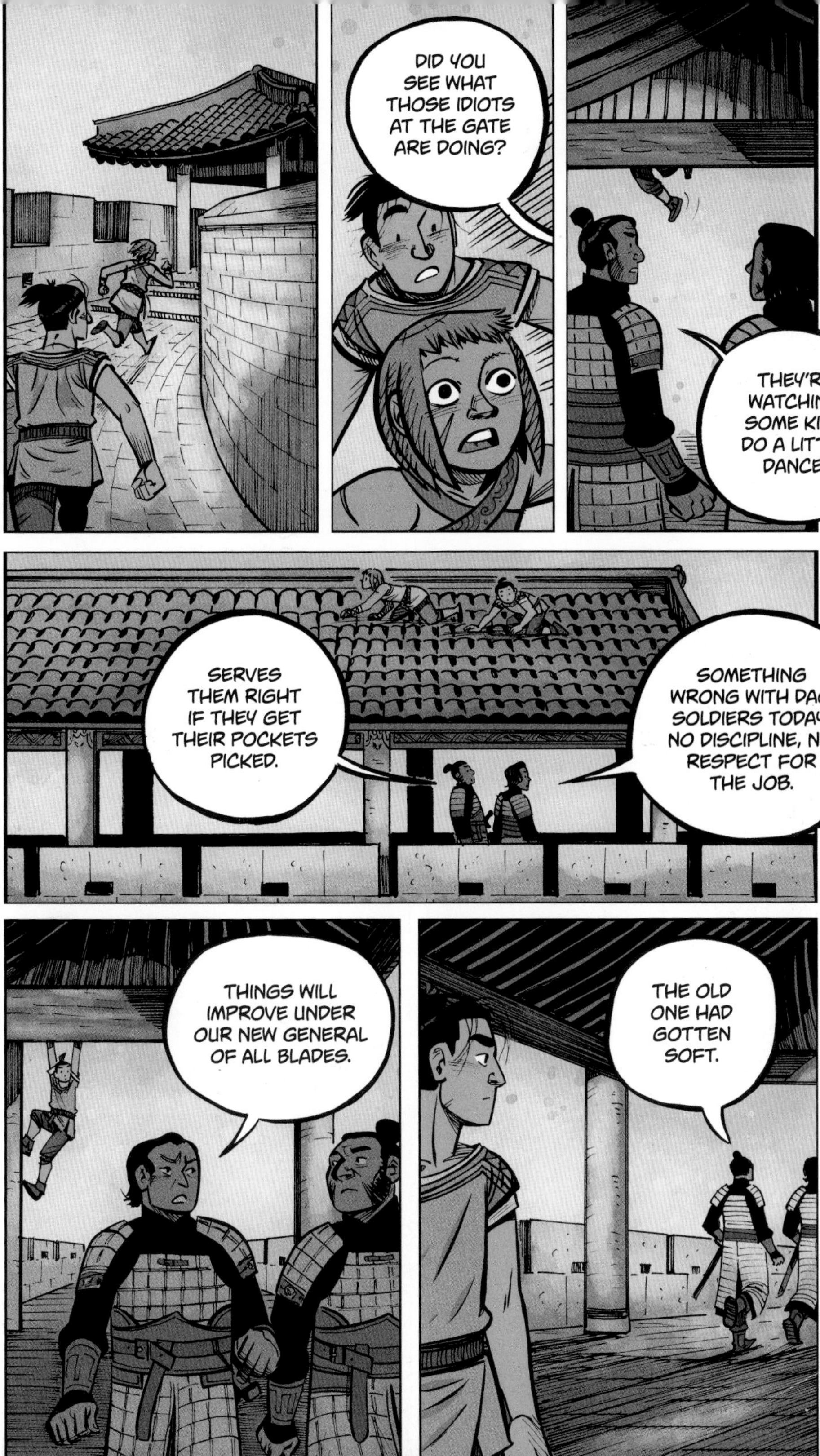
DID YOU SEE WHAT THOSE IDIOTS AT THE GATE ARE DOING?
THEY'RE WATCHING SOME KIDS DO A LITTLE DANCE.
SERVES THEM RIGHT IF THEY GET THEIR POCKETS PICKED.
SOMETHING WRONG WITH DAO SOLDIERS TODAY. NO DISCIPLINE, NO RESPECT FOR THE JOB.
THINGS WILL IMPROVE UNDER OUR NEW GENERAL OF ALL BLADES.
THE OLD ONE HAD GOTTEN SOFT.

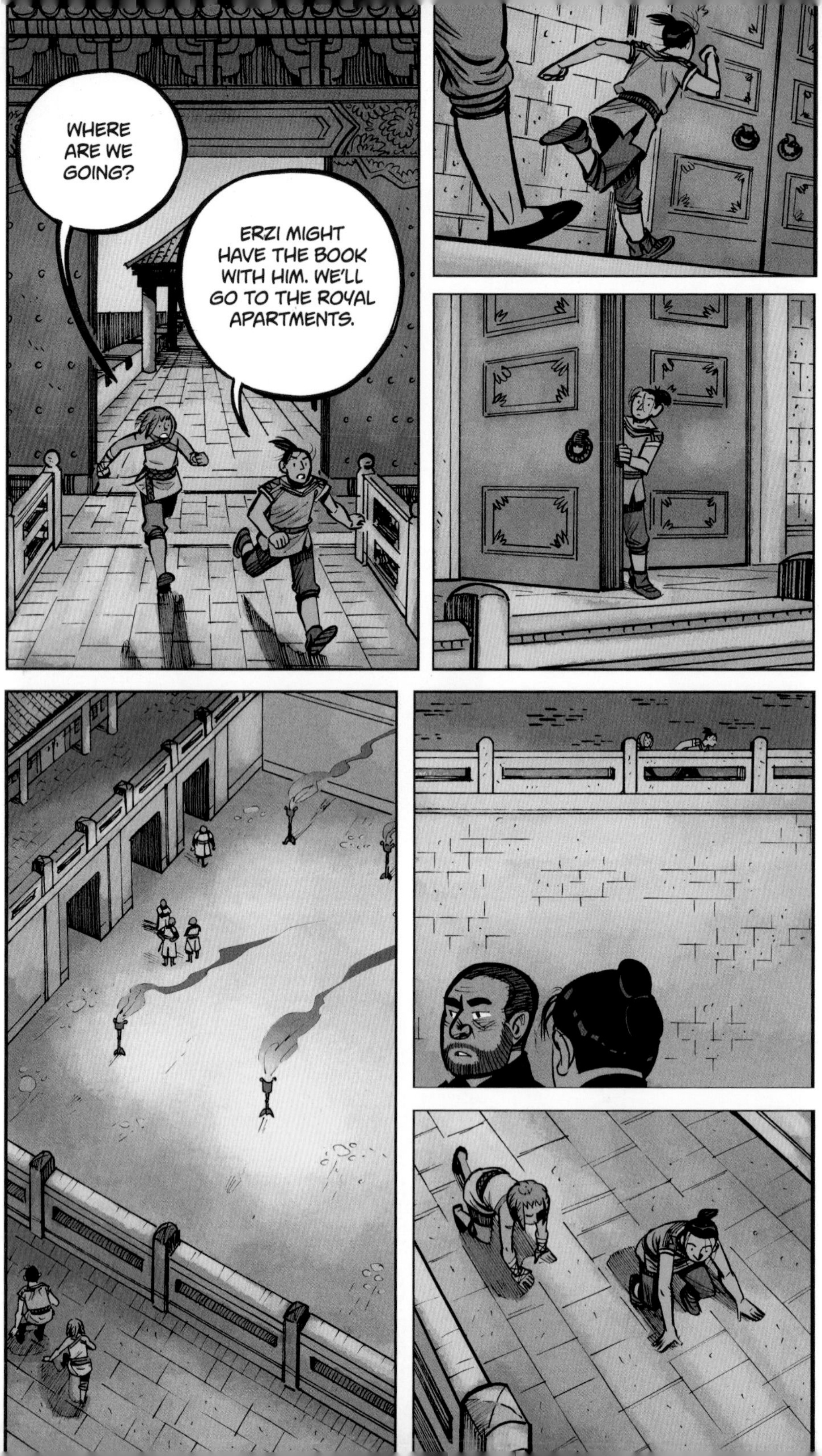
WHERE ARE WE GOING?
ERZI MIGHT HAVE THE BOOK WITH HIM. WE'LL GO TO THE ROYAL APARTMENTS.

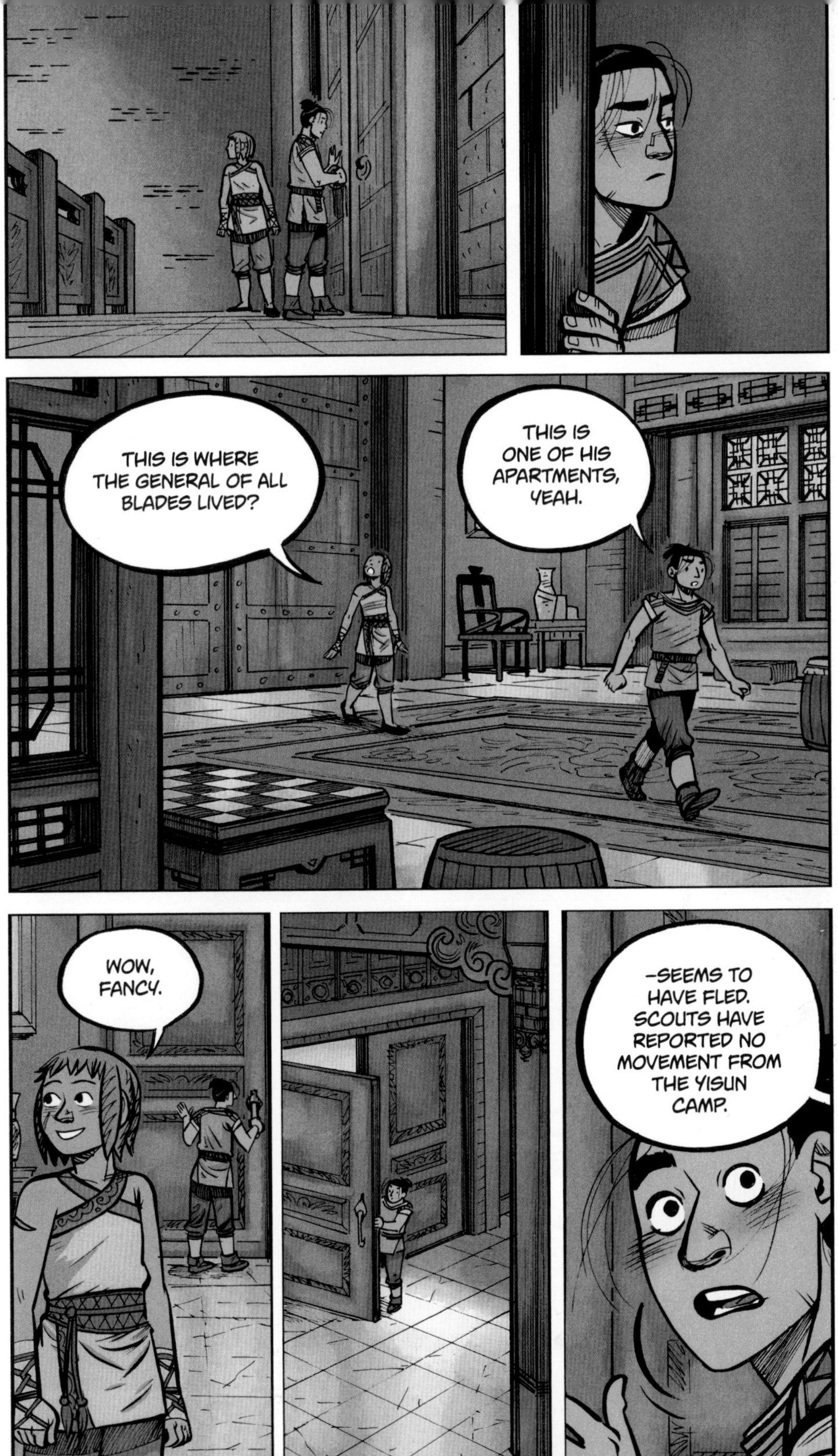
THIS IS WHERE THE GENERAL OF ALL BLADES LIVED?
THIS IS ONE OF HIS APARTMENTS, YEAH.
WOW, FANCY.
–SEEMS TO HAVE FLED. SCOUTS HAVE REPORTED NO MOVEMENT FROM THE YISUN CAMP.

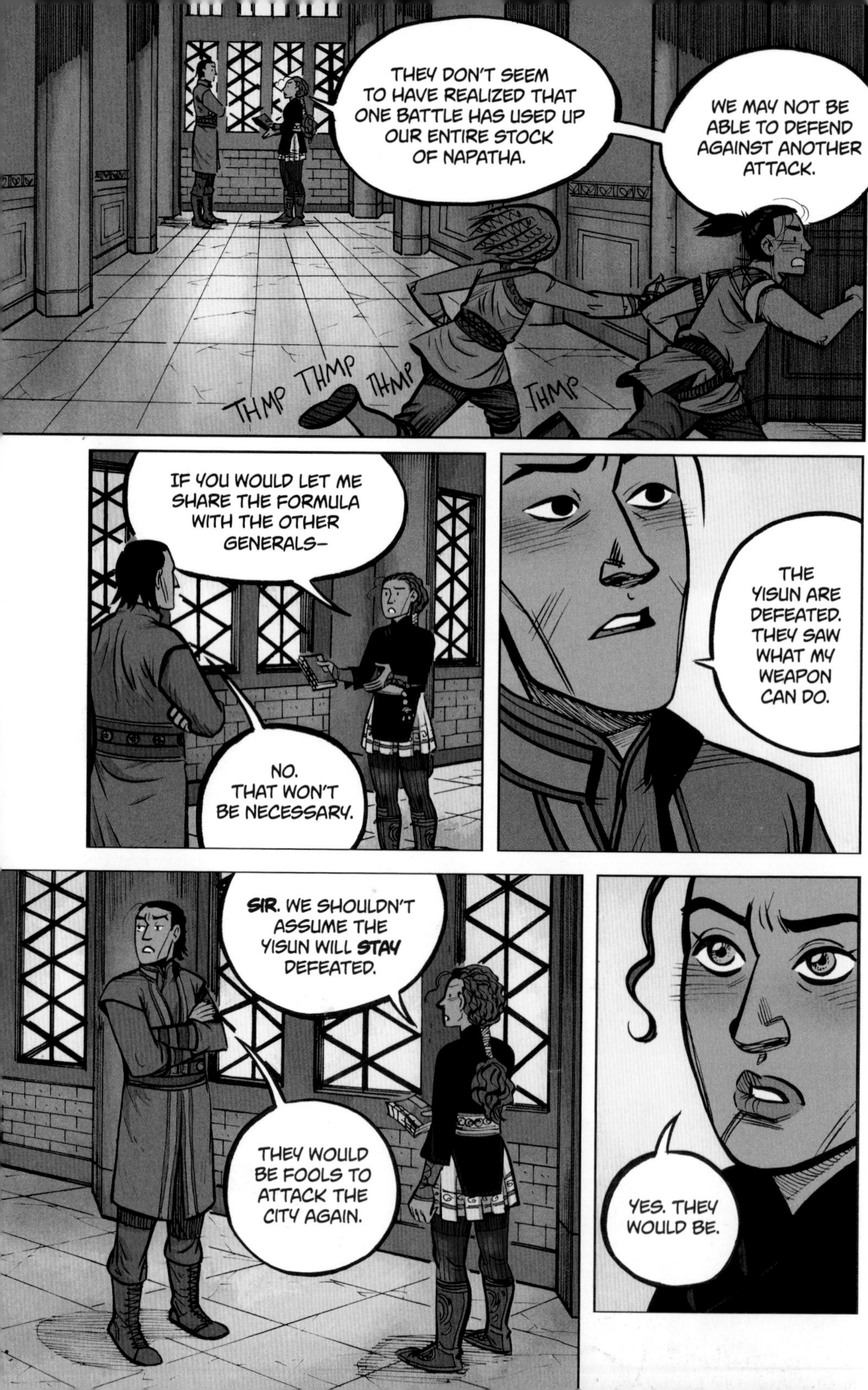
THEY DON'T SEEM TO HAVE REALIZED THAT ONE BATTLE HAS USED UP OUR ENTIRE STOCK OF NAPATHA.
WE MAY NOT BE ABLE TO DEFEND AGAINST ANOTHER ATTACK.
THMP THMP THMP THMP
IF YOU WOULD LET ME SHARE THE FORMULA WITH THE OTHER GENERALS–
NO. THAT WON'T BE NECESSARY.
THE YISUN ARE DEFEATED. THEY SAW WHAT MY WEAPON CAN DO.
SIR. WE SHOULDN'T ASSUME THE YISUN WILL STAY DEFEATED.
THEY WOULD BE FOOLS TO ATTACK THE CITY AGAIN.
YES. THEY WOULD BE.

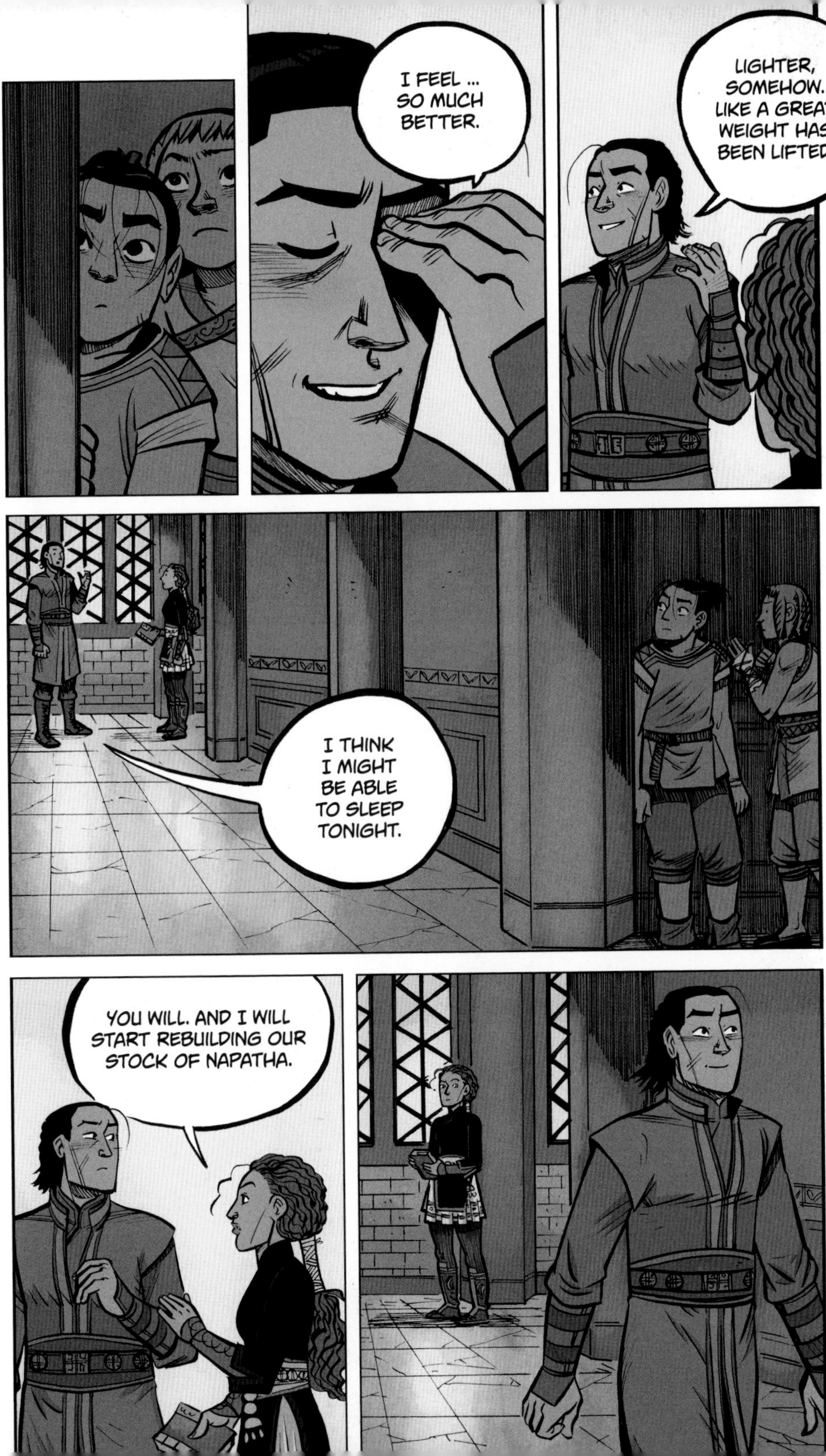
I FEEL ... SO MUCH BETTER.
LIGHTER, SOMEHOW. LIKE A GREAT WEIGHT HAS BEEN LIFTED.
I THINK I MIGHT BE ABLE TO SLEEP TONIGHT.
YOU WILL. AND I WILL START REBUILDING OUR STOCK OF NAPATHA.

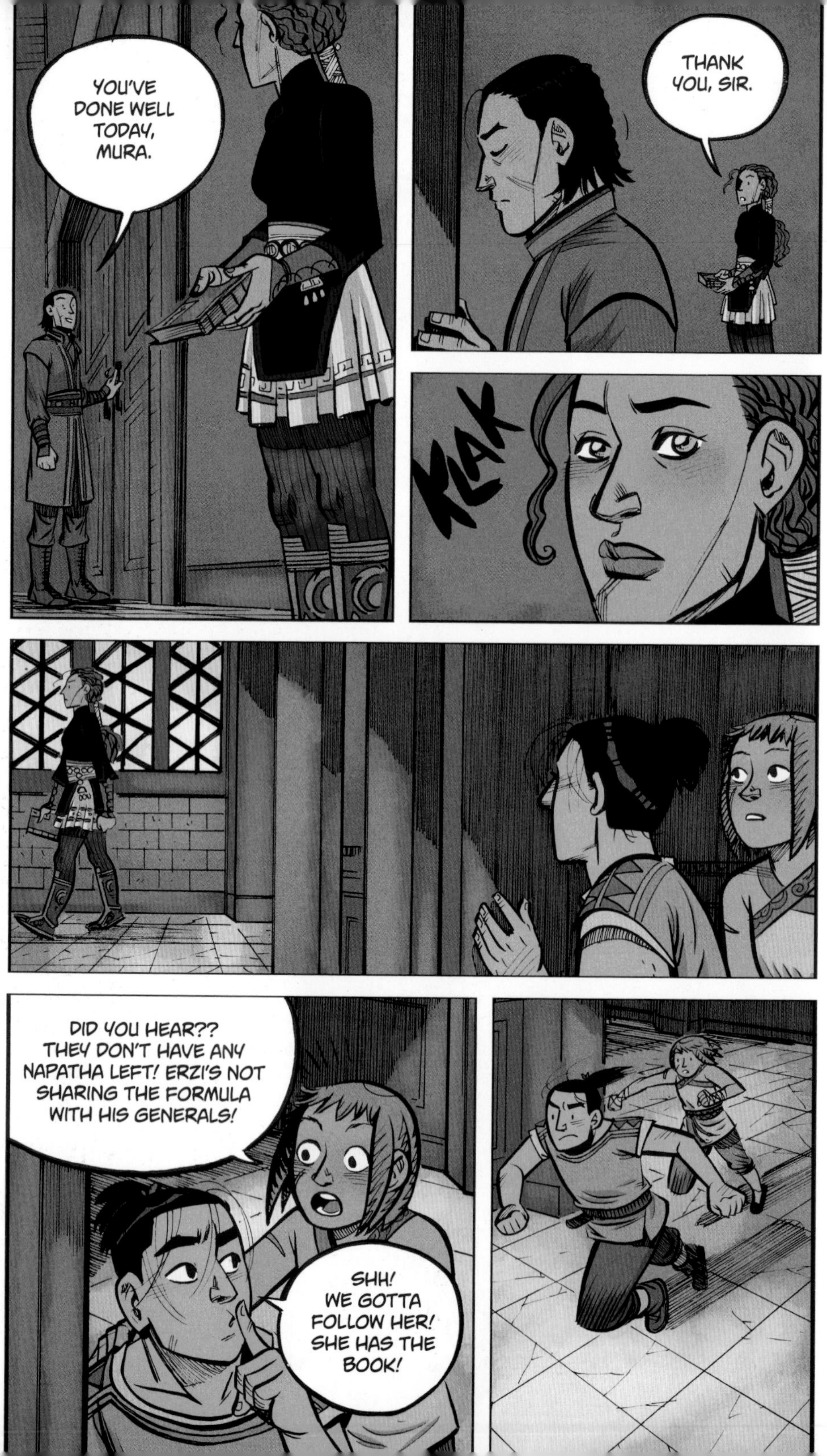
YOU'VE DONE WELL TODAY, MURA.
THANK YOU, SIR.
KLAK
DID YOU HEAR?? THEY DON'T HAVE ANY NAPATHA LEFT! ERZI'S NOT SHARING THE FORMULA WITH HIS GENERALS!
SHH! WE GOTTA FOLLOW HER! SHE HAS THE BOOK!

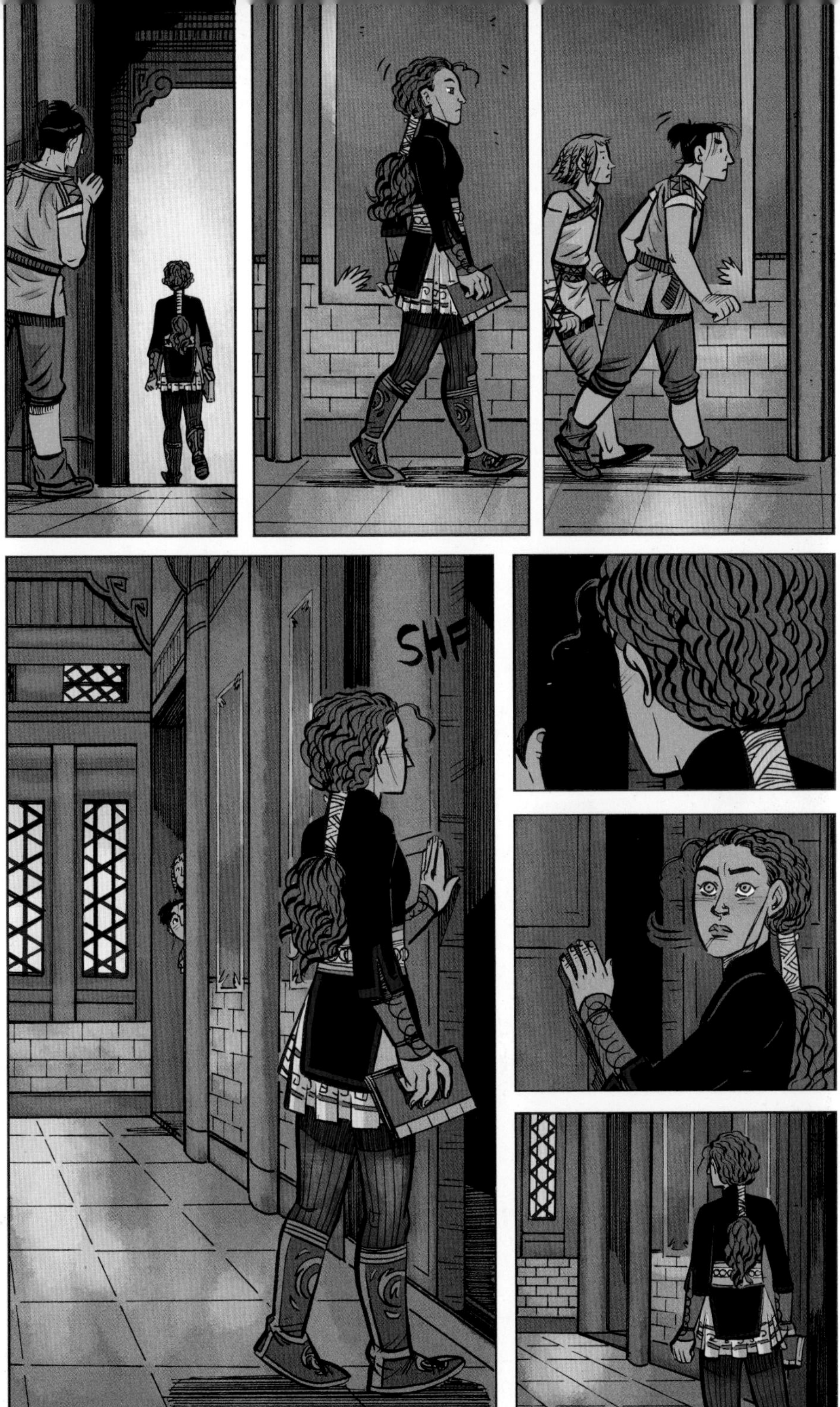
SHF

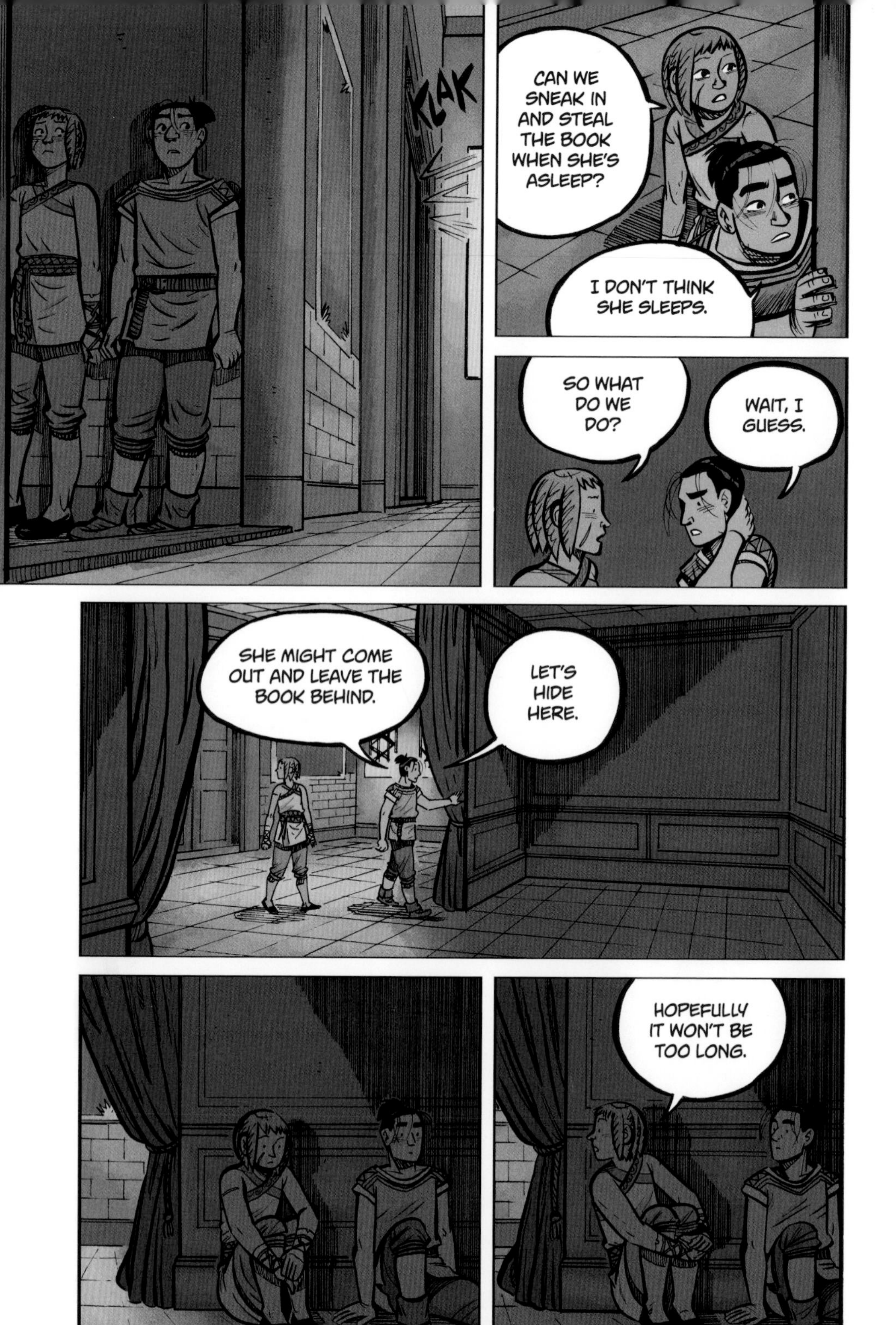
KLAK
CAN WE SNEAK IN AND STEAL THE BOOK WHEN SHE'S ASLEEP?
I DON'T THINK SHE SLEEPS.
SO WHAT DO WE DO?
WAIT, I GUESS.
SHE MIGHT COME OUT AND LEAVE THE BOOK BEHIND.
LET'S HIDE HERE.
HOPEFULLY IT WON'T BE TOO LONG.

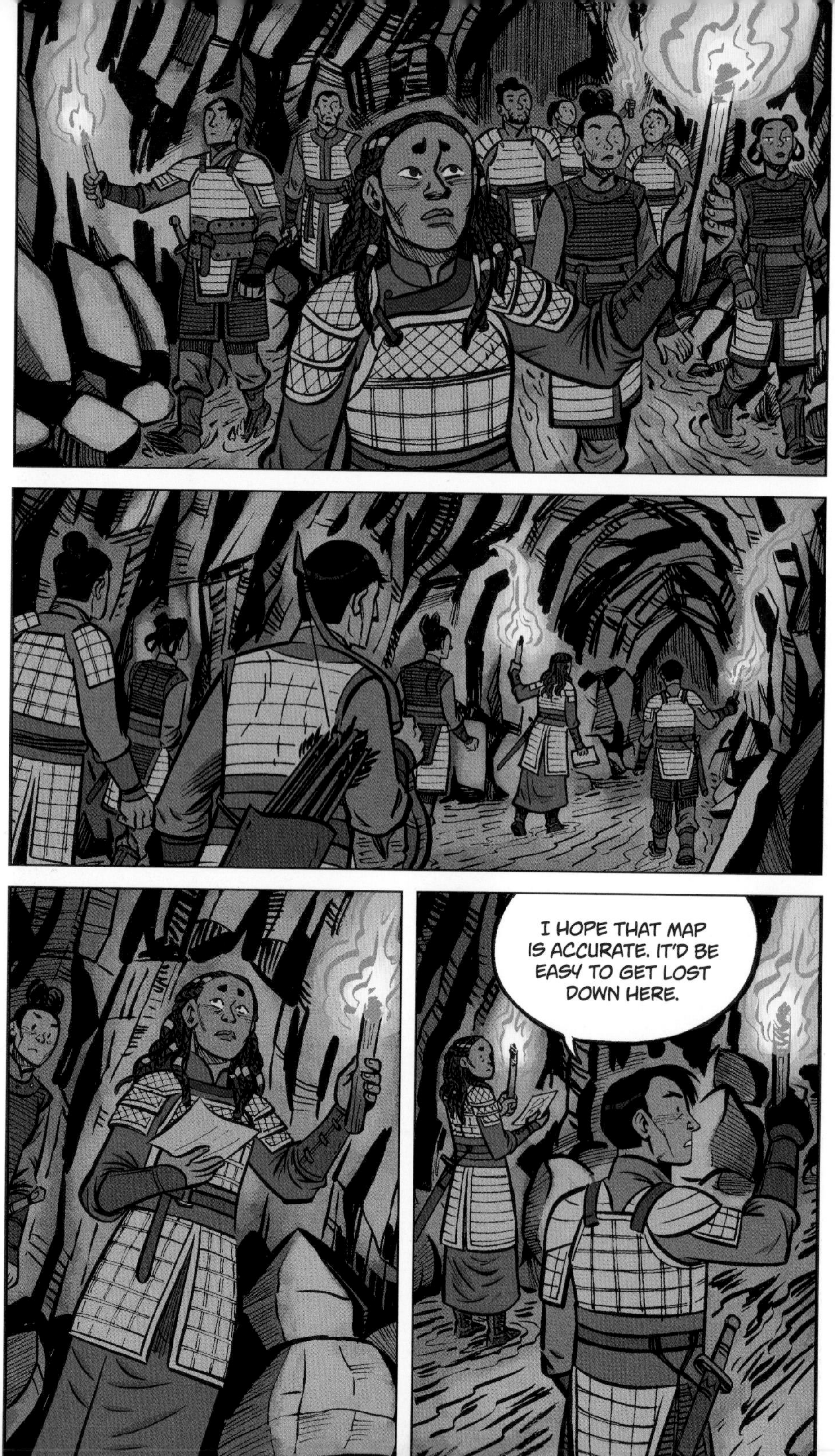
I HOPE THAT MAP IS ACCURATE. IT'D BE EASY TO GET LOST DOWN HERE.

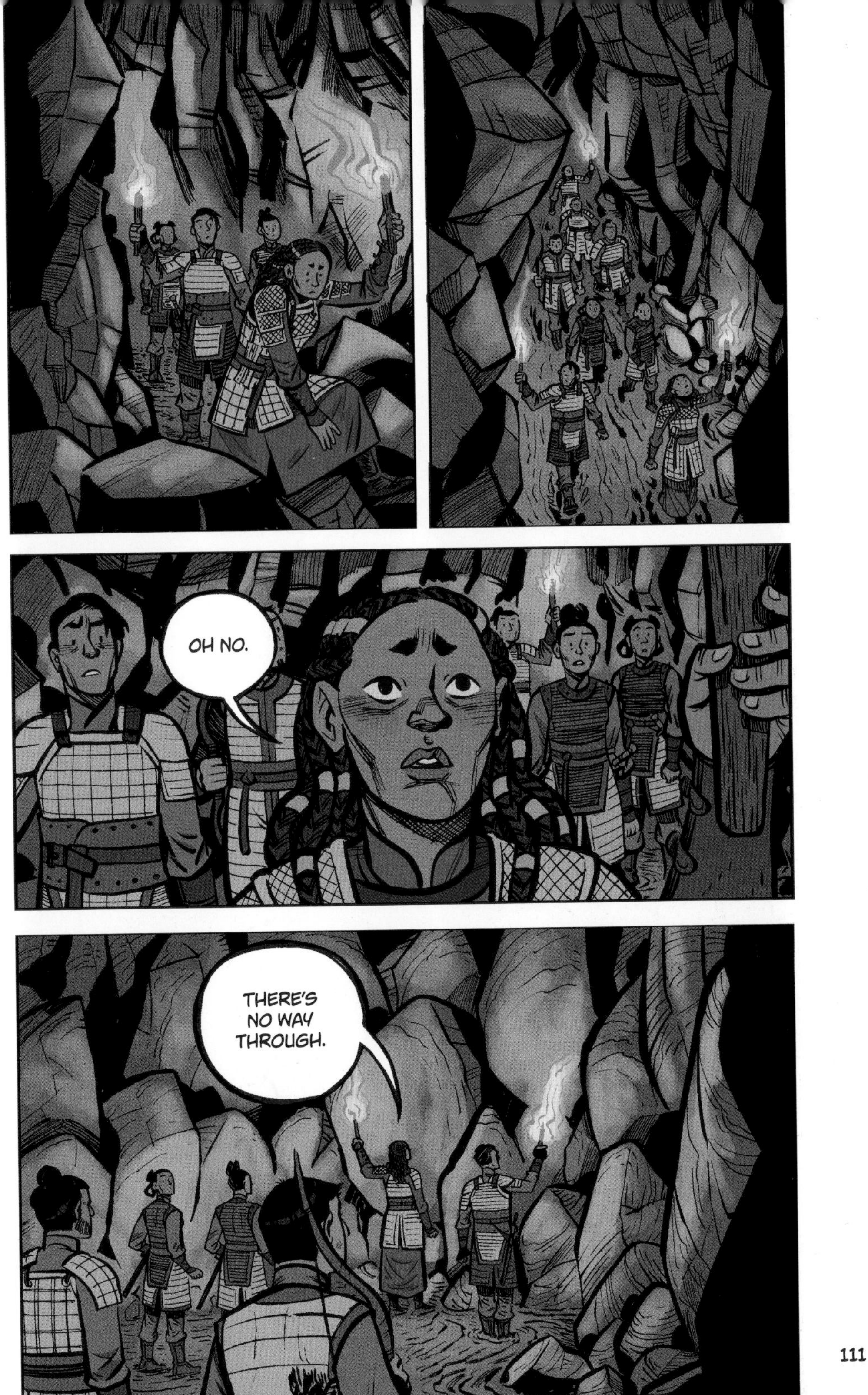
OH NO.
THERE'S NO WAY THROUGH.

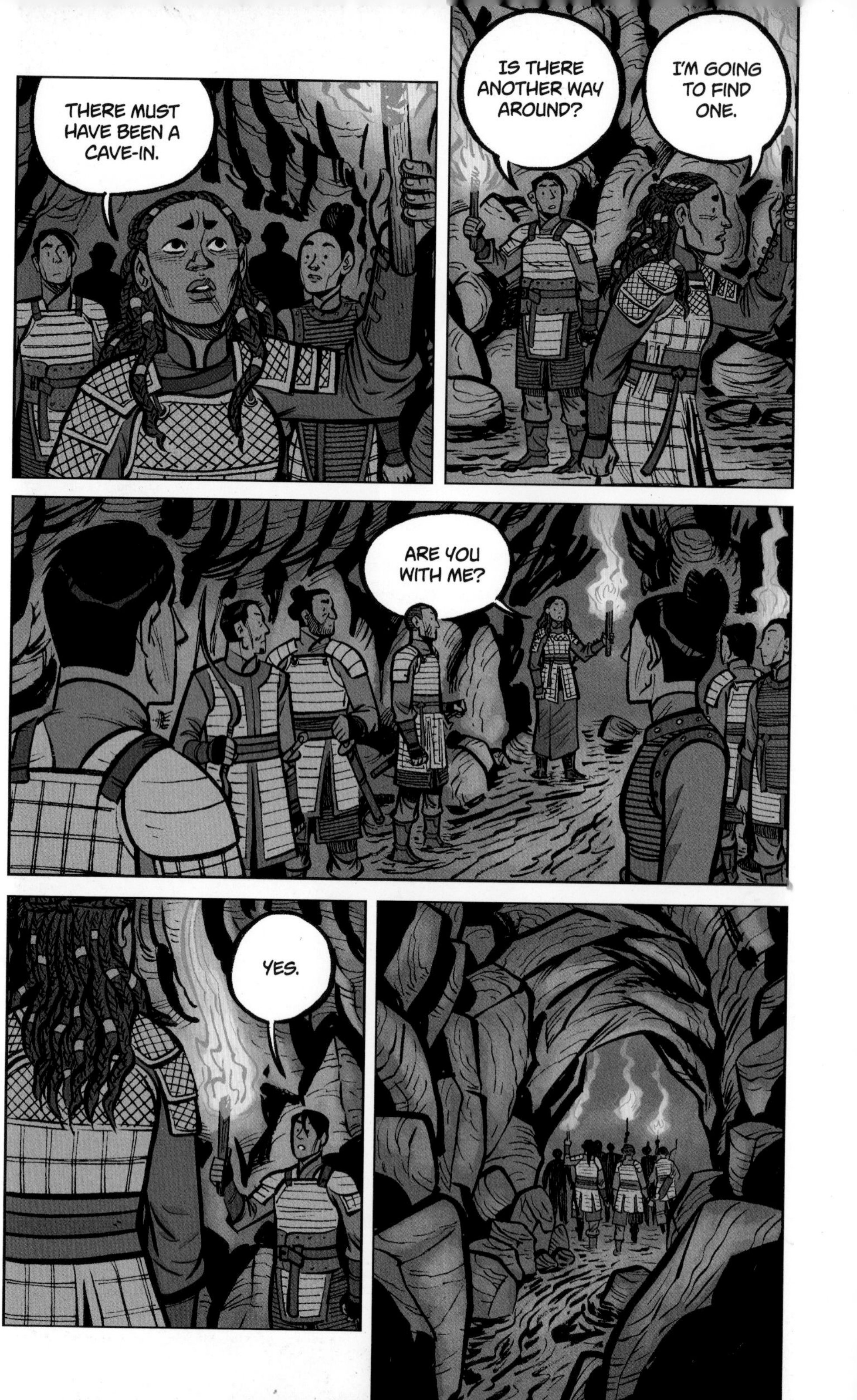
THERE MUST HAVE BEEN A CAVE-IN.
IS THERE ANOTHER WAY AROUND?
I'M GOING TO FIND ONE.
ARE YOU WITH ME?
YES.

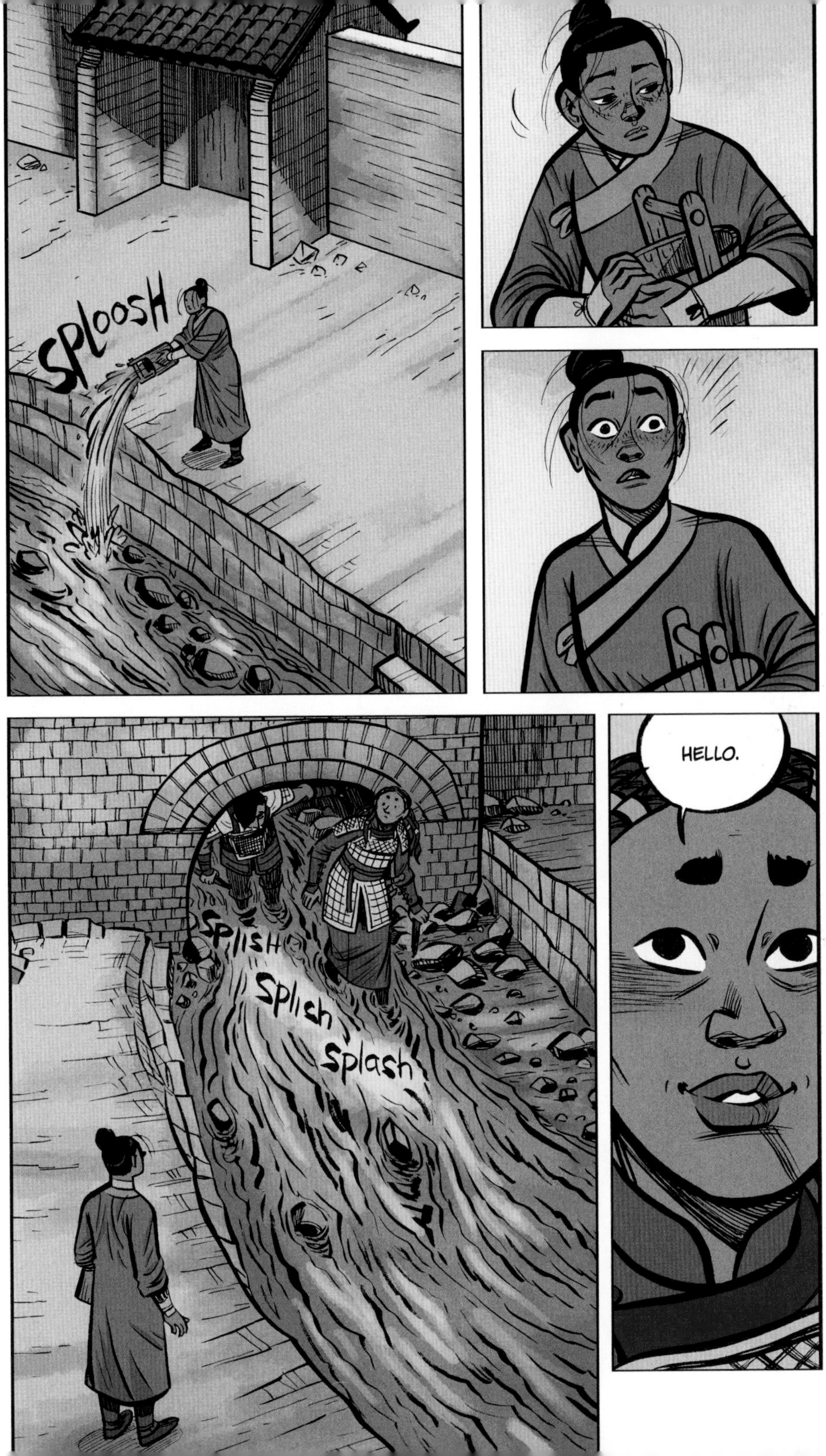
SPLOOSH
Splish
Splish
Splash
HELLO.

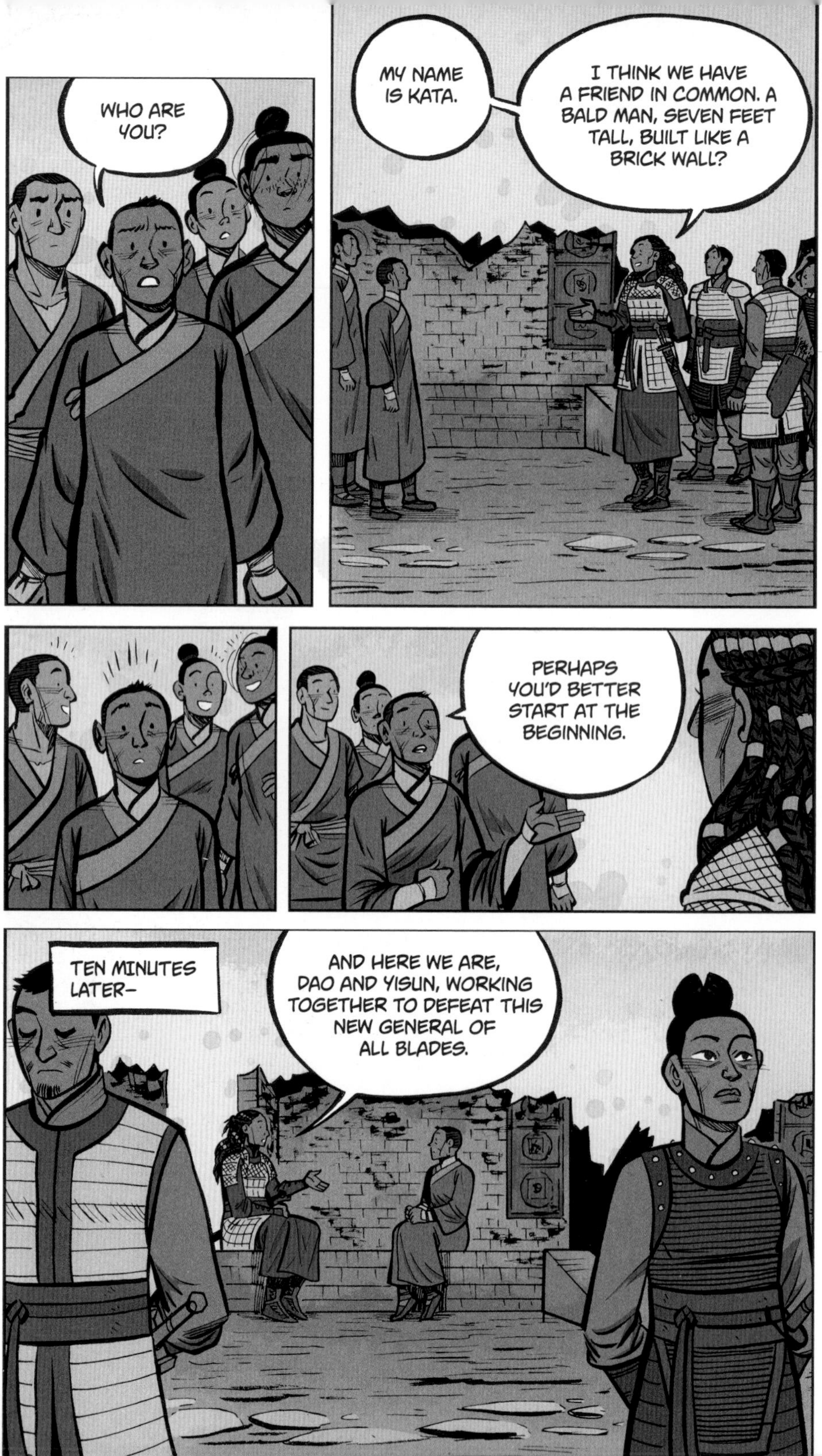
WHO ARE YOU?
MY NAME IS KATA.
I THINK WE HAVE A FRIEND IN COMMON. A BALD MAN, SEVEN FEET TALL, BUILT LIKE A BRICK WALL?
PERHAPS YOU'D BETTER START AT THE BEGINNING.
TEN MINUTES LATER—
AND HERE WE ARE, DAO AND YISUN, WORKING TOGETHER TO DEFEAT THIS NEW GENERAL OF ALL BLADES.

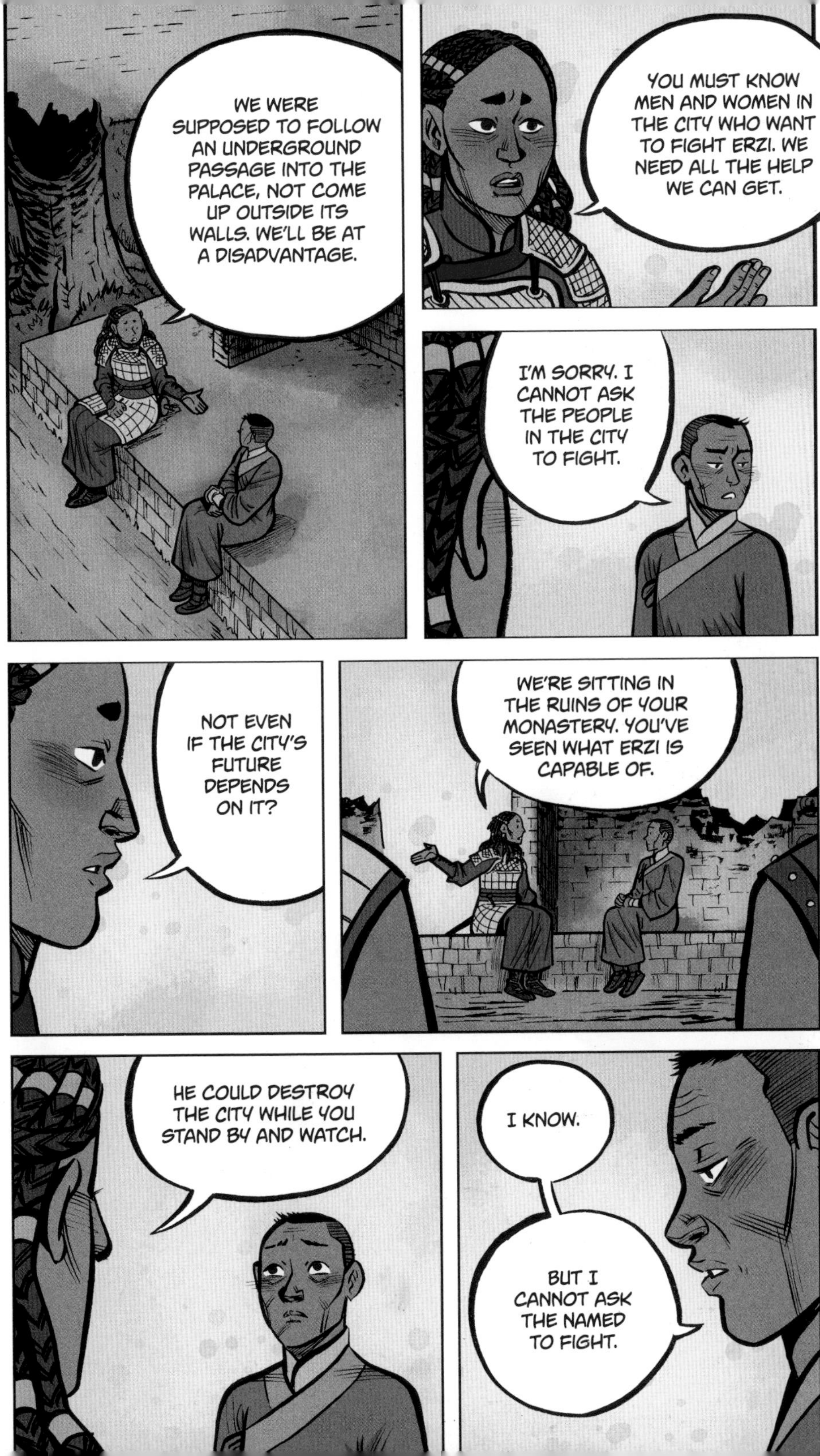
WE WERE SUPPOSED TO FOLLOW AN UNDERGROUND PASSAGE INTO THE PALACE, NOT COME UP OUTSIDE ITS WALLS. WE'LL BE AT A DISADVANTAGE.
YOU MUST KNOW MEN AND WOMEN IN THE CITY WHO WANT TO FIGHT ERZI. WE NEED ALL THE HELP WE CAN GET.
I'M SORRY. I CANNOT ASK THE PEOPLE IN THE CITY TO FIGHT.
NOT EVEN IF THE CITY'S FUTURE DEPENDS ON IT?
WE'RE SITTING IN THE RUINS OF YOUR MONASTERY. YOU'VE SEEN WHAT ERZI IS CAPABLE OF.
HE COULD DESTROY THE CITY WHILE YOU STAND BY AND WATCH.
I KNOW.
BUT I CANNOT ASK THE NAMED TO FIGHT.

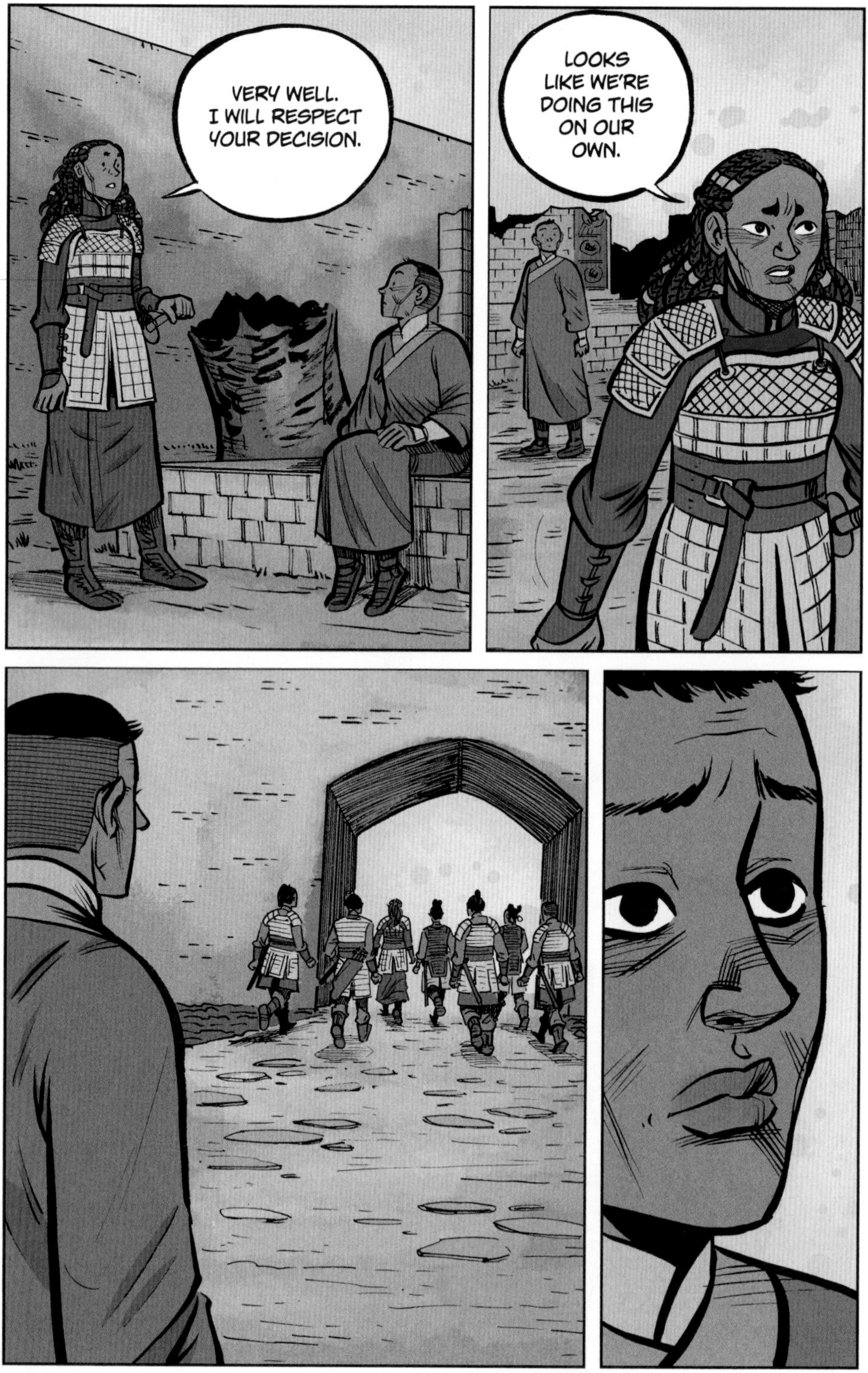
VERY WELL. I WILL RESPECT YOUR DECISION.
LOOKS LIKE WE'RE DOING THIS ON OUR OWN.

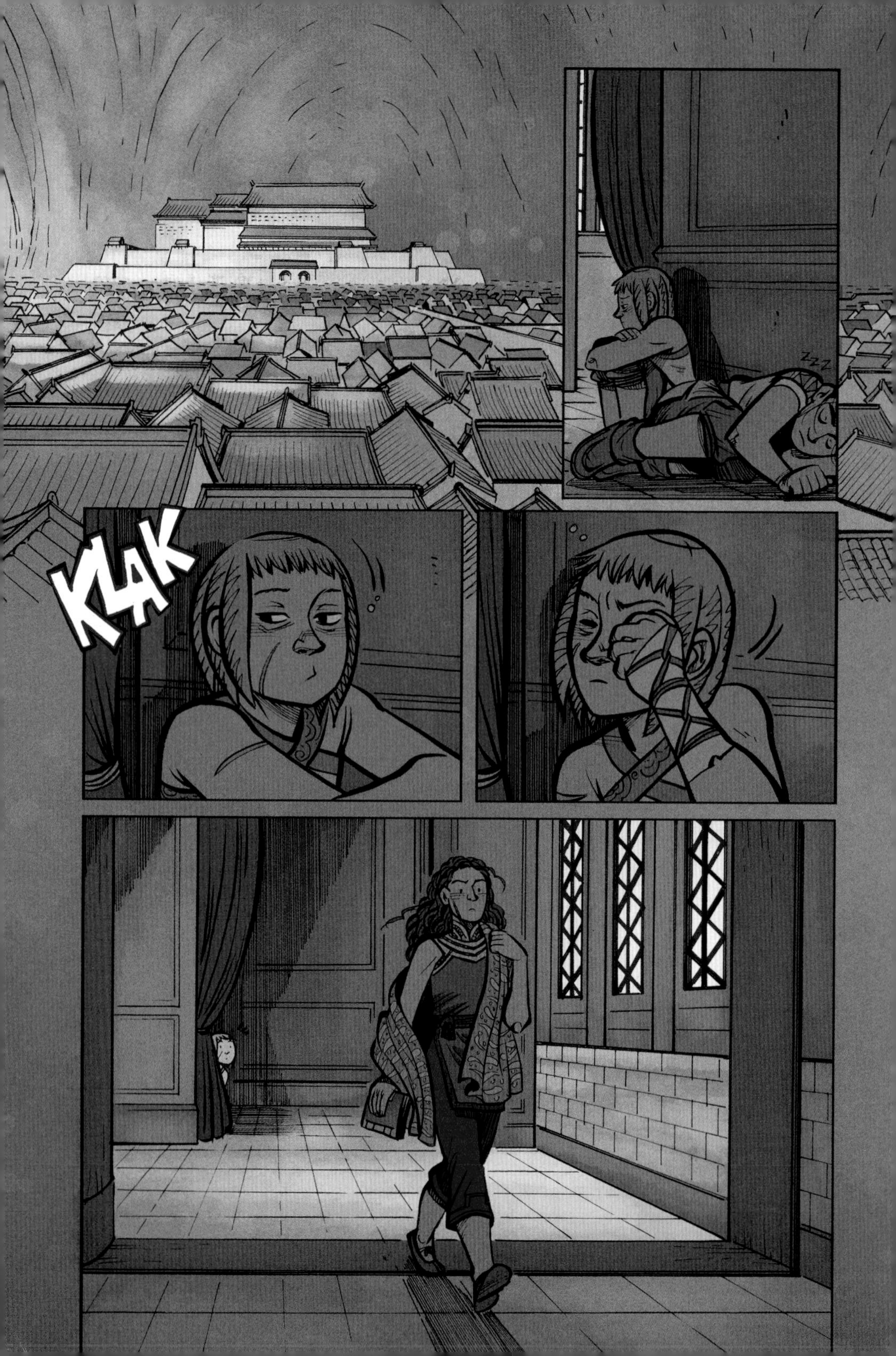
ZZZ
KLAK

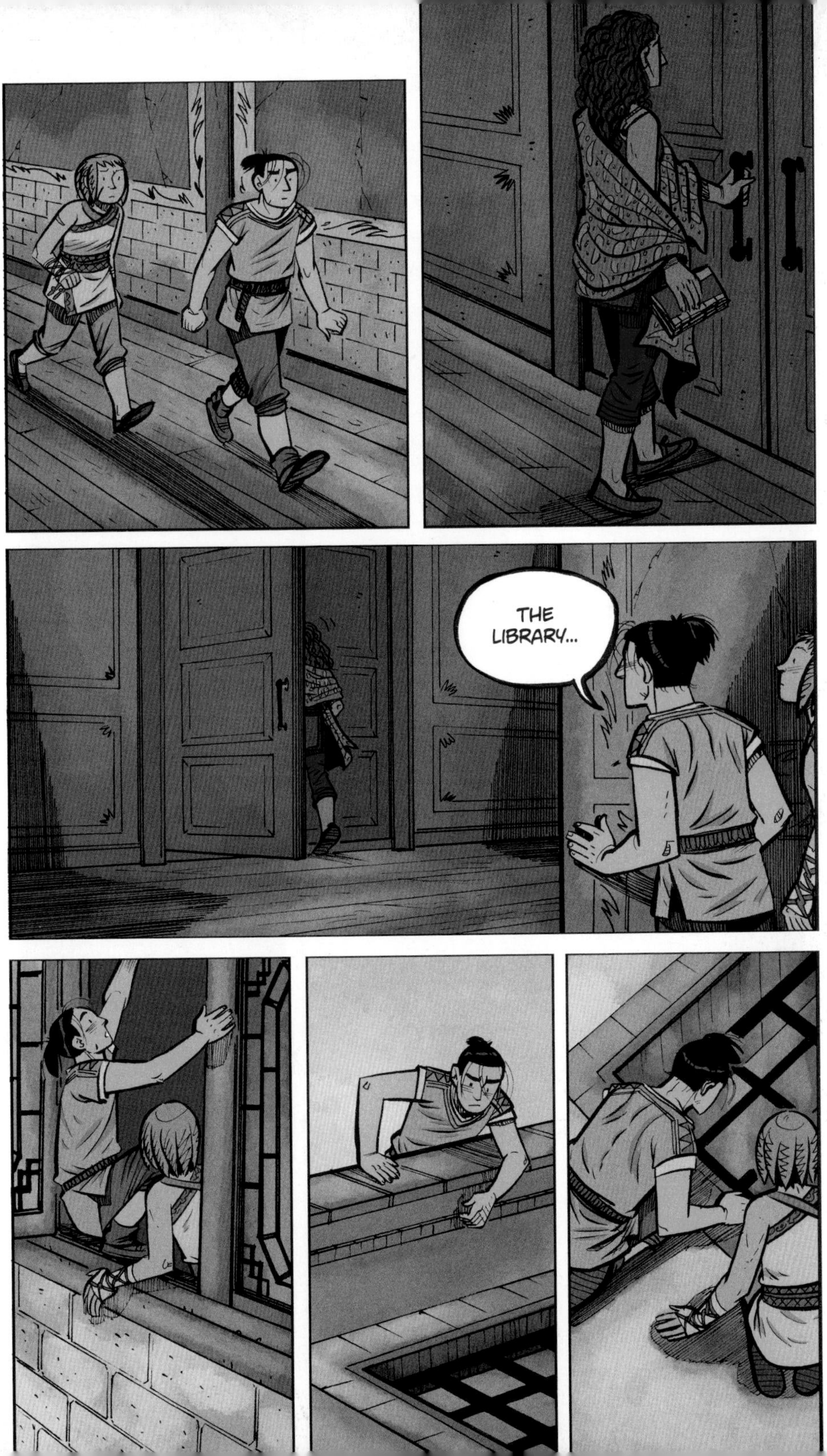
THE LIBRARY...

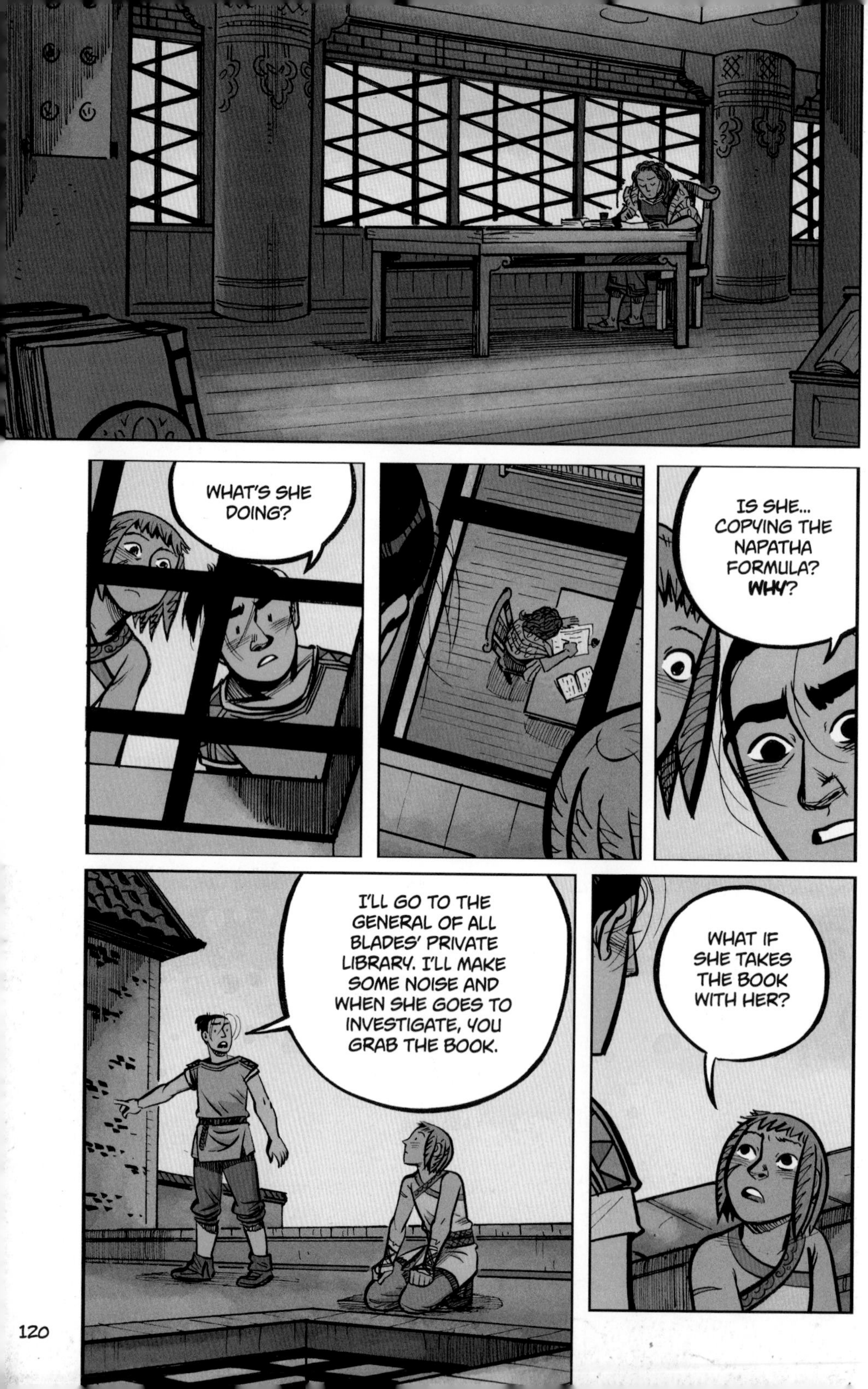
WHAT'S SHE DOING?
IS SHE... COPYING THE NAPATHA FORMULA? **WHY**?
I'LL GO TO THE GENERAL OF ALL BLADES' PRIVATE LIBRARY. I'LL MAKE SOME NOISE AND WHEN SHE GOES TO INVESTIGATE, YOU GRAB THE BOOK.
WHAT IF SHE TAKES THE BOOK WITH HER?

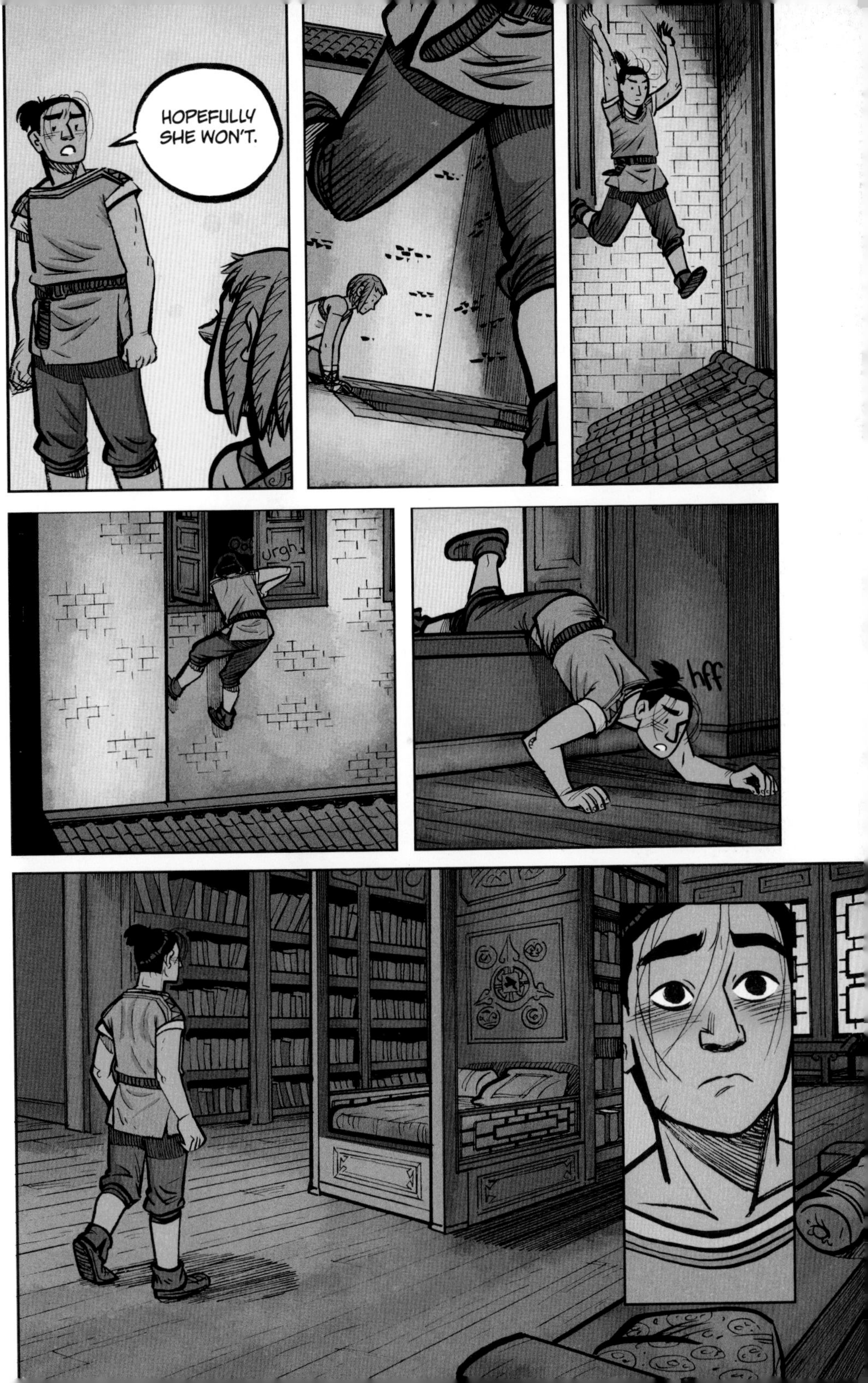
HOPEFULLY SHE WON'T.
urgh
hff

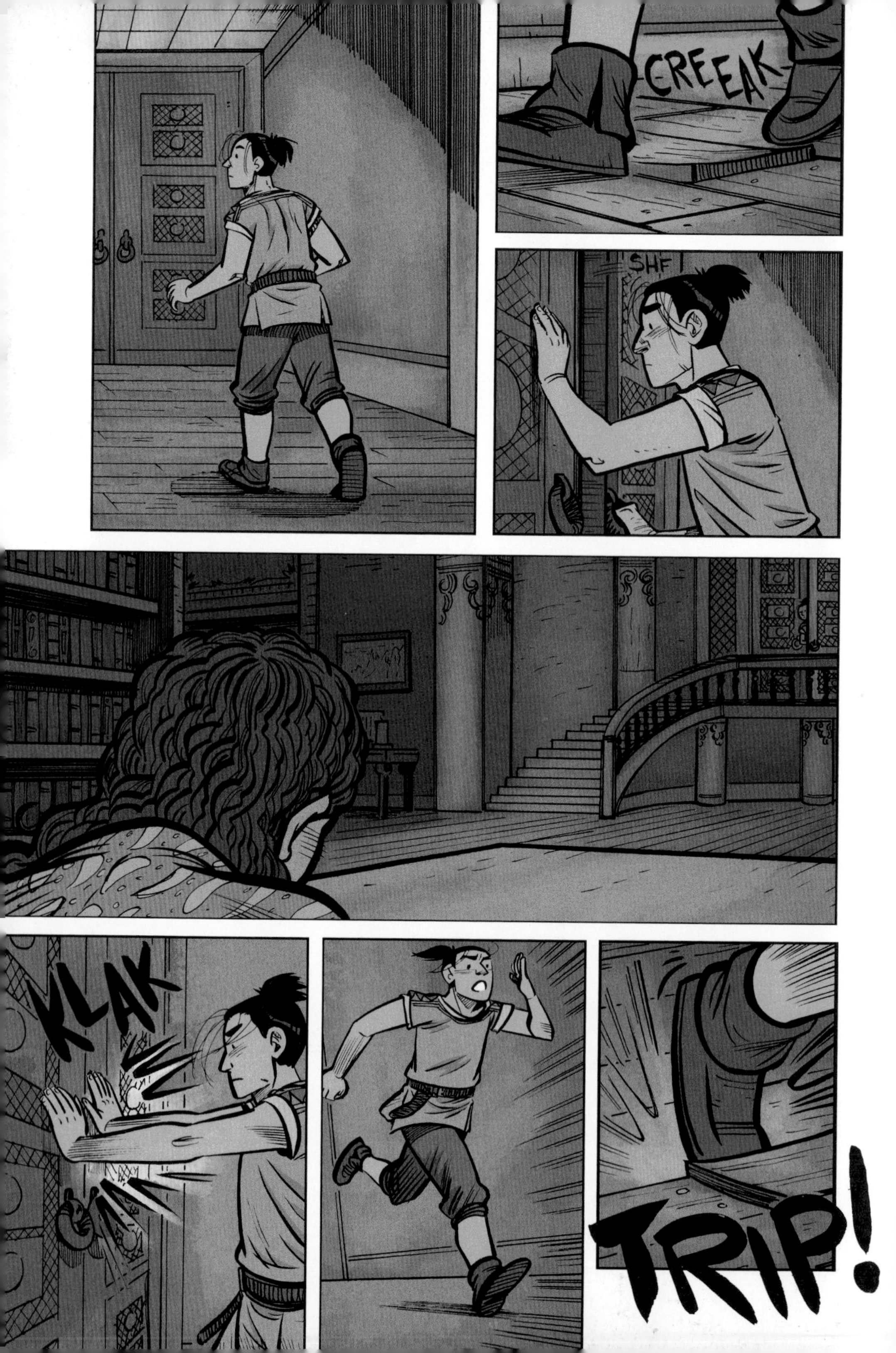
CREEAK
SHF
KLAK
TRIP!

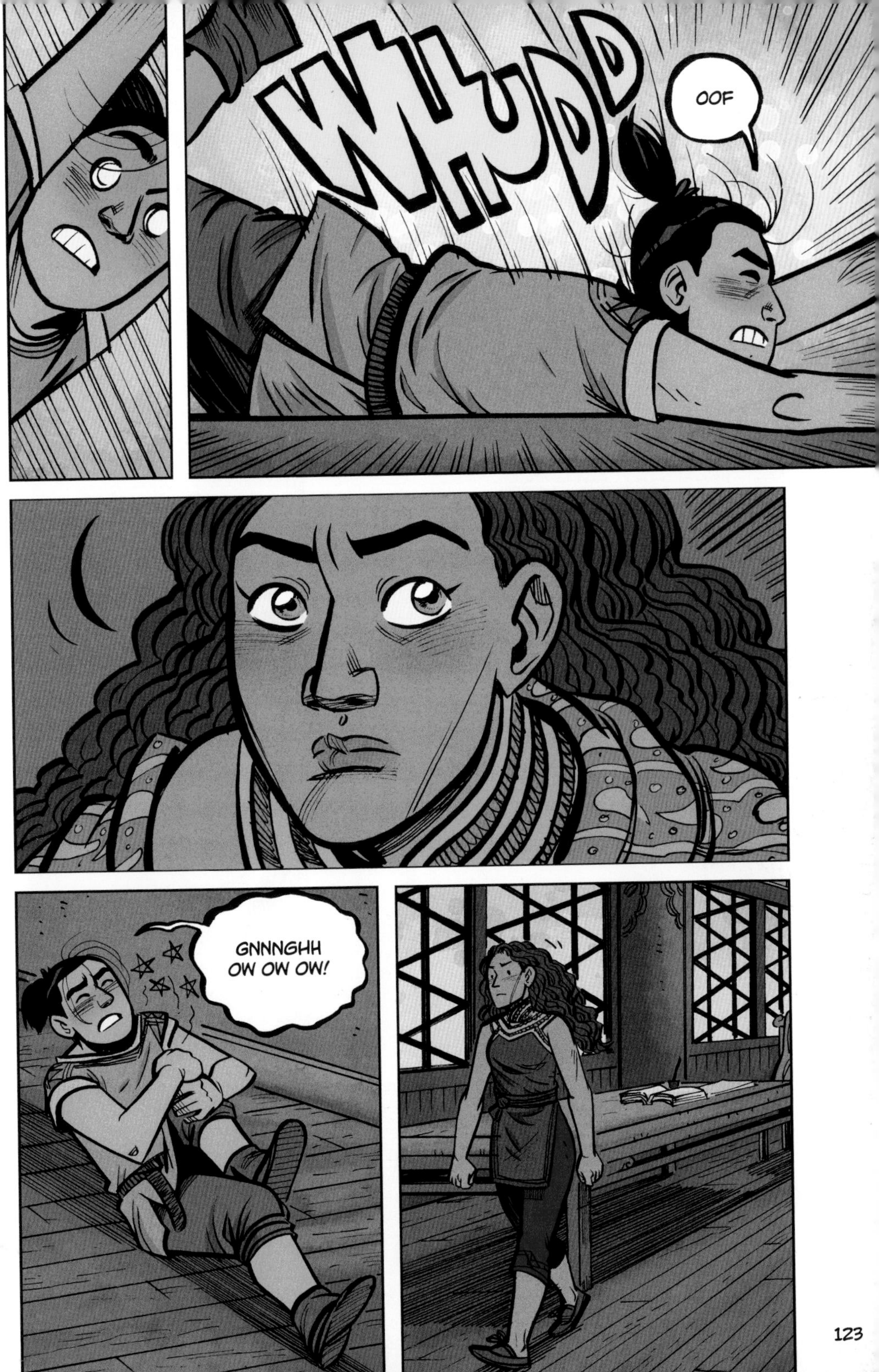
WHUDD
OOF
GNNNGHH OW OW OW!

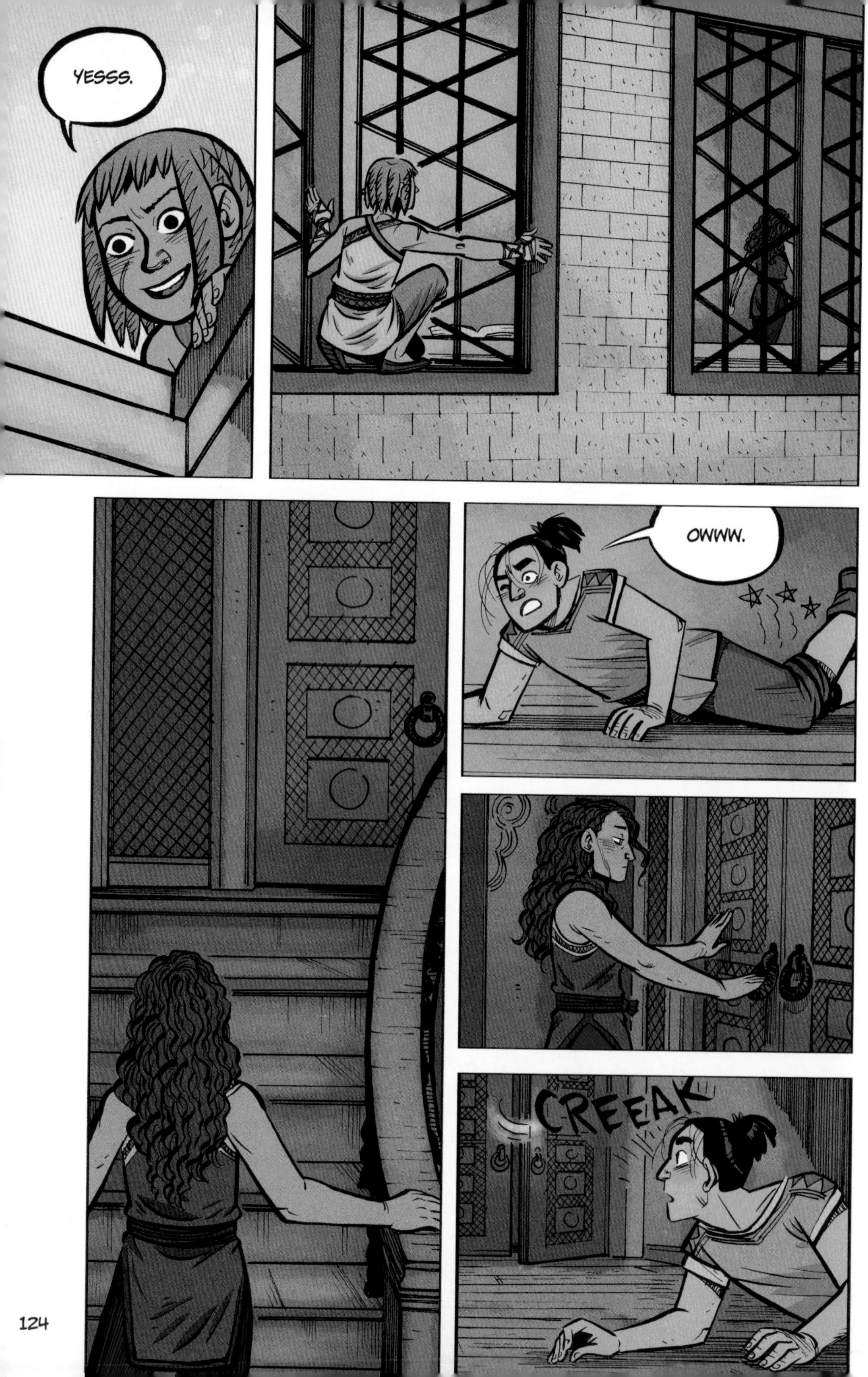
YESSS.
OWWW.
CREEAK

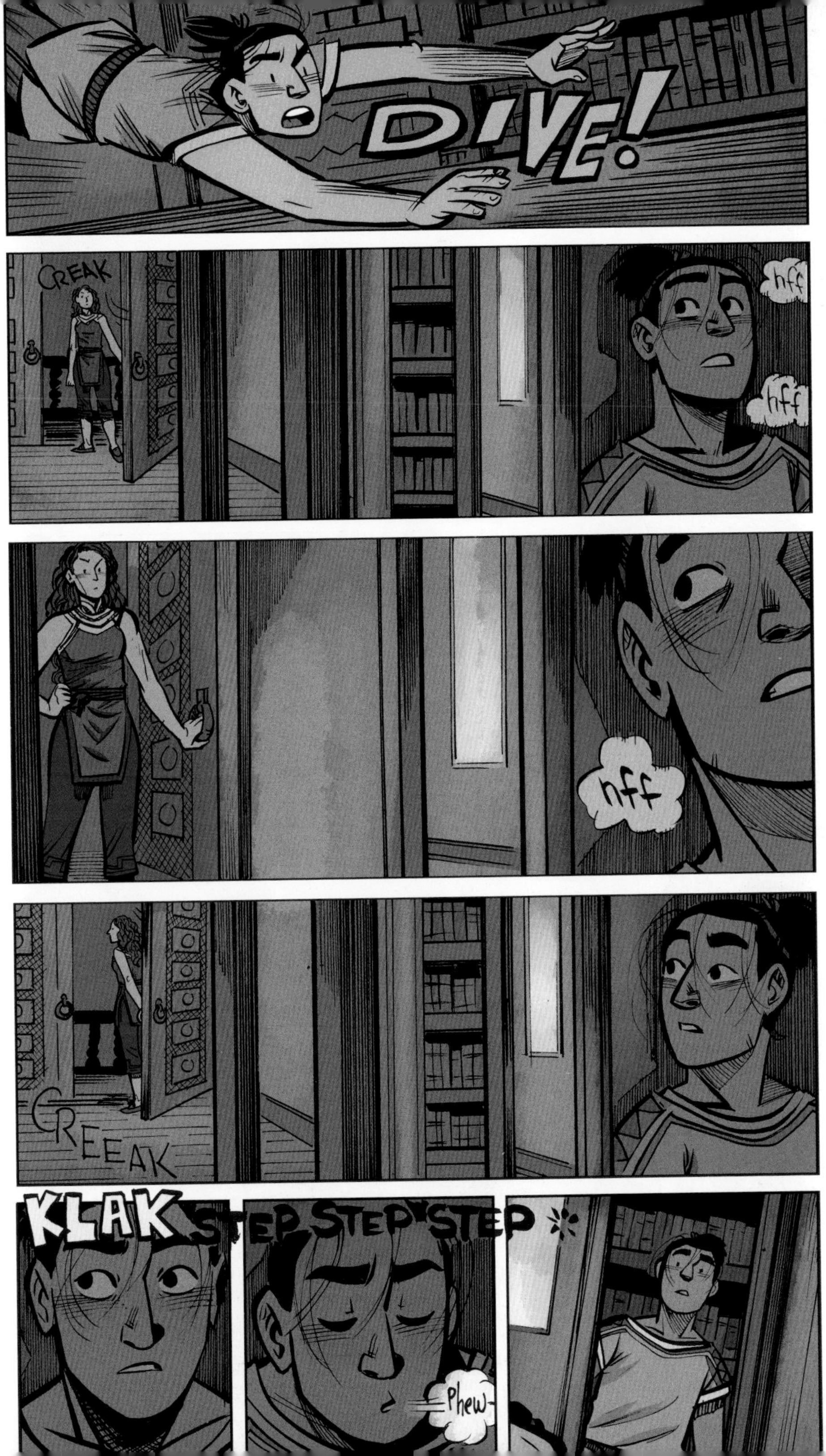
DIVE!
CREAK
hff
hff
hff
CREEAK
KLAK
STEP STEP STEP
Phew

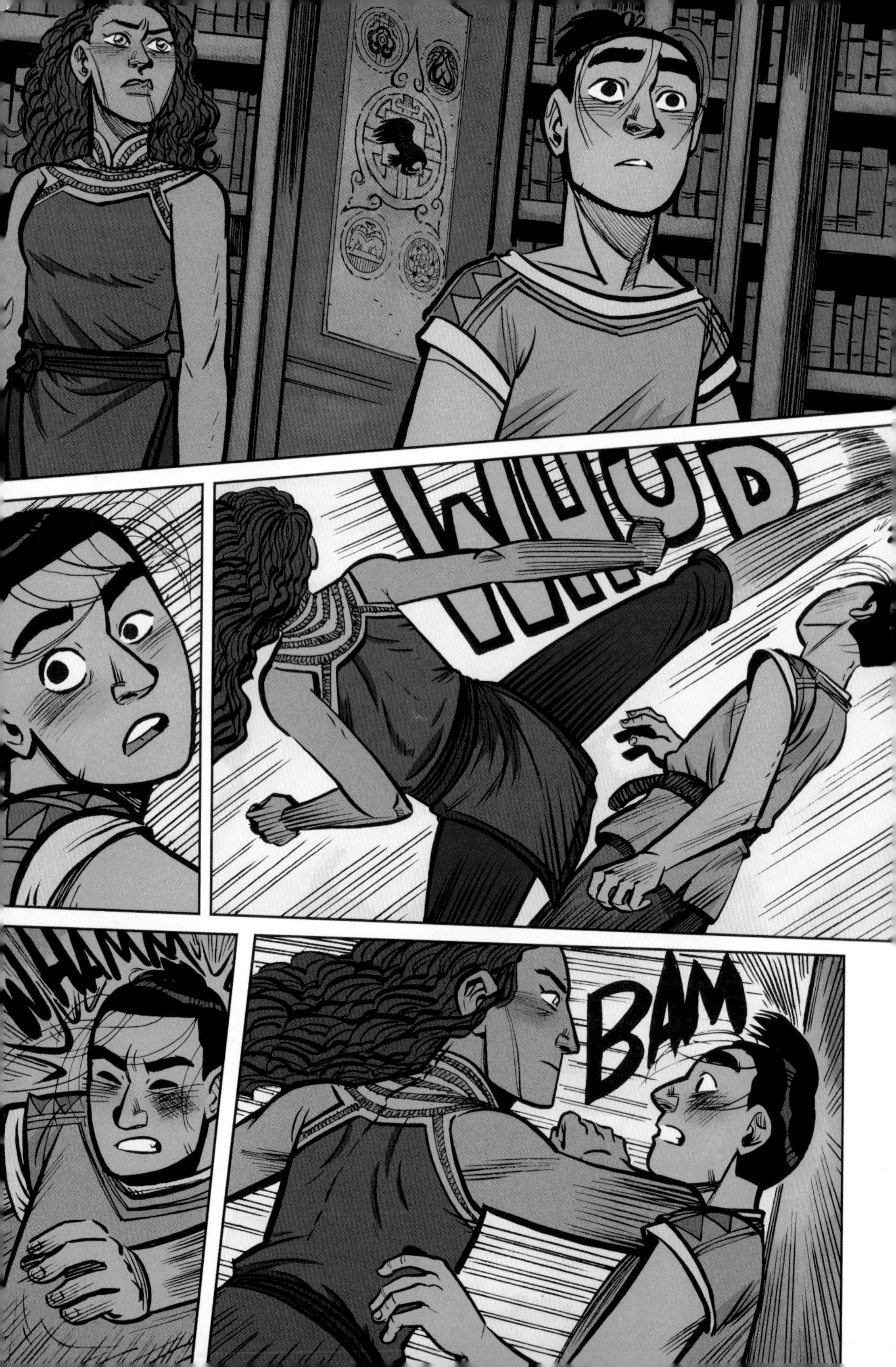
WHAMM
BAM

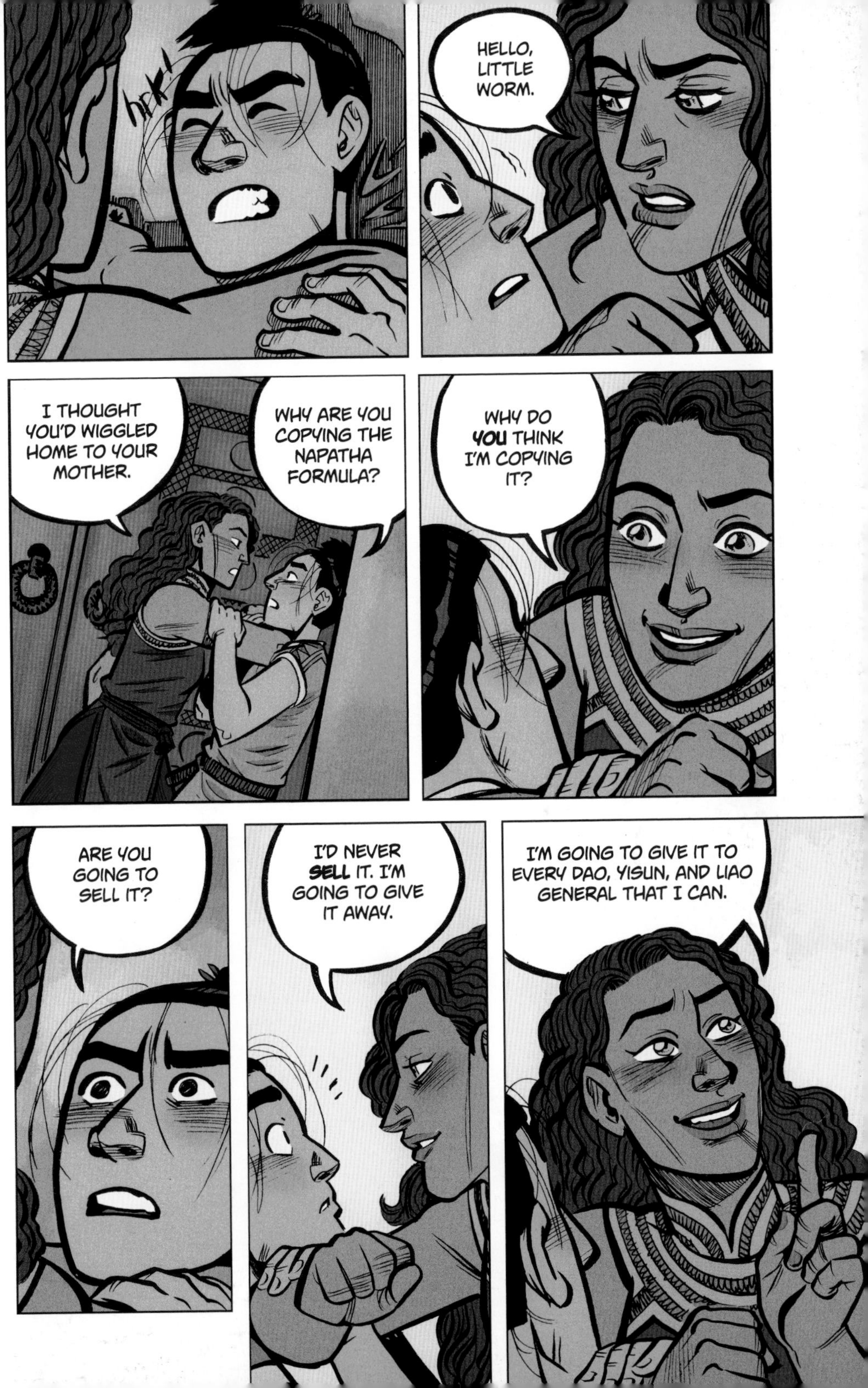
HRK!
HELLO, LITTLE WORM.
I THOUGHT YOU'D WIGGLED HOME TO YOUR MOTHER.
WHY ARE YOU COPYING THE NAPATHA FORMULA?
WHY DO **YOU** THINK I'M COPYING IT?
ARE YOU GOING TO SELL IT?
I'D NEVER **SELL** IT. I'M GOING TO GIVE IT AWAY.
I'M GOING TO GIVE IT TO EVERY DAO, YISUN, AND LIAO GENERAL THAT I CAN.

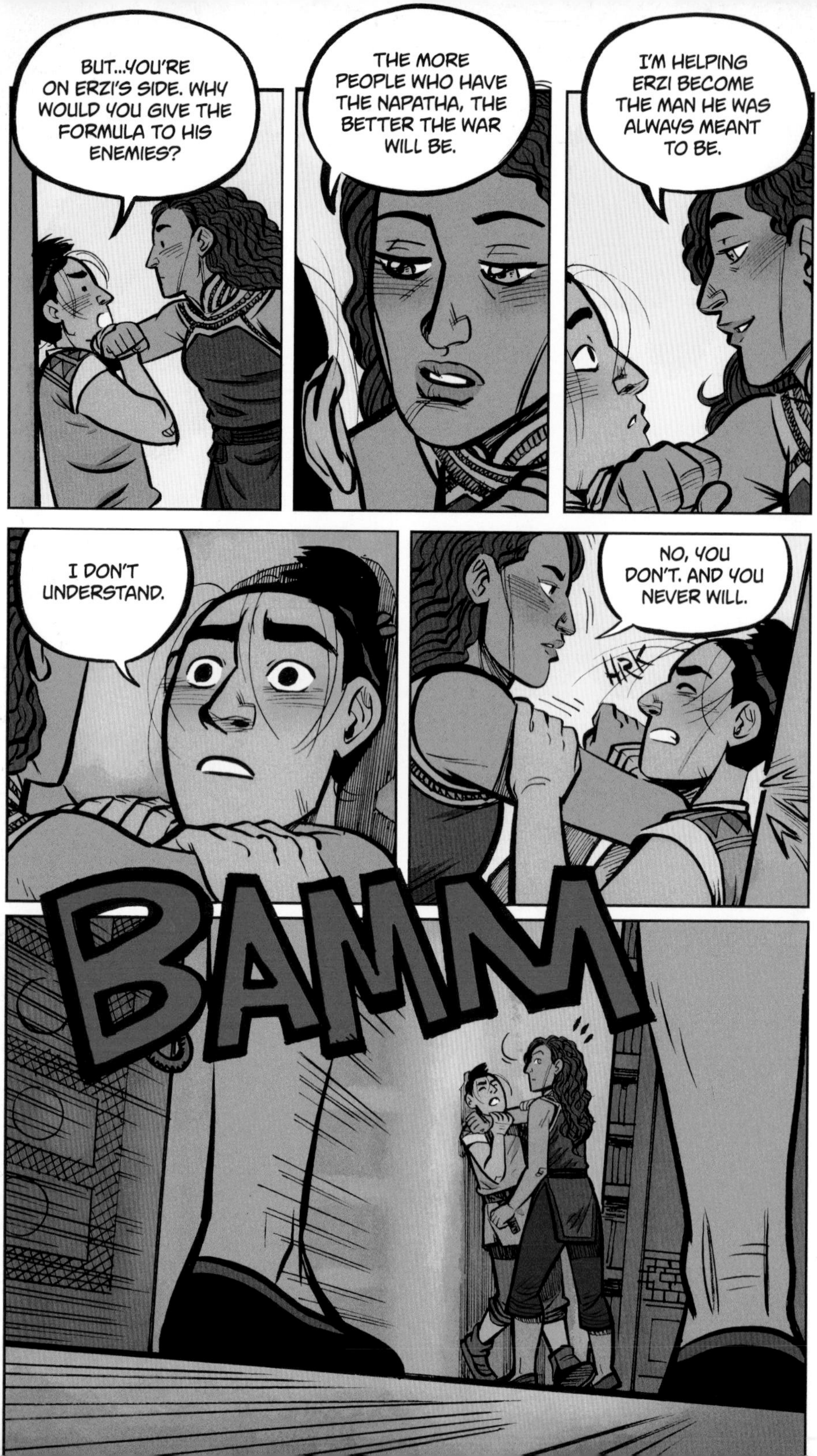
BUT...YOU'RE ON ERZI'S SIDE. WHY WOULD YOU GIVE THE FORMULA TO HIS ENEMIES?
THE MORE PEOPLE WHO HAVE THE NAPATHA, THE BETTER THE WAR WILL BE.
I'M HELPING ERZI BECOME THE MAN HE WAS ALWAYS MEANT TO BE.
I DON'T UNDERSTAND.
NO, YOU DON'T. AND YOU NEVER WILL.
HRK
BAMM

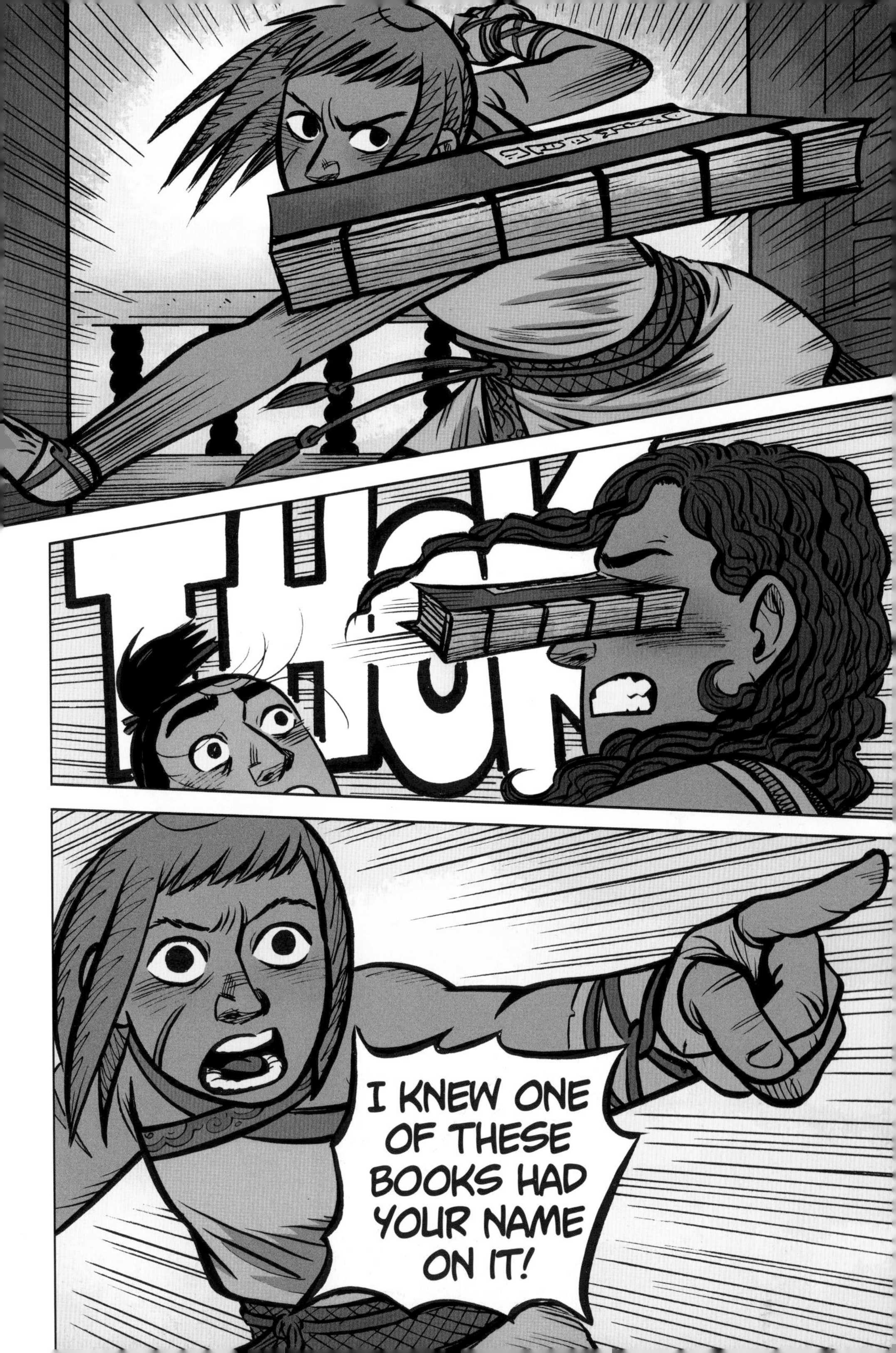
I KNEW ONE OF THESE BOOKS HAD YOUR NAME ON IT!

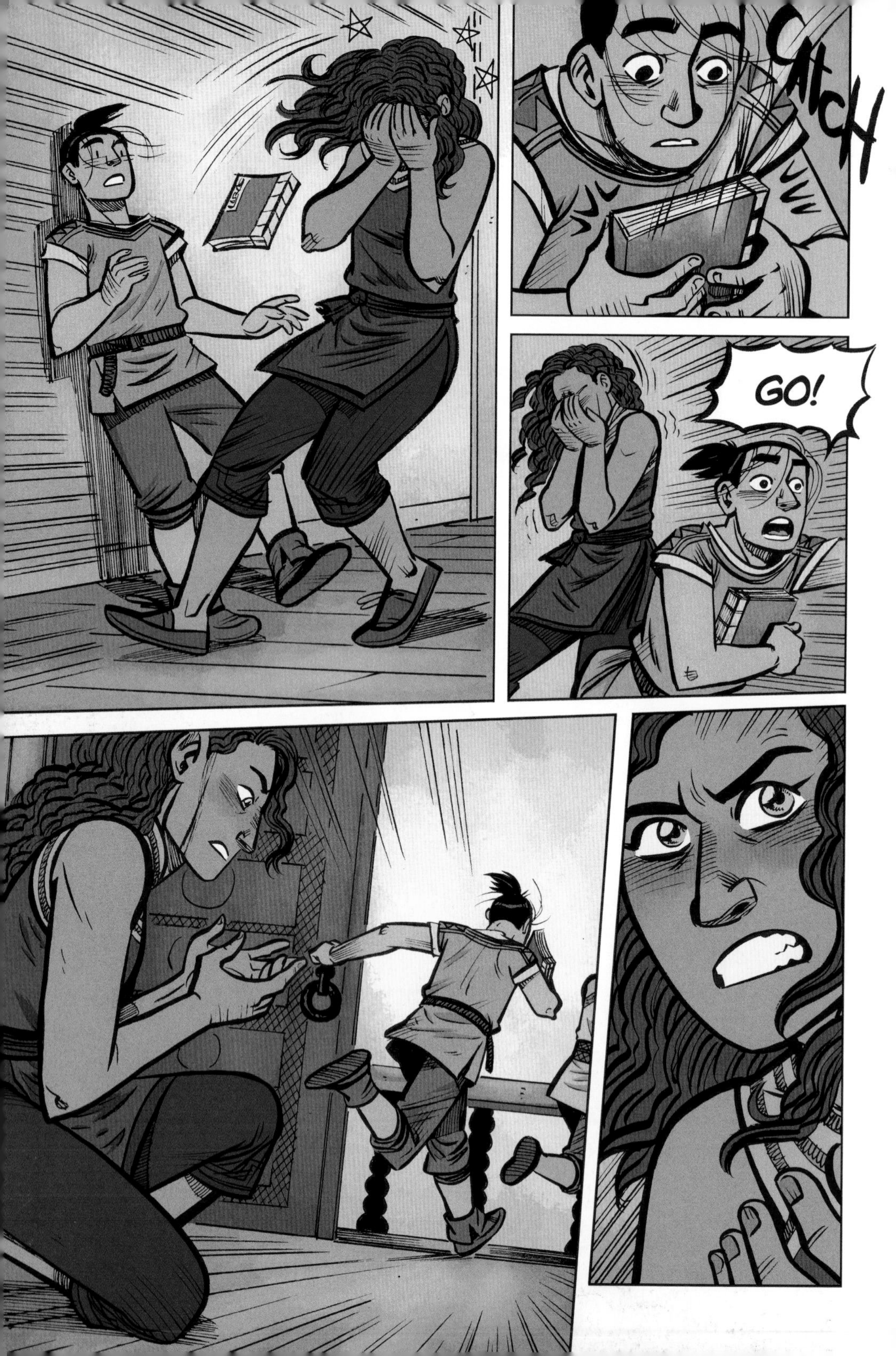
CATCH
GO!

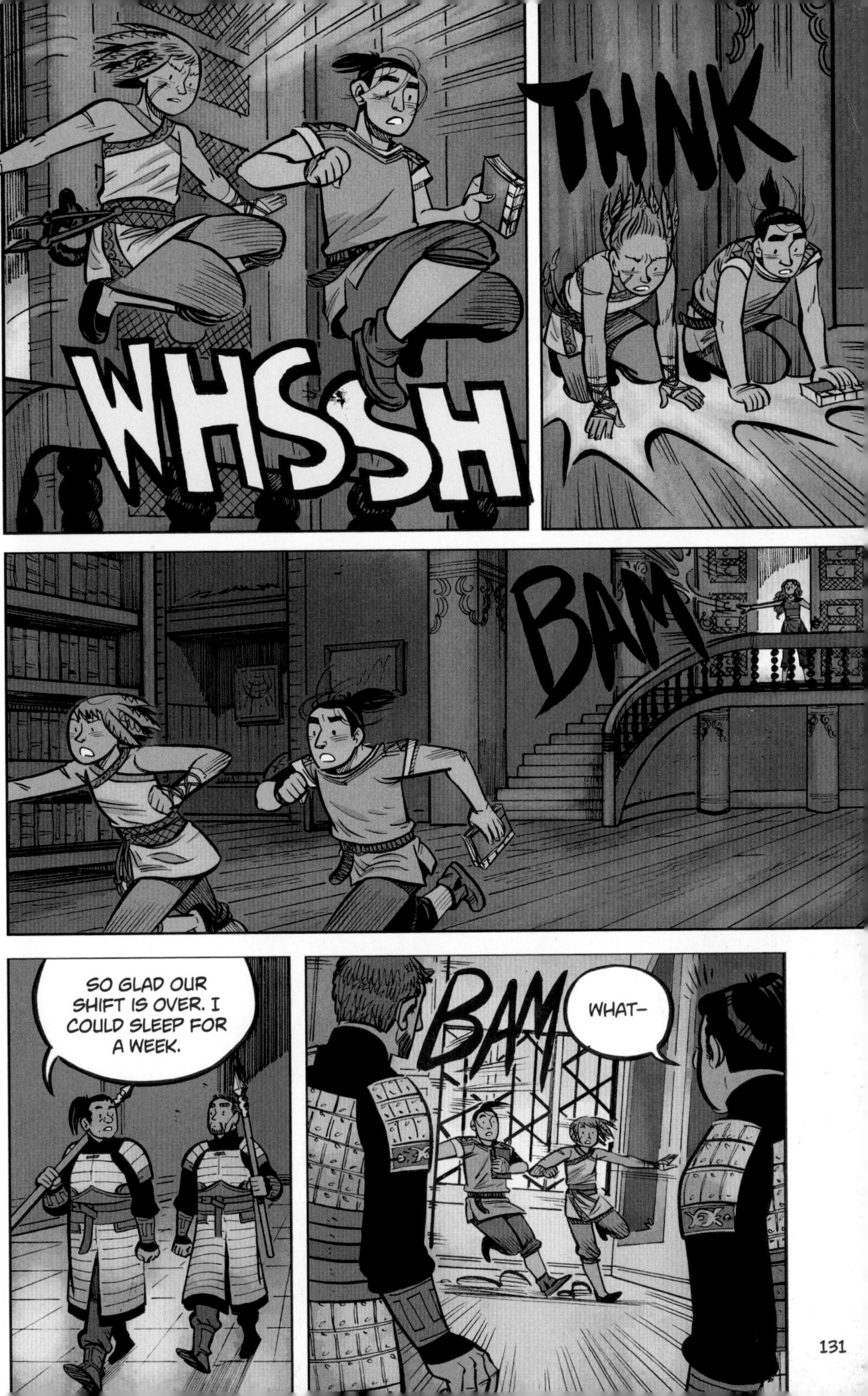
WHSSH
THNK
BAM
SO GLAD OUR SHIFT IS OVER. I COULD SLEEP FOR A WEEK.
BAM
WHAT-

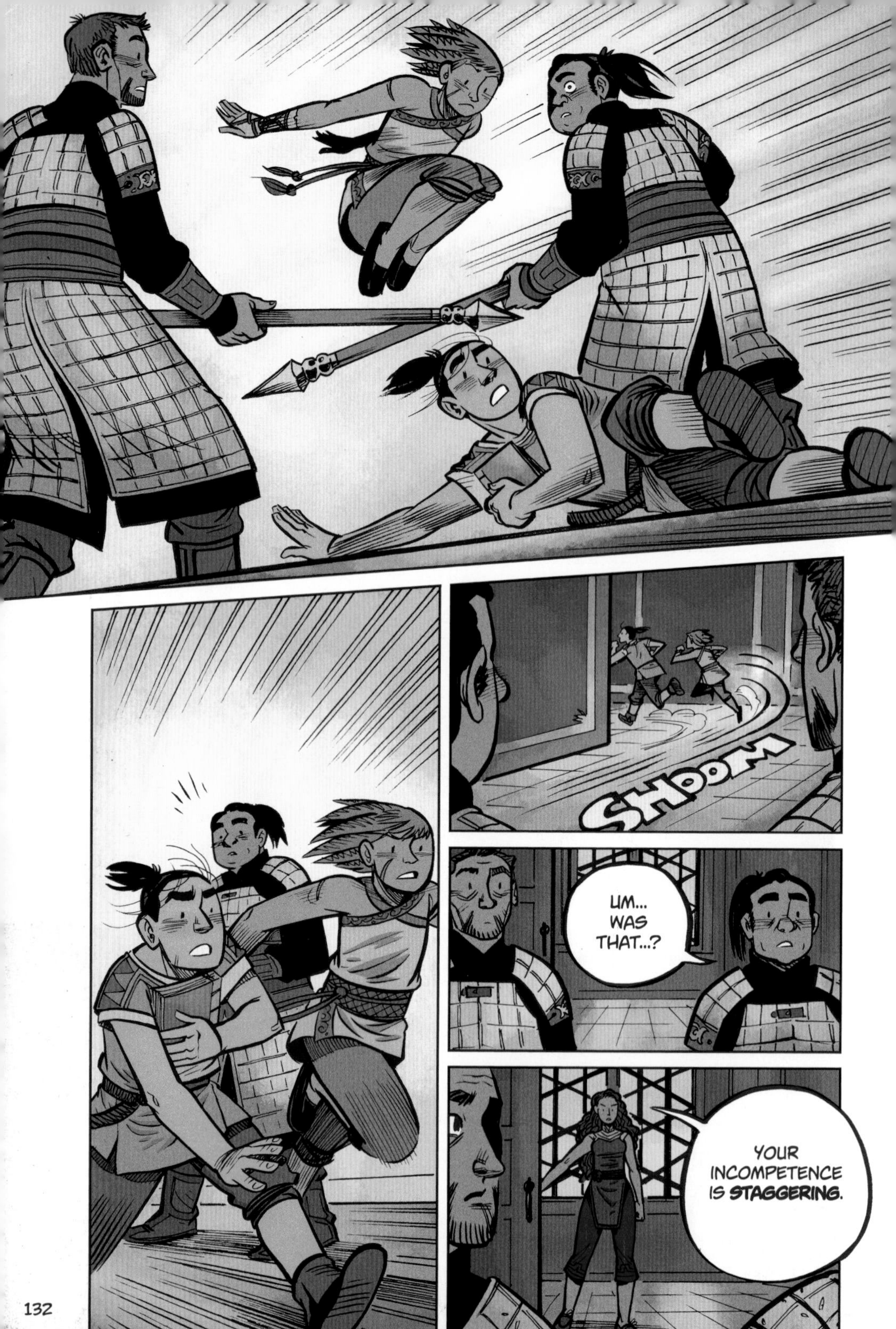
SHOOM
UM... WAS THAT...?
YOUR INCOMPETENCE IS **STAGGERING**.

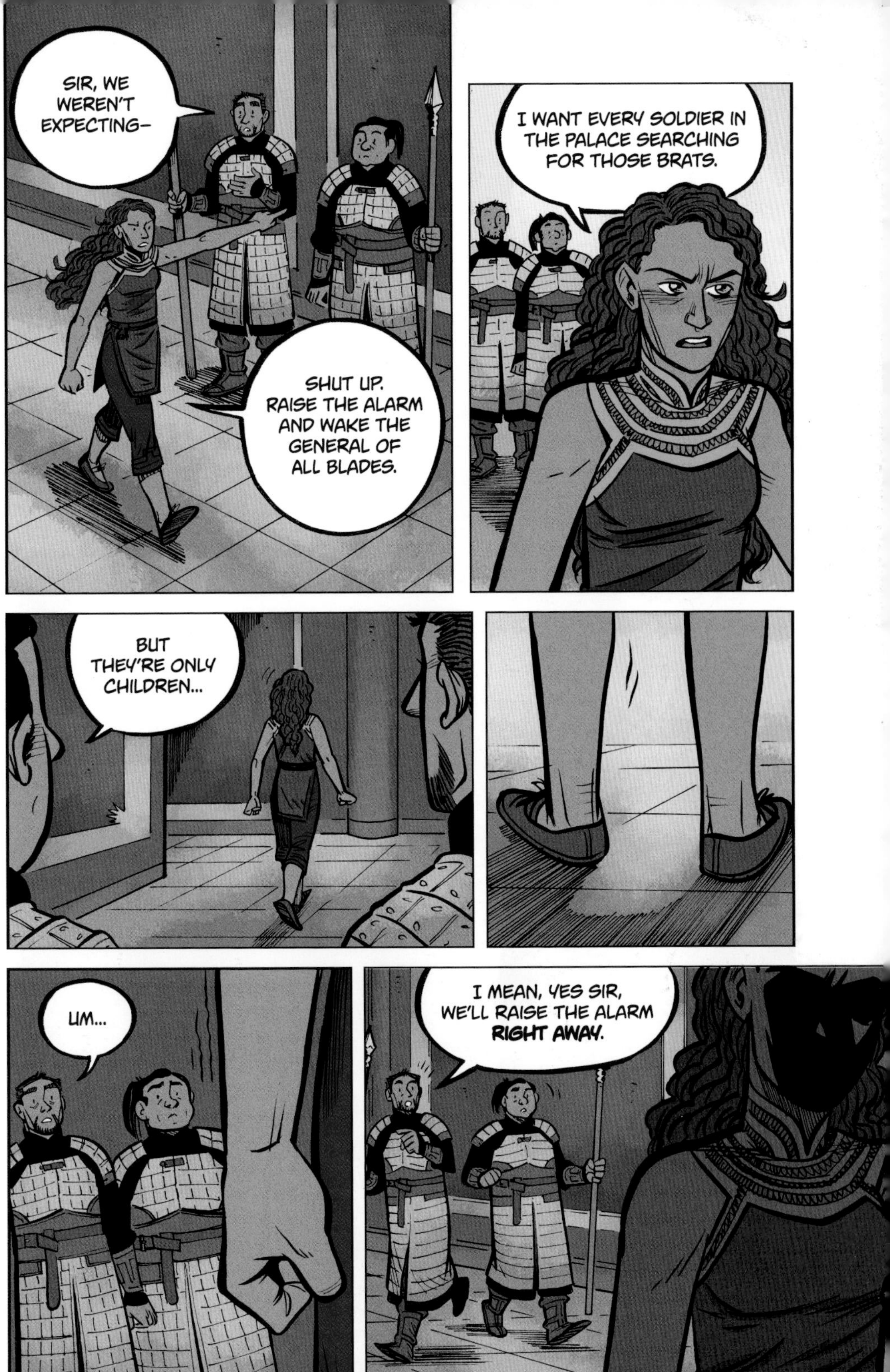
SIR, WE WEREN'T EXPECTING–
SHUT UP. RAISE THE ALARM AND WAKE THE GENERAL OF ALL BLADES.
I WANT EVERY SOLDIER IN THE PALACE SEARCHING FOR THOSE BRATS.
BUT THEY'RE ONLY CHILDREN...
UM...
I MEAN, YES SIR, WE'LL RAISE THE ALARM **RIGHT AWAY.**

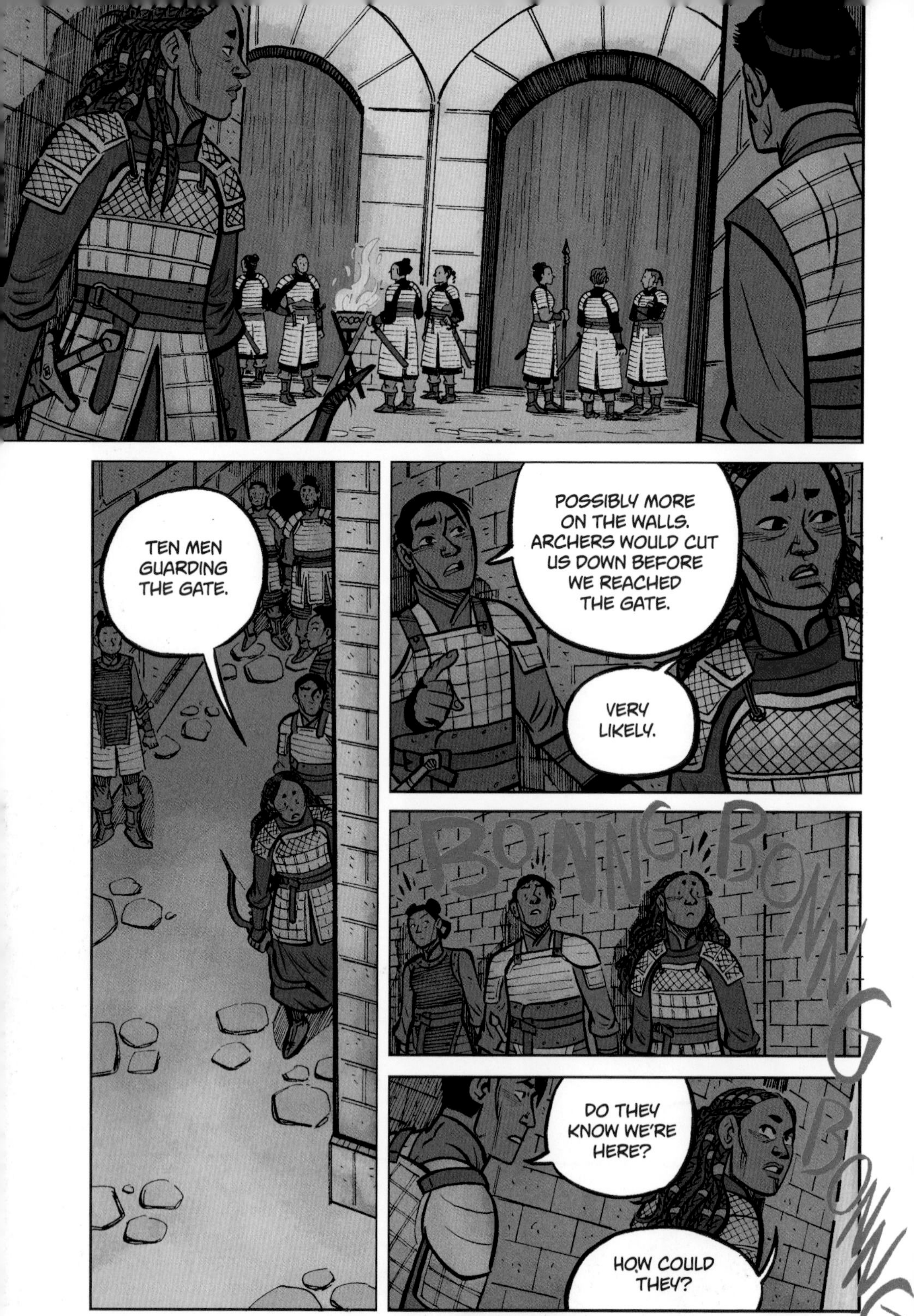
TEN MEN GUARDING THE GATE.
POSSIBLY MORE ON THE WALLS. ARCHERS WOULD CUT US DOWN BEFORE WE REACHED THE GATE.
VERY LIKELY.
BONNG BONNG BONNG BONNG
DO THEY KNOW WE'RE HERE?
HOW COULD THEY?

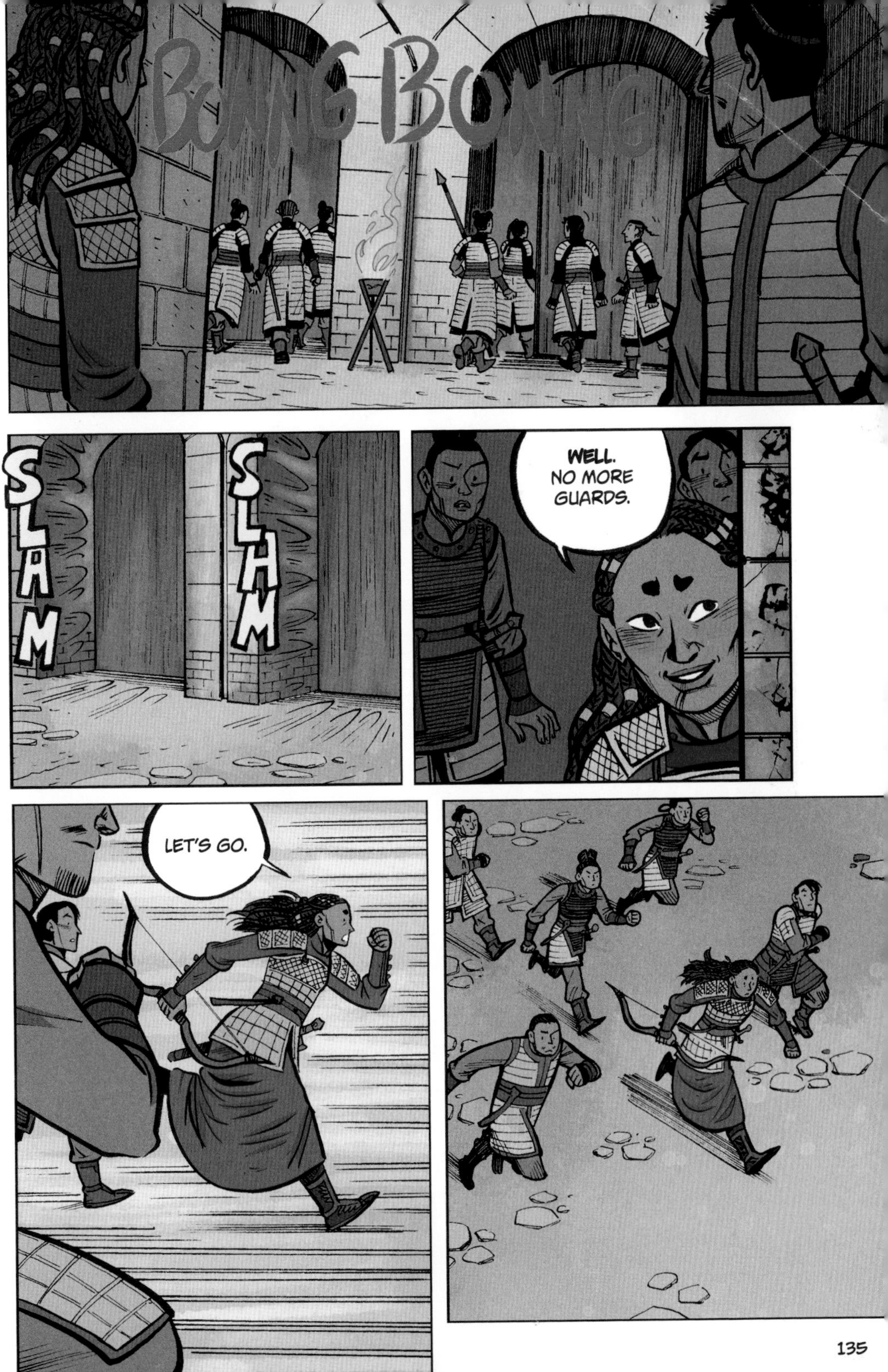
BUWNG BUWNG
SLAM
SLAM
WELL. NO MORE GUARDS.
LET'S GO.

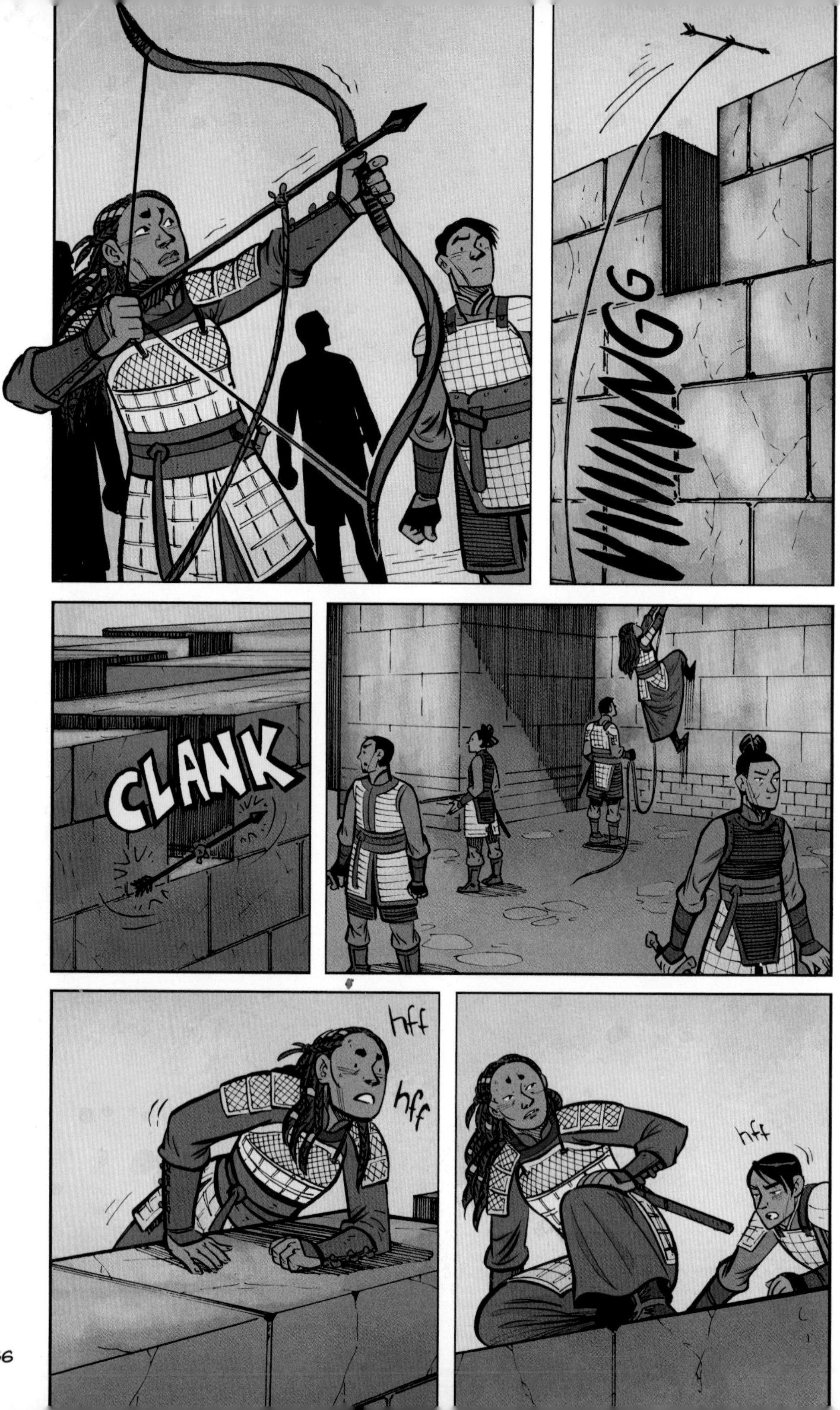
VVVVNNNNGG
CLANK
hff
hff
hff

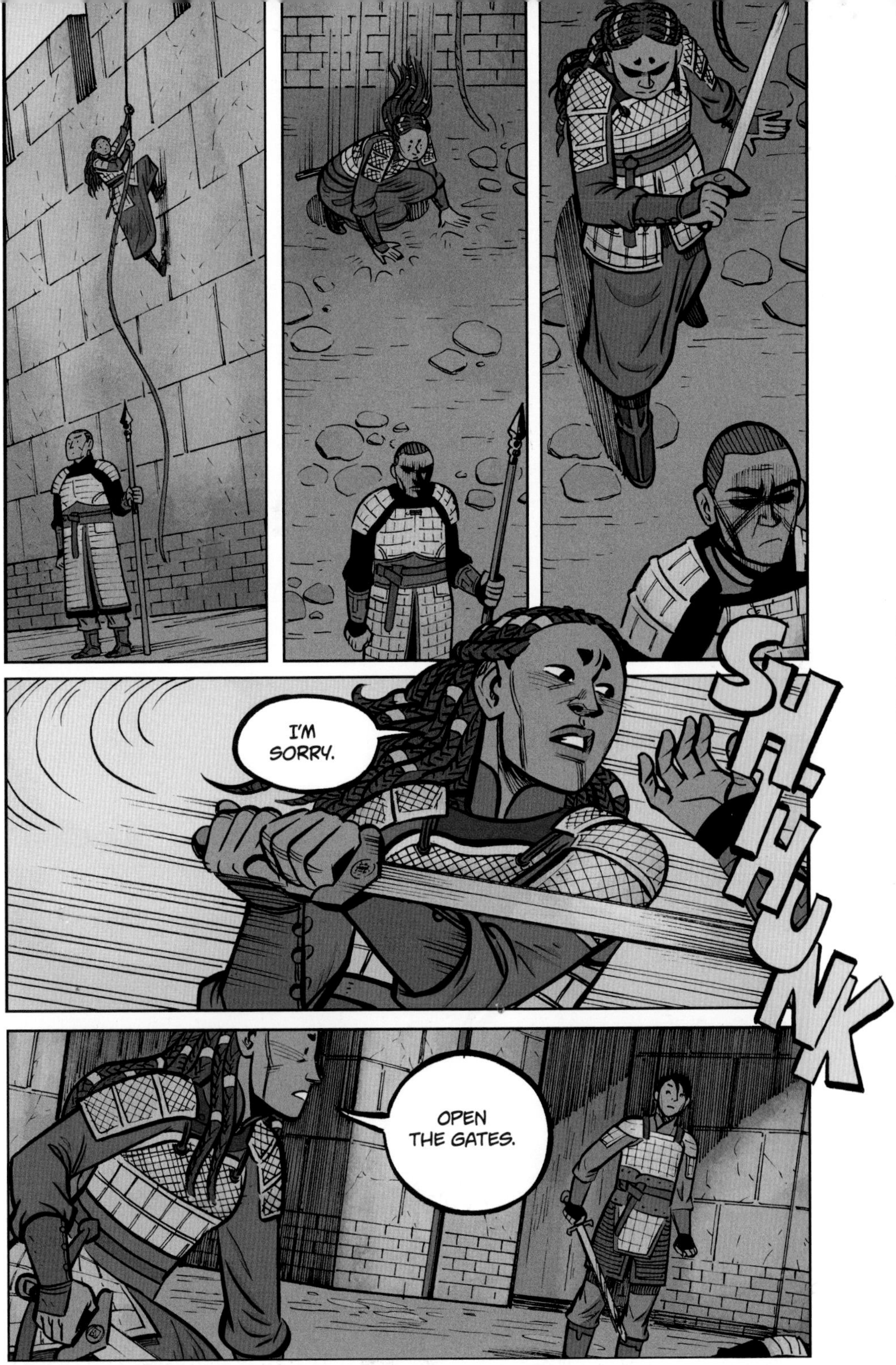
I'M SORRY.
SHHUNK
OPEN THE GATES.

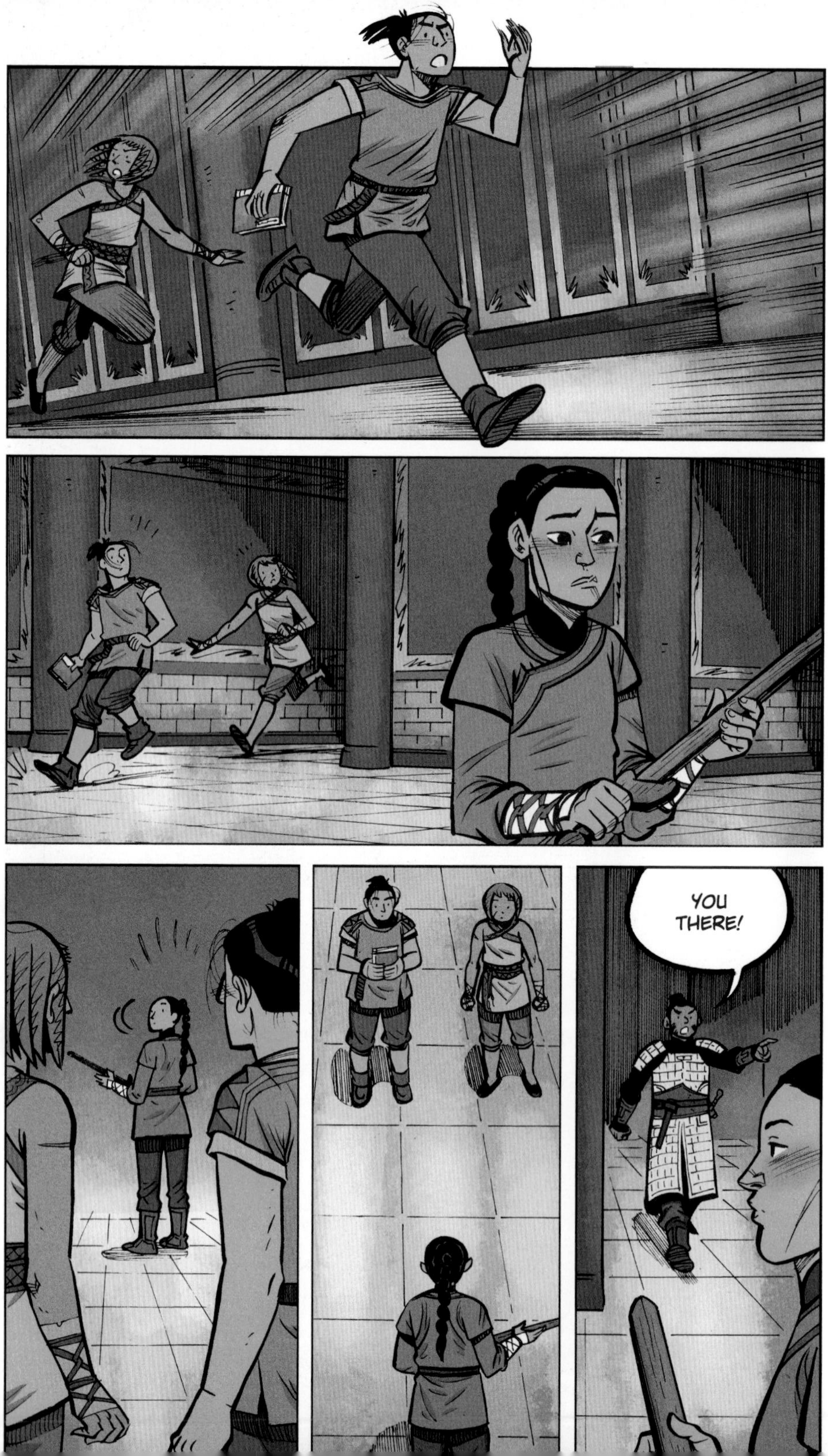
YOU THERE!

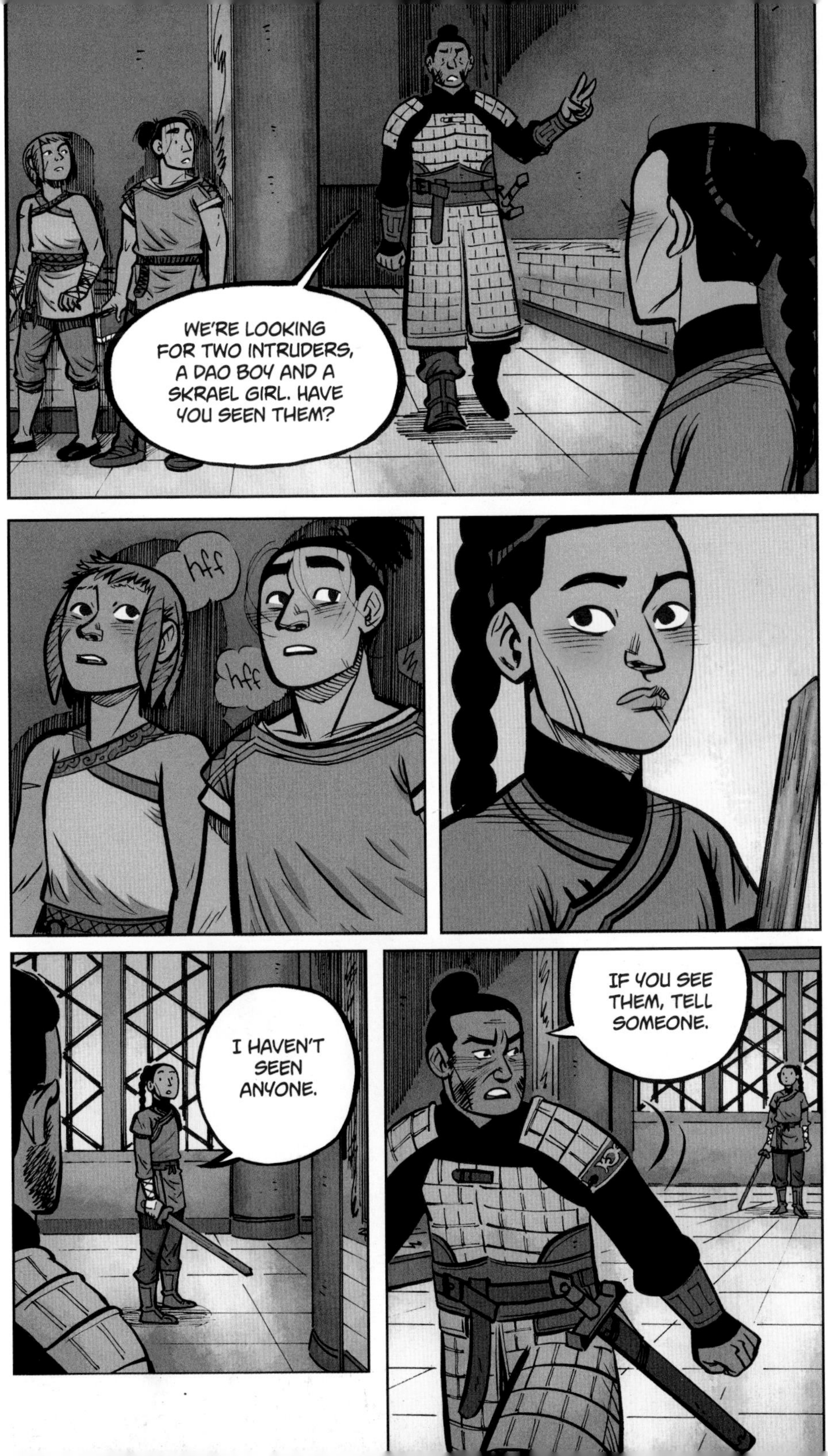

WE'RE LOOKING FOR TWO INTRUDERS, A DAO BOY AND A SKRAEL GIRL. HAVE YOU SEEN THEM?
hff
hff
I HAVEN'T SEEN ANYONE.
IF YOU SEE THEM, TELL SOMEONE.

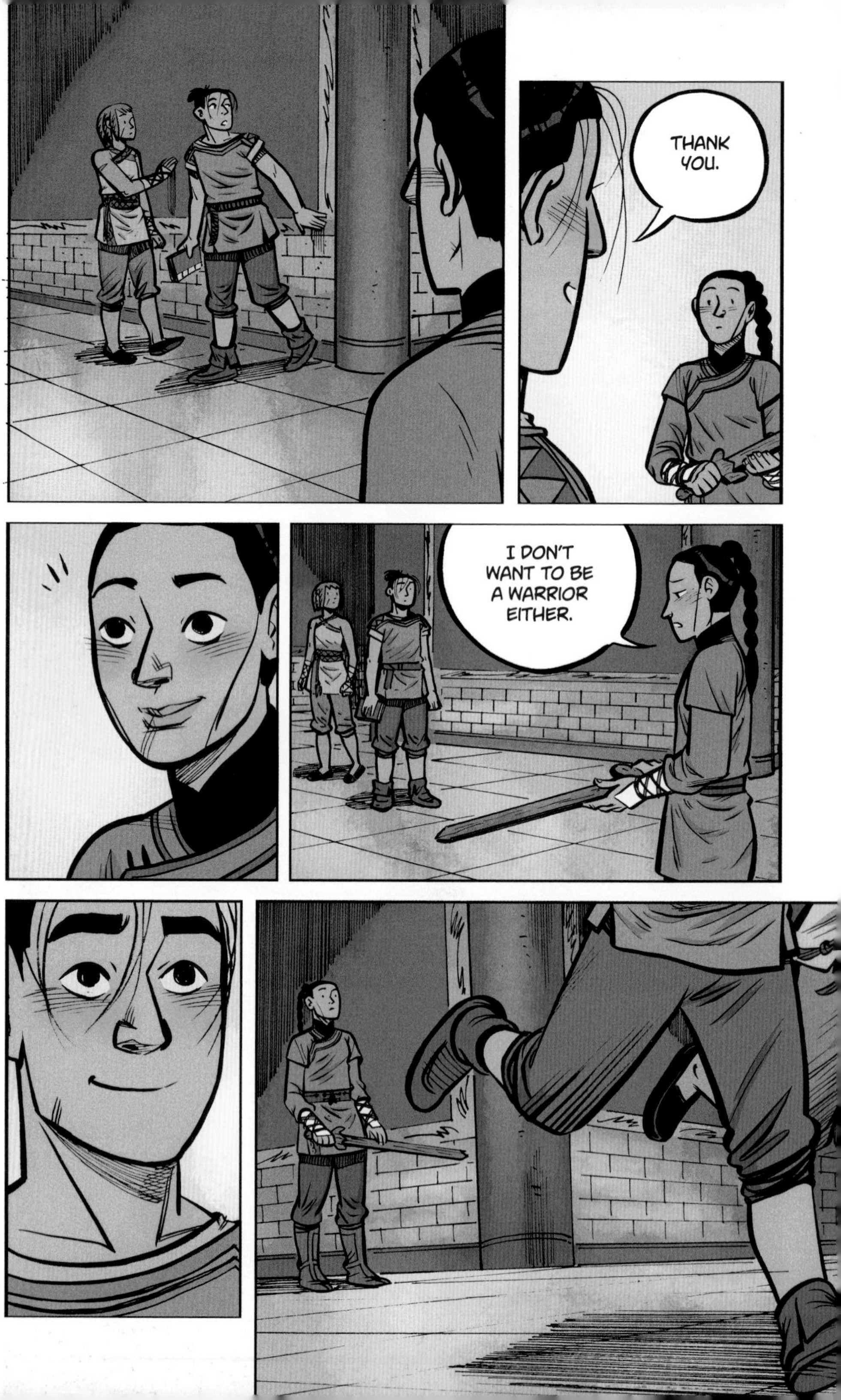
THANK YOU.
I DON'T WANT TO BE A WARRIOR EITHER.

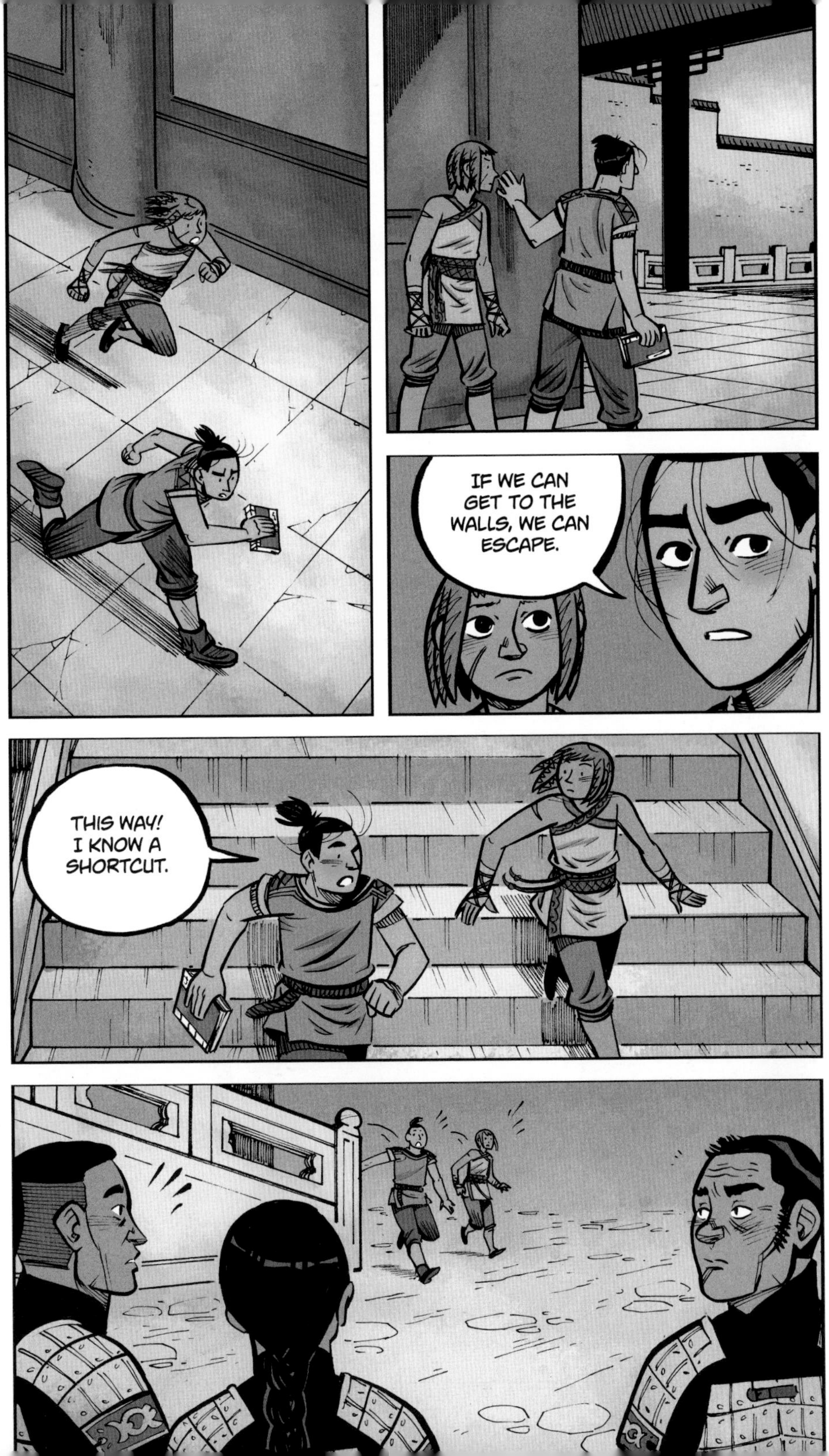
IF WE CAN GET TO THE WALLS, WE CAN ESCAPE.
THIS WAY! I KNOW A SHORTCUT.

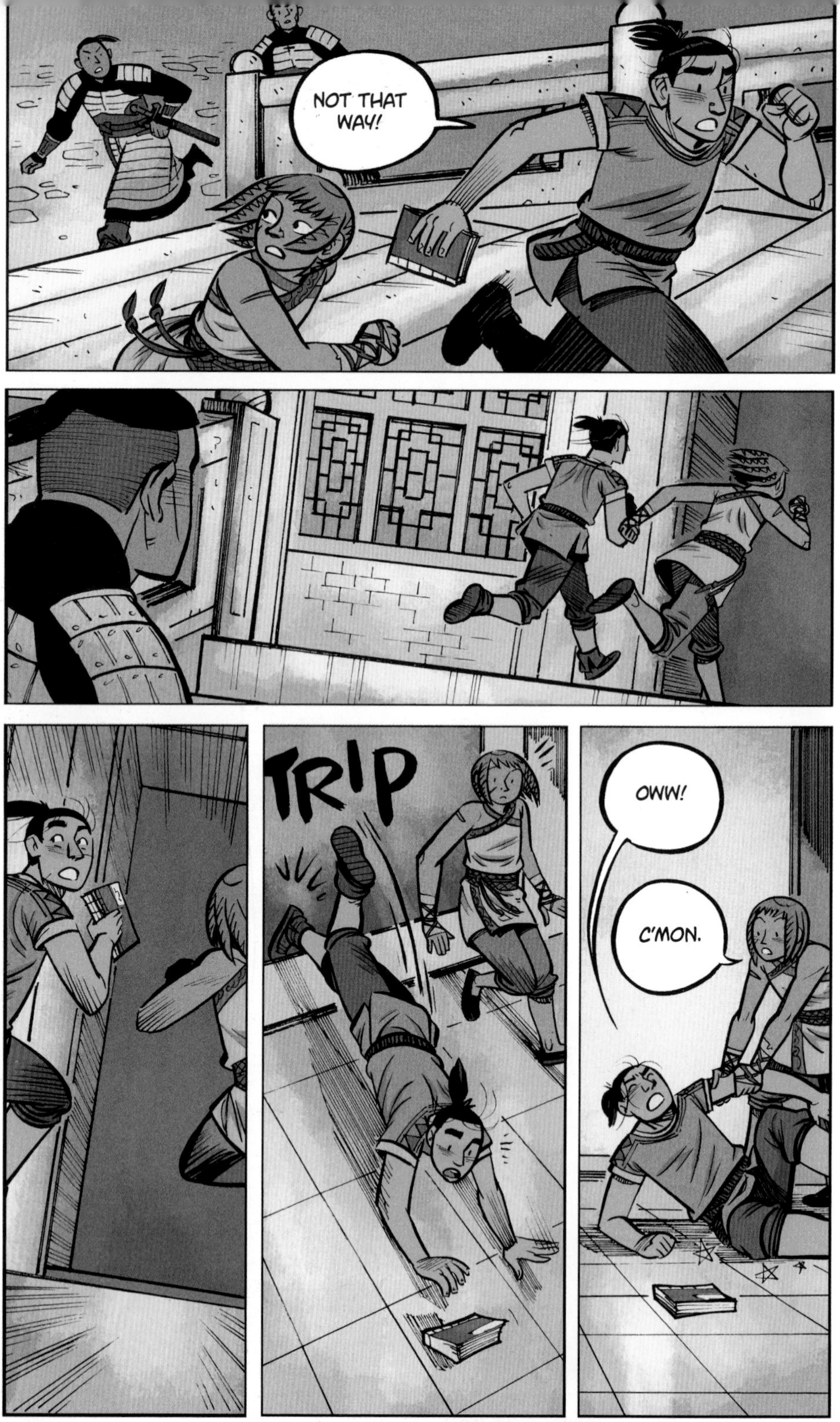
NOT THAT WAY!
TRIP
OWW!
C'MON.

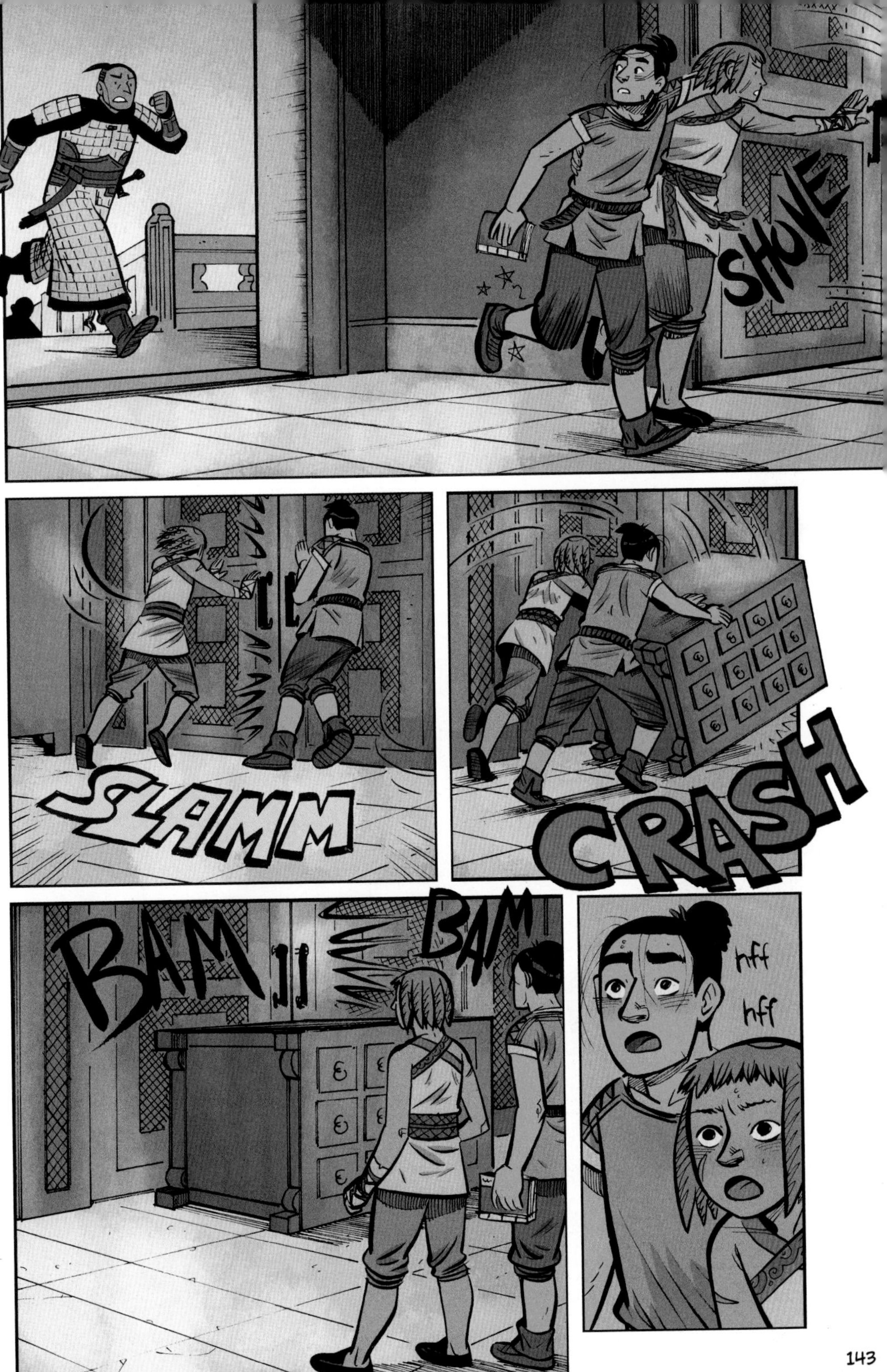
SHOVE
SLAMM
CRASH
BAM
BAM
hff
hff

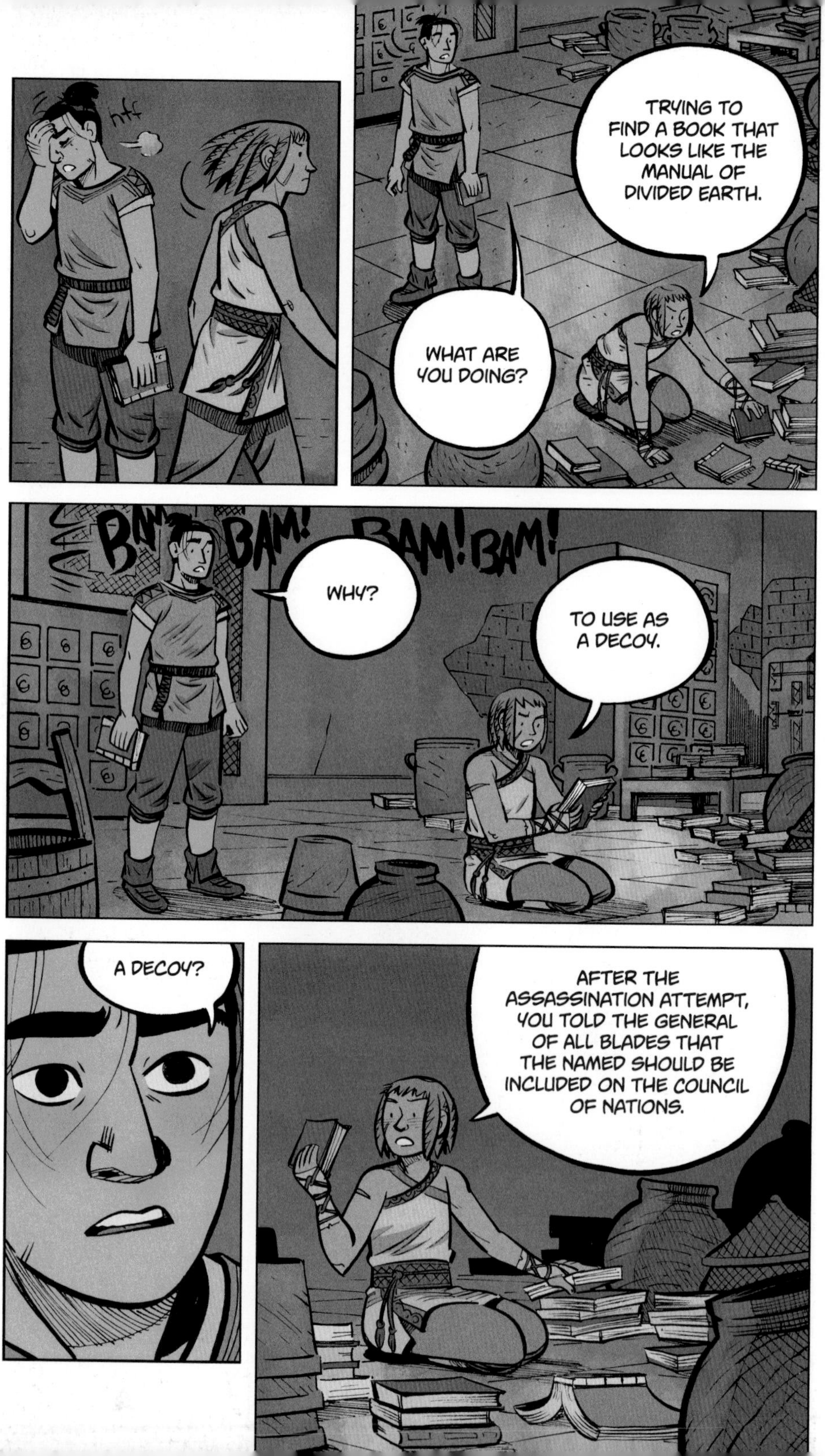

hff
WHAT ARE YOU DOING?
TRYING TO FIND A BOOK THAT LOOKS LIKE THE MANUAL OF DIVIDED EARTH.
BAM! BAM! BAM! BAM!
WHY?
TO USE AS A DECOY.
A DECOY?
AFTER THE ASSASSINATION ATTEMPT, YOU TOLD THE GENERAL OF ALL BLADES THAT THE NAMED SHOULD BE INCLUDED ON THE COUNCIL OF NATIONS.

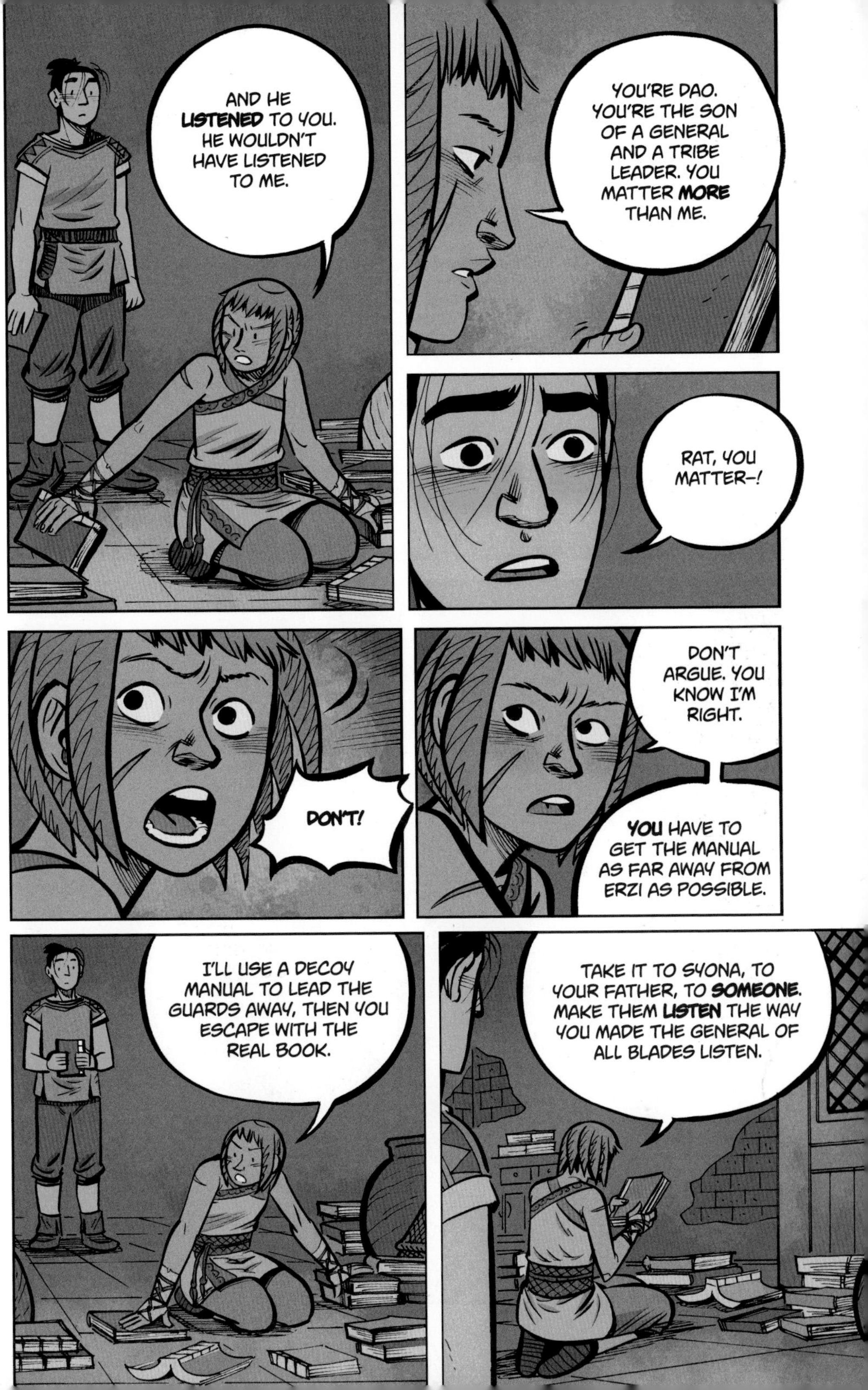
AND HE LISTENED TO YOU. HE WOULDN'T HAVE LISTENED TO ME.
YOU'RE DAO. YOU'RE THE SON OF A GENERAL AND A TRIBE LEADER. YOU MATTER MORE THAN ME.
RAT, YOU MATTER-!
DON'T!
DON'T ARGUE. YOU KNOW I'M RIGHT.
YOU HAVE TO GET THE MANUAL AS FAR AWAY FROM ERZI AS POSSIBLE.
I'LL USE A DECOY MANUAL TO LEAD THE GUARDS AWAY, THEN YOU ESCAPE WITH THE REAL BOOK.
TAKE IT TO SYONA, TO YOUR FATHER, TO SOMEONE. MAKE THEM LISTEN THE WAY YOU MADE THE GENERAL OF ALL BLADES LISTEN.

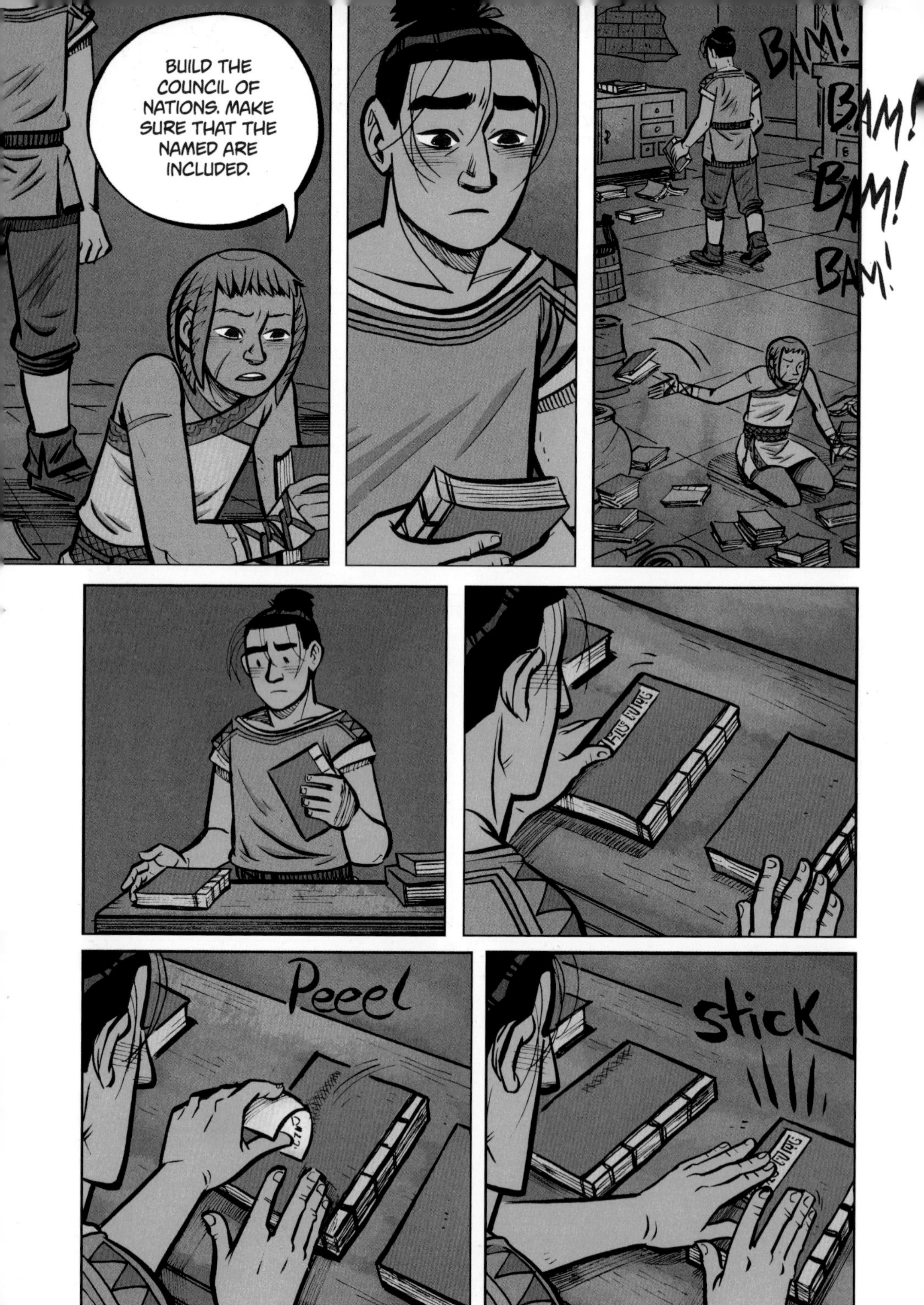
BUILD THE COUNCIL OF NATIONS. MAKE SURE THAT THE NAMED ARE INCLUDED.
BAM! BAM! BAM! BAM!
Peeel
stick

RAT, I FOUND A DECOY BOOK.

GOOD. GIVE IT TO ME.

B AM!

KRAK!

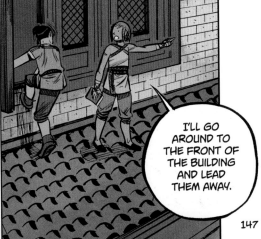

I'LL GO AROUND TO THE FRONT OF THE BUILDING AND LEAD THEM AWAY.

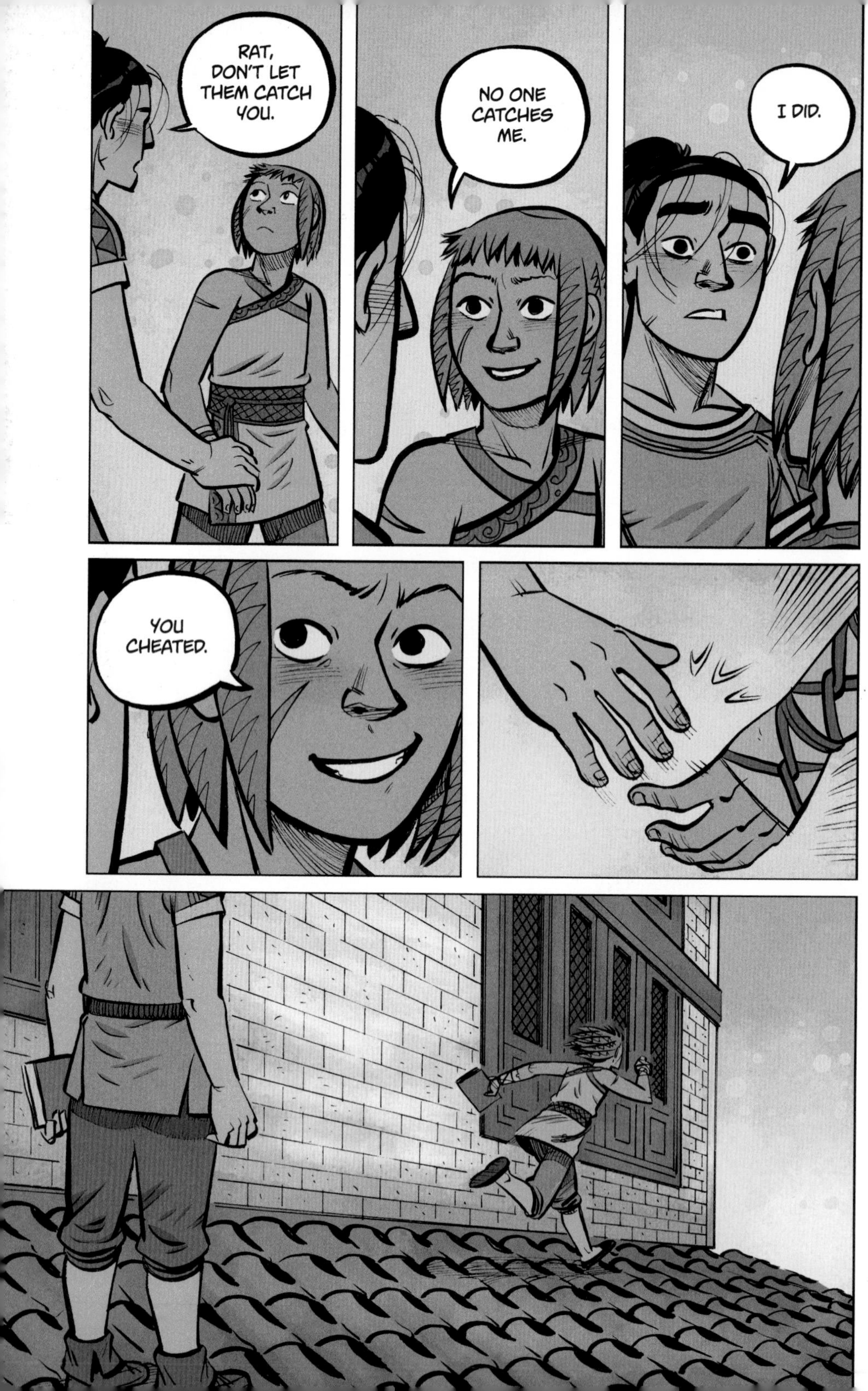
RAT, DON'T LET THEM CATCH YOU.
NO ONE CATCHES ME.
I DID.
YOU CHEATED.

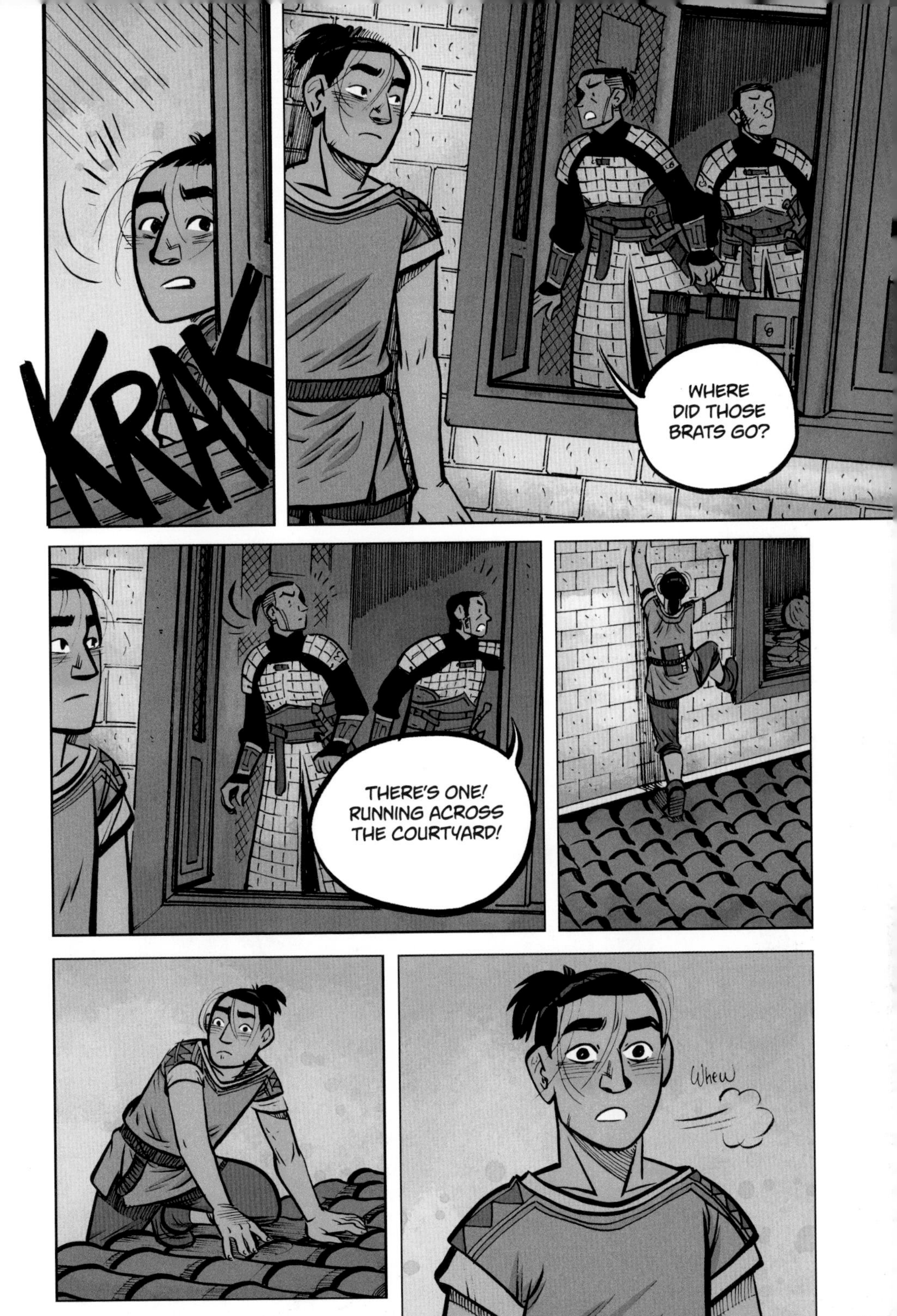
KRAK
WHERE DID THOSE BRATS GO?
THERE'S ONE! RUNNING ACROSS THE COURTYARD!
Whew

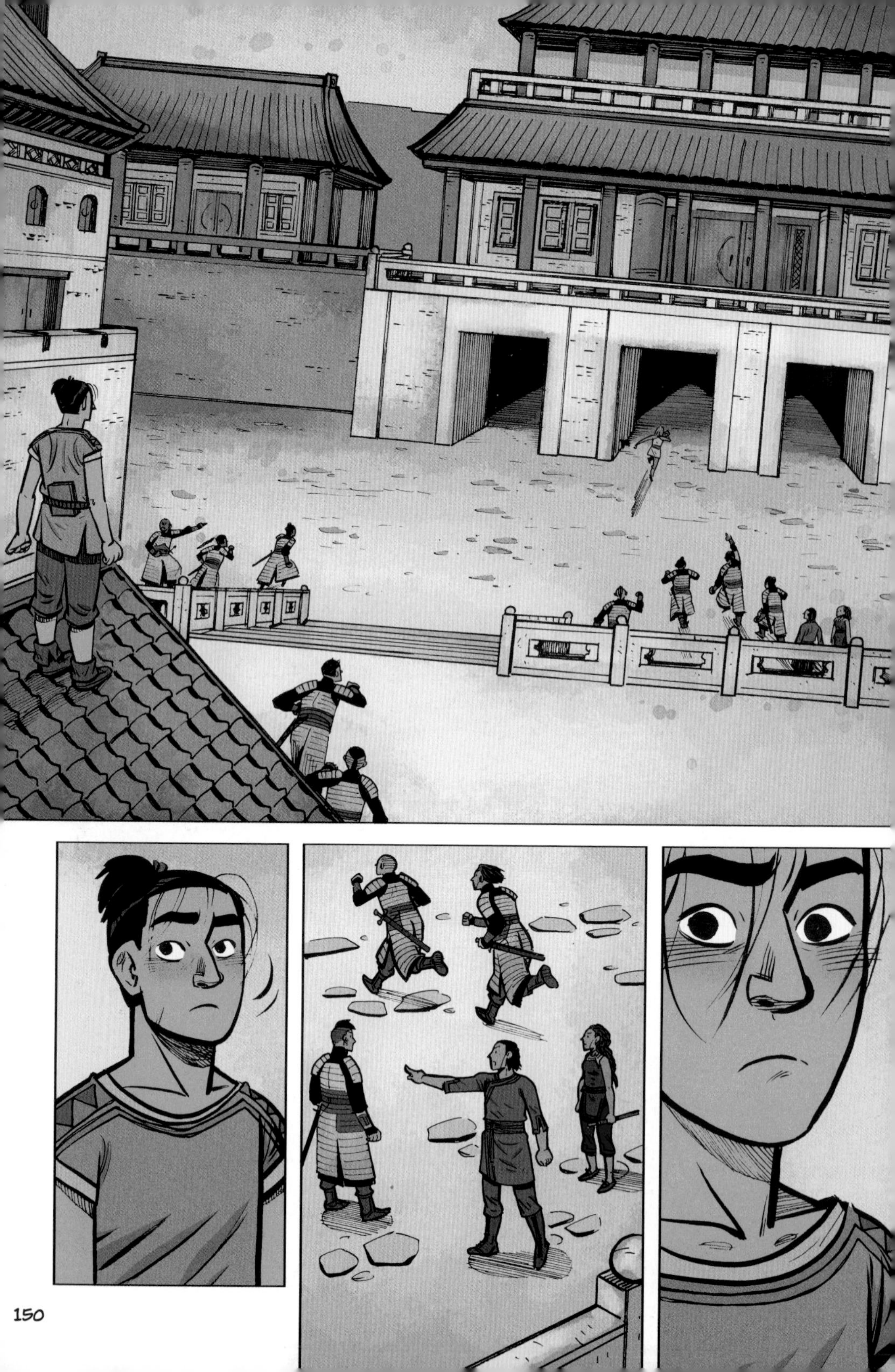

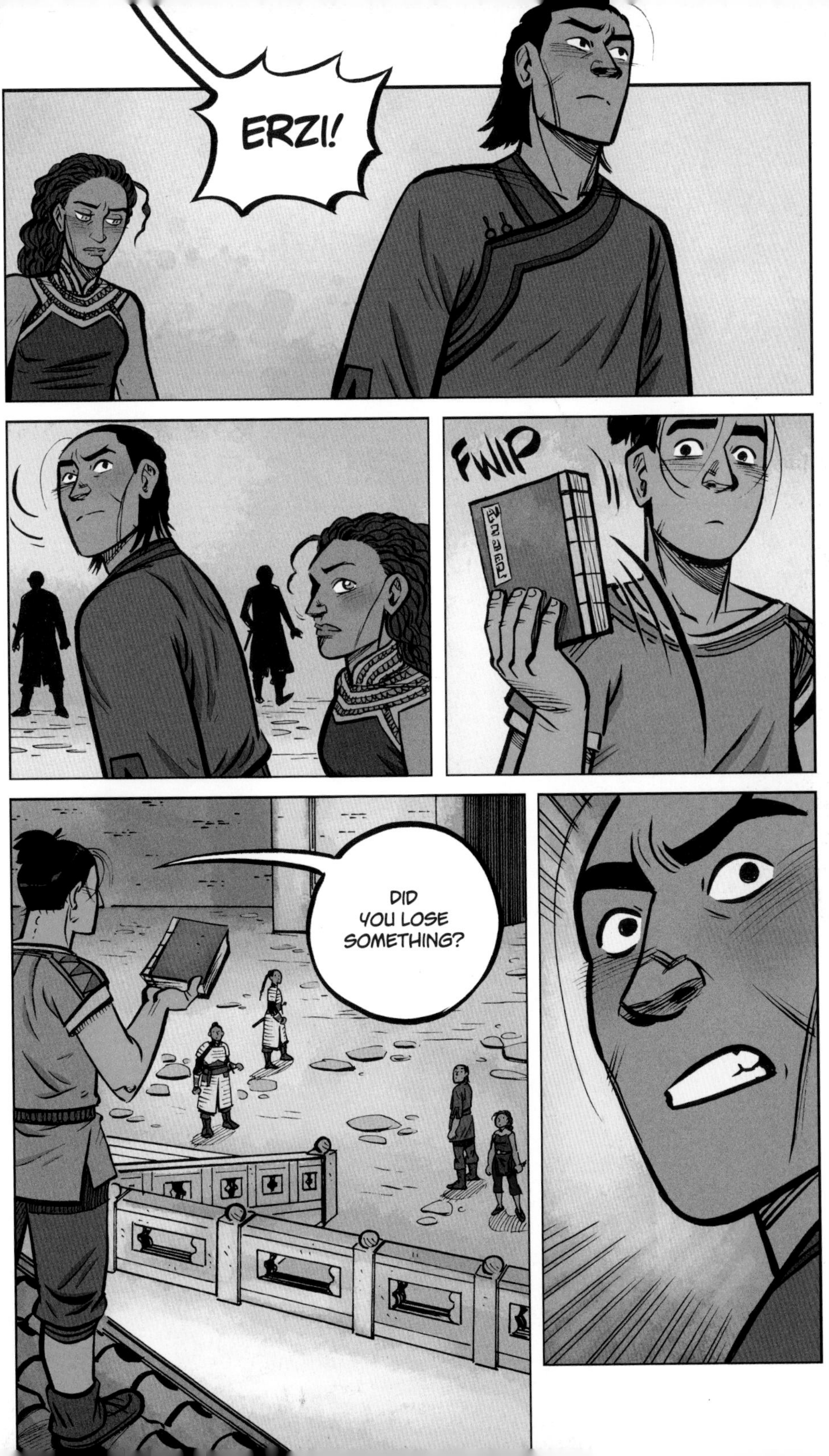
ERZI!
FWIP
DID YOU LOSE SOMETHING?

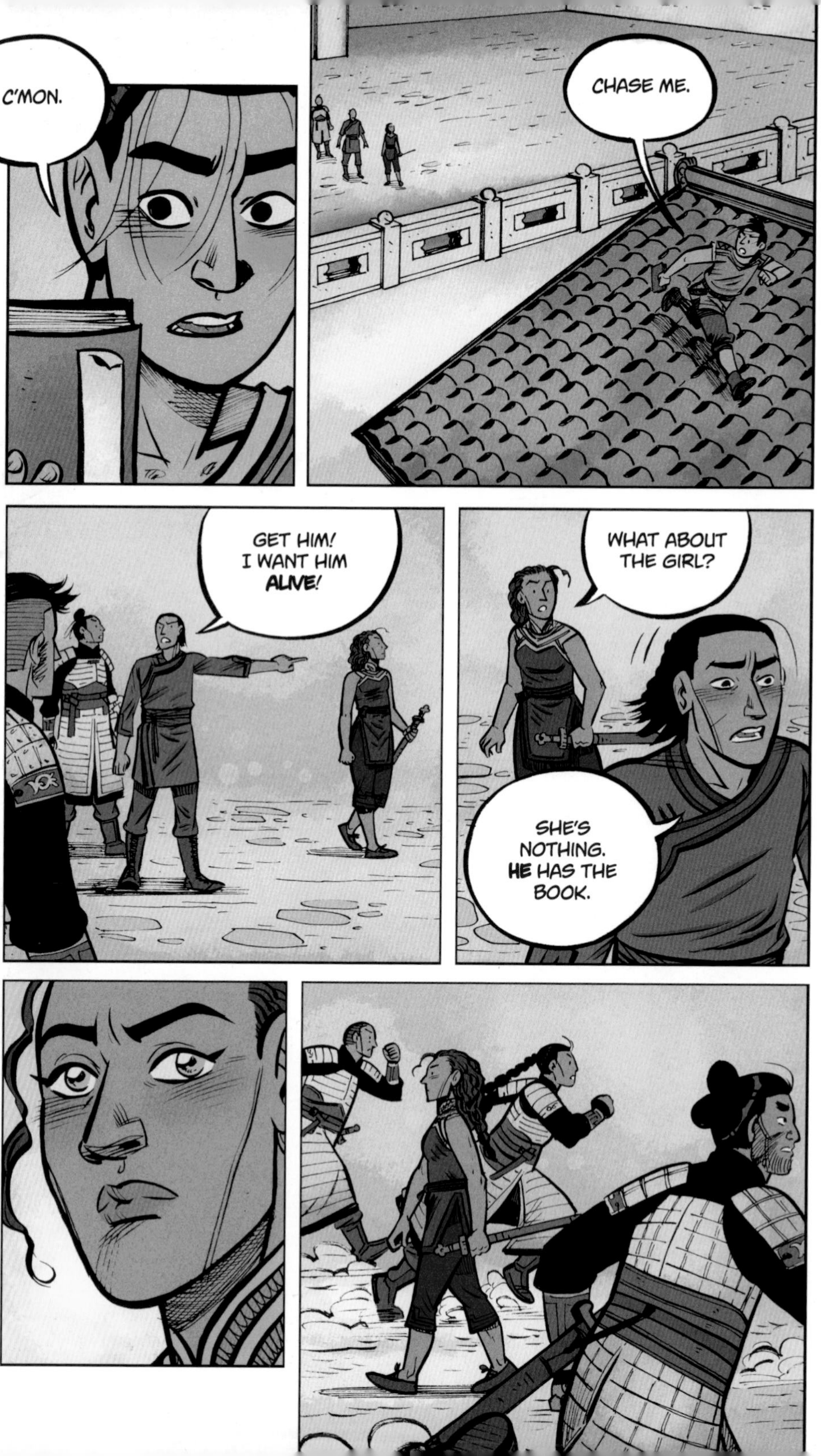
C'MON.
CHASE ME.
GET HIM! I WANT HIM ALIVE!
WHAT ABOUT THE GIRL?
SHE'S NOTHING. HE HAS THE BOOK.

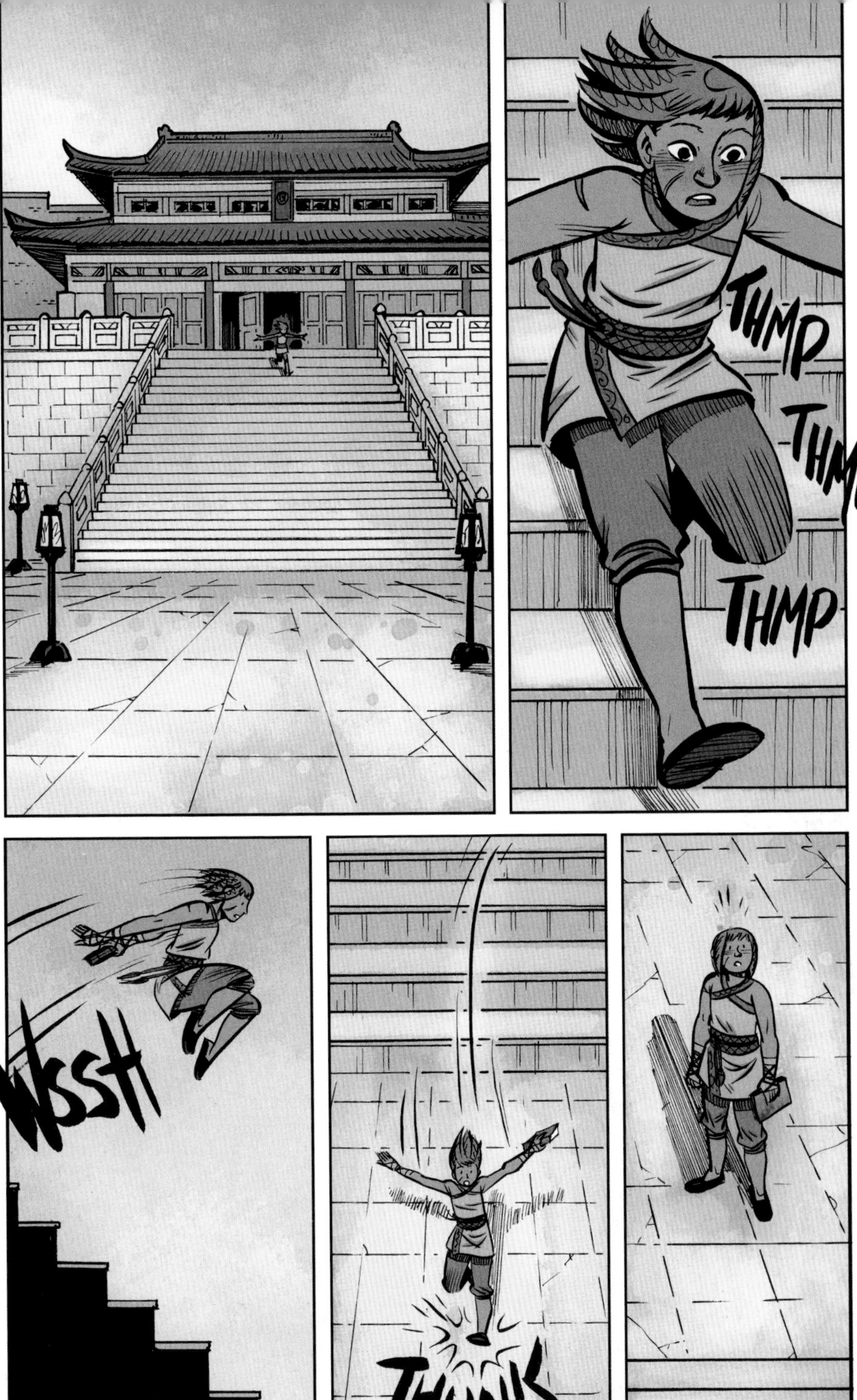
THMP
THMP
THMP
WSSH
THUNK

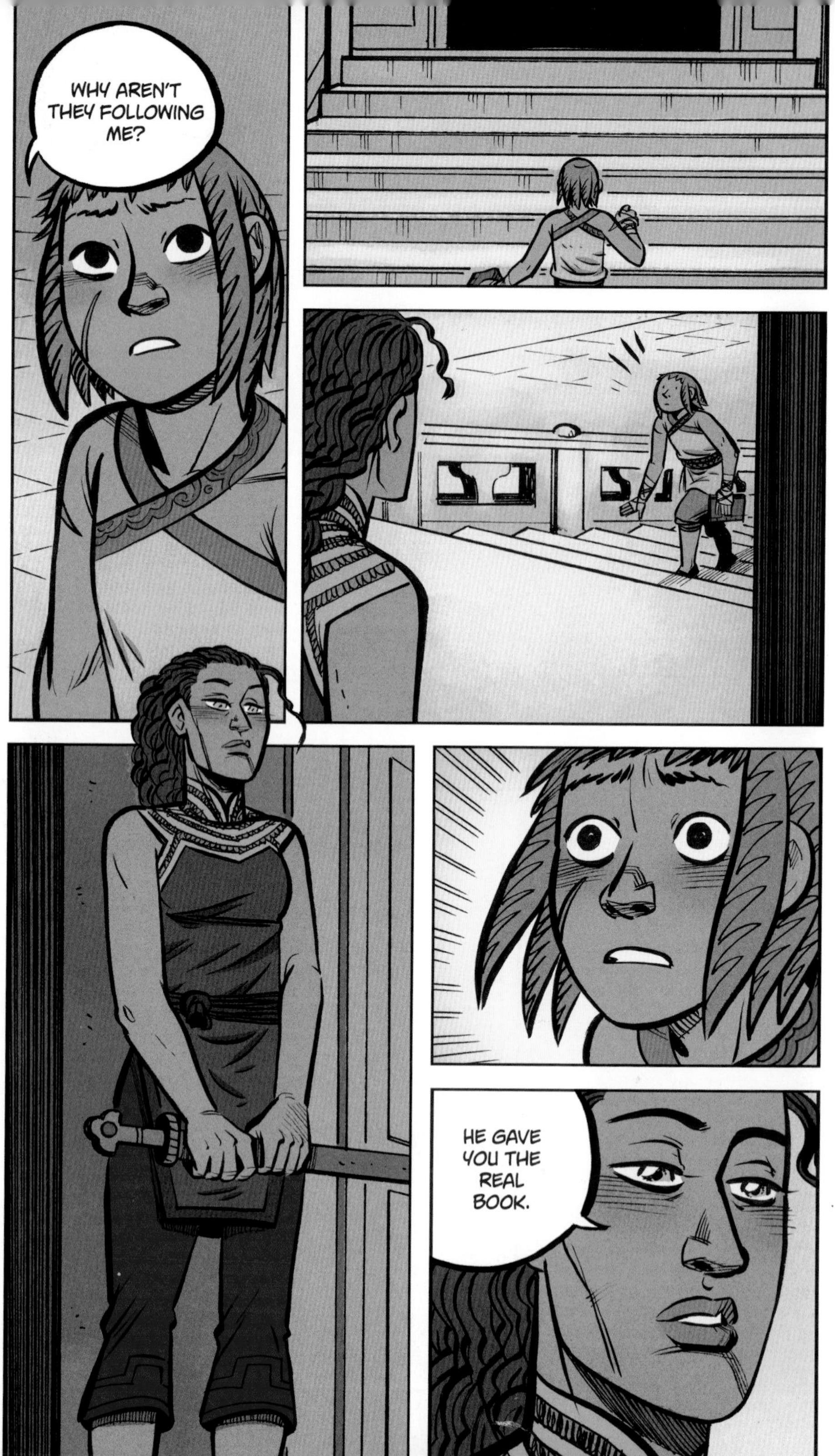

WHY AREN'T THEY FOLLOWING ME?
HE GAVE YOU THE REAL BOOK.

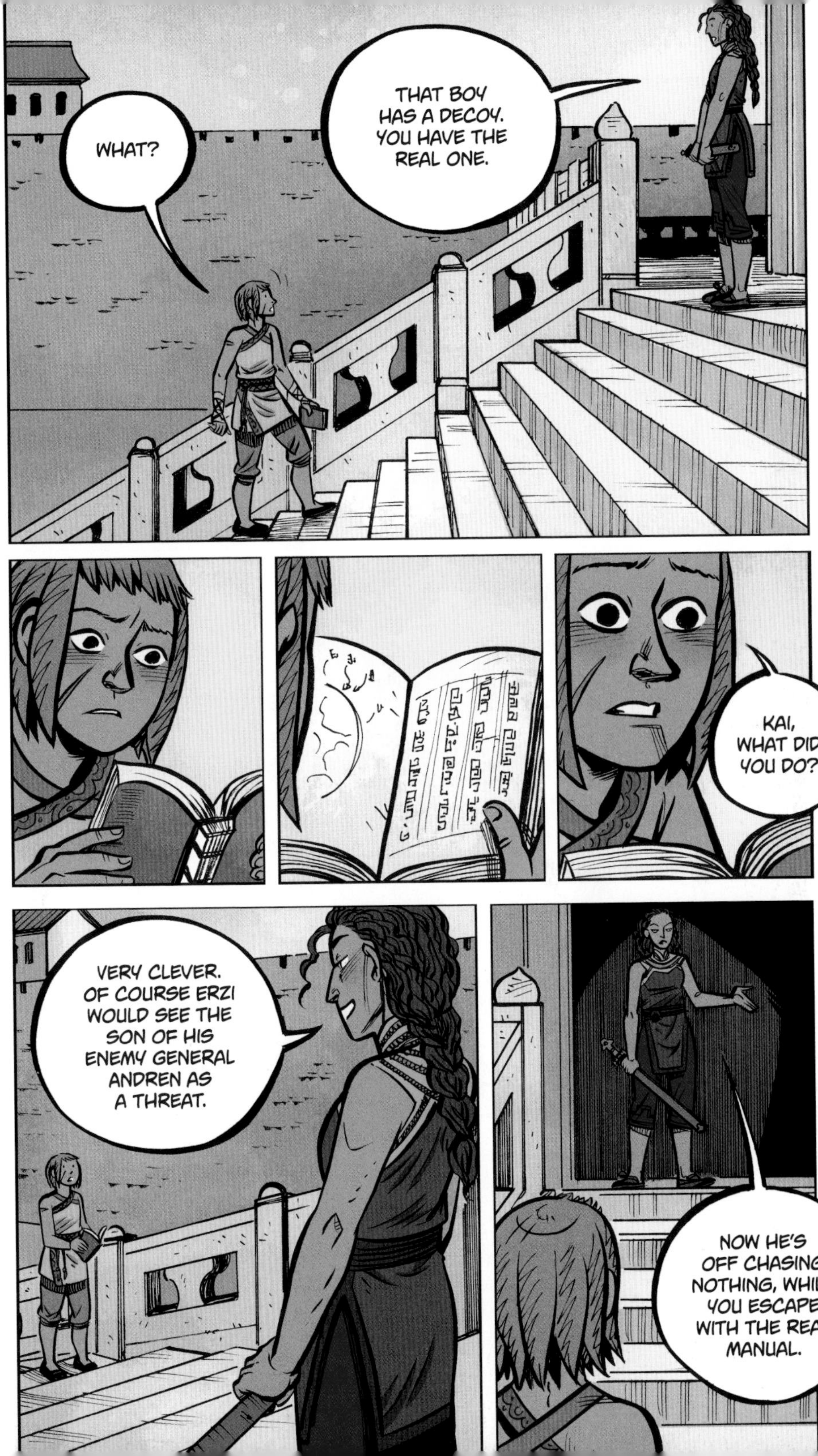
THAT BOY HAS A DECOY. YOU HAVE THE REAL ONE.
WHAT?
KAI, WHAT DID YOU DO?
VERY CLEVER. OF COURSE ERZI WOULD SEE THE SON OF HIS ENEMY GENERAL ANDREN AS A THREAT.
NOW HE'S OFF CHASING NOTHING, WHILE YOU ESCAPE WITH THE REAL MANUAL.

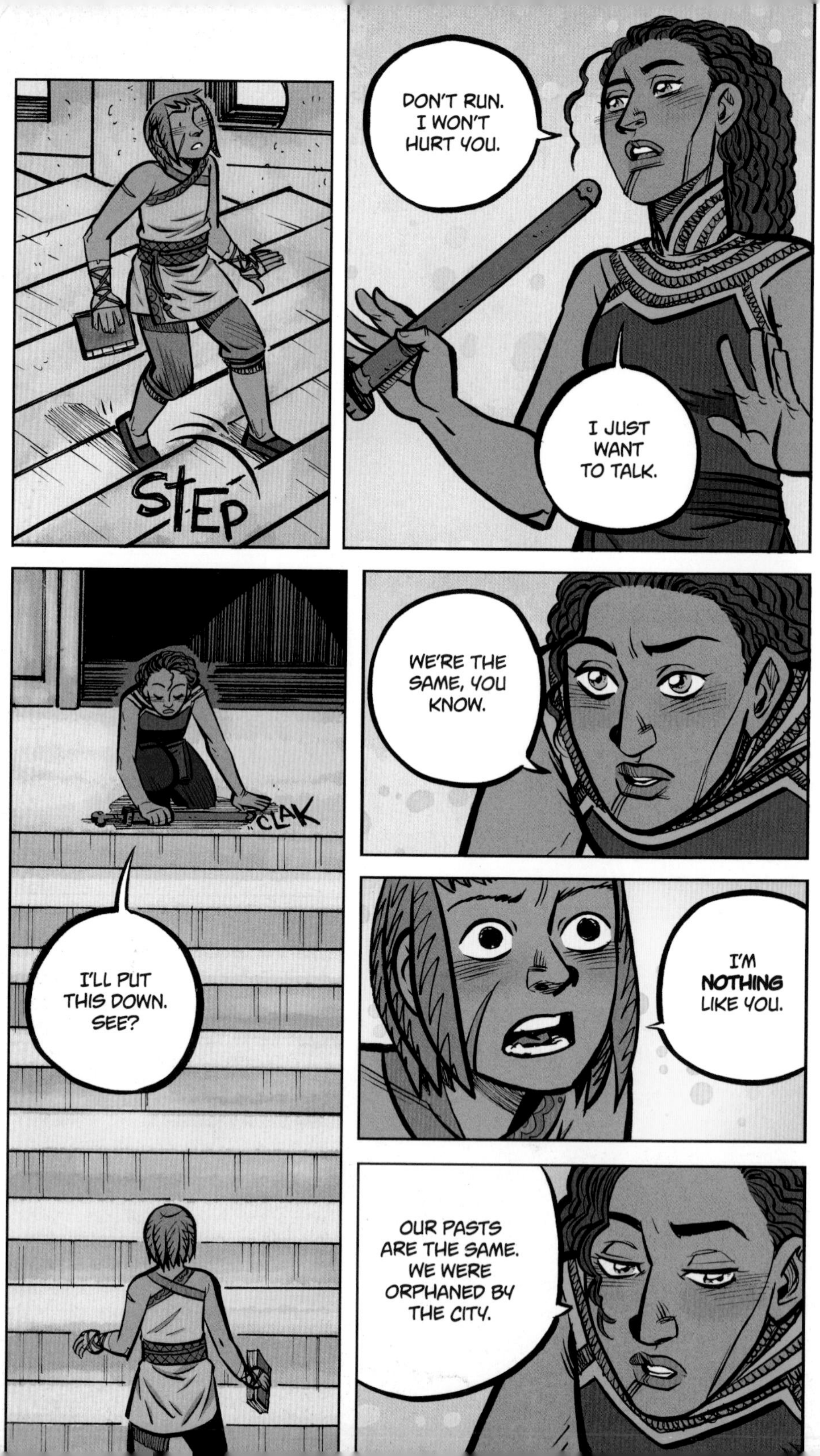
STEP
DON'T RUN. I WON'T HURT YOU.
I JUST WANT TO TALK.
CLAK
I'LL PUT THIS DOWN. SEE?
WE'RE THE SAME, YOU KNOW.
I'M **NOTHING** LIKE YOU.
OUR PASTS ARE THE SAME. WE WERE ORPHANED BY THE CITY.

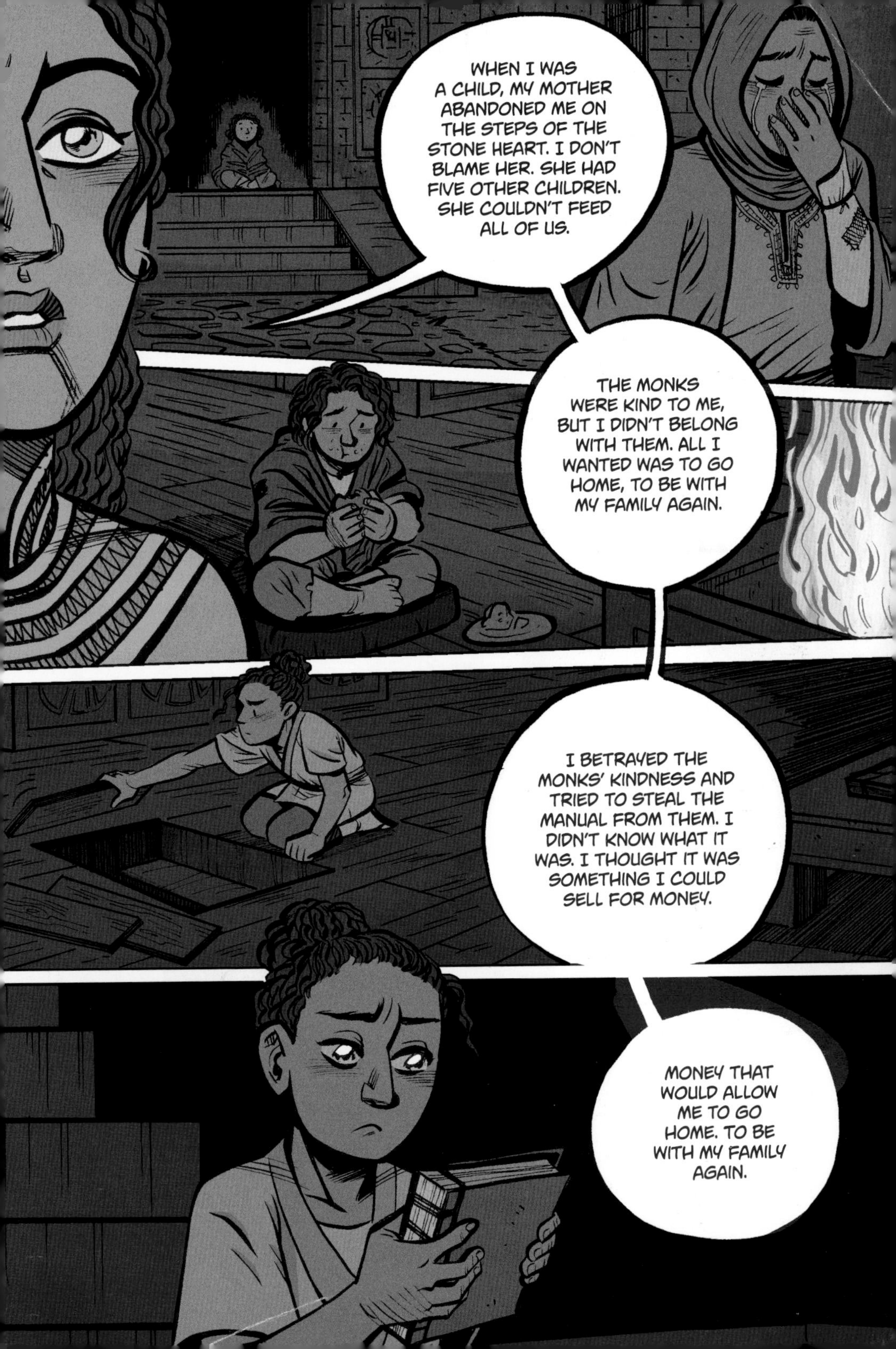
WHEN I WAS A CHILD, MY MOTHER ABANDONED ME ON THE STEPS OF THE STONE HEART. I DON'T BLAME HER. SHE HAD FIVE OTHER CHILDREN. SHE COULDN'T FEED ALL OF US.
THE MONKS WERE KIND TO ME, BUT I DIDN'T BELONG WITH THEM. ALL I WANTED WAS TO GO HOME, TO BE WITH MY FAMILY AGAIN.
I BETRAYED THE MONKS' KINDNESS AND TRIED TO STEAL THE MANUAL FROM THEM. I DIDN'T KNOW WHAT IT WAS. I THOUGHT IT WAS SOMETHING I COULD SELL FOR MONEY.
MONEY THAT WOULD ALLOW ME TO GO HOME. TO BE WITH MY FAMILY AGAIN.

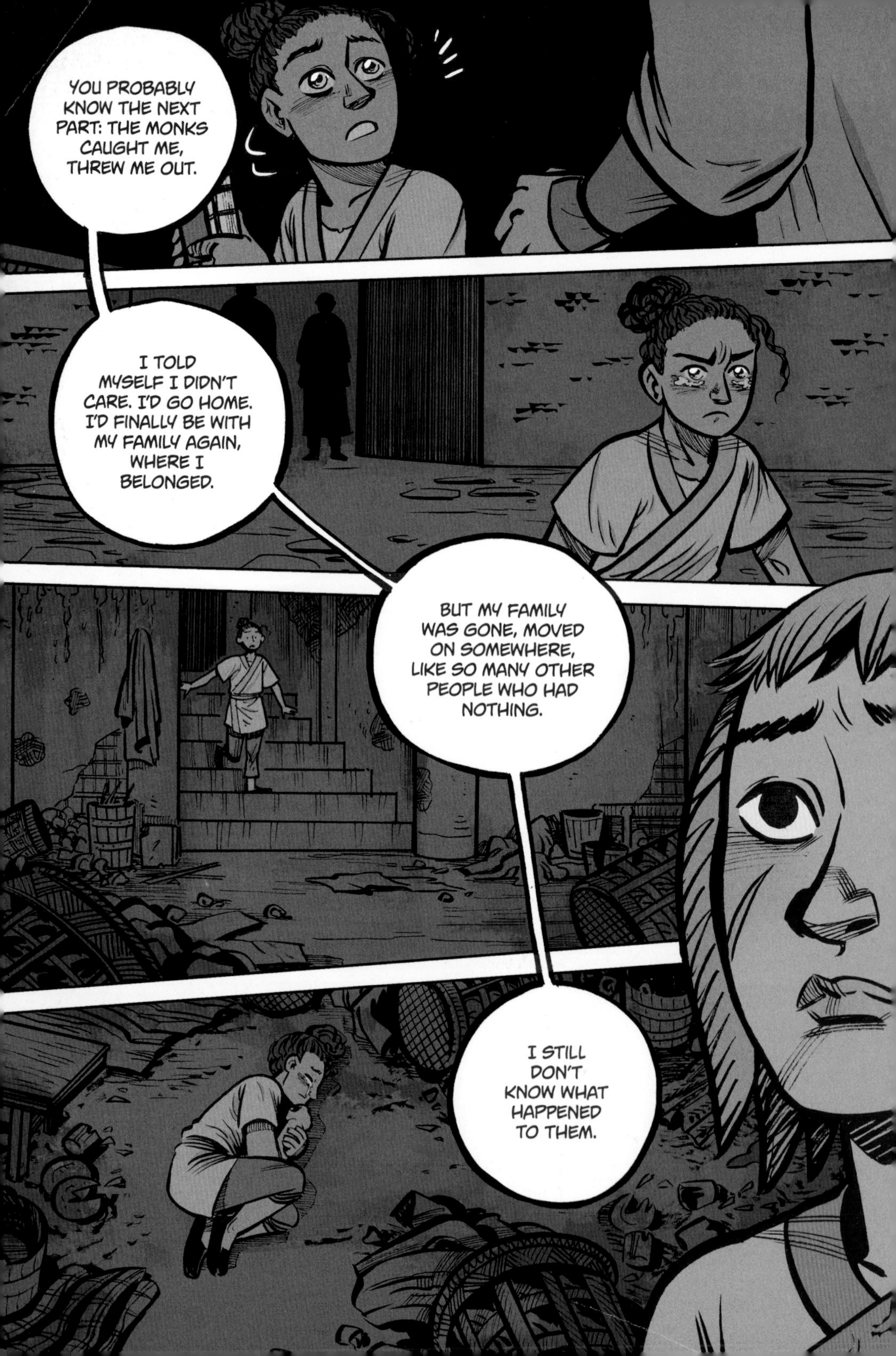
YOU PROBABLY KNOW THE NEXT PART: THE MONKS CAUGHT ME, THREW ME OUT.
I TOLD MYSELF I DIDN'T CARE. I'D GO HOME. I'D FINALLY BE WITH MY FAMILY AGAIN, WHERE I BELONGED.
BUT MY FAMILY WAS GONE, MOVED ON SOMEWHERE, LIKE SO MANY OTHER PEOPLE WHO HAD NOTHING.
I STILL DON'T KNOW WHAT HAPPENED TO THEM.

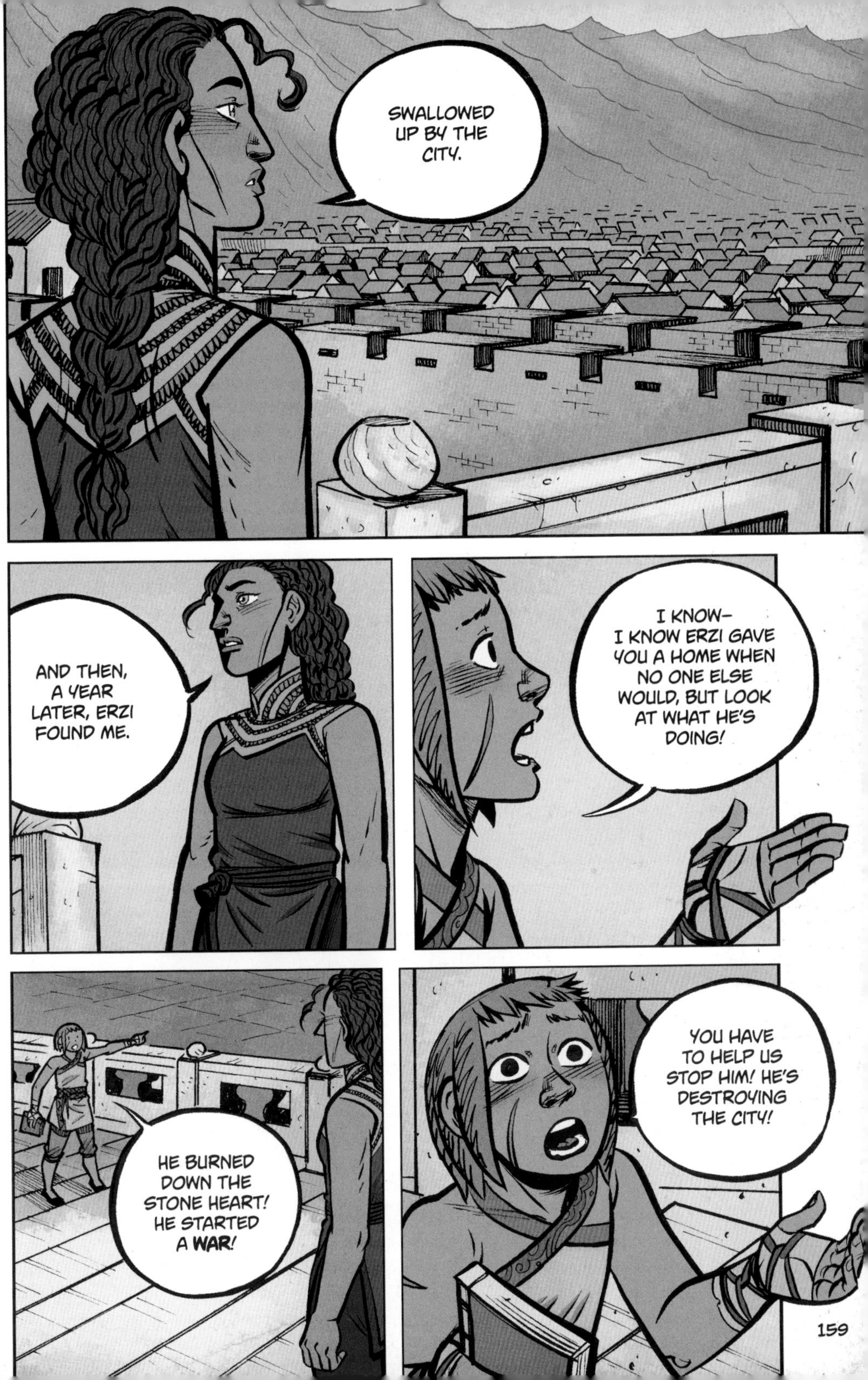
SWALLOWED UP BY THE CITY.
AND THEN, A YEAR LATER, ERZI FOUND ME.
I KNOW— I KNOW ERZI GAVE YOU A HOME WHEN NO ONE ELSE WOULD, BUT LOOK AT WHAT HE'S DOING!
HE BURNED DOWN THE STONE HEART! HE STARTED A **WAR**!
YOU HAVE TO HELP US STOP HIM! HE'S DESTROYING THE CITY!

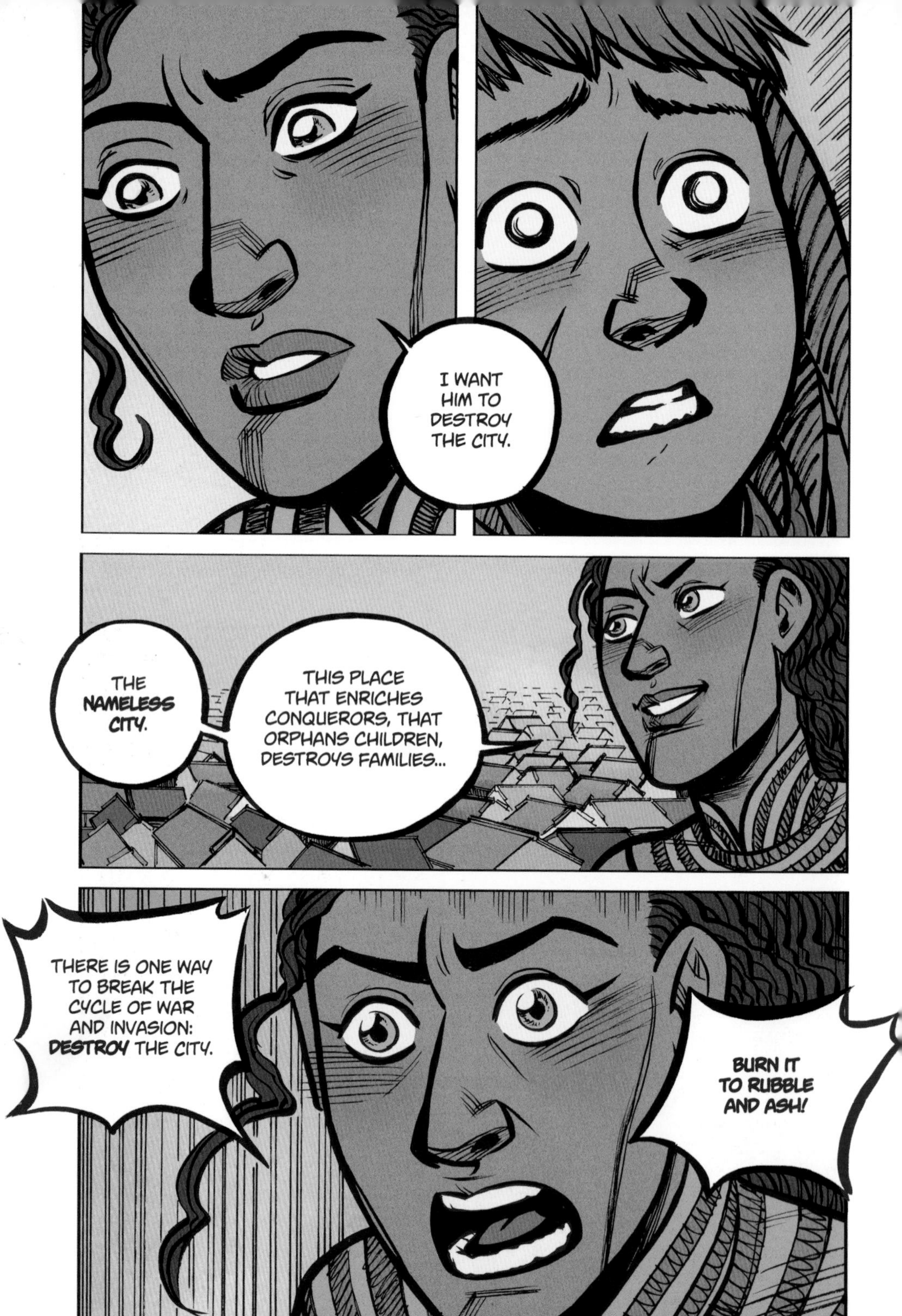

I WANT HIM TO DESTROY THE CITY.
THE NAMELESS CITY.
THIS PLACE THAT ENRICHES CONQUERORS, THAT ORPHANS CHILDREN, DESTROYS FAMILIES...
THERE IS ONE WAY TO BREAK THE CYCLE OF WAR AND INVASION: DESTROY THE CITY.
BURN IT TO RUBBLE AND ASH!

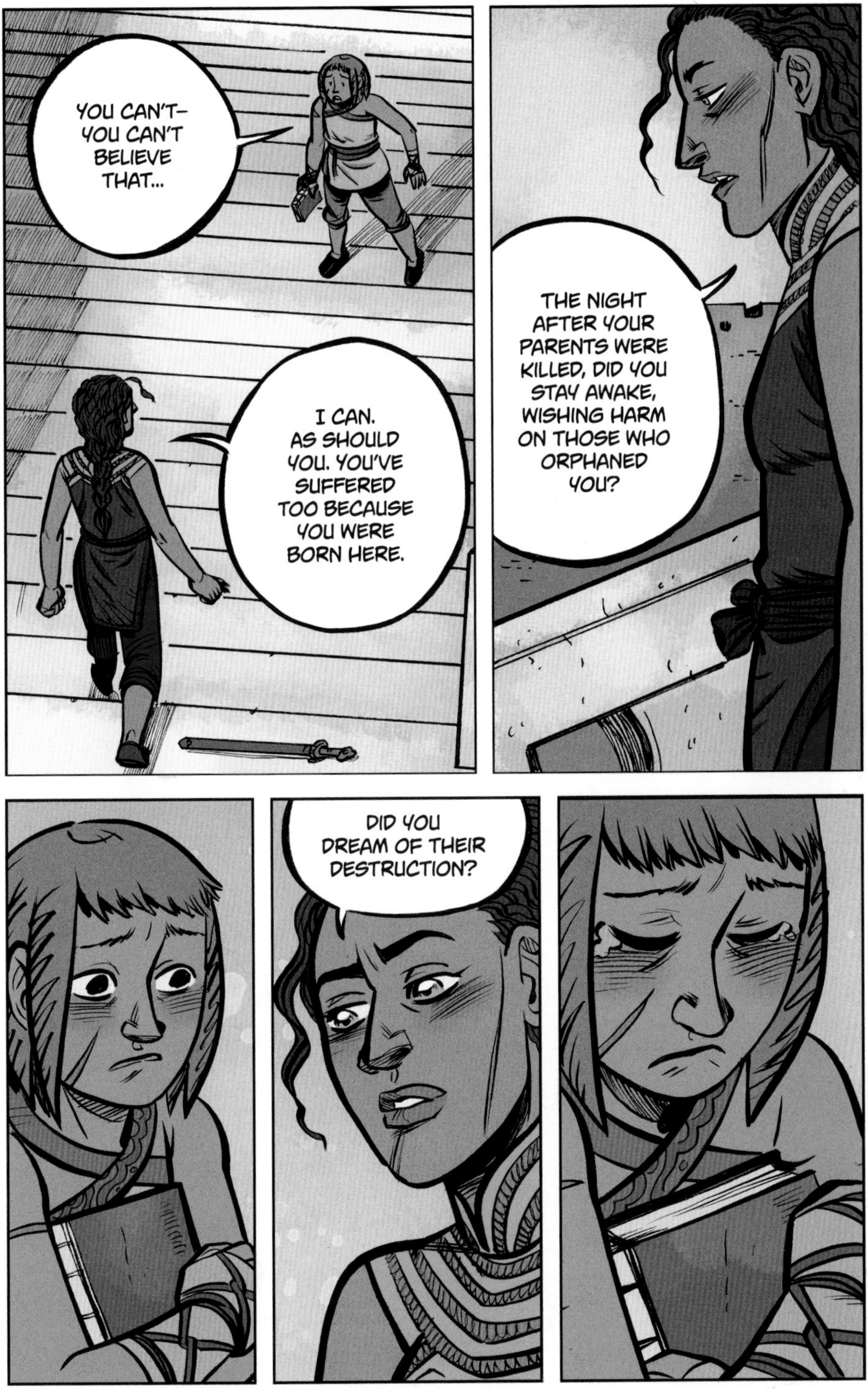
YOU CAN'T–
YOU CAN'T
BELIEVE
THAT...
I CAN.
AS SHOULD
YOU. YOU'VE
SUFFERED
TOO BECAUSE
YOU WERE
BORN HERE.
THE NIGHT
AFTER YOUR
PARENTS WERE
KILLED, DID YOU
STAY AWAKE,
WISHING HARM
ON THOSE WHO
ORPHANED
YOU?
DID YOU
DREAM OF THEIR
DESTRUCTION?

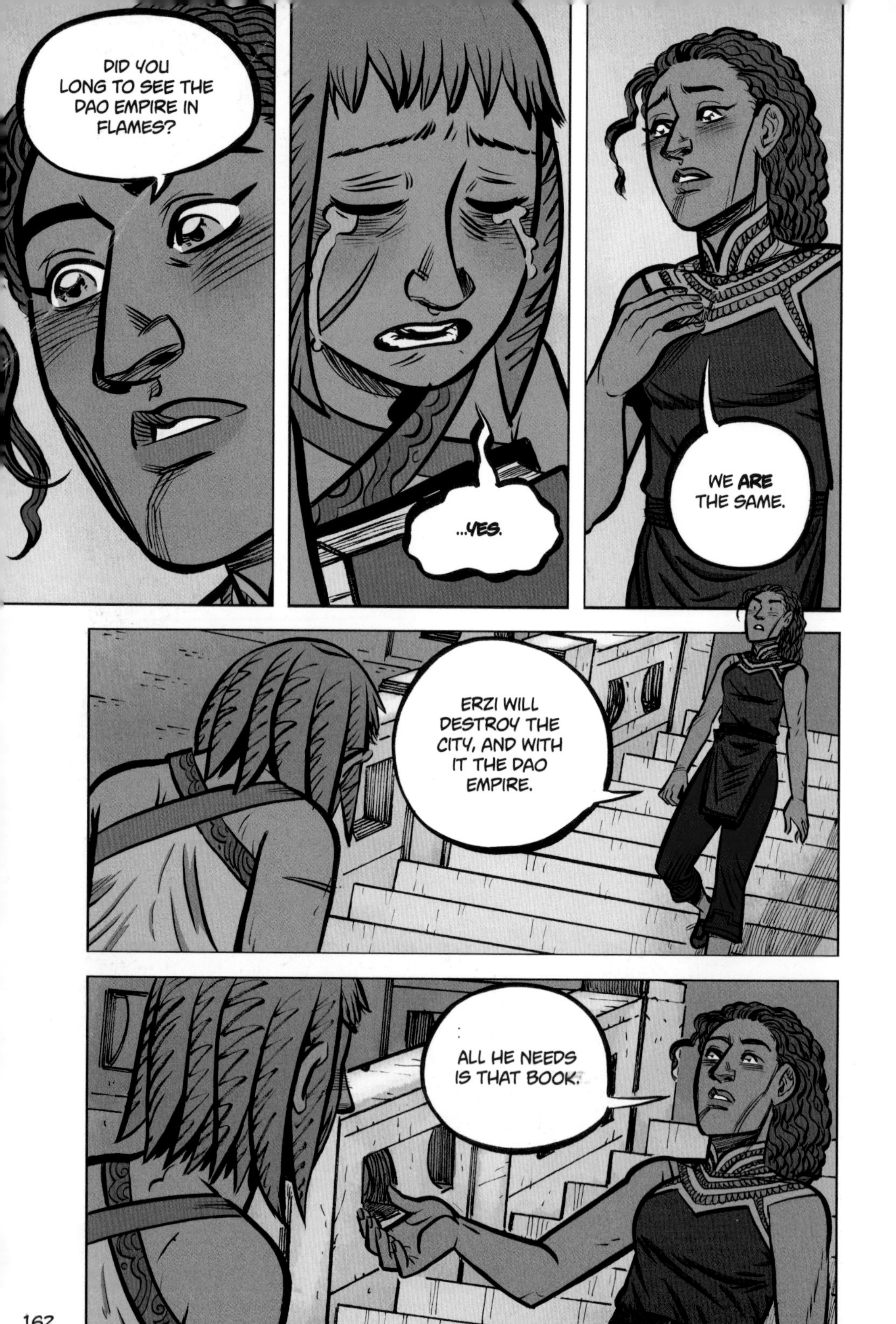
DID YOU LONG TO SEE THE DAO EMPIRE IN FLAMES?
...YES.
WE **ARE** THE SAME.
ERZI WILL DESTROY THE CITY, AND WITH IT THE DAO EMPIRE.
ALL HE NEEDS IS THAT BOOK.

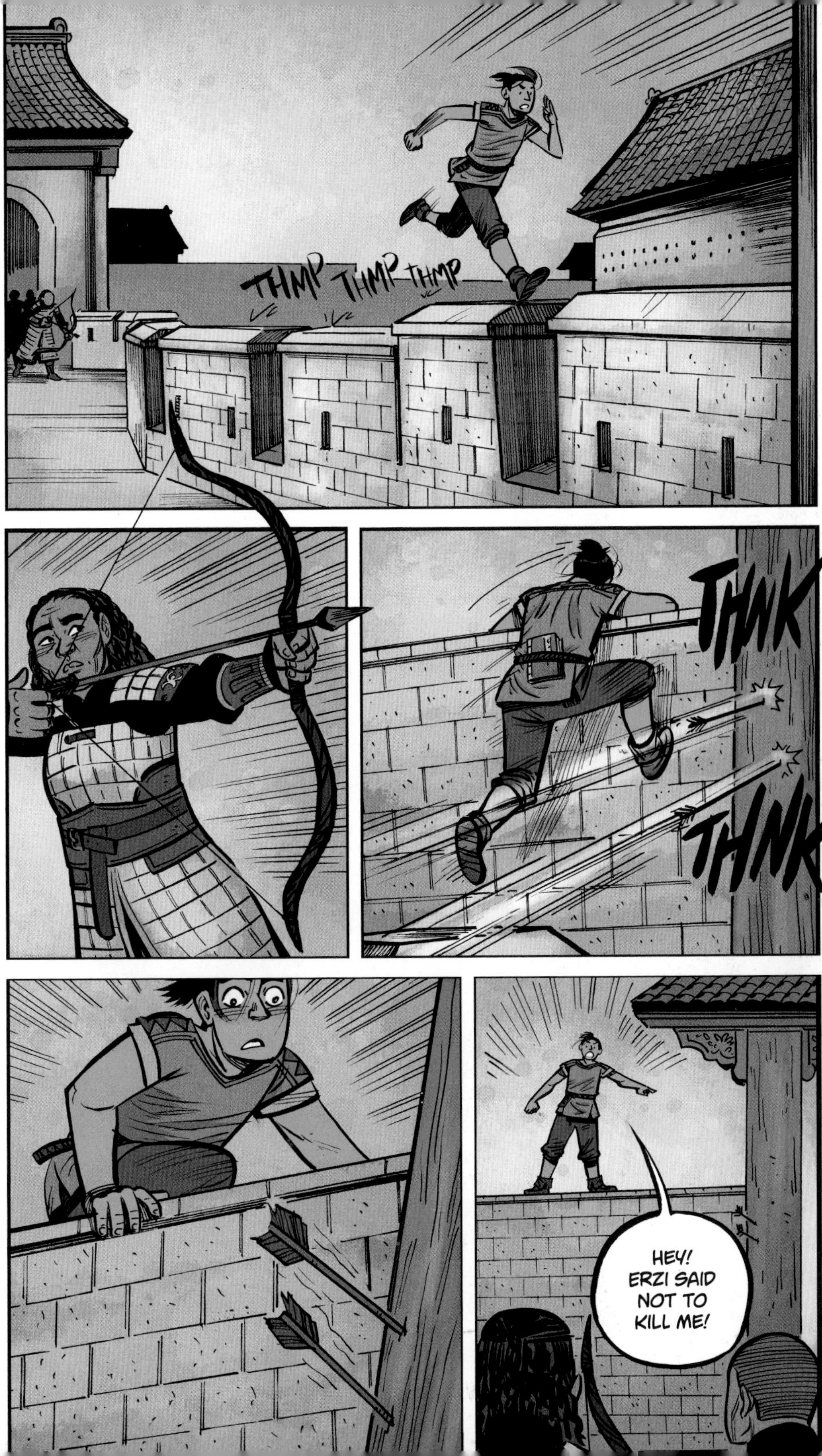
THMP THMP THMP
THNK
THNK
HEY! ERZI SAID NOT TO KILL ME!

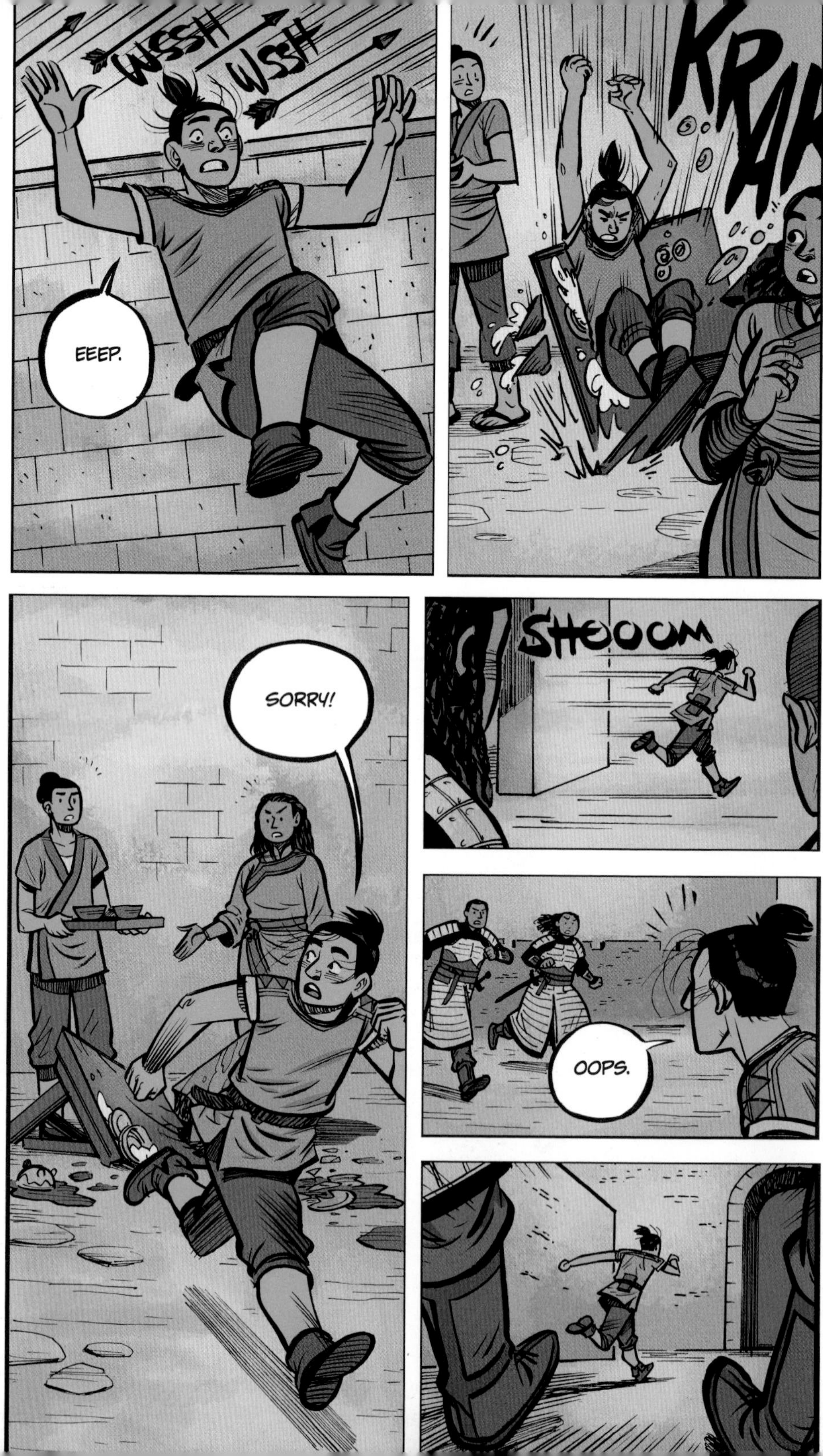
WSSH
WSSH
EEEP.
KRAK
SORRY!
SHOOOM
OOPS.

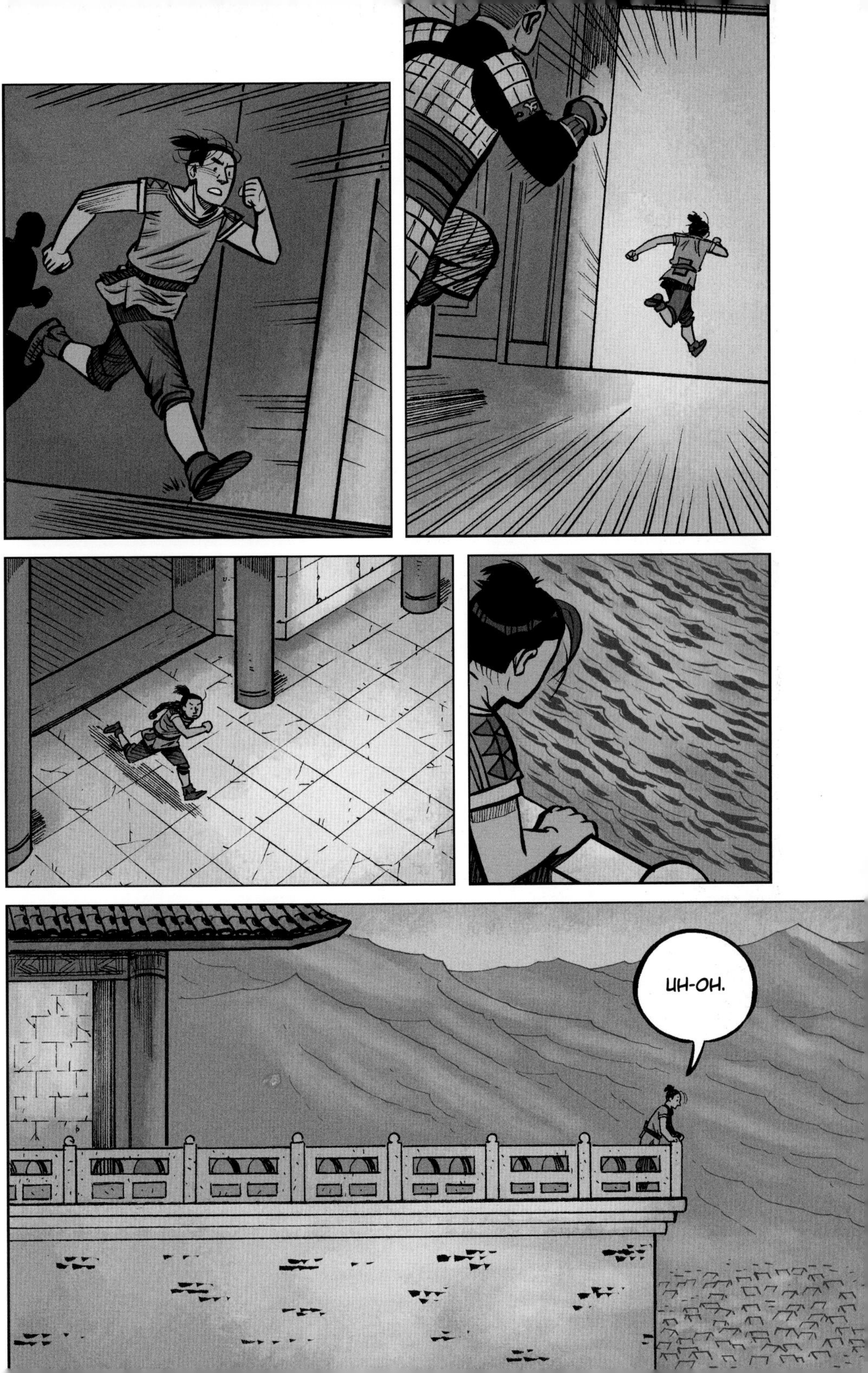
UH-OH.

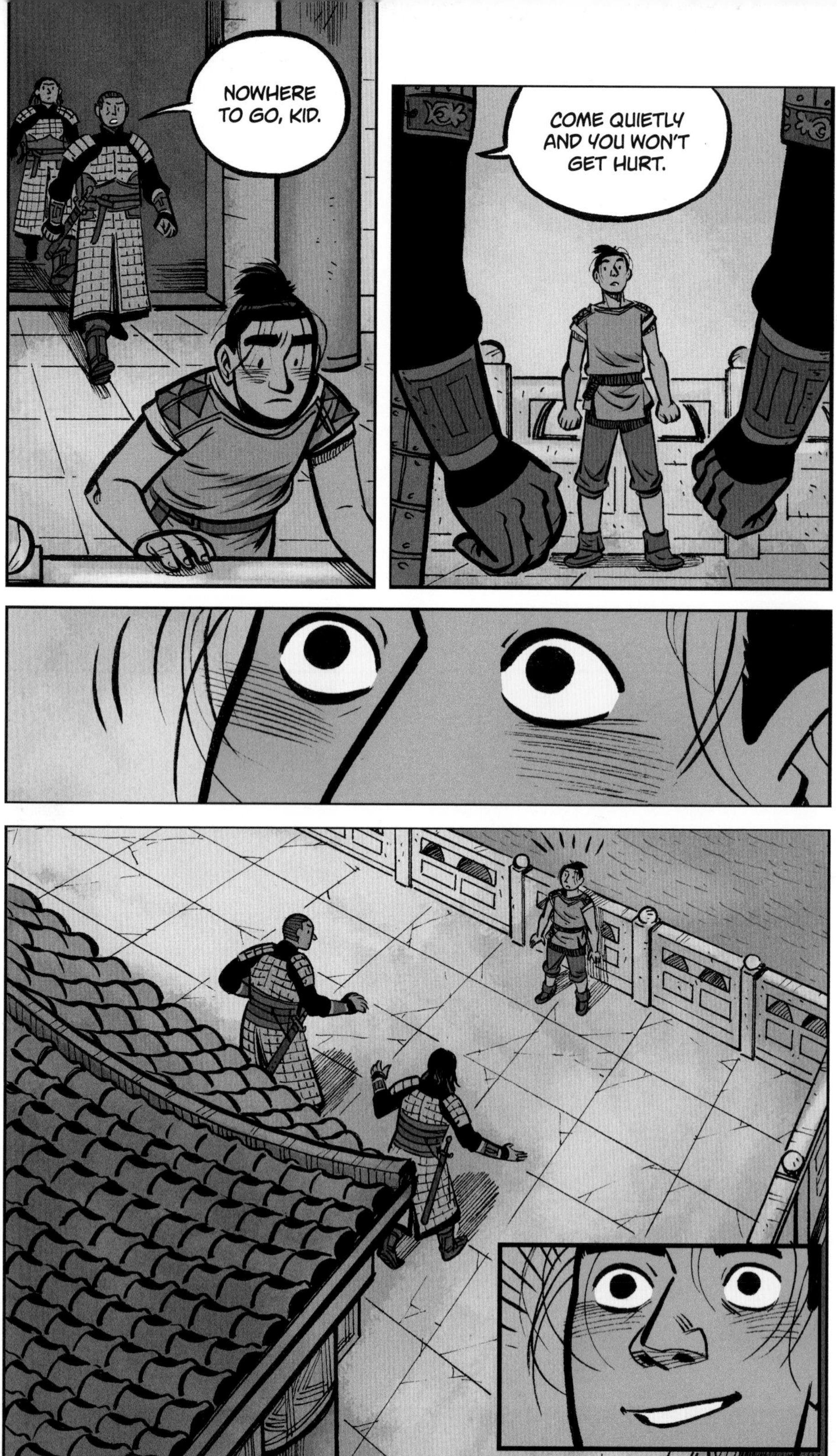
NOWHERE TO GO, KID.
COME QUIETLY AND YOU WON'T GET HURT.

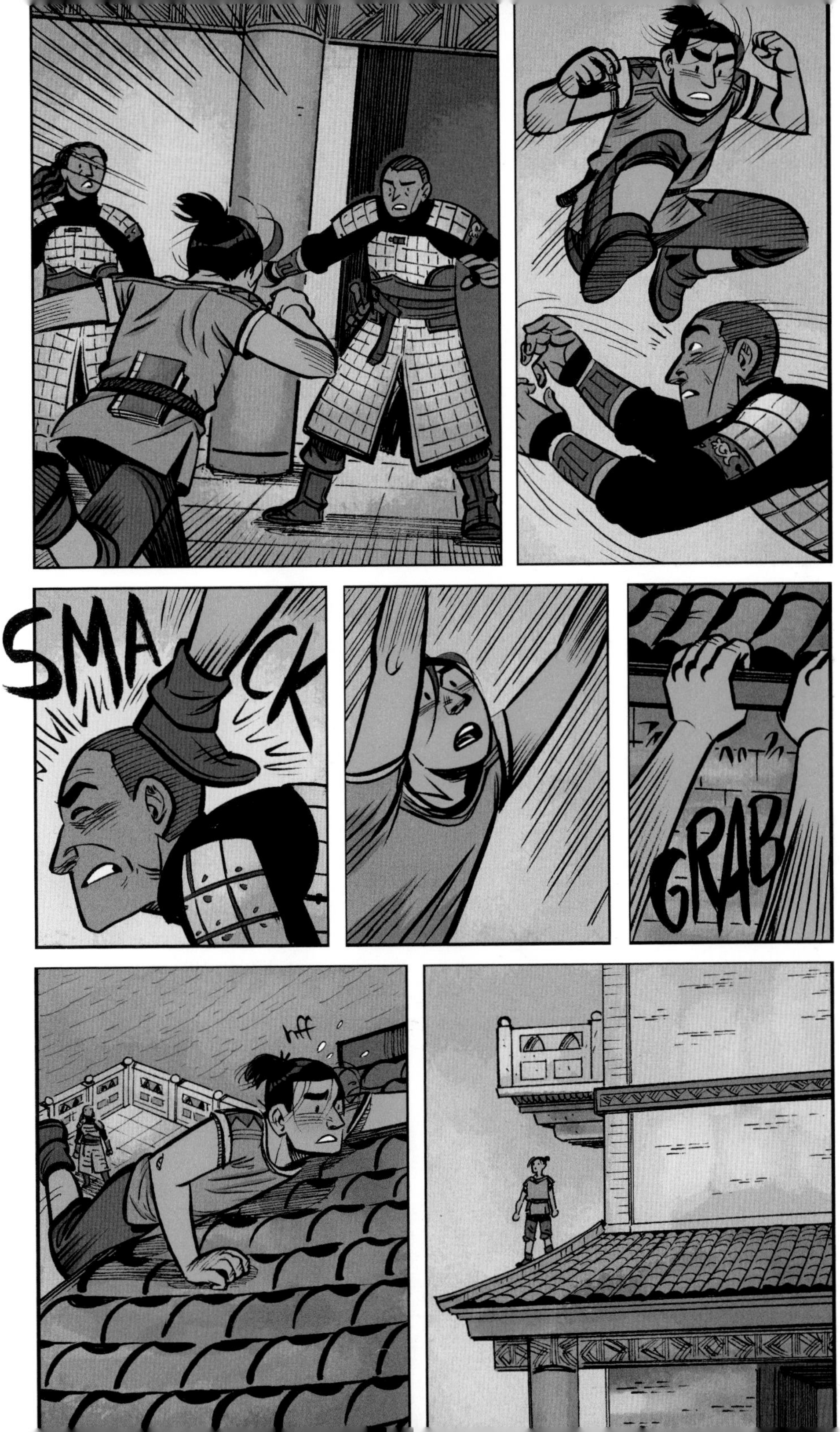
SMACK
GRAB
hff

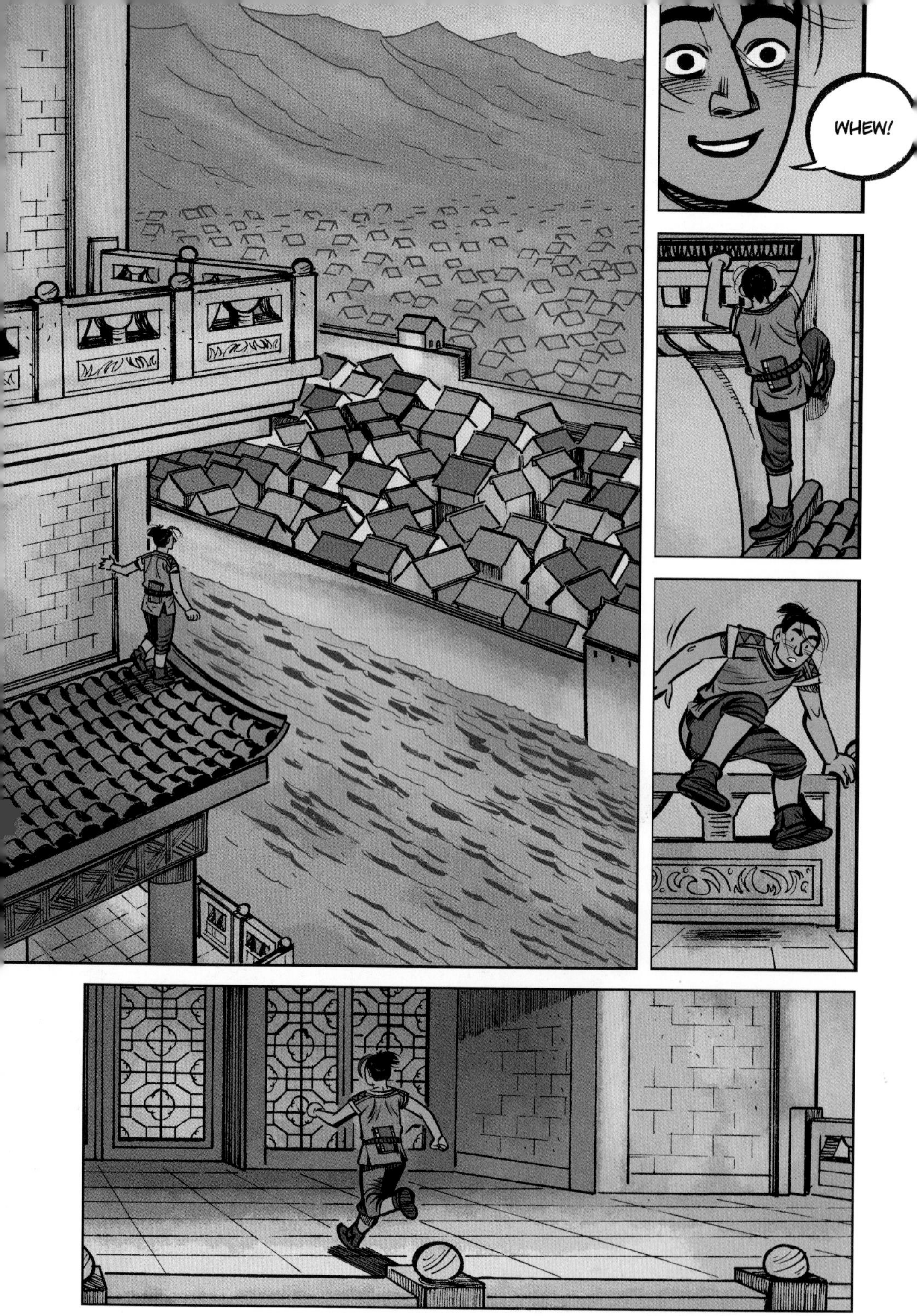
WHEW!

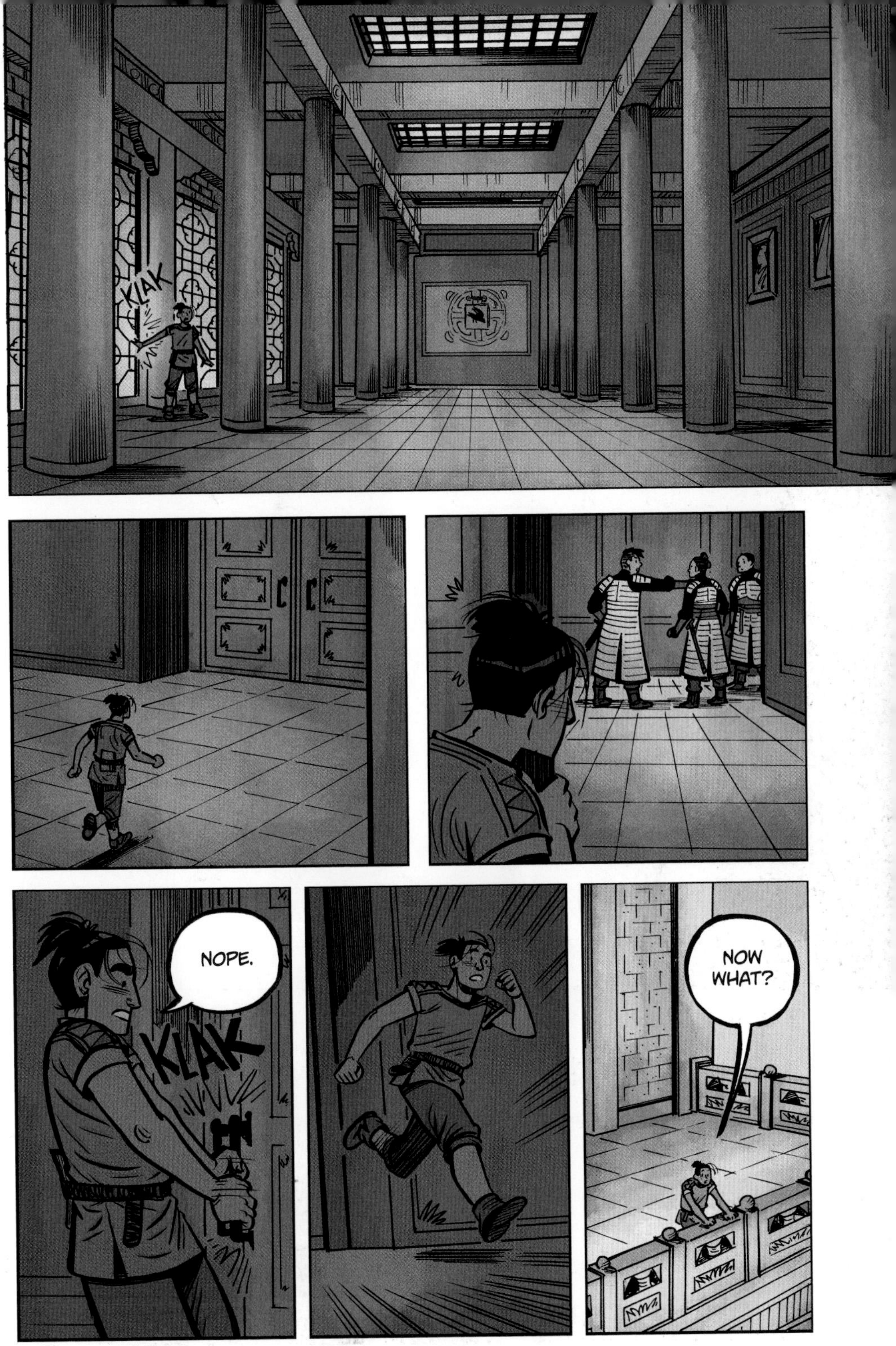
KLAK
NOPE.
KLAK
NOW WHAT?

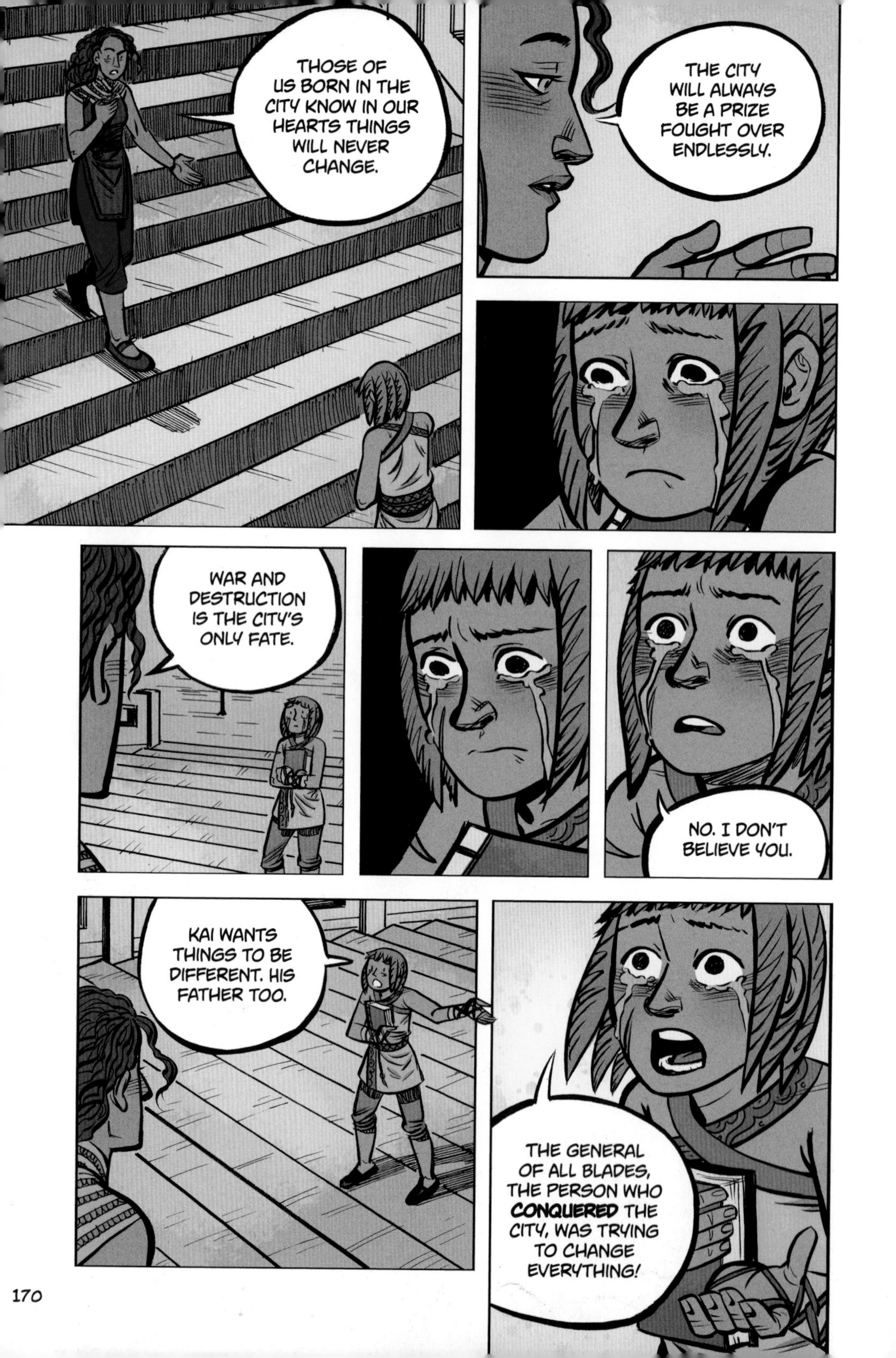
THOSE OF US BORN IN THE CITY KNOW IN OUR HEARTS THINGS WILL NEVER CHANGE.
THE CITY WILL ALWAYS BE A PRIZE FOUGHT OVER ENDLESSLY.
WAR AND DESTRUCTION IS THE CITY'S ONLY FATE.
NO. I DON'T BELIEVE YOU.
KAI WANTS THINGS TO BE DIFFERENT. HIS FATHER TOO.
THE GENERAL OF ALL BLADES, THE PERSON WHO **CONQUERED** THE CITY, WAS TRYING TO CHANGE EVERYTHING!

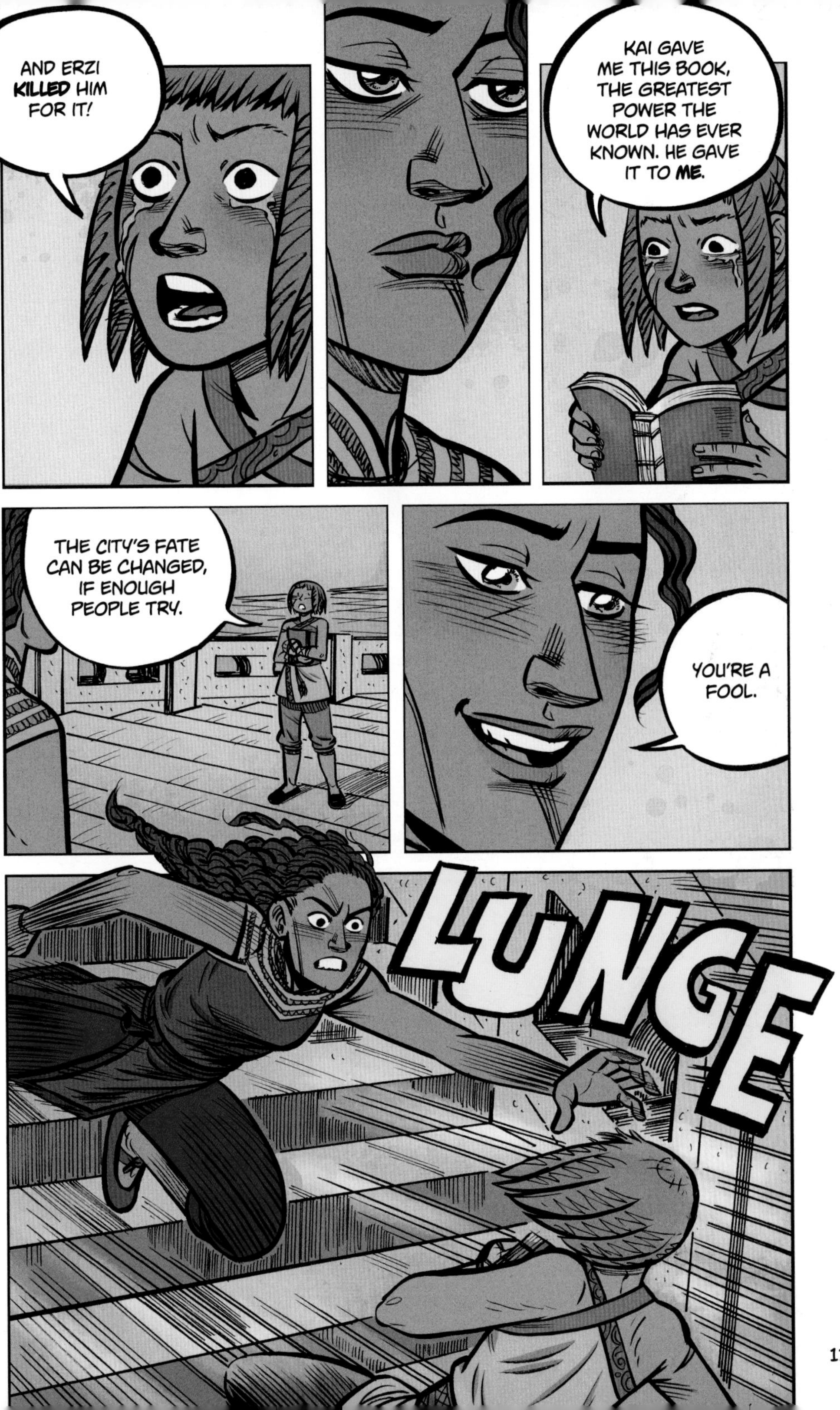
AND ERZI **KILLED** HIM FOR IT!
KAI GAVE ME THIS BOOK, THE GREATEST POWER THE WORLD HAS EVER KNOWN. HE GAVE IT TO **ME**.
THE CITY'S FATE CAN BE CHANGED, IF ENOUGH PEOPLE TRY.
YOU'RE A FOOL.
LUNGE

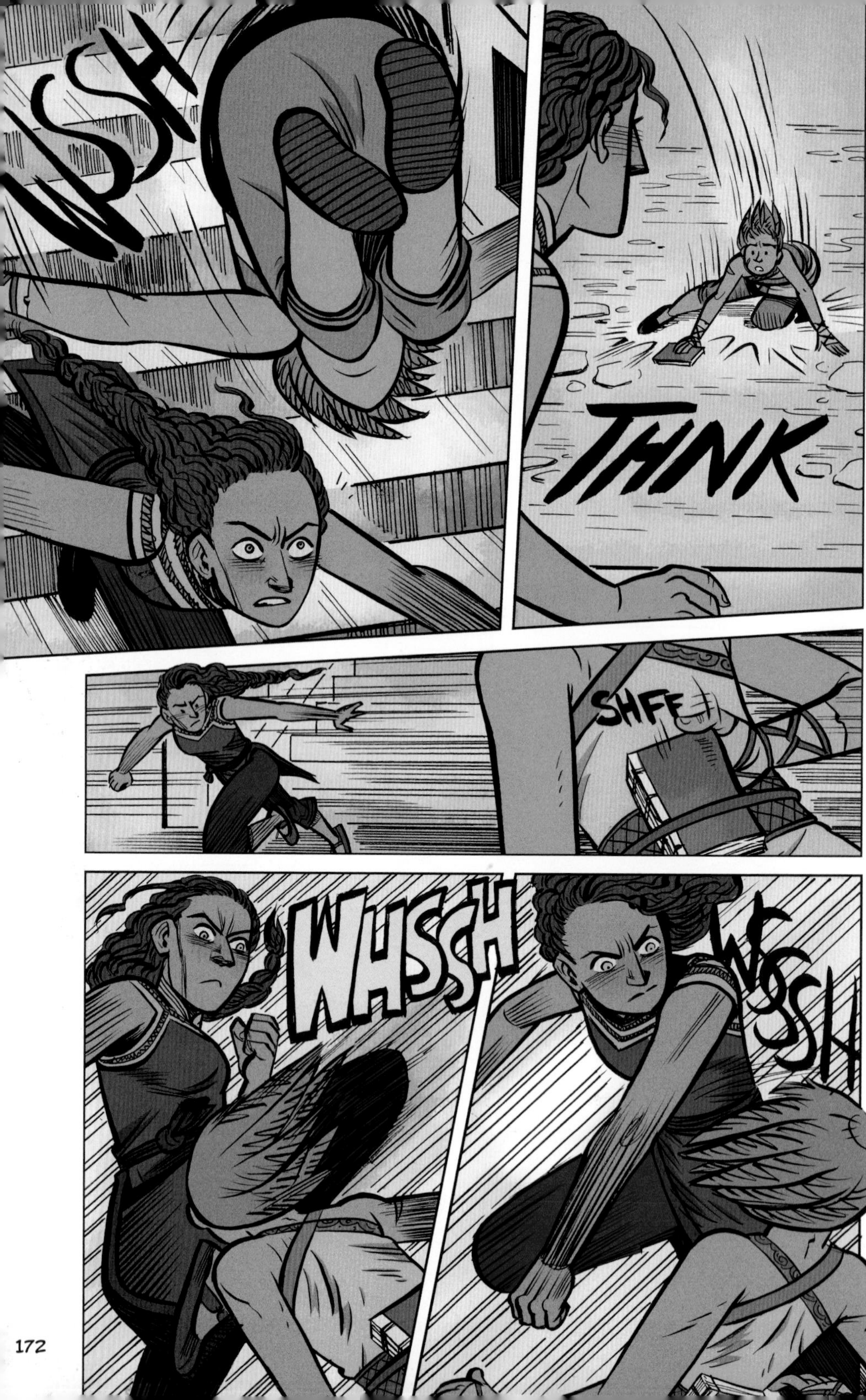
WSH
THNK
SHFF
WHSSH
WSSH

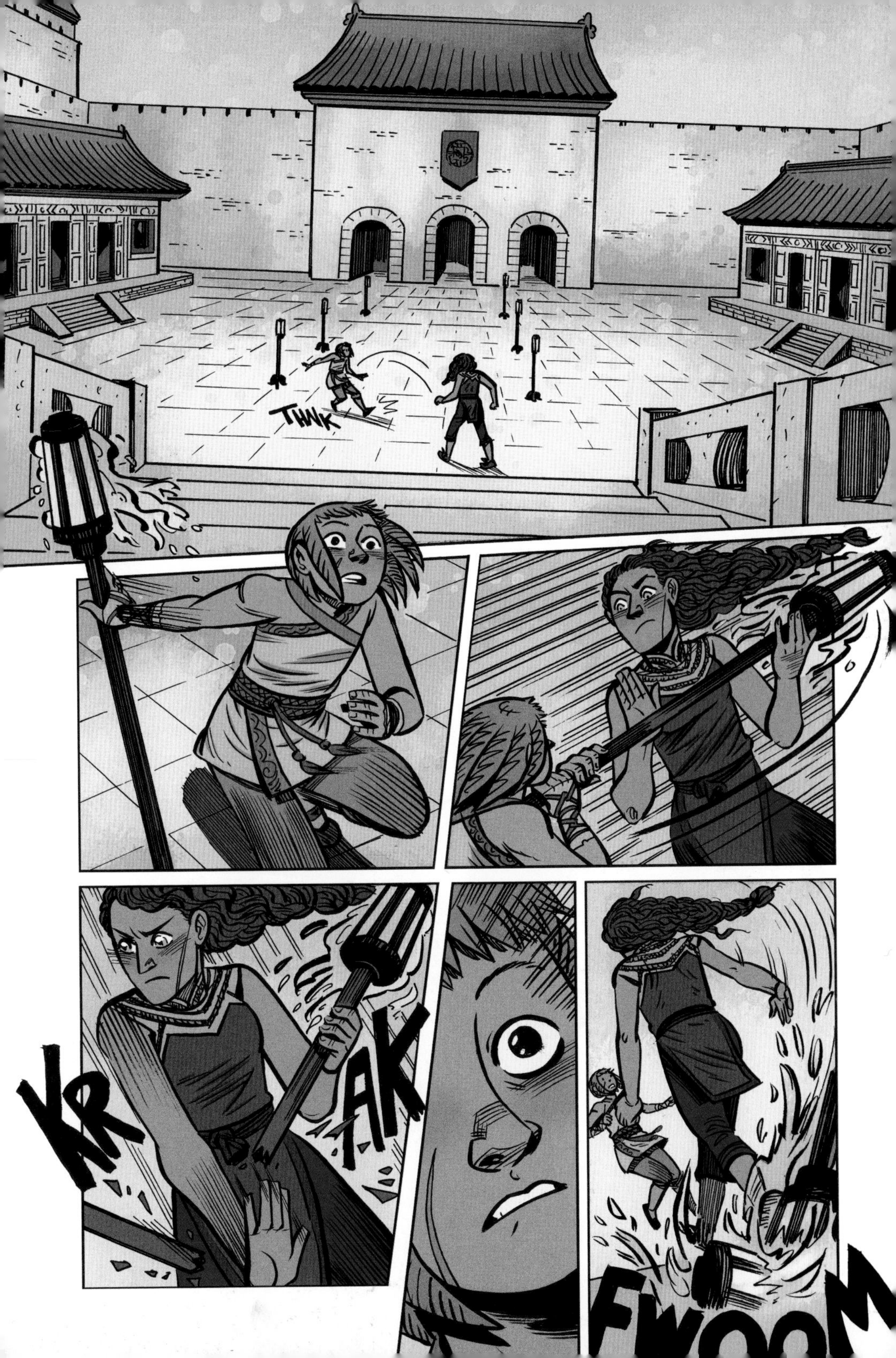
THNK
KR
AK
FWOOM

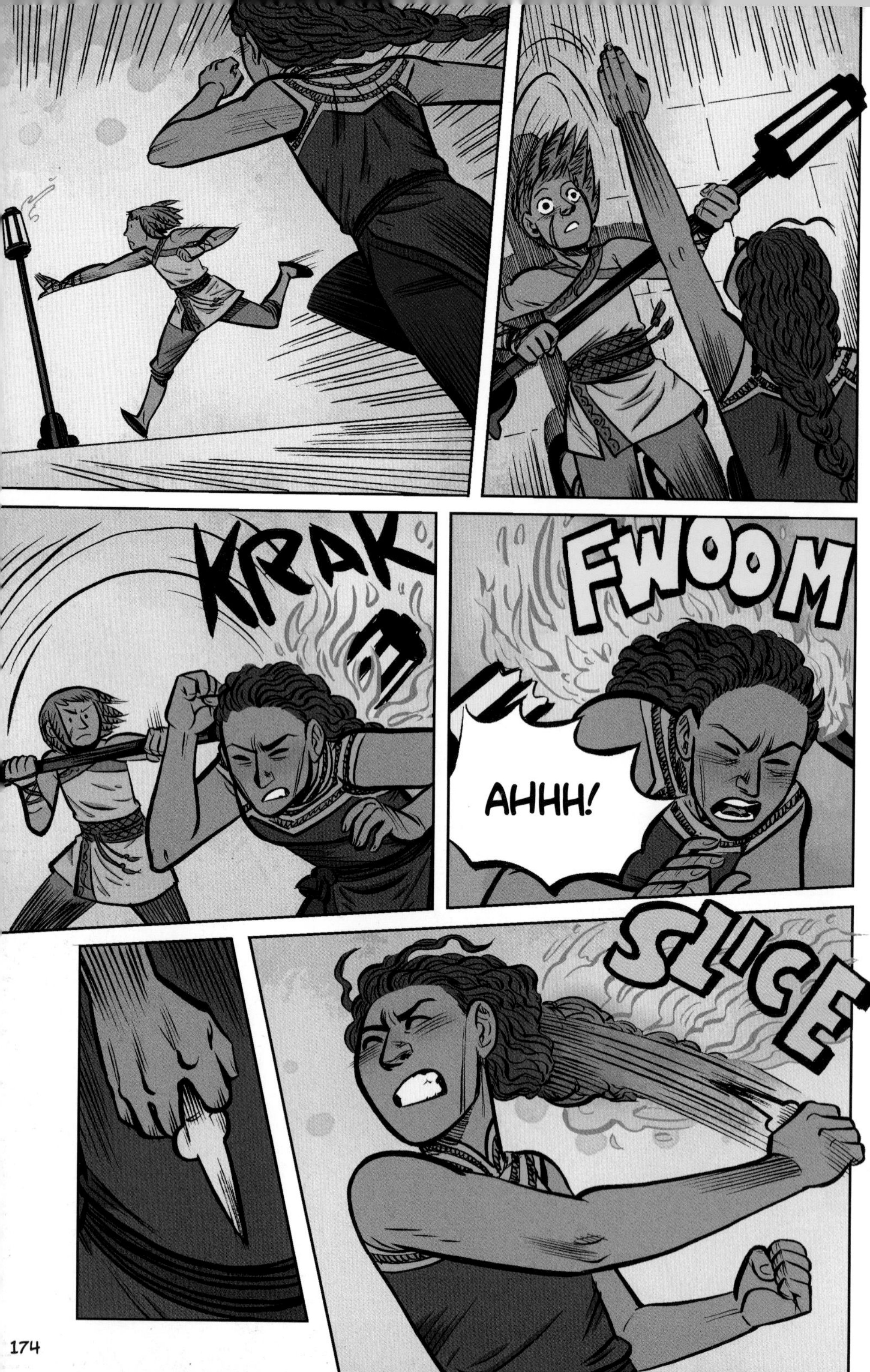
KRAK
FWOOM
AHHH!
SLICE

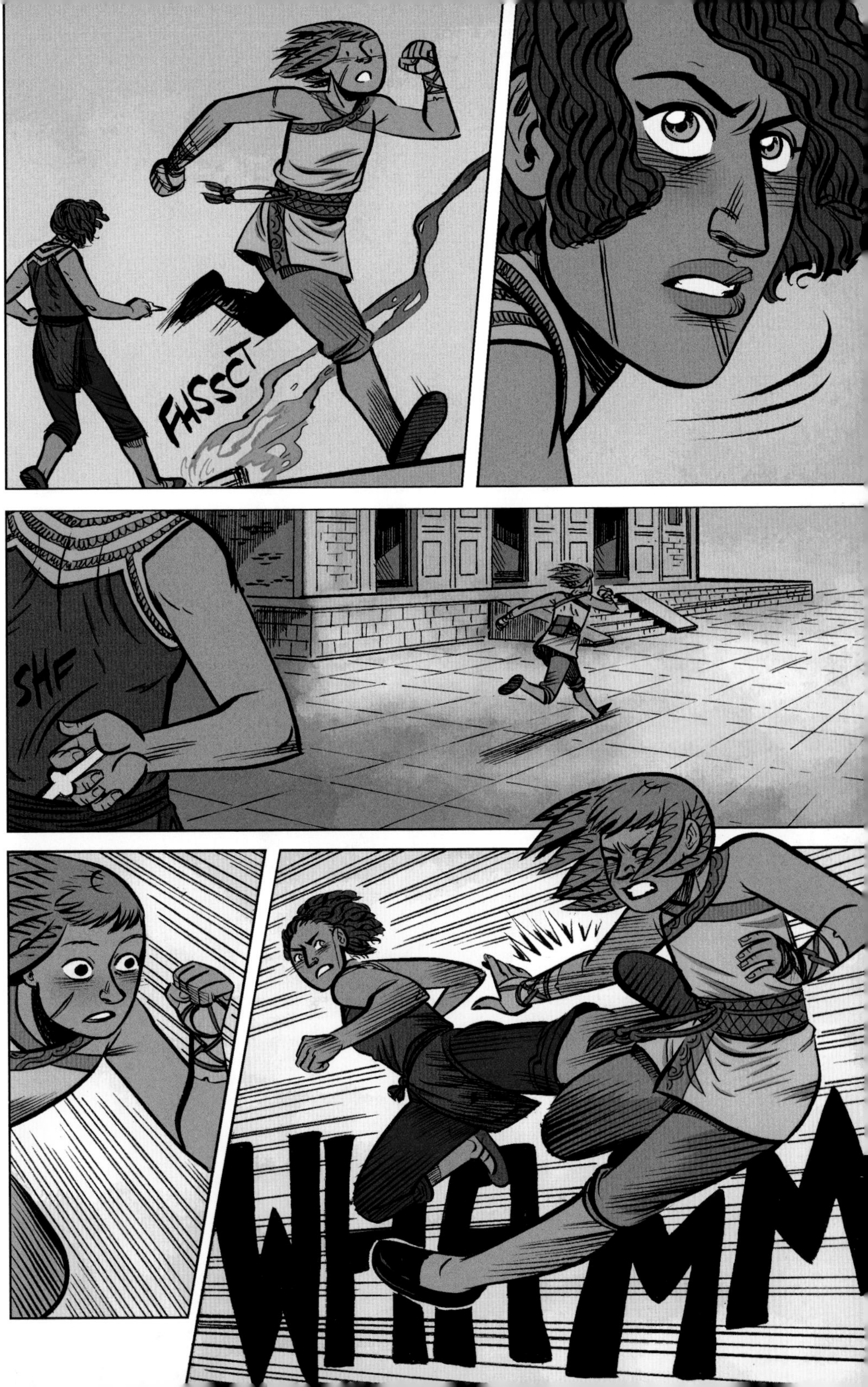
FHSSCT
SHF
WHHMM

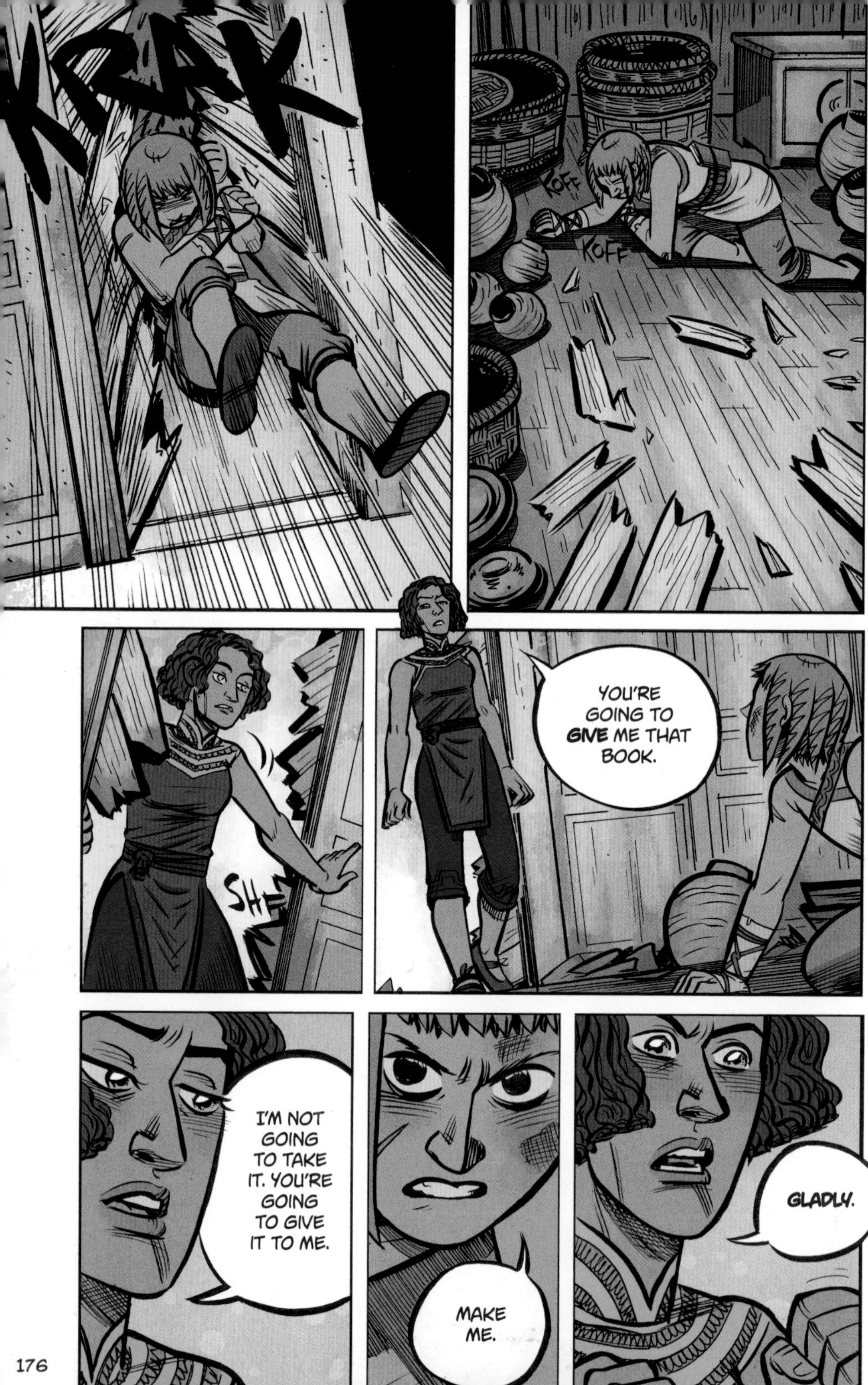
KRAK
KOFF
KOFF
SHF
YOU'RE GOING TO GIVE ME THAT BOOK.
I'M NOT GOING TO TAKE IT. YOU'RE GOING TO GIVE IT TO ME.
MAKE ME.
GLADLY.

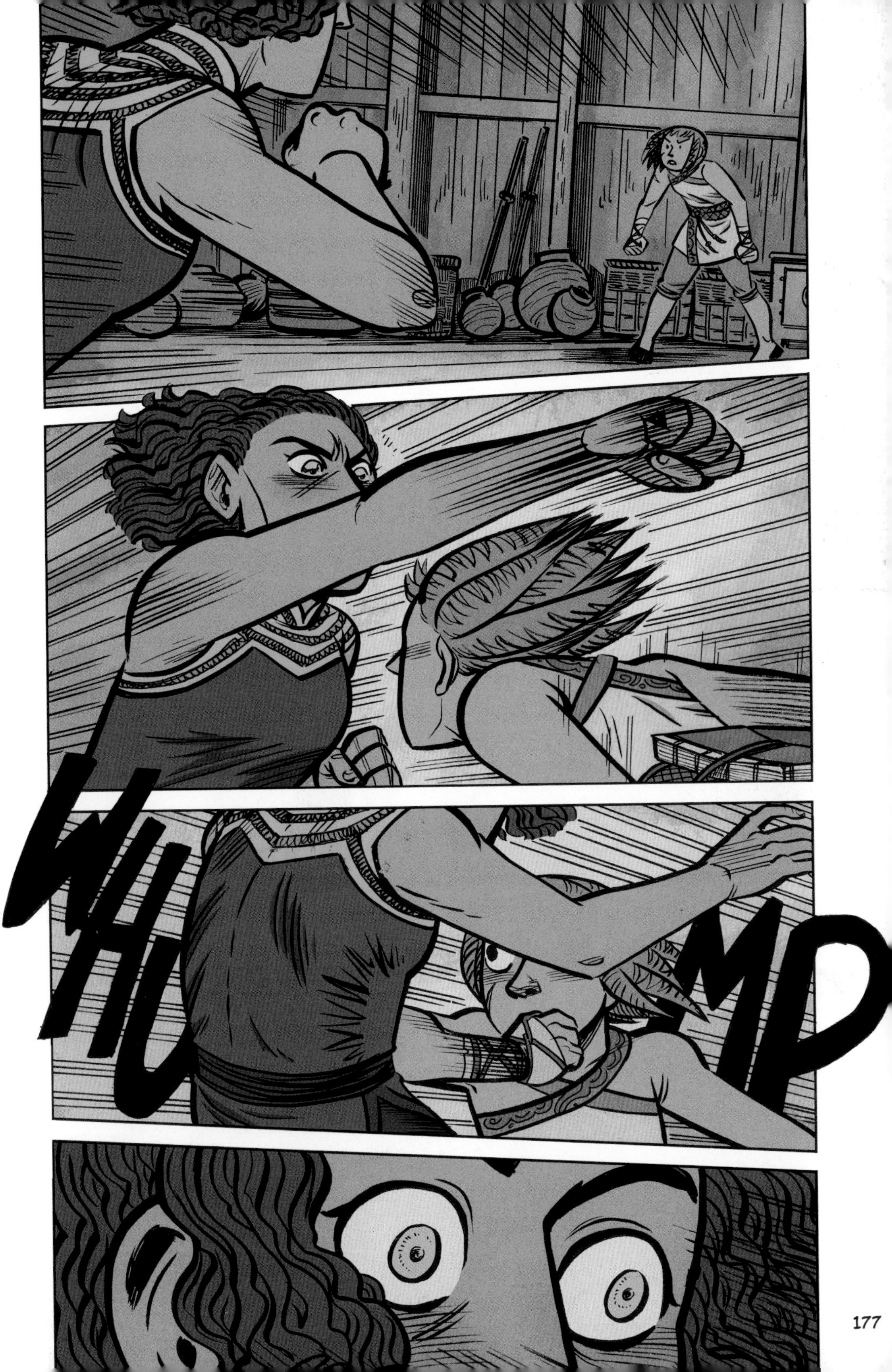
WHU
MP

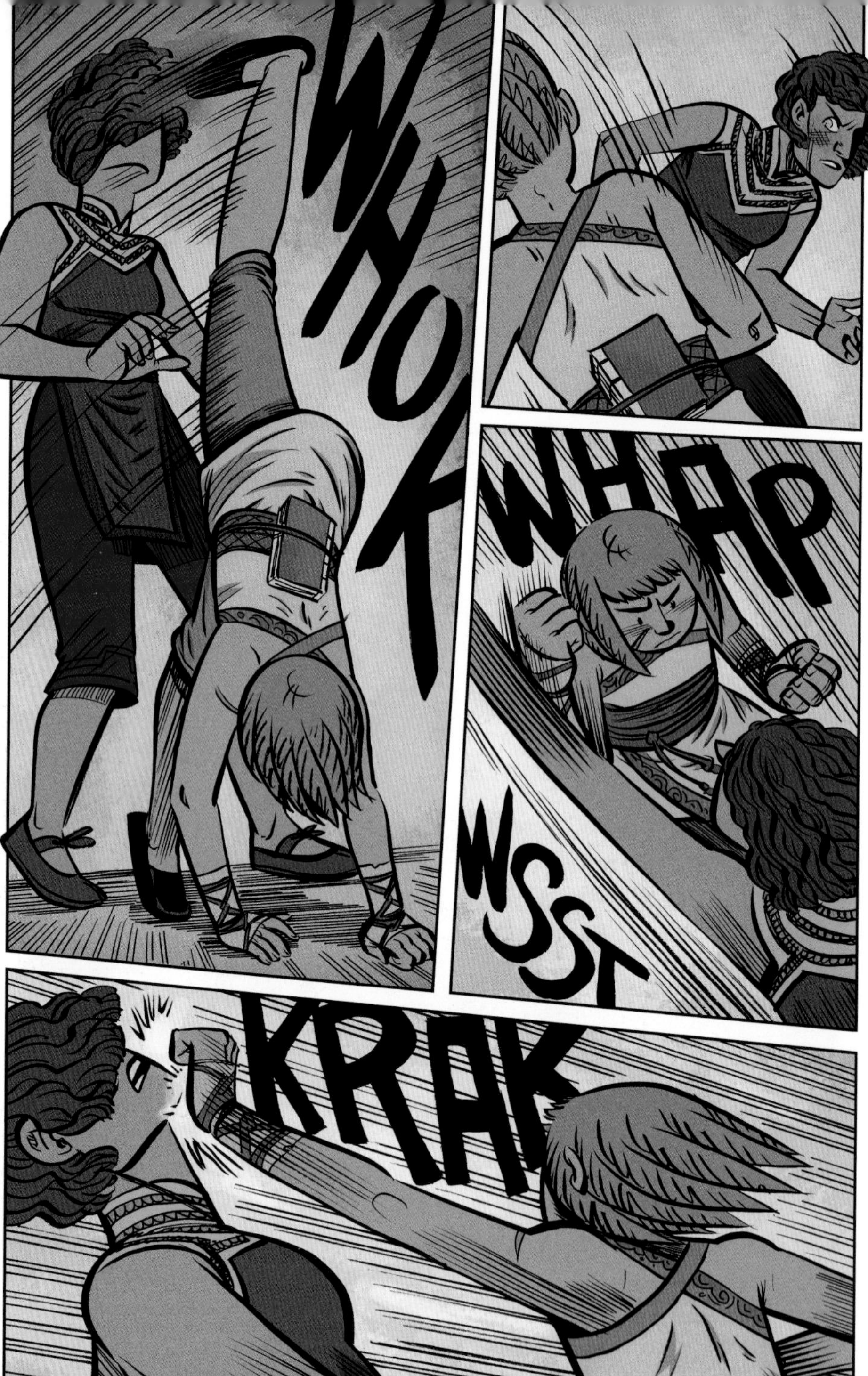
WHOK
WHAP
WSST
KRAK

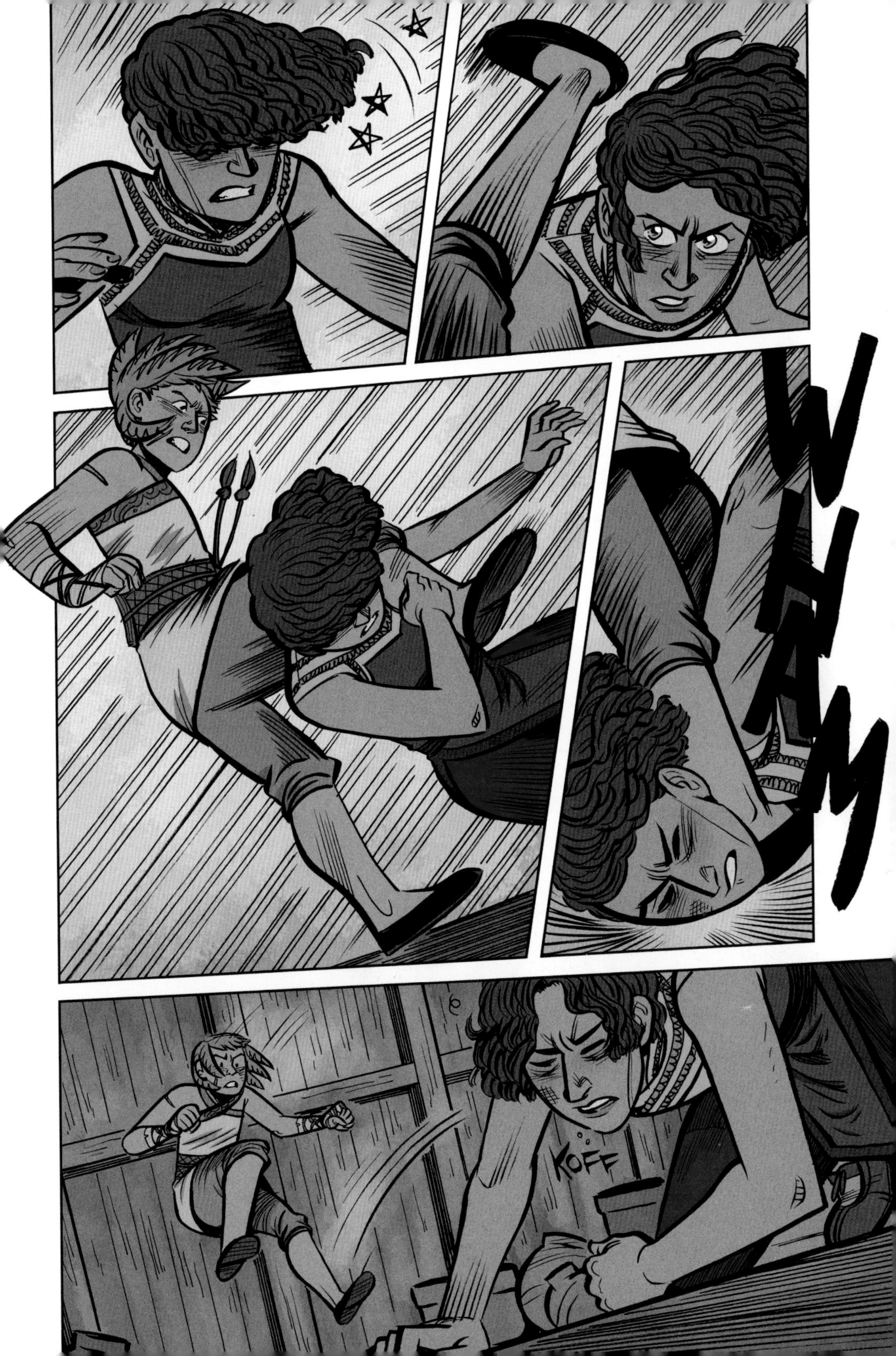
WHAM
KOFF

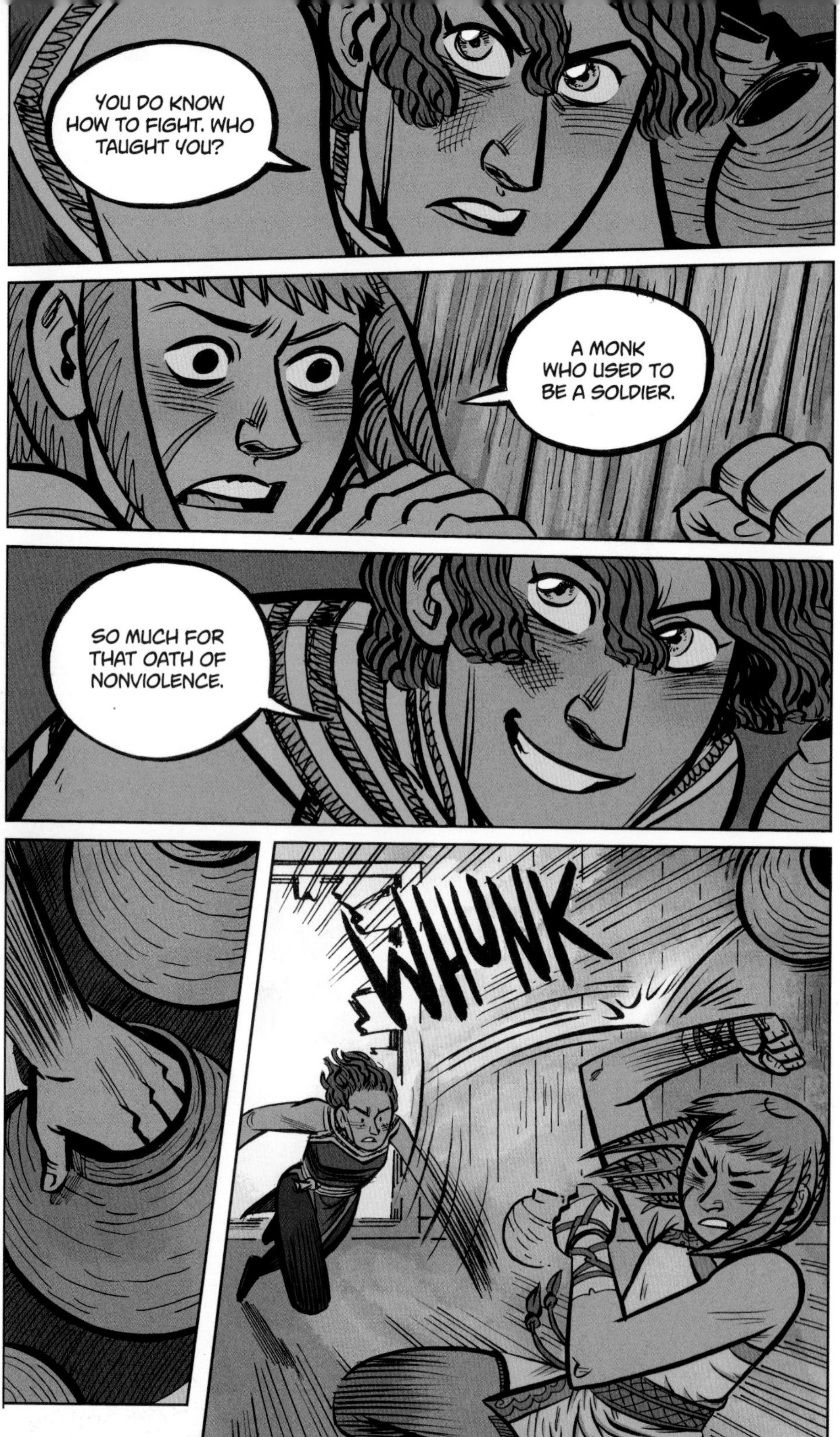
YOU DO KNOW HOW TO FIGHT. WHO TAUGHT YOU?
A MONK WHO USED TO BE A SOLDIER.
SO MUCH FOR THAT OATH OF NONVIOLENCE.
WHUNK

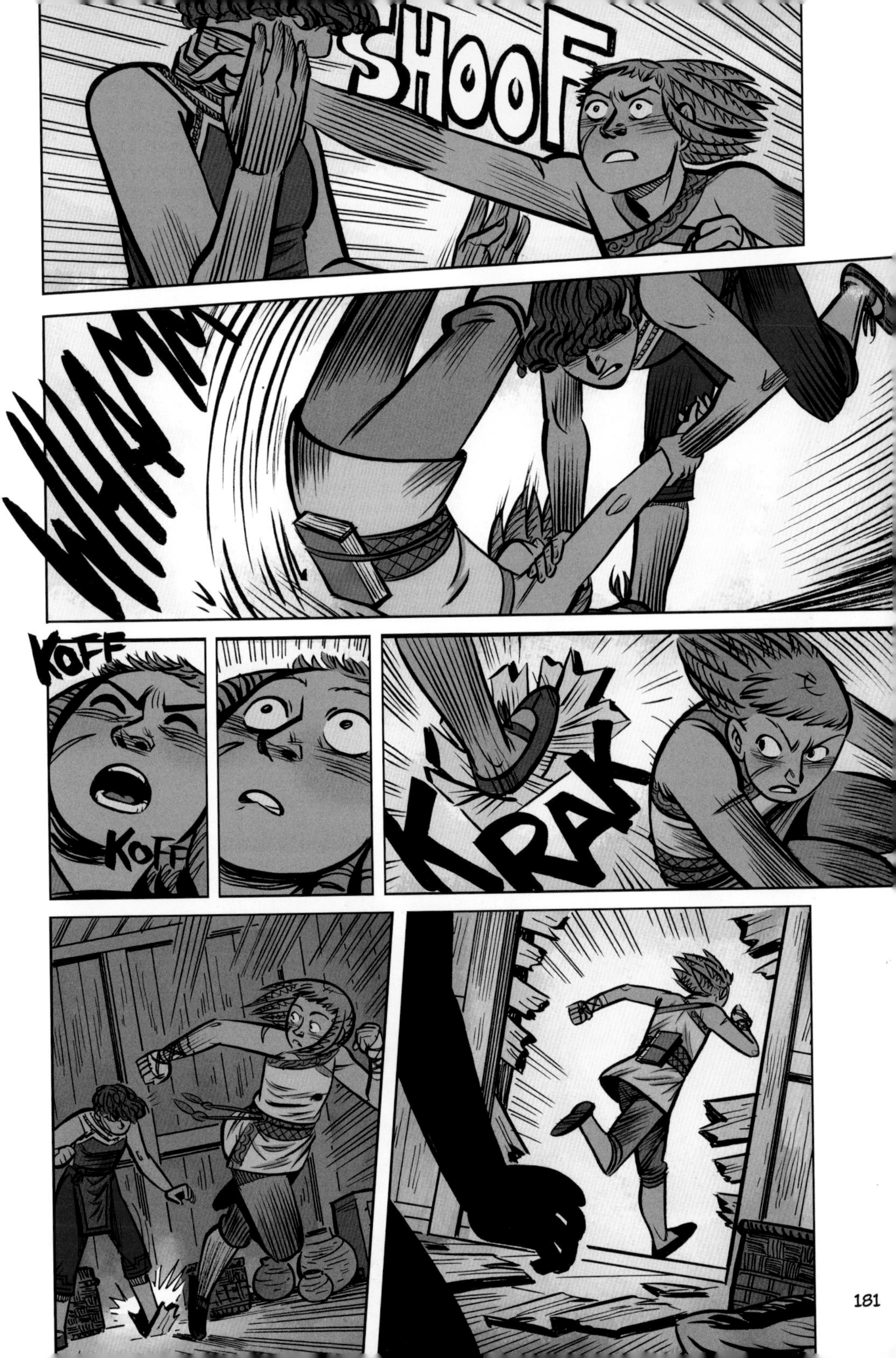
SHOOF
WHAM
KOFF
KOFF
KRAK

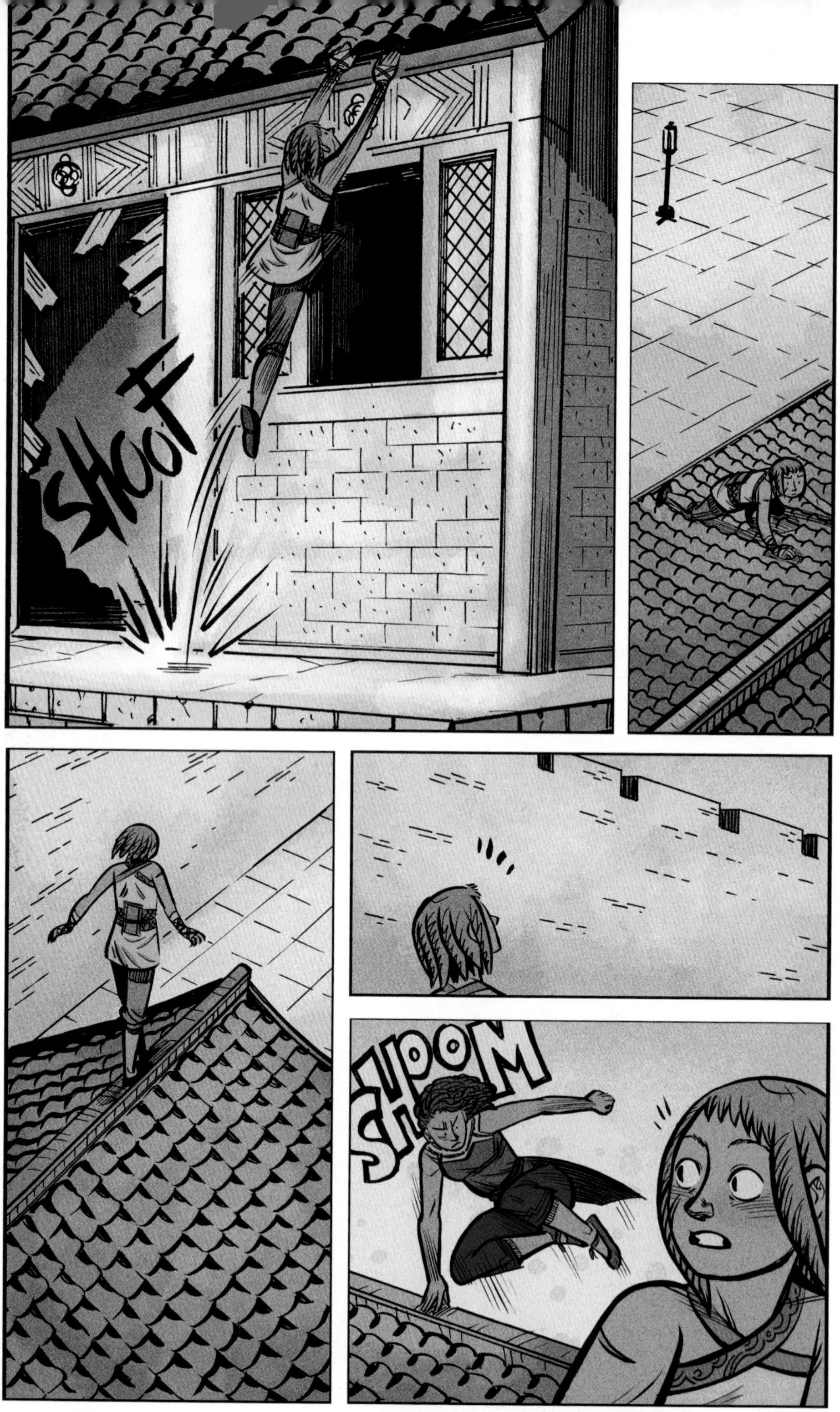
SHOOF
SHOOM

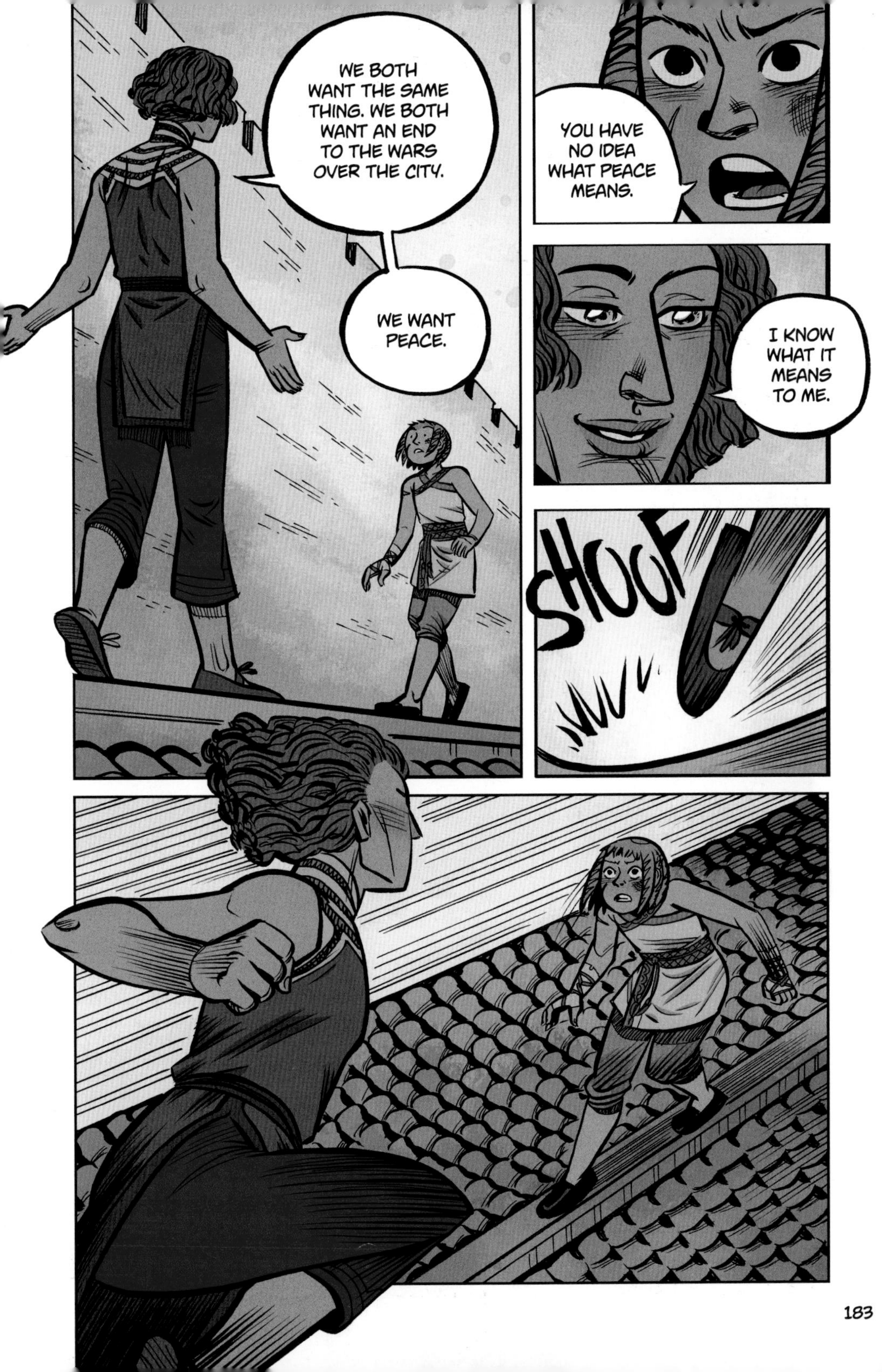
WE BOTH WANT THE SAME THING. WE BOTH WANT AN END TO THE WARS OVER THE CITY.
WE WANT PEACE.
YOU HAVE NO IDEA WHAT PEACE MEANS.
I KNOW WHAT IT MEANS TO ME.
SHOOF

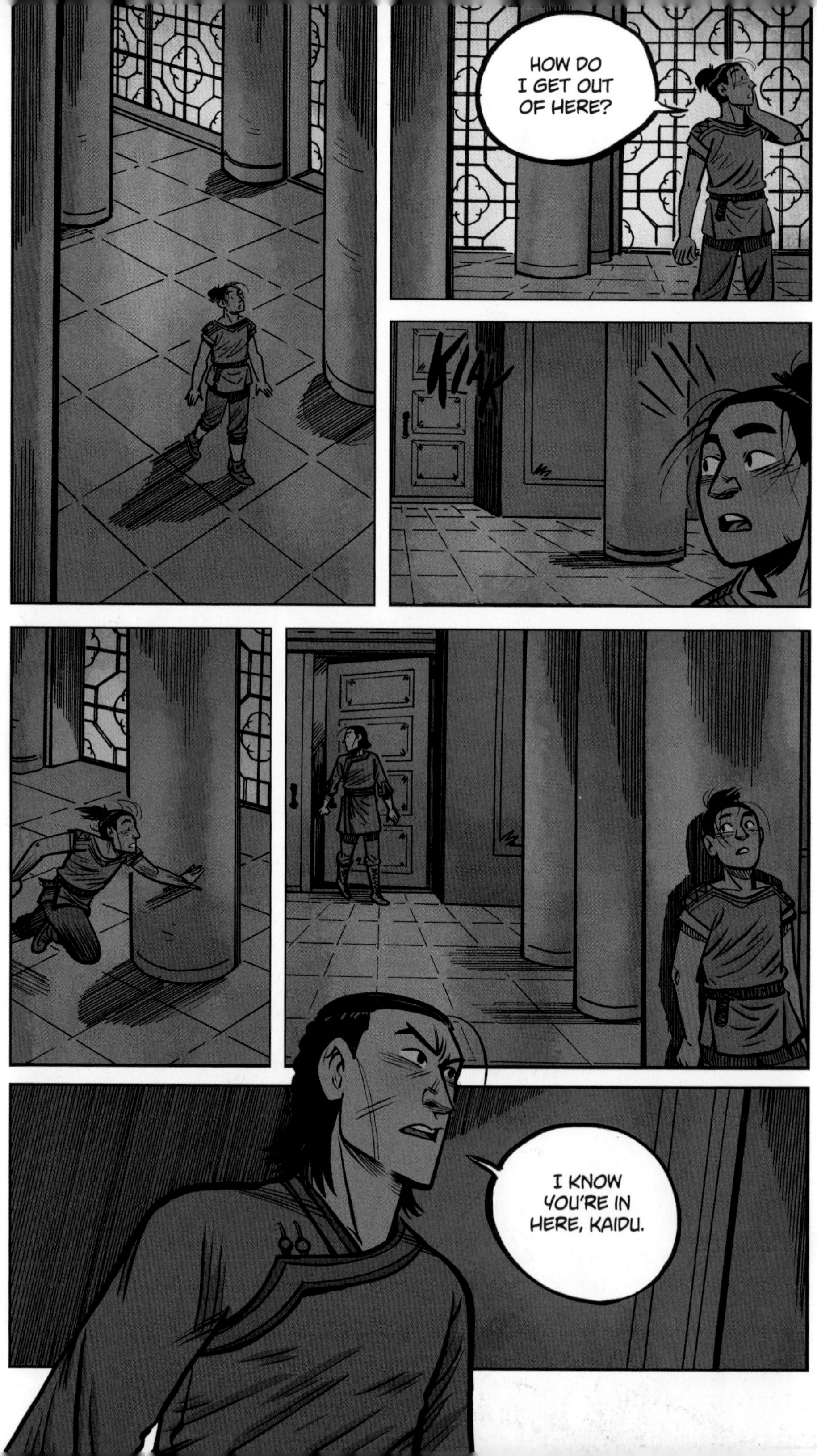
HOW DO I GET OUT OF HERE?
KIAK
I KNOW YOU'RE IN HERE, KAIDU.

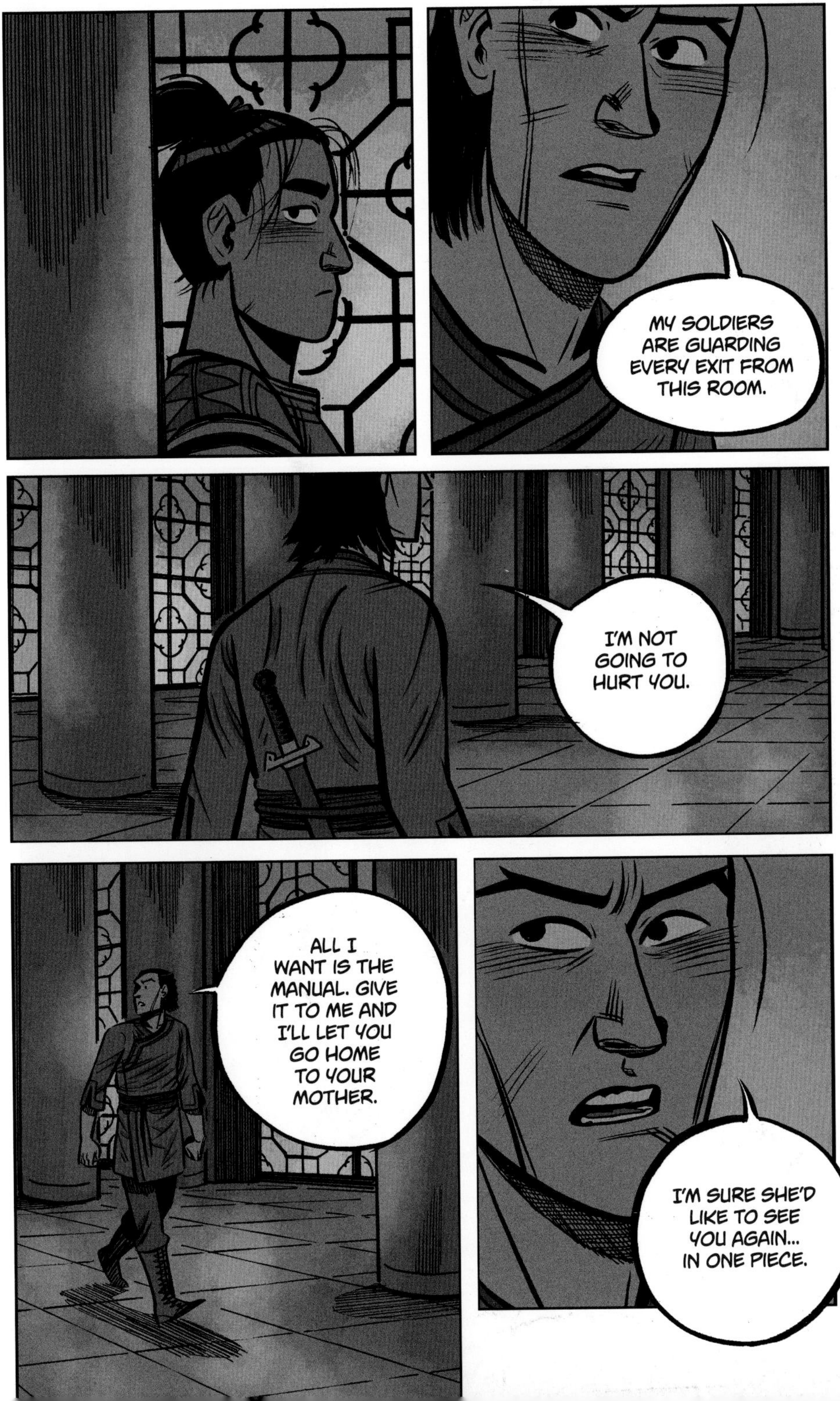
MY SOLDIERS ARE GUARDING EVERY EXIT FROM THIS ROOM.
I'M NOT GOING TO HURT YOU.
ALL I WANT IS THE MANUAL. GIVE IT TO ME AND I'LL LET YOU GO HOME TO YOUR MOTHER.
I'M SURE SHE'D LIKE TO SEE YOU AGAIN... IN ONE PIECE.

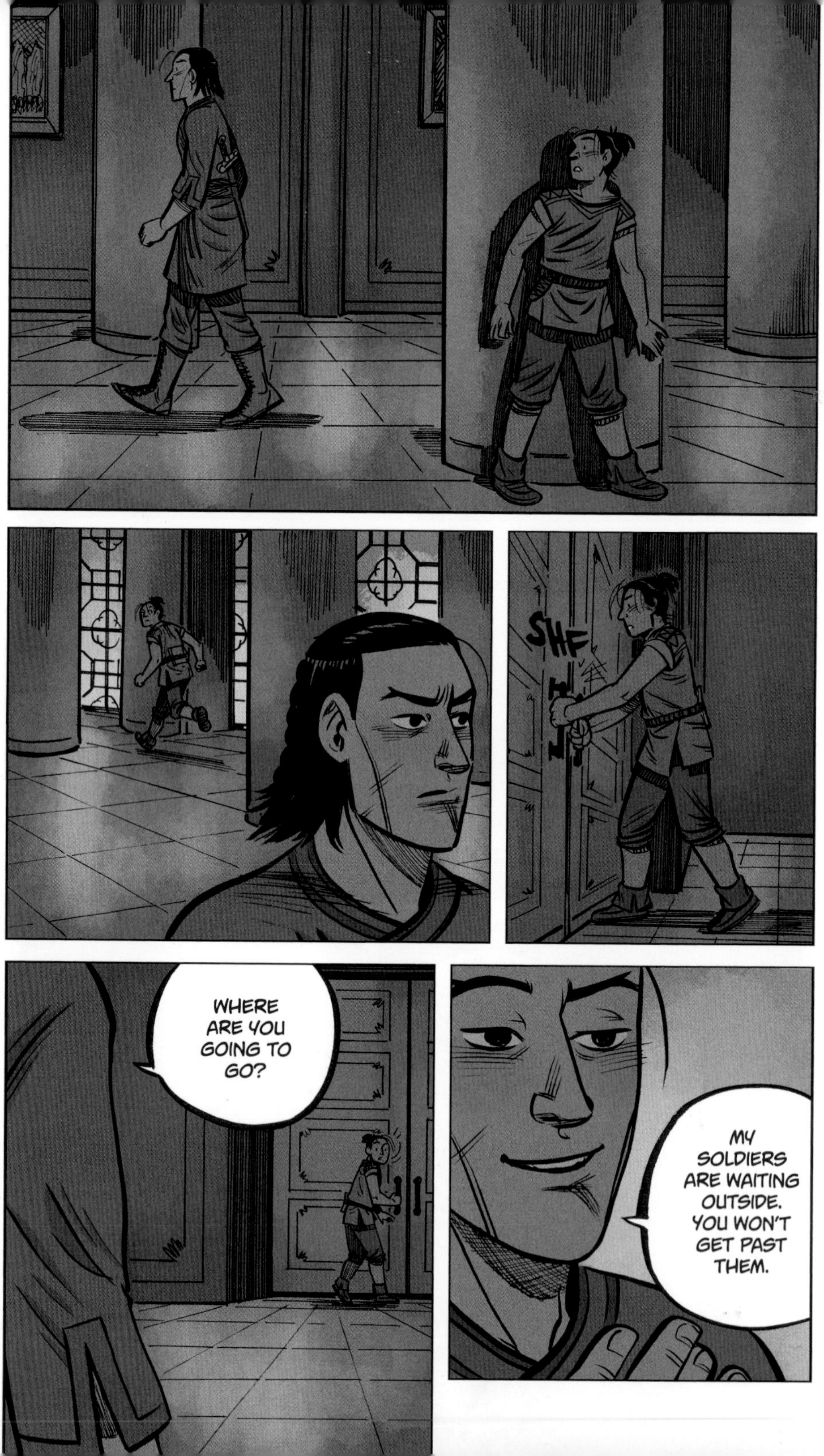
SHF
WHERE ARE YOU GOING TO GO?
MY SOLDIERS ARE WAITING OUTSIDE. YOU WON'T GET PAST THEM.

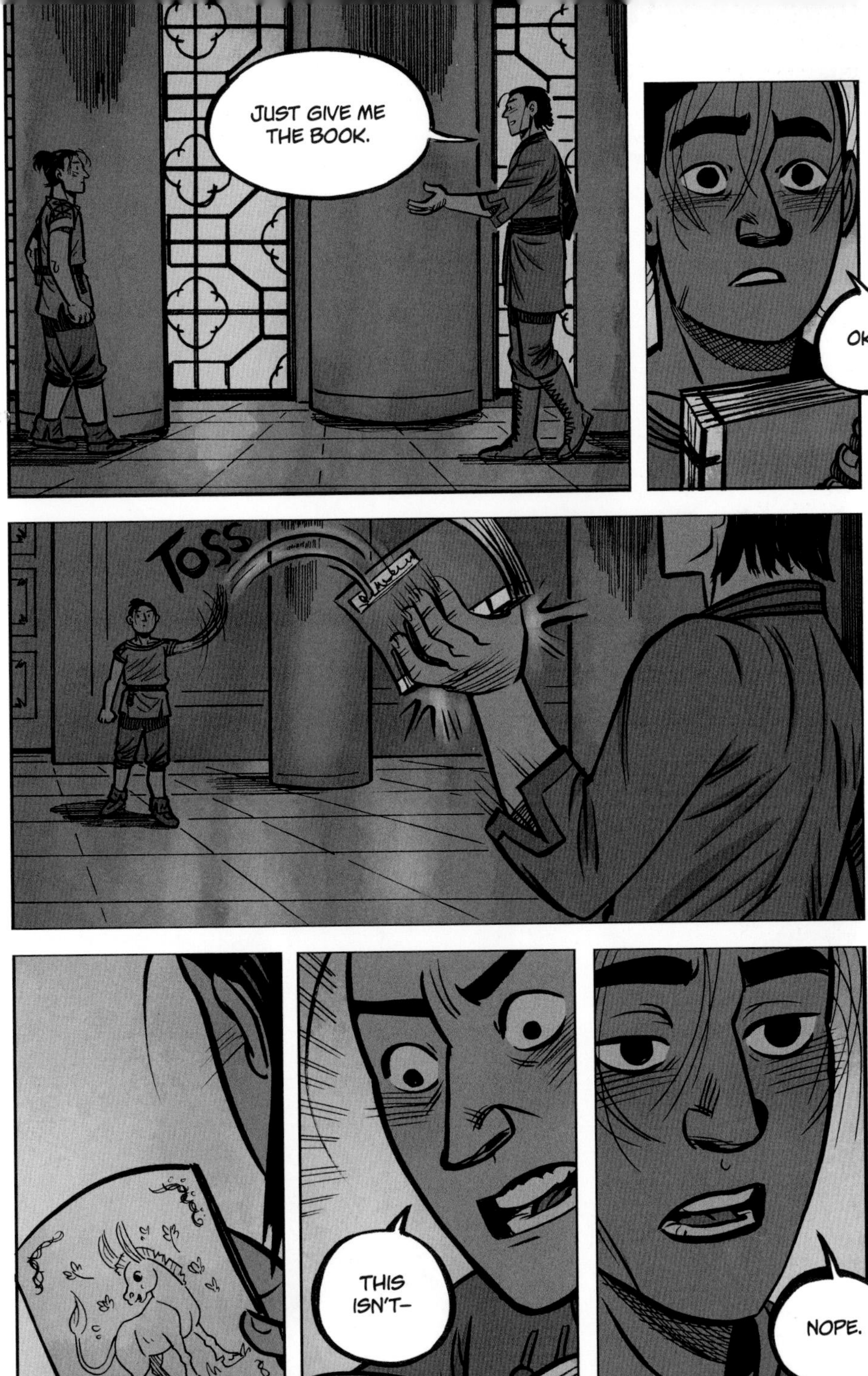
JUST GIVE ME THE BOOK.
OKAY.
TOSS
THIS ISN'T-
NOPE.

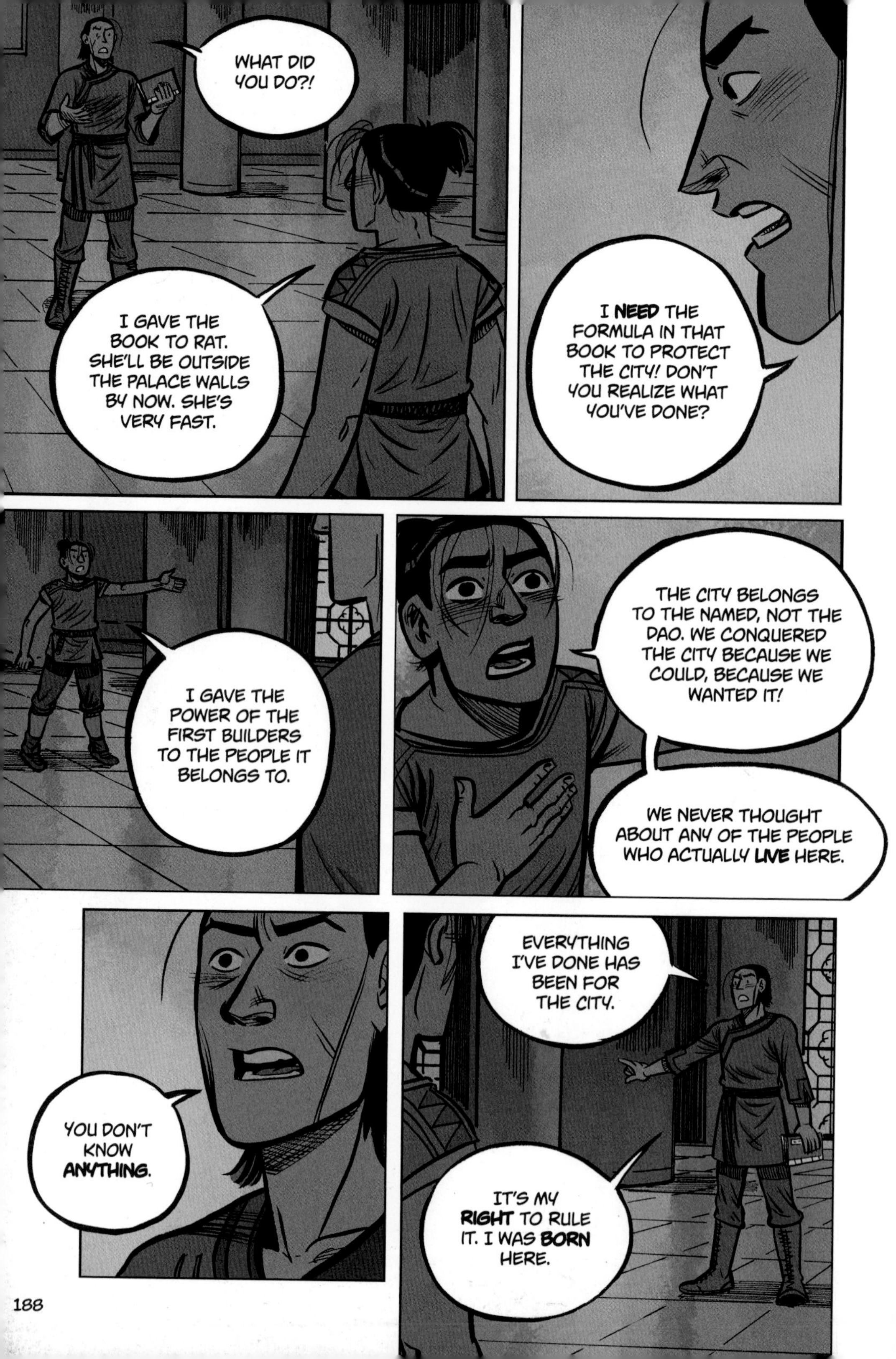
WHAT DID YOU DO?!
I GAVE THE BOOK TO RAT. SHE'LL BE OUTSIDE THE PALACE WALLS BY NOW. SHE'S VERY FAST.
I **NEED** THE FORMULA IN THAT BOOK TO PROTECT THE CITY! DON'T YOU REALIZE WHAT YOU'VE DONE?
I GAVE THE POWER OF THE FIRST BUILDERS TO THE PEOPLE IT BELONGS TO.
THE CITY BELONGS TO THE NAMED, NOT THE DAO. WE CONQUERED THE CITY BECAUSE WE COULD, BECAUSE WE WANTED IT!
WE NEVER THOUGHT ABOUT ANY OF THE PEOPLE WHO ACTUALLY **LIVE** HERE.
YOU DON'T KNOW **ANYTHING**.
EVERYTHING I'VE DONE HAS BEEN FOR THE CITY.
IT'S MY **RIGHT** TO RULE IT. I WAS **BORN** HERE.

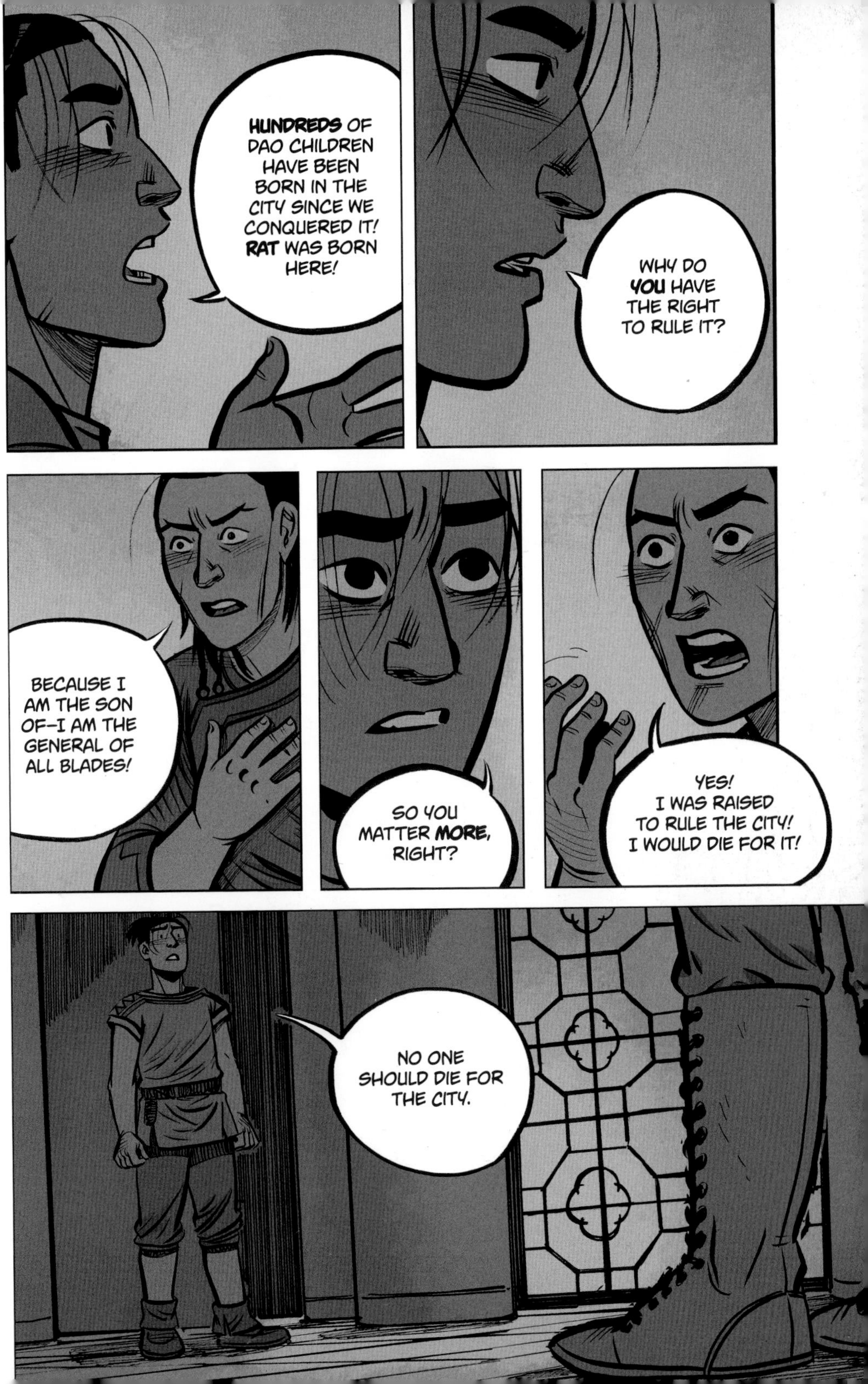
HUNDREDS OF DAO CHILDREN HAVE BEEN BORN IN THE CITY SINCE WE CONQUERED IT! **RAT** WAS BORN HERE!
WHY DO **YOU** HAVE THE RIGHT TO RULE IT?
BECAUSE I AM THE SON OF--I AM THE GENERAL OF ALL BLADES!
SO YOU MATTER **MORE**, RIGHT?
YES! I WAS RAISED TO RULE THE CITY! I WOULD DIE FOR IT!
NO ONE SHOULD DIE FOR THE CITY.

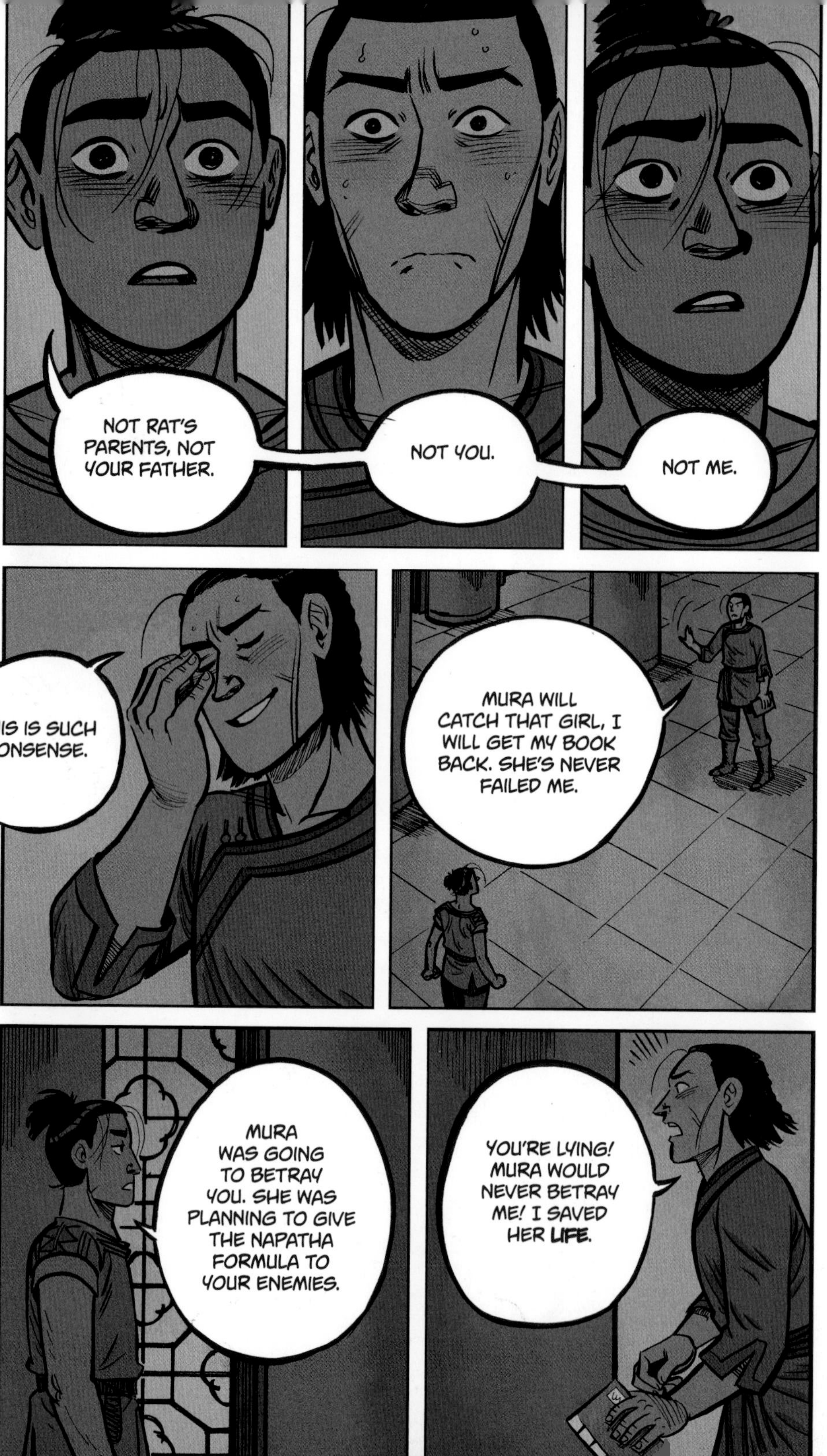
NOT RAT'S PARENTS, NOT YOUR FATHER.
NOT YOU.
NOT ME.
THIS IS SUCH NONSENSE.
MURA WILL CATCH THAT GIRL, I WILL GET MY BOOK BACK. SHE'S NEVER FAILED ME.
MURA WAS GOING TO BETRAY YOU. SHE WAS PLANNING TO GIVE THE NAPATHA FORMULA TO YOUR ENEMIES.
YOU'RE LYING! MURA WOULD NEVER BETRAY ME! I SAVED HER **LIFE**.

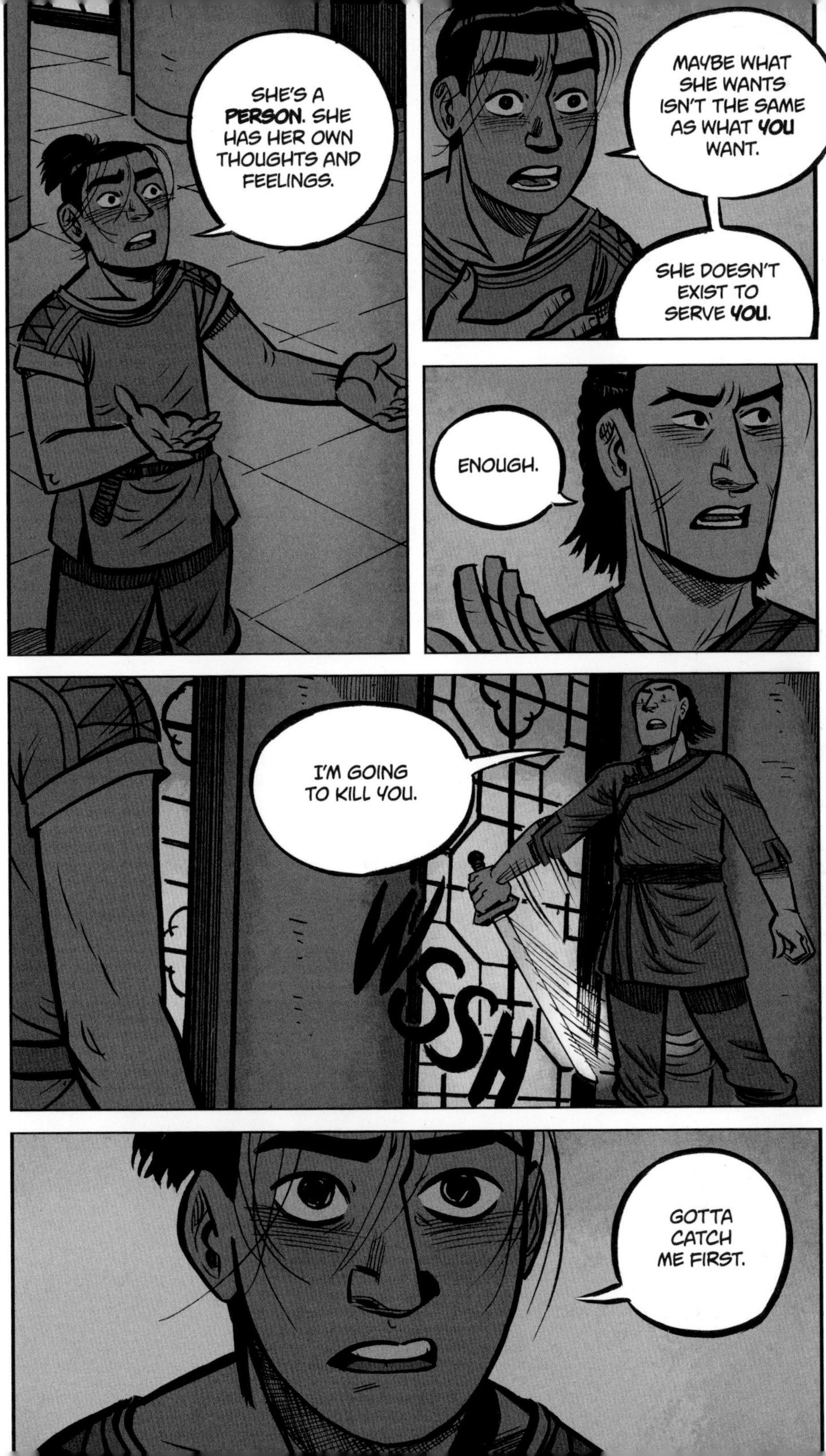
SHE'S A **PERSON**. SHE HAS HER OWN THOUGHTS AND FEELINGS.
MAYBE WHAT SHE WANTS ISN'T THE SAME AS WHAT **YOU** WANT.
SHE DOESN'T EXIST TO SERVE **YOU**.
ENOUGH.
I'M GOING TO KILL YOU.
WSSH
GOTTA CATCH ME FIRST.

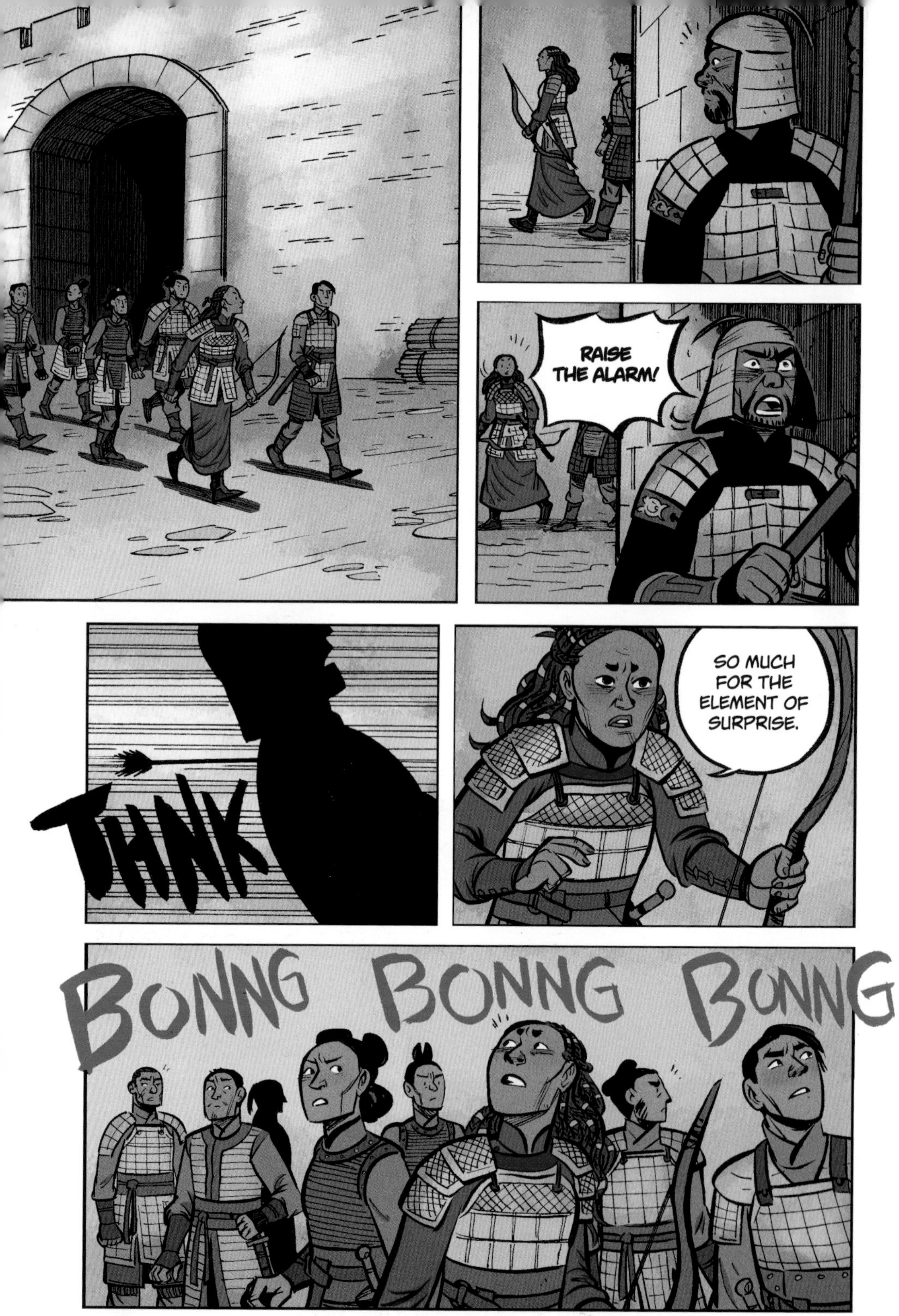
RAISE THE ALARM!
THNK
SO MUCH FOR THE ELEMENT OF SURPRISE.
BONNG BONNG BONNG

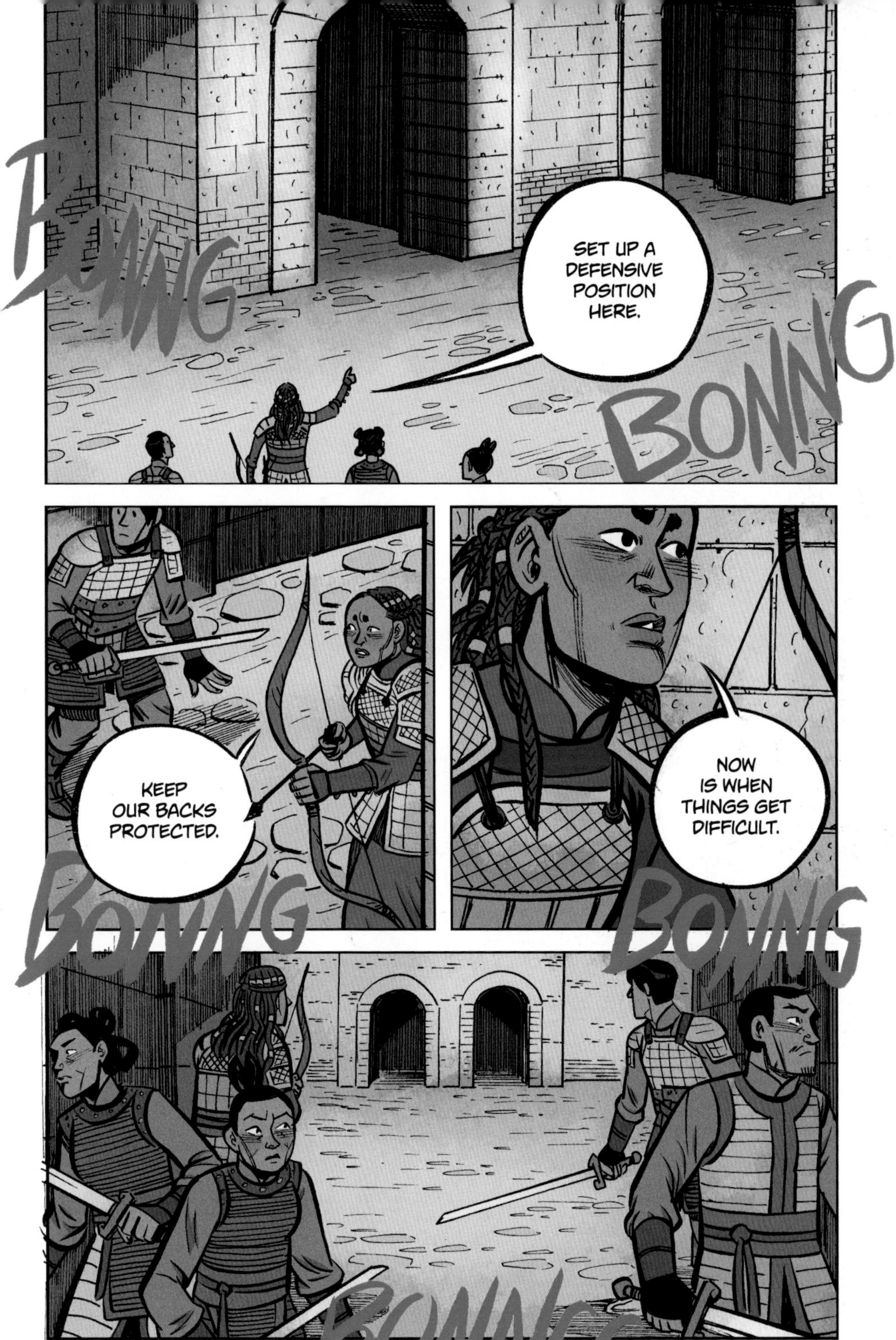
BONNG
SET UP A DEFENSIVE POSITION HERE.
BONNG
KEEP OUR BACKS PROTECTED.
BONNG
NOW IS WHEN THINGS GET DIFFICULT.
BONNG
BONNGG

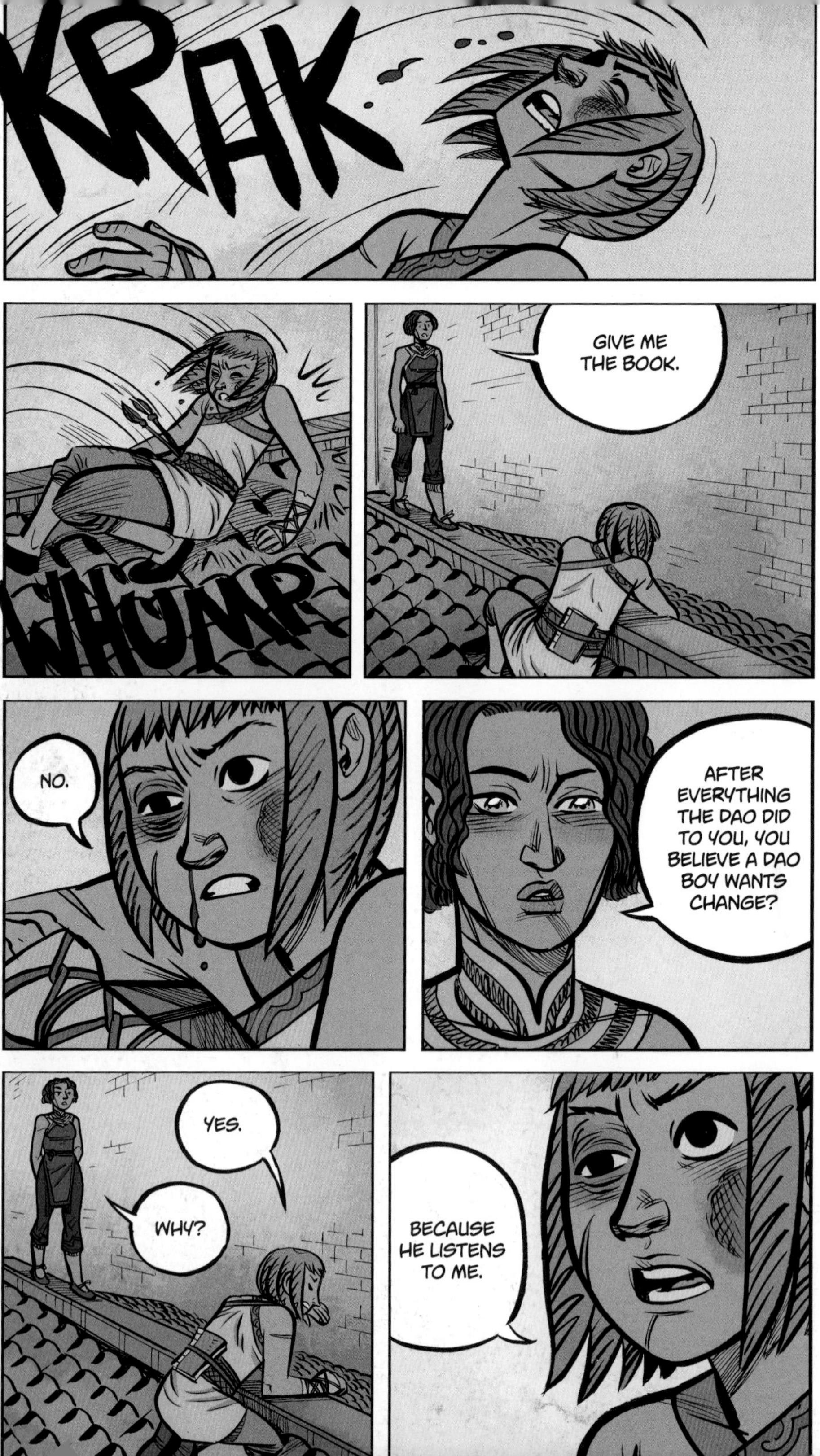

KRAK
WHUMP
GIVE ME THE BOOK.
NO.
AFTER EVERYTHING THE DAO DID TO YOU, YOU BELIEVE A DAO BOY WANTS CHANGE?
YES.
WHY?
BECAUSE HE LISTENS TO ME.

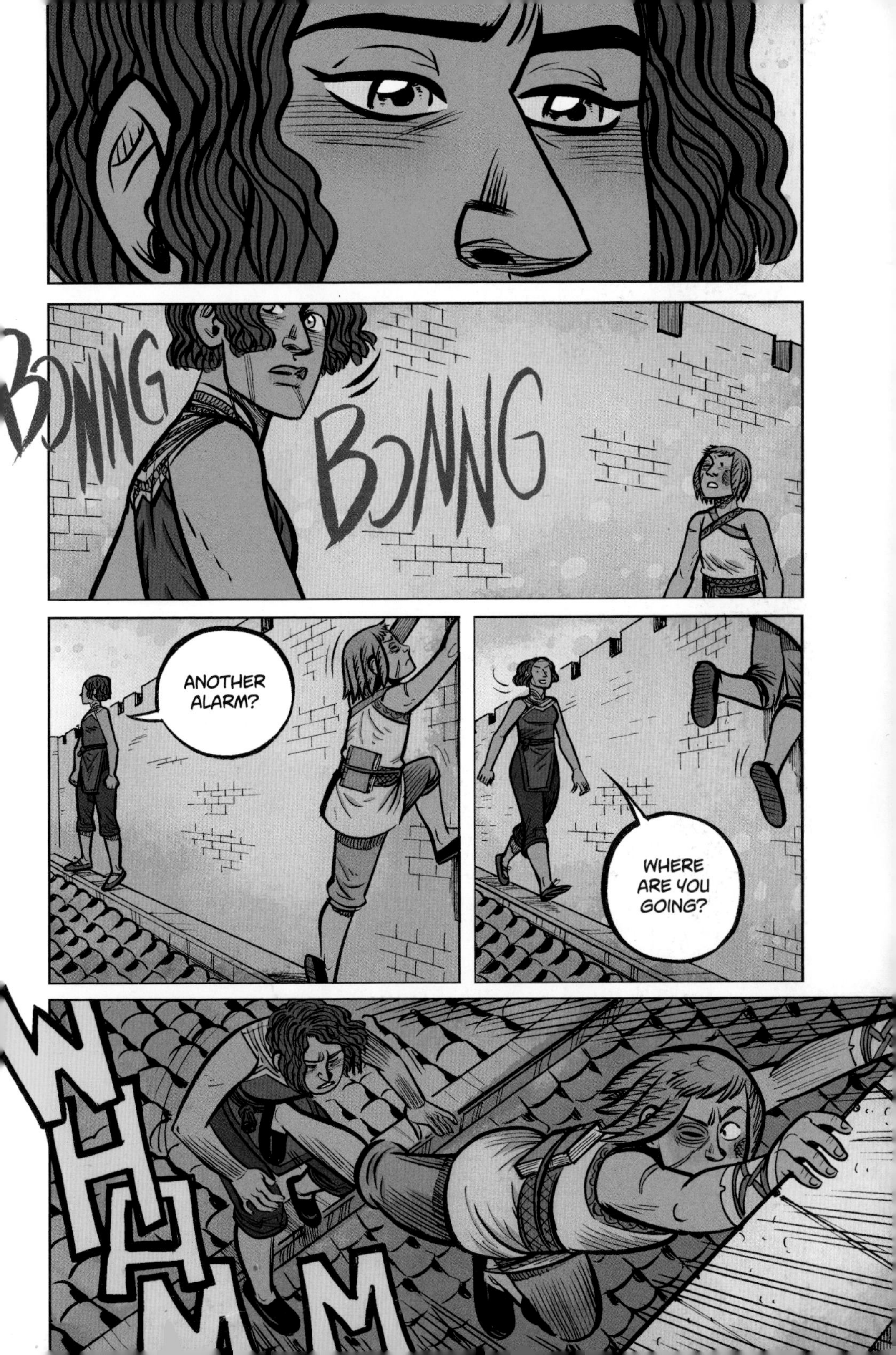
BONNG
BONNG
ANOTHER ALARM?
WHERE ARE YOU GOING?
WHAM

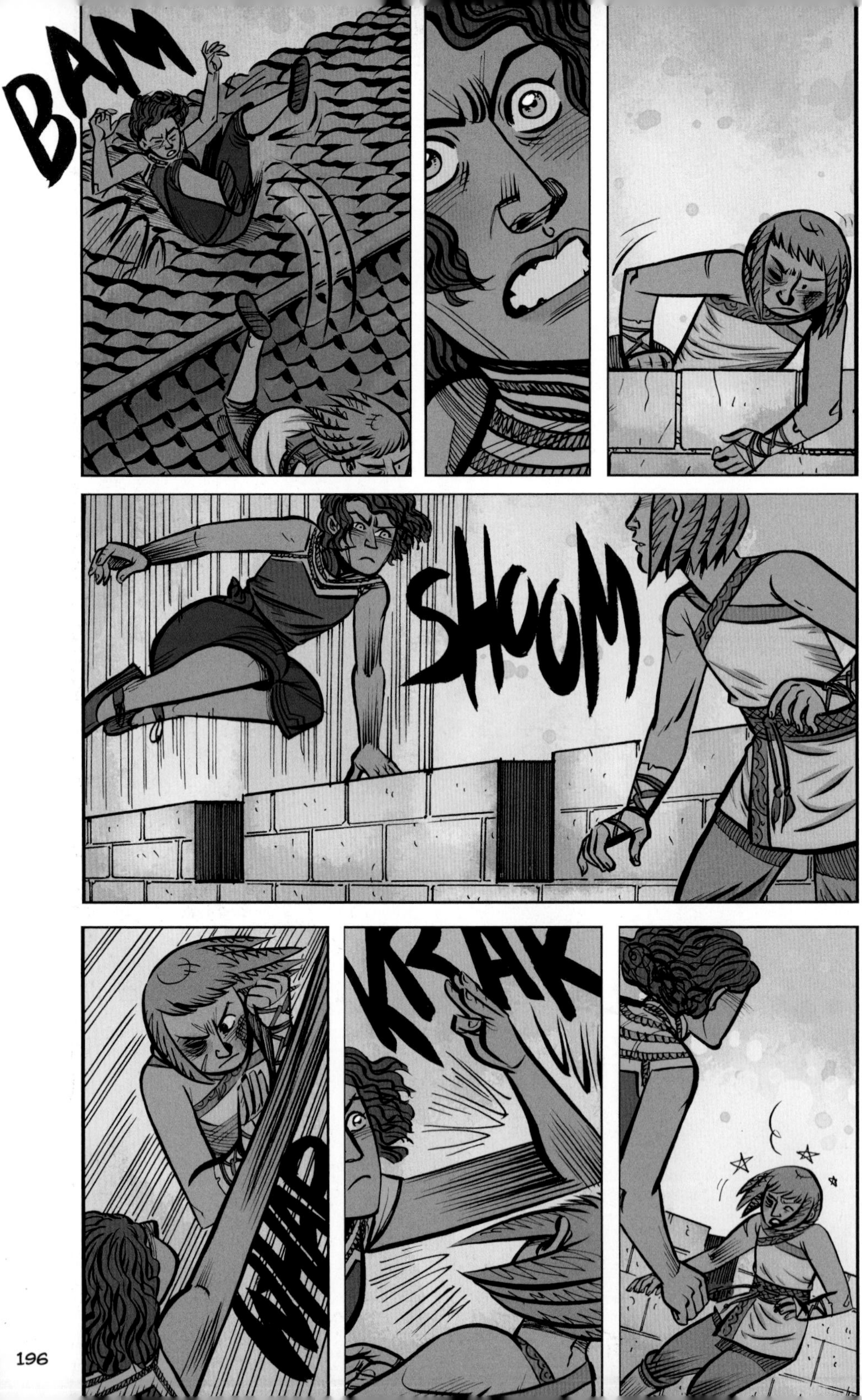
BAM
SHOOM
WHAP
KRAK

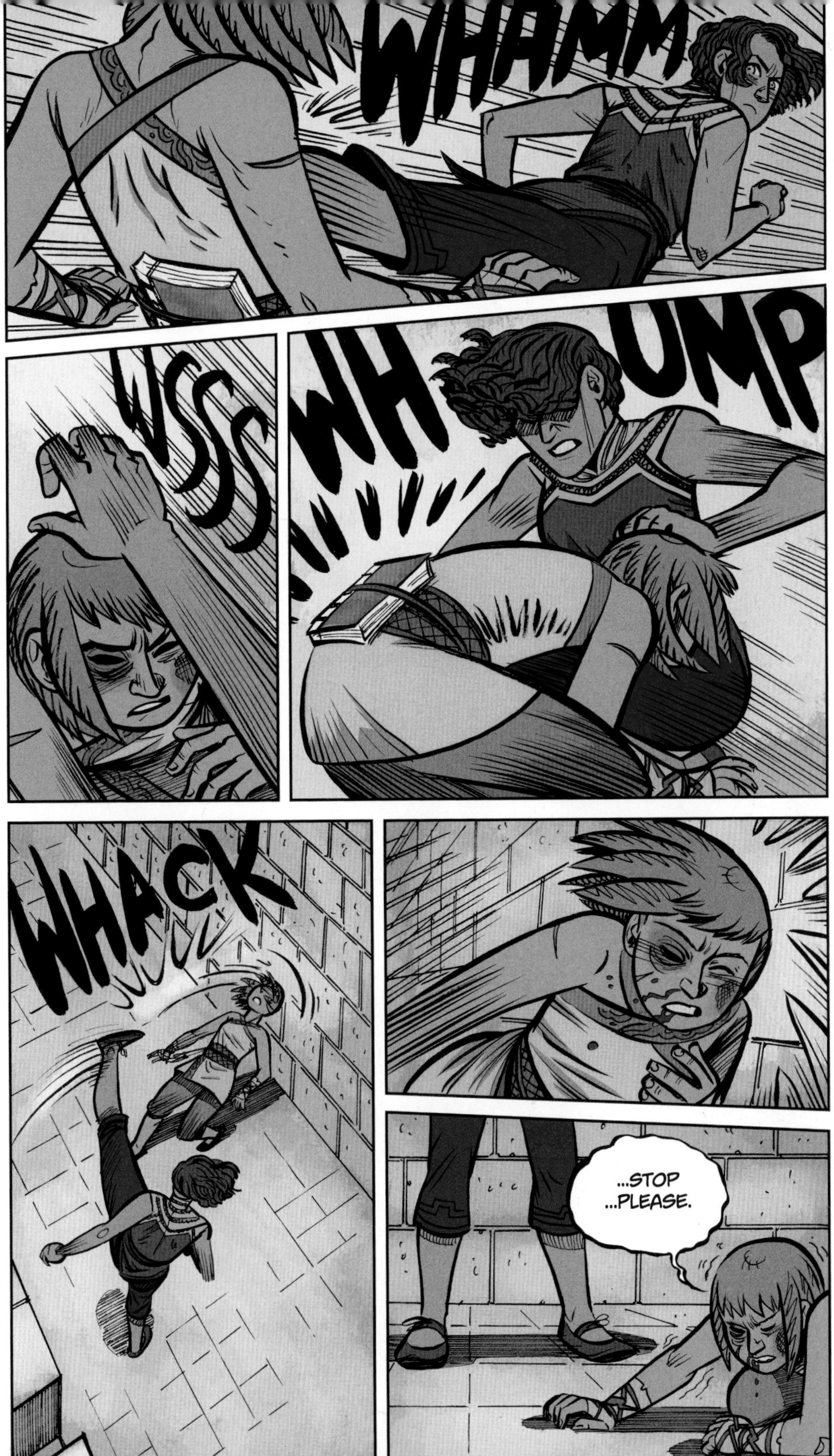
WHAMM
WSSS
WHUMP
WHACK
...STOP
...PLEASE.

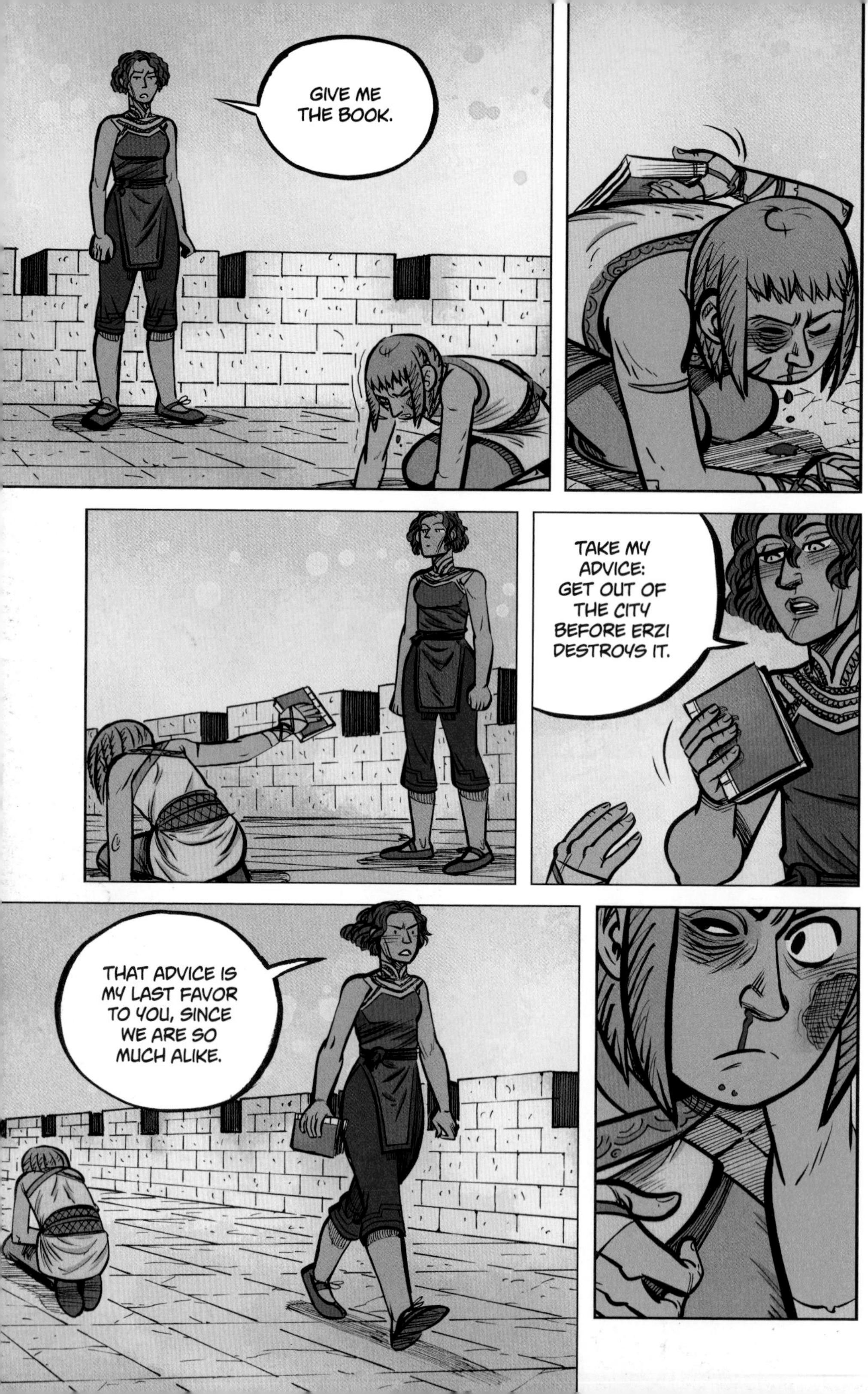
GIVE ME THE BOOK.
TAKE MY ADVICE: GET OUT OF THE CITY BEFORE ERZI DESTROYS IT.
THAT ADVICE IS MY LAST FAVOR TO YOU, SINCE WE ARE SO MUCH ALIKE.

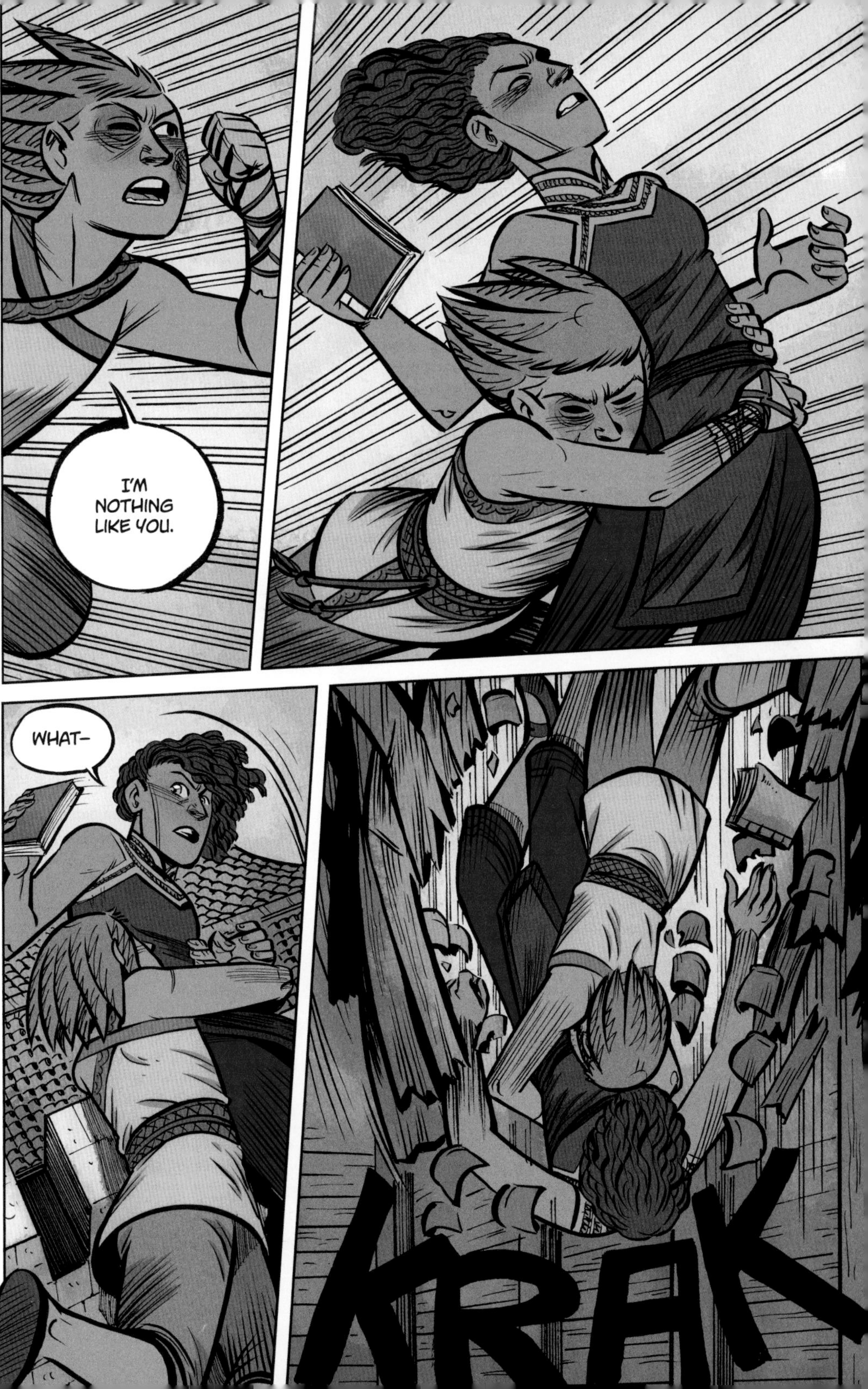
I'M NOTHING LIKE YOU.
WHAT-
KRAK

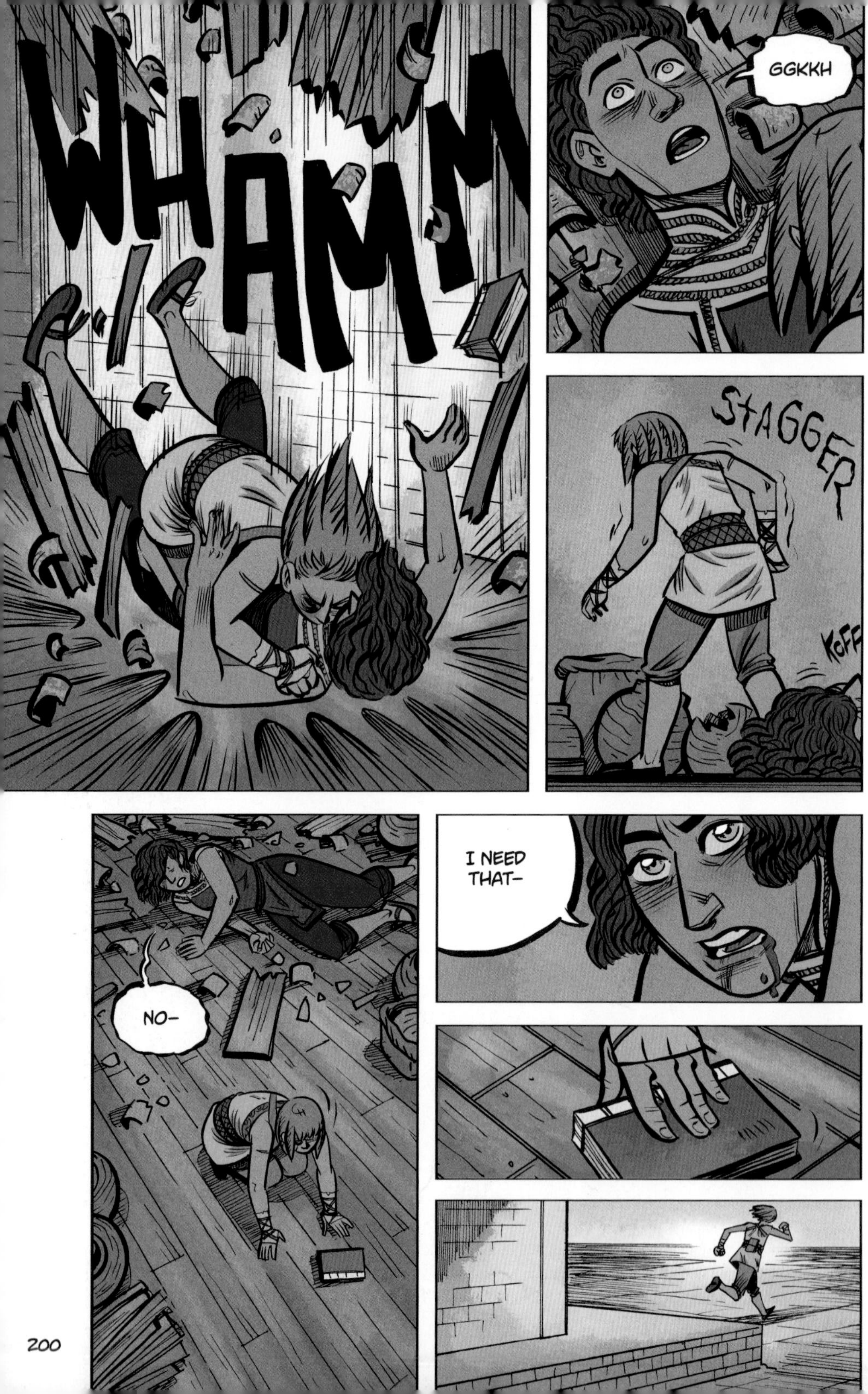

WHAMM
GGKKH
STAGGER
KOFF
I NEED THAT-
NO-

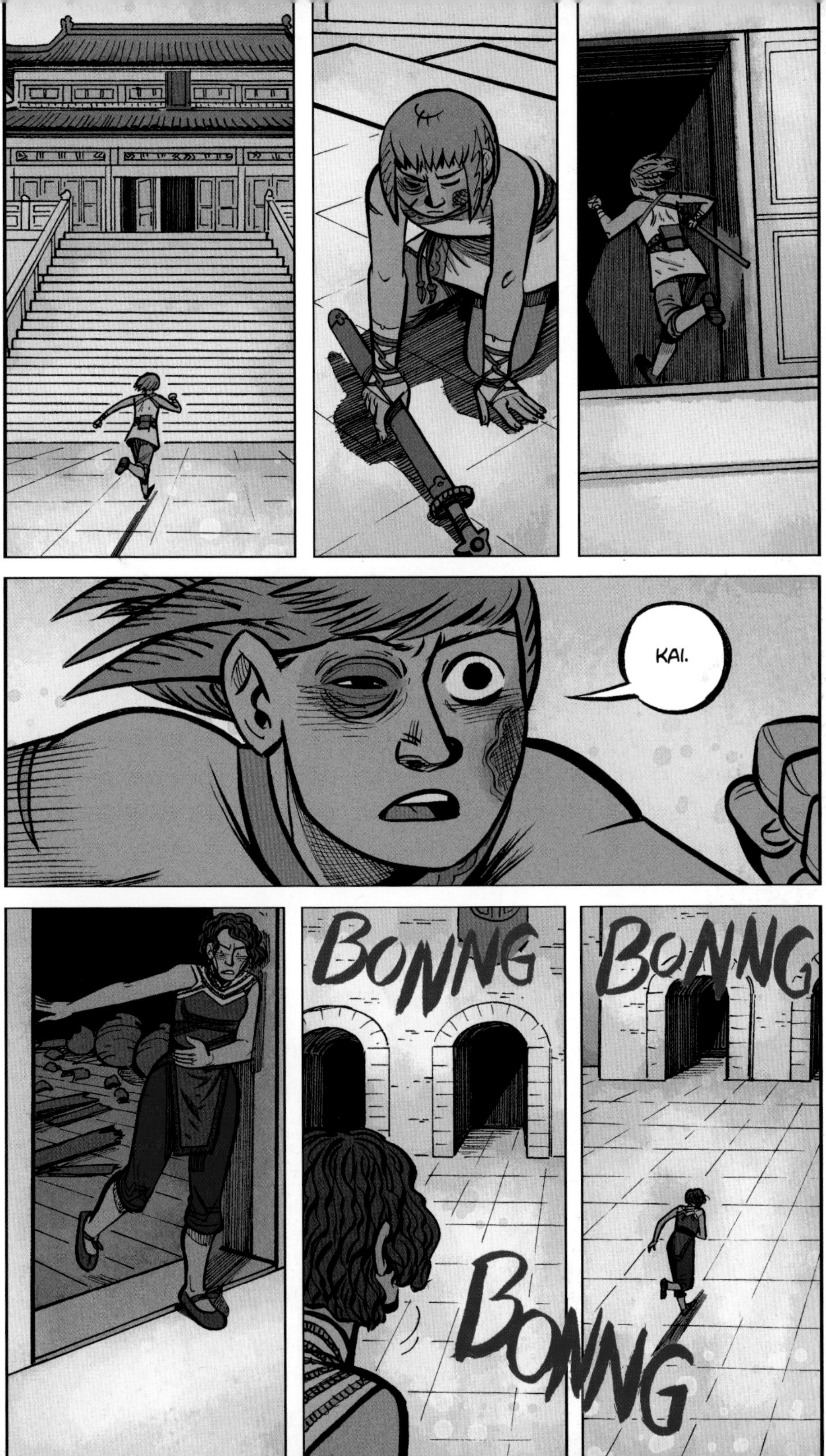
KAI.
BONNG
BONNG
BONNG

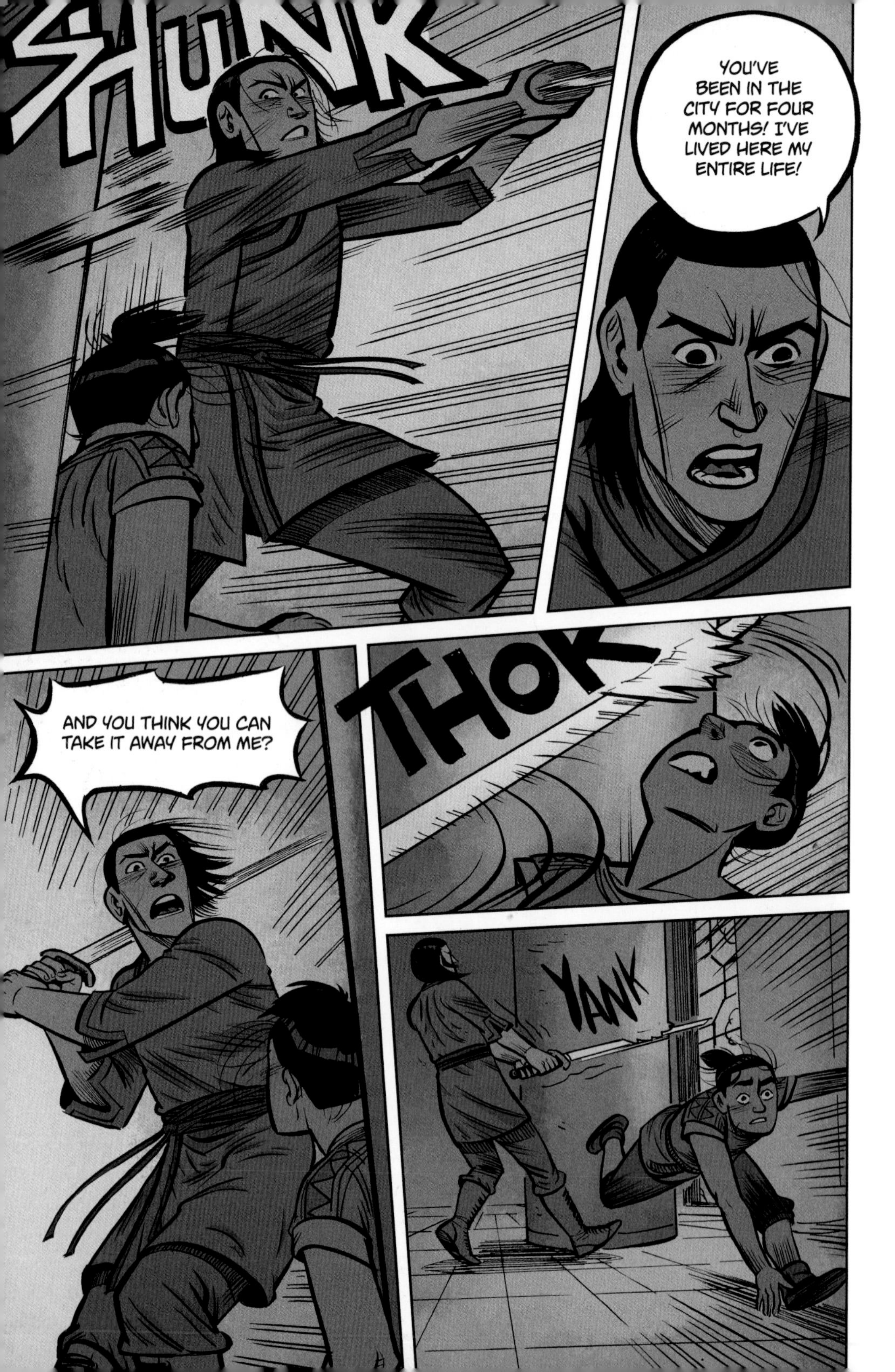
SHUNK
YOU'VE BEEN IN THE CITY FOR FOUR MONTHS! I'VE LIVED HERE MY ENTIRE LIFE!
AND YOU THINK YOU CAN TAKE IT AWAY FROM ME?
THOK
YANK

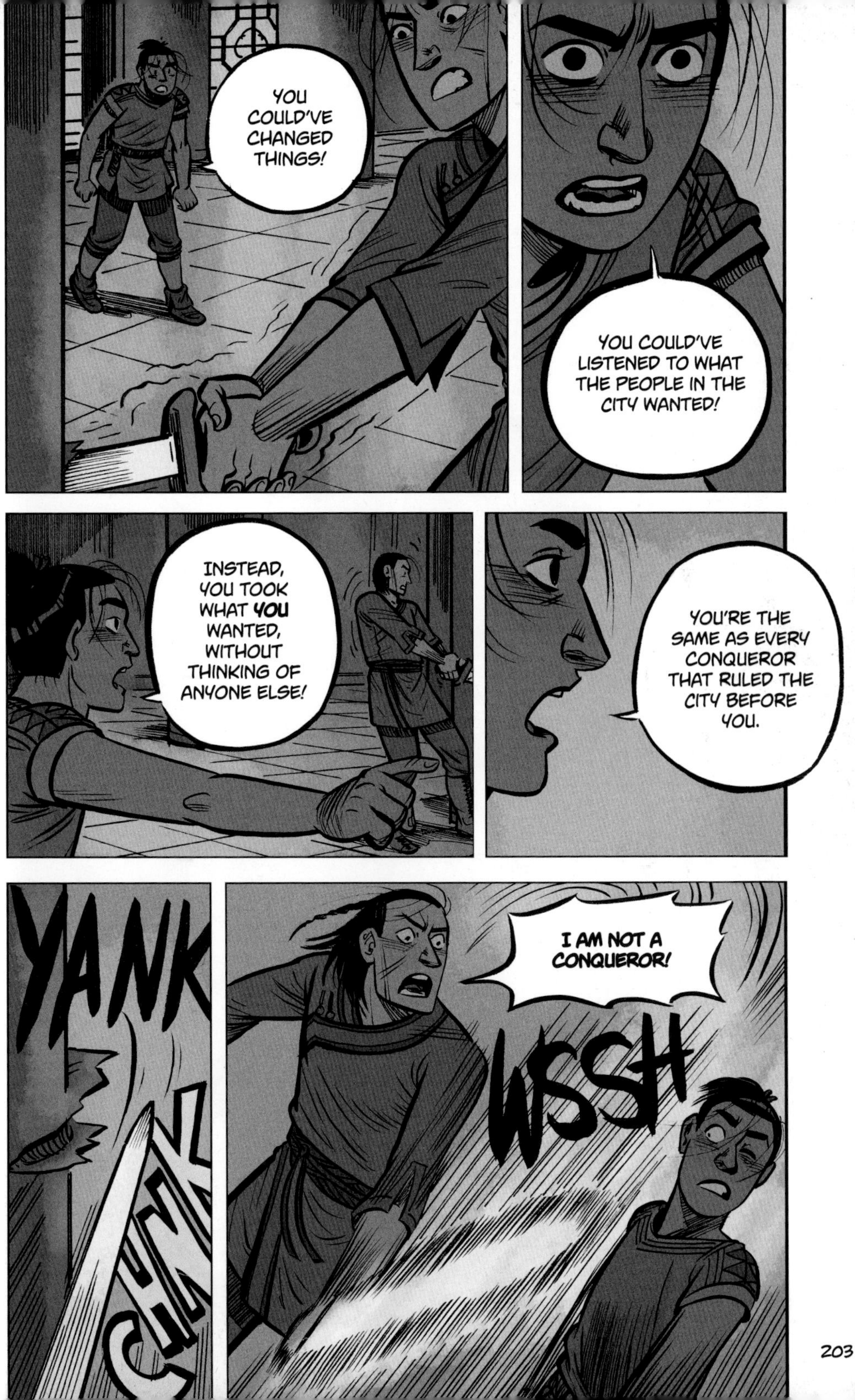
YOU COULD'VE CHANGED THINGS!
YOU COULD'VE LISTENED TO WHAT THE PEOPLE IN THE CITY WANTED!
INSTEAD, YOU TOOK WHAT **YOU** WANTED, WITHOUT THINKING OF ANYONE ELSE!
YOU'RE THE SAME AS EVERY CONQUEROR THAT RULED THE CITY BEFORE YOU.
YANK
CHUNK
I AM NOT A CONQUEROR!
WSSH

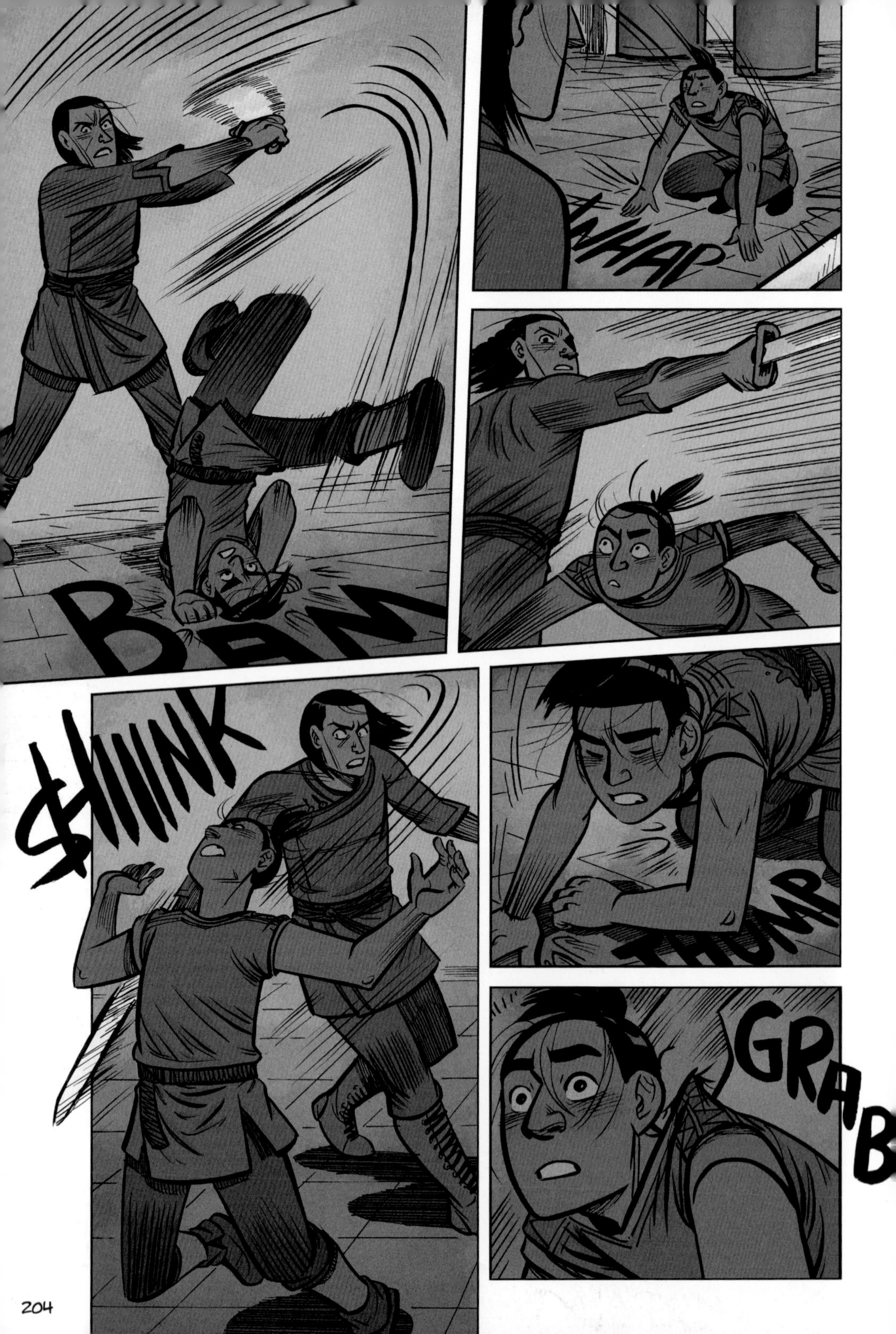
BAM
WHAP
SHIIINK
THUMP
GRAB

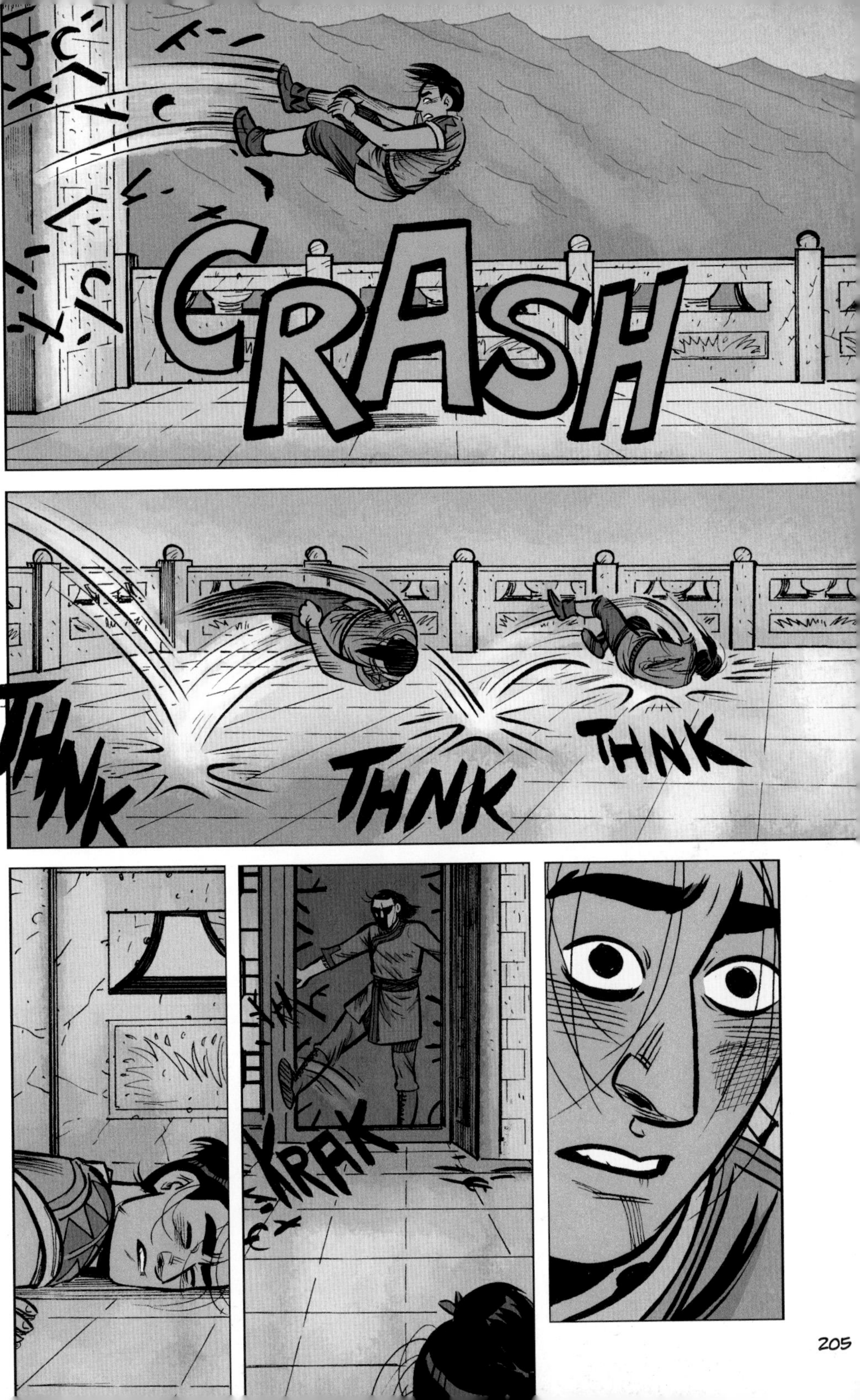
CRASH
THNK
THNK
THNK
KRAK

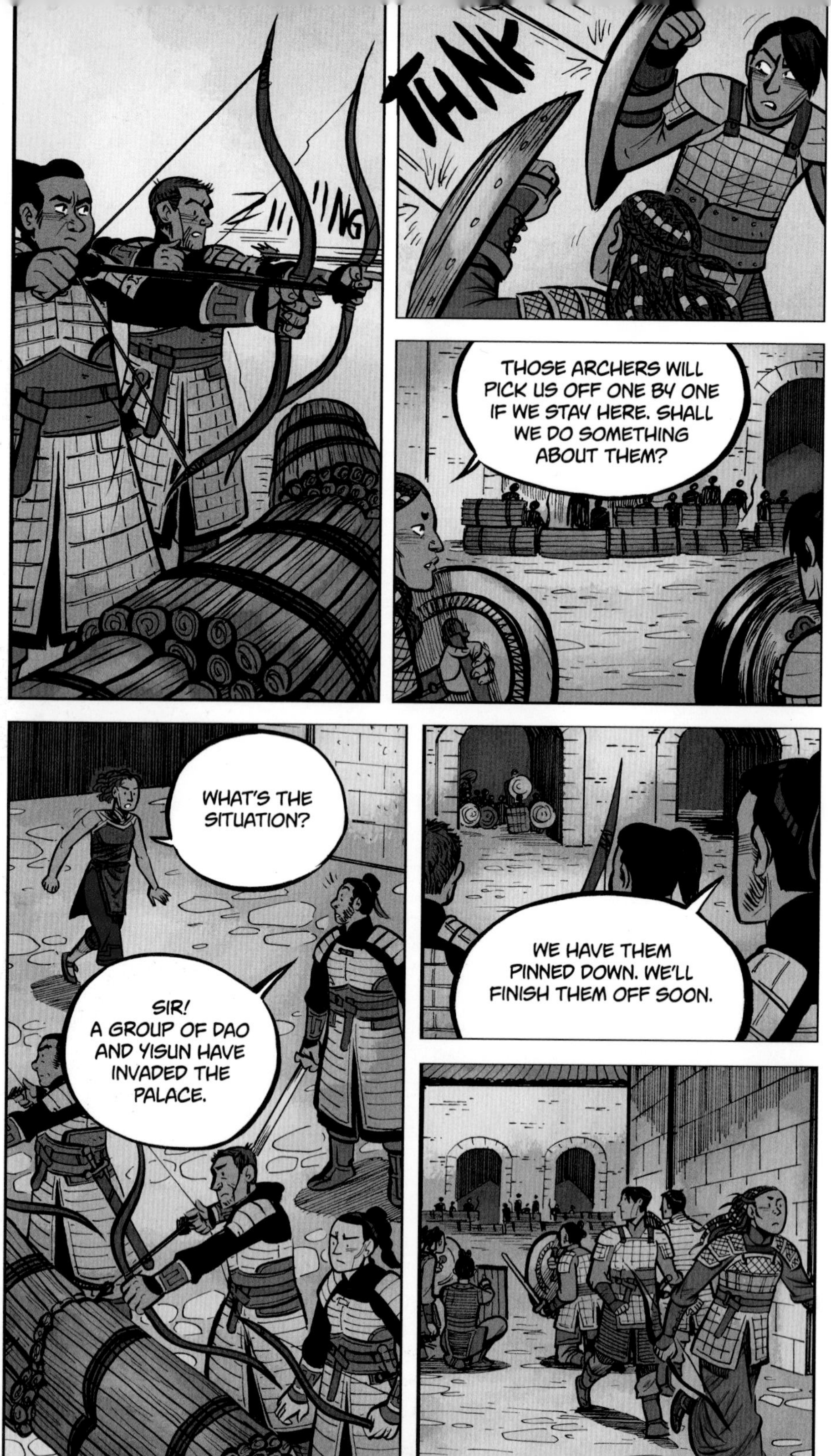
ZIIIING
THNK
THOSE ARCHERS WILL PICK US OFF ONE BY ONE IF WE STAY HERE. SHALL WE DO SOMETHING ABOUT THEM?
WHAT'S THE SITUATION?
SIR! A GROUP OF DAO AND YISUN HAVE INVADED THE PALACE.
WE HAVE THEM PINNED DOWN. WE'LL FINISH THEM OFF SOON.

ZIIING

hff

THNK

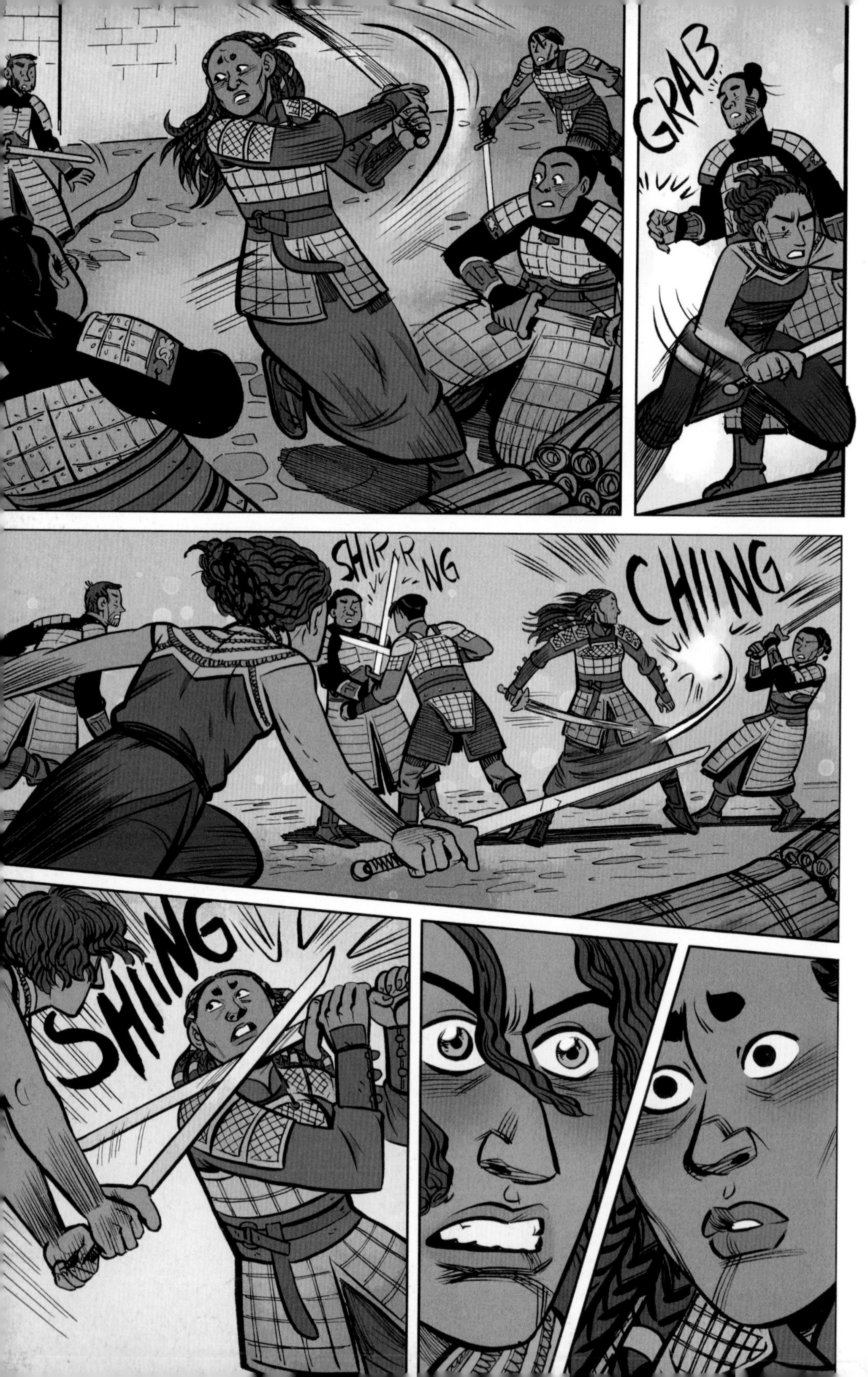
GRAB
SHIRRING
CHING
SHIING

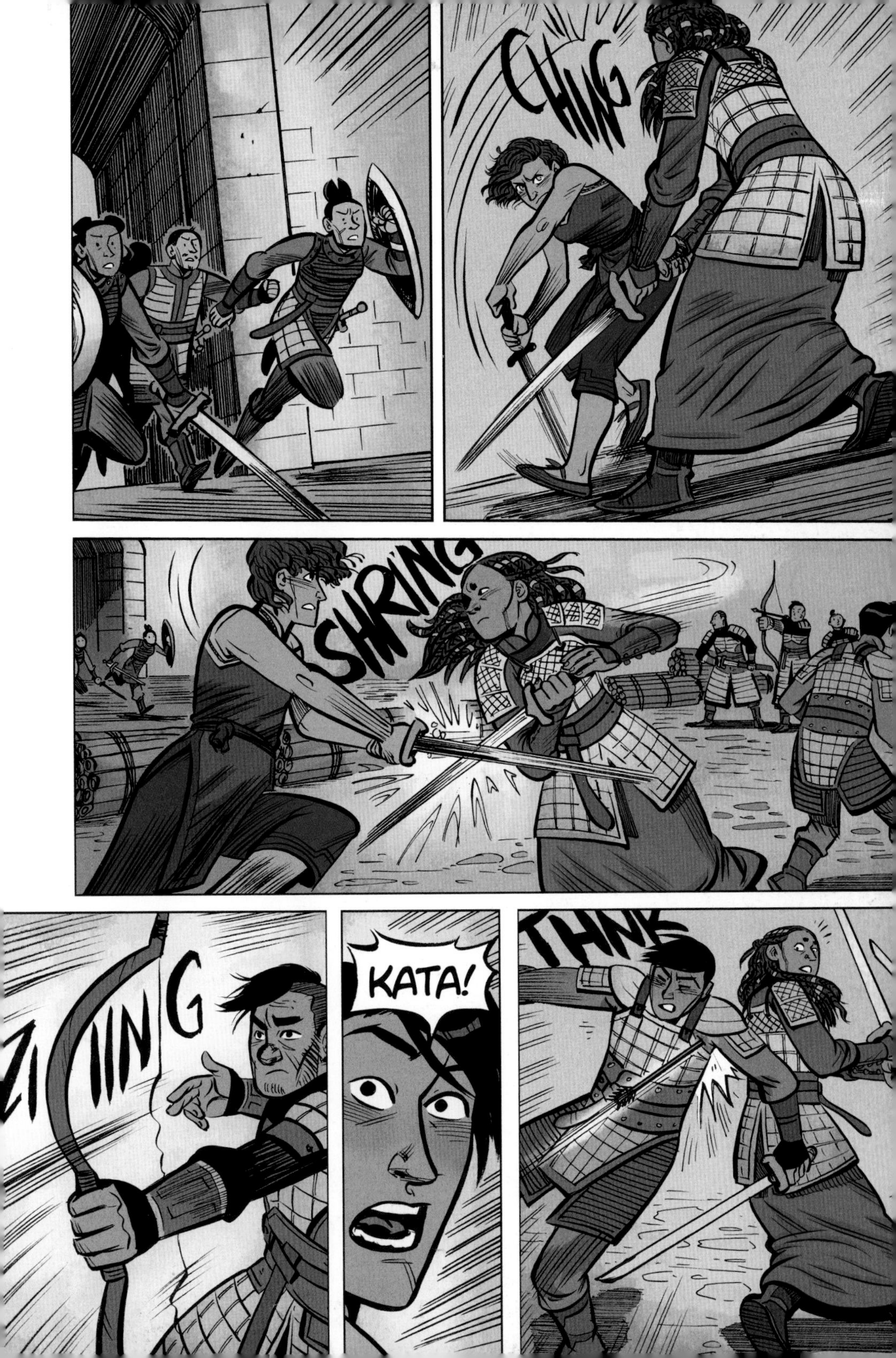
CHING
SHRING
ZIIING
KATA!
THNK

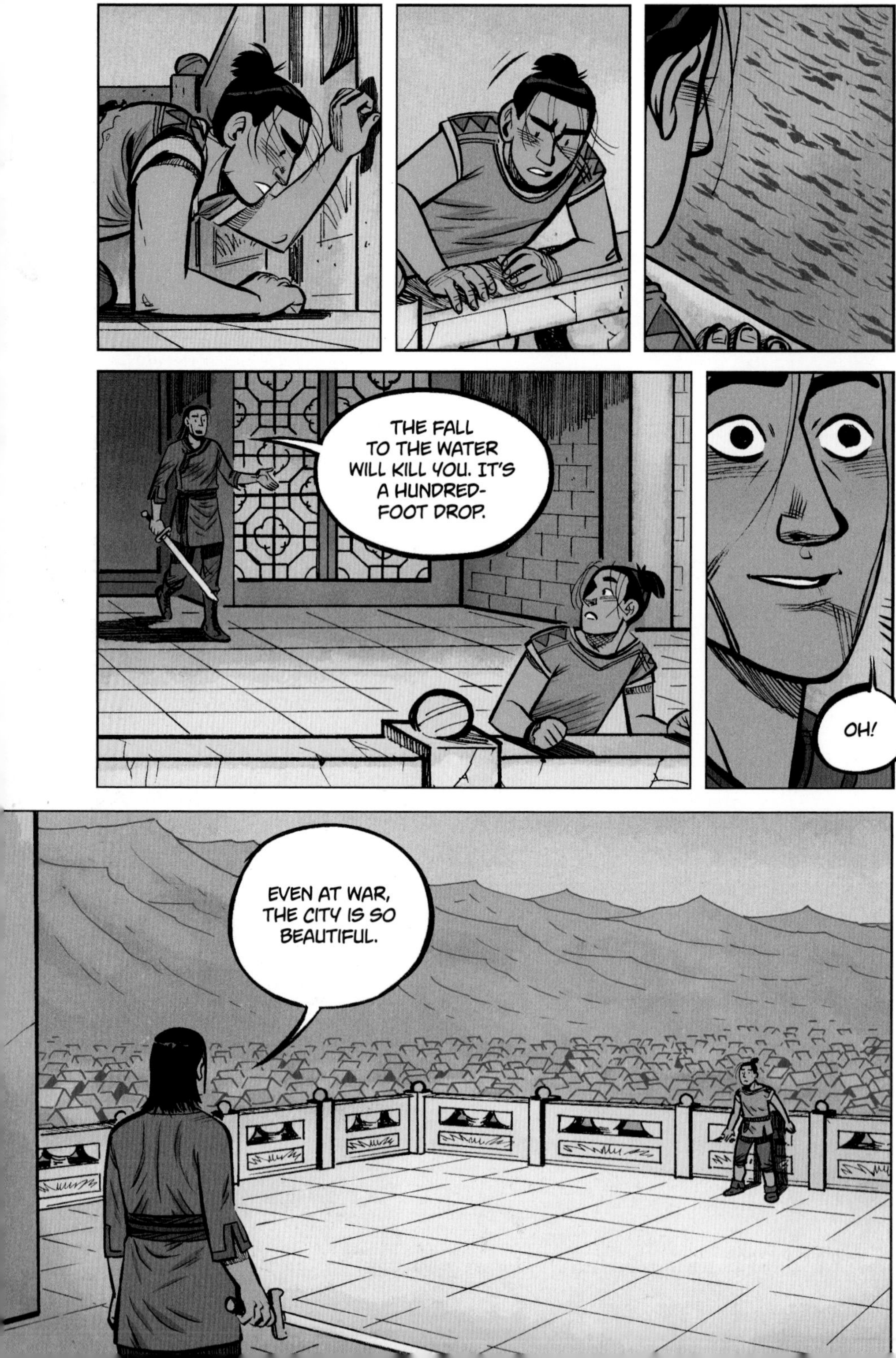
THE FALL TO THE WATER WILL KILL YOU. IT'S A HUNDRED-FOOT DROP.
OH!
EVEN AT WAR, THE CITY IS SO BEAUTIFUL.

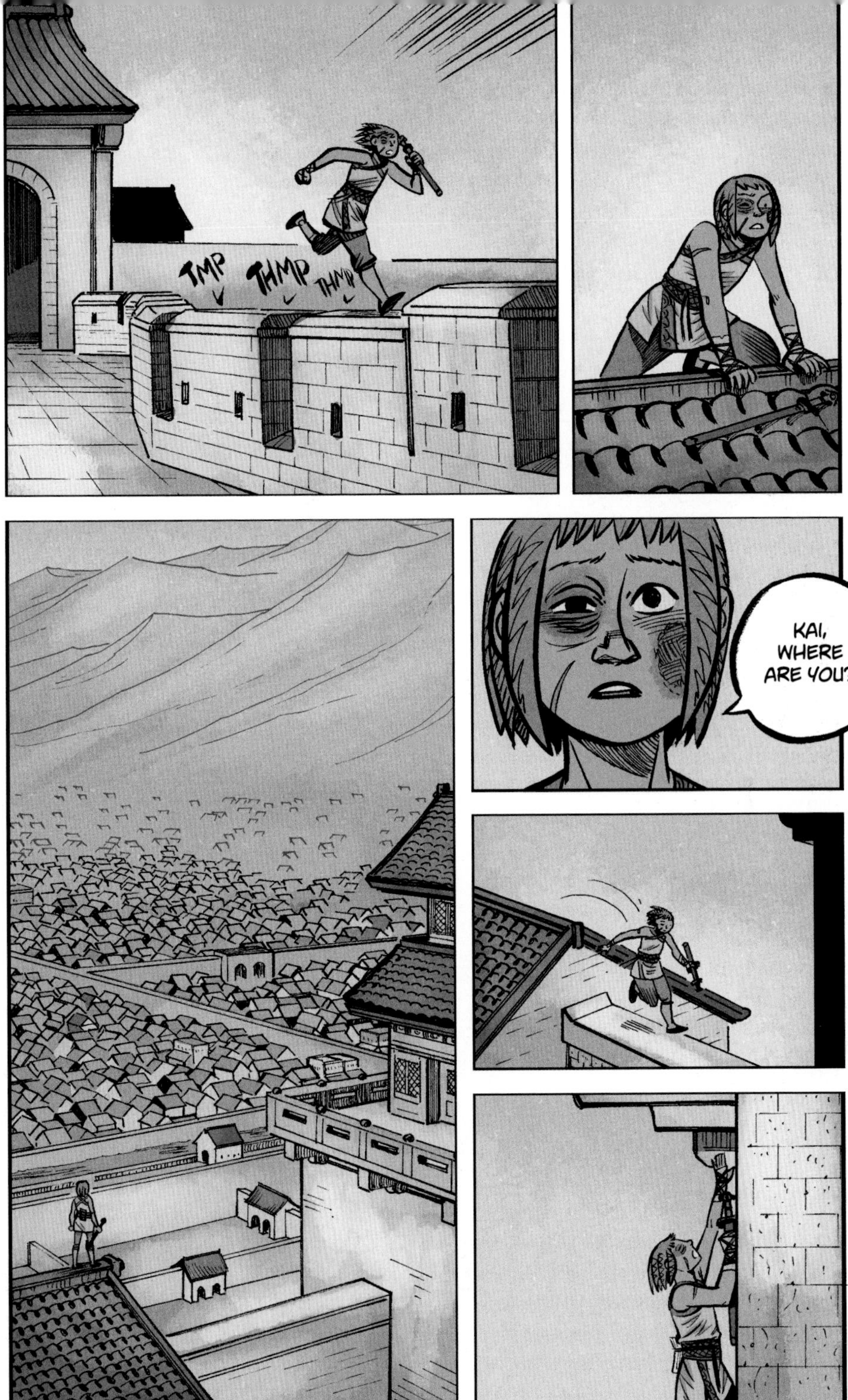
TMP
THMP
THMP
KAI, WHERE ARE YOU?

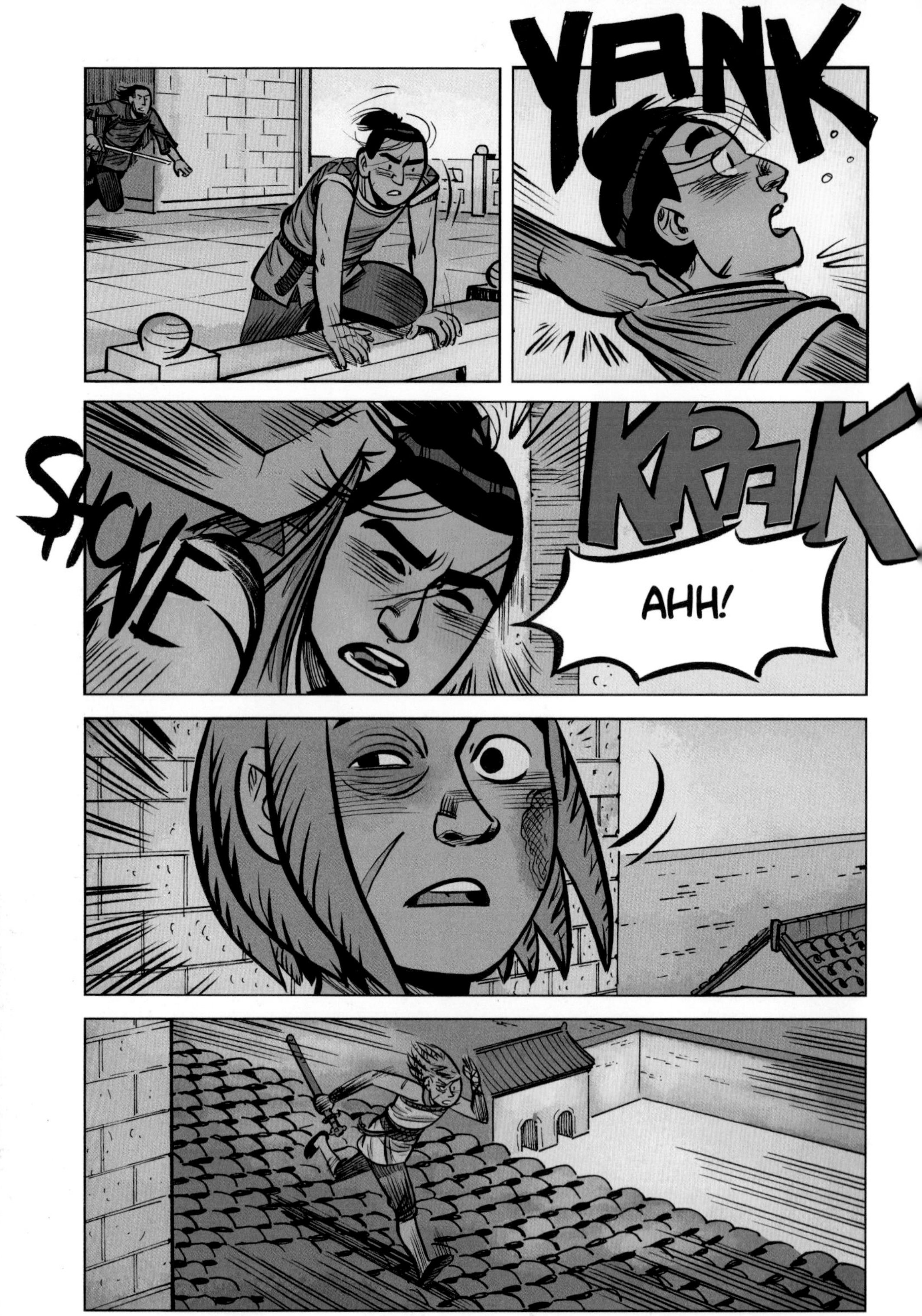
YANK
SHOVE
KRAK
AHH!

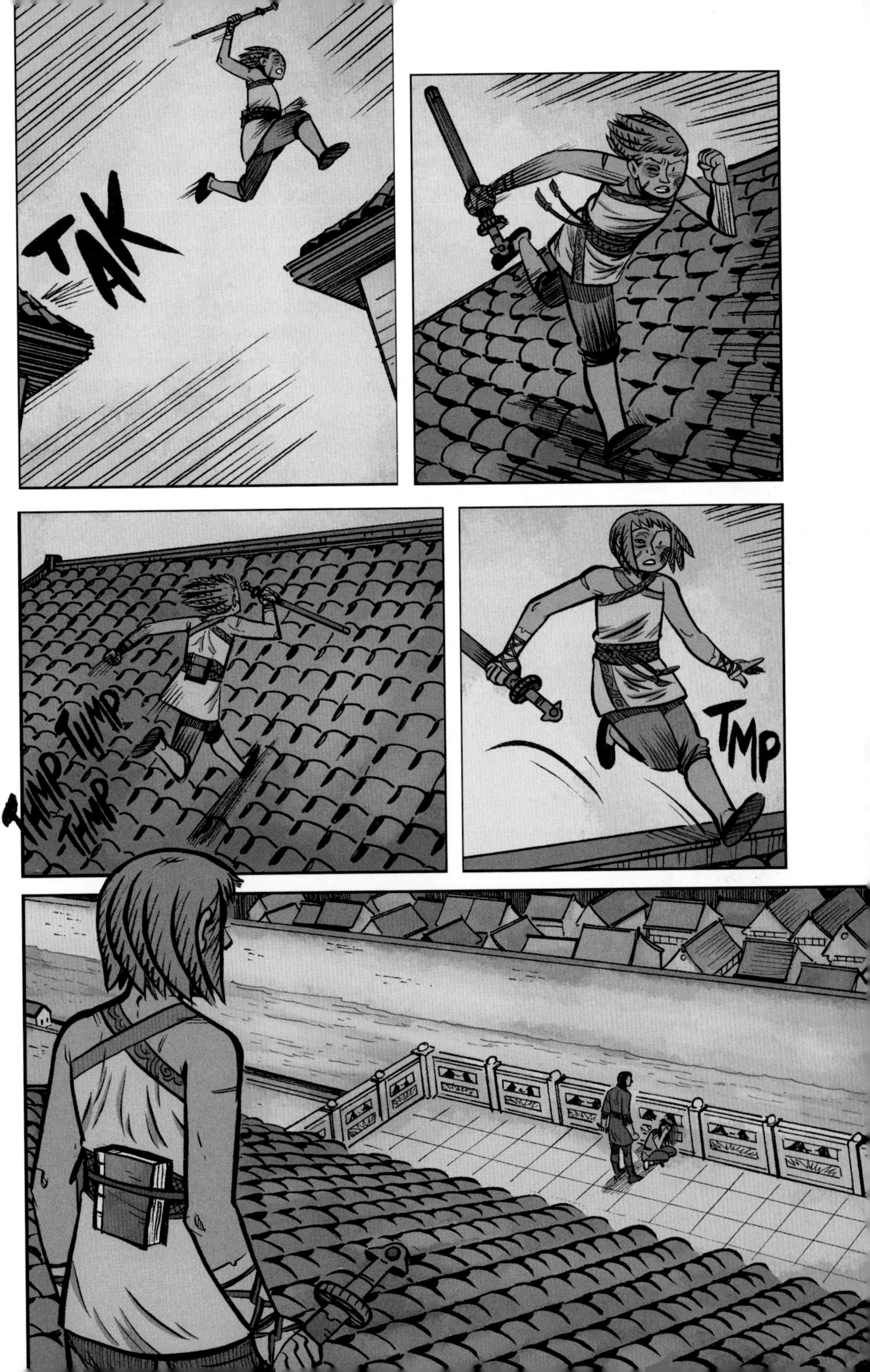
TAK
THMP THMP THMP
TMP

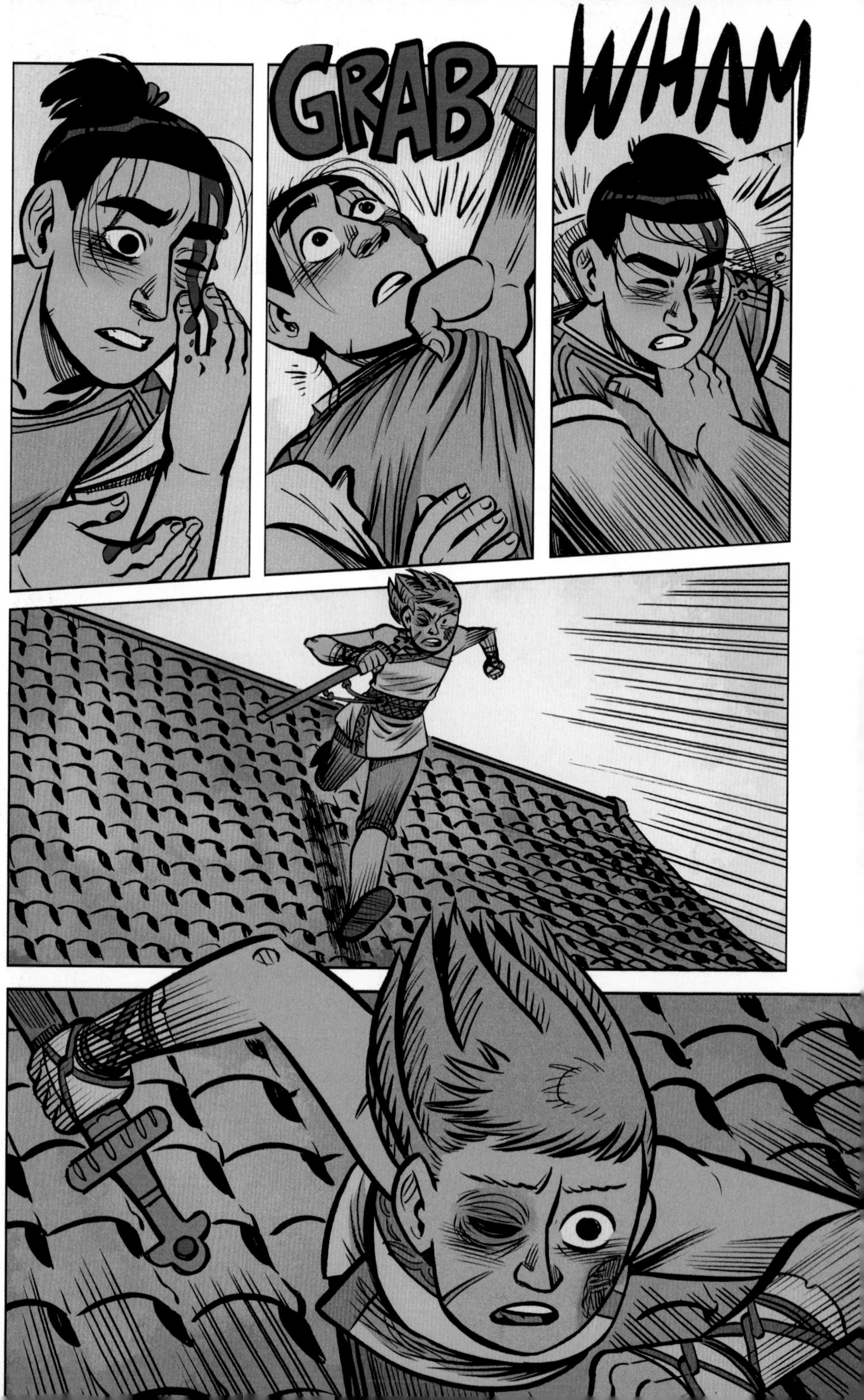
GRAB
WHAM

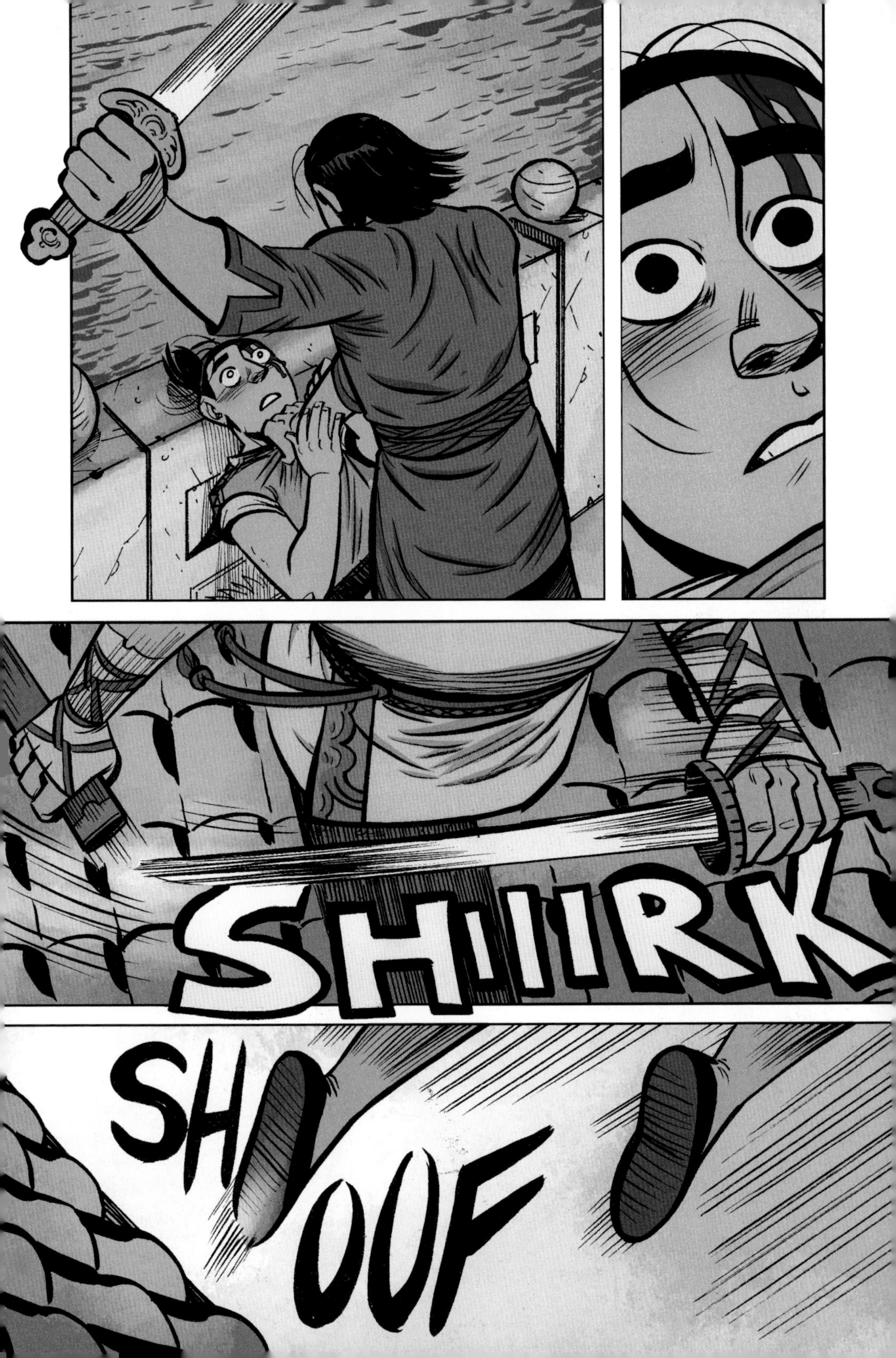
SHIIIRK
SHOOF

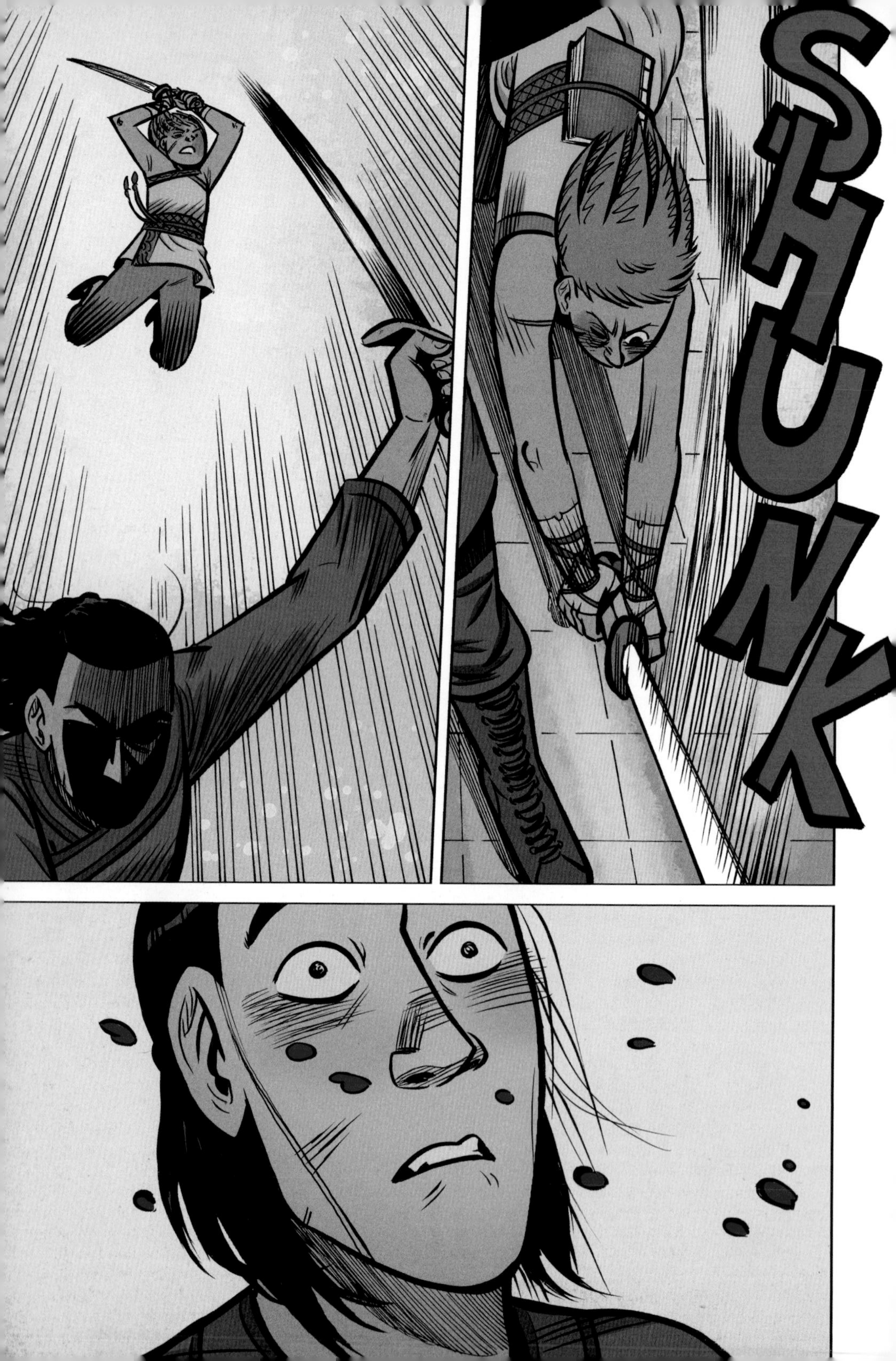
SHUNK

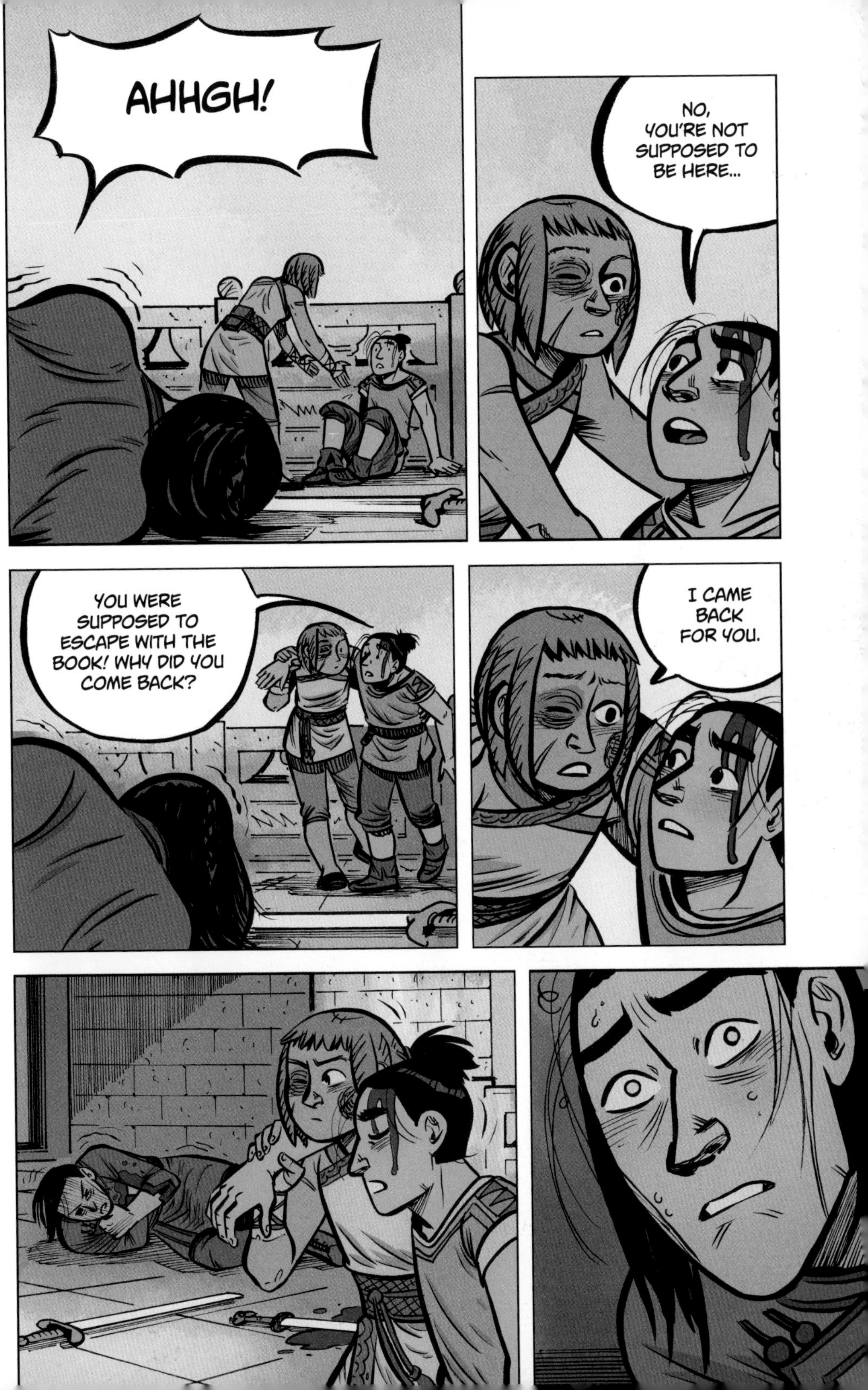
AHHGH!
NO, YOU'RE NOT SUPPOSED TO BE HERE...
YOU WERE SUPPOSED TO ESCAPE WITH THE BOOK! WHY DID YOU COME BACK?
I CAME BACK FOR YOU.

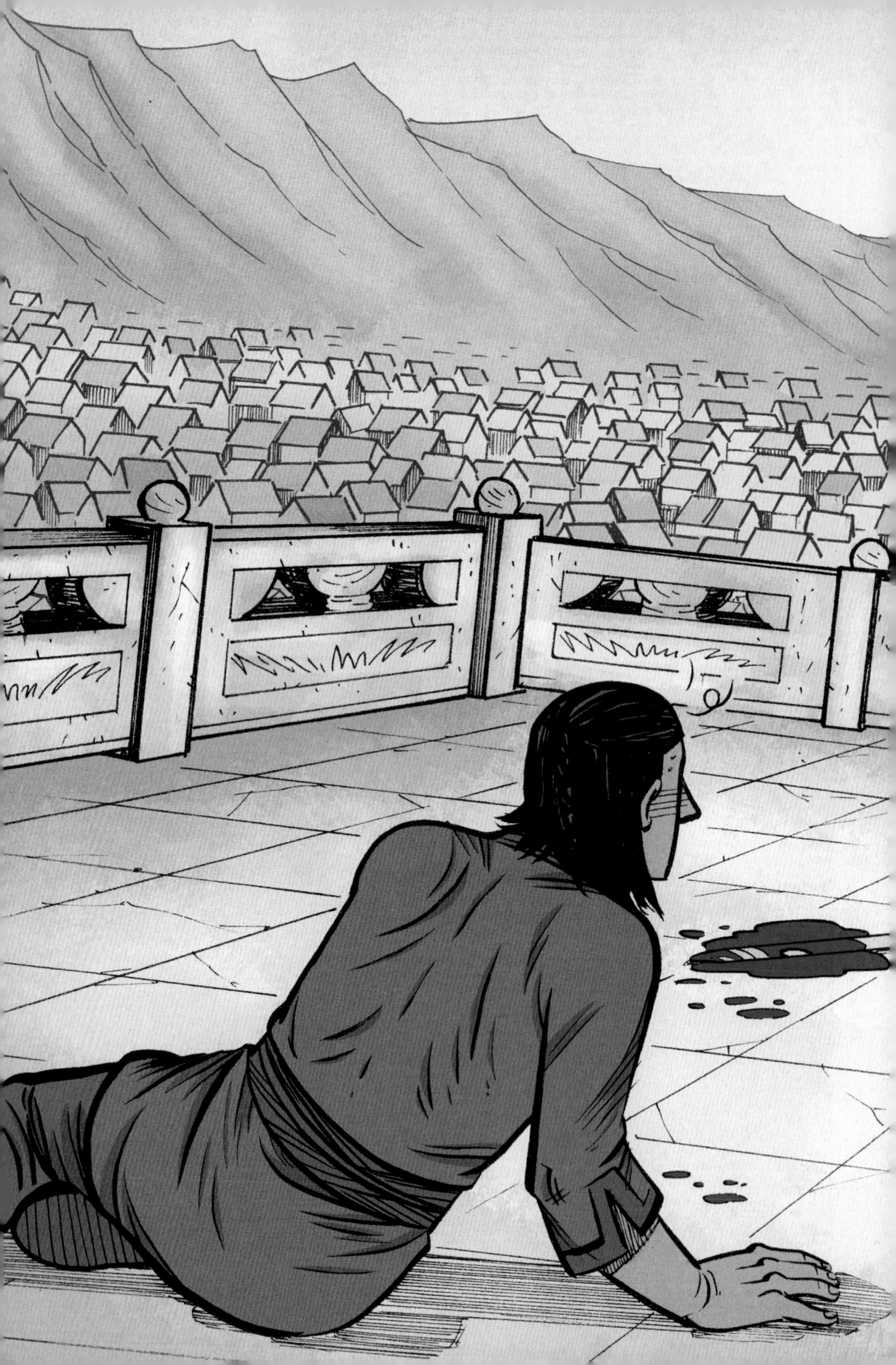

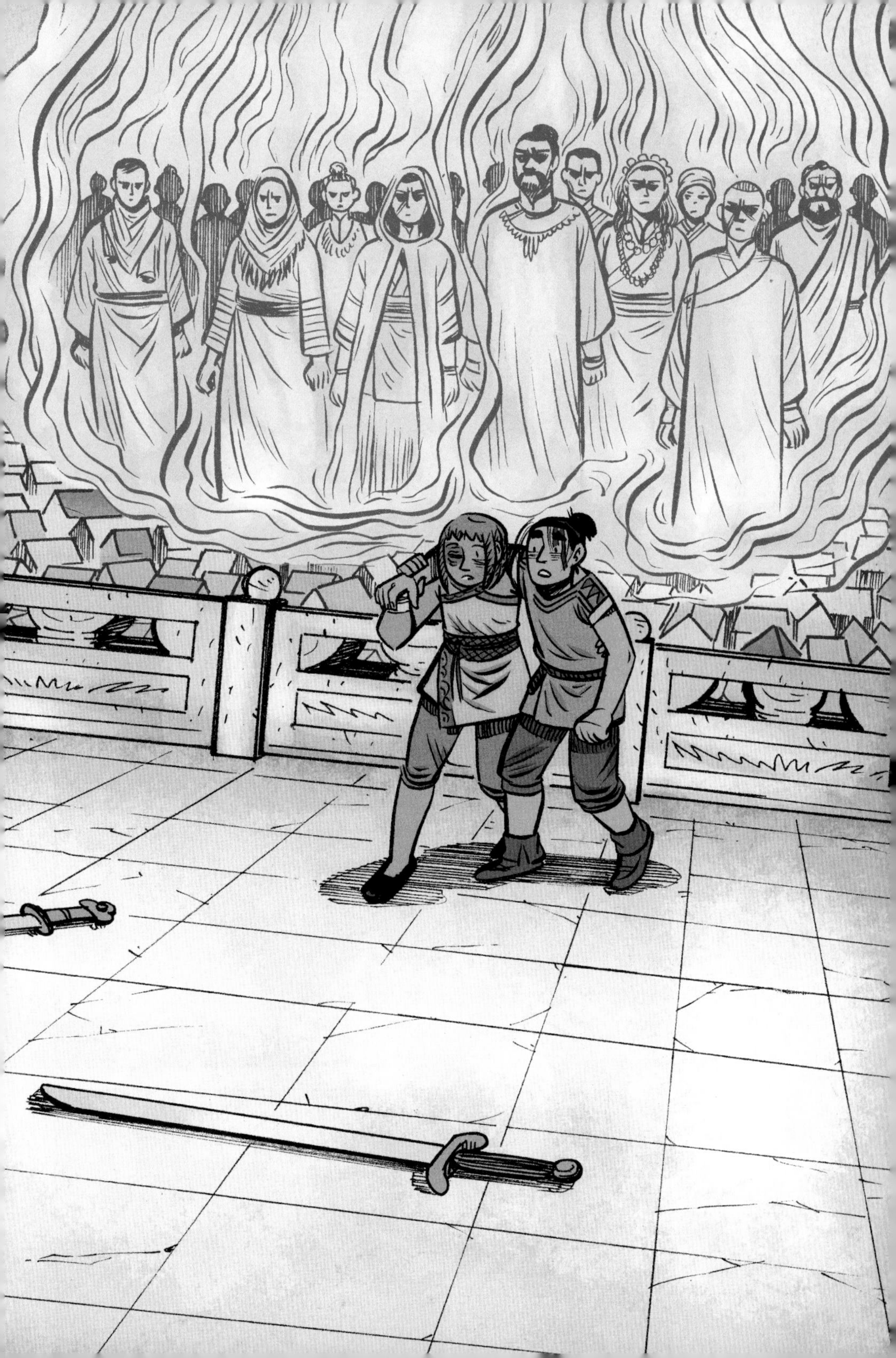

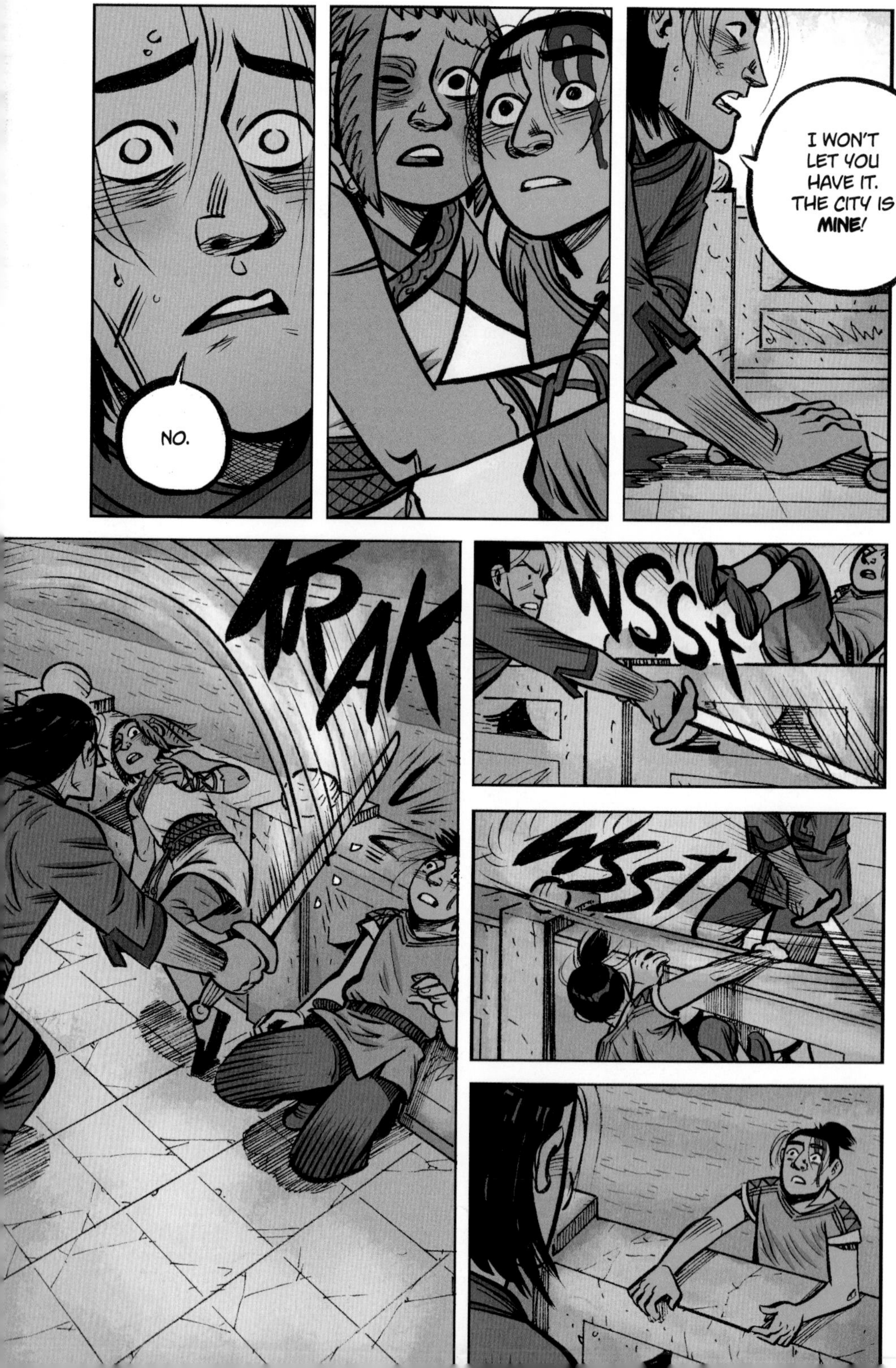
NO.
I WON'T LET YOU HAVE IT. THE CITY IS MINE!
KRAK
WSST
WSST

SHIIIING

NO!

MY REAL NAME
IS SETU.

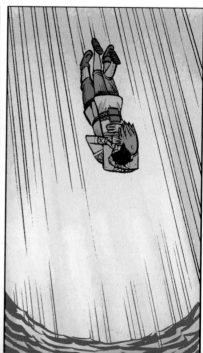

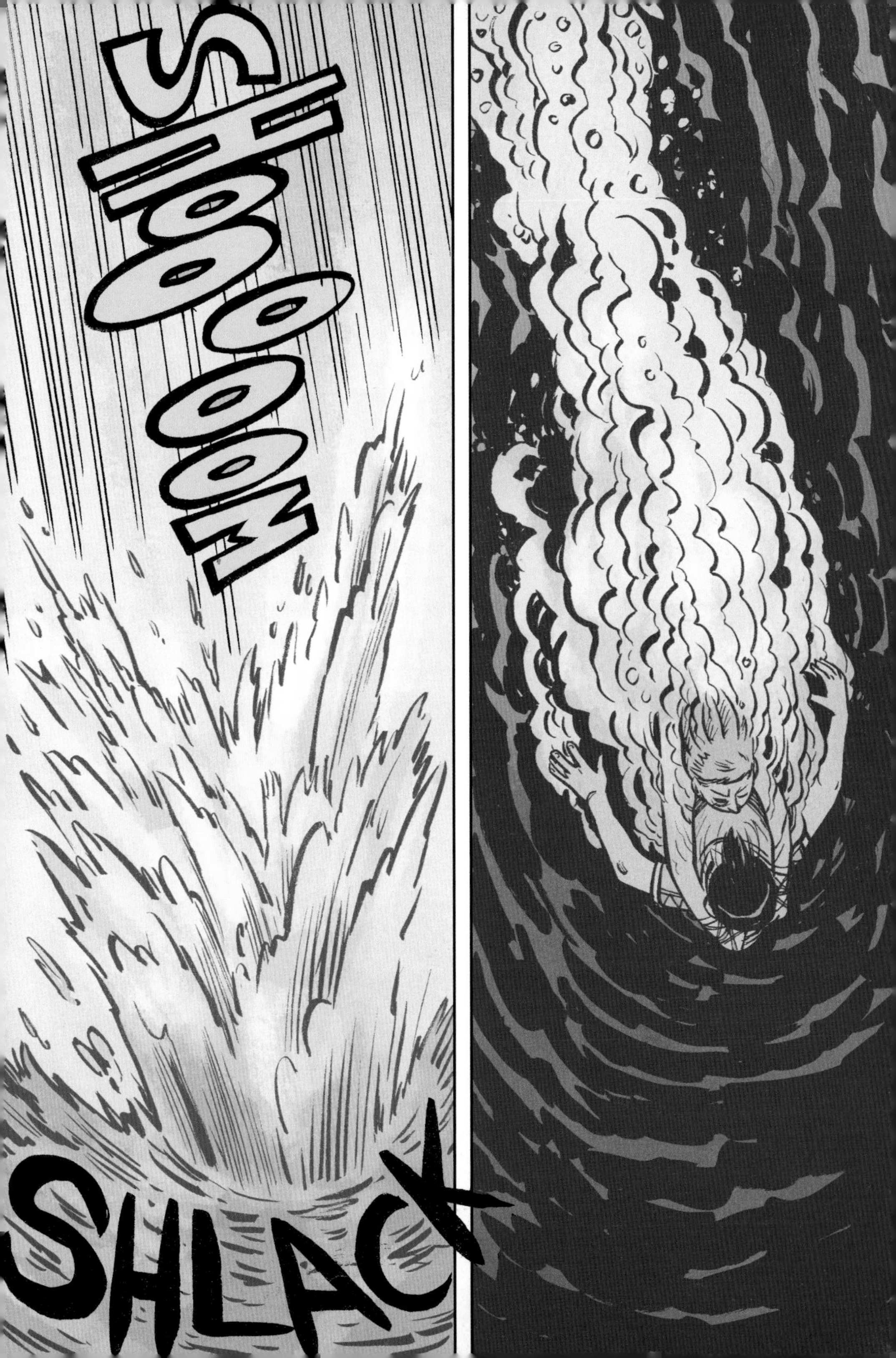
SHOOOOOOM
SHLACK

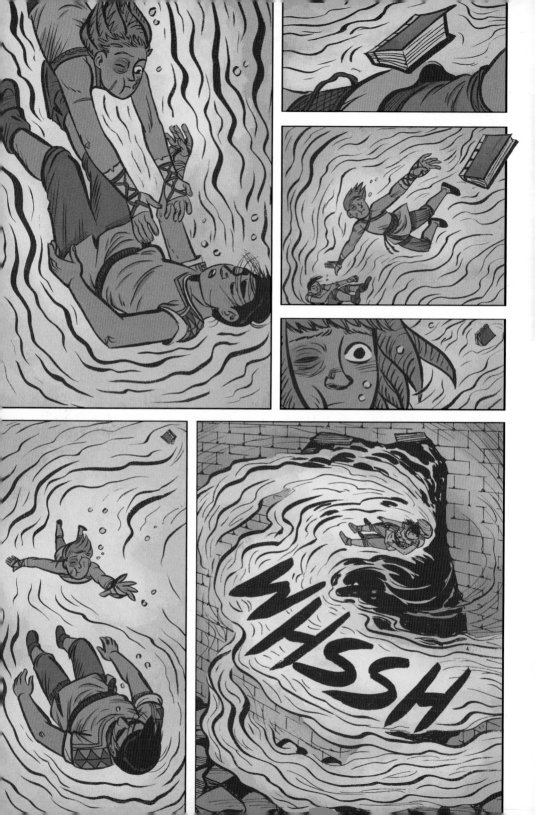

WHSSH

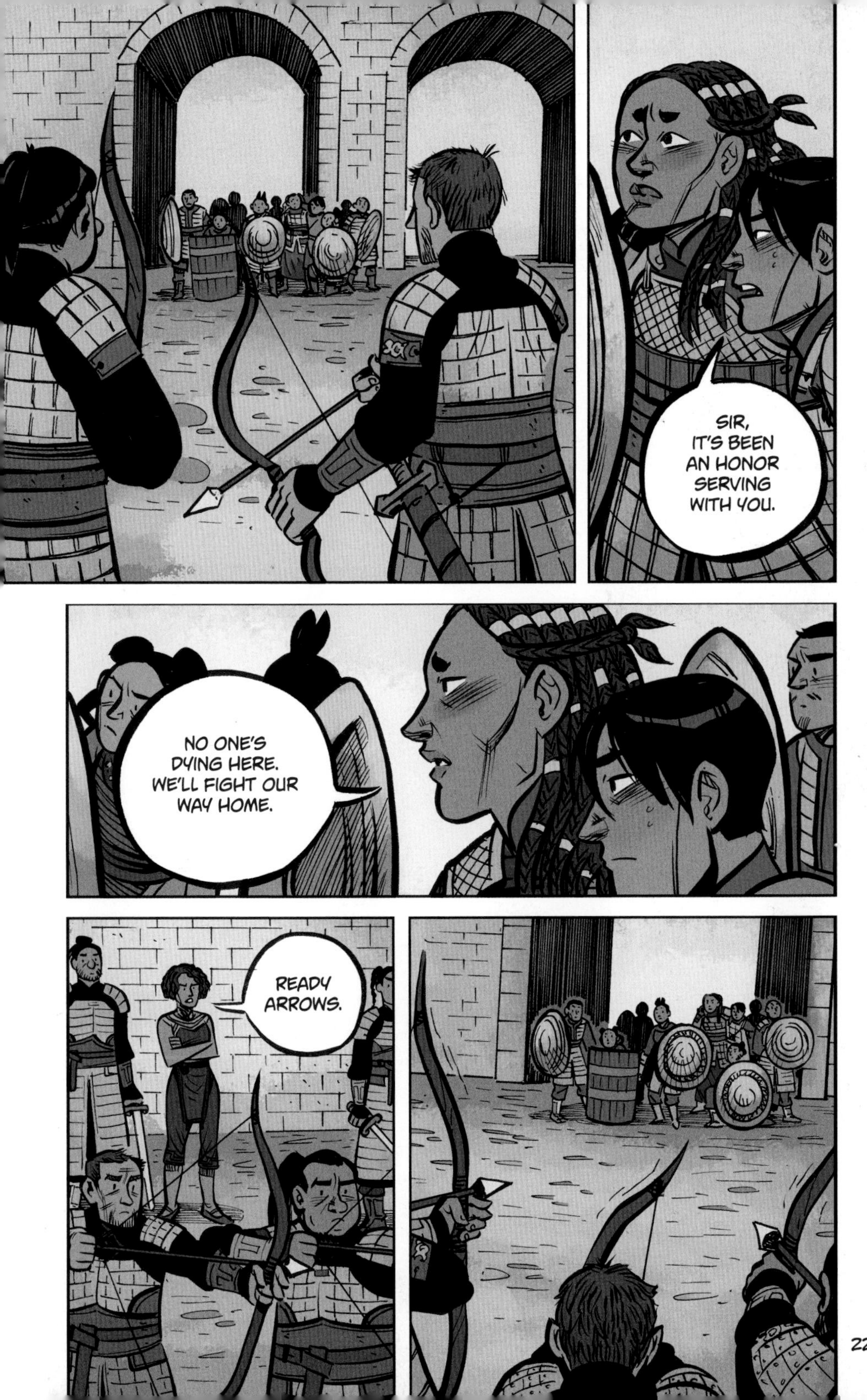
SIR, IT'S BEEN AN HONOR SERVING WITH YOU.
NO ONE'S DYING HERE. WE'LL FIGHT OUR WAY HOME.
READY ARROWS.

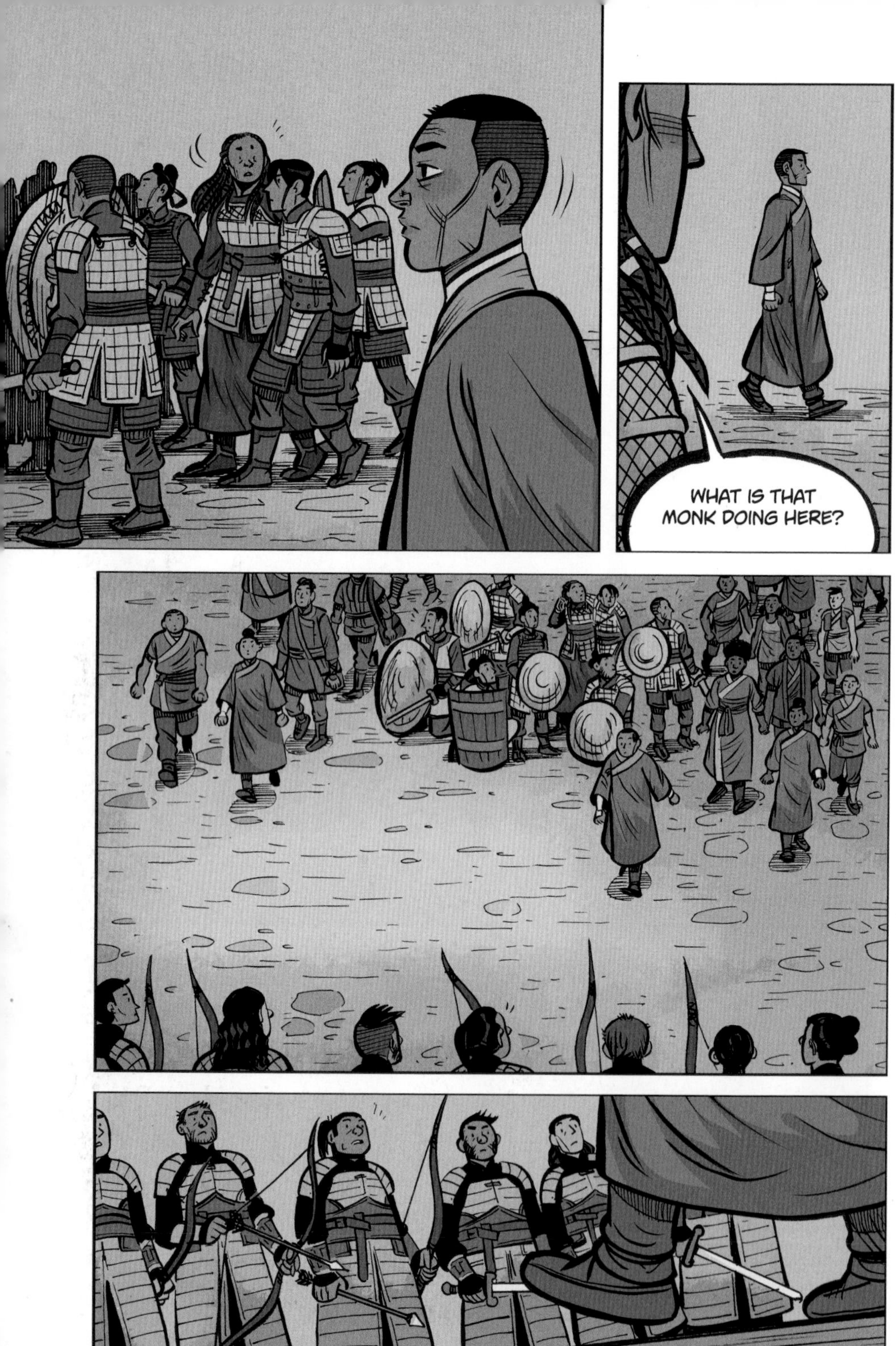
WHAT IS THAT
MONK DOING HERE?

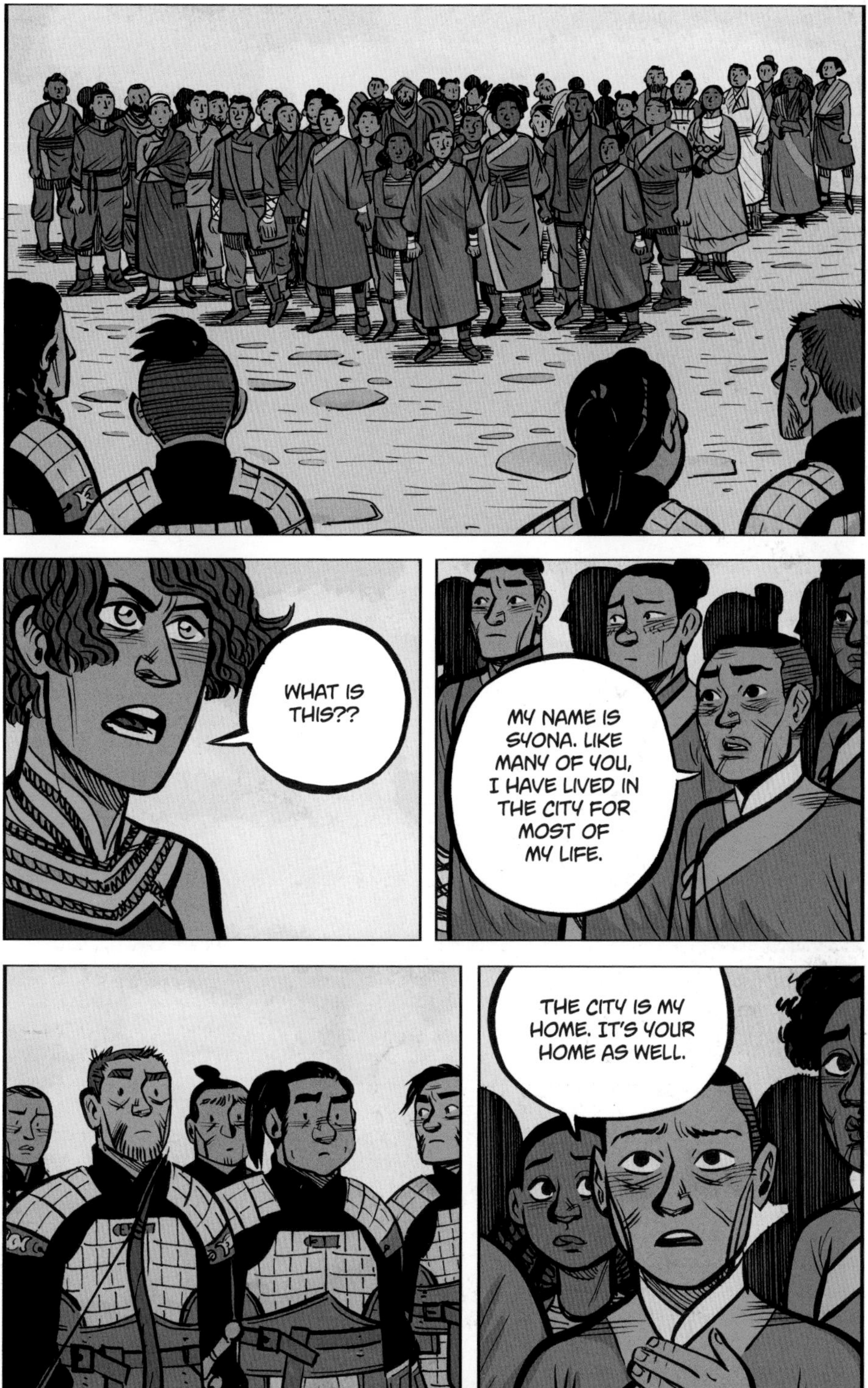
WHAT IS THIS??
MY NAME IS SYONA. LIKE MANY OF YOU, I HAVE LIVED IN THE CITY FOR MOST OF MY LIFE.
THE CITY IS MY HOME. IT'S YOUR HOME AS WELL.

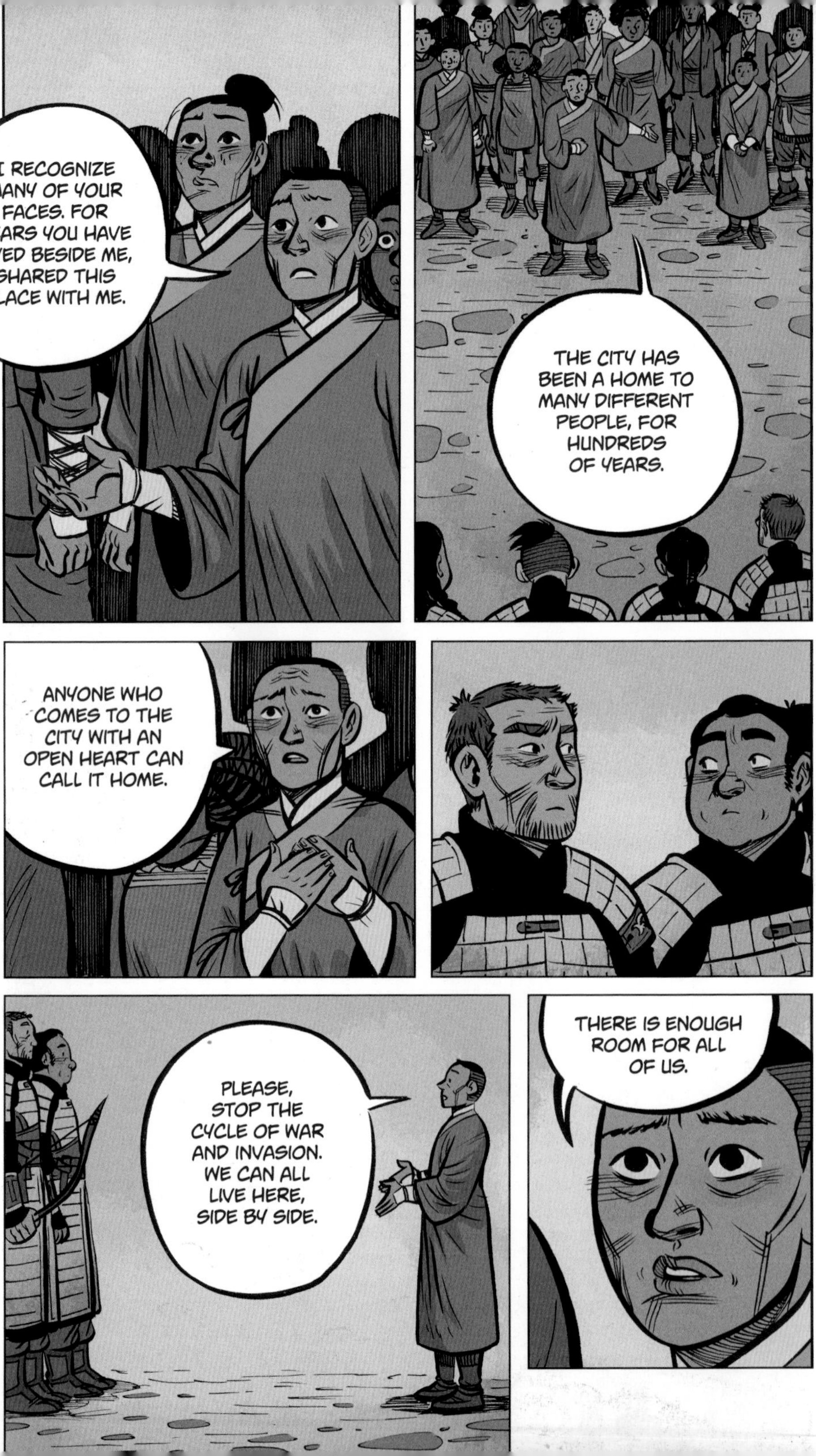
I RECOGNIZE MANY OF YOUR FACES. FOR YEARS YOU HAVE LIVED BESIDE ME, SHARED THIS PLACE WITH ME.
THE CITY HAS BEEN A HOME TO MANY DIFFERENT PEOPLE, FOR HUNDREDS OF YEARS.
ANYONE WHO COMES TO THE CITY WITH AN OPEN HEART CAN CALL IT HOME.
PLEASE, STOP THE CYCLE OF WAR AND INVASION. WE CAN ALL LIVE HERE, SIDE BY SIDE.
THERE IS ENOUGH ROOM FOR ALL OF US.

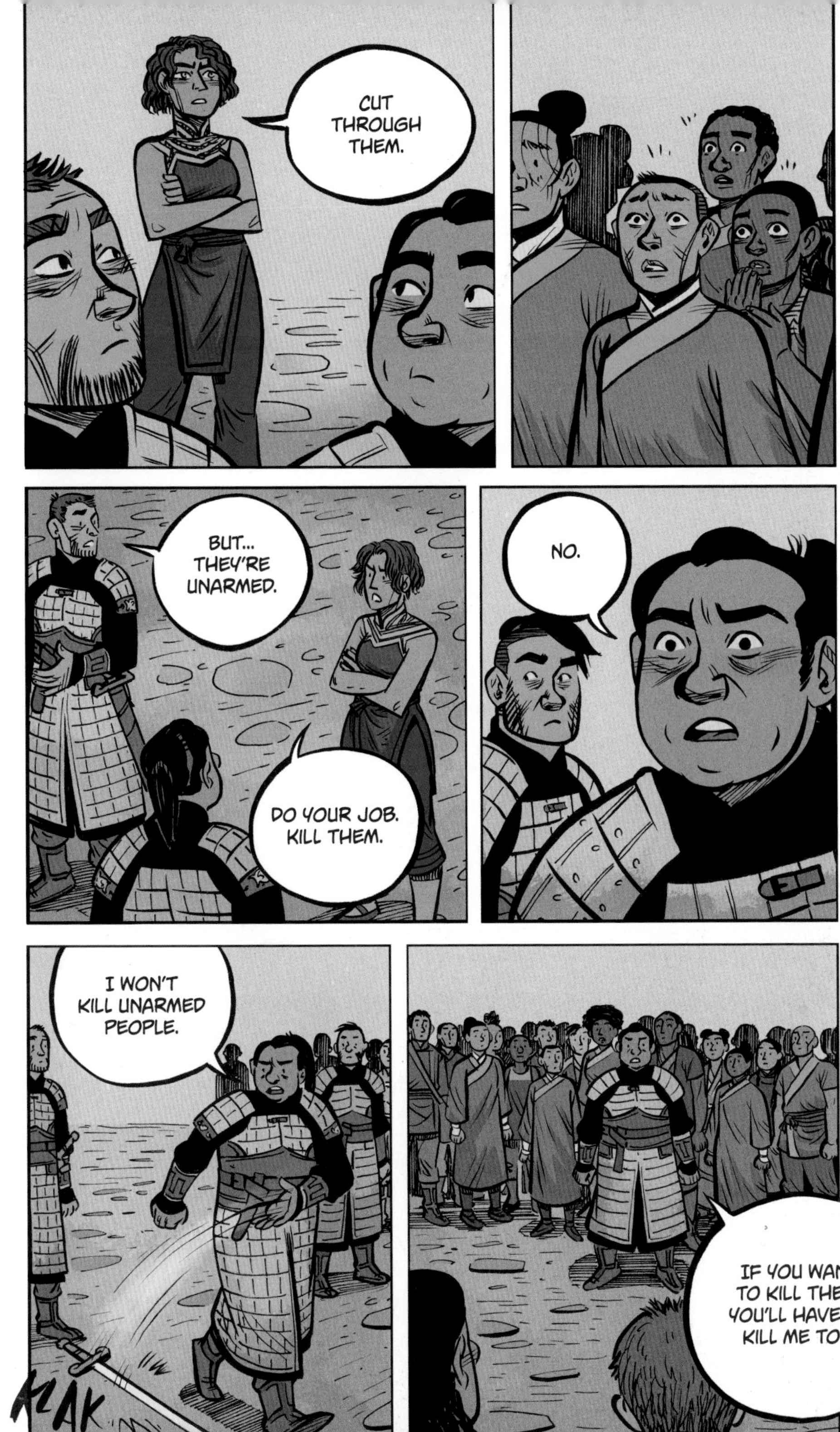
CUT THROUGH THEM.
BUT... THEY'RE UNARMED.
DO YOUR JOB. KILL THEM.
NO.
I WON'T KILL UNARMED PEOPLE.
KLAK
IF YOU WANT TO KILL THEM, YOU'LL HAVE TO KILL ME TOO.

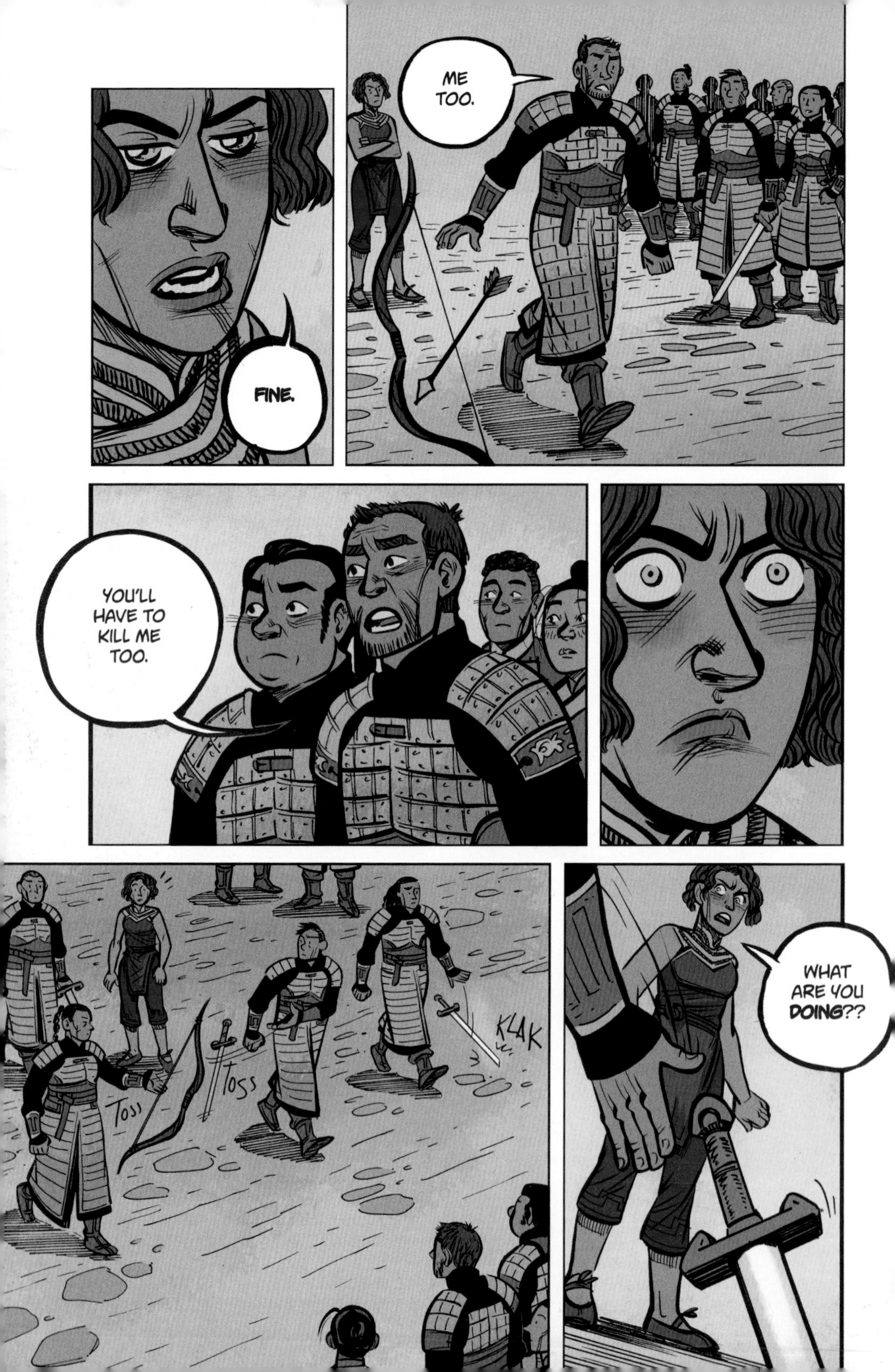
FINE.
ME TOO.
YOU'LL HAVE TO KILL ME TOO.
TOSS
TOSS
KLAK
WHAT ARE YOU **DOING**??

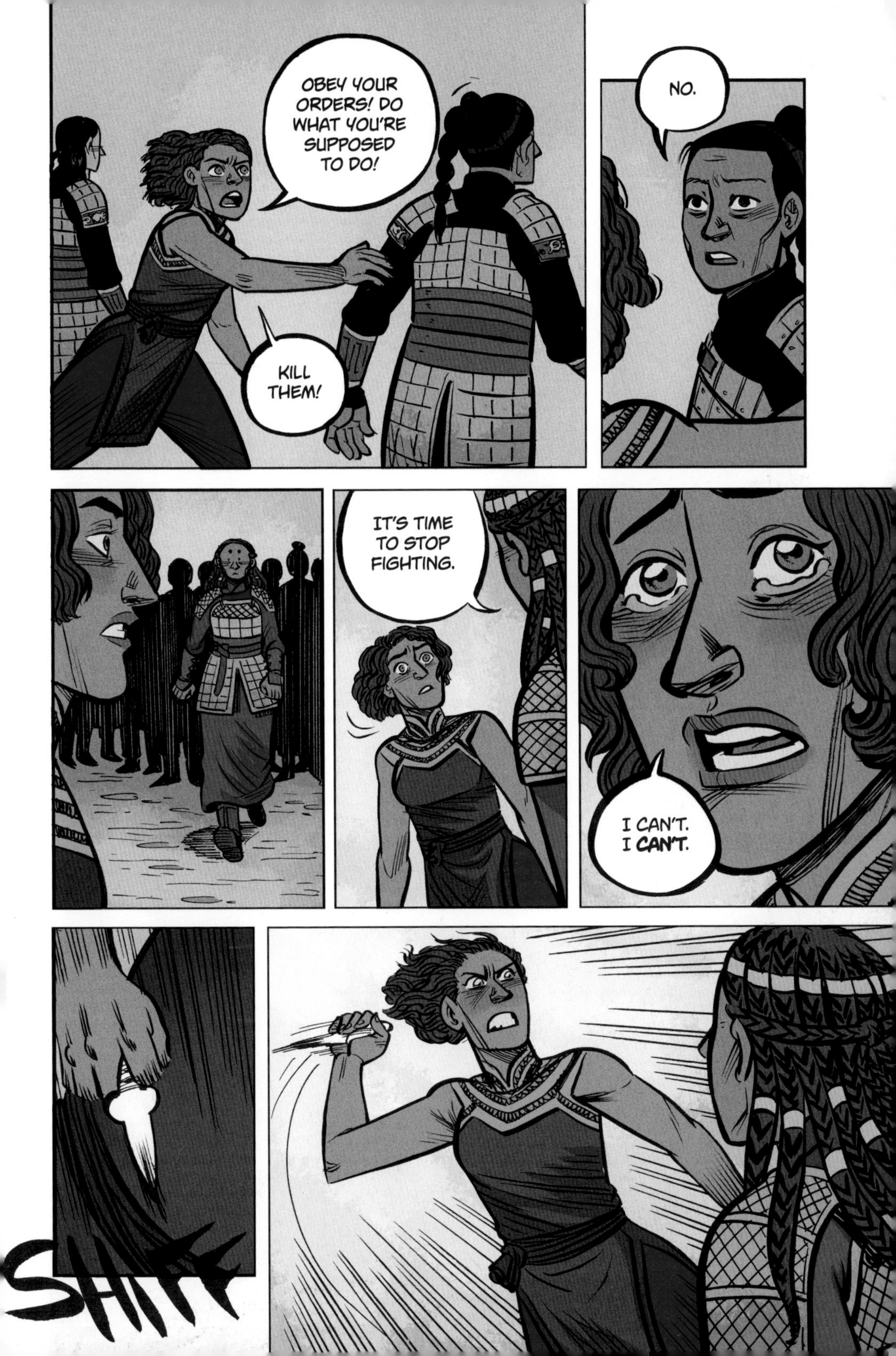
OBEY YOUR ORDERS! DO WHAT YOU'RE SUPPOSED TO DO!
KILL THEM!
NO.
IT'S TIME TO STOP FIGHTING.
I CAN'T. I **CAN'T**.
SHIFF

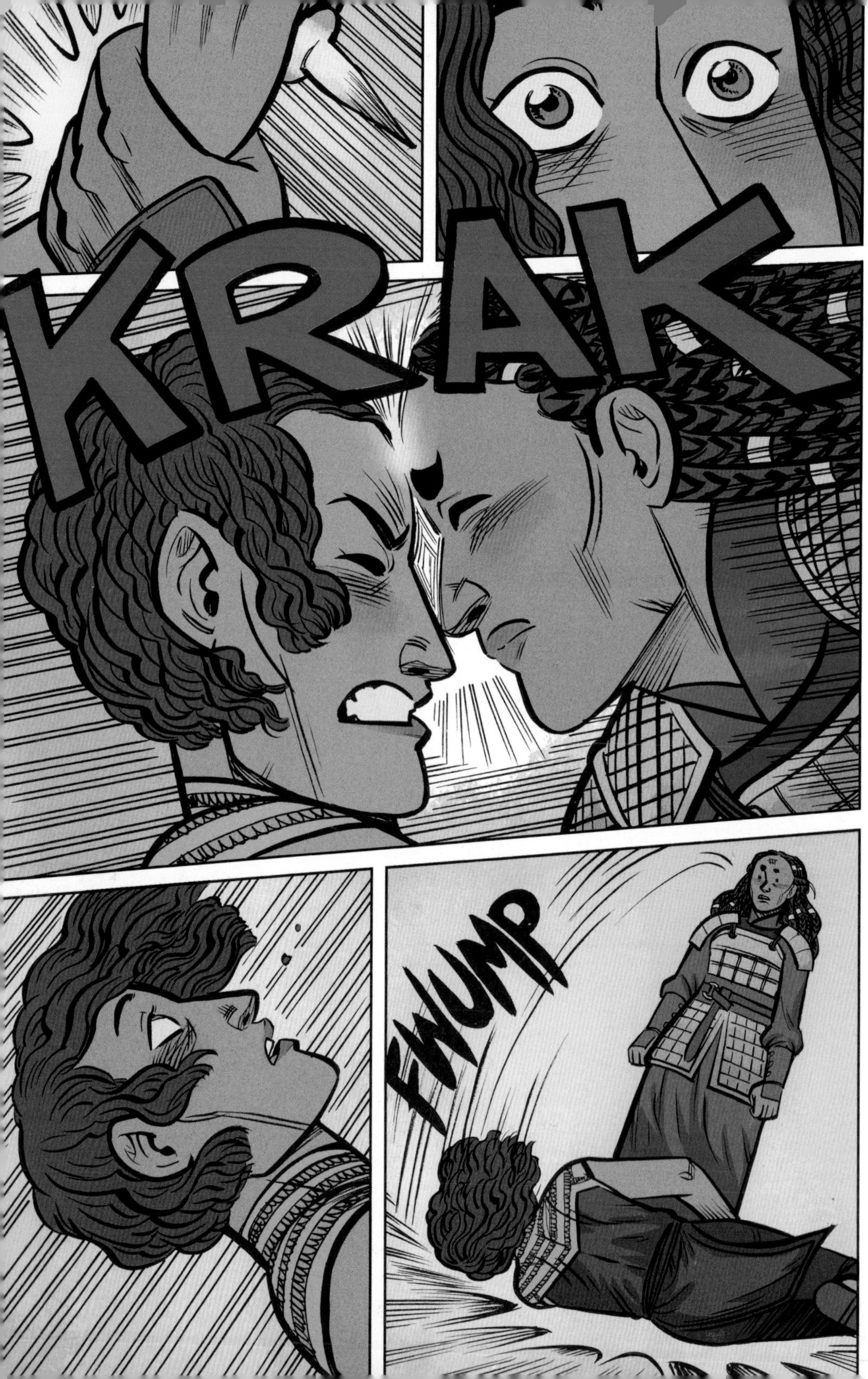
KRAK
FWUMP

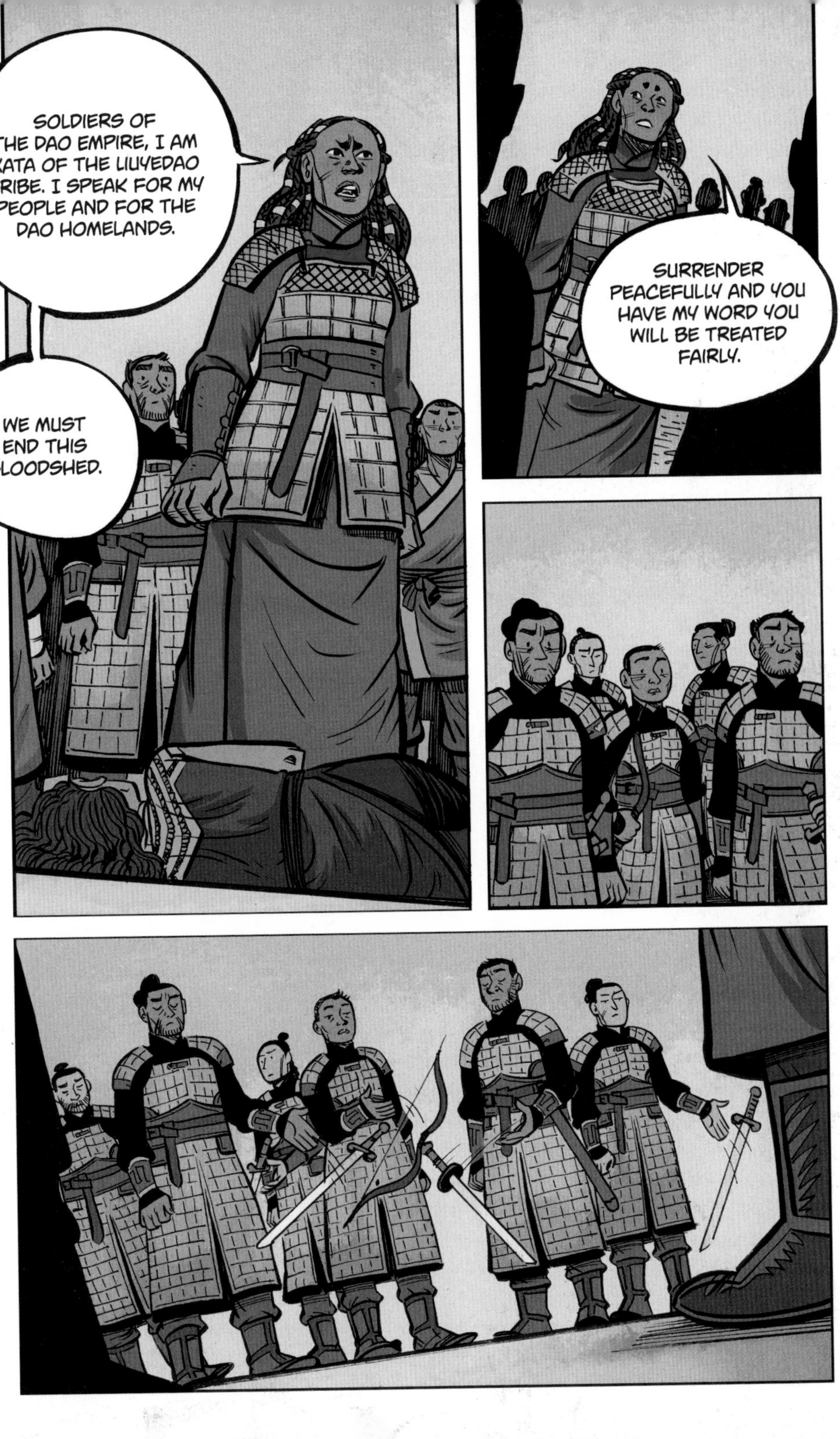
SOLDIERS OF THE DAO EMPIRE, I AM KATA OF THE LIUYEDAO TRIBE. I SPEAK FOR MY PEOPLE AND FOR THE DAO HOMELANDS.
WE MUST END THIS BLOODSHED.
SURRENDER PEACEFULLY AND YOU HAVE MY WORD YOU WILL BE TREATED FAIRLY.

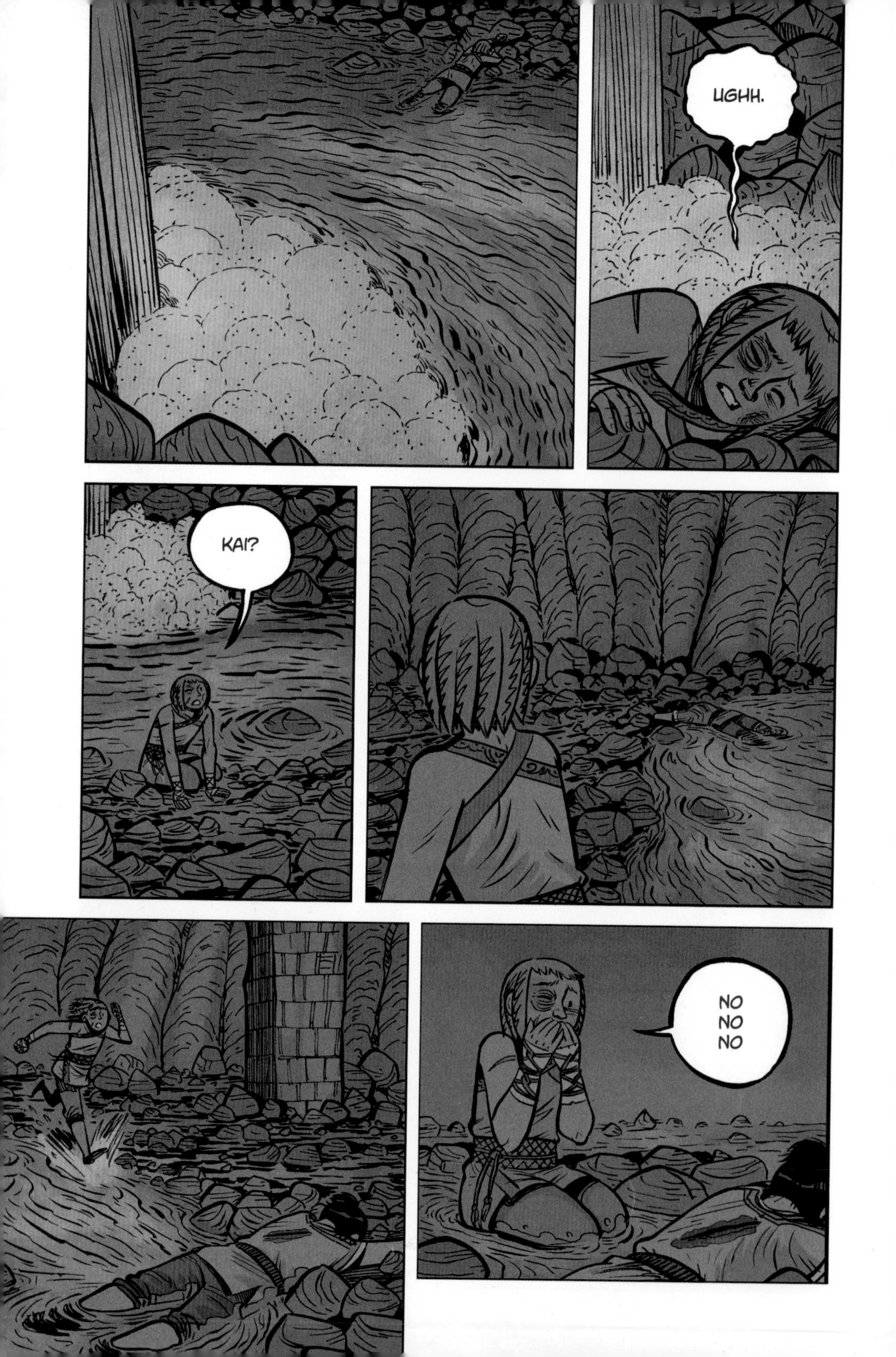
UGHH.
KAI?
NO
NO
NO

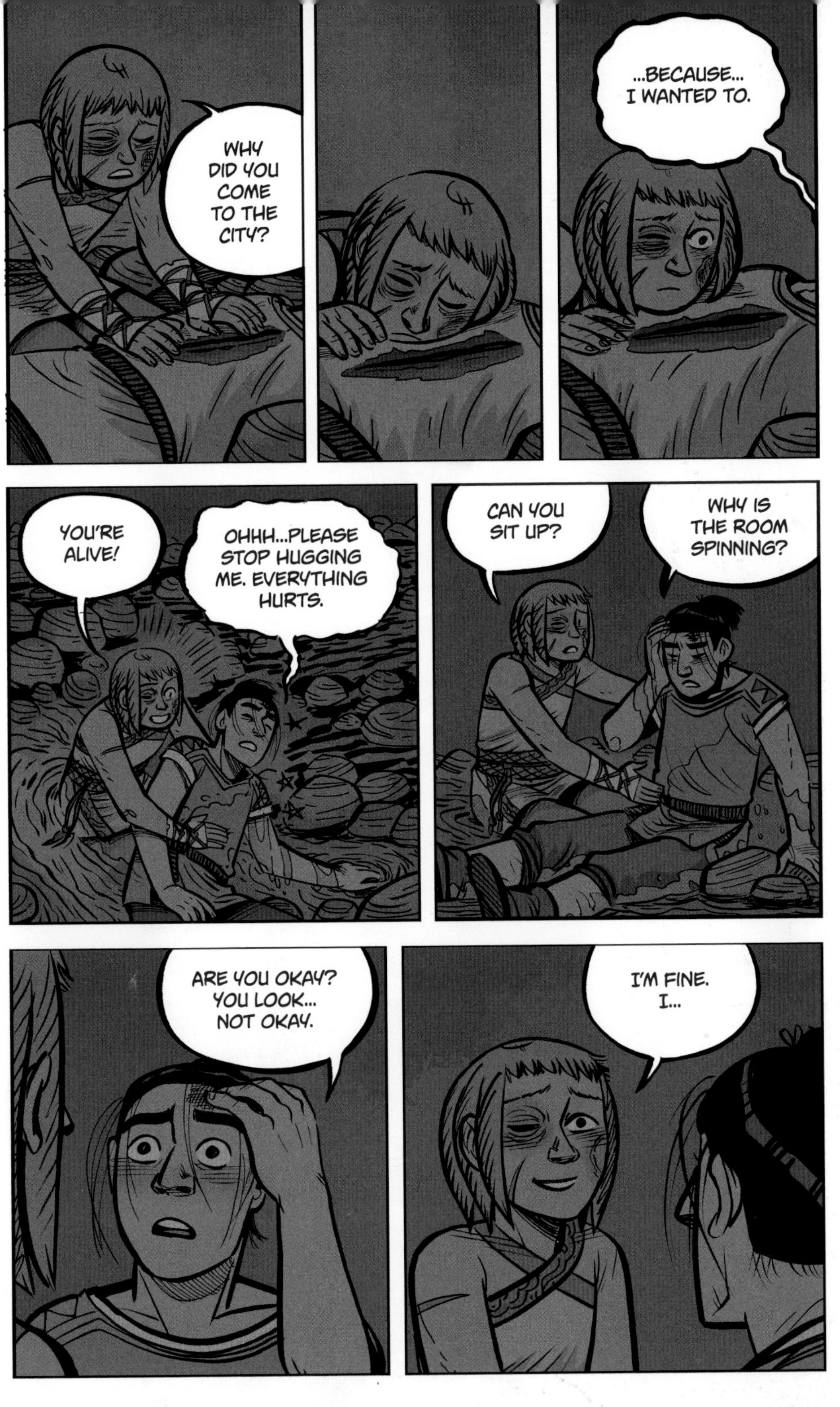
WHY DID YOU COME TO THE CITY?
...BECAUSE... I WANTED TO.
YOU'RE ALIVE!
OHHH...PLEASE STOP HUGGING ME. EVERYTHING HURTS.
CAN YOU SIT UP?
WHY IS THE ROOM SPINNING?
ARE YOU OKAY? YOU LOOK... NOT OKAY.
I'M FINE. I...

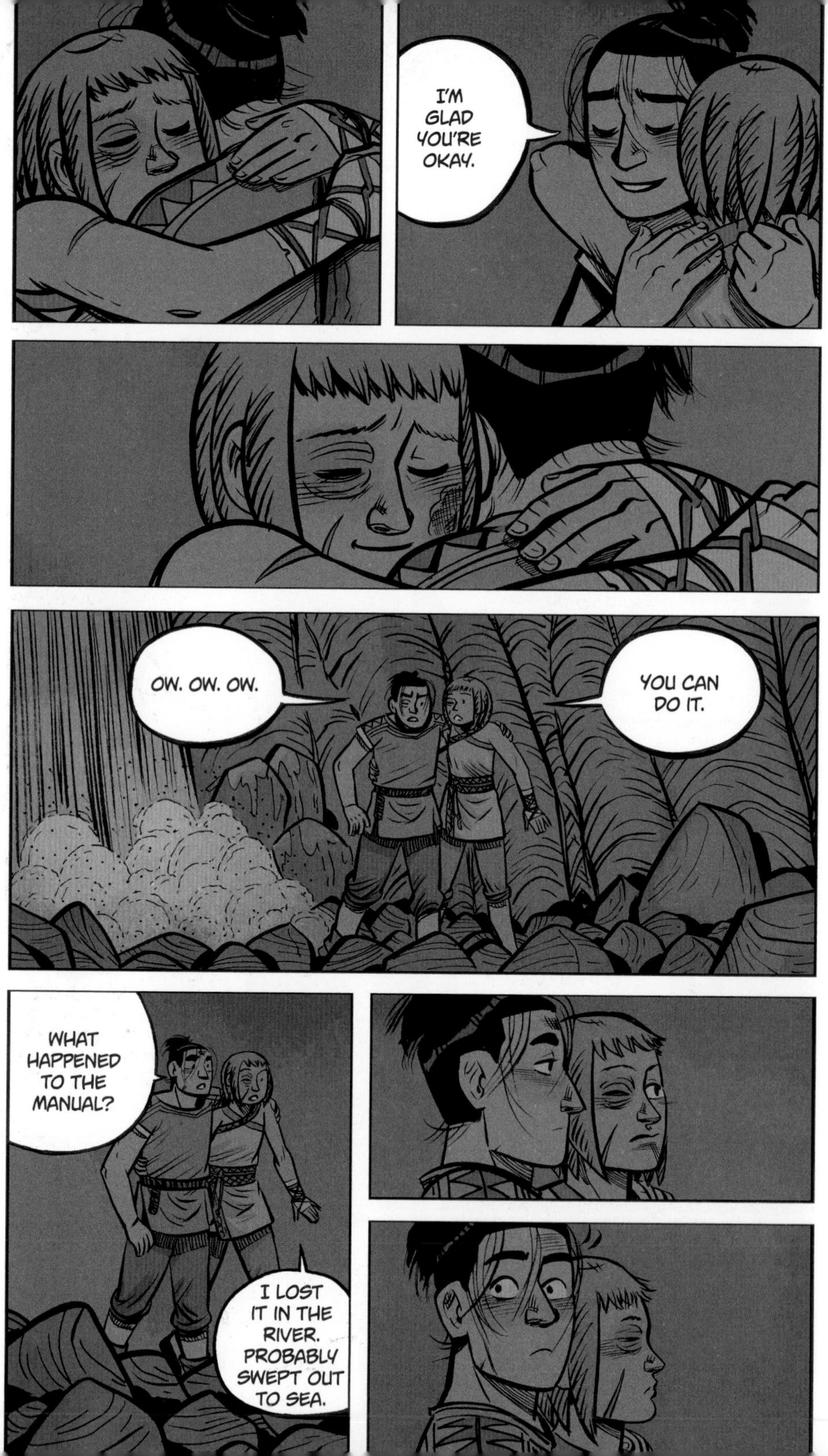
I'M GLAD YOU'RE OKAY.
OW. OW. OW.
YOU CAN DO IT.
WHAT HAPPENED TO THE MANUAL?
I LOST IT IN THE RIVER. PROBABLY SWEPT OUT TO SEA.

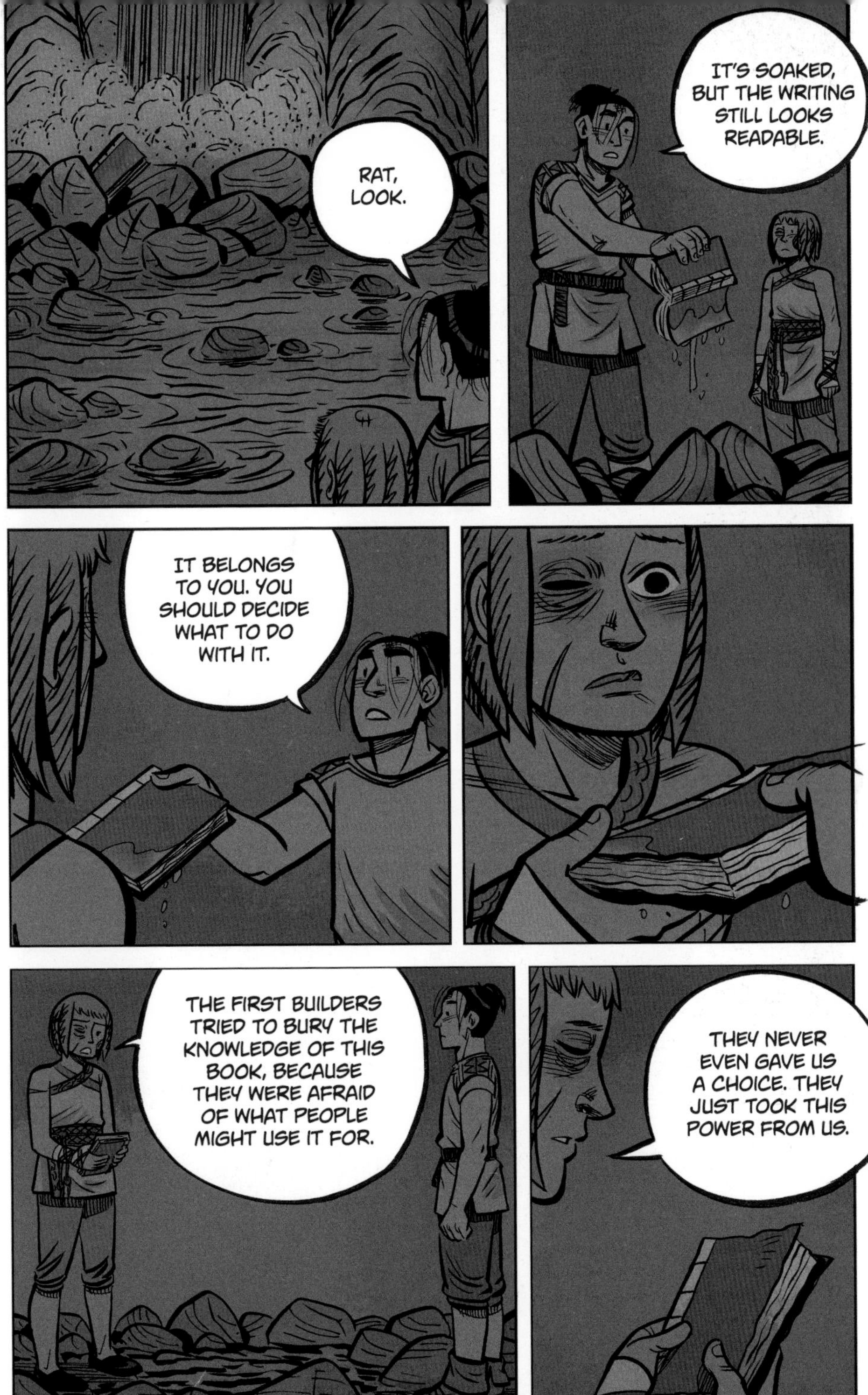
RAT, LOOK.
IT'S SOAKED, BUT THE WRITING STILL LOOKS READABLE.
IT BELONGS TO YOU. YOU SHOULD DECIDE WHAT TO DO WITH IT.
THE FIRST BUILDERS TRIED TO BURY THE KNOWLEDGE OF THIS BOOK, BECAUSE THEY WERE AFRAID OF WHAT PEOPLE MIGHT USE IT FOR.
THEY NEVER EVEN GAVE US A CHOICE. THEY JUST TOOK THIS POWER FROM US.

THERE WILL ALWAYS BE MEN LIKE ERZI, PEOPLE WHO WANT TO USE THIS POWER FOR WAR.

BUT I THINK THERE ARE MORE PEOPLE WHO WANT TO USE IT FOR PEACE.

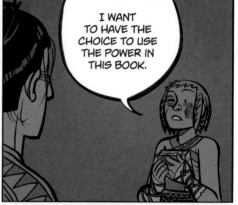

I WANT TO HAVE THE CHOICE TO USE THE POWER IN THIS BOOK.

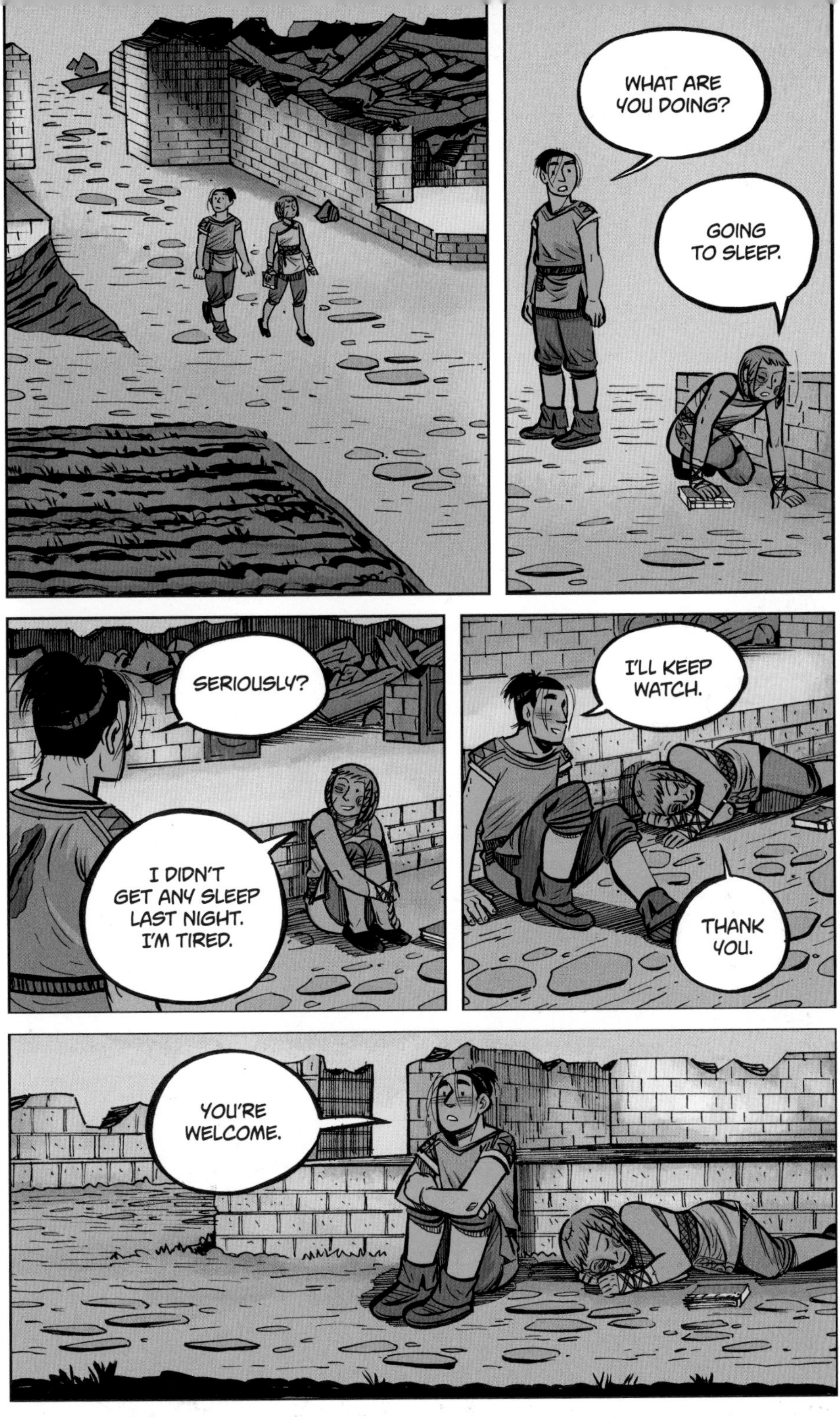
WHAT ARE YOU DOING?
GOING TO SLEEP.
SERIOUSLY?
I DIDN'T GET ANY SLEEP LAST NIGHT. I'M TIRED.
I'LL KEEP WATCH.
THANK YOU.
YOU'RE WELCOME.

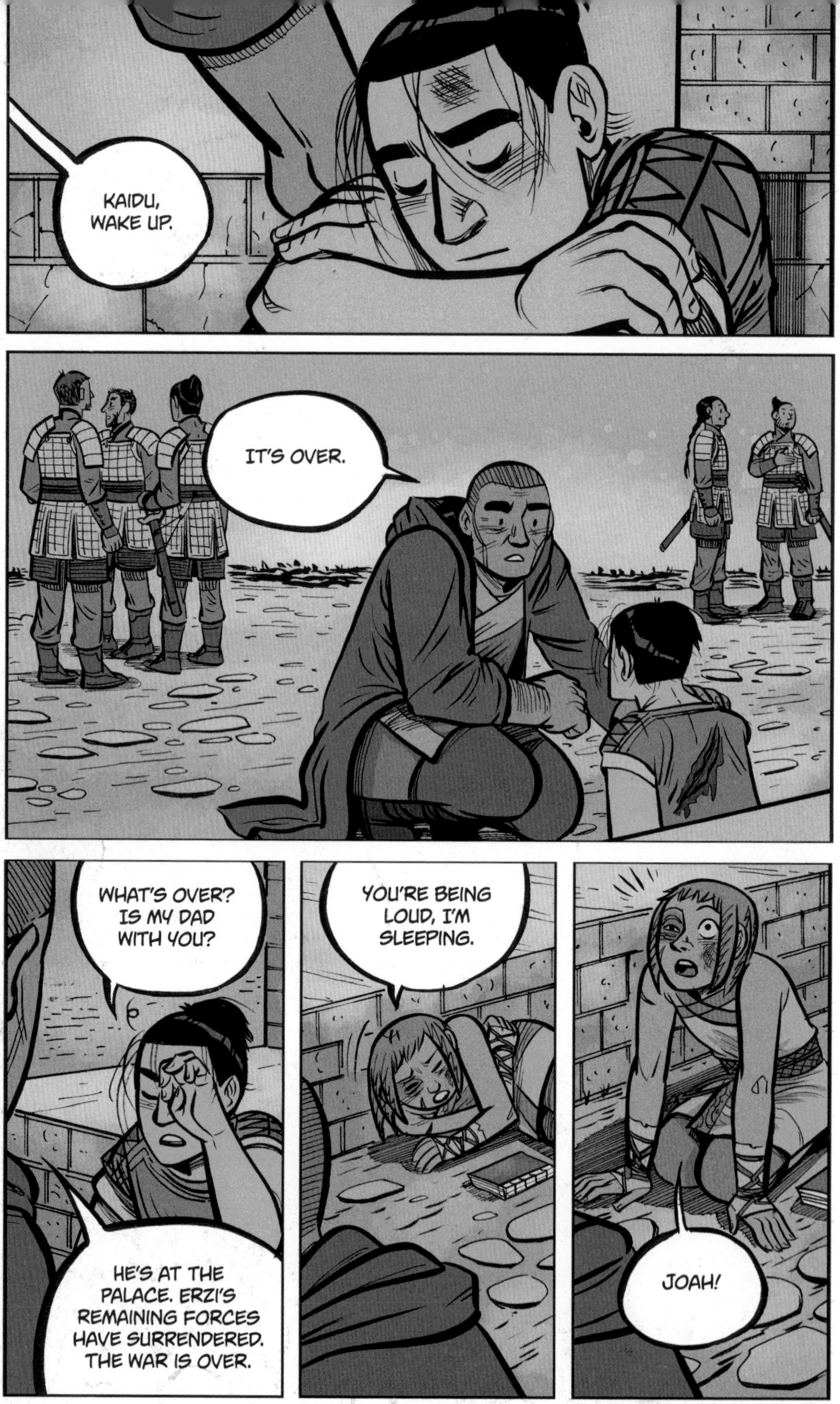
KAIDU, WAKE UP.
IT'S OVER.
WHAT'S OVER? IS MY DAD WITH YOU?
HE'S AT THE PALACE. ERZI'S REMAINING FORCES HAVE SURRENDERED. THE WAR IS OVER.
YOU'RE BEING LOUD, I'M SLEEPING.
JOAH!

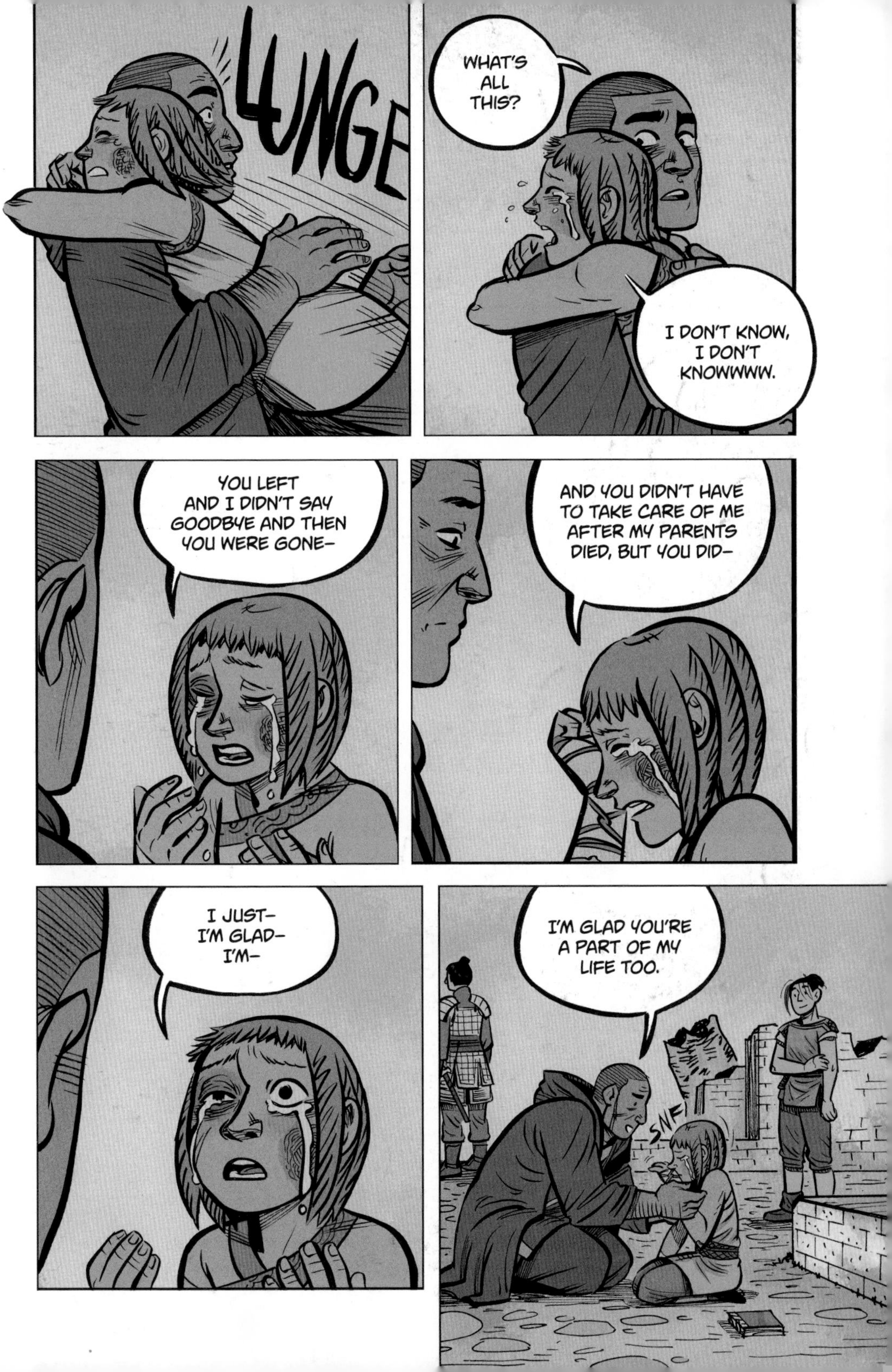
LUNGE
WHAT'S ALL THIS?
I DON'T KNOW, I DON'T KNOWWWW.
YOU LEFT AND I DIDN'T SAY GOODBYE AND THEN YOU WERE GONE–
AND YOU DIDN'T HAVE TO TAKE CARE OF ME AFTER MY PARENTS DIED, BUT YOU DID–
I JUST– I'M GLAD– I'M–
I'M GLAD YOU'RE A PART OF MY LIFE TOO.
SNF

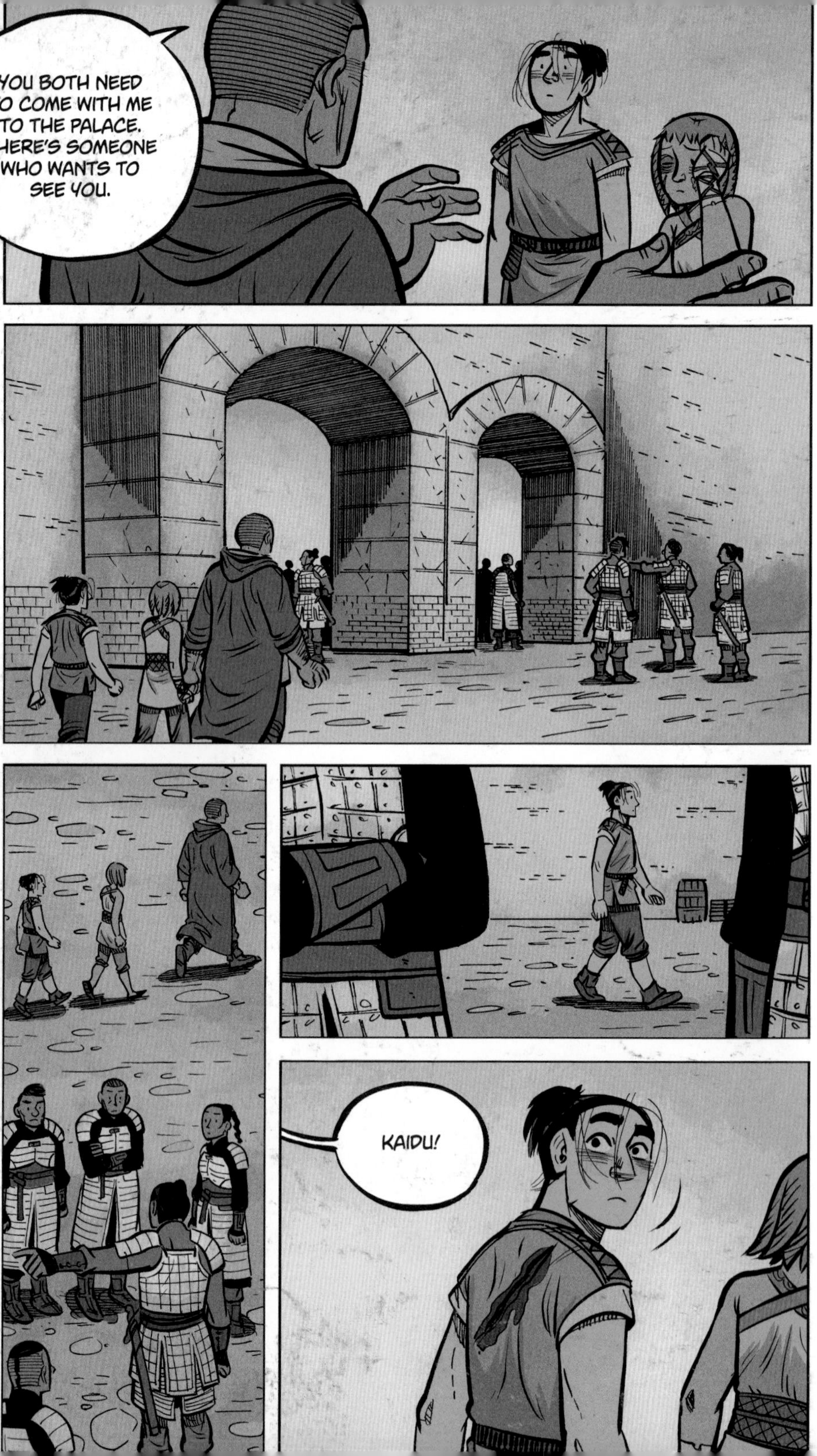
YOU BOTH NEED TO COME WITH ME TO THE PALACE. THERE'S SOMEONE WHO WANTS TO SEE YOU.
KAIDU!

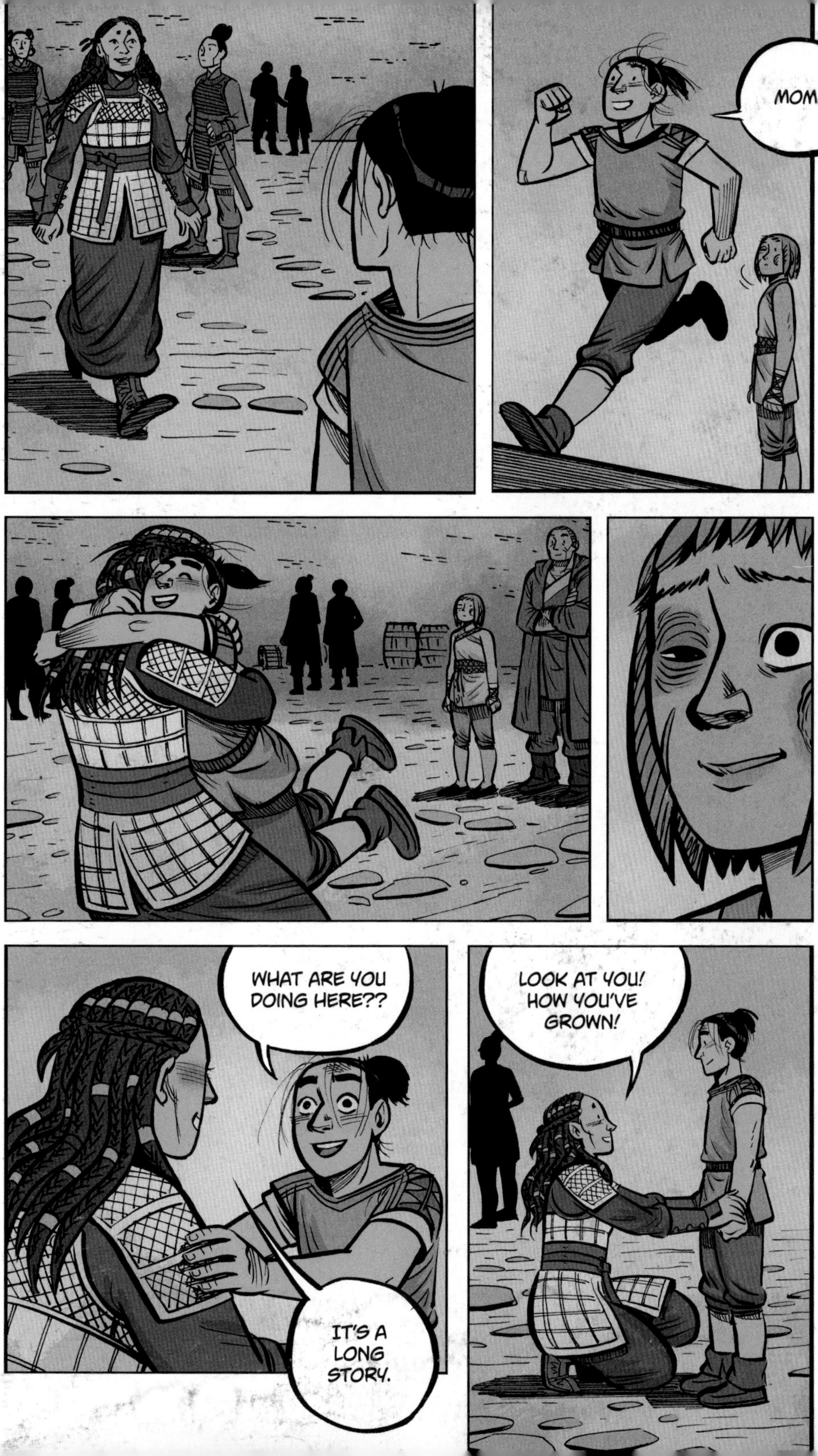
MOM!
WHAT ARE YOU DOING HERE??
IT'S A LONG STORY.
LOOK AT YOU! HOW YOU'VE GROWN!

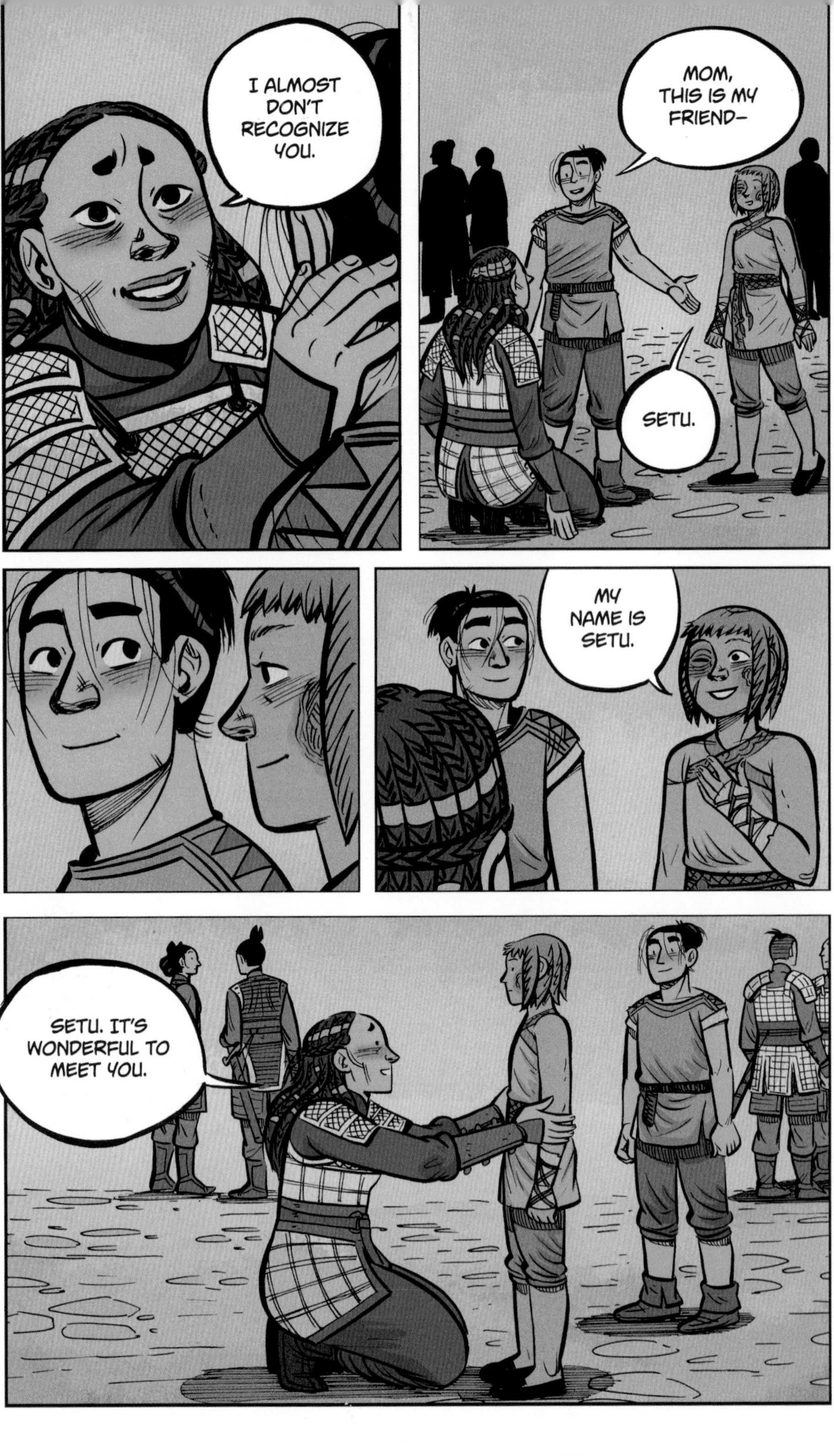
I ALMOST DON'T RECOGNIZE YOU.
MOM, THIS IS MY FRIEND–
SETU.
MY NAME IS SETU.
SETU. IT'S WONDERFUL TO MEET YOU.

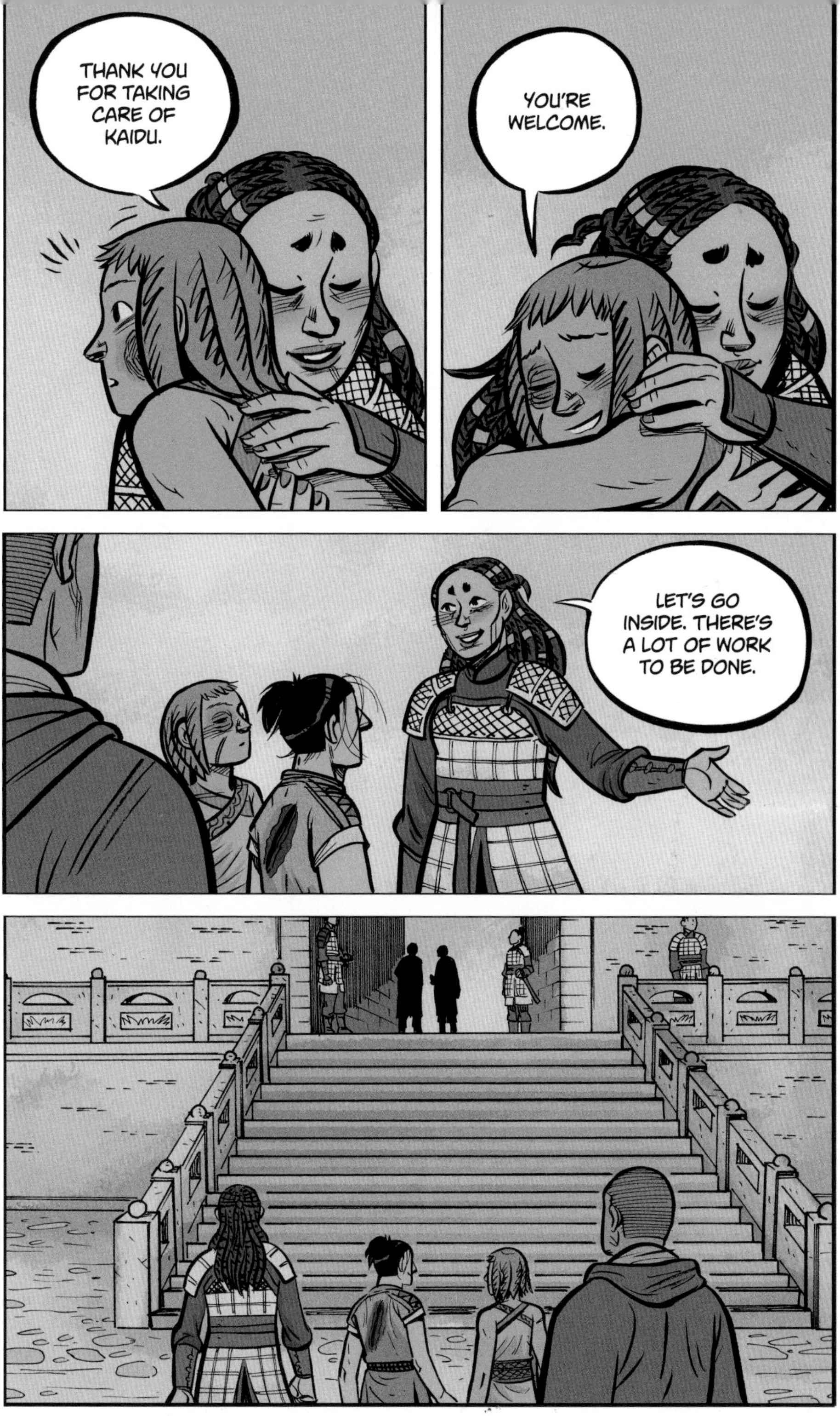
THANK YOU FOR TAKING CARE OF KAIDU.
YOU'RE WELCOME.
LET'S GO INSIDE. THERE'S A LOT OF WORK TO BE DONE.

DAY 10

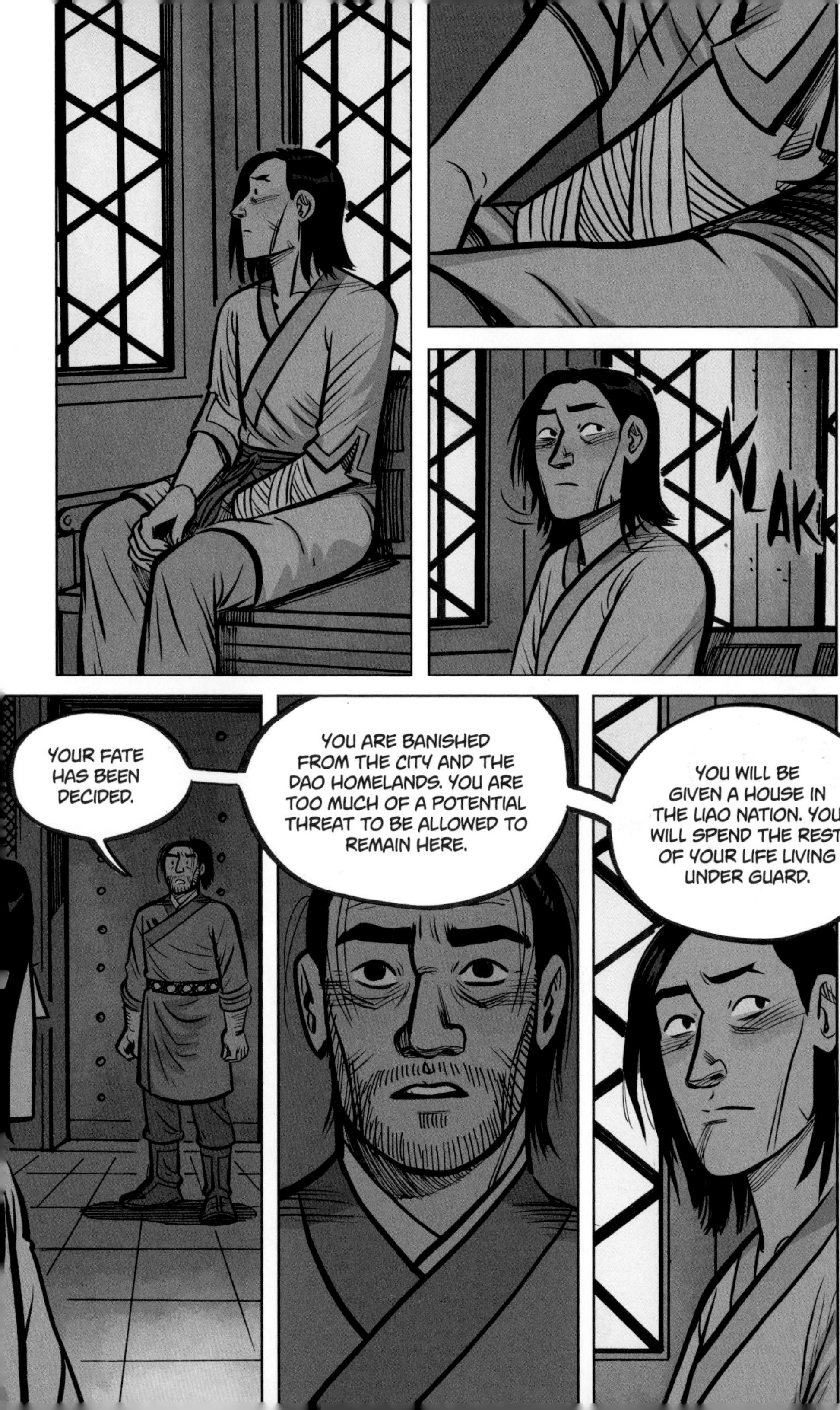
KLAK
YOUR FATE HAS BEEN DECIDED.
YOU ARE BANISHED FROM THE CITY AND THE DAO HOMELANDS. YOU ARE TOO MUCH OF A POTENTIAL THREAT TO BE ALLOWED TO REMAIN HERE.
YOU WILL BE GIVEN A HOUSE IN THE LIAO NATION. YOU WILL SPEND THE REST OF YOUR LIFE LIVING UNDER GUARD.

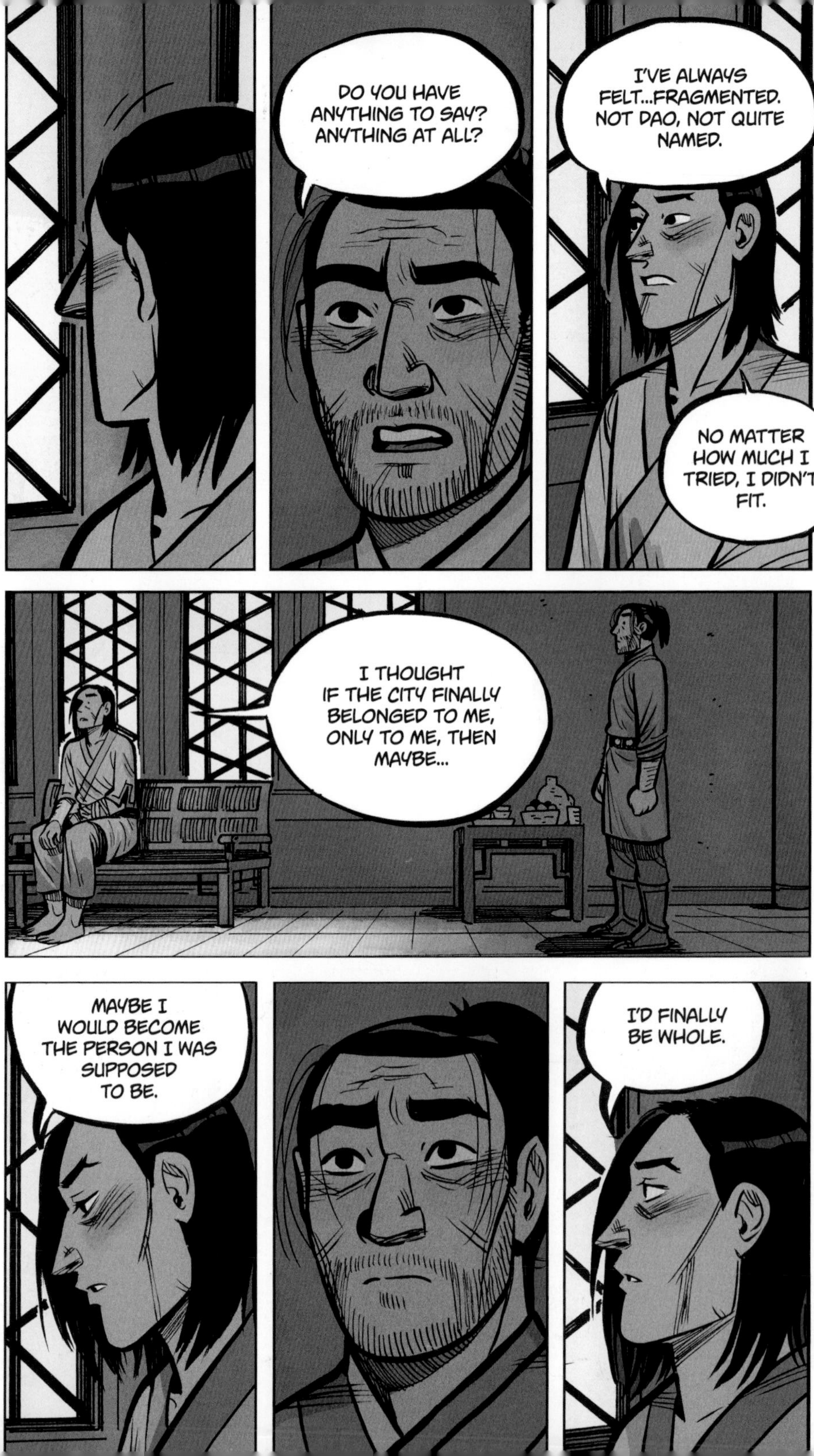
DO YOU HAVE ANYTHING TO SAY? ANYTHING AT ALL?
I'VE ALWAYS FELT...FRAGMENTED. NOT DAO, NOT QUITE NAMED.
NO MATTER HOW MUCH I TRIED, I DIDN'T FIT.
I THOUGHT IF THE CITY FINALLY BELONGED TO ME, ONLY TO ME, THEN MAYBE...
MAYBE I WOULD BECOME THE PERSON I WAS SUPPOSED TO BE.
I'D FINALLY BE WHOLE.

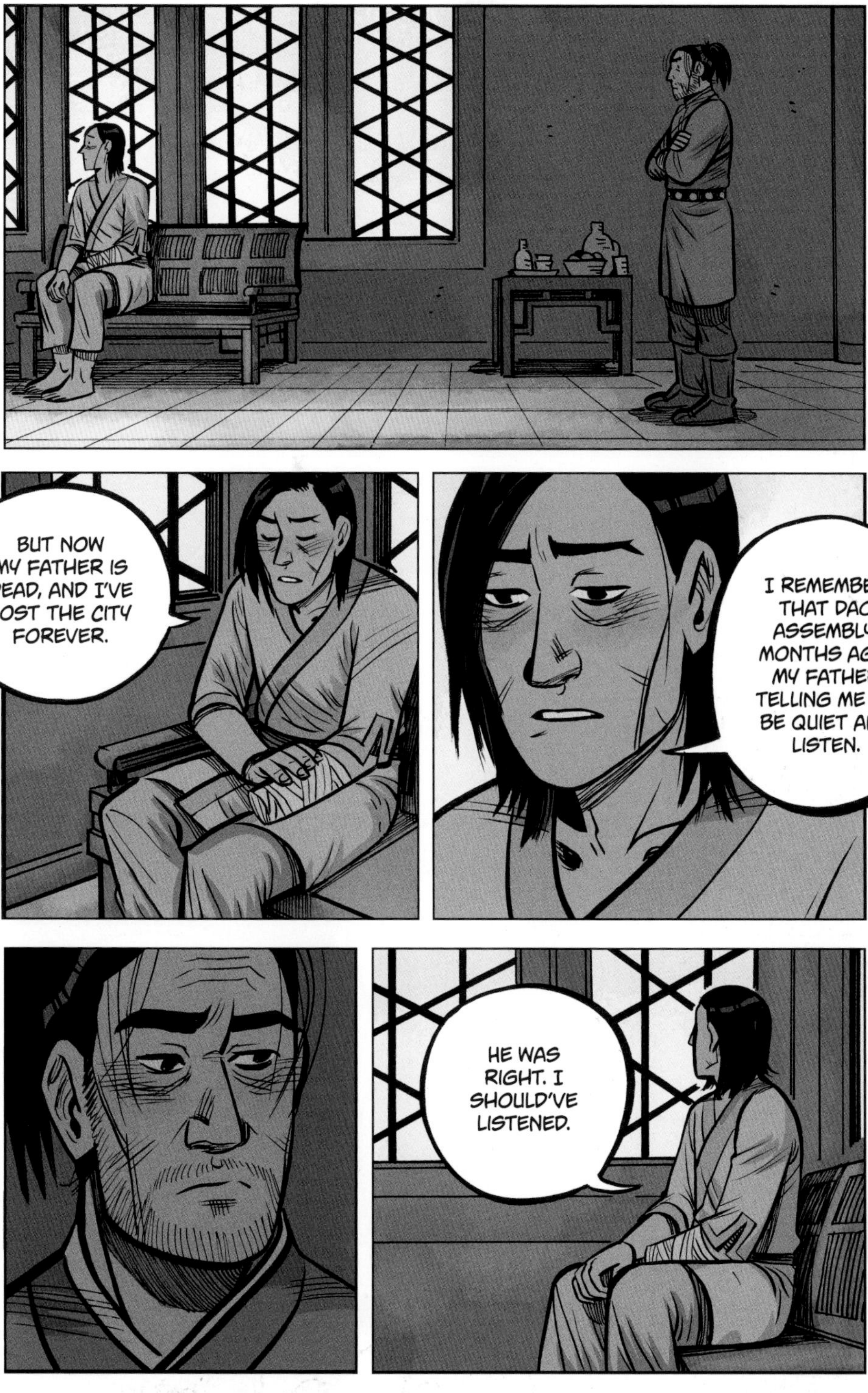
BUT NOW MY FATHER IS DEAD, AND I'VE LOST THE CITY FOREVER.
I REMEMBER THAT DAO ASSEMBLY, MONTHS AGO. MY FATHER TELLING ME TO BE QUIET AND LISTEN.
HE WAS RIGHT. I SHOULD'VE LISTENED.

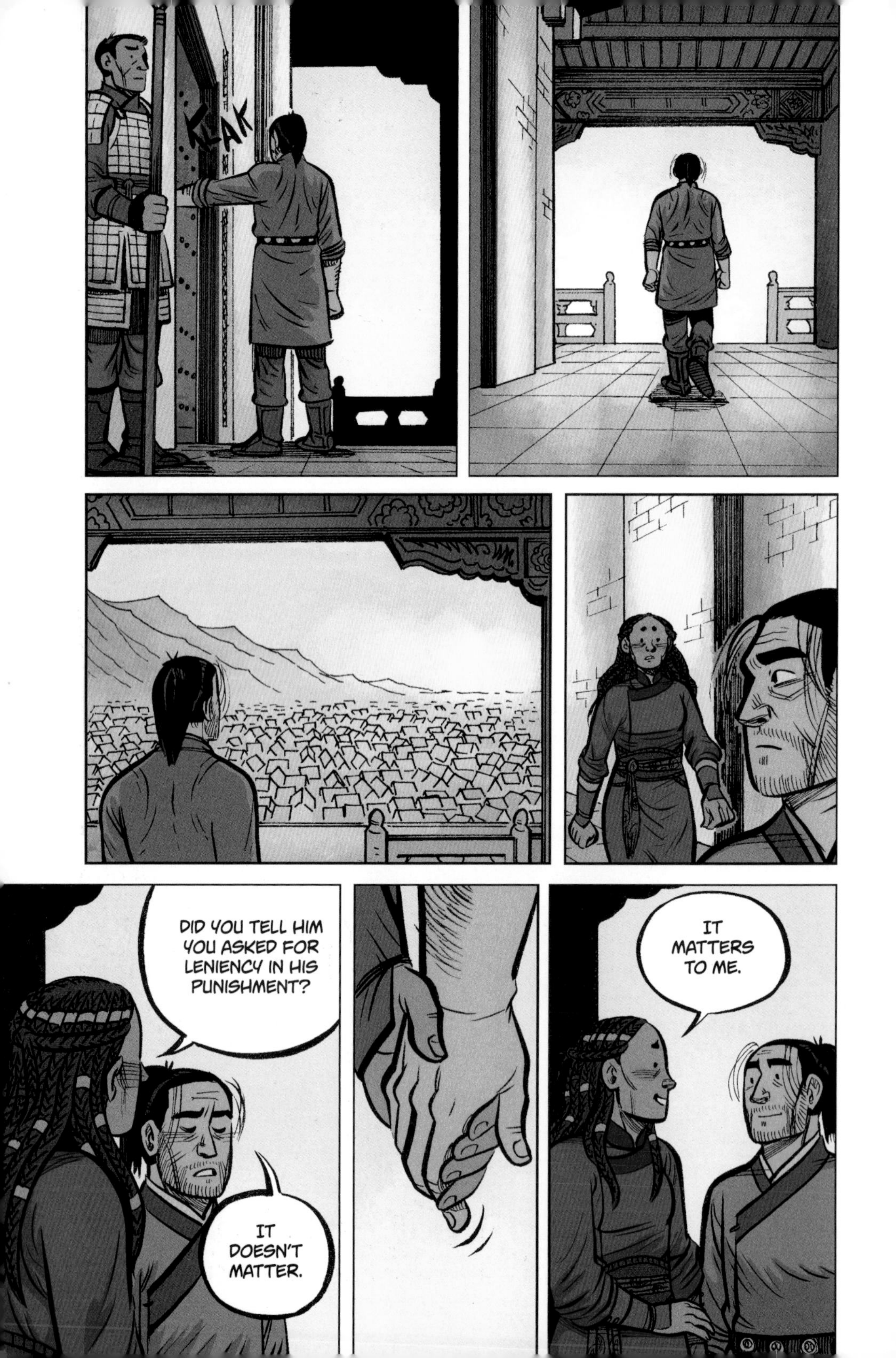
KLAK
DID YOU TELL HIM YOU ASKED FOR LENIENCY IN HIS PUNISHMENT?
IT DOESN'T MATTER.
IT MATTERS TO ME.

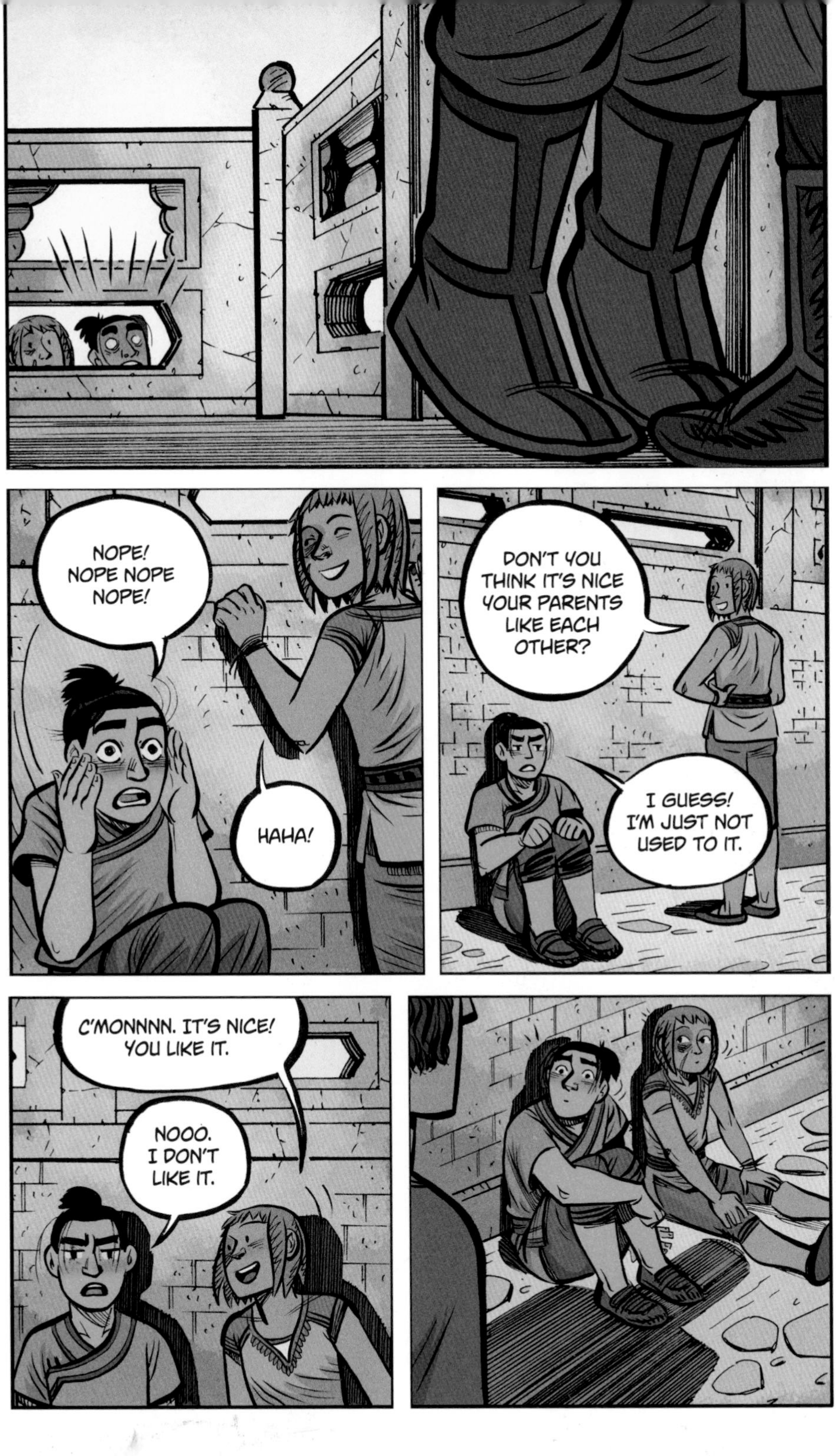
NOPE! NOPE NOPE NOPE!
HAHA!
DON'T YOU THINK IT'S NICE YOUR PARENTS LIKE EACH OTHER?
I GUESS! I'M JUST NOT USED TO IT.
C'MONNNN. IT'S NICE! YOU LIKE IT.
NOOO. I DON'T LIKE IT.

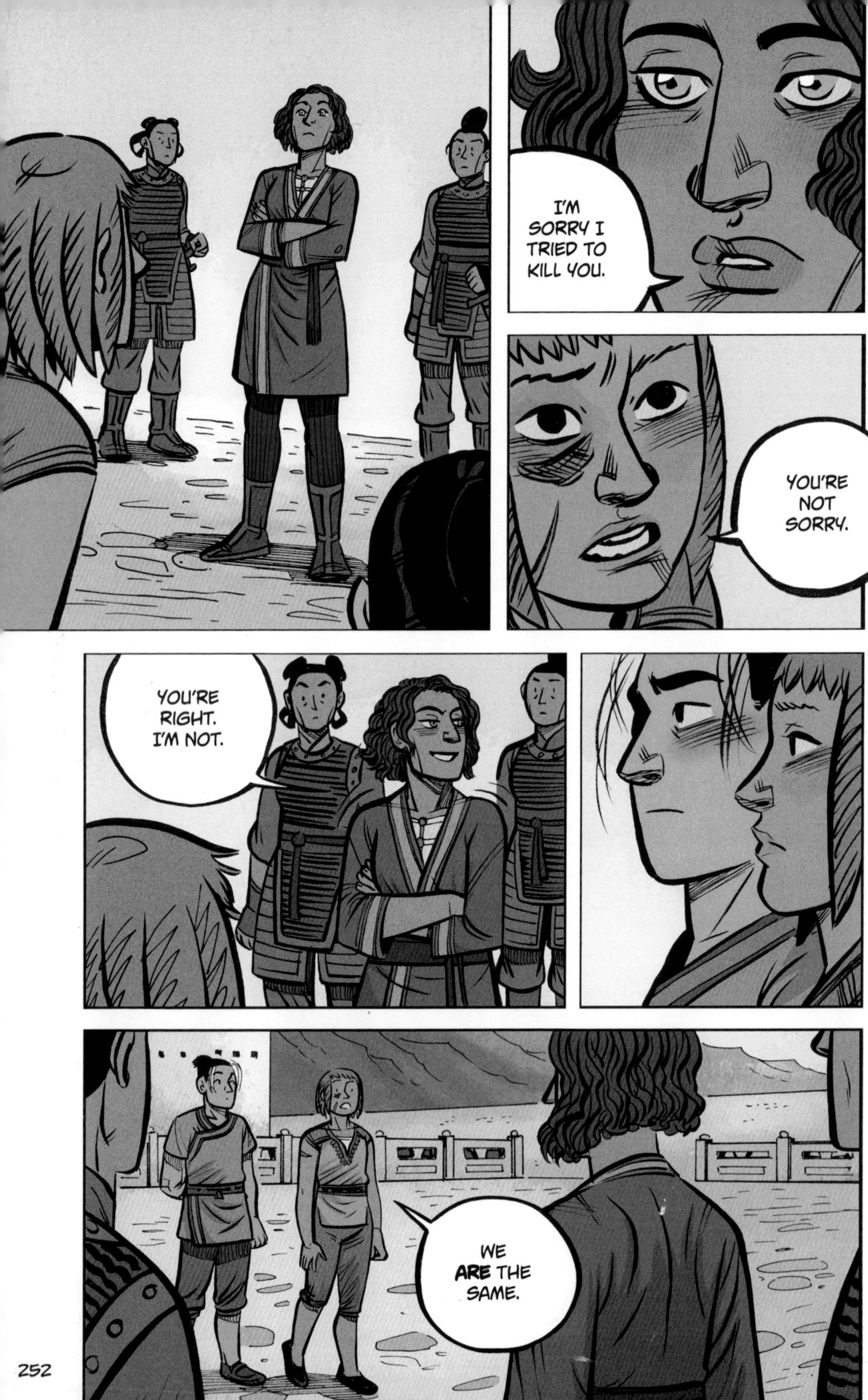
I'M SORRY I TRIED TO KILL YOU.
YOU'RE NOT SORRY.
YOU'RE RIGHT. I'M NOT.
WE **ARE** THE SAME.

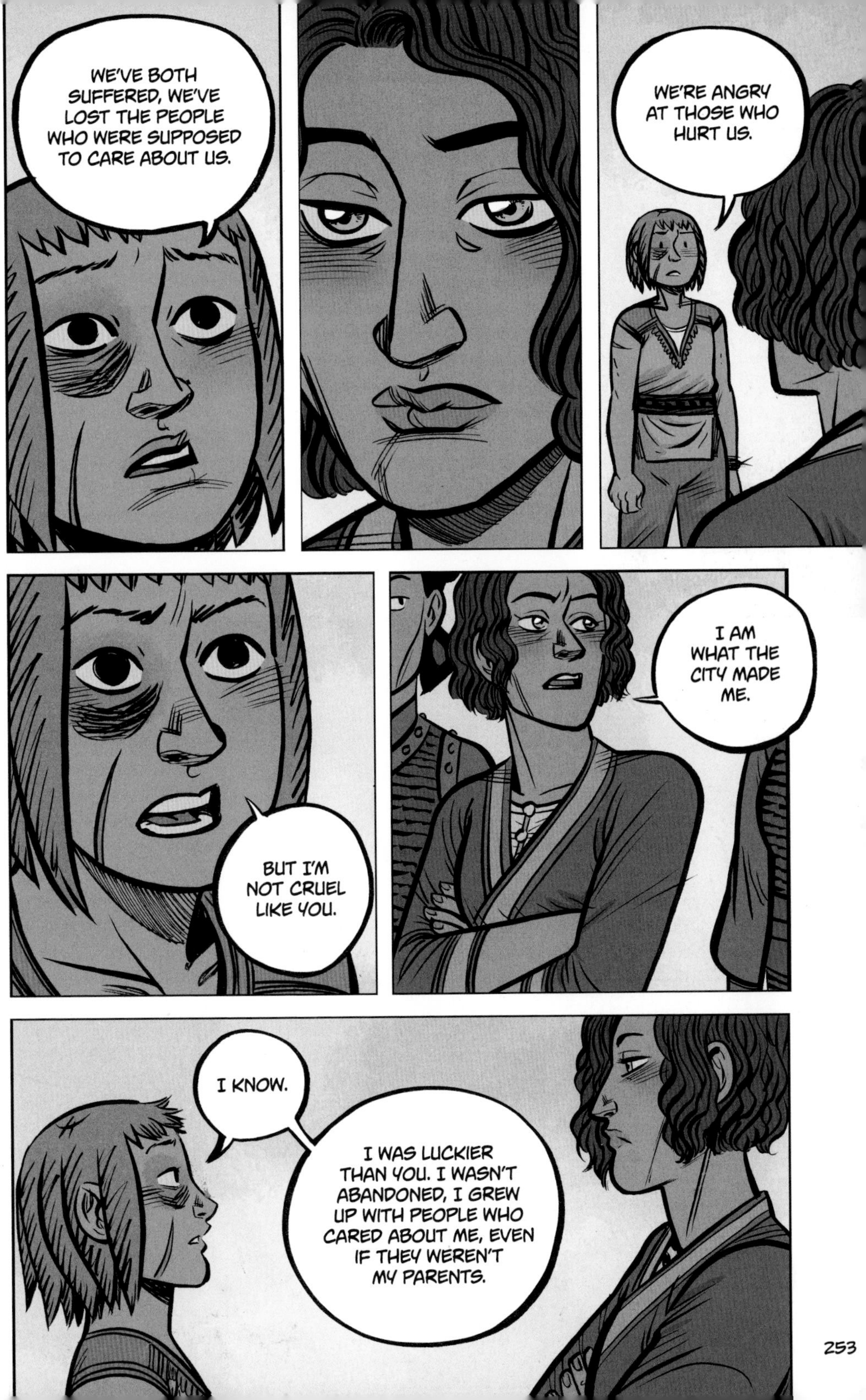
WE'VE BOTH SUFFERED, WE'VE LOST THE PEOPLE WHO WERE SUPPOSED TO CARE ABOUT US.
WE'RE ANGRY AT THOSE WHO HURT US.
BUT I'M NOT CRUEL LIKE YOU.
I AM WHAT THE CITY MADE ME.
I KNOW.
I WAS LUCKIER THAN YOU. I WASN'T ABANDONED, I GREW UP WITH PEOPLE WHO CARED ABOUT ME, EVEN IF THEY WEREN'T MY PARENTS.

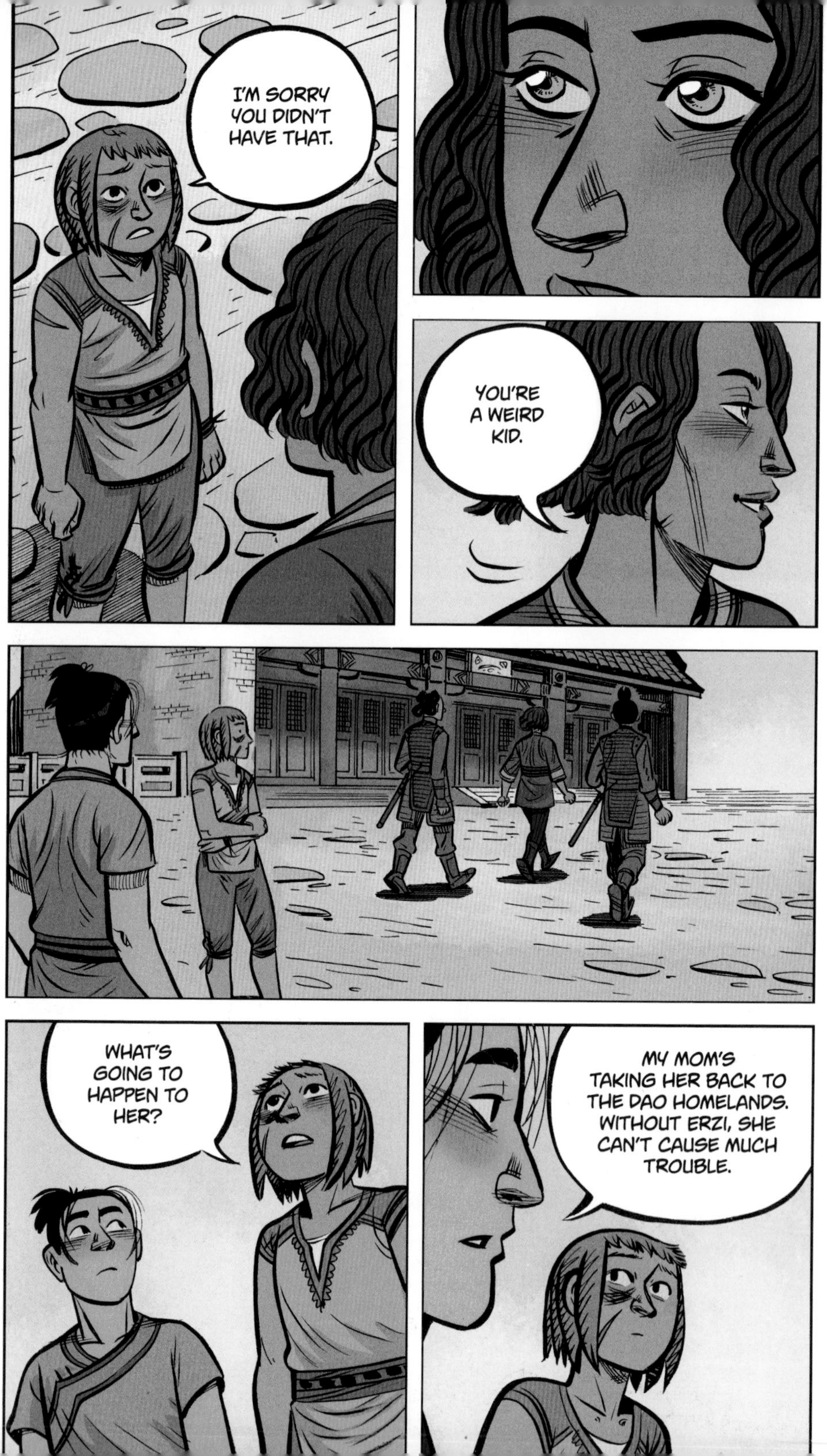
I'M SORRY YOU DIDN'T HAVE THAT.
YOU'RE A WEIRD KID.
WHAT'S GOING TO HAPPEN TO HER?
MY MOM'S TAKING HER BACK TO THE DAO HOMELANDS. WITHOUT ERZI, SHE CAN'T CAUSE MUCH TROUBLE.

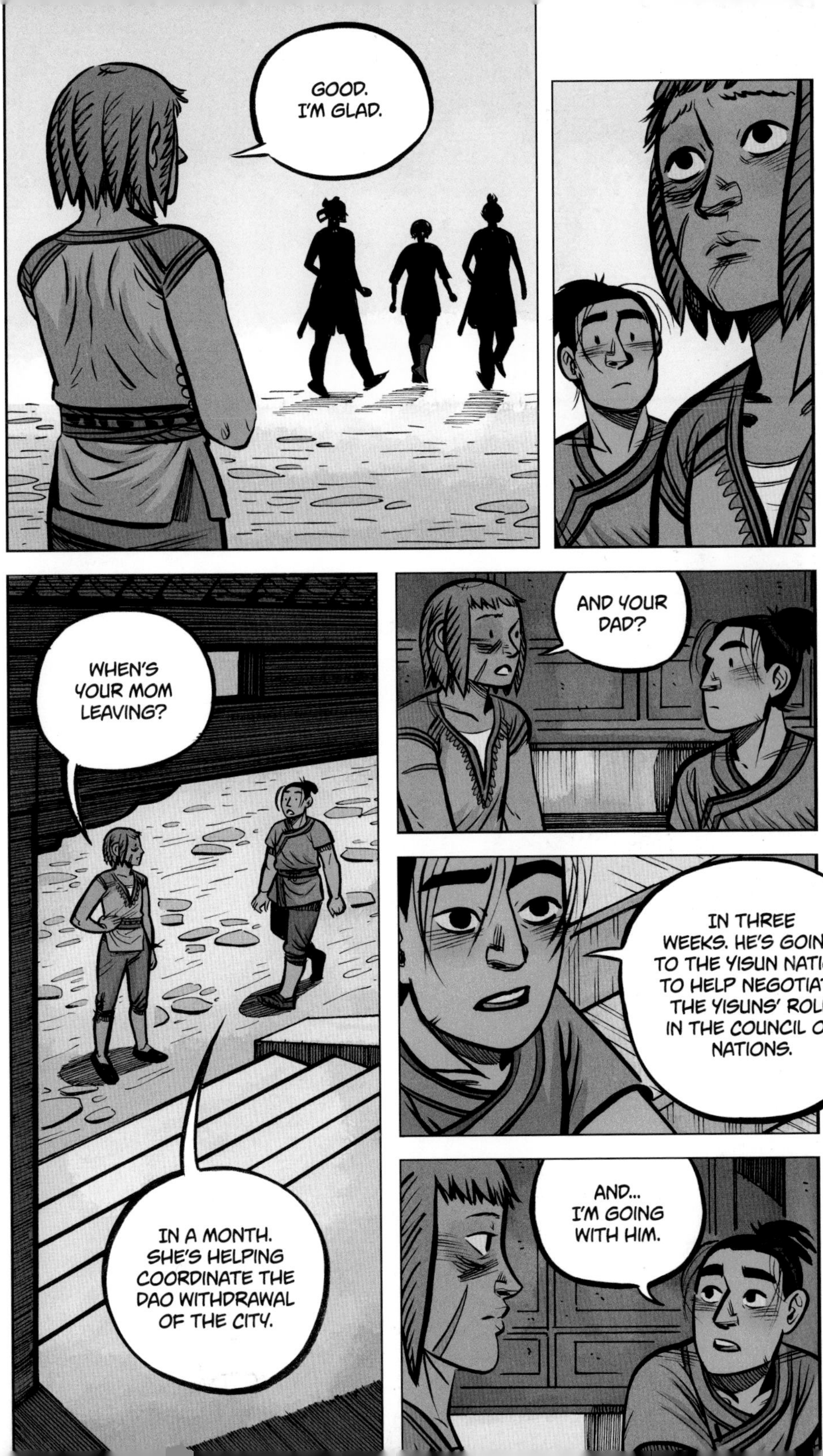
GOOD. I'M GLAD.
WHEN'S YOUR MOM LEAVING?
IN A MONTH. SHE'S HELPING COORDINATE THE DAO WITHDRAWAL OF THE CITY.
AND YOUR DAD?
IN THREE WEEKS. HE'S GOING TO THE YISUN NATION TO HELP NEGOTIATE THE YISUNS' ROLE IN THE COUNCIL OF NATIONS.
AND... I'M GOING WITH HIM.

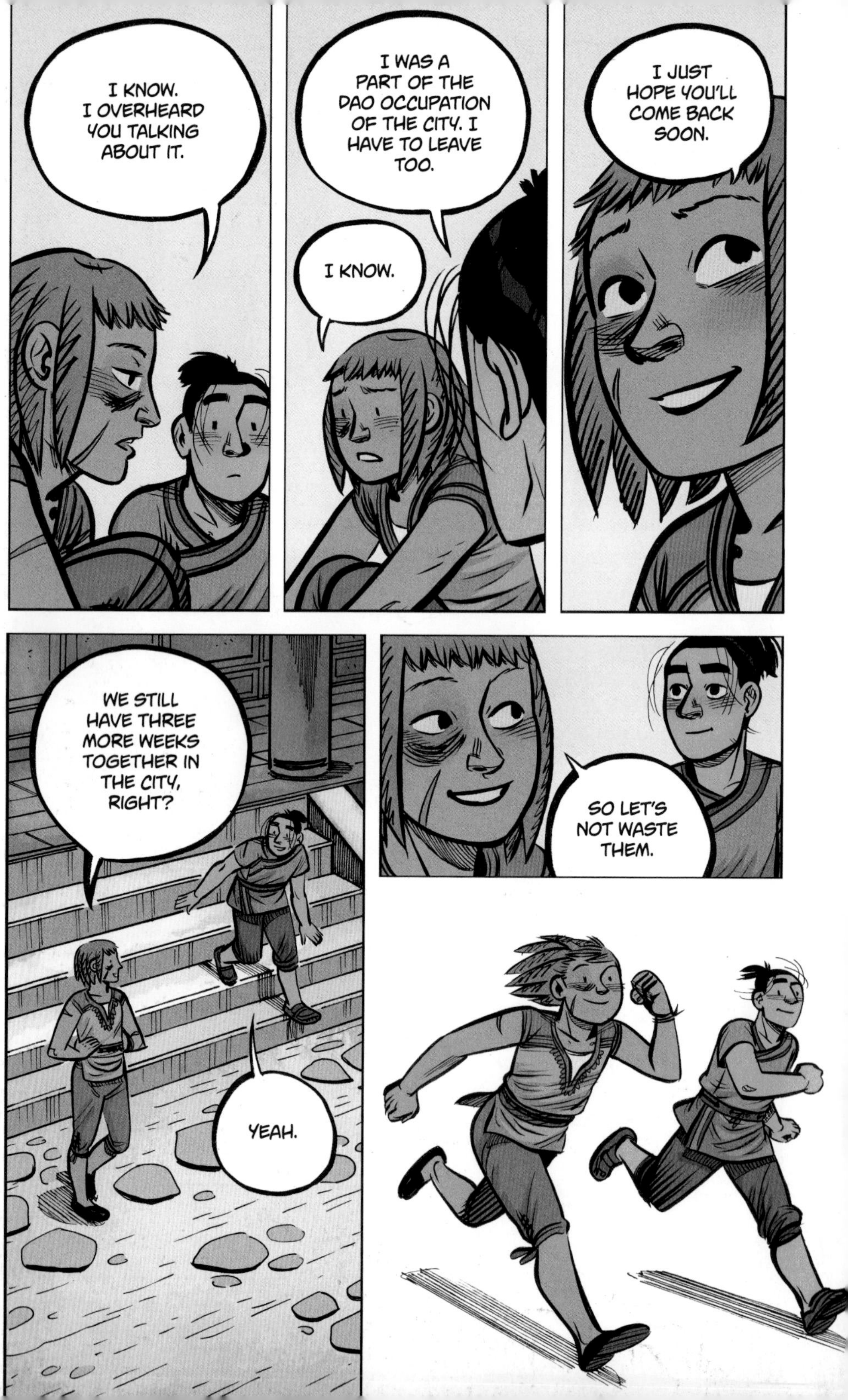
I KNOW. I OVERHEARD YOU TALKING ABOUT IT.
I WAS A PART OF THE DAO OCCUPATION OF THE CITY. I HAVE TO LEAVE TOO.
I KNOW.
I JUST HOPE YOU'LL COME BACK SOON.
WE STILL HAVE THREE MORE WEEKS TOGETHER IN THE CITY, RIGHT?
YEAH.
SO LET'S NOT WASTE THEM.

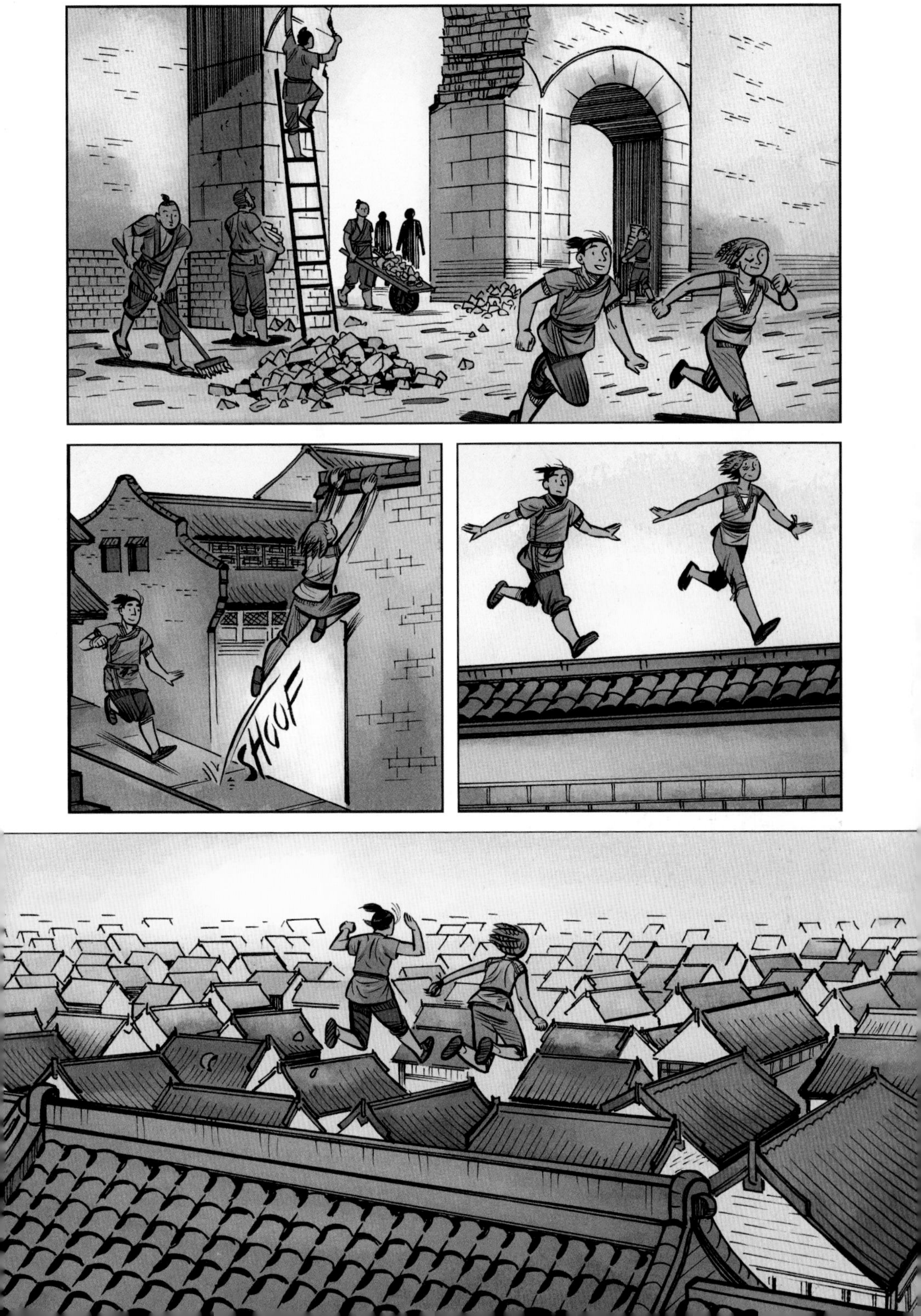
SHOOF

THREE YEARS LATER

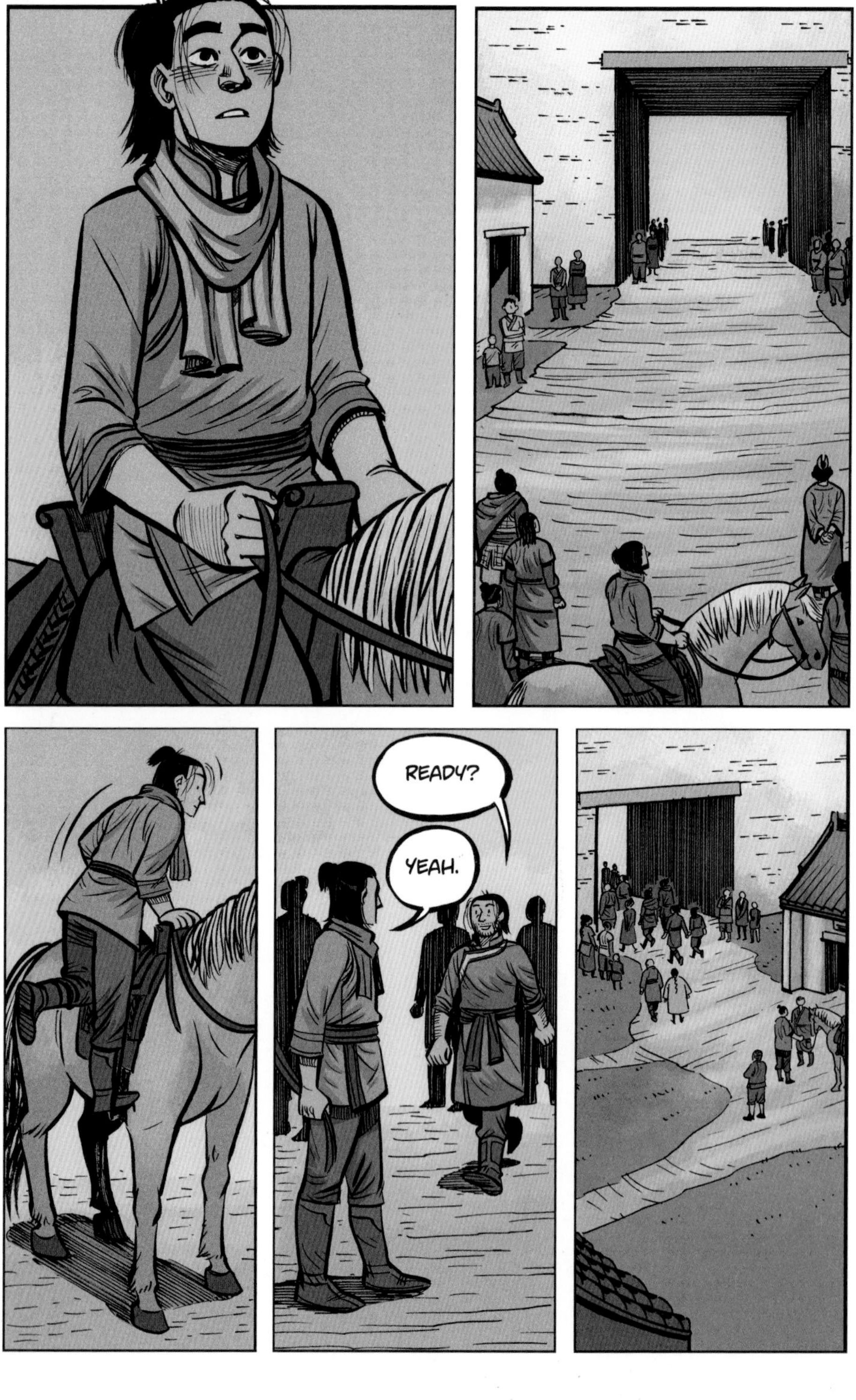
READY?
YEAH.

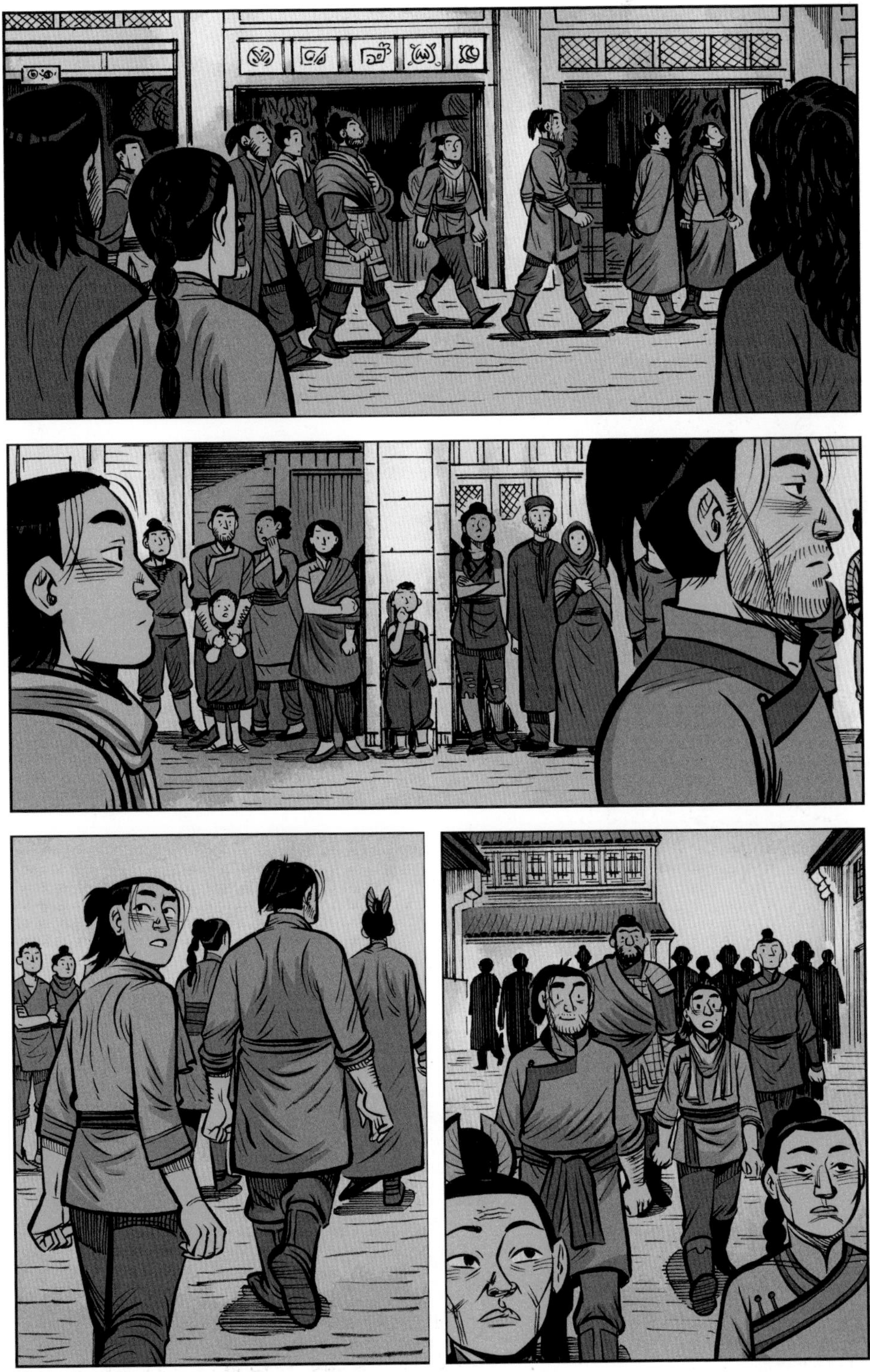

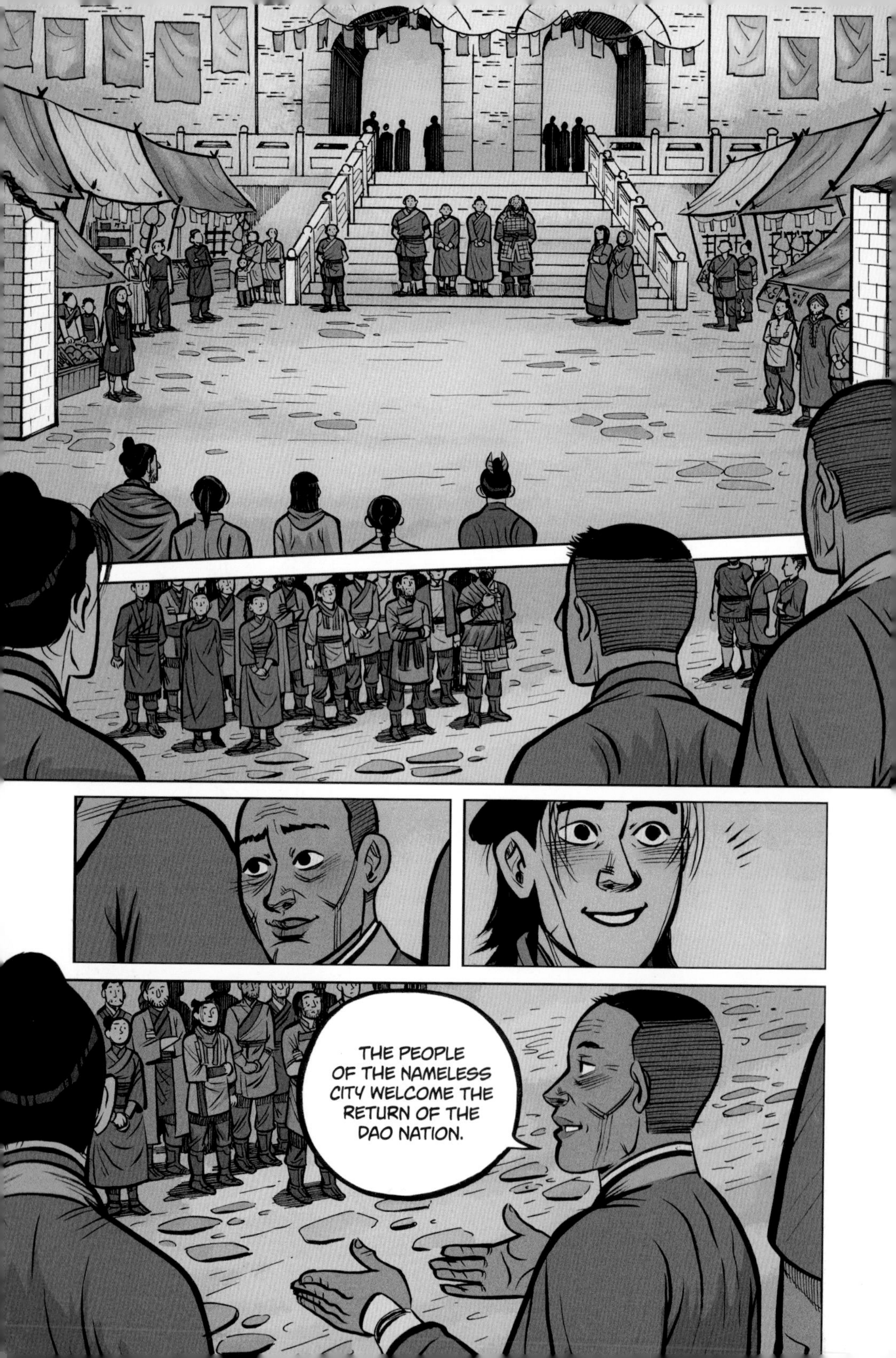
THE PEOPLE OF THE NAMELESS CITY WELCOME THE RETURN OF THE DAO NATION.

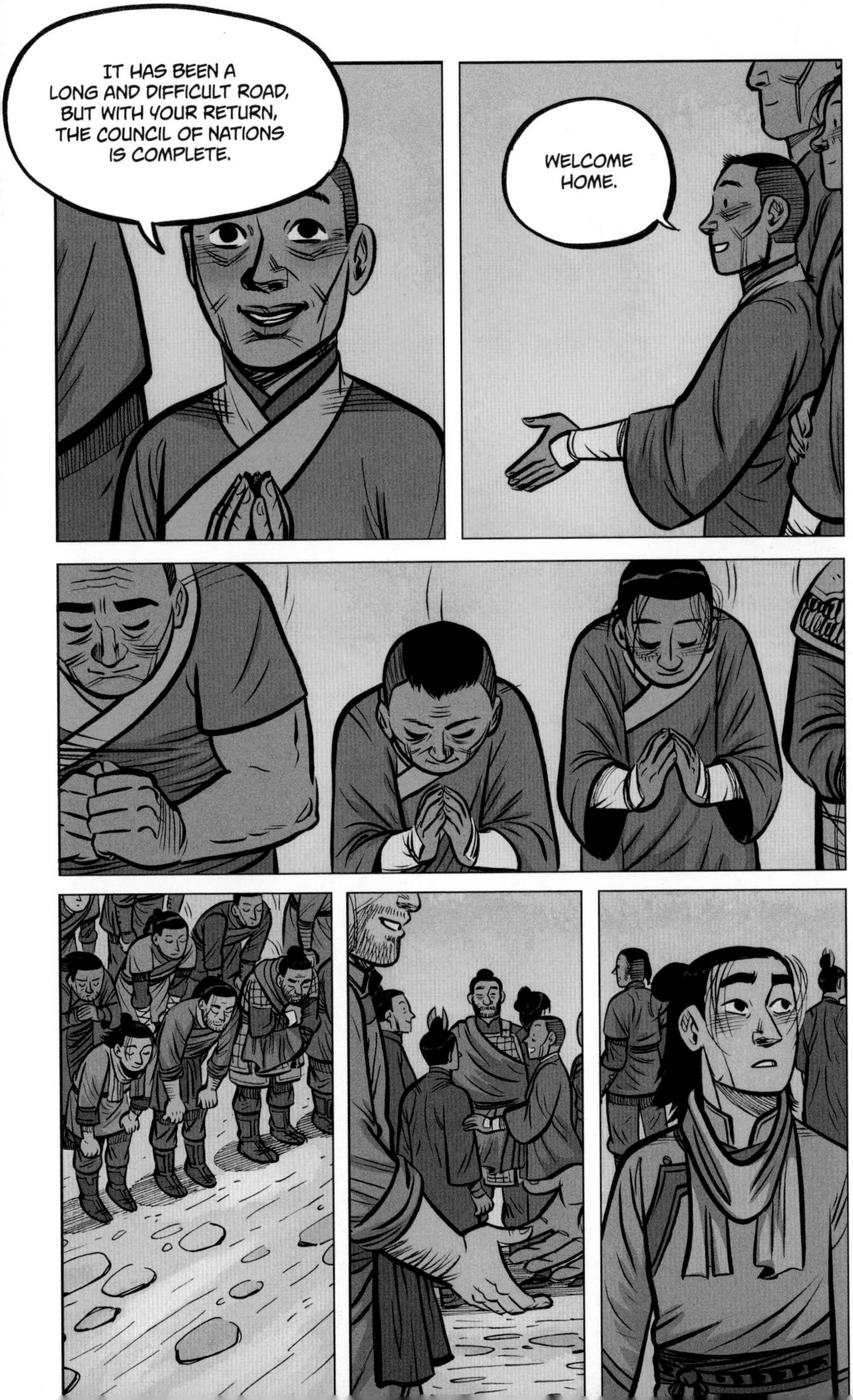
IT HAS BEEN A LONG AND DIFFICULT ROAD, BUT WITH YOUR RETURN, THE COUNCIL OF NATIONS IS COMPLETE.
WELCOME HOME.

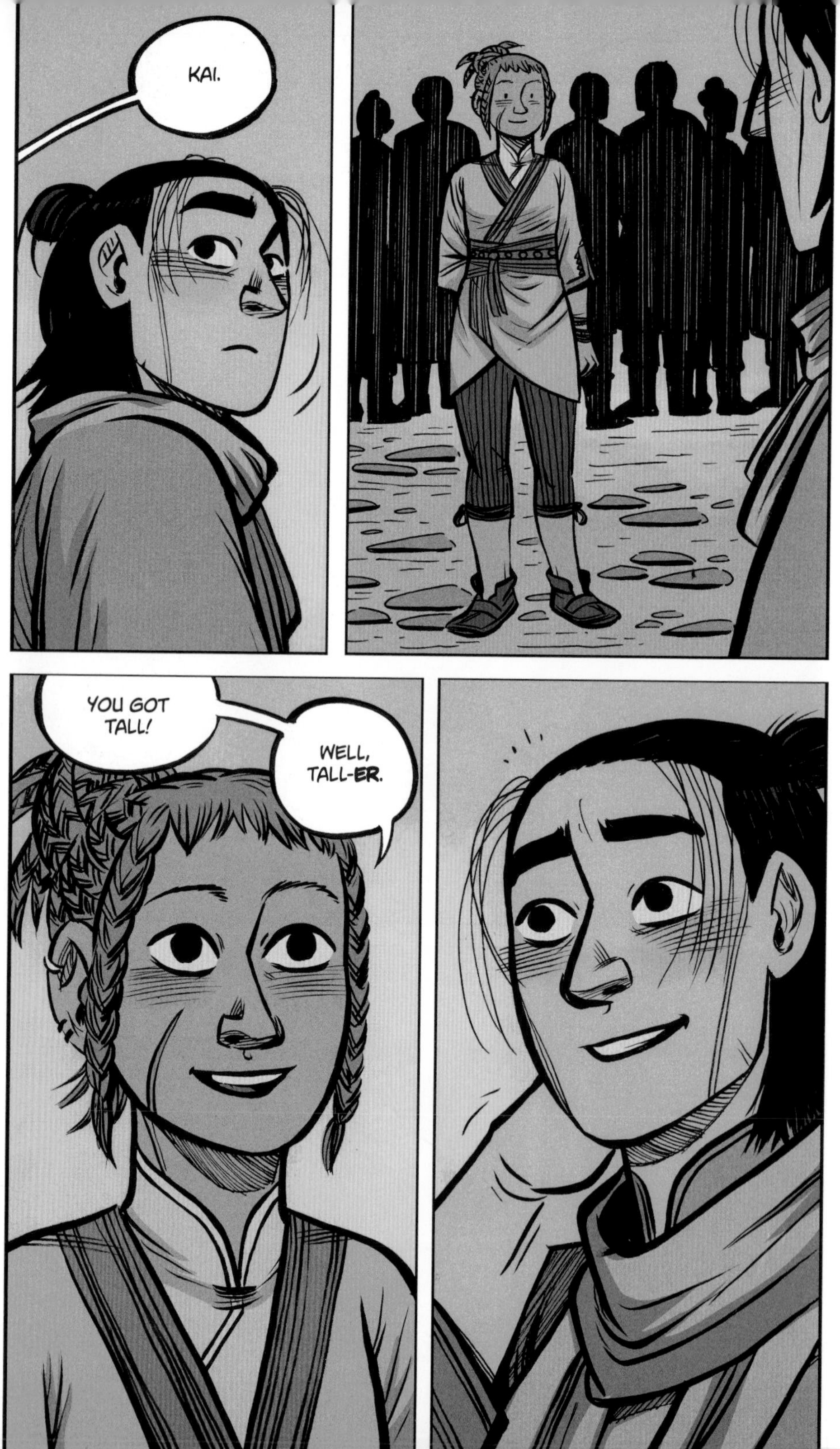
KAI.
YOU GOT TALL!
WELL, TALL-**ER**.

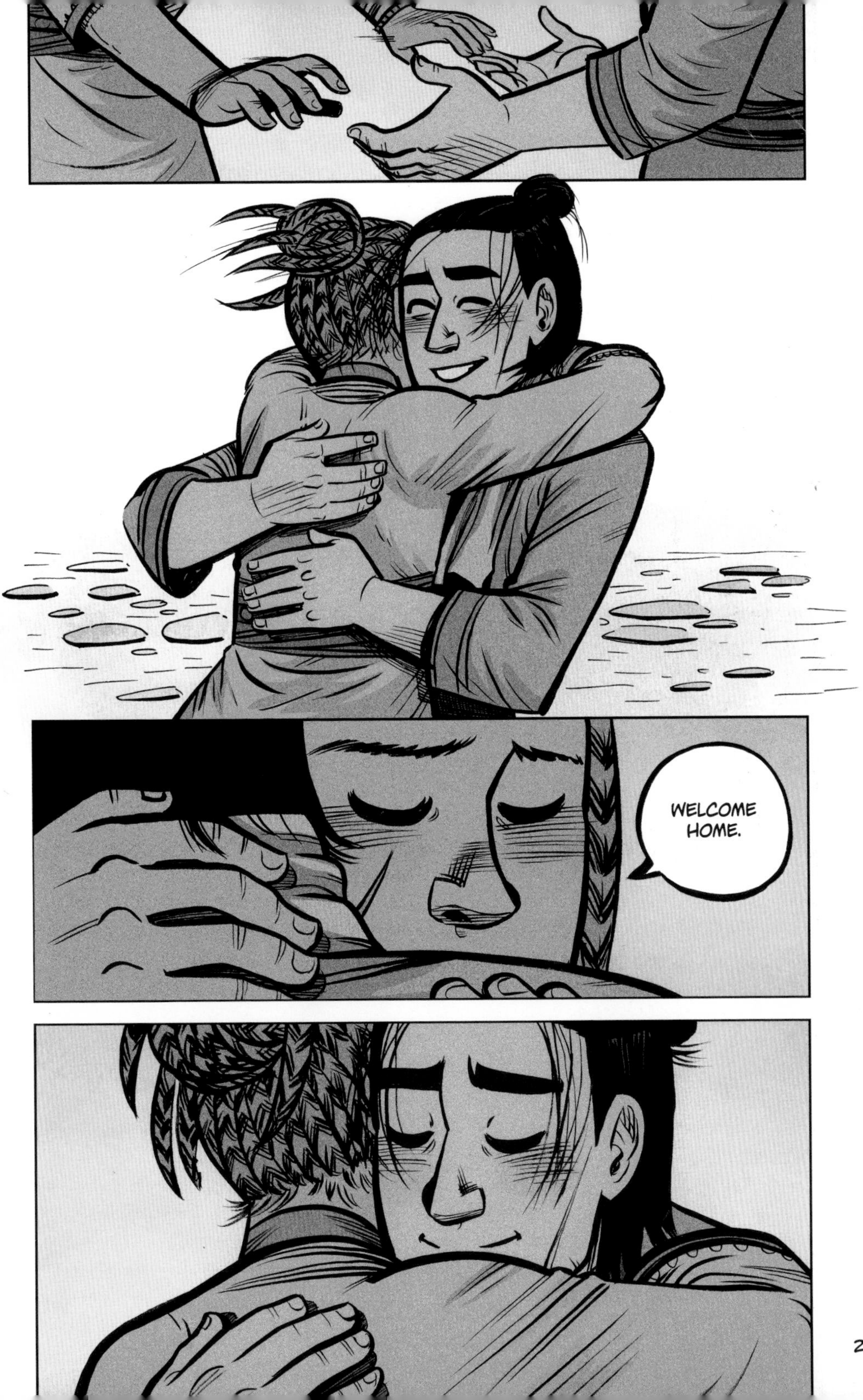
WELCOME HOME.

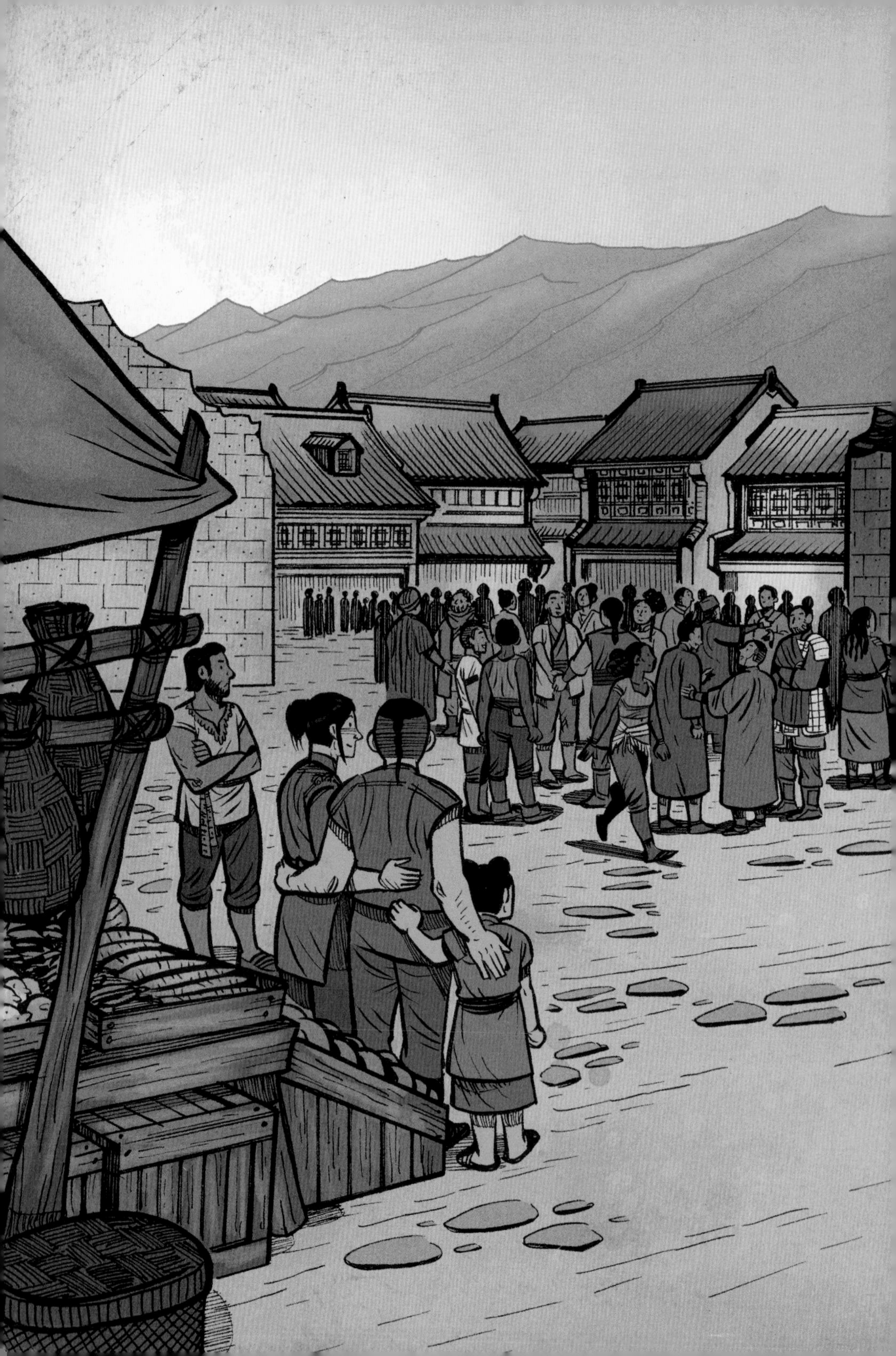

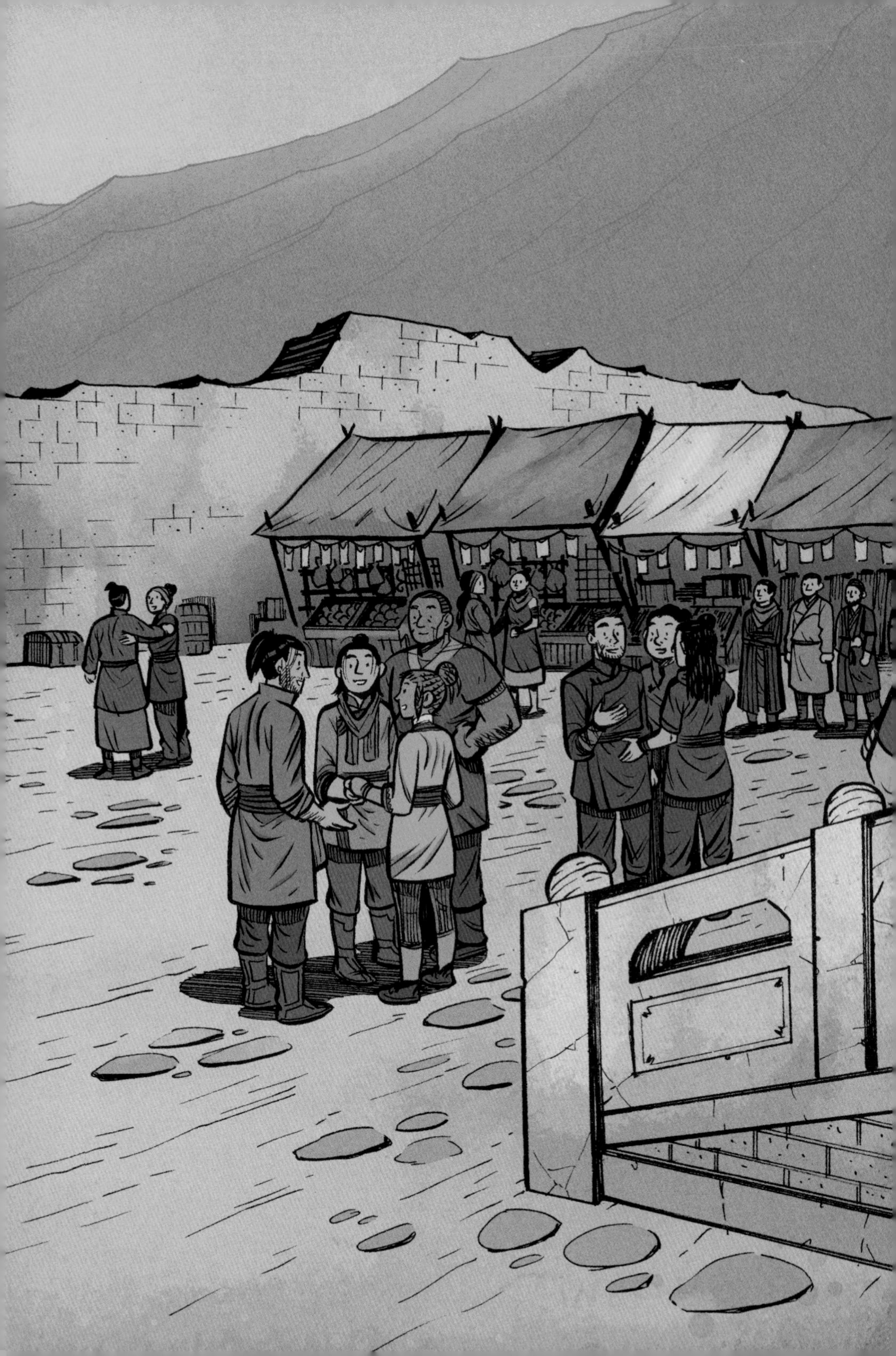

Faith Erin Hicks acknowledges the support of the Canada Council for the Arts, which last year invested $153 million to bring the arts to Canadians throughout the country.

Faith Erin Hicks remercions le Conseil des arts du Canada de son soutien. L'an dernier, le Conseil a investi 153 millions de dollars pour mettre de l'art dans la vie des Canadiennes et des Canadiens de tout le pays.

First Second

Copyright © 2018 by Faith Erin Hicks

Published by First Second
First Second is an imprint of Roaring Brook Press, a division of Holtzbrinck Publishing Holdings Limited Partnership
175 Fifth Avenue, New York, NY 10010
All rights reserved

Library of Congress Control Number: 2017957143

Hardcover ISBN: 978-1-62672-161-6
Paperback ISBN: 978-1-62672-160-9

Our books may be purchased in bulk for promotional, educational, or business use. Please contact your local bookseller or the Macmillan Corporate and Premium Sales Department at (800) 221-7945 ext. 5442 or by e-mail at MacmillanSpecialMarkets@macmillan.com.

First edition, 2018

Interior art colored by Jordie Bellaire
Cover art colored by Braden Lamb and Shelli Paroline
Book design by Angela Boyle
Printed in China by 1010 Printing International Limited, North Point, Hong Kong

Hardcover: 10 9 8 7 6 5 4 3 2 1
Paperback: 10 9 8 7 6 5 4 3 2 1

Penciled digitally in Manga Studio on a Wacom Cintiq. Inked traditionally with a Raphaël Kolinsky watercolor brush.

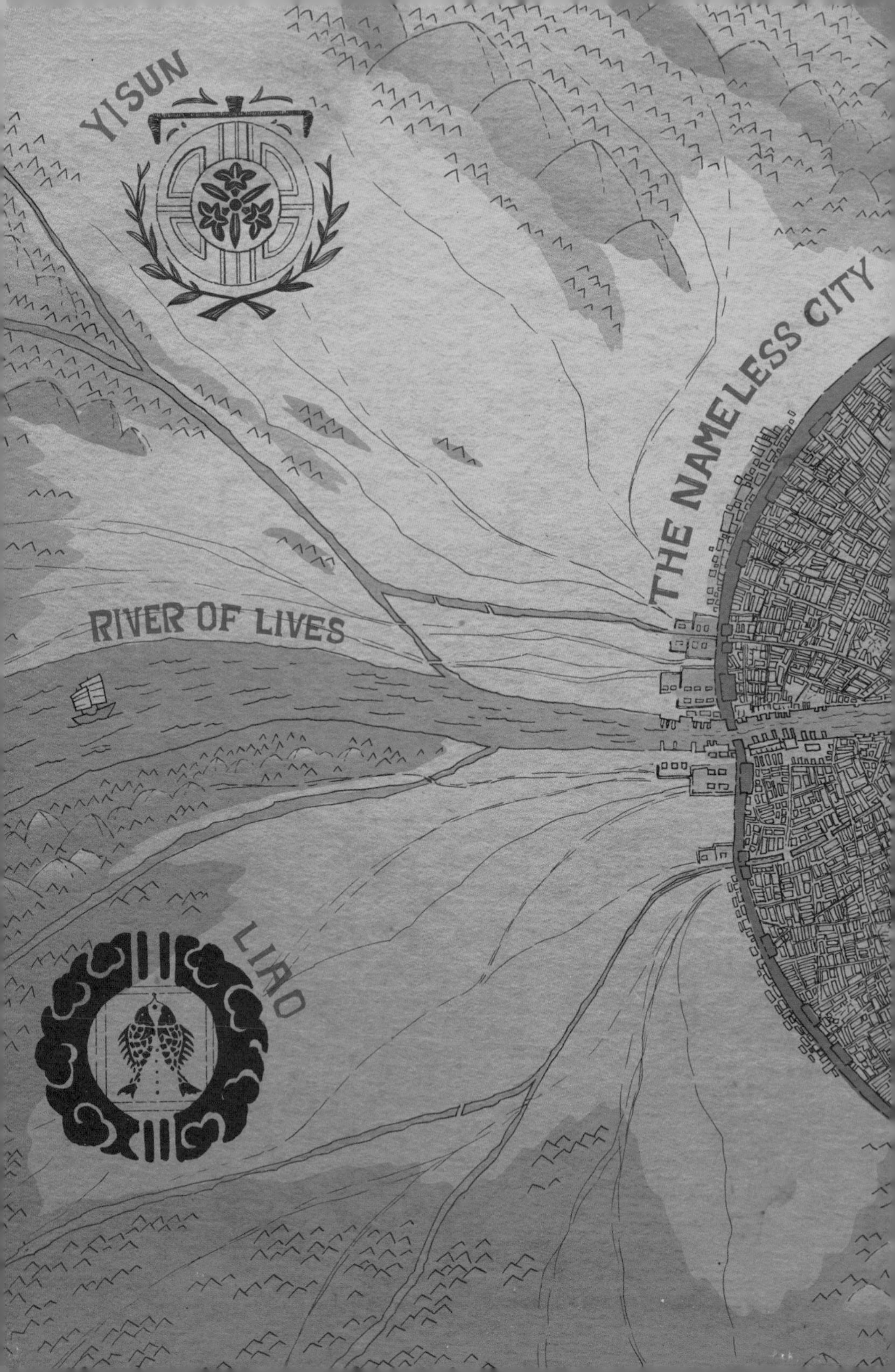
YISUN
THE NAMELESS CITY
RIVER OF LIVES
LIAO